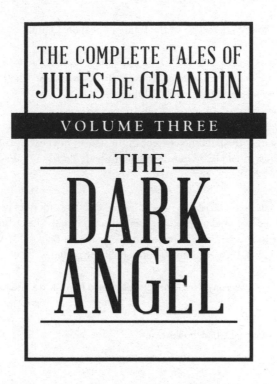

THE COMPLETE TALES OF JULES DE GRANDIN

VOLUME THREE

THE DARK ANGEL

SEABURY QUINN

EDITED BY GEORGE A. VANDERBURGH

Night Shade Books
New York

Night Shade books may be purchased in bulk at special discounts for sales promotion, corporate gifts, fund-raising, or educational purposes. Special editions can also be created to specifications. For details, contact the Special Sales Department, Night Shade Books, 307 West 36th Street, 11th Floor, New York, NY 10018 or info@skyhorsepublishing.com.

Night Shade Books® is a registered trademark of Skyhorse Publishing, Inc.®, a Delaware corporation.

Visit our website at www.nightshadebooks.com.

10 9 8 7 6 5 4 3 2 1

Library of Congress Cataloging-in-Publication Data

Names: Quinn, Seabury, 1889-1969, author. | Vanderburgh, George A., editor.
Title: The dark angel / Seabury Quinn ; edited by George A. Vanderburgh.
Description: New York : Night Shade Books, [2018] | Series: The complete tales of Jules de Grandin ; Volume three |
Identifiers: LCCN 2017043728 (print) | LCCN 2017046090 (ebook) | ISBN 9781597809450 (Ebook) | ISBN 9781597809443 (hardback : alk. paper)
Subjects: LCSH: Detective and mystery stories, American. | Paranormal fiction, American.
Classification: LCC PS3533.U69 (ebook) | LCC PS3533.U69 A6 2018 (print) | DDC 813/.52--dc23
LC record available at https://lccn.loc.gov/2017043728

Cover illustration by Donato Giancola
Cover design by Claudia Noble

Printed in the United States of America

TABLE OF CONTENTS

^Cover by Curtis C. Senf
*Cover by Margaret Brundage

THE COMPLETE TALES OF Jules de Grandin is dedicated to the memory of Robert E. Weinberg, who passed away in fall of 2016. Weinberg, who edited the six-volume paperback series of de Grandin stories in the 1970s, also supplied many original issues of *Weird Tales* magazine from his personal collection so that Seabury Quinn's work could be carefully scanned and transcribed digitally. Without his knowledge of the material and his editorial guidance, as well as his passion for Quinn's work over a long period of time (when admirers of the Jules de Grandin stories were often difficult to come by), this series would not have been possible, and we owe him our deepest gratitude and respect.

Introduction

by George A. Vanderburgh and Robert E. Weinberg

W EIRD TALES, THE SELF-DESCRIBED "Unique Magazine," and one of the most influential Golden Age pulp magazines in the first half of the twentieth century, was home to a number of now-well-recognized names, including Robert Bloch, August Derleth, Robert E. Howard, H. P. Lovecraft, Clark Ashton Smith, and Manly Wade Wellman.

But among such stiff competition was another writer, more popular at the time than all of the aforementioned authors, and paid at a higher rate because of it. Over the course of ninety-two stories and a serialized novel, his most endearing character captivated pulp magazine readers for nearly three decades, during which time he received more front cover illustrations accompanying his stories than any of his fellow contributors.

The writer's name was Seabury Quinn, and his character was the French occult detective Jules de Grandin.

Perhaps you've never heard of de Grandin, his indefatigable assistant Dr. Trowbridge, or the fictional town of Harrisonville, New Jersey. Perhaps you've never even heard of Seabury Quinn (or maybe only in passing, as a historical footnote in one of the many essays and reprinted collections of Quinn's now-more-revered contemporaries). Certainly, de Grandin was not the first occult detective—Algernon Blackwood's John Silence, Hodgson's Thomas Carnacki, and Sax Rohmer's Moris Klaw preceded him—nor was he the last, as Wellman's John Thunstone, Margery Lawrence's Miles Pennoyer, and Joseph Payne Brennan's Lucius Leffing all either overlapped with the end of de Grandin's run or followed him. And without doubt de Grandin shares more than a passing resemblance to both Sir Arthur Conan Doyle's Sherlock Holmes (especially with his Dr. Watson-like sidekick) and Agatha Christie's Hercule Poirot.

Indeed, even if you were to seek out a de Grandin story, your options over the years would have been limited. Unlike Lovecraft, Smith, Wellman, Bloch, and other *Weird Tales* contributors, the publication history of the Jules de Grandin tales is spotty at best. In 1966, Arkham House printed roughly 2,000 copies of *The Phantom-Fighter*, a selection of ten early works. In the late 1970s, Popular Library published six paperback volumes of approximately thirty-five assorted tales, but they are now long out of print. In 2001, the specialty press The Battered Silicon Dispatch Box released an oversized, three-volume hardcover set of every de Grandin story (the first time all the stories had been collected), and, while still in production, the set is unavailable to the general trade.

So, given how obscure Quinn and his character might seem today, it's justifiably hard to understand how popular these stories originally were, or how frequently new ones were written. But let the numbers tell the tale: from October 1925 (when the very first de Grandin story was released) to December 1933, a roughly eight-year span, de Grandin stories appeared in an incredible sixty-two of the ninety-six issues that *Weird Tales* published, totaling well-over three-quarters of a million words. Letter after letter to the magazine's editor demanded further adventures from the supernatural detective.

If Quinn loomed large in the mind of pulp readers during the magazine's hey-day, then why has his name fallen on deaf ears since? Aside from the relative unavailability of his work, the truth is that Quinn has been successfully marginalized over the years by many critics, who have often dismissed him as simply a hack writer. The de Grandin stories are routinely criticized as being of little worth, and dismissed as unimportant to the development of weird fiction. A common argument, propped up by suspiciously circular reasoning, concludes that Quinn was not the most popular writer for *Weird Tales*, just the most prolific.

These critics seem troubled that the same audience who read and appreciated the work of Lovecraft, Smith, and Howard could also enjoy the exploits of the French ghostbuster. And while it would be far from the truth to suggest that the literary merits of the de Grandin stories exceed those of some of his contemporaries' tales, Quinn was a much more skillful writer, and the adventures of his occult detective more enjoyable to read, than most critics are willing to acknowledge. In the second half of the twentieth century, as the literary value of some pulp-fiction writers began to be reconsidered, Quinn proved to be the perfect whipping boy for early advocates attempting to destigmatize weird fiction: He was the hack author who churned out formulaic prose for a quick paycheck. Anticipating charges that a literary reassessment of Lovecraft would require reevaluating the entire genre along with him, an arbitrary line was quickly drawn in the sand, and as the standard-bearer of pulp fiction's popularity, the creator of Jules de Grandin found himself on the wrong side of that line.

First and foremost, it must be understood that Quinn wrote to make money, and he was far from the archetypal "starving artist." At the same time that his Jules de Grandin stories were running in *Weird Tales,* he had a similar series of detective stories publishing in *Real Detective Tales.* Quinn was writing two continuing series at once throughout the 1920s, composing approximately twenty-five thousand words a month on a manual typewriter. Maintaining originality under such a grueling schedule would be difficult for any author, and even though the de Grandin stories follow a recognizable formula, Quinn still managed to produce one striking story after another. It should also be noted that the tendency to recycle plots and ideas for different markets was very similar to the writing practices of *Weird Tales's* other prolific and popular writer, Robert E. Howard, who is often excused for these habits, rather than criticized for them.

Throughout his many adventures, the distinctive French detective changed little. His penchant for amusingly French exclamations was a constant through all ninety-three works, as was his taste for cigars and brandy after (and sometimes before) a hard day's work, and his crime-solving styles and methods remained remarkably consistent. From time to time, some new skill or bit of knowledge was revealed to the reader, but in most other respects the Jules de Grandin of "The Horror on the Links" was the same as the hero of the last story in the series, published twenty-five years later.

> He was a perfect example of the rare French blond type, rather under medium height, but with a military erectness of carriage that made him look several inches taller than he really was. His light-blue eyes were small and exceedingly deep-set, and would have been humorous had it not been for the curiously cold directness of their gaze. With his wide mouth, light mustache waxed at the ends in two perfectly horizontal points, and those twinkling, stock-taking eyes, he reminded me of an alert tomcat.

Thus is de Grandin described by Dr. Trowbridge in the duo's first meeting in 1925. His personal history is dribbled throughout the stories: de Grandin was born and raised in France, attended medical school, became a prominent surgeon, and in the Great War served first as a medical officer, then as a member of the intelligence service. After the war, he traveled the world in the service of French Intelligence. His age is never given, but it's generally assumed that the occult detective is in his early forties.

Samuel Trowbridge, on the other hand, is a typical conservative small-town doctor of the first half of the twentieth century (as described by Quinn, he is a cross between an honest brother of George Bernard Shaw and former Chief Justice of the United States Charles Evans Hughes). Bald and bewhiskered, most—if not all—of his life was spent in the same town. Trowbridge is old-fashioned and somewhat conservative, a member of the Knights Templar, a vestryman in the Episcopal Church, and a staunch Republican.

While the two men are dissimilar in many ways, they are also very much alike. Both are fine doctors and surgeons. Trowbridge might complain from time to time about de Grandin's wild adventures, but he always goes along with them; there is no thought, ever, of leaving de Grandin to fight his battles alone. More than any other trait, though, they are two men with one mission, and perhaps for that reason they remained friends for all of their ninety-three adventures and countless trials.

The majority of Quinn's de Grandin stories take place in or near Harrison-ville, New Jersey, a fictional community that rivals (with its fiends, hauntings, ghouls, werewolves, vampires, voodoo, witchcraft, and zombies) Lovecraft's own Arkham, Massachusetts. For more recent examples of a supernatural-infested community, one need look no further than the modern version of pulp-fiction narratives . . . television. *Buffy the Vampire Slayer*'s Sunnydale, California, and *The Night Strangler*'s Seattle both reflect the structural needs of this type of super-natural narrative.

Early in the series, de Grandin is presented as Trowbridge's temporary house guest, having travelled to the United States to study both medicine and mod-ern police techniques, but Quinn quickly realized that the series was due for a long run and recognized that too much globe-trotting would make the stories unwieldy. A familiar setting would be needed to keep the main focus of each tale on the events themselves. Harrisonville, a medium-sized town outside New York City, was completely imaginary, but served that purpose.

Most of the de Grandin stories feature beautiful girls in peril. Quinn discov-ered early on that Farnsworth Wright, *Weird Tales*'s editor from 1924 to 1940, believed nude women on the cover sold more copies, so when writing he was careful to always feature a scene that could translate to appropriately salacious artwork. Quinn also realized that his readers wanted adventures with love and romance as central themes, so even his most frightening tales were given happy endings (. . . of a sort).

And yet the de Grandin adventures are set apart from the stories they were published alongside by their often explicit and bloody content. Quinn predated the work of Clive Barker and the splatterpunk writers by approximately fifty years, but, using his medical background, he wrote some truly terrifying horror stories; tales like "The House of Horror" and "The House Where Time Stood Still" feature some of the most hideous descriptions of mutilated humans ever set down on paper. The victims of the mad doctor in "The House of Horror" in particular must rank near the top of the list of medical monstrosities in fiction.

Another element that set Quinn's occult detective apart from others was his pioneering use of modern science in the fight against ancient superstitions.

De Grandin fought vampires, werewolves, and even mummies in his many adventures, but oftentimes relied on the latest technology to save the day. The Frenchman put it best in a conversation with Dr. Trowbridge at the end of "The Blood-Flower":

> "And wasn't there some old legend to the effect that a werewolf could only be killed with a silver bullet?"
>
> "Ah, bah," he replied with a laugh. "What did those old legend-mongers know of the power of modern firearms? . . . When I did shoot that wolfman, my friend, I had something more powerful than superstition in my hand. *Morbleu*, but I did shoot a hole in him large enough for him to have walked through."

Quinn didn't completely abandon the use of holy water, ancient relics, and magical charms to defeat supernatural entities, but he made it clear that de Grandin understood that there was a place for modern technology as well as old folklore when it came to fighting monsters. Nor was de Grandin himself above using violence to fight his enemies. Oftentimes, the French occult investigator served as judge, jury and executioner when dealing with madmen, deranged doctors, and evil masterminds. There was little mercy in his stories for those who used dark forces.

While sex was heavily insinuated but rarely covered explicitly in the pulps, except in the most general of terms, Quinn again was willing to go where few other writers would dare. Sexual slavery, lesbianism, and even incest played roles in his writing over the years, challenging the moral values of the day.

In the end, there's no denying that the de Grandin stories are pulp fiction. Many characters are little more than assorted clichés bundled together. De Grandin is a model hero, a French expert on the occult, and never at a loss when battling the most evil of monsters. Dr. Trowbridge remains the steadfast companion, much in the Dr. Watson tradition, always doubting but inevitably following his friend's advice. Quinn wrote for the masses, and he didn't spend pages describing landscapes when there was always more action unfolding.

The Jules de Grandin stories were written as serial entertainment, with the legitimate expectation that they would not be read back to back. While all of the adventures are good fun, the best way to properly enjoy them is over an extended period of time. Plowing through one story after another will lessen their impact, and greatly cut down on the excitement and fun of reading them. One story a week, which would stretch out this entire five-volume series over two years, might be the perfect amount of time needed to fully enjoy these tales of the occult and the macabre. They might not be great literature, but they don't pretend to be. They're pulp adventures, and even after seventy-five years, the stories read well.

Additionally, though the specific aesthetic values of *Weird Tales* readers were vastly different than those of today's readers, one can see clearly see the continuing allure of these types of supernatural adventures, and the long shadow that they cast over twentieth and early twenty-first century popular culture. Sure, these stories are formulaic, but it is a recipe that continues to be popular to this day. The formula of the occult detective, the protector who stands between us and the monsters of the night, can be seen time and time again in the urban fantasy and paranormal romance categories of commercial fiction, and is prevalent in today's television and movies. Given the ubiquity and contemporary popularity of this type of narrative, it's actually not at all surprising that Seabury Quinn was the most popular contributor to *Weird Tales*.

We are proud to present the first of five volumes reprinting every Jules de Grandin story written by Seabury Quinn. Organized chronologically, as they originally appeared in *Weird Tales* magazine, this is the first time that the collected de Grandin stories have been made available in trade editions.

Each volume has been graced by tremendous artwork from renowned artist Donato Giancola, who has given Quinn's legendary character an irresistible combination of grace, cunning and timelessness. We couldn't have asked for a better way to introduce "the occult Hercule Poirot" to a new generation of readers.

Finally, if Seabury Quinn is watching from above, and closely scrutinizing the shelves of bookstores, he would undoubtedly be pleased as punch, and proud as all get-out, to find his creation, Dr. Jules de Grandin, rising once again in the minds of readers around the world, battling the forces of darkness . . . wherever, whoever, or whatever the nature of their evil might be.

When the Jaws of Darkness Open,
Only Jules de Grandin Stands in Satan's Way!

Robert E. Weinberg
Chicago, Illinois, USA

and

George A. Vanderburgh
Lake Eugenia, Ontario, Canada

23 September 2016

Jules de Grandin:
"The Pillar of *Weird Tales*"

by Darrell Schweitzer

F OR SOMEONE WHO PLAYED such an important role in the magazine's hey-day, there is surprisingly little information available about Seabury Quinn and his behind-the-scenes relationship with *Weird Tales*. Author and pulp magazine contributor E. Hoffmann Price, among the memoirs in his *Book of the Dead* (Arkham House, 2001), profiles Quinn, but doesn't say much about him in connection to *Weird Tales*. Price also profiles *WT* editor Farnsworth Wright, but doesn't mention Quinn. Price could be an insightful biographer, and he esteemed both men highly, but given that Price regarded pulp writing as purely a trade—something done for the money, the same as carpentry or brick-laying—it isn't surprising that he skimps on the working details, which to him were unimportant.

It *is* clear enough that Quinn, who lived in Brooklyn until mid-1937, when he lost his job as editor of the mortician's journal *Casket and Sunnyside* and moved to Washington, D.C., was not a member of Wright's social circle. The *Weird Tales* office was in Chicago. So Quinn could hardly have been one of the "Varnished Vultures"—an informal club of writers, editors, and artists associated with the magazine who regularly met in Wright's apartment (Price was a member)—or someone who stopped by on occasion to help read manuscripts. To my knowledge, Wright and Quinn never met—at least, I've yet to find someone who can confirm they did.

We do know that Quinn met H.P. Lovecraft on several occasions when Lovecraft was visiting New York. Lovecraft thought well of him, but not of his work, and it is not hard to find comments about him in the various volumes of Lovecraft's letters. For example, HPL wrote the following to author J. Vernon Shea on July 30, 1931:

> I met Quinn twice during my stay in N.Y. & find him exceedingly intelligent and likeable. He is 44 years old but looks rather less than that. Increasingly stocky, dark, with a closely-clipped moustache. He is first of all a shrewd business man & freely affirms that he manufactures hokum to order for market demands—in contrast to the artist, who seeks sincere expression as the result of an obscure inward necessity.

This was not the only time Lovecraft spoke poorly of Quinn's contributions to the magazine. To author Robert Bloch he wrote, in mid-November 1934, that "de Grandin is merely a puppet moulded according to cheap popular demand—he represents nothing of Quinn." To writer Natalie H. Wooley, on November 22, 1934, he bemoaned the "devolution" of various writers—including Quinn, Price, Edmond Hamilton, A. Merritt, and many others—who succumbed to the "insidious cheapness of the pulp magazine tradition" so that they lost their status as "sincere writers" and came across as mere "herd-caterers." And again, to Bloch on May 9, 1934, he said: "Quinn, also, has frankly sold his soul to Mammon—but he could turn out magnificent stuff if he would." And so on in a similar vein. There is no need to quote any more.

Since we tend to view the entire *Weird Tales* scene through a Lovecraftian lens, it has become perceived wisdom over the years that Quinn was a disinterested craftsman who just typed out his stories and sent them in, and Farnsworth Wright bought them like yard-goods. No interaction, just pure business.

What's wrong with this picture is that it is not entirely true. It is not even mostly true. Fortunately, we *do* get a glimpse from Quinn's point of view in a series of letters he wrote to the artist Virgil Finlay between January and October of 1937. This correspondence takes up thirty-two pages in *Fantasy Collector's Annual, 1975*, edited and published by Gerry de la Ree.

The personality revealed in the letters is not quite what we'd expect from the dignified figure we see in the few surviving photos of Quinn. He is informal, slangy, maybe even a little pushy. He uses words like "feller" and signs himself with his initials, always drawing little smiley faces inside the "Q." He also has a fairly large ego. The correspondence is prefaced with a letter from Quinn to Farnsworth Wright, in which he extolls the virtues of "The Globe of Memories" (one of his first non-de Grandin stories during the period in which he took a brief "vacation" from the mercurial Frenchman's adventures) in no uncertain terms:

Dear Wright:

Ambrose Bierce might have written

<u>THE GLOBE OF MEMORIES</u>

but he didn't. I did!

He then asks that Finlay be allowed to illustrate it, at which point his correspondence with Finlay ensues.

The letters are full of revelations, about Quinn, *Weird Tales*, and de Grandin. For all Quinn claims—"Because of my inability to visualize my characters as pictures [. . .] I don't really know what [de Grandin] looks like"—he most definitely *does* know, and later includes a drawing (that looks like it was cut from a comic strip) to specify *exactly* what his hero looks like, down to the right kind of moustache – "needle," not "fish-hook." In fact, Finlay eventually found Quinn a little irritating and a micro-manager. Sometimes Quinn says that Finlay should follow his own imagination, but at other times he is specifying how many people are in a scene, in what poses, with what costumes, etc.

What is *very* clear from these letters from the author is that de Grandin is more than the "puppet" Lovecraft supposed, caring quite a bit for how his characters were portrayed. Of course, Quinn did make a substantial amount of money from the adventures of de Grandin and Trowbridge. "For that reason, if no other, I should be fond of them," he writes. "But my liking goes deeper. I really regard them as personal friends, and it's sometimes a shock to me to realize that there is no Harrisonville, NJ, no Dr. Samuel Trowbridge, no Jules de Grandin."

That doesn't sound like a mere hack writer, does it?

Quinn was very pleased with the portraits of de Grandin and Trowbridge that Finlay produced, which were used as a standard feature for most of the pair's later appearances in *Weird Tales*. He also acquired some of Finlay's cover paintings and decorated his office with them. (These he received from Wright as gifts, since in those days pulp artists sold their work to publishers outright, never imagining it would have any resale value.)

We learn some other intriguing details: While there is no evidence that Wright ever asked for revisions, or worked with Quinn on the content of the de Grandin stories very much, we do learn that "Frozen Beauty" was originally entitled "The Snow Queen," presumably as an allusion to the fairy tale. Wright changed that. He thought it was too "highbrow."

In one of the earlier letters Quinn expresses more than passing interest in *Weird Tales* itself, repeating to Finlay in detail what he must have previously written to Wright. He wanted to redesign the magazine entirely, transforming it into a quality digest on semi-glossy paper like *Coronet* or *Reader's Digest,* which would appeal to a more general audience. He had very exact ideas about what kinds of art should be used, how they should be placed, etc. There's no record of how Wright responded, but in any case, most of Quinn's suggestions came to nothing. *Weird Tales* remained a pulp, its appearance (largely thanks to Finlay) steadily improving in the late '30s, but another of Quinn's ideas did come to fruition. It was he who suggested to Wright that Finlay should be given a full page each issue to illustrate a scene or image from famous fantastic or weird poems. Finlay's "poetry page" soon became one of the most popular features in *Weird Tales*.

Of course, one of the reasons *Weird Tales* never transcended the pulp category was lack of money. Quinn was fully aware of the privations the magazine had suffered in the depths of the Depression. It was, he explained to Finlay (who was younger, and had not been involved with the magazine at the time), "a minor miracle" that Wright and his associates were able to keep *Weird Tales* going at all.

How *Weird Tales* survived this crisis is a particularly dramatic story, which Quinn didn't tell Finlay. The details were only discovered recently, and described in an essay by scholar Scott Connors, "*Weird Tales* and the Great Depression," which was published in *The Robert E. Howard Reader*, an anthology I edited in 2010. It seems that, in order to pay printing bills as the magazine was struggling to establish itself, publisher J.C. Henneberger sold the majority interest in *Weird Tales* to the printer, one B. Cornelius. The understanding was that once the magazine became profitable, Cornelius would be repaid and he would return the stock to Henneberger.

Then the Depression hit. But, believing the claims of then-president Herbert Hoover that prosperity was "just around the corner," Henneberger and his editor Farnsworth Wright instead decided to double down, launching a companion magazine, *Oriental Stories*, with its first issue dated October-November 1930. Customarily, distributors held back payments for three issues of a magazine, and so they wouldn't pay for any sales of *Oriental Stories* until a fourth issue was delivered. Until that fourth issue, *Weird Tales* would have to earn enough to support both itself and *Oriental*.

Cornelius, the printer who had been sold a majority interest in *Weird Tales*, had been patient. Depression-era pulp printers often had to run on credit because otherwise they might have nothing to print and not even the promise of income, and would have to let their employees go. But enough was enough, and sometime in late 1931, Cornelius ordered Henneberger and Wright to shut *Weird Tales* down. That could very well have been the end of the magazine, except that Wright was able to convince Cornelius that he had in inventory two serials strong enough to save the magazine.

One was *Tam, Son of Tiger* an imitation Tarzan novel by Otis Adelbert Kline, which in theory could draw some buyers away from *Argosy*, where that sort of thing usually appeared.

The other was *The Devil's Bride* by Seabury Quinn, easily the longest Jules de Grandin story ever written, which was ultimately stretched out over six issues, February to July 1932. In Quinn's story was something reliably popular enough to keep *Weird Tales* going, and it eventually did make it through, if only barely, to the other side of the Great Depression. When you consider that Robert E. Howard still had his best *Weird Tales* material in front of him (the first Conan story, "The Phoenix on the Sword," appeared in the December 1932 issue), and that all of the *Weird Tales* work of C.L. Moore, Robert Bloch, and many others was yet to come, it is worth pausing to reflect on how much fantastic literature owes to Seabury Quinn's excitable Frenchman.

The Devil's Bride is, of course, quintessential pulp fiction. Here Quinn pulls out all the stops. Yet another imperiled society girl (a standby in the de Grandin series) is kidnapped at her wedding rehearsal by a truly fiendish cult of Yezidees, Satanists, Communists, and who knows what else. There ensue gory murders, a raid on a Black Mass, and, at the climax, a police and army raid on an even larger cult orgy in West Africa, which is conducted with such violence that it makes Inspector Legrasse's adventure in the Louisiana swamp, from Lovecraft's "The Call of Cthulhu," look like the issuance of a parking ticket. Don't forget the family curse. The girl in question is the descendant of a Yezidee promised to Satan. A family heirloom, a "bridal girdle," is partially composed of human skin. Various young ladies end up unclad throughout the course of the story (Quinn certainly knew how to get his tales featured on the covers of *Weird Tales*, which in this period almost always featured nudes).

What more could any pulp reader want? *The Devil's Bride* is lurid as all get-out, containing weird cultism, thrilling action, kidnappings, escapes, a sinister wolf-master, a naked lady found crucified in a convent garden, jungle adventure, massive slaughter . . . just about everything short of dinosaurs and a giant ape. There is also more characterization than usual. If we are to be in the company of Jules de Grandin for six issues, we must inevitably learn more about him, including the surprising tale of the lost love of his youth.

It might not have been "literature," but it was certainly what kept the customers coming back, month after month. *The Devil's Bride* was an important expansion of the character's universe for readers, as well as a well-timed financial life preserver for the magazine. The Jules de Grandin series in general was unquestionably one of the major pillars of *Weird Tales*, and new tales of the

Frenchman appeared so frequently that he very much helped to define what *Weird Tales* was.

Seabury Quinn *was*, of course, a professional writer. He did this for a living, particularly after he lost his *Casket and Sunnyside* gig. Times were hard. We know that after the worst of the Depression he, along with many other writers, took a pay cut and was sometimes paid late. He explained to Finlay in 1937 that he was no longer enjoying the luxurious rates he had in 1928. He wrote for other magazines, too—detective stories, jungle stories, a few historicals for *Golden Fleece* in the late '30s—but it's clear that for Quinn, *Weird Tales* and Jules de Grandin were something special.

They still are. That is why you are holding this volume in your hands. This isn't throw-away writing. It has survived.

THE
DARK
ANGEL

The Lost Lady

1. The Stranger from Cambodia

FOUR MILES AWAY, WHERE Hopkins Point light thrust its thin rapier of luminance into the relentless advance of the sea-mist, a fog-horn hooted with dolorous persistence. Half a mile out, rising and falling rhythmically with the undulation of an ocean which crept forward with a flat, oily swell, a bell-buoy sounded a warning mournful as a funeral toll. "Clank-a-clang—clang-a-clang!" it repeated endlessly.

Moneen McDougal glanced at the fog-obscured window, half in annoyance, half in what seemed nervous agitation. "I wish it would stop," she exclaimed petulantly; "that everlasting clang-clang is getting on my nerves. A storm would be preferable to that slow, never-ending tolling. I can't stand it!" She shook her narrow shoulders in a shudder of repugnance.

Her big husband smiled tolerantly. "Don't let it get you, old dear," he counseled. "We'll have a cupful of wind before morning, that'll change the tempo for you. This fog won't last; never does this time o' year." To us he added in explanation:

"Moneen's all hot and bothered tonight, her colored boy friend—"

"Dougal!" his wife cut in sharply. "I tell you he wasn't a Negro. He was a Chinaman—an Oriental of some kind, at any rate. Ugh!" she trembled at the recollection. "He sickened me!"

Turning to me, she continued, "I drove into Harrisonville this afternoon, Doctor Trowbridge, and just as I was leaving Braunstein's he stepped up to me. I felt something pawing at my elbow without realizing what it was; then a hand gripped my arm and I turned round. A tall, thin man with a perfect death's-head face was bending forward, grinning right into my eyes. I started back, and he tightened his grip on my arm with one hand and reached the other out to stroke my face. Then I screamed. I couldn't help it, for the touch of those long, bony fingers fairly sickened me.

"Fortunately the doorman happened to notice us just then, and came running to my assistance. The strange man leaned over and whispered something I couldn't understand in my ear, then made off through the crowd of shoppers before the doorman could lay hold of him. *B-r-r-rh!*" she shuddered again; "I can't get the memory of that face out of my mind. It was too dreadful."

"Oh, he was probably just some harmless nut," Dougal McDougal consoled with a laugh. "You should feel complimented, my dear. Cheerio, Christmas is coming. Licker up!" He poured himself a glassful of Napoleon brandy and raised it toward us with a complimentary gesture.

Jules de Grandin replaced his demitasse on the low tabouret of Indian mahogany and decanted less than a thimbleful of the brandy into a tiny crystal goblet. "*Exquis*," he pronounced, passing the little glass beneath his narrow nostrils, savoring the ruby liquor's bouquet as a languishing poet might inhale a rose from his lady-love's girdle. "*C'est sans comparaison. Madame, Monsieur*—to you. May you have a truly *Joyeux Noël*." He inclined his head toward our hostess and host in turn, then drained his glass with ritualistic solemnity.

"Oh, but it won't be Christmas for three whole days yet, Doctor de Grandin," Moneen protested, "and Dougal—the horrid old thing—won't tell me what my gift's to be!"

"Night after tomorrow is *la veille de Noël*," de Grandin reminded with a smile as he refilled his glass, "and we can not be too forehanded with good wishes, *Madame*."

Dougal McDougal and his bride sat opposite each other across the resined logs that blazed in the wide, marble-manteled fireplace—the cunningly modernized fireplace from a vandalized French château—he, tall, long-limbed, handsome in a dark, bleak, discontented fashion (a trick of nature and heredity, for by temperament he was neither); she, a small, slight wisp of womanhood, the white, creamy complexion of some long-forgotten Norse ancestor combining charm with her Celtic black hair and pansy eyes, clad in a scanty *eau-de-Nil* garment, swinging one boyishly-slim leg to display its perfection of cobweb silken sheath and Paris slipper. The big, opulent living-room matched both of them. Electric lamps under painted shades spilled pools of light on bizarre little tables littered with unconsidered trifles—cigarette boxes, bridge-markers, ultra-modern magazines—the deep mahogany bookshelves occupying recesses each side of the mantelpieces hoarded current bestsellers and standard works of poetry indiscriminately, a grand piano stood in the deep oriel window's bay, the radio was cunningly camouflaged in a charming old cabinet of Chinese Chippendale; here and there showed the blurred blue, mulberry and red of priceless old china and the dwarfed perfection of exquisitely chosen miniatures in frames of carved and heavily gilded wood. The room was obviously the shrine of these two, bodying forth their community of treasures, tastes and personalities.

"Give me a cigarette, darling," Moneen, curled up in her deep chair like a Persian kitten on its cushion, extended a bare, scented arm toward her big, handsome husband.

Dougal McDougal proffered her a hammered silver tray of Deities, while de Grandin, not to be outdone in gallantry, leaped nimbly to his feet, snapped his silver pocket lighter into flame and held the blue-blazing wick out to her till she set her cigarette aglow.

"Beg pardon, sir," Tompkins, McDougal's irreproachable butler, bowed deferentially from the arched doorway, "there's a gentleman here—a foreign gentleman—who insists on seeing Doctor de Grandin at once. He won't give his name, sir,—"

Quick steps sounded on the polished floor of the hall and an undersized individual shouldered the butler aside with a lack of ceremony I should never have essayed, then glanced menacingly about the room.

On second glance I realized my impression of the visitor's diminutive stature was an error. Rather, he was a giant in miniature. His very lack of height gave the impression of material equilibrium and tremendous physical force. His shoulders were unusually broad and his chest abnormally deep. One felt instinctively that the thews of his arms were massive as those of a gladiator and his torso sheathed in muscle like that of a professional wrestler. A mop of iron-gray hair was brushed back in a pompadour from his wide brow, and a curling white mustache adorned his upper lip, while a wisp of white imperial depended from his sharply pointed chin. But the most startling thing about him was his cold, pale face—a face with the pallor of a statue—from which there burned a pair of big, deep-set dark eyes beneath horizontal parentheses of intensely black and bushy brows.

Once more the stranger gazed threateningly about; then, as his glowing eyes rested on de Grandin, he announced ominously: "I am here!"

Jules de Grandin's face went blank with amazement, almost with dismay, then lit up with an expression of diabolical savagery. "*Morbleau*, it is the assassin!" he exclaimed incredulously, leaping from his seat and putting himself in a posture of defense.

"*Apache!*" the stranger ground the insult between strong, white teeth which flashed with animal-like ferocity.

"Stealer of superannuated horses!" de Grandin countered, advancing a threatening step toward the other.

"Pickpocket, burglar, highwayman, cut-throat, everything which is execrable!" shouted the intruder with a furious scowl as he shook clenched fists in de Grandin's face.

"*Embrasse moi!*" they cried in chorus, and flung themselves into each other's arms like sweethearts reunited after long parting. For a moment they embraced, kissing each other's cheeks, pounding each other's shoulders with affectionate fists, exchanging the deadliest insults in gamin French. Then, remembering himself, de Grandin put the other from him and turned to us with a ceremonious bow.

"Monsieur and Madame McDougal, Doctor Trowbridge," he announced with stilted formality, "I have the very great honor to present Monsieur Georges Jean Joseph Marie Renouard, *Inspecteur du Service de Sûreté Général*, and the cleverest man in all the world—except myself. Georges, abominable stealer-of-blind-men's sous that you are, permit that I introduce Monsieur and Madame Dougal McDougal, my host and hostess, and Doctor Samuel Trowbridge, skilled physician and as noble a fellow as ever did honor to the sacred name of friend. It is with him I have lived since coming to this country."

Inspecteur Renouard bent forward in a jack-knife bow as he raised Moneen's hand to his lips, bowed again to McDougal, then took my hand in a grip which nearly paralysed the muscle of my forearm.

"I am delight'," he assured us. "Monsieur Trowbridge, your taste in permitting this one to reside beneath your roof is execrable, no less, but he is clever—almost as clever as I—and doubtless he has imposed on you to make you think him an honest fellow. *Eh bien*, I have arrived at last like Nemesis to spoil his little game. Me, I shall show him in his true colors, no less!" Having thus unburdened himself, he lapsed into a seat upon the divan, accepted a liqueur, folded his large white hands demurely in his lap and gazed from one of us to the other with a quick, bird-like glance which seemed to take minute inventory of everything it fell upon.

"And what fortunate wind blows you here, *mon brave?*" de Grandin asked at length. "Well I know it is no peaceful mission you travel on, for you were ever the stormy petrel. Tell me, is excitement promised? I grow weary of this so uneventful American life."

"*Tiens*," Renouard laughed. "I think we shall soon see much excitement—plenty—*mon petit coq*. As yet I have not recovered my land legs after traveling clear about the earth in search of one who is the Devil's other self, but tomorrow the hunt begins afresh, and then—who knows? Yes. Certainly." He nodded gravely to us in turn; then: "Clear from Cambodia I come, my friend, upon the trail of the cleverest and wickedest of clever-wicked fellows—and a lady."

"A lady?" de Grandin's blue eyes lit up with interest. "You amaze me."

"Prepare for more amazement, then, *mon vieux*; she is a runaway lady, young, beautiful, *ravissante*"—he gathered his fingers at his lips and wafted a kiss gently toward the ceiling—"a runaway *bayadère* from the great temple of Angkor, no less!"

"*Mordieu*, you excite me! What has she done?"

"Run away, decamped; skipped!"

"*Précisément*, great stupid-head; but why should you, an inspector of the secret police, pursue her?"

"She ran away from the temple—" Renouard began again, and:

"*Bête*, repeat that so senseless statement but one more time and I shall give myself the pleasure of twisting your entirely empty head from off your deformed shoulders!" de Grandin broke in furiously.

"—and he whom I seek ran after her," his colleague continued imperturbably. "*Voilà tout*. It is once again a case of *cherchez la femme*."

"Oh, how interesting!" Moneen exclaimed. "Won't you tell us more, Inspector Renouard?"

Frenchmen are seldom importuned in vain by pretty women. The Inspector was no exception. "Do you know Cambodia, by any unhappy chance?" he asked, flashing his gleaming eyes appreciatively at the length of silk-sheathed leg Moneen displayed as she sat one foot doubled under her, the other hanging toward the floor.

We shook our heads, and he continued: "It is the hottest spot upon the earth, *mes amis*—hot and wet. Always the humidity hovers near one hundred per cent. Your clothes are soaked with perspiration in a few minutes, and will not dry out overnight. Sheets and bedding are useless for the same reason, and one learns to sleep on tightly stretched matting on bare boards. Clothing mildews and wounds never heal. It is the only land where snakes large enough to kill by constriction are also venomous, and its spiders' bites make that of the tarantula seem harmless by comparison. The natives sleep all day and emerge at night like bats, cats and owls. It is a land unfit for white men."

"But this temple dancer—this Oriental girl?" Moneen insisted. "Why do you follow her here?"

"She is no Oriental, *Madame*; she, too, is white."

"White? A temple dancing-girl? How—"

The Inspector lit a cigarette before replying: "The Angkor temple is the great cathedral of Buddhism in Southern Asia. But it is a Buddhism gone to seed and overgrown with strange rites, even as the Lamist Buddhism of Tibet is bastardized. Very well. This temple of Angkor is a vast stone structure with sculptured terraces, fountains and houses for the priests and sacred dancers. All ceremonies are held outdoors, the terraces being the scene of the rites. The debased Buddhism is a religion of the dance. Its services are largely composed of most beautiful and extremely intricate dances which often last for days on end, nor are they meaningless or merely ritualistic. By no means. Like those of the devil-dancers of the North, these ceremonies of the South have meaning—definite meaning. Every movement of arms, legs, head, eye and lips, down to the very angle of hands and feet, conveys a word or phrase or sentence to those who watch and understand as clearly as the soldier's semaphore flags convey a meaning to the military observer. It is kind of stenography of motion.

"Now it can easily be imagined that such skill is not acquired overnight. No, the dancers are trained almost from the cradle. They are under the absolute control of the priests. The smallest infraction of a temple rule, or even the whim of a holy man, and sentence is forthwith passed and the unfortunate dancer dies slowly and in circumstances of great elaboration and discomfort.

"So much by way of prologue. Now for this runaway young lady: Twenty years ago a young and earnest man from your country named Joseph Crownshield came to Cambodia to preach the Word of God as expounded by authority of the Mennonite Church to the benighted followers of Buddha. *Hélas*, while his zeal was great, his judgment was small. He committed two great errors, first in coming to Cambodia at all, second in having with him his young wife.

"The priests of Angkor did not relish the things which this Monsieur Crownshield said. They relished even less what he did, for he was earnest, and began to convert the natives, and gifts for the great temple were less plentiful.

"The young man died. A snake bit him as he was about to enter his bath. Snakes have no business in the bathroom, but—his household servants were, of course, Cambodians, and the priesthood numbered expert snake-charmers among its personnel. At any rate, he died.

"Misfortunes seldom come singly. Two days later the church and parsonage burned down, and in the smoking ruins was found the body of a woman. Madame Crownshield? Perhaps. Who can say? At all events, the body was interred beside the missionary's and life went on as usual. But sixteen years later came rumors to the French *gendarmerie* of a dancer in the temple, a girl who danced like a flame in the wind, like a moonbeam on flowing water, like the twinkling of a star at midnight. And, rumor said, though her hair was black it was fine as split-silk, not coarse like that of the native women, and her skin was fair as milk and her eyes blue as violets in springtime.

"Devotees of the temple are not supposed to speak to outsiders; the penalty of an unguarded tongue is lingering death, but—the ear of the *Sûreté* is keen and its arm is very long. We learned that rumor was well founded. Within the temple there was such a one, and she was even as rumor described her. Though she never emerged from her dwelling-place within the sacred edifice, her presence there was definitely established. Unquestionably she was white; equally beyond question she had no business where she was, but—" He paused, spreading his hands and puffing our his cheeks. "It is not wise to trifle with the religion of the natives," he ended simply.

"But who *was* she?" Moneen asked.

"*Parbleu*, I would give my tongue to the cat if I could answer you," the Inspector returned. "The *Sûreté* found itself against a wall of stone more stubborn than that of which the temple was composed. In that God-detested land we learn much. If one fasts long enough he will hear voices and see visions. The poisons of certain drugs and the toxins of certain fevers have the same effect. Occasionally 'the Spirit of Budda' permeates the soul of a white man—more frequently a white woman—in the tropics. The accumulated toxic effect of the climate leads him—or her—to give up the materialistic, cleanly civilization of the West and retire to a life of squalor, filth and contemplation as a devotee of some Eastern faith. Had this happened here? Was this girl self-devoted as a dancer in the temple? Had her mother, perhaps, devoted herself years ago, and had the child been born and reared in the shadow of the temple idols? One wonders."

"But surely you investigated?" Moneen pursued.

"But naturally, *Madame*. I am Renouard; I do not do things by the half. No.

"To the Angkor temple I went and demanded sight of her. 'There is no such person here,' I was assured.

"'You lie,' I answered courteously, 'and unless you bring her to me forthwith, I shall come in for her.'

"*Eh bien, Messieurs*," he turned to us with a chuckle, "the Frenchman is logical. He harbors no illusions about the love of subject peoples. Nor does he seek to conciliate them. Love him they may not, but fear and respect him they must. My hint was sufficient—especially as two platoons of *gendarmerie*, a howitzer and machine-guns were there to give it point. The lady whose existence had been denied so vehemently, a moment before was straightway brought to me.

"Beyond doubt she was pure European. Her hair was black and gently waved, her skin was white as curdled cream, her eyes were blue as—*Parbleu*, *Madame*"—he gazed at Moneen McDougal with wide-open eyes, as though he saw her for the first time—"she was much like you!"

I thought I saw a shiver of terror ripple through Moneen's lithe form, but her husband's hearty laugh relieved the tension. "Well, who was she?" he asked.

"*Le bon Dieu* knows," Renouard returned. "Although I made the ape-faced priests retire so that we might converse unheard, they had either terrified the girl that she dared not speak or she was actually unable to inform me. I spoke to her in every language that I know—and they are many—but only the lingo of the Khmer could she understand or speak. Her name, she said, was Thi-bah, she was a sacred dancer in the temple, and she remembered no other world. She had always lived there. Of her parentage she could not speak, for father or mother she had never known. And at the end she joined hands together palm to palm, the fingers pointing downward—which is the symbol of submission—and begged I would permit her to go back to her place among the temple women. *Sacré nom!* What is one to do in such circumstances? Nothing!

"That is what I did. I retired in chagrin and she returned to her cell within the temple."

"*Bien oui*," de Grandin tweaked the needle points of his little blond mustache and grinned impishly at the Inspector, "but a tale half told is poorly told, my friend. What of this other one, this so clever-devilish fellow whom you trail while he trails the runaway lady? *Hein?*"

Renouard joined his square-tipped fingers end to end and pursed his lips judicially. "*Oui-da*," he admitted, "that is the other half of the tale, indeed. Very well; *regardez-moi bien*: In Cochin China in the days before the Great War there lived a certain gentleman named Sun Ah Poy. He was, as you may gather from his name, Chinese, but his family had been resident in Saigon for generations. The Sun family is so numerous in China that to bear the name means little more than for a Frenchman to be called DuPont, or an Englishman Smith or an Irishman Murphy. Nevertheless, all these names have had their famous representatives, as you will recall when you think of your great colonizer, Captain John Smith, and the illustrious Albert of the present generation. Also you will remember China's first president was Doctor Sun Yat Sen.

"This Sun Ah Poy was no shopkeeping son of a coolie father, he was an educated gentleman, a man of great wealth, taught by private tutors in the learning of the East and holding a diploma from the Sorbonne. His influence with the native population was phenomenal, and his opinions were eagerly sought and highly regarded by the *conseil privé*. He wore the ribbon of the Legion of Honor for distinguished service to the Republic. This, then, was the man who a few days before the Armistice went up-country to supervise an elephant hunt.

"A savage old tusker had been roped between two trained beasts and was being led into the stockade when, without warning, he broke his fetters and charged. The elephant on which Doctor Sun was seated was directly in the maddened brute's path. In a moment the runaway beast had seized the unfortunate man in his trunk, snatched him from his saddle and hurled him forty feet through the air, crashing him into the wall of the stockade.

"Medicine and surgery did their best. Sun Ah Poy lived, *hélas!* When he rose from his hospital bed it was with body and mind hopelessly crippled. The physical injury was apparent to all, the mental ailment we were to find out to our cost. Insubordination broke out among the natives, French officers were openly disobeyed, criminals were permitted to escape from prison, laborers on the public works were assaulted and beaten, sometimes killed; the process of criminal jurisprudence broke down completely, for witnesses could not be made to testify; *gendarmes* went forth to make arrests and came back feet first; examining magistrates who prosecuted investigations with honest thoroughness died mysteriously, and most opportunely for the criminals—official records of the police disappeared from their files overnight. It was all too obvious that outlawry had raised its red standard and hurled defiance at authority.

"In Paris this would have been bad. In Asia it was unspeakable, for the white man must keep his prestige at all costs. Once he 'loses face' his power over the natives is gone. What was he to do?

"At length, like men of sound discretion, the Government put the case in my charge. I considered it. From all angles I viewed it. What did I see? A single dominating intelligence seemed guiding all the lawlessness, an intelligence which knew beforehand what plans Government made. I cast about for suspects, and my eye fell on three, Sun Ah Poy and two others. He seemed least likely of the three, but he enjoyed our confidence, and it lay within his power to thwart our plans if he so desired. Therefore I laid my trap. I called three councils of war, to each of which a different suspect was invited. At these councils I outlined my plans for raiding certain known centers of the criminal elements. The first two raids were successful. We caught our game red-handed. The third raid was a glorious failure. Only a brightly glowing campfire and a deserted encampment waited for the *gendarmes*. It was of this raid I had spoken to Doctor Sun.

"Proof? Not in English courts, nor American; but this was under French jurisdiction. We do not let the guilty escape through fear of affronting the possibly innocent. No. I issued a warrant for Doctor's Sun's apprehension.

"That evening, as I sat within my cabinet, I heard a clicking-scratching on the matting-covered floor. *Sapristi!* Toward me there charged full-tilt a giant tarantula, the greatest, most revolting-looking spider I had ever seen! Now, it is seldom that these brutes attack a man who does not annoy them; that they should deliberately attack an inoffensive, passive person is almost beyond experience; yet though I sat quiescent at my table, this one made for me as though he had a personal feud to settle. Fortunately for me, I was wearing my belt, and with a single motion I leaped upon the table, drew my pistol and fired. My bullet crushed the creature and I breathed again. But that night as I rode home to my quarters a second poison-spider dropped from a tree-bough into my rickshaw. I struck it with my walking-stick, and killed it, but my escape was of the narrowest. When I went into my bathroom I found a small but very venomous serpent coiled, ready to receive me.

"It struck. I leaped. *Grand Dieu*, I leaped like a monkey-on-a-stick, and came down with my heels upon its head. I triumphed, but my nerves were badly shaken.

"My men returned. Sun Ah Poy was nowhere to be found. He had decamped. Who warned him? My native clerk? Perhaps. The tenacles of this octopus I sought to catch stretched far, and into the most unexpected places.

"I walked in constant terror. Everywhere I went I carried my revolver ready; even in my house I went about with a heavy cane in my hand, for I knew not what instant silent death would come striking at my feet or dropping on me from the ceiling.

"At length my spies reported progress. A new priest, a crippled man, was in the Angkor temple. He was enamored of the white dancer, they said. It was well. Where the lioness lairs the lion will surely linger. I went to take him, nor did I confide my plans to any but Frenchmen.

"*Hélas*, the love which makes the world to move also spoiled my coup.

"The Khmer are an effeminate, lascivious, well-nigh beardless race. All traces of virility have vanished from them, and craft had replaced strength in their dealings. Thi-bak, the white-girl dancer, had lived her life within the confines of the temple, and except myself, I doubt that she had seen a single white man in her whole existence—till Monsieur Archibald Hildebrand appeared. He was young, handsome, vigorous, mustached—all that the men she knew were not. Moreover, he was of her race, and like calls to like in Cambodia as in other places. How he met her I do not know, nor how he made himself understood, for she spoke no English, he no Khmer; but a gold key unbars all doors, and the young man from America had gold in plenty. Also love makes mock of lexicons and speaks its own language, and they had love, these two. *Enfin*, they met, they loved; they eloped.

"It may seem strange that this could be, for the whole world knows that temple-women of the East are well-nigh as carefully guarded as inmates of the zenana. Elsewhere, yes; but in Cambodia, no! There night is day and day is night. In the torrid, steaming heat of day the population sleeps, or tries to, and only fleeing criminals and foreigners unaccustomed to the land are abroad. One might mount the temple terraces and steal the head from off a carven Buddha and never find a temple guard to say him nay, provided he went by daylight. So it was here. Thi-bah the dancer had but to creep forth from her cell on soft-stepping, unshod feet, meet her lover in the sunlight and go away.

"Two days before I arrived at Angkor with handcuffs already warmed to fit the wrists of him I sought, Monsieur Hildebrand and this Thi-bah set sail from Saigon on a *Messageries Maritimes* steamship. One day later Doctor Sun Ah Poy shook the dust of Cochin China from his feet. He did it swiftly, silently. He dropped down the Saigon River in a sampan, was transferred to a junk at sea and vanished—where, whither?"

"Here?" we asked in breathless chorus.

"Where else? The man is crazed with love, or passion, or whatever you may choose to call it. He is fabulously rich, infinitely resourceful, diabolically wicked and inordinately vain, as all such criminal lunatics are. Where the moth of his desire flutters the spider will not be long absent. Although he did not travel as quickly as the fleeing lovers, he will soon arrive. When he does I have grave fears for the health of Monsieur Hildebrand and his entire family. They are thorough, these men from the East, and their blood feuds visit the sins of the sons upon the ancestors unto the third and fourth generation."

"Can that be *our* Archy Hildebrand, Doctor Trowbridge?" Moneen asked.

Inspector Renouard drew forth a small black-leather notebook and consulted it. "Monsieur Archibald Van Buren Hildebrand, son of Monsieur Van Rensselaer Hildebrand," he read. "Address of house: 1937 *Rue* Passaic"—he pronounced it "Pay-sa-ay"—"Harrisonville, New Jersey, E.U.A."

"Why, that *is* Archy!" Moneen exclaimed. "Oh, I hope nothing happens to—"

"Nonsense, dear," her husband cut in brusquely. "What could happen here? This is America, not Cochin China. The police—"

"*Tiens, Monsieur*," de Grandin reminded frigidly, "they also have police in Cambodia."

"Oh, yes; of course, but—"

"I hope you are correct," the little Frenchman interrupted. "Me, I do not discount anything which Inspector Renouard may say. He is no alarmist, as I very well know. *Eh bien*, you may be right. But in the meantime, a little preparedness can do no harm."

2. Doctor Sun Leaves His Card

AT MY INVITATION THE Inspector agreed to make my house his headquarters, and it was arranged that he and de Grandin share the same room. Midnight had long since struck when we bid the McDougals adieu, and began our twenty-mile drive to the city. "Remember, you're all invited here Christmas evening," Moneen reminded us at parting. "I'm expecting my sister Avis down from Holyoke and I know she'd love to meet you."

We left the fog behind us as we drove northward from the ocean, and the night was clear and cold as we whizzed through Susquehanna Avenue to my house.

"That's queer," I muttered as I bent to insert my latchkey in the lock. "Somebody must know you're here, Inpector. Here's a note for you." I picked up the square, white envelope which had dropped as I thrust the door open and put it in his hand.

He turned the folder over and over, inspecting the clear-cut, boldly written inscription, looking in vain for a clue to the sender. "Who can know—who could suspect that I am arrived?" he began wonderingly, but de Grandin interrupted with a chuckle.

"You are incurably the detective, *mon* Georges" he rallied. "You receive a letter. '*Parbleu*, who can have sent this?' you ask you, and thereupon you examine the address, you take tests of the ink, you consult handwriting experts. 'This is from a lady,' you say to yourself, 'and from the angle of the letters in her writing I am assured she is smitten by my manly beauty.' Thereupon you open the note, and find what? That it is a bill for long-overdue charges on your laundry, *cordieu!* Come, open it, great stupidhead. How otherwise are you to learn from whom it comes?"

"Silence, magpie!" Renouard retorted, his pale face flushing under de Grandin's mockery. "We shall see—*mon Dieu*, look!"

The envelope contained a single sheet of dull white paper folded in upon itself to form a sort of frame in which there rested a neatly engraved gentleman's visiting-card:

DR. SUN AH POY
Saigon

That was all, no other script, or print.

"*Eh bien*, he is impudent, that one!" de Grandin exclaimed, bending over his friend's shoulder to inspect the missive. "*Parbleu*, he laughs at our faces, but I think all the cards are not yet played. We shall see who laughs at whom before this game is ended, for—"

He broke off abruptly, head thrown back, delicate nostrils contracting and expanding alternately as he sniffed the air suspiciously. "Do you, too, get it?" he asked, turning from Renouard to me inquiringly.

"I think I smell of perfume, but I can't quite place it—" I began, but his exclamation cut me short.

"Drop it, *mon vieux*—unhand it, right away, at once; immediately!" he cried, seizing Renouard's wrist and fairly shaking the card from his grasp. "Ah—so; permit it to remain there," he continued, staring at the upturned square of pasteboard. "Trowbridge, Renouard, *mes amis*, I suggest you stand back—mount chairs—keep your feet well off the floor. So! That is better!"

We stared at him in open-mouthed astonishment as he barked his staccato orders, but as he matched command with obedience and mounted a chair himself after the manner of a timid housewife who sights a mouse, we followed suit.

From the shaft of his gold-headed ebony opera cane he drew the slender, wire-like sword-blade and swished it once or twice through the air, as though to test its edge. "Attend me," he commanded, fixing his level, unwinking stare on us in turn. "Like you, Friend Georges, I have lived in Cambodia. While you were still among the Riffs in Africa I went to nose out certain disaffections in Annam, and while there I kept eyes, ears and nose wide open. Certainly. Tell me, my friend—think back, think carefully—just what happened that night in Saigon when you were beset by spiders?"

Renouard's bright dark eyes narrowed in concentration. "My laundry was delayed that day," he answered at length, "the messenger had good excuses, but my white uniforms did not arrive until—*nom d'une pipe*—yes! Upon the freshly starched-and-ironed drill there hung a faint perfume, such as we smell here and now!"

"*Exactement*," de Grandin nodded. "Me, I recognized him almost immediately. He is a concentrated extract, or a synthetic equivalent for the scent excreted by a great—and very poisonous—Cambodian spider to attract its mate. I damn suspected something of the kind when you related your experience at Monsieur McDougal's, but I did not put you to the cross-examination then lest I frighten our pretty hostess, who had already received one shock today, of which I must inform you, but this, my friends; *regardez!*"

Something squat and obscene, something like a hand amputated at the wrist, long mummified and overgrown with spiny prickles, but now endued with some kind of ghastly after-life which enabled it to flop and crawl upon bent fingers, came sliding and slithering across the floor of the hall, emerging from the darkness of my consulting-room.

"Ah-ha; ah-ha-ha, *Monsieur la Tarentule*, you have walked into *our* parlor, it would seem!" de Grandin cried exultantly. The razor-edged, needle-pointed sword whistled through the air as he flung it from his vantage-point upon the chair, stabbing through the crawling creature's globular body and pinning it to the floor. But still the dry, hairy legs fought and thrashed as the great spider sought to drag itself toward the scented card which lay a yard or so beyond it. "Wriggle, *parbleu*," de Grandin, invited mockingly as he dropped from his refuge on the chair and advanced toward the clawing monster, "wriggle, writhe and twist. Your venom will not find human flesh to poison this night. No, *pardieu!*" With a quick stamp of his heel he crushed the thing, withdrew the sword which pinioned it to the floor and wiped the steel upon the rug.

"It was fortunate for us that my nose and memory co-operated," he remarked. "He was clever, your friend Sun, *mon brave*, I grant you. The card, all smeared with perfume as it was, was addressed to you. Naturally your hands would be the first to touch it. Had we not acted as we did, you would have been a walking invitation to that one"—he nodded toward the spider's carcass—"and I do not think he would have long delayed responding. No. Assuredly you would have moved when he leaped on you and *pouf!* tomorrow, or the next day, or the next day after that at latest, we should have had the pleasure of attending a solemn high mass of requiem for you, for his bite is very poisonous."

"You don't suppose any more of those things are hiding 'round the house, do you?" I asked uncomfortably.

"I doubt it," he returned. "Renouard's friend could not have had time to pack an extensive kit before he left, and spiders and reptiles of the tropics are difficult to transport, especially in this climate. No, I think we need have small fear of a repetition of that visit, tonight, a least. Also, if there be others, the center of attraction will be the scented card. They will not trouble us unless we tread on them."

For several minutes after we had entered the study he sat in silent thought. At last: "They can not know for sure what rooms you will occupy, *mon* Georges," he remarked, "but the bathroom is always easily identified. Trowbridge, my friend, do you happen to possess such a thing as a sheet of fly-paper at this time?"

"Fly-paper?" I asked, astonished.

"But certainly, the stuff with which one catches flies," he answered, going through the pantomime of a luckless fly alighting on a sheet of tanglefoot and becoming enmeshed on it.

"I hardly think so," I replied, "but we can look in the pantry. If Nora had any left over in the autumn she probably stored it there."

We searched the pantry shelves as prospectors might hunt the hills for gold. At last, "*Triomphe*," de Grandin called from his perch upon the step-ladder. "*Eureka*, I have found it!" From the uppermost shelf he dragged a packet of some half a dozen sticky sheets.

We warmed the stuff at the furnace door, and when its adhesive surface was softened to his satisfaction de Grandin led us to the bathroom. Stealthily he pushed the door open, dropped a double row of fly-paper on the tiled floor, then with the handle of a mop, began exploring the recesses beneath the tub and behind the washstand.

We had not long to wait. Almost at the second thrust of the mop-handle a faint almost soundless hissing noise like steam escaping from a gently boiling kettle came to us, and as he probed again something like a length of old-fashioned hair watch-chain seemed to uncoil itself upon the white-tile floor and slither with the speed of light across the room. It was a dainty little thing, no thicker than a lead-pencil and scarcely longer, prettily marked with alternating bands of black, yellow and red.

"*Sacré nom!*" Renouard exclaimed. "*Le drapeau Allemand!*"

De Grandin bent still farther forward, thrust his stick fairly at the tiny, writhing reptile and endeavored to crush its small, flat head against the wall. The thing dodged with incredible quickness, and so swiftly I could scarcely follow its motion with my eye, struck once, twice, three times at the wood, and I watched it wonderingly, for it did not coil to strike, but bent its head quickly from side to side, like a steel spring suddenly set vibrating by the touch of a finger.

"You see?" he asked simply, still prodding at the flashing, scaly thing.

Although his efforts to strike it were unsuccessful, his strategy was well planned, for though it dodged his flailing stick with ease, the snake came ever nearer to the barricade of fly-paper which lay before the door. At last it streaked forward, passed fairly over the sticky paper, then gradually slowed down, writhed impotently a moment, then lay still, its little red mouth gaping, lambent tongue flickering from its lips like a wind-blown flame, low, almost inaudible hisses issuing from its throat.

"You have right, my friend, it is 'the German flag,' so called because it bears the German national colors in its markings," he told Renouard. "A tiny thing it is, yet so venomous that the lightest prick of its fangs means certain death, for aid can not be given quickly enough to counteract its poison in the blood. Also it can strike, as you noticed, and strike again without necessity for coiling. One has but to step on or near it in darkness or in light, for that matter—and he is lucky if its venom allows him time to make his tardy peace with heaven. It is of the order *elapidæ*, this little, poison thing, a small but worthy cousin of the king cobra, the death adder and the tiger snake of Australia."

He bore the fly-paper with its helpless prisoner to the cellar and flung it into the furnace. "*Exeunt omnes,*" he remarked as the flames destroyed the tiny cylinder of concentrated death. "Die you must eventually, Friend Georges, but it was not written that you should die by snake-bite this night. No. Your friend Doctor Sun is clever, but so is Jules de Grandin, and I am here. Come, let us go to bed. It is most fatiguing, this oversetting of Doctor Sun's plans for your American reception, my friend."

3. A Lost Lady

THE DAY DAWNED CRISP and cold, with a tang of frost and hint of snow in the air. My guests were in high spirits, and did ample justice to the panned sole, waffles and honey in the comb which Nora McGinnis had prepared for breakfast. Renouard, particularly, was in a happy mood, for the joy the born man-hunter takes in his work was fairly overflowing in him as he contemplated the game of hide-and-seek about to commence.

"First of all," he announced as he scraped the last remaining spot of honey from his plate, "I shall call at the *préfecture de police* and present my credentials. They will help me; they will recognize me. Yes."

"Undoubtlessly they will recognize you, *mon enfant*," de Grandin agreed with a nod. "None could fail to do so." Renouard beamed, but I discerned the hidden meaning of de Grandin's statement, and had all I could do to keep a sober face. Innate good taste, cosmopolitan experience and a leaning toward the English school of tailoring marked Jules de Grandin simply as a more than ordinarily well-dressed man wherever he might be; Renouard, by contrast, could never be mistaken for other than what he was, an efficient officer of the *gendarmerie* out of uniform, and the trade mark of his nationality was branded indelibly on him. His rather snugly fitting suit was that peculiarly horrible shade of blue beloved of your true Frenchman, his shirt was striped with alternate bands of blue and white, his cravat was a thing to give a haberdasher a violent headache, and his patent leather boots with their round rubber heels tapered to sharp and most uncomfortable-looking points.

"But of course," he told us, "I shall say to them, *Messieurs*, if you have here a stout fellow capable of assisting me, I beg you will assign him to this case. I greatly desire the assistance of—"

"Sergeant Costello," Nora McGinnis announced as she appeared in the breakfast room door, the big, red-headed Irish detective towering behind her.

"Ah, welcome, *mon vieux*," de Grandin cried, rising and extending a cordial hand to the caller. "A Merry Christmas to you."

"An' th' same to ye sor, an' ye, too, gentlemen," Costello returned, favoring Renouard and me with a rather sickly grin.

"How now? You do not say it heartily," de Grandin said as he turned to introduce Renouard. "You are in trouble? Good. Tell us; we shall undoubtlessly be able to assist you."

"I'm hopin' so, sor," the Sergeant returned as he drew up a chair and accepted a cup of steaming coffee. "I'm afther needin' help this mornin'."

"A robbery, a murder, blackmail, kidnaping?" de Grandin ran through the catalogue of crime. "Which is it, or is it a happy combination of all?"

"Mebbe so, sor, I'm not quite sure yet meself," Costello replied. "Ye see, 'twas early this mornin' it happened, an' I ain't got organized yet, so to speak. It were like this, sor:

"A Miss Brindell come over to Harrisonville on th' six o'clock train. She wuz comin' to visit her sister who lives down on the South Shore, an' they hadn't expected her so early, so there's no one to meet her when she gits to th' station. She knows about where her brother-in-law's house is over to Mary's Landin', so she hops in a taxi an' starts there. 'Twere a twenty-mile drive, sor, but she's satisfied wid th' price, so, th' cabby don't argue none wid her.

"Well, sors, th' taxi has hardly started from th' depot when alongside runs another car, crowds 'im to th' curb an' dishes his wheel. Th' cabby ain't too well pleased wid that, ye may be sure, so he starts to get down an' express his opinion o' th' felly as done it when *wham!* sumpin hits him on th' coco an' he goes down fer th' count."

"The *comte?*" Renouard interjected. "Where was this nobleman, and why should the chauffeur descend for him?"

"Silence, *mon brave*, it is an American idiom, I will explain later," de Grandin bade. To Costello: "Yes, my Sergeant, and what then?"

"Well, sor, th' next thing th' pore felly knows he's in Casualty Horspittle wid a bandage round his head an' his cab's on th' way to th' police pound. He tells us he had a second's look at th' guy that crowned 'im, an—"

"I protest!" Renouard broke in. "I understood you said he was struck with a *massue*, now I am told he was crowned. It is most confus—"

"*Imbécile*, be silent!" de Grandin ordered savagely. "Because you speak the English is no reason for you to flatter yourself that you understand American. Later I shall instruct you. Meantime, keep fast hold upon your tongue while we talk. Proceed, Sergeant, if you please."

"He got a glimpse o' th' felly that K.O.'d him, sor, an' he swore it were a Chinaman. We're holdin' 'im, sor, for his story seems fishy to me. I've been on th' force, harness bull an' fly cop, since th' days when Teddy Roos-velt—God rest his noble soul!—wuz President, an' though we've a fair-sized Chinatown here an' th' monks gits playful now an' then an' shoots each other up or carves their initials in each other wid meat-cleavers, I've never known 'em to mix it wid white folks, an' never in me livin' days have I heard of 'em stealin' white gur-rls, sor. I know they tells some funny tales on 'em, but me personal experience has been that th' white gur-rls as goes wid a Chinaman goes o' their own free will an' accord an' not because annybody steals 'em. So—"

"What is it you say, she was kidnaped?" de Grandin interrupted.

"Looks kind o' that way, sor. We can't find hide nor hair o' her, an'—"

"But you know her name. How is that?"

"That's part o' th' funny business, sor. Her grips an' even her handbag wuz all in th' taxi when we went through it, an' in 'em we found letters to identify her as Miss Avis Brindell, who'd come to visit her brother-in-law an' sister, Mr. an' Mrs. Dougal McDougal, at their house at Mary's Landin'; so—"

"*Nom d'un chou-fleur*, do you tell me so?" de Grandin gasped. "Madame McDougal's sister kidnaped by Orientals? *Ha*, can it be possible? One wonders."

"What's that, sor?"

"I think your taximan is innocent, my friend, but I am glad you have him readily available," de Grandin answered. "Come, let us go interview him right away, immediately; at once."

Mr. Sylvester McCarty, driver of Purple Cab 188672, was in a far from happy frame of mind when we found him in the detention ward of Casualty Hospital. His day had started inauspiciously with the wreck of his machine, the loss of a more than usually large fare, considerable injury to his person, finally with the indignity of arrest. "It's a weepin' shame, that's what it is!" he told us as he finished the recital of his woes. "I'm an honest man, sir, an'—"

"Agreed, by all means," de Grandin interrupted soothingly. "That is why we come to you for help, my old one. Tell us, if you will, just what occurred this morning—describe the cowardly miscreant who struck you down before you had a chance to voice your righteous indignation. I am sure we can arrange for your release from durance."

McCarty brightened. "It's hard to tell you much about it, sir," he answered, "fer it all happened so quick-like I hardly had time to git me bearin's. After I'm crowded to th' curb an' me wheel's dished, I sees th' other car is jammed right smack agin me, an' just as I turns round I hears me fare holler, 'Leave me be; take yer hands off'n me!'

"Wid that I jumps down an' picks up me crank-handle, fer if there's goin to be a argyment, I figures on bein' prepared. I on'y gits one eye-flash at 'em, though, sir. There's a queer-lookin' sort o' gink settin' at th' wheel o' th' other car—a brown-faced guy, not colored nor yet not quite like a Chinee, but more like some o' them Fillypinos ye see around sometimes, ye know. He's all muf-fled up in a fur coat wid th' collar turned up around his chin an' his cap pulled down over his eyes, so I can't git much of a slant on him. But just as I starts in to tell him what sort o' people I think his family wuz, up hops another coffee-an'-cream-colored son-of-a-gun an' *zingo!* let's me have a bop over th' bean that makes me see all th' stars there is, right in broad daylight. I goes over like th' kingpin when a feller rolls a strike, but just before I goes to sleep I sees th' guy that smacked me down an' another one hustlin' th' young lady out o' me cab into th' other car; then th' chauffeur steps on her an' rolls away, leavin' me flat-ter'n a pancake. Then I goes out like a light an' th' next thing I knows I'm layin' here in th' horsepittle wid a bandage round me dome an' th' nurse is sayin', 'Sit up, now, an' drink this.'"

"U'm?" de Grandin regarded him gravely. "And did you notice the make of car which fouled you?"

"Not rightly, sir. But it was big an' long—a limousine. I thought it wuz a Rolls, though it might o' been a Renault or Issorta—I don't think it wuz an American car."

"Very good. And one presumes it is too much to hope you had opportunity to note the number?"

"I *did* that, sir. We gits camera-eyed in this racket, an' th' first thing we do when anyone fouls us is to look at his number. It's second nature."

"Ah, fine, excellent, *parfait*. Tell me—"

"X11—7734, sir. Jersey plates."

"Ah, my prince of chauffeurs, I salute you! Assuredly, it was nobly done! Sergeant, you will surely let him go now?"

"Sure," Costello grunted. "You can run along, feller; but don't try any hide-away business. We'll know where to git ye when we want ye, don't forgit."

"Sure, you will," Mr. McCarty assured him earnestly. "Right by th' depot, chief. I'm there ter meet all th' trains."

"An' now fer th' number," Costello chuckled. "Bedad, Doctor de Grandin, sor, this case is easier than I thought. I'm sorry I bothered ye wid it, now."

"Not too fast, my friend," the Frenchman counseled. "The prudent cat does not mistake all that is white for milk."

Five minutes later Costello returned from a telephone conversation with the license bureau. "I reckon I wuz all wet, Doctor de Grandin," he admitted ruefully. "X11—7734 is th' plate o' Gleason's Grocery car. It's a Ford delivery truck, an' its plates wuz stolen last night whilst it was standin' in front o' th' store."

4. Poltergeist?

FOR A MOMENT WE stared at each other in blank consternation. "*Que diable?*" swore Renouard, grasping his tuft of beard and jerking it so violently that I feared for his chin.

"Looks that way," Costello nodded dismally, understanding the French-man's tone, if not his words.

"*Sacré nom de dix mille sales cochons!*" de Grandin exclaimed. "Why do we stand here looking ourselves out of countenance like a convention of petrified bullfrogs in the *Musée de l'Histoire Naturelle*? Let us be doing!"

"Sez you," Costello responded. "Doin' what, sor?"

"Finding them, *pardieu*. Consider: Their appearance was bizarre enough to be noted by the excellent Monsieur McCarty, even in the little minute between the collision of their vehicle and his and the blow which struck him senseless. Very well. Will not others notice them likewise? I think so. They have not been here long, there has been small time to acquire a base of operations, yet they must have one. They must have a house, probably not far from here. Very good. Let us find the house and we shall have found them and the missing lady, as well."

"All right I'll bite," Costello offered. "What's th' answer to that one?"

"*Cordieu*, it is so simple even you should see it!" the Frenchman retorted. "It is like this: They have scarcely had time to consummate a purchase; besides, that would be wasteful, for they require only a temporary abode. Very well, then, what have they done? Rented a house, *n'est-ce-pas?* I think likely. We have, then, but to set a corps of energetic investigators to the task of soliciting the realty agents of the city, and when one tells us he has let a house to an Oriental gentleman—*voilà*, we have him in our net. Certainly."

"Sure, it sounds O.K.," Costello agreed, "but th' only thing wrong wid it is it won't work. Just because th' assistant villains who kidnaped th' pore little lady this mornin, wuz a lot o' monkey-faced chinks is no sign th' head o' th' gang's one, too. 'Tis more likely he's a white man usin' Chinese to do his dirty work so's he'll not be suspected, an'—"

"And it is entirely probable that pigs would fly like birds, had they the necessary wings," de Grandin interrupted bitingly. "I say no! Me, I know—at least I damn suspect—what all this devil's business means, and I am sure an Oriental is not only the head, but the brains of this crew of *apaches*, as well. Come, *mon fils*, do as I say. We shall succeed. We must succeed."

Dubiously Costello agreed, and two officers at headquarters were given copies of the classified telephone directory and bidden go down the list of real estate agents systematically, 'phoning each and inquiring whether he had rented a dwelling to a Chinese gentleman during the past week or ten days. Meantime de Grandin smoked innumerable cigarettes and related endless risqué stories to the great edification of the policemen lounging in the squad room. I excused myself and hurried to the office, for consulting hours had come, and I could not neglect my practise.

THE SEASONAL NUMBER OF coryza cases presented themselves for treatment and I was wondering whether I might cut short the consultation period, since no more applicants for Seiler's solution and Dover's powder seemed imminent, when a young man hurried into the office. Tall, lean, sun-bitten till he almost resembled a Malay, he was the kind of chap one took to instantly. A scrubbed-with-coldwater cleanliness and vigor showed in every line of his spare face and figure, his challenging, you-be-damned look was softened by the humorous curve of the wide, thin-lipped mouth beneath his dark, close-clipped mustache. Only the lines of habit showed humor now, however, for an expression of keen anxiety was on his features as he advanced toward me. "I don't know whether you'll remember me or not, Doctor Trowbridge," he opened while still ten feet from me, "but you're one of my earliest recollections. I'm Archy Hildebrand. My father—"

"Why, surely I remember you, son," I returned, "though I don't know I'd have recognized you. We were talking about you last night."

"Were, eh?" he answered grimly. "Suppose you particularized concerning how many different kinds of a fool I've made of myself? Well, let me tell you—"

"Not at all," I cut in as I noted the quick anger hardening in his eyes. "A French gentleman from Saigon was out to McDougal's last night, and he happened to mention your romance, and we were all greatly interested. He seemed to think—"

"Was he a policeman?" Archy interrupted eagerly.

"Why—er—yes, I suppose you might call him that. He's an inspector in the *Sûreté Général*, and—"

"Thank the Lord! Maybe he'll be able to help us. But I need you, first, sir."

"What's the matter?" I began, but he literally dragged me toward the door.

"It's Thi-bah, my wife, sir. I met her in Cambodia and married her in France. No time to go into particulars now, but she—she's in a bad way, sir, and I wish you'd see her as soon as you can. It seems like some sort of eruption, and it's dreadfully painful. Won't you come now, right away?"

"*Mais certainement*, right away, immediately," de Grandin assured him, appearing with the abruptness of a phantom at the consulting-room door. "We shall be most happy to place ourselves at the entire disposal of *Madame*, your wife, young *Monsieur*."

As Hildebrand stared at him in open-mouthed astonishment he explained: "I have but just entered the house, and it was impossible for me not to overhear what you said to Doctor Trowbridge. I have had much experience with the obscure diseases of the Orient, whence Madame Hildebrand came, and I am sure I shall be of assistance to Friend Trowbridge, if you do not object to my entering the case with him?" He paused on a questioning note and regarded Archy with a frank, disarming smile.

"Delighted to have you," I put in before the younger man could express an opinion. "I know you'll be glad of Doctor de Grandin's assistance, too, Archy," I added.

"Certainly," he agreed. "Only hurry, please, gentlemen. She may be suffering another attack right now, and she's so lonely without me—I'm the only one who understands her, you see."

We nodded sympathetically as we left the house, and a moment later I had headed the car toward the Hildebrand mansion.

"Perhaps you can give us a description of *Madame's* malady?" de Grandin asked as we spun along.

Archy flushed beneath his coat of tar. "I'm afraid it'll be hard to tell you," he returned slowly. "You know"—he paused a moment, then continued in evident embarrassment—"if such a thing were possible, I'd say she's the victim of a *poltergeist*."

"Eh, what is it you say?" the Frenchman demanded sharply.

The young man misunderstood his query. "A *poltergeist*," he returned. "I've seen what they declared to be their work in the Black Forest district of Germany, and I assure you it's very mystifying. A person, usually a child or young woman, will become the victim of a malignant spirit, the peasants believe, and this pelting ghost, or *poltergeist*, as they call it in German, will follow the poor thing about, fling dishes and light articles of furniture at her, snatch the bedclothes off her while she sleeps, and bite, pinch and scratch her. I've seen severe skin-wounds inflicted on unfortunate children who'd been selected by a *poltergeist* as its victim, and the parents assured me the injuries appeared by magic, while others looked on in broad daylight, yet no one could see the hand that inflicted the scratches or the teeth which bit the afflicted person. I'd set the whole business down as superstitious nonsense, but since I saw what happened to my wife this morning, I'm not so certain I wasn't laughing out of turn when I grinned at those German peasants."

"Say on, *Monsieur*, I listen," de Grandin answered.

"My wife was dressing this morning when she suddenly let out a shrill scream and half fell across the bench before her vanity. I ran to her, and when I reached her I saw across the white skin of her shoulders the distinct wale of a whip. I've seen just such marks on laborers in Cochin China when the overseer had lashed them. She was almost fainting when I got to her, and babbling something in Khmer which I couldn't understand. I picked her up and started to carry her toward the bed, and as I did so she emitted another cry, and crossing the first diagonal mark was a second wale, so heavy this time that I could see the little spots of blood starting through the skin where it had been bruised to the point of rupture.

"I laid her on the bed and ran into the bathroom to soak a towel in witch hazel to put across her shoulders." He paused a moment and looked challengingly at us. "Please remember she was lying on her back in bed," he continued with slow emphasis. "Her shoulders were pressing directly on the sheet; nothing, not even a bullet from a high-power rifle could have struck her from beneath through the thick layers of cotton-felt of the mattress, yet even as I was crossing the room to her she screamed a third time, and when I reached her there was another whip-mark crossing the first two at an angle on her shoulders. This happened just as I'm telling you," he concluded, then regarded us with an almost threatening glance as he awaited our expressions of polite incredulity.

"*Mais oui*, I believe you, my friend," de Grandin told him. "It is entirely possible. Indeed, I am not at all surprised. No. On the contrary.

"Are we arrived? Good, we shall examine these so strange marks upon your poor lady and do what we can to relieve her suffering.

"By the way," he added as we mounted the porch steps, "at what time did this most unpleasant experience befall *Madame?*"

Hildebrand considered a moment. "About eight o'clock, as near as I can remember," he answered. "We usually breakfast at eight, but we'd overslept this morning and were hurrying to get down to the dining-room before Rumsen, the cook, presented her resignation. She usually resigns if she has to wait a meal more than half an hour, and we were dressing with one eye on the clock when Thi-bah felt the first pain and the first mark showed on her skin."

"Eight o'clock," de Grandin repeated musingly. "At six they take her, at eight the phenomenon is observed. *Eh bien*, they wasted little time, those ones. Yes, it all fits together admirably. I was sure before, now I am certain."

"What's that?" Archy asked.

"I did but confirm my diagnosis, *Monsieur*. It is seldom that I am mistaken. This time, it seems, I am less so than usual. Lead us to *Madame* your wife, if you please."

"**W**HY—" I EXCLAIMED AS we entered the pleasant, chintz-hung room where young Mrs. Hildebrand lay, then stared at the girl in fatuous, hang-jawed amazement.

"*Nom d'un parapluie rose!*" de Grandin exclaimed softly. "I suspected it, now I know. Yes. Of course. Observe her, my friend."

I did. I couldn't help it. I knew it could not be, yet there on the bed before me lay Moneen McDougal, or her twin sister, and stared at us with the wide, hopeless gaze of a dumb thing taken in a trap and waiting in mute terror for the hunter's knife across its throat.

"*Madame*," de Grandin began softly, deferentially, "we have heard of your trouble and are come to aid you."

A tiny parenthesis of puzzled wrinkles formed between the girl's arched black brows, but no sign of understanding showed in her pale face.

"*Madame*," he essayed again, "*je suis un médecin français, et—*"

Still no sign of understanding in the wide, frightened gaze.

He paused a moment, his little, round blue eyes narrowed in concentrated thought, then launched forth a series of queer-sounding, singsong words which reminded me of the gibberish with which Chinese laundrymen address each other.

Instant recognition shone in her dark eyes and she answered in a torrent of droning, oddly inflected phrases.

He motioned me forward, still conversing in the outlandish dialect, and together we approached the bed, turned down the coverlet and bent to examine her. Like most modern young women she wore as her sole under-garment above the waist a knitted-silk bandeau about her bosoms, and as she had dressed only in her lingerie when the curious illness overtook her, we had no difficulty in observing the lashmarks across her cream-satin shoulders. High, angry-looking wales they were, as though freshly laid on by a heavy whip in the hands of a brutally strong tormentor. "*Cher Dieu!*" de Grandin swore, then bent to question her again, but stopped abruptly as she stiffened suddenly and gave a short, terrified exclamation; the sort a patient undergoing odontotrypy might emit; and under our very eyes there rose across her shoulders another scourge mark, red, ecchymosed, swollen. It was as if the skin were inflated from beneath, for a mound like a miniature molehill rose as we watched, and the white skin turned bright, blood-sweating red.

Again she trembled in our grasp and again a red and angry welt showed on her shoulders. From scapula to scapula her back showed a wicked criss-cross of ugly, livid wales.

"Quick, *mon ami*, your hypo, and some morphine, if you please!" he cried. "This will continue intermittently until—we must give her surcease of her pain at once!"

I prepared the mercy-bearing syringe with trembling hands and drove the needle deep into her quivering arm, then shot the plunger home, and as the opiate took hold upon her tortured nerves she relaxed from her rigid pose and sank back slowly on the bed, but as she did so another lash-track appeared on her shoulder, and now the fragile skin was broken through, and a stain of bright capillary blood spread on the linen bedclothes.

"Good heavens, what is it, some obscure form of hemophilia?" I asked.

"Neither obscure nor hemophilia," de Grandin answered grimly. "It is devilment, my friend; but devilment we can do nothing to palliate until Costello finds the one we seek."

"Costello?" I echoed in amazement. "What has he to do with this poor child's—"

"Everything, *pardieu!*" the Frenchman interrupted. "Now, if we do prepare a bandage pack and soak it well with leadwater and laudanum, we shall have done all possible until—"

"Until?" I prompted, as he ceased speaking and proceeded to prepare the soothing dressing for the girl's lacerated back.

"Until the leaden-footed Costello bestirs himself," he returned sharply. "Have I not said it? Certainly.

"Renew the dressing every hour, my friend," he bade young Hildebrand as we prepared to leave. "If her attacks return with frequency, administer these codeine tablets, but never more than one in each half-hour. *Au revoir*, we shall return, and when we do she will have ceased to suffer."

"You mean she'll be—" Archy choked, then stopped, afraid to name the dread eventuality.

"By no means; no," de Grandin cheered him. "She will survive, *mon vieux*, nor will she suffer much meantime, but though we do our work away from here you may be sure that we shall not be idle."

As the young man looked at him bewildered he added, "For ailments such as this some laboratory work is necessary," then smiled as a light of understanding broke in the tortured husband's face.

"The plausible explanation is always best," he murmured as we entered my car and turned toward home.

"Have you really an idea what's wrong with her?" I asked. "It's the strangest case I've ever seen."

"But yes, my ideas are most certain," he returned, "although I can not set them forth in full just now. You are perhaps familiar with stigmata?"

"Only indirectly," I answered. "I've never seen a case of stigmata, but from what I've read I understand it's a physical manifestation of a condition of hysteria. Aren't certain religious fanatics supposed to work themselves into a state of ecstasy and then show marks approximating wounds on their hands and feet, in simulation of the Savior's crucifixion-marks?"

"*Précisément*," he agreed with a nod. "And hysteria is a condition of psychoneurosis. Normal inhibitions are broken down, the conscious mind is in abeyance. You have doubtless seen in psychological laboratories the hypnotist bid the blood leave the subject's hand, and thereupon have observed the hand in question go corpse-pale as the vital fluid gradually receded?"

"Of course," I answered, "but what the deuce are you driving at, anyway?"

"I formulate an hypothesis. Anon we shall put it to the test, I hope."

5. Sympathetic Magic

DETECTIVE SERGEANT JEREMIAH COSTELLO was pacing gloomily back and forth across my study when we returned, a worried look in his blue eyes, a worried frown between his brows, his hands sunk elbow-deep in his trousers pockets.

"What news, *mon brave?*" de Grandin asked eagerly as he espied the big Irishman.

"Plenty, sor, such as it is," the detective returned. "Misther Dougal McDougal's been down to headquarters raisin' partic'lar hell wid everybody from th' Commissioner down. He's threatenin' to see th' Mayor an' petition congress an' call out th' Marines if we don't find his wife's sister before dark."

"*Dites*, and have you been successful in the search for the mysterious Oriental gentleman as yet?" de Grandin asked.

"No, sor. 'Twas a crack-brained idea ye had there, if ye'll excuse me sayin' so. We'd have no more chance o' findin' 'em that way than we'd have o' meetin' up wid a needle in a haystack, as th' felly says, sor. Now, if 'twas me—"

"*Triomphe, victoire, je suis couronné de succès!*" Inspector Renouard burst into the room, his dark eyes fairly blazing with excitement, his beard and mustaches bristling electrically. "All the way from the *préfecture* I have run—as fast as a taximeter could carry me! Behold, we have found him! Those peerless realtors, Sullivan, Dorsch & Doerr have but recently rented a mansion to one Chinese gentleman, a fine, large, furnished house with commodious garage attached. He particularly desired a garage, as he possessed an automobile of noble size in which he drove to the house agent's office, accompanied by a chauffeur and footman, also Orientals. Yes, of course. The gentlemen of real estate noticed this particularly, since such customers are of the rarest at their office. In lieu of references he paid them three months' rent in cash—in golden *louis*—no, what is it the American gold coin is called? Bucks? Yes, in golden bucks he paid one thousand berries—the *gendarme* at headquarters told me.

"How much in dollars is a thousand berries, my friend?" he turned bright, inquiring eyes upon Costello.

"T'ell wid stoppin' to translate now; let's git busy an' find *him!*" Costello roared. "Are ye wid me, Doctor de Grandin, sor?"

"*Cordieu*, when was I ever otherwise in such a case, *mon vieux?*" the little Frenchman answered in a perfect fever of excitement. "Quick, make haste, my friend!"

Of Renouard he asked: "And where may one find this so superbly furnished house and garage the Oriental gentleman rented, *petit frère?*"

"At 68 Hamilton Avenue of the West," the other returned, consulting his black-leather pocketbook. "Where is Friend Costello? He has not yet computed the berries into dollars for me."

Sergeant Costello had no time to explain the vagaries of American slang to the excited Inspector. With tight-lipped mouth pressed close to the transmitter of my office telephone he was giving directions to some one at police headquarters in a low and ominously calm voice. "Yeah," he murmured, "tear-bombs, that's what I said. An' a couple o' choppers, an' some fire-axes, an' riot guns, an' every man wid his nightstick. Git me? O.K., be 'round here *pronto*, an' if anny one rings th' bell or sounds th' siren on th' way I'll beat 'im soft wid me own two fists. Git *that*, too. Come on, now, shake a leg; I'm waitin', but I ain't waitin' long. See?"

THE EARLY DECEMBER DARK had descended, though the moon was not yet high enough to illuminate the streets as the police car set out for Hamilton Avenue. Obedient to Costello's fiercely whispered injunction, gong and siren were silent, and we slipped through the dusk as silently as a wraith.

The house we sought stood well back on a quarter-acre plot of land planted with blue spruce, Japanese maples and rhododendron. As far as we could see, the place was deserted, for no gleam of light showed anywhere and an atmosphere of that utterly dead silence which seems the peculiar property of tenantless buildings wrapped it like a blanket.

"Spooky," Costello declared as he brought the car to a halt half-way down the block and marshaled his forces. "Gilligan, you and Schultz take th' back," he ordered. "See no one gits out that way, an' put th' nippers on anny one that tries to make a break. Sullivan, you an' Esposito git posted be th' front—take cover behind some bushes, an' hit th' first head that shows itself out th' front door. I'm leavin' ye th' job o' seein' no one gits out that way. Norton, cover th' garage. No one's to go in there till I give th' word. Git it?" The men nodded assent, and:

"All right," he continued. "Hornsby, you an' Potansky bring th' choppers an' come wid us. All ready, gentlemen?" he swept Renouard, de Grandin and me with an inquiring glance.

"More than ready, *mon brave*, we are impatient," de Grandin answered. "Lead on; we come."

From a shoulder-holster slung beneath his left armpit Inspector Renouard drew a French-army revolver almost as large as a field gun and spun its cylinder appraisingly. "*Bien*," he murmured, "let us go." The two patrolmen with their vicious little submachine-guns fell in on either side of us, and we advanced across the lawn at a run.

"I've got th' warrant here," Costello whispered as we paused before the veranda. "Think I'd better knock an'—"

"By no means," de Grandin cut in. "Let us enter at once. If our presence is protested, the warrant will give it validity. Meantime, there is much value in surprise, for each moment of delay threatens death for two unfortunate ladies."

"*Two* women?" Costello asked in wonder. "How d'ye figure—"

"*Zut!* Action now, my friend; explanations can wait.

"*Permettez-moi*," he added as Costello drew back to thrust his shoulder at the door. "This is better, I think." He felt quickly in his pocket, producing a ring on which half a dozen keys dangled, and sinking to his knees began trying first one, then another in the door. The first three trials were failures, but the fourth key sprung the lock, and with a muttered exclamation of satisfaction he swung back the door and motioned us in.

"Bedad, what an illigant burglar wuz spoilt when you decided to go straight!" Costello commented admiringly as we stepped across the threshold.

Thick rugs ate up the sound of our footfalls as we entered the darkened hall, and a blackness almost tangible surrounded us while we paused to take our bearings. "Shall I give 'em a call?" the Sergeant whispered.

"Not at all," de Grandin denied. "If we advertise our presence we have assuredly lost what advantage we have thus far gained, and—"

Somewhere, faint and far-away seeming, as though strained through several tight-locked doors, there came to us a faint, shrill, eery note, a piping, quavering cry like the calling of a screech-owl heard a long way off, and, answering it, subtly, like an echo, another wail.

"Howly Mither, what's that?" Costello asked. "Which way did it come from?"

"From under us, I think," de Grandin answered, "and it is devilment of the most devilish sort, my friend. Come, let us hasten; there is no time to waste!"

We tiptoed down the hall, guided by an occasional flash from Costello's pocket light, crept softly through the kitchen, paused a moment at the basement door to reassure ourselves we followed the right track, then swung the white enameled door back and passed quietly down the stairs.

At the turn of the stairway we paused, fairly petrified by the scene below us.

Draperies of heavy silk had been hung at all the basement windows, effectively cutting off all telltale gleams of light to the outside world. A heavy Chinese rug, gorgeous with tones of blue and gold and deep rust-red, was spread upon the floor, and at its four corners stood tall vases with perforated tops through which there slowly drifted writhing gray coils of heavy incense. Robed in yellow, a parody of a man squatted cross-legged in the center of the rug, and it needed no second glance to see he was terribly deformed. One arm was a mere shriveled relic of its former self, one shoulder was a full half-foot higher than the other, his spine was dreadfully contorted, and his round buffer-head thrust forward, like that of a vulture contemplating a feast of carrion. His cheeks were sunken, eye-sockets so depressed that they appeared mere hollow caverns, and the yellow skin was drawn drum-tight over his skull so that the lips were retracted from the uneven, discolored teeth studding his gums. "A very death's-head of a face!" I thought.

But this bizarre, uncanny figure squatting between the incense pots was but a stage property of the show.

Nude and fainting, a young girl was lashed face-forward to a pillar in the floor. Her feet were raised a foot or more above the cement, and round the pillar and her ankles was passed turn after turn of finely knit silken cord, knotting her immovably to the beam and forcing her entire weight upon the thongs which bit so cruelly into her white and shrinking flesh. Her arms were drawn around the post, the wrists crossed and tied at the farther side, but this did little to relieve the strain upon the cords encircling her ankles.

As we came to pause at the turning of the stairs a short and slender brown-skinned man clad in a sort of apron of yellow silk, but otherwise quite naked, stepped forward from the shadows, raised his right hand and swung a scourge of plaited leather mercilessly, dragging the lash diagonally across the girl's defenseless back.

She screamed and trembled and drew herself convulsively closer to the post to which she was bound, as though she sought to gain protection from her tormentor by forcing her body into the very substance of the pillar.

And at her trembling scream the seated monstrosity laughed silently, and from her other side another yellow-aproned man stepped forth and struck her with a leather lash, and as she screamed again a third attendant who squatted on the floor lifted a reed flute to his lips and with the cunning fidelity of a phonograph mocked her agonized. cry with a trilling, quavering note.

As such things will flash through the mind unbidden in times of stress, I could not help comparing her despairing cry and the mockery of the flute to that composition called *Le Roitelet* in which a coloratura soprano sings a series of runs, trills and diversions while a flute accompaniment blends so perfectly with the voice that the listener could hardly say which is human note and which the note of woodwind instrument.

But my random thought was quickly dissipated by de Grandin's sharp whisper to Renouard: "The one at the right for you, the other one for me, my friend!"

Their weapons spoke in unison, and once again the noises harmonized, for the deep roar of Renouard's revolver was complemented by the spiteful, whip-like crack of de Grandin's automatic as a tenor complements a bass, and the two whip-wielding torturers pitched forward on the gorgeous rug as though an unseen giant had pushed them from behind.

The flutist half rose from his seat on the floor, but crumpled impotently in the grasp of one of the policemen, while Inspector Renouard fairly hurled himself upon the deformed man and bore him backward.

"*Ah-ha* you pig-swine, I have you now!" he cried exultantly. "You would kill my men and mock the laws of France, and run off to the temple and think you hid successfully from me! You would follow those escaping lovers to America and put snakes and spiders where they could bite me to death, *hein*? You would torture this poor one here until she screamed for mercy while your so detestable musician made mockery of her suffering? Very well; you have had your laugh; now comes mine, *parbleu!* I think my laugh is best!"

He rose, dragging the other with him, and we saw the gleam of steel upon the cripple's wrists. "Sun Ah Poy," he announced formally, "I arrest you for wilful murder, for sedition and subornation of sedition, and for stirring up rebellion against the Republic of France.

"He is your prisoner, Sergeant," he added to Costello. "Look well to him, and on tomorrow morning I shall begin the extradition proceedings."

Costello nodded curtly. "Take 'em out, Hornsby," he ordered with a gesture toward Sun and the other prisoner. "Tell Sullivan an' Esposito to ring for th' van an' run 'em down to headquarters, an' call th' other boys in. We're goin' through this joint." He motioned to the other patrolmen to precede him up the stairs, then turned to us. "Annything I can do, gentlemen?" he asked, and I realized the innate delicacy of the man as I noticed how he conscientiously kept his glance averted from the nude, limp form which de Grandin cut down from the pillar of torture.

"I think not," the little Frenchman answered, looking up from his task with a quick, friendly smile. "We will join you upstairs anon, *mon brave*."

Together we bent above the unconscious girl. Her white back showed a lattice-work of crossed whip-welts, and in several places the skin had ruptured, letting out the blood where the lash-marks crossed. At de Grandin's mute command I gathered her in my arms and bore her up the stairs to a bedroom, laid her under the covers, then went to help him search the bathroom for boric acid. "It is not much use," he admitted as we applied the powder to her ugly-looking bruises, "but it must do till we can secure opium wash at your house, my friend."

Headed by Costello and Renouard the police searched the house from foundation to ridgepole, but no sign of other occupants could be found, and the Sergeant went to the telephone to tell the city morgue of the bodies lying in the basement. "Will ye be afther comin' along now, sors?" he asked, halting in the doorway to the room where we treated Avis Brindell's hurts.

"But certainly," de Grandin agreed, taking a blanket from the bed and wrapping the girl in it. "Will you set us down at Doctor Trowbridge's, please? We must give this poor one further attention."

WITH THE GIRL'S INJURED back well rubbed with soothing medicine and carefully bandaged, a powerful hypnotic administered to assure her several hours' restful sleep, de Grandin and I joined Costello and Renouard in the study.

"She will do nicely," he pronounced. "By tomorrow morning the hurt will have vanished from her bruises; Christmas night she will assuredly be able to attend her sister's dinner party, though it will be some time before she may again wear décolleté gowns without some slight embarrassment. However"—he raised eyebrows and shoulders in an expressive shrug—"things might have been much worse, n'est-ce-pas?

"Sergeant, mon brave camarade"—he looked affectionately at Costello—"I would suggest you telephone Monsieur and Madame McDougal and tell them the lost lady has been found."

He helped himself to a cigar and smoked in thoughtful silence while the big Irishman went to make his report.

"She much resembles her so charming sister, this Madame Avis, does she not?" he asked apropos of nothing as Detective Sergeant Costello rejoined us.

"Yes," I agreed, "the resemblance is remarkable. Indeed, I never recall seeing three women looking more alike than—"

"Précisément," he interrupted. "It is there the explanation lies.

"When first the possibilities of this case appealed to me was when Inspector Renouard told Madame McDougal that this Thi-bah, the missing temple-dancer, resembled her," he added.

"Remember, Friend Trowbridge, Madame's nerves were all on edge last night because a strange man, a skull-faced Oriental, had accosted her in the streets of Harrisonville? 'That are outrageous!' I told me, but I thought no more about it until the good Renouard pops up like a jack-in-the-box from Cambodia and tells us this story of the runaways from the Angkor temple. When he informs Madame McDougal that the missing Thi-bah resembles her, something goes *click* in this so clever brain of mine—I begin to foresee complications; I also damn suspect why this Oriental with a face like a skeleton's has taken special note of a strange lady in an American city. Yes; Jules de Grandin is like that.

"Now, as you know, I, too, have sojourned in Cambodia; the secrets of that land are not strange to me. By no means. Of the ways of her people I have inquired deeply, and this I have learned: Should a slave run off from those who own him, or a lady leave her lawful wedded spouse, or the man who claims her without the benefit of clergy, for that matter, the deserted one will seek to find the fugitive, but if he can not do so, he will resort to sympathetic magic to compel the runaway's return.

"You know how in the ancient days, and more recent times, too, the wizards and the witches were wont to make a waxen image of one whom they desired to be rid of, then place the figurine before the fire so it would slowly melt, and as it melted, the original would slowly pine away and die? Of course. Occasionally they would vary their technique by thrusting pins through the image in a vital spot, and as they did so, the poor unfortunate whose effigy the image was, was seized with insupportable pains in the same region as that through which the pin was thrust.

"It does sound childish, I admit," he told us with a smile, "but magic is a most real thing, especially if it be believed in, and there is quite reliable evidence that deaths have actually been caused thus.

"Now, the Cambodians have a somewhat similar practise, though it entails double suffering: They procure some person who bears a real or fancied resemblance to the runaway, and thereupon they treat him most discourteously. Sometimes they beat the substitute—that is the usual manner of beginning. If that mild treatment fails they progress to branding with white-hot irons, to cutting off fingers and toes, hands and feet, ears, nose, breast and tongue, with dull knives. Then comes the interesting process of gouging out the eyes with iron hooks, finally complete evisceration while the unfortunate one still lives and breathes.

"Preposterous? Not necessarily. I, myself, have seen Cambodians' hands wither, as though with leprosy, for no apparent reason, I have seen feet become useless, and seen eyes grow dim and blind. I sought to find some medical explanation and was told there was none. It was simply that some enemy was working sympathetic magic somewhere at a place unknown, and somewhere another poor unfortunate was undergoing excruciating torture that the hated one might also suffer.

"Remember, my friends, the Cambodians *believe* this to be possible, believe it implicitly; that makes a world of difference. So it was with Thi-bah; she who is now Madame Hildebrand. For all of her short life she had been subject to those monkey-faced priests, she was taught to believe in their fell powers, that they might not be able to do all they claimed had never once been entertained in her thought. Undoubtlessly she had seen such cases in the past, had seen unfortunate women tortured that some fugitive might suffer, had seen other unfortunates grow crippled, despair and die because somewhere an enemy worked magic on them.

"When we heard Mademoiselle Avis had been kidnaped and that she was Madame McDougal's sister, the reason for the crime at once leaped to my eye. That she bore family resemblance to her sister, who had been said to much resemble Thi-bah, I made no doubt. What the so amiable Doctor Sun would do in the circumstances I also could assume without great trouble. Therefore we set about finding him and finding him in haste, lest harm befall his unfortunate involuntary guest.

"I was on the point of asking Friend Trowbridge to accompany me to Monsieur Hildebrand's to interview his bride when the young man saved me the trouble by appearing so opportunely. *Alors*, to his house we went; there we beheld his young and pretty wife, and saw the whip-scars take form upon her back, even as we looked. These scars were psychic force physically manifested, of course, but they were none the less painful for that reason. Also, Mademoiselle Brindell, who served as substitute for her whom Doctor Sun would have liked to torment in person, was no less tortured because she suffered through no fault of hers. There is the answer and the explanation, my friends."

"But—" I began.

"*Excusez-moi*," he broke in, "I must inquire after Madame Hildebrand."

"And she rests easily?" he asked when his connection had been made and Archy had reported favorably. "*Très bien—ha*, do you tell me so! Excellent, *Monsieur*, I am most happy.

"Monsieur Archy reports," he told us as he replaced the receiver in the hook, "that *Madame* his wife not only rests easily, but that the whip-marks have almost entirely disappeared. A miraculously quick cure for bruises such as we observed this afternoon, *n'est-ce-pas*, Friend Trowbridge?"

"It certainly is," I agreed, "but—"

"And the day after tomorrow we dine with Monsieur and Madame McDougal, and the so charming Mademoiselle Avis," he interrupted. "Sergeant, you must go, too. The party would be dismal without you. Me, I devoutly hope they have procured a turkey of noble proportions. At present I could eat one as great as an elephant."

Again he faced us with one of his quick, elfin smiles. "Sergeant, Friend Trowbridge, will you be good enough to excuse *Inspecteur* Renouard and me for the remainder of the evening?" he asked.

"Come, Renouard, *mon petit singe*, we must do that which we have not done together since the days of the War."

"*Qu'est-ce que c'est?*" demanded the Inspector, but the anticipatory gleam in his bright, dark eyes gave me the cue, even before de Grandin answered:

"What? You ask me what? What, indeed, except to get most vilely and abominably drunk, *mon copain?*"

The Ghost Helper

"Non, my friend, I mean it," Jules de Grandin persisted. "You Americans are a gloomy people; even in your pleasures you are melancholy!"

I grinned at him despite myself. The Chez Pantoufle Dorée certainly showed no signs of melancholia which I could see. Waiters scurried here and there between the rows of softly illuminated tables; the air was heavy with the odor of well-cooked food, warm, perfumed woman-flesh and the smoke of excellent tobacco; the muted clatter of china and table silver mingled with the hum of conversation, lilting, flirtatious laughter and the syncopated overtone of the jazz band's throbbing appeal to elemental passion. "Not much evidence of gloom here, is there?" I queried, attacking the Welsh rabbit the waiter placed before me and decanting a mugful of illegal but most enjoyable ale.

"But yes," he nodded, "that is what I mean, *précisément*. Observe these people; they are typical. How is it your popular song says? 'I Dance With the Tear in My Eye?' That is it. The gayety is forced, unnatural. They are like a group of pallbearers telling each other funny stories while they ride to the cemetery; like little boys whistling to tell themselves how brave they are as they walk quick past the graveyard after dark. 'See us,' they say, 'we are devils of fellows; gay, carefree, debonair; we care for nothing, we fear nothing!' But always they look fearfully across their shoulders, and always in the shadows behind they see the hovering, disapproving ghosts of Calvin, Knox and Wesley, of Cotton Mather and William Jennings Bryan. So they are *triste*. Yes.

"Take those ones, by example"—he nodded to the tenants of a table somewhat to our left—"*c'est un couple bien assorti, n'est-ce-pas?* They should have every mark of happiness upon them, and yet observe—is not discomfort, even fear, written in their faces? I think yes. *Que diable?* Is that the way of joyousness?"

Waiting a decent interval, I turned my head and followed his critical glance. The man was tall, slender, stoop-shouldered, thin-faced and studious-looking, a perfect example of American gentleman with generations of Anglo-Saxon heritage behind him. His duplicate could be found on all our college faculties, in half our law offices and experimental laboratories, in many of the higher branches of our Government departments. Calm, level-headed and efficient, but without the blatant hall-mark of the "go-getter" on him, he showed the ideal combination of seriousness and humor which has enabled science and the arts to keep alive amid the hustle of our New World tempo—and to find practical application in the usages of business.

His companion was a sight to draw the eye in any company. Long-bodied and long-limbed in build, graceful as a panther, with a small, proud head crowned with a skull-cap of close-cut hair the shade of ripened maize, long, insolent eyes of darkest blue set under almost horizontal brows of startling blackness, straight-nosed, firm-chinned, thin-lipped, her skin as white as pearl and seemingly almost transparent, she, too, was eloquent of breeding, but her ancestors had bred their women-folk for physical appeal. However fine her mind might be, no man could forget her brilliant body and allure even for a moment, and though she might show gentleness at times, I knew it would be but the mildness of a cat-creature whose claws are only thinly masked in velvet paws.

I took them in with one swift glance, then turned back to de Grandin. "Why, it's Idris Breakstone and his wife," I said.

"You know them?"

"I know him. I ought to. I helped bring him to Harrisonville thirty-six years ago, and I'd treated his parents for five years before that. The woman I don't know. He married her out of town. She's his second wife, and—"

"U'm?" his murmured comment cut me short. "And is that look—that air of malaise which he and his so charming lady display—entirely natural to them?"

I looked again. The little Frenchman was right. In both Idris' face and that of his companion there was a look of vague fear, a sort of haunted expression which a fugitive from justice might wear when strangers were about and any moment might bring the tapping hand and grim announcement of arrest. "No-o," I answered slowly. "I don't think it is. Now you mention it, they *do* look ill at ease, but—"

"Perhaps that one is to blame?" De Grandin cast his glance beyond the Breakstones' table to a man sitting alone. "He looks like Nemesis's twin—or Satan's. Observe how he regards the lady. *Pardieu*, were she a mouse and he a cat, I should not care to undertake insuring her life!"

I followed the direction of his gaze. Seated in an angle of the wall was a man of slight, boyish build with almost feminine, delicate hands idly toying with his watch chain in a listless, indolent fashion. His old face, long, hard-shaven like a priest's or actor's, was in odd contrast to his youthful body, and in the aged, wrinkle-etched countenance there burned a pair of great, sorrowful eyes—eyes like Lucifer's as he broods upon the high estate from which he fell—which gazed steadfastly and unchangingly at the smoothly brushed blond hair above the nape of Mrs. Breakstone's creamy neck.

I shook my head and wrinkled my brow in distaste. It seemed to me that every atom of liquor-heated masculine desire in the room had been merged into the fixed, unwavering stare of those two sad yet pitiless eyes set in that old, wicked face which topped the lithe, incongruously youthful body of the stranger.

"What do you make of him?" de Grandin prompted as I held my peace.

I shook off the sort of trance which held me. For a moment I had been deaf to the *café's* clatter, blind to its softly glowing lights, unmindful of the food which cooled before me as a single thought-desire seemed to overwhelm me—an almost uncontrollable desire to rise and cross the floor and dash my knotted fist into that old and sinful face, bruise those sorrowful, steadfast eyes and trample that frail, boyish body underfoot.

"Eh?" I returned as I emerged from my fog of primordial fury like a sleeper coming out of sleep. "Oh—excuse me; I was thinking."

"*Exactement*; I think I know your thoughts; I have the same," de Grandin answered with a laugh. "But ere we give way to desire and slay that unclean-looking person, tell me what you think of him. Is he the cause of Monsieur and Madame Breakstone's perturbation?"

"No," I returned, "I do not think so. I doubt if they realize he's there. If she did, she'd surely tell her husband, and if Idris saw him looking at his wife that way—well, I think our impulse would be translated into action, and without much delay."

The little Frenchman nodded understandingly. "I agree," he told me. "Come, let us eat and go, my friend. If we remain much longer I shall most certainly do that one an injury—and I have no desire to be embroiled with the police so late at night."

THE NUMBING COLD OF the evening had abated somewhat and a fine, crisp snow had fallen, covering streets and lawns with an inch or so of gleaming veneer; but the snow had ceased and the moon had risen and silvered the sleeping city with an overlay of nacre when the shrilling of my bedside telephone summoned me from sleep. The biting caress of the light, early-morning wind filtering through the stripped trees made me shiver as I snatched up the instrument and growled a sleepy "Hullo?"

"Idris Breakstone speaking, Doctor Trowbridge," the caller responded. "Can you come over? Muriel—my wife—she's—please hurry; this is urgent!"

"H'm, it had better be!" I murmured grimly as I reached for the clothes which a lifetime of experience as a general practitioner had taught me to keep in order on the bedside chair against such emergencies as this. "Confounded nuisance, knocking a man out of bed like this. Why—"

"What is it, my friend?" Wrapped in a mauve-silk dressing-gown, purple kid slippers on his womanishly small feet, a pink-and-lavender muffler about his throat, Jules de Grandin appeared at the bedroom door, all trace of sleep banished from his little, round blue eyes as he surveyed me with an elfish grin.

"Oh? It woke you too, eh?" I countered, jamming my foot into a shoe and fumbling with the lacings. "Well, misery loves company. No, I doubt it's important; it's Muriel Breakstone, the girl we saw in the night club, you know—her husband just 'phoned, and"—I tied the knot of my second shoe and drew on my waistcoat and jacket—"and she's probably got indigestion from too much rich food or some of that funny liquor they serve there. Little fool! If she'd had sense enough to stick to good, wholesome beer—"

"Await me, my old one; I hasten, I rush, I fly!" de Grandin interrupted as he swung about and raced down the hall toward his room. "The lady will surely not expire if you delay until I dress; and I damn think anything concerning her should interest us. Oh, undoubtlessly, yes."

He was dressed in less time than it took me to go to the garage for my car, and was waiting, my medicine kit beneath his arm, as I drove round to the front door.

I gave him a curious sidelong glance as we swung out into the quiet snow-muffled street. "What's up?" I asked. "I know you can smell a mystery as far as a Scotsman can scent a bargain, but—"

"Hélas, I can not tell you with assurance," he replied. "I have only what you call a hunch to go on; but this so attractive lady with her ill-at-ease manner, and that old-young one who watched her so intently, they intrigue me. I damn think we shall hear more of them, and meantime I would keep in touch with the situation—"

"Well, here's your chance," I interrupted as I brought the car to a halt. "Here we are."

The wide front door of Breakstone's house swung back as we mounted the porch steps, letting a path of warmth and lamplight stream out across the snow. Idris himself let us in and hurried us across the hall with its pavement of turf-soft rugs. "It happened half an hour ago," he told, us, and from the way his lips trembled and his firm, deft chin quivered, we could see that panic fear was tugging at his nerves. "We were out late tonight, and stayed up talking after we got back. We went to bed only a little while ago, and I don't think either of us had more than just gone to sleep when—come up and see her, gentlemen. Do what you can for her—then I'd like to talk with you."

I glanced curiously at his stooped shoulders as we followed him up the stairs. I'd known Idris from his first second of life, and this nervous, trembling, incoherent man was a stranger to me.

A bandeau of black lace held Muriel Breakstone's smoothly, shingled and marcelled blond hair in place, and her diaphanous black lace-and-chiffon night-robe disclosed low breasts and arms and shoulders white and dimpled as a baby's. I bent to feel her pulse, and noted with a start that it was weak and feeble. Her flesh was cold as clay, despite the double blanket of thick camel's hair and the down-filled comforter upon the bed, and all along her hands and forearms there showed the tiny hummocks of horripilation. Her eyes were wide and glassy, and about her nose where it joined the cheeks were the faint-drawn lines of exhaustion. As I leaned forward to listen at her heart her breath struck my cheek, cold and damp as a draft from a cellar—or a mausoleum.

"Pain?" I asked sententiously, laying my left hand palm-down across her right iliac fossa and tapping its back gently with the fingers of my right. To de Grandin I muttered: "Subnormal temperature, light, increased pulsation, low vitality. Almost too soon for para-appendicitis, but—"

"No," the patient answered feebly, fumbling listlessly with the hemstitched edge of the pale-pink linen sheet, "I'm not suffering any, only—terribly—frightened—Doctor. Please—" her voice trailed off to an inaudible whisper, and again a light shudder ran through her, while the goose-flesh on her arms became more pronounced.

"She woke up screaming something had her by the throat," Idris broke in. "At first she was hysterical, but she's been like this since just before I called you, and—"

"Get me an electric pad, or a hot water bottle, if you haven't that," I interrupted. "What d'ye say, de Grandin? Shock?"

"*Mais oui,*" he agreed with a nod. "I concur. External heat, a little ether, some brandy later, perhaps, then a sedative. Undoubtlessly it is shock, as you say, my friend. Yes."

We gave our treatment quickly, and when the patient rested in a light, calm sleep, trooped down the stairs to the library.

"Now, what's the cause of this?" I asked as Idris preceded us into the luxurious room and switched on the lights. "What did she eat at the Pantoufle Dorée tonight? I'm convinced this comes from a nightmare induced by indigestion, though I'm willing to admit I found no evidences of dyspepsia. Still—"

"*Zut,* my old one, we are here to listen, not to talk," de Grandin reminded. Then, to Idris:

"You wished to speak with us, *Monsieur?*"

The young man took a turn across the room, lighted a cigarette, crushed its fire out against the bottom of a cloisonné ash-tray, then snapped his lighter as he set a second one aglow. "Doctor Trowbridge," he began, expelling a twin column of smoke from his nostrils, "do you believe in ghosts?"

"Eh, do I believe in—Lord bless my soul!" I answered.

"*Monsieur*," de Grandin added, "despite the admonitions of the elder churchmen, that man is a fool who states his implicit belief in anything—likewise his unqualified disbelief—we have the open mind. What is it you would tell us?"

Idris tossed his cigarette aside half smoked, then mechanically lit another. He studiously avoided glancing at us as he replied slowly:

"I think this house is haunted."

"Eh?" de Grandin answered sharply. "Do you say it?"

"Nonsense!" I scoffed. "That's just silly, boy. For one thing, the place isn't old enough. It hasn't been finished more than half a year, has it?"

"All right," the young man answered with a trace of dogged stubbornness in his voice, "let's put it another way. Suppose I say we—Muriel and I—are haunted?"

"Oh—" I began, but Jules de Grandin's quick reply cut through my mocking rejoinder:

"How is that, *Monsieur?* We are interested. Tell us everything. There are no unconsidered trifles in cases such as this."

Idris dropped into an easy-chair, crossed his left knee over his right leg, then his right knee over his left, lifted the top from a cigarette box and replaced it slightly awry, then straightened it with meticulous care. "Do you remember Marjorie?" he asked irrelevantly.

"Humph!" I grunted. Was I likely to forget the sweet, old-fashioned girl he married on his return from France, the joy I'd wished them on their wedding day and the pang his marriage to the exotic creature lying upstairs had caused me when all my skill proved unavailing to keep Marjorie alive? "Yes, I remember her," I answered shortly.

"And who was she?" de Grandin asked, leaning slightly forward in his chair and fixing a level, unwinking stare on Idris.

"My wife."

"Ah? And—"

"Anything I say tonight is told you under the seal of your profession?" Idris asked.

"But certainly, in strictest confidence. Say on, *Monsieur*."

"Marjorie Denham and I were born within a city block and a single month of each other. Right, Doctor Trowbridge? You ought to know, you officiated at both our—"

"Get on with it," I ordered with a curt nod. "You're right."

"We grew up together," he continued listlessly, "made mud-pies together, played together. I never teased her or pulled her hair, or hurt her in any way, for even as a savage little brat of a boy I was too fond of her for that. We went to school together, and I carried her books back and forth. We went to our first party together, and it was I she went out with when she wore her first long dress and put her hair up for the first time. She never had a beau, I never had a sweet heart—we weren't lovers, you see, just good, intimate friends, but each filled the other's needs for comradeship so fully that the want of other companions never seemed to enter our thoughts.

"I joined up early when the war broke out, made the first training-camp and went across in the fall of '17. Marjorie came round to the house to see me off and brought me a sweater and helmet. She cried a little, and I was pretty close to tears myself, but we didn't kiss. It just didn't occur to us—to me, at any rate.

"Every mail—every mail that was delivered, that is—brought me news of home from Marjorie. They weren't love letters; just good, long, gossipy letters of happenings around town, and they were like visits home to me.

"I got it in the lungs at Saint-Mihiel when we wiped out the salient—good stiff dose of chlorine gas that almost did me in. It put me in hospital and a convalescent home at Biarritz for almost a year. They thought I'd turn out to be a lunger, after all, but I fooled 'em—worse luck.

"It was while I was convalescing at the home I heard—through Marjorie, of course—of my parents' death. Flu sent Dad west just after the Armistice, and Mother went early in '19. Broken heart, I guess. There are such things, you know.

"There wasn't any reception committee or brass band waiting at the station when I came back to Harrisonville. Everybody was too busy making money while the chance was good to care about a demobbed soldier then, and besides, no one knew I was coming, for I hadn't written. The camp surgeon's office—out at Dix didn't make up its mind to give me a discharge till the last minute, and I didn't know whether it would be Harrisonville, New Jersey, or Nogales, Arizona, I'd be headed for an hour before my papers came through the personnel adjutant's office.

"I was in civvies, and no one seemed to notice me when I got off the train. You can't imagine how strange the town where I'd been born seemed as I stood in the station that afternoon, gentlemen," he continued, "and when I realized my home was closed, and no one there to welcome me, I felt like lying down and crying, right there on the platform."

"*Mon pauvre!*" de Grandin murmured sympathetically.

Idris turned his head aside and winked his eyes several times, as though to clear them of a film of tears. "There was just one place I wanted to go—one place that seemed like home," he continued, lighting a cigarette and puffing it slowly. "That was our family plot in Shadow Lawns. So I jumped in a taxi and went out there.

"It was something after four o'clock in a November afternoon, and dusk was already settling when I walked up the drive leading to their graves—my father's and mother's. I wanted to tell them, 'I'm here at last, dear old people,' and maybe kneel in the grass and whisper something intimate in Mother's grave. But—"

He paused again and drew a handkerchief from the pocket of his lounging-robe, dabbed unashamed at his eyes, and continued: "But there was some one already there when I arrived. It was Marjorie, and she'd brought two bouquets of fresh-cut flowers, one for Mother's grave, one for Dad's.

"Then, gentlemen, I knew. Just as Saul of Tarsus saw the light when the scales dropped from his eyes at the house of Judas in the street called Straight, I saw Marjorie as she really was. I'd always thought her a nice-looking girl with fine eyes and a clear skin, but from that moment she has seemed beautiful to me. All the happiness I'd had from her companionship, all the unvarying kindness she'd shown me throughout our lives, all the dear things she'd meant to me since we were babies suddenly came home to me as I stood beside my parents' graves that afternoon.

"There wasn't any formal proposal. I just opened my arms to her and said, 'My dear!' and:

"'I've always loved you, Idris, and I always shall,' she told me as I held her in my arms and she turned her lips up to mine and gave and took the first kiss of her life—the first kiss she'd ever had from any man outside her family.

"We were married the next week, you remember, Doctor Trowbridge.

"Poor Marjorie! I hadn't much but love to give her. The war that made 'most everybody rich had ruined my father. He was an importer of aniline dyes, and war with Germany killed his business. All he left me, except a few receipted bills, was something like a hundred dollars cash and a formula he'd worked out for making dyes. He'd died just after perfecting it; they said he'd have had more chance with the flu if he hadn't weakened himself working nights in his little laboratory on that formula.

"I got a job and Marjorie and I set up housekeeping. Dad's old place had been sold to pay his debts, so we started living in a three-room flat. Between times, when I wasn't working in the company's laboratory, I tried to market Dad's dye formula, but nobody seemed interested. The German patents had been sequestered anyway, and with the treaty signed new importations were coming in from Europe, so no one had much time for home-made products in the dye industry.

"Then the baby—little Bobby, named for Dad, you know—came, and we had it harder than ever. Marjorie—God rest her soul!—even took in sewing to help ends meet, but—well, you know what happened, Doctor Trowbridge. Tuberculosis wouldn't touch these gas-burned lungs of mine, but it fastened on my wife like a wolf upon a lamb. Sending her away was out of the question. We didn't have carfare to take us west of Camden! Marjorie wouldn't hear of leaving me, anyway; 'We've waited so long for each other, Idris,' she told me, 'please let me have you till the last moment.'

"We'd been married with a double-ring ceremony, and on the inside of her ring and mine was engraved '*Forever*.' A few days before she died she asked me, 'Idris, dear, you'll always love me, always love me more than anyone, and never, never forget me?'

"I could hardly answer for the sobs that filled my throat, but I put my lip against her ear and told her, 'Always, dear love; always and forever.'

"You know what happened, Doctor Trowbridge. All my love and all hers, and all your years of experience couldn't keep her, so she left me, and her last words were: 'Promise you'll remember, Idris.'

"The irony of it! Marjorie had hardly been buried in the Breakstone plot— certainly the funeral bill was nowhere near paid—when I struck it. The Claven- der Company, that had turned me down cold two years before, bid in my patent formula and gave me such a royalty contract as I'd never had the nerve to think of asking. I've had more money than I've known what to do with ever since, and when Bobby grows up he'll be one of the richest young men in the state. And half, a tenth, a twentieth of the money I get for doing nothing every half-year now would have kept her with me!

"I haven't known what to do with either my money or myself these last few years. I've given away more than I ever hoped to own, splashed it around like dishwater, squandered it; still it kept coming in faster than I could spend it. I bought a hundred thousand shares of wildcat mining stock at two dollars. The stuff looked so worthless it wouldn't even do for wallpaper. I forgot it, but it didn't forget me. Within a year it shot up to a hundred, and, of course, I sold. Next month the bottom fell out, and the stock became utterly worthless, but I'd made a fortune in it. That's the sort of luck I've had—now that it doesn't matter any more.

"Last winter I met Muriel Maidstone on a Mediterranean cruise. You've seen her; you know her appeal. I was lonesome as Lucifer cast out of heaven, and—well, we were married. That's that.

"It wasn't long before I realized what a fool I'd been. She came from a good Southern family; poor as church mice. Like so many old families with fine tradi- tions and scarcely any money to carry them on, they'd come to worship wealth as Deity. The mere possession of money seemed to them—and her—an end in itself. Wealth was its own justification, and luxury the only thing worth while. A racketeer with unlimited money at his disposal was greater in their estima- tion than Galileo and Darwin and Huxley, all together.

"Fool! I married her because she set my blood on fire and stole my thought and made me forget the emptiness of life with her Circe-lure. I learned later I could have had all she had to give—to sell, rather—without the formality of marriage, provided I'd been willing to pay enough. It was for *that* I took off the little, cheap, plain-gold ring with '*Forever*' written in it, that Marjorie had put upon my finger when we married! God pity me!

"I said money was Muriel's god, but that's only half the truth. Money's first, of course, but power's a close second. When her arms are round a man she can make him swear his soul away and never know it. And she loves to use that power. She kept at me everlastingly, making me vow my love for her, swear I loved her more than anything, finally, declare I loved her above everything in this world *or the next*.

"I haven't had a moment's peace since I took that perjured oath. My conscience has tormented me unceasingly, for I've felt I've been untrue to Marjorie—*and Marjorie knows!*

"I've felt her near me, felt her presence, just as I used to in the old, poor, happy days together, while I shave or dress, or sit here reading in the library, and Muriel's felt it, too. She says the house is spooky and uncanny and wants to sell it; but she feels a queer, pursued sensation even when she's away. It's always with her, it's almost always with me.

"Muriel hasn't much use for Bobby, you know. She hardly ever sees him and never speaks a word to him when she can avoid it. Two nights ago we went out, and, though I didn't know it, she gave the servants the night off. Bobby was left here alone. I was nearly frantic with remorse when we got back, and rushed up to the nursery to apologize to him and say I hadn't realized he was deserted that way.

"'Oh, that's all right, Daddy,' he answered. 'Mother's been here. She often is.'

"No amount of argument could make him change his story. I tried to tell him Mother was in heaven, and folks up there don't come back to earth, but he persisted.

"'She comes to see me nearly every night,' he said. 'Sometimes she holds me in her lap and sings to me; sometimes she just sits by the bed and holds my hand until I go to sleep. One time a noise outside frightened me, and I cried, and she bent over me and smoothed my hair and kissed me and told me, "Don't be afraid, Bobbycums. Mother won't ever let *anything* hurt you; anything or anyone!"'

"I didn't tell you this upstairs; I couldn't; but tonight when we came home from the theater and the supper club Bobby was restless. He called me several times, and finally I went into the nursery and sat with him. Muriel was furious. She called me once or twice, then came after me. When Bobby protested at my leaving she slapped his face. An hour later she woke up screaming something had her by the throat, went into hysterics, then fell into that semi-coma in which you found her.

"No, Doctor Trowbridge," he concluded, "it wasn't anything she'd eaten that caused that nightmare-fright. *I* know what—*who*—it was. *So does Muriel!*"

I forbore to look at Idris. Obviously the youngster was convinced of everything he told us, and to remonstrate with him would have been as unkind as arguing a child out of his belief in Santa Claus.

Jules de Grandin suffered no such reticence. "What you tell us is entirely credible, my friend," he assured young Breakstone. "As to any dereliction of faith on your part, do not reproach yourself too harshly. The weakness of men where women are concerned is equaled only by the weakness of women where men are involved. *Madame*, your *cidevant* wife, she understands and makes allowances, I am sure. Love may transcend death, but jealousy? I do not think so; for perfect understanding and jealousy can not exist together. No."

THE NEXT DAY WAS a busy one for me. The customary gluttony attendant on the Christmas season produced its usual results, and I nearly suffered writer's cramp penning prescriptions for bismuth salicylate and magnesium calcinate. I was dog-tired by dinner time and ready for bed at nine.

How long I lay in the quiet slumber of exhaustion I do not know, but that I sat bolt-upright in my bed, all vestiges of sleep departed, I well remember. I had not dreamed, I know that; yet through the muffling curtains of sleep I had distinctly heard a voice which called me by name to rise and dress and go somewhere, although the destination was not plain. Now that I was awake, the summons still persisted, though it was no longer an actual, oral order, but rather a voice heard "inside my head" as one is conscious of the phrasing of a thought or of that subjective sound of ringing bells in the ears which follows an overdose of quinine.

"What?" I asked, as though an actual voice addressed me.

"Eh, you have heard it, too?" de Grandin's query came from the darkened hall. "Then it is an actuality!"

"What d'ye mean?" I asked, snapping on the bedside light and blinking at him.

"A moment hence," he replied, "I woke from sleep with the strong impression that some one—a woman, by the voice—called me and urgently requested that I proceed forthwith to 195 Leight Street. Is there, perhaps, such an address?"

"Oh, yes," I answered. "There's such a number, and it's a pretty shabby neighborhood, too; but—"

"And did you wake in similar circumstances?" he interrupted.

"Yes, I did," I admitted, "but—"

"Then there are no buts, my friend. Come, let us go."

"Go? Where?"

"Where in Satan's name but to that Leight Street address," he returned. "Come, make haste; we must hurry."

Grumbling, I heaved myself from the bed and began to don my clothes, the little Frenchman's admonitions to speed ringing in my ears.

Leight Street, as I had told him, was a shabby neighborhood. Once, years ago, it had been fashionable; now it was like an old duchess in poverty. Drab, dismal rows of shabby old houses faced it north and south, their broken windows and weather-scarred, almost paintless, doors like rheumy eyes and broken teeth in old and hopeless faces. Damp, bleak winds blew through the narrow thoroughfare from the bay, bearing a freight of dust and tattered newspapers and the heavy, unwholesome smell of coarse and poorly cooked food—the cheap boarding-house smell, redolent of human misery and degradation as the fetor from a jail or madhouse. Before the old, decrepit houses stood low, rust-bitten iron fences enclosing little yards once used as gardens, but barren of any vegetation save the hardiest of weeds for many years. Somehow, they reminded me of the little fences one sometimes sees about old, neglected graves in country churchyards. Of all the melancholy houses in the melancholy, shabby-genteel street, 195 seemed most wretched. A small, fly-specked sign displayed behind the cracked panes of its French windows advised the passerby that lodgers were accommodated there, and a flickering gas flame burned anemically in the shelter of a cracked red-glass globe in the shabby hall behind the shabby vestibule.

We halted before the decrepit gate while de Grandin viewed the place reflectively. "Of all the crazy, crack-brained things—" I began indignantly, but he cut me short with a quick gesture.

"A light burns yonder," he whispered; "let us investigate." Fearing the rusty hinges of the gate might give warning of our entrance, we stepped across the yard's iron fence and tiptoed toward the tall windows which lighted the English basement. Shades were lowered behind the panes, but a wrinkle in the linen made a tiny opening at one side through which one might look into the room by applying his eye to the glass.

Protesting, I followed him, paused at the tiny areaway before the window and looked round guiltily while he bent forward shamelessly to spy into the house.

"Ah?" I heard him murmur. "A-a-ah? See, look, observe, Friend Trowbridge. What is it we have here?"

Reluctantly I glued my eye to the chink between the blind and window-frame and looked into the room. The contrast between the drab, down-at-the-heel exterior of the house and the apartment into which I gazed almost took my breath. A bright fire blazed behind polished brass fire-dogs in the open fireplace, an Oriental rug of good quality was on the floor, the furniture was substantial and expensive, well-rubbed mahogany, tastefully upholstered, a fine Winthrop desk, a table spread with spotless linen and glistening with silver and cut glass; most incongruous of all, a silver girandole with a bouquet of fresh-cut flowers. Half facing us, but with his odd, sad eyes steadfastly fixed on Muriel Breakstone, sat the queer, old-young man we had noticed in the supper club the evening before. As he came into my line of vision he was in the act of pouring some colorless liquid into a small phial. His lips moved, though no sound came to us. Muriel, her pale, clear-cut face a shade paler than usual, faced him; her eyes were wide with fear, but the man's long, deeply wrinkled countenance betrayed no more emotion than if it had been graven out of stone. I turned to Jules de Grandin with a question, but the words died stillborn on my tongue, for:

"Here, here, now, what are youse two guys up to?" demanded a truculent voice as the street-lamp's rays glistened on the polished shield and buttons of a policeman.

The little Frenchman leaped back from the window as though its glass had suddenly become white-hot, then turned to the patrolman. "*Monsieur,*" he began, but paused with a quick smile of recognition. "Ah, is it truly you, my friend?" he asked, advancing with extended hand.

"Why, it's Doctor de Grandin!" Officer Hornsby exclaimed with an answering grin. "I didn't recognize ye, sir. What's doin'? Can I help ye? Detective Sergeant Costello told me th' other night that if ye ever called on me for help, 'twas just th' same as if he done it hisself."

The Frenchman chuckled. "It is well to be so highly thought of by the force," he answered, then: "Advance, my friend, but cautiously, for we must not advertise our presence. Look through the gap in yonder curtain and tell me who it is you see. That man, you know him, perhaps?"

"Holy Mike, I'll say I know him!" Patrolman Hornsby ejaculated, backing away from the window and fumbling for his gun. "That's 'Poker Face Louis,' th' quickest-shootin' racketeer in th' game. He's been hidin' out these last three weeks, 'count of a little shootin' bee he had with some state troopers. Wanted for murder, an' a few other things, that bird is. Well, well, so this is his hideout, eh? You just wait here, sir, while I go get a couple o' more boys to help me run this baby in. Some one's goin' to get hurt before we finish th' job, but—"

"Why go for help? I am here," de Grandin answered. "Let us take him here and now, my friend. Think of the admiration you will receive for such a feat."

"We-el," obviously, Officer Hornsby wavered between desire for praise and the likelihood of coming out of the encounter with a bullet in him, "a'right, sir; I'm game if you are."

"But we saw that man last night in a supper club," I protested. "Surely, if he's been wanted by the police, he wouldn't dare—"

"You don't know 'Poker Face,' Doctor Trowbridge, sir," Hornsby interrupted. "Puttin' stockings on a eel is a cinch compared with tryin' to arrest him. Of course you seen him in a club. He's got half th' waiters in town on his payroll, an' they slip 'im through th' back doors—an' out th' same way—th' moment anything that looks like a policeman comes in sight. All ready, sir?" he asked de Grandin.

"In a moment," the other answered, stepped back to the boundary of the yard and pried a piece of paving-stone from the loose earth beneath the iron fence. A moment later he heaved it through a window letting out of the front parlor which occupied the building's first floor, and as the glass fell crashing before his missile, leaped forward with Officer Hornsby, straight at the shaded window of the room where "Poker Face Louis" and Muriel Breakstone sat.

Cap pulled down, overcoat collar up about his neck to fend off flying glass, Hornsby crashed through the window like a tank through barbed wire, Jules de Grandin at his elbow. "Poker Face" leaped from his seat with the agility of a startled cat and, thrust one hand into his dinner jacket, but before he could snatch his weapon from his shoulder holster, de Grandin's deadly little automatic pistol was thrust against his temple. "Hands up—and keep them there, if you please, *petit porc*," the Frenchman ordered sharply. "Me, I do not greatly admire that face of yours; it would require small inducement for me to change its appearance with a bullet. Examine him, Friend Hornsby; unless I miss my guess, he wears an arsenal on him."

He did. Under Hornsby's expert search a revolver, two automatic pistols and a murderous, double-edged stiletto were removed from the prisoner's clothes.

"Why, you damned, dirty little Frog, you—" the captive began, but:

"Softly, my friend, there is a lady present, and your language is not suited to her ears," de Grandin admonished as Hornsby locked handcuffs on the prisoner's wrists. "*Madame*," he turned toward Muriel's chair, "I much regret our so unceremonious intrusion, but—*mon Dieu*, she is gone!"

Taking advantage of our preoccupation with her companion, Muriel Breakstone had vanished.

"After her, Friend Trowbridge!" he cried. "Hasten, rush; fly! We must overtake her before she reaches home—*we must!*"

"What's it all about?" I panted as we reached my car and set out in pursuit of the vanished woman. "If—"

"If we are too late I shall never cease reproaching myself," he interrupted. "Can not you see it all? Madame Breakstone is enamored of this criminal. It is not the first time that gently brought-up women have succumbed to such fascinations. No. She is tired of her good, respectable husband, and thinks only of getting rid of him. *Ha*, and that one with the unchanging face, he is not averse to helping her. That liquor we saw him give her undoubtlessly was poison; could you not read fear of murder in her face as she received the bottle from him? But that will not deter her. No. Like a pantheress she is, cruel and passionate as a she-cat. Unquestionably she will administer the drug to Monsieur Idris, unless we can arrive in time to warn him, and—*Dieu de Dieu*, is Satan in league with them?"

The warning clang-clang of a locomotive bell sounded as he spoke, and I clapped my brakes down sharply, stopping us within two feet of the lowered crossing-gate as a seventy-car freight train rumbled past. De Grandin beat his knuckles on the windshield, pulled at his mustache till I thought he would tear hair and skin away in one tremendous tug, and swore venomously in mingled French and English while the train crawled past. When the gates were finally raised we had lost the better part of fifteen minutes, and to make matters worse a broken bottle tossed in the street by some one who had patronized a neighboring bootlegger with more generosity than wisdom cut our front tire to ribbons as I put on speed.

Taxicabs were non-existent in that poverty-stricken neighborhood, and no service station was available for half a mile. We limped along on a flopping, ruined tire, finally found a place where a new one could be had, but lost three-quarters of an hour in the search.

"It is hardly worth while hurrying now," de Grandin told me with a fatalistic shrug as we resumed our way. "However, we might as well continue; Monsieur Martin the coroner, will be pleased to have us sign some sort of statement, I suppose."

Lights blazed in Breakstone's house, when we drew up before the door, and servants followed each other about in futile, hysterical circles.

"Oh, thank Gawd, you've come, sir!" the butler greeted us. "I telephoned you immediately it happened, but they told me you were out, and Doctor Chapman was out, too, so—"

"*Ha*, it has occurred, then?" de Grandin cut in sharply. "Where is he?"

The servant gazed at him in awe-struck wonder, but swallowed his amazement as he turned to lead us to the library.

Idris Breakstone lay supine on the leather couch, one hand trailing to the floor, the other folded peacefully across his breast. A single look confirmed our fears. No need to tell us! Death's trade mark can not be counterfeited, and physicians recognize it all too well. His eyes were partly closed and brilliant with a set, fixed, glassy stare, his lips were slightly parted, and light flecks of whitish foam were at the corners of his mouth.

The Frenchman turned from the body almost indifferently, took up the empty glass upon the table, and held it to his nose, sniffing lightly once or twice, then passed it to me with a shrug. Faint, but still perceptible the odor of peach-kernels hung about the goblets rim, "Hydrocyanic acid," he pronounced. "Less than one grain is fatal, and death is almost instantaneous. They were stupid, those two, for all their fancied cleverness. A child could not be deceived by this, and—"

"But see here," I remonstrated. "You're set on the theory of murder, I know, but, there's a slim chance this might be suicide, de Grandin. We know Idris was—well, talking strangely, to say the least, last night, and we know he was a broken spirited, disillusioned man. He might have done this thing himself. Plain justice demands we take that into consideration. It's true we saw that queer-faced man give Muriel something in a bottle, but we didn't hear what they said and we don't really know it was poison, so—"

"*Précisément*," he nodded grimly. "You have right, my friend. We do not yet know it was poison he gave her, or that she administered it, so we shall interview Madame Breakstone and hear the truth from her lovely, guilty lips. Come; we are not men dealing with a woman, now, but agents of justice with a criminal." He strode to the door, flung it open and beckoned to the butler. "Your mistress," he ordered curtly. "Take us to her."

"Ye-es sir. She's upstairs, sir. I thought you'd like to see her as soon as you were through with the master. Will you come this way, sir?"

"Assuredly," the Frenchman agreed, and fell into step beside the servant. "No noise," he warned in a threatening whisper "If you advise her of our coming—"

"Sir?" the other interrupted with a shocked expression.

"Exactly, precisely, quite so; I have said it," de Grandin, returned sharply. "Your hearing is of the best, my friend. Proceed."

THE SOUND OF A woman sobbing softly came to us as we approached Muriel's bedroom door. "*Tiens, Madame*, tears will avail you nothing," the Frenchman muttered. "Justice knows neither sex nor gallantry; neither does Jules de Grandin in such a case as this." He rapped sharply on the white-enameled panels, then, as the door swung back:

"*Grand Dieu*—what is this?" he asked in blank amazement.

Upon the bed lay Muriel Breakstone, a coverlet drawn over her, leaving only her quiet face exposed. A maid, red-eyed with weeping, rose from her chair and motioned us toward the still form. "You're the doctors?" she queried between sobs. "It's awful, gentlemen. I was down th' hall by Master Bobby's door when I heard Mrs. Breakstone come running upstairs and into her room as if some one was after her. She screamed once, and I came as quickly as I could, but when I got here she was—oh, I was so scared, I didn't know what to do—I couldn't even scream, for a minute! I got her to the bed and drew the cover over her, then got her smelling-salts, but—"

"*Précisément*, it was useless; I perceive," de Grandin interrupted. "You did your best, Mademoiselle, and as your nerves have had a shock, I suggest you go below stairs and give yourself a cup of tea. You will find it restful." He motioned toward the door, and as the trembling girl crept out he turned down the coverlet and stared intently in the dead woman's face.

"And what do you make of this, Friend Trowbridge?" he asked, tapping Muriel's throat with the tip of a well-manicured forefinger. Upon the right side of the smooth, white neck was already forming an elongated patch of discoloration, while the left side showed four long, parallel, reddish lines reaching toward the back from a point midway between the tip and angle of the jaw.

"Why—er—" I began, but he waved me to silence, took my hand in his and pressed my first two fingers against the neck in the receding angle below the chin. Only soft flesh opposed the pressure.

"You see?" he remarked. "The right horn of the hyoid bone is fractured. It is often so in cases of strangulation—throttling by the hand. Yes; of course; I have seen it more than once in the Paris morgue.

"B-but who did it—who could have done it?" I stammered. "D'ye suppose Idris could have been seized with a fit of homicidal madness, strangled Muriel, then, returning to sanity and realizing what he'd done, committed suici—"

"*Zut!*" he exclaimed impatiently. "Your question slanders the helpless dead, my friend. That poor one downstairs was murdered, foully murdered. As to who performed the deed for this one—one wonders." But from the expression on his face I knew he had arrived at a decision.

He was strangely silent on the homeward drive, nor would he respond to any of my attempts at conversation.

T HEY BURIED IDRIS AND Muriel Breakstone on New Year's Eve. The coroner's jury returned a verdict of suicide while of unsound mind in Idris' case, and of murder by throttling at the hands of some person or persons unknown in the case of Muriel. At de Grandin's request Coroner Martin, in his private and unofficial capacity of funeral director, saw that the little, plain-gold ring with "*Forever*" engraved on its inner surface was slipped on the third finger of Idris' hand before the body was placed in the casket. The tall, gray-haired mortician and the little Frenchman were fast friends, and though the coroner asked no questions, he nodded sympathetically when de Grandin gave him the ring and asked that he see it was put on the body.

Darkness had fallen and the old year was dying in a flurry of light, feathery snow when Jules de Grandin and I stopped at Breakstone's house, the Frenchman with a great bundle of toys and a gigantic box of chocolates under his arm.

"I bring them for *petit* Monsieur Bobby—*le pauvre enfant!*" he told the child's grandmother, who, with her husband, had agreed to occupy the house until Idris' estate could be settled and permanent arrangements made for the little boy.

"Your daughter, Monsieur Breakstone's first wife, she would have wished that you take charge of her little one in such circumstances," de Grandin whispered as he ascended the stairs to the nursery. "It is well that you are here.

"We shall not waken him if he is sleeping," he added as we halted before the nursery door, "but I should like to look at him, if I may, and leave these gifts where he can find them when he rises in the morning. However, if you think—"

He broke off abruptly, while he and Mr. Denham and I stared at each other in blank amazement. From the darkened nursery there came to us distinctly the sound of voices—happy voices!—of a child's light laughter, the deeper laugh of a man and the soft, lilting laughter of a woman. Then: "Good night, little son, happy dreams; sleep tight!" a woman said, and, "Good night!" a childish treble answered.

Mr. Denham pushed back the door and stared about the room. Save for the little boy, snugly cuddled in his crib, the nursery was empty. "Why"—the grandfather began—"I thought—"

"Hello, Grandpa," the youngster greeted sleepily, smiling at the old gentleman, "Mother's been here, and Daddy, too. They told me good-night just a moment—"

"Why, Bobby, that can't be!" his grandfather cut in. "Your Mother and Daddy are—"

"Say it, *Monsieur*," de Grandin challenged fiercely, his little, round blue eyes glazing as they rested on the older man, "say it, and, *parbleu*, I shall pull your nose!"

To Bobby he announced: "Of course they were here, *mon petit*, and they shall come to you many, many more times in future, and he who says otherwise is a foul, depraved liar. Moreover, he must fight with Jules de Grandin who would tell you they may not come. Yes; I have said it." He bent and kissed the youngster on the brow, then laid his gifts upon the table. "They are for you, my little cabbage," he said. "Tomorrow, when you rise, you shall have them all, and—my love to your dear parents when next they come to you, my little one!"

"I WONDER WHAT IT WAS we heard in there?" I asked as we drove home from the theater some hours later. "I could have sworn we heard a man's voice—and a woman's, too—but that's impos—"

"You could have sworn!" he interrupted, something like incredulity in his tone. "*Pardieu*, I shall swear it; I have sworn it; upon a pile of Holy Scriptures high as that Monsieur Woolworth's so beautiful tower I will affirm it before all the world. 'Whom did we hear?' you ask. *Barbe d'un chou-fleur*, who should be in the little man's nursery at sleepy-time but those who loved him in life; who but she who summoned us to witness the perfidy of the false wife and her paramour, and to learn the truth about the poison which took Monsieur Breakstone's life? Who but the one who wreaked swift vengeance on the false-hearted murderess even as she gloated over her success? Who, indeed, *parbleu*?

"Death is strong, but love is stronger, my friend, and woman fights for the man she loves. The false one had but short time to enjoy her triumph, while as for her lover—*ha*, did not the spirit of dear Madame Marjorie, which led us to that house in Leight Street, indirectly cause his apprehension, and must he not now answer for his misdeeds before the bar of justice? But certainly.

"Attend me, my friend: Women, children and dogs know their friends instinctively. So, it would seem, do disembodied spirits. When Madame Marjorie sought one on this earthly plane to help her in her work, whom should she choose but Jules de Grandin? In times gone past he has been known as a ghost-breaker. These last few nights, I damn think, he has essayed a new rôle, that of ghost-helper. Yes, *par la barbe d'un taureau*, and it is a rôle he has liked exceedingly well!"

"But see here," I expostulated, "you don't seriously believe that Marjorie's spirit was responsible for all this?"

Across the city, down by the water works, a whistle hooted hoarsely, another took up the cry, in a moment the night was full of shrieking, cheering whistles and clamoring bells. The carillon in St. Chrysostom's belfry began to sing a joyous peal:

"Ring out the false, ring in the true,

Ring, happy bells, across the snow . . ."

Jules de Grandin removed the white-silk handkerchief from the left cuff of his dinner jacket and wiped his eyes upon it, unashamed. "My friend," he assured me solemnly, "I do believe it; I believe it with all my heart. Come, let us hurry."

"Why, what's the hurry now?"

"The Old Year dies. I would greet the New Year fittingly—with a drink," he answered.

Satan's Stepson

1. The Living Dead

"HORNS OF A LITTLE blue devil!" Jules de Grandin bent his head against the sleet-laden February wind and clutched madly at my elbow as his feet all but slipped from under him. "'We are three fools, my friends. We should be home beside our cheerful fire instead of risking our necks going to this *sacré* dinner on such a night."

"*Comment ça va, mon Jules*," demanded Inspector Renouard, "where is your patriotism? Tonight's dinner is in honor of the great General Washington, whose birthday it is. Did not our own so illustrious Marquis de Lafayette—"

"*Monsieur le Marquis* is dead, and we are like to be the same before we find our way home again," de Grandin cut in irritably. "As for the great Washington, I think no more of him for choosing this so villainous month in which to be born. Now me, I selected May for my *début*; had he but used a like discretion—"

"*Misère de Dieu*, see him come! He is a crazy fool, that one!" Renouard broke in, pointing to a motor car racing toward us down the avenue.

We watched the vehicle in open-mouthed astonishment. To drive at all on such a night was risking life and limb, yet this man drove as though contending for a record on the racing track. Almost abreast of us, he applied his brakes and swerved sharply to the left, seeking to enter the cross street. The inevitable happened. With a rending of wood and metal the car skidded end for end and brought up against the curb, its right rear wheel completely dished, its motor racing wildly as the rimless spokes spun round and round.

"*Mordieu*, you are suicidal, my friend!" de Grandin cried, making his way toward the disabled vehicle with difficulty. "Can I assist you? I am a physician, and—"

A woman's hysterical scream cut through his offer. "Help—save me—they're—" Her cry died suddenly as a hand was clapped over her mouth, and a hulking brute of a man in chauffeur's leather coat and vizored cap scrambled from the driver's cab and faced the Frenchman truculently. "*Yékhat!* Be off!" he ordered shortly. "We need no help, and—"

"Don't parley with him, Dimitri!" a heavy voice inside the tonneau commanded. "Break his damned neck and—"

"'*Cré nom!* With whose assistance will you break my neck, *cochon?*" de Grandin asked sharply. "Name of a gun, make but one step toward me, and—"

The giant chauffeur needed no further invitation. As de Grandin spoke he hurled himself forward, his big hands outstretched to grasp the little Frenchman's throat. Like a bouncing ball de Grandin rose from the ground, intent on meeting the bully's rush with a kick to the pit of the stomach, for he was an expert at the French art of foot-boxing, but the slippery pavement betrayed him. Both feet flew upward and he sprawled upon his back, helpless before the larger man's attack.

"À *moi, mon Georges!*" he called Renouard. "*Je suis perdu!*"

Practical policeman that he was, Renouard lost no time in answering de Grandin's cry. Reversing the heavy walking-stick which swung from his arm he brought its lead-loaded crook down upon the chauffeur's head with sickening force, then bent to extricate his friend from the other's crushing bulk.

"The car, into the *moteur*, my friend!" de Grandin cried. "A woman is in there; injured, perhaps; perhaps—"

Together they dived through the open door of the limousine's tonneau, and a moment later there came the sound of scuffling and mingled grunts and curses as they fought desperately with some invisible antagonist.

I rushed to help them, slipped upon the sleet-glazed sidewalk, and sprawled full length as a dark body hurtled from the car, cannoned into me and paused a moment to hurl a missile, then sped away into the shadows with a mocking laugh.

"Quick, Friend Trowbridge, assist me; Renouard is hit!" de Grandin emerged from the wrecked car supporting the Inspector on his arm.

"*Zut!* It is nothing—a scratch!" Renouard returned. "Do you attend to her, my friend. Me, I can walk with ease. Observe—" he took a step and collapsed limply in my arms, blood streaming from a deeply incised wound in his left shoulder.

Together de Grandin and I staunched the hemorrhage as best we could, then rummaged in the ruined car for the woman whose screams we had heard when the accident occurred.

"She is unconscious but otherwise unhurt, I think," de Grandin told me. "Do you see to Georges; I will carry her—*prie-Dieu* I do not slip and kill us both!"

"But what about this fellow?" I asked, motioning toward the unconscious chauffeur. "We oughtn't leave him here. He may freeze or contract pneumonia—"

"*Eh bien*, one can but hope," de Grandin interrupted. "Let him lie, my friend. The sleet may cool his ardor—he who was so intent on breaking Jules de Grandin's neck. Come, it is but a short distance to the house. Let us be upon our way; *allez-vous-en!*"

A RUGGED CONSTITUTION AND THE almost infinite capacity for bearing injury which he had developed during years of service with the *gendarmerie* stood Inspector Renouard in good stead. Before we had reached the house he was able to walk with my assistance; by the time he had had a proper pack and bandage applied to his wound and absorbed the better part of a pint of brandy he was almost his usual debonair self.

Not so our other patient. Despite our treatment with cold compresses, sal volatilis and aromatic ammonia it was nearly half an hour before we could break the profound swoon in which she lay, and even then she was so weak and shaken we forbore to question her.

At length, when a slight tinge of color began to show in her pale cheeks de Grandin took his station before her and bowed as formally as though upon a ballroom floor. "*Mademoiselle*," he began, "some half an hour since we had the happy privilege of assisting you from a motor wreck. This is Doctor Samuel Trowbridge, in whose office you are; I am Doctor Jules de Grandin, and this is our very good friend, Inspector Georges Jean Jacques Joseph-Marie Renouard, of the *Sûreté Générale*, all of us entirely at your service. If *Mademoiselle* will be so kind as to tell us how we may communicate with her friends or family we shall esteem it an honor—"

"Donald!" the young woman interrupted breathlessly. "Call Donald and tell him I'm all right!"

"*Avec plaisir*," he agreed with another bow. "And this Monsieur Donald, he is who, if you please?"

"My husband."

"Perfectly, *Madame*. But his name?"

"Donald Tanis. Call him at the Hotel Avalon and tell him that I—that Sonia is all right, and where I am, please. Oh, he'll be terribly worried!"

"But certainly, *Madame*, I fully understand," he assured her. Then:

"You have been through a most unpleasant experience. Perhaps you will be kind enough to permit that we offer you refreshment—some sherry and biscuit—while *Monsieur* your husband comes to fetch you? He is even now upon his way."

"Thank you so much," she nodded with a wan little smile, and I hastened to the pantry in search of wine and biscuit.

Seated in an easy-chair before the study fire, the girl sipped a glass of Duff Gordon and munched a pilot biscuit while de Grandin, Renouard and I studied her covertly. She was quite young—not more than thirty, I judged—and lithe and slender in stature, though by no means thin, and her hands were the whitest I had ever seen. Ash-blond her complexion was, her skin extremely fair and her hair that peculiar shade of lightness which, without being gray, is nearer silver than gold. Her eyes were bluish gray, sad, knowing and weary, as though they had seen the sorrow and futility of life from the moment of their first opening.

"You will smoke, perhaps?" de Grandin asked as she finished her biscuit. As he extended his silver pocket lighter to her cigarette the bell shrilled imperatively and I hastened to the front door to admit a tall, dark young man whose agitated manner labeled him our patient's husband even before he introduced himself.

"My dear!" he cried, rushing across the study and taking the girl's hand in his, then raising it to his lips while de Grandin and Renouard beamed approvingly.

"Where—how—" he faltered in his question, but his worshipful glance was eloquent.

"Donald," the girl broke in, and though the study was almost uncomfortably warm she shuddered with a sudden chill, "*it was Konstantin!*"

"Wha—*what?*" he stammered in incredulous, horrified amazement. "My dear, you surely can't be serious. Why, he's *dead!*"

"No, dear," she answered wearily, "I'm not jesting. It was Konstantin. There's no mistaking it. He tried to kidnap me.

"Just as I entered the hotel dining-room a waiter told me that a gentleman wanted to see me in the lobby; so, as I knew you had to finish dressing, I went out to him. A big, bearded man in a chauffeur's leather uniform was waiting by the door. He told me he was from the Cadillac agency; said you had ordered a new car as a surprise for my birthday, but that you wanted me to approve it before they made delivery. It was waiting outside, he said, and he would be glad if I'd just step out and look at it.

"His accent should have warned me, for I recognized him as a Russian, but there are so many different sorts of people in this country, and I was so surprised and delighted with the gift that I never thought of being suspicious. So I went out with him to a gorgeous new limousine parked about fifty feet from the porte-cochère. The engine was running, but I didn't notice that till later.

"I walked round the car, admiring it from the outside; then he asked if I'd care to inspect the inside of the tonneau. There seemed to be some trouble with the dome light when he opened the door for me, and I was half-way in before I realized some one was inside. Then it was too late. The chauffeur shoved me in and slammed the door, then jumped into the cab and set the machine going in high gear. I never had a chance to call for help.

"It wasn't till we'd gone some distance that my companion spoke, and when he did I almost died of fright. There was no light, and he was so muffled in furs that I could not have recognized his face anyway, but his voice—and those corpse-hands of his—I knew them! It was Konstantin.

"'*Jawohl, meine liebe Frau,*' he said—he always loved to speak German to torment me—'it seems we meet again, *nicht wahr?*'

"I tried to answer him, to say something—anything—but my lips and tongue seemed absolutely paralyzed with terror. Even though I could not see, I could feel him chuckling in that awful, silent way of his.

"Just then the driver tried to take a curve at high speed and we skidded into the curb. These gentlemen were passing and I screamed to them for help. Konstantin put his hand over my mouth, and at the touch of his cold flesh against my lips I fainted. The next I knew I was here and Doctor de Grandin was offering to call you, so—" She paused and drew her husband's hand down against her cheek. "I'm frightened, Donald—terribly frightened," she whimpered. "Konstantin—"

Jules de Grandin could stand the strain no longer. During Mrs. Tanis' recital I could fairly see his ungovernable curiosity bubbling up within him; now he was at the end of his endurance.

"*Pardonnez-moi, Madame,*" he broke in, "but may one inquire who this so offensive Konstantin is?"

The girl shuddered again, and her pale cheeks went a thought paler.

"He—he is my husband," she whispered between blenched lips.

"But, *Madame,* how can it be?" Renouard broke in. "Monsieur Tanis, he is your husband, he admits it, so do you; yet this Konstantin, he is also your husband. *Non,* my comprehension is unequal to it."

"But Konstantin is *dead,* I tell you," her husband insisted. "I saw him die—I saw him in his coffin—"

"Oh, my darling," she sobbed, her lips blue with unholy terror, "you saw *me* dead—coffined and buried, too—but I'm living. Somehow, in some way we don't understand—"

"*Comment?*" Inspector Renouard took his temples in his hands as though suffering a violent headache. "Jules, my friend, tell me I can not understand the English," he implored. "You are a physician; examine me and tell me my faculties are failing, my ears betraying me! I hear them say, I think, that Madame Tanis has died and been buried in a grave and coffin; yet there she sits and—"

"Silence, *mon singe,* your jabbering annoys one!" de Grandin cut him short. To Tanis he continued:

"We should be grateful for an explanation, if you care to offer one, for *Madame's* so strange statement has greatly puzzled us. It is perhaps she makes the pleasantry at our expense, or—"

"It's no jest, I assure you, sir," the girl broke in. "I *was* dead. My death and burial are recorded in the official archives of the city of Paris, and a headboard, marks my grave in Saint Sébastien, but Donald came for me and married—"

"*Eh bien, Madame,* either my hearing falters or my intellect is dull," de Grandin exclaimed. "Will you repeat your statement once again, slowly and distinctly, if you please? Perhaps I did not fully apprehend you."

2. Inferno

DESPITE HERSELF THE GIRL smiled. "What I said is literally true," she assured him. A pause, then: "We hate to talk of it, for the memory horrifies us both, but you gentlemen have been so kind I think we owe you an explanation.

"My name was Sonia Malakoff. I was born in Petrograd, and my father was a colonel of infantry in the Imperial Army, but some difficulty with a superior officer over the discipline of the men led to his retirement. I never understood exactly what the trouble was, but it must have been serious, for he averted court-martial and disgrace only by resigning his commission and promising to leave Russia forever.

"We went to England, for Father had friends there. We had sufficient property to keep us comfortable, and I was brought up as an English girl of the better class.

"When the War broke out Father offered his sword to Russia, but his services were peremptorily refused, and though he was bitterly hurt by the rebuff, he determined to do something for the Allied cause, and so we moved to France and he secured a noncombatant commission in the French Army. I went out as a V.A.D. with the British.

"One night in '16 as our convoy was going back from the advanced area an air attack came and several of our ambulances were blown off the road. I detoured into a field and put on all the speed I could. As I went bumping over the rough ground I heard some one groaning in the darkness. I stopped and got down to investigate and found a group of Canadians who had been laid out by a bomb. All but two were dead and one of the survivors had a leg blown nearly off, but I managed to get them into my van with my other *blessés* and crowded on all the gas I could for the dressing-station.

"Next day they told me one of the men—the poor chap with the mangled leg—had died, but the other, though badly shell-shocked, had a good chance of recovery. They were very nice about it all, gave me a mention for bringing them in, and all that sort of thing. Captain Donald Tanis, the shell-shocked man, was an American serving with the Canadians. I went to see him, and he thanked me for giving him the lift. Afterward they sent him to a recuperation station on the Riviera, and we corresponded regularly, or as regularly as people can in such circumstances, until—" she paused a moment, and a slight flush tinged her pallid face.

"*Bien oui*," de Grandin agreed with a delighted grin. "It was love by correspondence, *n'est-ce-pas, Madame?* And so you were married? Yes?"

"Not then," she answered. "Donald's letters became less frequent, and— and of course I did what any girl would have done in the circumstances, made mine shorter, cooler and farther apart. Finally our correspondence dwindled away entirely.

"The second revolution had taken place in Russia and her new masters had betrayed the Allies at Brest-Litovsk. But America had come into the war and things began to look bright for us, despite the Bolsheviks' perfidy. Father should have been delighted at the turn events were taking, but apparently he was disappointed. When the Allies made their July drive in '18 and the Germans began retreating he seemed terribly disturbed about something, became irritable or moody and distrait, often going days without speaking a word that wasn't absolutely necessary.

"We'd picked up quite a few friends among the émigrés in Paris, and Father's most intimate companion was Alexis Konstantin, who soon became a regular visitor at our house. I always hated him. There was something dreadfully repulsive about his appearance and manner—his dead-white face, his flabby, fish-cold hands, the very way he dressed in black and walked about so silently—he was like a living dead man. I had a feeling of almost physical nausea whenever he came near me, and once when he laid his hand upon my arm I started and screamed as though a reptile had been put against my flesh.

"When Donald's letters finally ceased altogether, though I wouldn't admit it, even to myself, my heart was breaking. I loved him, you see," she added simply.

"Then one day Father came home from the War Department in a perfect fever of nervousness. 'Sonia,' he told me, 'I have just been examined by the military doctors. They tell me the end may come at any time, like a thief in the night. I want you to be provided for in case it comes soon, my dear. I want you to be married.'

"'But Father, I don't want to marry,' I replied. 'The war's not over yet, though we are winning, and I've still my work to do with the ambulance section. Besides, we're well enough off to live; there's no question of my having to marry for a home; so—'

"'But that's just it,' he answered. 'There is. That is exactly the question, my child. I—I've speculated; speculated and lost. Every kopeck we had has gone.

I've nothing but my military pay, and when that stops, as it must stop directly the war is won, we're paupers.'

"I was surprised, but far from terrified. 'All right,' I told him, 'I'm strong and healthy and well educated, I can earn a living for us both.'

"'At what?' he asked sarcastically. 'Typing at seventy shillings a week? As nursery governess at five pounds per month with food and lodging? No, my dear, there's nothing for it but a rich marriage, or at least a marriage with a man able to support us both while I'm alive and keep you comfortably after that.'

"I thought I saw a ray of hope. 'We don't know any such man,' I objected. 'No Frenchman with sufficient fortune to do what you wish will marry a dowerless girl, and our Russian friends are all as poor as we, so—'

"'Ah, but there *is* such a man,' he smiled. 'I have just the man, and he is willing—no, anxious—to make you his wife.'

"My blood seemed to go cold in my arteries as he spoke, for something inside me whispered the name of this benefactor even before Father pronounced it: Gaspardin Alexis Konstantin!

"I wouldn't hear of it at first; I'd sooner wear my fingers out as seamstress, scrub tiles upon my knees or walk the pavements as a *fille de joie* than marry Konstantin, I told him. But though I was English bred I was Russian born, and Russian women are born to be subservient to men. Though I rebelled against it with every atom of my being, I finally agreed, and so it was arranged that we should marry.

"Father hurried me desperately. At the time I thought it was because he didn't want me to have time to change my mind, but—

"It was a queer wedding day; not at all the kind I'd dreamed of. Konstantin was wealthy, Father said, but there was no evidence of wealth at the wedding. We drove to and from the church in an ancient horse-drawn taximeter cab and my father was my only attendant. An aged *papa* with one very dirty little boy as acolyte performed the ceremony. We had only the cheap silver-gilt crowns owned by the church—none of our own—and not so much as a single spray of flowers for my bridal bouquet."

"The three of us came home together and Konstantin sent the *concierge* out for liquor. Our wedding breakfast consisted of brandy, raw fish and tea! Both Father and my husband drank more than they ate. I did neither. The very sight of Konstantin was enough to drive all desire of food away, even though the table had been spread with the choicest dainties to be had from a fashionable caterer.

"Before long, both men were more than half tipsy and began talking together in low, drunken mutterings, ignoring me completely. At last my husband bade me leave the room, ordering me out without so much as looking in my direction.

"I sat in my bedroom in a sort of chilled apathy. I imagine a condemned prisoner who knows all hope of reprieve is passed waits for the coming of the hangman as I waited there.

"My half-consciousness was suddenly broken by Father's voice. 'Sonia, Sonia!' he called, and from his tone I knew he was beside himself with some emotion.

"When I went into the dining-room my father was trembling and wringing his hands in a perfect agony of terror, and tears were streaming down his cheeks as he looked imploringly at Konstantin. 'Sonia, my daughter,' he whispered, 'plead with him. Go on your knees to him, my child, and beg him—pray him as you would pray God, to—'

"'Shut up, you old fool,' my husband interrupted. 'Shut up and get out—leave me alone with my bride.' He leered drunkenly at me.

"Trembling as though with palsy, my father rose humbly to obey the insolent command, but Konstantin called after him as he went out: 'Best take your *pistolet, mon vieux*. You'll probably prefer it to *le peloton d'exécution*.'

"I heard Father rummaging through his chest in the bedroom and turned on Konstantin. 'What does this mean?' I asked. 'Why did you say he might prefer his own pistol to the firing-party?'

"'Ask him,' he answered with a laugh, but when I attempted to join my father he thrust me into a chair and held me there. 'Stay where you are,' he ordered. 'I am your master, now.'

"Then my British upbringing asserted itself. 'You're not my master; no one is!' I answered hotly. 'I'm a free woman, not a chattel, and—'

"I never finished. Before I could complete my declaration he'd struck me with his fist and knocked me to the floor, and when I tried to rise he knocked me down again. He even kicked me as I lay there.

"I tried to fight him off, but though he was so slightly built he proved strong as a prize-fighter, and my efforts at defense were futile. They seemed only to arouse him to further fury, and he struck and kicked me again and again. I screamed to my father for help, but if he heard me he made no answer, and so my punishment went on till I lost consciousness.

"My bridal night was an inferno. Sottish with vodka and drunk with passion, Konstantin was a sadistic beast. He tore—actually ripped—my clothing off; covered me with slobbering, drunken caresses from lips to feet, alternating maudlin, obscene compliments with scurrilous insults and abuse, embracing and beating me by turns. Twice I sickened under the ordeal and both times he sat calmly by, drinking raw vodka from the bottle and waiting till my nausea passed, then resumed my torment with all the joy a mediæval Dominican might have found in torturing a helpless heretic.

"It was nearly noon next day when I woke from what was more a stupor of horror and exhaustion than sleep. Konstantin was nowhere to be seen, for which I thanked God as I staggered from the bed and sought a nightrobe to cover the shameless nudity he had imposed on me.

"'I'll not stand it,' I told myself as, my self-respect somewhat restored by the garment I'd slipped on, I prepared a bath to wash the wounds and bruises I'd sustained during the night.

"Then all my new-found courage evaporated as I heard my husband's step outside, and I cringed like any odalisk before her master as he entered—groveled on the floor like a dog which fears the whip.

"He laughed and tossed me a copy of the Paris edition of *The Daily Mail*. 'You may be interested in that obituary,' he told me, 'the last paragraph in the fourth column.'

"I read it, and all but fainted as I read, for it told how my father had been found that morning in an obscure street on the left bank. A bullet wound in the head pointed to suicide, but no trace of the weapon had been found, for thieves had taken everything of value and stripped the body almost naked before the gendarmes found it.

"They gave him a military funeral and buried him in a soldier's grave. His service saved him from the Potter's Field, but the army escort and I were his only mourners. Konstantin refused to attend the services and forbade my going till I had abased myself and knelt before him, humbly begging for permission to attend my father's funeral and promising by everything I held sacred that I would be subservient to him in every act and word and thought forever afterward if only he would grant that one poor favor.

"That evening he was drunk again, and most ill-natured. He beat me several times, but offered no endearments, and I was glad of it, for his blows, painful as they were, were far more welcome than his kisses.

"Next morning he abruptly ordered me to rejoin my unit and write him every day, making careful note of the regiments and arms of service to which the wounded men I handled belonged, and reporting to him in detail.

"I served two weeks with my unit, then the Commandant sent for me and told me they were reducing the personnel, and as I was a married woman they deemed it best that I resign at once. 'And by the bye, Konstantin,' she added as I saluted and turned to go, 'you might like to take these with you—as a little souvenir, you know.' She drew a packet from her drawer and handed it to me. It was a sheaf of fourteen letters, every one I'd written to my husband. When I opened them outside I saw that every item of intelligence they contained had been carefully blocked out with censor's ink.

"Konstantin was furious. He thrashed me till I thought I'd not have a whole bone left.

"I took it as long as I could; then, bleeding from nose and lips, I tried to crawl from the room.

"The sight of my helplessness and utter defeat seemed to infuriate him still further. With an animal-snarl he fairly leaped on me and bore me down beneath a storm of blows and kicks.

"I felt the first few blows terribly; then they seemed to soften, as if his hands and feet were encased in thick, soft boxing-gloves. Then I sank face-downward on the floor and seemed to go to sleep.

"WHEN I AWOKE—IF YOU can call it that—I was lying on the bed, and everything seemed quiet as the grave and calm as Paradise. There was no sensation of pain or any feeling of discomfort, and it seemed to me as if my body had grown curiously lighter. The room was in semi-darkness, and I noticed with an odd feeling of detachment that I could see out of only one eye, my left. 'He must have closed the right one with a blow,' I told myself, but, queerly, I didn't feel resentful. Indeed, I scarcely felt at all. I was in a sort of semi-stupor, indifferent to myself and everything else.

"A scuffle of heavily booted feet sounded outside; then the door was pushed open and a beam of light came into the room, but did not reach to me. I could tell several men had entered, and from their heavy breathing and the scraping sounds I heard, I knew they were lugging some piece of heavy furniture.

"'Has the doctor been here yet?' one of them asked.

"'No,' some one replied, and I recognized the voice of Madame Lespard, an aged widow who occupied the flat above. 'You must wait, gentlemen, the law—'

"'À bas the law!' the man replied. 'Me, I have worked since five this morning, and I wish to go to bed.'

"'But gentlemen, for the love of heaven, restrain yourselves!' Madame Lespard pleaded. 'La pauvre belle créature may not be—'

"'No fear,' the fellow interrupted. 'I can recognize them at a mile. Look here.' From somewhere he procured a lamp and brought it to the bed on which I lay. 'Observe the pupils of the eyes,' he ordered, 'see how they are fixed and motionless, even when I hold the light to them.' He brought the lamp within six inches of my face, flashing its rays directly into my eye; yet, though I felt its luminance, there was no sensation of being dazzled.

"Then suddenly the light went out. At first I thought he had extinguished the lamp, but in a moment I realized what had actually happened was that my eyelid had been lowered. Though I had not felt his finger on the lid, he had drawn it down across my eye as one might draw a curtain!

"'And now observe again,' I heard him say, and the scratch of a match against a boot-sole was followed by the faint, unpleasant smell of searing flesh.

"Forbear, Monsieur!" old Madame Lespard cried in horror. "Oh, you are callous—inhuman—you gentlemen of the pompes funèbres!"

"Then horrifying realization came to me. A vague, fantasmal thought which had been wafting in my brain, like an unremembered echo of a long-forgotten verse, suddenly crystallized in my mind. These men were from the *pompes funèbres*—the municipal undertakers of Paris—the heavy object they had lugged in was a coffin—*my coffin!* They thought me dead!

"I tried to rise, to tell them that I lived, to scream and beg them not to put me in that dreadful box. In vain. Although I struggled till it seemed my lungs and veins must burst with effort, I could not make a sound, could not stir a hand or finger, could not so much as raise the eyelid the undertaker's man had lowered!

"'Ah, *bon soir, Monsieur le Médicin!*' I heard the leader of the crew exclaim. 'We feared you might not come tonight, and the poor lady would have to lie un-coffined till tomorrow.'

"The fussy little municipal doctor bustled up to the bed on which I lay, flashed a lamp into my face and mumbled something about being overworked with *la grippe* killing so many people every day. Then he turned away and I heard the rustle of papers as he filled in the blanks of my certificate of death. If I could have controlled any member of my body I would have wept. As it was, I merely lay there, unable to shed a single tear for the poor unfortunate who was being hustled, living, to the grave.

"Konstantin's voice mingled with the others'. I heard him tell the doctor how I had fallen head-first down the stairs, how he had rushed wildly after me and borne me up to bed, only to find my neck was broken. The lying wretch actually sobbed as he told his perjured story, and the little doctor made perfunctory, clucking sounds of sympathy as he listened in attentively and wrote the death certificate—the warrant which condemned me to awful death by suffocation in the grave!

"I felt myself lifted from the bed and placed in the pine coffin, heard them lay the lid above me and felt the jar as they drove home nail after nail. At last the task was finished, the *entrepreneurs* accepted a drink of brandy and went away, leaving me alone with my murderer.

"I heard him take a turn across the room, heard the almost noiseless chuckle which he gave whenever he was greatly pleased, heard him scratch a match to light a cigarette; then, of a sudden, he checked his restless walk and turned toward the door with a short exclamation.

"'Who comes?' he called as a measured tramping sounded in the passageway outside.

"'The military police!' his hail was answered. 'Alexis Konstantin, we make you arrested for espionage. Come!'

"He snarled like a trapped beast. There was the *click* of a pistol-hammer, but the gendarmes were too quick for him. Like hounds upon the boar they leaped on him, and though he fought with savage fury—I had good cause to know how strong he was!—they overwhelmed him, beat him into submission with fists and saber-hilts and snapped steel bracelets on his wrists.

"All fight gone from him, cursing, whining, begging for mercy—to be allowed to spend the last night beside the body of his poor, dead wife!—they dragged him from the room and down the stairs. I never saw him again—until tonight!"

The girl smiled sadly, a trace of bitterness on her lips. "Have you ever lain awake at night in a perfectly dark room and tried to keep count of time?" she asked. "If you have, you know how long a minute can seem. Imagine how many centuries I lived through while I lay inside that coffin, sightless, motionless, soundless, but with my sense of hearing abnormally sharpened. For longer years than the vilest sinner must spend in purgatory I lay there thinking—thinking. The rattle of carts in the streets and a slight increase in temperature told me day had come, but the morning brought no hope to me. It meant only that I was that much nearer the Golgotha of my Via Dolorosa.

"At last they came. 'Where to?' a workman asked as rough hands took up my coffin and bore me down the stairs.

"'Saint Sébastien,' the *premier ouvrier* returned, 'her husband made arrangements yesterday. They say he was rich. *Eh bien*; it is likely so; only the wealthy and the poor dare have funerals of the third class.'

"Over the cobbles of the streets the little, one-horse hearse jolted to the church, and at every revolution of the wheels my panic grew. 'Surely, *surely* I shall gain my self-control again,' I told myself. 'It can't be that I'll lie like this until—' I dared not finish out the sentence, even in my thoughts.

"The night before, the waiting had seemed endless. Now it seemed the shambling, half-starved nag which drew the hearse was winged like Pegasus and made the journey to the cemetery more swiftly than the fastest airplane.

"At last we halted, and they dragged me to the ground, rushed me at breakneck speed across the cemetery and put me down a moment while they did something to the coffin. What was it? Were they making ready to remove the lid? Had the municipal doctor remembered tardily how perfunctory his examination had been, and conscience-smitten, rushed to the cemetery to snatch me from the very jaws of the grave?

"'We therefore commit her body to the earth—earth to earth, ashes to ashes, dust to dust—' the priest's low sing-song came to me, muffled by the coffin-walls. Too late I realized the sound I heard had been only the knotted end of the lowering-rope falling on the coffin top as the workmen drew a loop about the case.

"The priest's chant became fainter and fainter. I felt myself sinking as though upon a slowly descending lift, while the ropes sawed and rasped against the square edges of the coffin, making noises like the bellow of a cracked bass viol, and the coffin teetered crazily from side to side and scraped against the raw edges of the grave. At last I came to rest. A jolt, a little thud, a final scraping noise, and the lowering-ropes were jerked free and drawn underneath the coffin and out of the grave. The end had come, there was no more—

"A terrible report, louder than the bursting of a shell, exploded just above my chest, and the close, confined air inside the coffin shook and trembled like the air in a dugout when hostile flyers lay down an air-barrage. A second shock burst above my face—its impact was so great I knew the coffin lid must surely crack beneath it—then a perfect drum-fire of explosions as clod on roaring clod struck down upon the thin pine which coffined me. My ears were paralyzed with the continuous detonations, I could feel the constantly increasing weight of earth pressing on my chest, my mouth, my nostrils. I made one final effort to rouse myself and scream for help; then a great flare, like the bursting of a star-shell, enveloped me and the last shred of sensation went amid a blaze of flame and roar of thunder.

"SLOWLY I FOUGHT BACK to consciousness. I shuddered as the memory of my awful dream came back to me. I'd dreamed that I was dead—or, rather, in a trance—that men from the *pompes funèbres* came and thrust me into a coffin and buried me in Saint Sébastien, and I had heard the clods fall on the coffin lid above me while I lay powerless to raise a hand.

"How good it was to lie there in my bed and realize that it had only been a dream! There, with the soft, warm mattress under me, I could lie comfortably and rest till time had somewhat softened the terror of that nightmare; then I would rise and make a cup of tea to soothe my frightened nerves; then go again to bed and peaceful sleep.

"But how dark it was! Never, even in those days of air-raids, when all lights were forbidden, had I seen a darkness so absolute, so unrelieved by any faintest ray of light. I moved my arms restlessly. To right and left were hard, rough wooden walls that pressed my sides and interfered with movement. I tried to rise, but fell back with a cry of pain, for I had struck my brow a violent blow. The air about me was very close and damp; heavy, as though confined under pressure.

"Suddenly I knew. Horror made my scalp sting and prickle and the awful truth ran through me like an icy wave. It was no dream, but dreadful fact. I had emerged from the coma which held me while preparations for my funeral were made; at last I was awake, mistress of my body, conscious and able to move and scream aloud for help—but none would ever hear me. I was coffined, shut up beneath a mound of earth in Saint Sébastien Cemetery—buried alive!

"I called aloud in agony of soul and body. The dreadful reverberation of my voice in that sealed coffin rang back against my ears like thunder-claps tossed back by mountain peaks.

"Then I went mad. Shrieking, cursing the day I was born and the God Who let this awful fate befall me, I writhed and twisted, kicked and struggled in the coffin. The sides pressed in so closely that I could not raise my hands to my head, else I had torn my hair out by the roots and scratched my face to the bone, but I dug my nails into my thighs through the flimsy drapery of my shroud and bit my lips and tongue until my mouth was choked with blood and my raving cries were muted like the gurglings of a drowning man. Again and yet again I struck my brow against the thin pine wood, getting a fierce joy from the pain. I drew up my knees as far as they could go and arched my body in a bow, determined to burst the sepulcher which held me or spend my faint remaining spark of life in one last effort at escape. My forehead crashed against the coffin lid, a wave of nausea swept over me and, faint and sick, I fell back to a merciful unconsciousness.

"The soft, warm sunlight of September streamed through an open window and lay upon the bed on which I lay, and from the table at my side a bowl of yellow roses sent forth a cloud of perfume. 'I'm surely dead,' I told myself. 'I'm released from the grave at last. I've died and gone—where? Where was I? If this were heaven or paradise, or even purgatory, it looked suspiciously like earth; yet how could I be living, and if I were truly dead, what business had I still on earth?

"Listlessly I turned my head. There, in American uniform, a captain's bars gleaming on his shoulders, stood Donald, my Donald, whom I'd thought lost to me forever. 'My dear,' I whispered, but got no farther, for in a moment his arms were round me and his lips were pressed to mine."

Sonia paused a moment, a smile of tenderest memory on her lips, the light that never was on sea or land within her eyes. "I didn't understand at all," she told us, "and even now I only know it second-hand. Perhaps Donald will tell you his part of the story. He knows the details better than I."

3. La Morte Amoureuse

THE LEAPING FLAMES BEHIND the andirons cast pretty highlights of red and orange on Donald Tanis and his wife as they sat hand in hand in the love seat beside the hearth rug. "I suppose you gentlemen think I was pretty precipitous in love-making, judging from the record Sonia's given," the young husband began with a boyish grin, "but you hadn't watched beside her bed while she hovered between sanity and madness as I had, and hadn't heard her call on me and say she loved me. Besides, when she looked at me that afternoon and said,

'My dear!' I knew she loved me just as well as though she'd taken all day long to tell me."

De Grandin and Renouard nodded joint and most emphatic approval. "And so you were married?" de Grandin asked.

"You bet we were," Donald answered. "There'd have been all sorts of red tape to cut if we'd been married as civilians, but I was in the army and Sonia wasn't a French citizeness; so we went to a friend of mine who was a padre in one of our outfits and had him tie the knot. But I'm telling this like a newspaper story, giving the ending first. To begin at the start:

"The sawbones in the hospital told me I was a medical freak, for the effect of the bursting 'coalbox' on me was more like the bends, or caisson disease, than the usual case of shell-shock. I didn't go dotty, nor get the horrors; I wasn't even deafened to any extent, but I did have the most God-awful neuralgic pains with a feeling of almost overwhelming giddiness whenever I tried to stand. I seemed as tall as the Woolworth tower the minute I got on my feet, and seven times out of ten I'd go sprawling on my face two seconds after I got out of bed. They packed me off to a convalescent home at Biarritz and told me to forget I'd ever been mixed up in any such thing as a war.

"I did my best to follow orders, but one phase of the war just wouldn't be forgotten. That was the plucky girl who'd dragged me in that night the Fritzies tried to blow me into Kingdom Come. She'd been to see me in hospital before they sent me south, and I'd learned her name and unit, so as soon as I was up to it I wrote her. Lord, how happy I was when she answered!

"You know how those things are. Bit by bit stray phrases of intimacy crept into our notes, and we each got so that the other's letters were the most important things in life. Then Sonia's notes became less frequent and more formal; finally they hinted that she thought I was not interested any more. I did my best to disabuse her mind of *that* thought, but the letters came farther and farther apart. At last I decided I'd better tell her the whole truth, so I proposed by mail. I didn't like the idea, but there I was, way down in the Pyrénées, unable to get about, except in a wheel-chair, and there she was somewhere on the west front. I couldn't very well get to her to tell her of my love, and she couldn't come to me—and I was dreadfully afraid I'd lose her.

"Then the bottom dropped out of everything. I never got an answer to that letter. I didn't care a hang what happened to me then; just sat around and moped till the doctors began to think my brain must be affected, after all.

"I guess about the only thing that snapped me out of it was America's coming in. With my own country sending troops across, I had a definite object in life once more; to get into American uniform and have a last go at the Jerries. So I concentrated on getting well.

"It wasn't till the latter part of July, though, that they let me go, and then they wouldn't certify me for duty at the front. 'One more concussion and you'll go blotto altogether, lad,' the commandant told me before I left the nursing-home, and he must have put a flea in G.H.Q's. ear, too, for they turned me down cold as caviar when I asked for combatant service.

"I'd made a fair record with the Canadians, and had a couple of good friends in the War Department, so I drew a consolation prize in the form of a captaincy of infantry with assignment to liaison duty with the *Censure Militaire*.

"The French officers in the bureau were first-rate scouts and we got along famously. One day one of 'em told me of a queer case they'd had passed along by the British M.I. It seemed there was a queer sort of bird, a Russian by the name of Konstantin, who'd been making whoopee for some time, but covering up his tracks so skillfully they'd never been able to put salt on his tail. He'd been posing as an *émigré* and living in the Russian colony in Paris, always with plenty of money, but no visible employment. After the way the Bolshies had let the Allies down everything Russian was regarded with suspicion, and this bird had been a source of several sleepless nights for the French Intelligence. Finally, it seemed, they'd got deadwood on him.

"An elderly Russian who'd been billeted in the censor's bureau and always been above suspicion had been found dead in the streets one morning, a suicide, and the police had hardly got his body to the morgue when a letter from him came to the chief. In it he confessed that he'd been systematically stealing information from censored documents and turning it over to Konstantin, who was really an agent for the Soviets working with the Heinies. Incidentally, the old fellow named several other Russians who'd been corrupted by Konstantin. It seemed his game was to lend them money when they were hard up, which they generally were, then get them to do a little innocuous spying for him in return for the loan. After that it was easy. He had only to threaten to denounce them in order to keep them in his power and make them go on gathering information for him, and of course the poor fish were more and more firmly entangled in the net with each job they did for him.

"Just why old Captain Malakoff chose to kill himself and denounce Konstantin wasn't clear, but the Frenchman figured that his conscience had been troubling him for some time and he'd finally gotten to the point where he couldn't live with it any longer.

"I'd been sitting back, not paying much attention to Lieutenant Fouchet's story, but when he mentioned the suicide's name my interest was roused. Of course, Malakoff isn't an unusual Russian name, but this man had been an officer in the Imperial army in his younger days, and had been taken in the French service practically as an act of charity. The details seemed to fit my case. 'I used to know a girl named Malakoff,' I said. 'Her father was in the censorship, too, I believe.'

"Fouchet smiled in that queer way he had, showing all his teeth at once beneath his little black mustache. I always suspected he was proud of the bridge work an American dentist had put in for him. 'Was the young lady's name Sonia, by any chance?' he asked.

"That brought me up standing. 'Yes,' I answered.

"'Ah? It is doubtless the daughter of our estimable suicide, in that case,' he replied. 'Attend me: Two weeks ago she married with this Konstantin while she was on furlough from her unit at the front. Almost immediately after her marriage she rejoined her unit, and each day she has written her husband a letter detailing minutely the regiments and arms of service to which the wounded men she carried have belonged. These letters have, of course, been held for us by the British, and *voilà*, our case is complete. We are prepared to spring our trap. Captain Malakoff we buried with full military honors; no one suspects he has confessed. Tonight or tomorrow we all arrest this Konstantin and his accomplices.' He paused and smiled unpleasantly; then: 'It is dull work for the troops stationed here in Paris,' he added. 'They will appreciate a little target practice.'

"'But—but what of Sonia—Madame Konstantin?' I asked.

"'I think that we can let the lady go,' he said. 'Doubtless she was but a tool in her husband's hands; the same influence which drove her father from his loyalty may have been exerted on her; he is a very devil with the women, this Konstantin. Besides, several of his aides have confessed, so we have ample evidence on which to send him to the firing-party without the so pitiful little spy-letters his wife wrote to him. She must be dismissed from the service, of course, and never may she serve in any capacity, either with the civil or military governments, but at least she will be spared a court-martial and public disgrace. Am I not kind, my friend?'

"A few days later he came to me with a serious face. 'The man Konstantin has been arrested,' he said, 'but his wife, *hélas*, she is no more. The night before last she died in their apartment—fell down the stairs and broke her lovely neck, I'm told—and yesterday they buried her in Saint Sébastien. Courage, my friend!' he added as he saw my face. 'These incidents are most regrettable, but—there is much sorrow in the world today—*c'est la guerre*.'

"He looked at me a moment; then: 'You loved her?' he asked softly.

"'Better than my life,' I answered. 'It was only the thought of her that brought me through—she dragged me in and saved my life one night out by Lens when the Jerries knocked me over with an air-bomb.'

"'*Mon pauvre garçon!*' he sympathized. Then: 'Consider me, my friend, there is a rumor—oh, a very unsubstantiated rumor, but still a rumor, that poor Madame Konstantin did not die an entirely natural death. An aged widow-neighbor of hers has related stories of a woman's cries for mercy, as though she were most brutally beaten, coming from the Konstantin apartment. One does not know this is a fact. The old talk much, and frequently without good reason, but—'

"'The dog!' I interrupted. 'The cowardly dog, if he hit Sonia I'll—'

"Fouchet broke in. 'I shall attend the execution tomorrow,' he informed me. 'Would not you like to do the same?'

"Why I said yes I've no idea, but something, some force outside me, seemed to urge me to accept the invitation, and so it was arranged that I should go.

"A few hooded street lamps were battling ineffectually with the foggy darkness when we arrived at the Santé Prison a little after three next morning. Several motor cars were parked in the quadrangle and a sergeant assigned us seats in one of them. After what seemed an interminable wait, we saw a little knot of people come from one of the narrow doors leading into the courtyard—several officers in blue and black uniforms, a civilian handcuffed to two gendarmes, and a priest—and enter a car toward the head of the procession. In a moment we were under way, and I caught myself comparing our motorcade to a funeral procession on its way to the cemetery.

"A pale streak of dawn was showing in the east, bringing the gabled roofs and towers out in faint silhouette as we swung into the Place de la Nation. The military chauffeurs put on speed and we were soon in the Cours de Vincennes, the historic old fortification looming gloomy and forbidding against the sky as we dashed noiselessly on to the *champ d'execution*, where two companies of infantry in horizon blue were drawn up facing each other, leaving a narrow lane between. At the farther end of this aisle a stake of two-by-four had been driven into the turf, and behind and a little to the left stood a two-horse black-curtained van, from the rear of which could be seen protruding the butt of a deal coffin, rough and unfinished as a hardware merchant's packing-case. A trio of unshaven workmen in black smocks lounged beside the wagon, a fourth stood at the horses' heads.

"As our party alighted a double squad of musicians stationed at the lower end of the files of troops tossed their trumpets upward with a triple flourish and began sounding a salute and the soldiers came to present arms. I could see the tiny drops of misty rain shining like gouts of sweat on the steel helmets and bayonet blades as we advanced between the rows of infantry. A chill of dread ran up my spine as I glanced at the soldiers facing us on each side. Their faces were grave and stern, their eyes harder than the bayonets on their rifles. Cold, implacable hatred, pitiless as death's own self, was in every countenance. This was a spy, a secret enemy of France, who marched to his death between their perfectly aligned ranks. The wet and chilly morning air seemed surcharged with an emanation of concentrated hate and ruthlessness.

"When the prisoner was almost at the stake he suddenly drew back against the handcuffs binding him to his guard and said something over his shoulder to the colonel marching directly behind him. The officer first shook his head, then consulted with a major walking at his left, finally nodded shortly. '*Monsieur le Capitaine*,' a dapper little sub-lieutenant saluted me, 'the prisoner asks to speak with you. It is irregular, but the colonel has granted permission. However, you may talk with him only in the presence of a French officer'—he looked coldly at me, as though suspecting I were in some way implicated in the spy's plots—'you understand that, of course?'

"'I have no wish to talk with him—' I began, but Fouchet interrupted.

"'Do so, my friend,' he urged. 'Who knows, he may have news of Madame Sonia, your *morte amoureuse*. Come.

"'I will act as witness to the conversation and stand surety for Captain Tanis,' he added to the subaltern with frigid courtesy.

"They exchanged polite salutes and decidedly impolite glares, and Fouchet and I advanced to where the prisoner and the priest stood between the guarding gendarmes.

"Even if I had known nothing of him—if I'd merely passed him casually on the boulevard—Konstantin would have repelled me. He was taller than the average and thin with a thinness that was something more than the sign of malnutrition; this skeletal gauntness seemed to have a distinct implication of evil. His hat had been removed, but from neck to feet he was arrayed in unrelieved black, a black shirt bound round the collar with a black cravat, a black serge suit of good cut and material, shoes of dull-black leather, even gloves of black kid on his long, thin hands. He had a sardonic face, long, smooth-shaven, its complexion an unhealthy yellowish olive. His eyes were black as carbon, and as lacking in luster, overhung by arched brows of intense, dead black, like his hair, which was parted in the middle and brushed sharply back from the temples, leaving a point at the center of the forehead. This inverted triangle led down to a long, hooked nose, and that to a long, sharp chin. Between the two there ran a wide mouth with thin, cruel lips of unnatural, brilliant red, looking, against the sallow face, as though they had been freshly rouged. An evil face it was, evil with a fathomless understanding of sin and passion, and pitiless as the visage of a predatory beast.

"He smiled briefly, almost imperceptibly, as I approached. 'Captain Donald Tanis, is it not?' he asked in a low, mocking voice.

"I bowed without replying.

"'*Monsieur le Capitaine*,' he proceeded, 'I have sent for you because I, of all the people in the world, can give you a word of comfort—and my time for disinterested philanthropy grows short. A little while ago I had the honor to take to wife a young lady in whom you had been deeply interested. Indeed I think we might make bold to say you were in love with her, *nicht wahr?'*

"As I still returned no answer he opened that cavernous, red-lipped mouth of his and gave a low, almost soundless chuckle, repulsive as the grinning of a skull.

"'*Jawohl*,' he continued, 'let us waive the tender confession. Whatever your sentiments were toward her, there was no doubt of hers toward you. She married me, but it was you she loved. The marriage was her father's doing. He was in my debt, and I pressed him for my pound of flesh, only in this instance it was a hundred pounds or so of flesh—his daughter's. He'd acted as an agent of mine at the *Censure Militaire* until he'd worn out his usefulness, so I threatened to denounce him unless he would arrange a marriage for me with the charming Sonia. Having gotten what I wanted, I had no further use for him. The sad-eyed old fool would have been a wet blanket on the ardor of my honeymoon. I told him to get out—gave him his choice between disposing of himself or facing a French firing-squad.

"'It seems now that he chose to be revenged on me at the same time he gave himself the happy dispatch. Dear, dear, who would have thought the sniveling old dotard would have had the spirit?

"'But we digress and the gentlemen grow impatient,' he nodded toward the file of troops. 'We Russians have a saying that the husband who fails to beat his wife is lacking in outward manifestation of affection.' He chuckled soundlessly again. 'I do not think my bride had cause for such complaint.

"'What would you have given,' he asked in a low, mocking whisper, 'to have stood in my place that night three weeks ago? To have torn the clothing off her shuddering body, to have cooled her fevered blushes with your kisses, then melted her maidenly coolness with burning lips—to have strained her trembling form within your arms, then, in the moment of surrender, to have thrust her from you, beaten her down, hurled her to the floor and ground her underfoot till she crept suppliant to you on bare and bleeding knees, holding up her bruised and bleeding face to your blows or your caresses, as you chose to give them—utterly submissive, wholly, unconditionally yours, to do with as you wished?'

"He paused again and I could see little runnels of sweat trickling down his high, narrow brow as he shook with passion at the picture his words had evoked.

"'*Nu*,' he laughed shortly. 'I fear my love became too violent at last. The fish in the pan has no fear of strangling in the air. I can tell you this without fear of increasing my penalty. Sonia's death certificate declares she died of a broken neck resulting from a fall downstairs. Bah! She died because I beat her! I beat her to death, do you hear, my fish-blooded American, my chaste, chivalrous worshiper of women, and as she died beneath my blows, she called on you to come and save her!

"'You thought she stopped her letters because she had grown tired? Bah, again. She did it out of pride, because she thought that you no longer cared. At my command her father intercepted the letters you sent to her Paris home—I read them all, even your halting, trembling proposal, which she never saw or even suspected. It was amusing, I assure you.

"'You've come to see me die, *hein*? Then have your fill of seeing it. *I* saw Sonia die; heard her call for help to the lover who never came, saw her lower her pride to call out to the man she thought had jilted her as I rained blow on blow upon her!'

"Abruptly his manner changed, he was the suave and smooth-spoken gentleman once more. '*Auf Wiedersehen, Herr Hauptmann!*' he bid me with a mocking bow.

"'I await your pleasure, *Messieurs*,' he announced, turning to the gendarmes.

"A detail of twelve soldiers under the command of a lieutenant with a drawn sword detached itself from the nearer company of infantry, executed a left wheel and came to halt about five meters away, their rifles at the order, the bayonets removed. The colonel stepped forward and read a summary of the death sentence, and as we drew back the gendarmes unlatched their handcuffs and bound the prisoner with his back against the post with a length of new, white rope. A handkerchief was bound about his eyes and the gendarmes stepped back quickly.

"'*Garde à vous!*' the firing-party commander's voice rang out.

"'*Adieu pour ce monde, mon Lieutenant*, do not forget the *coup de grâce!*' Konstantin called airily.

"The lieutenant raised his sword and swung it downward quickly; a volley rang out from the platoon of riflemen.

"The transformation in the prisoner was instant and horrible. He collapsed, his body sagging weakly at the knees, as a filled sack collapses when its contents are let out through a cut, then sprawled full length face-downward on the ground, for the bullets had cut the rope restraining him. But on the turf the body writhed and contorted like a snake seared with fire, and from the widely opened mouth there came a spate of blood and gurgling, strangling cries mingled with half-articulate curses.

"A corporal stepped forward from the firing-party, his heavy automatic in his hand. He halted momentarily before the widening pool of blood about the writhing body, then bent over, thrust the muzzle of his weapon into the long black hair which, disordered by his death agonies, was falling about Konstantin's ears, and pulled the trigger. A dull report, like the popping of a champagne cork, sounded, and the twisting thing upon the ground gave one convulsive shudder, then lay still.

"'This is the body of Alexis Konstantin, a spy, duly executed in pursuance of the sentence of death pronounced by the military court. Does anyone lay claim to it?' announced the commandant in a steady voice. No answer came, though we waited what seemed like an hour to me.

"'À vos rangs!' Marching in quick time, the execution party filed past the prostrate body on the blood-stained turf and rejoined its company, and at a second command the two units of infantry formed columns of fours and marched from the field, the trumpet sounding at their head.

"The black-smocked men dragged the coffin from the black-curtained van, dumped the mangled body unceremoniously into it, and the driver whipped his horses into a trot toward the cemetery of Vincennes where executed spies and traitors were interred in unmarked graves.

"'A queer one, that,' an officer of the party which had accompanied the prisoner to execution told us as we walked toward our waiting cars. 'When we left the Santé he was almost numb with fright, but when I told him that the coup de grâce—the mercy shot—was always given on occasions of this kind, he seemed to forget his fears and laughed and joked with us and with his warders till the very minute when we reached the field. Tiens, he seemed to have a premonition that the volley would not at once prove fatal and that he must suffer till the mercy shot was given. Do you recall how he reminded the platoon commander to remember the shot before the order to fire was given? Poor devil!'"

"Ah?" said Jules de Grandin. "A-ah? Do you report that conversation accurately, my friend?"

"Of course I do," young Tanis answered. "It's stamped as firmly on my mind as if it happened yesterday. One doesn't forget such things, sir."

"Précisément, Monsieur," de Grandin agreed with a thoughtful nod. "I did but ask for verification. This may have some bearing on that which may develop later, though I hope not. What next, if you please?"

Young Tanis shook his head as though to clear an unhappy memory from his mind. "Just one thought kept dinning in my brain," he continued. "'Sonia is dead—Sonia is dead!' a jeering voice seemed repeating endlessly in my ear. 'She called on you for help and you failed her!' By the time we arrived at the censor's bureau I was half mad; by luncheon I had formed a resolve. I would visit Saint Sébastien that night and take farewell of my dead sweetheart—she whom Fouchet had called my morte amoureuse.

"The light mist of the morning had ripened into a steady, streaming downpour by dark; by half-past eleven, when my fiacre let me down at Saint Sébastien, the wind was blowing half a gale and the rain drops stung like whip-lashes as they beat into my face beneath the brim of my field hat. I turned my raincoat collar up as far as it would go and splashed and waded through the puddles to the pentice of the tiny chapel beside the cemetery entrance. A light burned feebly in the intendant's cabin, and as the old fellow came shuffling to open the door in answer to my furious knocks, a cloud of super-heated, almost fetid air burst into my face. There must have been a one per cent concentration of carbon monoxide in the room, for every opening was tightly plugged and a charcoal brazier was going full blast.

"He blinked stupidly at me a moment; then: '*M'sieur l'Americain?*' he asked doubtfully, looking at my soaking hat and slicker for confirmation of his guess. '*M'sieur* has no doubt lost his way, *n'est-ce-pas?* This is the cemetery of Saint Sébastien—'

"'*Monsieur l'Americain* has not lost his way, and he is perfectly aware this is the cemetery of Saint Sébastien,' I assured him. Without waiting for the invitation I knew he would not give, I pushed by him into the stuffy little cabin and kicked the door shut. 'Would the estimable *fossoyeur* care to earn a considerable sum of money—five hundred—a thousand francs—perhaps?' I asked.

"'*Sacré Dieu*, he is crazy, this one,' the old man muttered. 'Mad he is, like all the Yankees, and drunk in the bargain. Help me, blessed Mother!'

"I took him by the elbow, for he was edging slowly toward the door, and shook a bundle of hundred-franc notes before his staring eyes. 'Five of these now, five more when you have fulfilled your mission, and not a word to anyone!' I promised.

"His little shoe-button eyes shone with speculative avarice. '*M'sieur* desires that I help him kill some one?' he ventured. 'Is it perhaps that M'*sieur* has outside the body of one whom he would have secretly interred?'

"'Nothing as bad as that,' I answered, laughing in spite of myself, then stated my desires baldly. 'Will you do it, at once?' I finished.

"'For fifteen hundred francs, perhaps—' he began, but I shut him off.

"'A thousand or nothing,' I told him.

"'*Mille tonnerres, M'sieur*, you have no heart,' he assured me. 'A poor man can scarcely live these days, and the risk I run is great. However,' he added hastily as I folded the bills and prepared to thrust them back into my pocket, 'however, one consents. There is nothing else to do.' He slouched off to a corner of the hut and picked up a rusty spade and mattock. 'Come, let us go,' he growled, dropping a folded burlap sack across his shoulders.

"The rain, wind-driven between the leafless branches of the poplar trees, beat dismally down upon the age-stained marble tombs and the rough, unsodded mounds of the ten-year concessions. Huddled by the farther wall of the cemetery, beneath their rows of ghastly white wooden signboards, the five- and three-year concessions seemed to cower from the storm. These were the graves of the poorer dead, one step above the tenants of the Potter's Field. The rich, who owned their tombs or graves in perpetuity, slept their last long sleep undisturbed; next came the rows of ten-year concessionaires, whose relatives had bought them the right to lie in moderately deep graves for a decade, after which their bones would be exhumed and deposited in a common charnel-house, all trace of their identity lost. The five-year concessionnaires' graves were scarcely deeper than the height of the coffins they enclosed, and their repose was limited to half a decade, while the three-year concessions, placed nearest the cemetery wall, were little more than mounds of sodden earth heaped over coffins sunk scarce a foot underground, destined to be broken down and emptied in thirty-six months. The sexton led the way to one of these and began shoveling off the earth with his spade.

"His tool struck an obstruction with a thud and in a moment he was wrenching at the coffin top with the flat end of his mattock.

"I took the candle-lantern he had brought and flashed its feeble light into the coffin. Sonia lay before me, rigid as though petrified, her hands tight-clenched, the nails digging into the soft flesh of her palms, little streams of dried blood running from each self-inflicted wound. Her eyes were closed—thank heaven!—her mouth a little open, and on her lips there lay a double line of bloody froth.

"'*Grand Dieu!*' the sexton cried as he looked past me into the violated coffin. 'Come away, quickly, *M'sieur*; it is a vampire that we see! Behold the life-like countenance, the opened mouth all bloody from the devil's breakfast, the hands all wet with human blood! Come, I will strike it to the heart with my pickax and sever its unhallowed head with my spade, then we shall fill the grave again and go away all quickly. O, *Sainte Vierge*, have pity on us! See, *M'sieur*, I do begin!' He laid the spur-end of his mattock against Sonia's left breast, and I could see the flimsy crêpe night robe she wore by way of shroud and the soft flesh beneath dimple under the iron's weight.

"'Stop it, you fool!' I bellowed, snatching his pickax and bending forward. 'You shan't—' Some impulse prompted me to rearrange the shroud where the muddy mattock had soiled it, and as my hand came into contact with the beloved body I started. *The flesh was warm.*

"I thrust the doddering old sexton back with a tremendous shove and he landed sitting in a pool of mud and water and squatted there, mouthing bleating admonitions to me to come away.

"Sinking to my knees beside the grave I put my hand against her breast, then laid a finger on her throat beneath the angle of the jaw, as they'd taught us in first-aid class. There was no doubt of it. Faint as the fluttering of a fledgling thrust prematurely from its nest and almost perished with exposure, but still perceptible, a feeble pulse was beating in her breast and throat.

"A moment later I had snatched my raincoat off, wrapped it about her, and, flinging a handful of banknotes at the screaming sexton, I clasped her flaccid body in my arms, sloshed through the mud to the cemetery wall and vaulted over it.

"I found myself in a sort of alley flanked on both sides by stables, a pale light burning at its farther end. Toward this I made, bending almost double against the driving rain in order to shield my precious burden from the storm and to present the poorest target possible if the sexton should procure a gun and take a pot-shot at me.

"It seemed as though I waded through the rain for hours, though actually I don't suppose I walked for more than twenty minutes before a prowling taxi hailed me. I jumped into the vehicle and told the man to drive to my quarters as fast as his old rattletrap would go, and while we skidded through the sodden streets I propped Sonia up against the cushions and wrapped my blouse about her feet while I held her hands in mine, chafing them and breathing on them.

"Once in my room I put her into bed, piled all the covers I could about her, heated water and soaked some flannel cloths in it and put the hot rolls to her feet, then mixed some cognac and water and forced several spoonfuls of it down her throat.

"I must have worked an hour, but finally my clumsy treatment began to show results. The faintest flush appeared in her cheeks, and a tinge of color came to the pale, wounded lips which I'd wiped clean of blood and bathed in water and cologne when I first put her into bed.

"As soon as I dared leave her for a moment I hustled out and roused the *concierge* and sent her scrambling for a doctor. It seemed a week before he came, and when he did he merely wrote me a prescription, looked importantly through his *pince-nez* and suggested that I have him call next morning.

"I pleaded illness at the bureau and went home from the surgeon's office with advice to stay indoors as much as possible for the next week. I was a sort of privileged character, you see, and got away with shameless malingering which would have gotten any other fellow a good, sound roasting from the sawbones. Every moment after that which I could steal from my light duties at the bureau I spent with Sonia. Old Madame Couchin, the *concierge*, I drafted into service as a nurse, and she accepted the situation with the typical Frenchwoman's aplomb.

"It was September before Sonia finally came back to full consciousness, and then she was so weak that the month was nearly gone before she could totter out with me to get a little sunshine and fresh air in the *bois*. We had a wonderful time shopping at the Galleries Lafayette, replacing the horrifying garments Madame Couchin had bought for us with a suitable wardrobe. Sonia took rooms at a little *pension*, and in October we were—

"*Ha, parbleu*, married at last!" Jules de Grandin exclaimed with a delighted chuckle. "*Mille crapauds*, my friend, I thought we never should have got you to the parson's door!"

"Yes, and so we were married," Tanis agreed with a smile.

The girl lifted her husband's hand and cuddled it against her cheek. "Please, Donald dear," she pleaded, "please don't let Konstantin take me from you again."

"But, darling," the young man protested, "I tell you, you must be mistaken. "Mustn't she, Doctor de Grandin?" he appealed. "If I saw Konstantin fall before a firing-party and saw the corporal blow his brains out, and saw them nail him in his coffin, he *must* be dead, mustn't he? Tell her she can't be right, sir!"

"But, Donald, you saw *me* in *my* coffin, too—" the girl began.

"My friends," de Grandin interrupted gravely, "it may be that you both are right, though the good God forbid that it is so."

4. Menace Out of Bedlam

DONALD AND SONIA TANIS regarded him with open-mouthed astonishment. "You mean it's possible Konstantin might have escaped in some mysterious way, and actually come here?" the young man asked at last.

The little Frenchman made no answer, but the grave regard he bent on them seemed more ominous than any vocally expressed opinion.

"But I say," Tanis burst out, as though stung to words by de Grandin's silence, "he can't take her from me. I can't say I know much about such things, but surely the law won't let—"

"*Ah bah!*" Inspector Renouard's sardonic laugh cut him short. "The law," he gibed, "what is it? *Parfum d'un chameau.* I think in this country it is a code devised to give the criminal license to make the long nose at honest men. Yes.

"A month and more ago I came to this so splendid country in search of one who has most richly deserved the kiss of Madame Guillotine, and here I catch him red-handed in most flagrant crime. 'You are arrest,' I tell him. 'For wilful murder, for sedition and subornation of sedition and for stirring up rebellion against the Republic of France I make you arrested.' *Voilà.*

"I take him to the Ministry of Justice. '*Messieurs*,' I say, 'I have here a very noted criminal whom I desire to return to French jurisdiction that he may suffer according to his misdoings.' Certainly.

"*Alors*, what happens? The gentlemen at the *Palais de Justice* tell me: 'It shall be even as you say.'

"Do they assist me? *Hélas*, entirely otherwise. In furtherance of his diabolical designs this one has here abducted a young American lady and on her has committed the most abominable assault. For this, say the American authorities, he must suffer.

"'How much?' I ask. 'Will his punishment be death?'

"'Oh, no,' they answer me. 'We shall incarcerate him in the *bastille* for ten years; perhaps fifteen.'

"'*Bien alors*,' I tell them, 'let us compose our differences amicably. Me, I have traced this despicable one clear across the world, I have made him arrested for his crimes; I am prepared to take him where a most efficient executioner will decapitate his head with all celerity. *Voilà tout*; a man dies but once, let this one die for the crime which is a capital offense by the laws of France, and which is not, but should be capital by American law. That way we shall both be vindicated.' Is not my logic absolute? Would not a three-year-old child of most deficient intellect be convinced by it? Of course; but these ones? *Non*.

"'We sympathize with you,' they tell me, 'but *tout la même* he stays with us to expiate his crime in prison.' Then they begin his prosecution.

"*Grand Dieu*, the farce that trial is! First come the lawyers with their endless tongues and heavy words to make fools of the jury. Next comes a corps of doctors who will testify to anything, so long as they are paid. 'Not guilty by reason of insanity,' the verdict is, and so they take him to a madhouse.

"Not only that," he added, his grievance suddenly becoming vocal again, "they tell me that should this despicable one recover from his madness, he will be discharged from custody and may successfully resist extradition by the Government of France. Renouard is made the fool of! If he could but once get his hands on this criminal, Sun Ah Poy, or if that half-brother of Satan would but manage to escape from the madhouse that I might find him unprotected by the attendants—"

Crash! I ducked my head involuntarily as a missile whistled through the sleet-drenched night, struck the study window a shattering blow and hurtled across the room, smashing against the farther wall with a resounding crack.

Renouard, the Tanises and I leaped to our feet as the egg-like object burst and a sickly-sweet smell permeated the atmosphere, but Jules de Grandin seemed suddenly to go wild. As though propelled by a powerful spring he bounded from the couch, cleared the six feet or so separating him from Sonia in a single flying leap and snatched at the trailing drapery of her dinner frock, ripping a length of silk off with a furious tug and flinging it veilwise about her head. "Out—for your lives, go out!" he cried, covering his mouth and nose with a wadded handkerchief and pushing the girl before him toward the door.

We obeyed instinctively, and though a scant ten seconds intervened between the entry of the missile and our exit, I was already feeling a stinging sensation in my eyes and a constriction in my throat as though a ligature had been drawn around it. Tears were streaming from Renouard's and Tanis' eyes, too, as we rushed pell-mell into the hall and de Grandin slammed the door behind us. "What—" I began, but he waved me back.

"Papers—newspapers—all you have!" he ordered hysterically, snatching a rug from the hall floor and stuffing it against the crack between the door and sill.

I took a copy of the *Evening News* from the hall table and handed it to him, and he fell to tearing it in strips and stuffing the cracks about the door with fierce energy. "To the rear door," he ordered. "Open it and breath as deeply as you may. I do not think we were exposed enough to do us permanent injury, but fresh air will help, in any event.

"I humbly beg your pardon, Madame Tanis," he added as he joined us in the kitchen a moment later. "It was most unconventional to set on you and tear your gown to shreds the way I did, but"—he turned to Tanis with a questioning smile—"perhaps *Monsieur* your husband can tell you what it was we smelled in the study a moment hence."

"I'll tell the world I can," young Donald answered. "I smelt that stuff at Mons, and it darn near put me in my grave. You saved us; no doubt about it, Doctor de Grandin. It's tricky, that stuff."

"*What* is?" I asked. This understanding talk of theirs got on my nerves.

"Name of a thousand pestiferous mosquitoes, yes, what was it?" Renouard put in.

"Phosgene gas—COCl2" de Grandin answered. "It was among the earliest of gases used in the late war, and therefore not so deadly as the others; but it is not a healthy thing to be inhaled, my friend. However, I think that in a little while the study will be safe, for that broken window makes a most efficient ventilator, and the phosgene is quickly dissipated in the air. Had he used mustard gas—*tiens*, one does not like to speculate on such unpleasant things. No."

"He?" I echoed. "Who the dickens are you talking—"

There was something grim in the smile which hovered beneath the upturned ends of his tightly waxed wheat-blond mustache. "I damn think Friend Renouard has his wish," he answered, and a light which heralded the joy of combat shone in his small blue eyes. "If Sun Ah Poy has not burst from his madhouse and come to tell us that the game of hide-and-go-seek is on once more I am much more mistaken than I think. Yes. Certainly."

The whining, warning *whe-e-eng!* of a police car's siren sounded in the street outside and heavy feet tramped my front veranda while heavy fists beat furiously on the door.

"Ouch, God be praised, ye're all right, Doctor de Grandin, sor!" Detective Sergeant Jeremiah Costello burst into the house, his greatcoat collar turned up round his ears, a shining film of sleet encasing the black derby hat he wore habitually. "We came here hell-bent for election to warn ye, sor," he added breathlessly. "We just heard it ourselves, an'—"

"*Tiens*, so did we!" de Grandin interrupted with a chuckle.

"Huh? What're ye talkin' of, sor? I've come to warn ye—"

"That the efficiently resourceful Doctor Sun Ah Poy, of Cambodia and elsewhere, has burst the bonds of bedlam and taken to the warpath, *n'est-ce-pas?*" de Grandin laughed outright at the Irishman's amazed expression.

"Come, my friend," he added, "there is no magic here. I did not gaze into a crystal and go into a trance, then say, 'I see it all—Sun Ah Poy has escaped from the asylum for the criminal insane and comes to this place to work his mischief.' Indeed no. Entirely otherwise. Some fifteen minutes gone the good Renouard expressed a wish that Doctor Sun might manage his escape so that the two might come to grips once more, and hardly had the words flown from his lips when a phosgene bomb was merrily tossed through the window, and it was only by a hasty exit we escaped the inconvenience of asphyxiation. I am not popular with many people, and there are those who would shed few tears at my funeral, but I do not know of one who would take pleasure in throwing a stink-bomb through the window to stifle me. No, such clever tricks as that belong to Doctor Sun, who loves me not at all, but who dislikes my friend Renouard even more cordially. *Alors*, I deduce that Sun Ah Poy is out again and we shall have amusement for some time to come. Am I correct?"

"Check an' double check, as th' felly says," Costello nodded. "'Twas just past dark this evenin' whilst th' warders wuz goin' through th' State Asylum, seein' everything wuz shipshape for th' night, sor, that Doctor Sun did his disappearin' act. He'd been meek as anny lamb ever since they took him to th' bughouse, an' th' orderlies down there had decided he warn't such a bad actor, afther all. Well, sor, th' turnkey passed his door, an' this Doctor Sun invites him in to see a drawin' he's made. He's a clever felly wid his hands, for all his bein' crippled, an' th' boys at th' asylum is always glad to see what he's been up to makin'.

"Th' pore chap didn't have no more chance than a sparry in th' cat's mouth, sor. Somewhere th' Chinese divil had got hold of a table-knife an' ground it to a razor edge. One swipe o' that across th' turnkey's throat an' he's floppin' round th' floor like a chicken wid its head cut off, not able to make no outcry for th' blood that's stranglin' him. A pore nut 'cross th' corridor lets out a squawk, an' Doctor Sun ups an' cuts *his* throat as cool as ye'd pare a apple for yer luncheon, sor. They finds this out from another inmate that's seen it all but had sense enough in his pore crazy head to keep his mouth shut till afther it's all over.

"Ye know th' cell doors ain't locked, but th' different wards is barred off from each other wid corridors between. This Doctor Sun takes th' warder's uniform cap as calm as ye please and claps it on his ugly head, then walks to th' ward door an' unlocks it wid th' keys he's taken from th' turnkey. Th' guard on duty in th' corridor don't notice nothin' till Sun's clear through th' door; then it's too late, for Sun stabs 'im to th' heart before he can so much as raise his club, an' beats it down th' corridor. There's a fire escape at th' other end o' th' passage—one o' them spiral things that works like a slide inside a sheet-iron cylinder, ye know. It's locked, but Sun has th' key, an' in a moment he's slipped inside, locked th' door behind him an' slid down faster than a snake on roller skates. He's into th' grounds an' over th' wall before they even know he's loose, an' he must o' had confederates waitin' for him outside, for they heard th' roar of the car runnin' like th' hammers o' hell whilst they're still soundin' th' alarm.

"O' course th' State Troopers an' th' local police wuz notified, but he seems to 'a' got clean away, except—"

"Yes, except?" de Grandin prompted breathlessly, his little, round blue eyes sparkling with excitement.

"Well, sor, we don't rightly *know* it wuz him, but we're suspectin' it. They found a trooper run down an' kilt on th' highway over by Morristown, wid his motorcycle bent up like a pretzel an' not a whole bone left in his body. Looks like Sun's worrk, don't it, sor?"

"Assuredly," the Frenchman nodded. "Is there more to tell?"

"Nothin' except he's gone, evaporated, vanished into thin air, as th' sayin' is, sor; but we figured he's still nursin' a grudge agin Inspector Renouard an' you, an' maybe come to settle it, so we come fast as we could to warn ye."

"Your figuring is accurate, my friend," de Grandin answered with another smile. "May we trespass on your good nature to ask that you escort Monsieur and Madame Tanis home? I should not like them to encounter Doctor Sun Ah Poy, for he plays roughly. As for us—Renouard, Friend Trowbridge and me—we shall do very well unguarded for tonight. Good Doctor Sun has shot his bolt; he will not be up to other tricks for a little time, I think, for he undoubtlessly has a hideaway prepared, and to it he has gone. He would not linger here, knowing the entire *gendarmerie* is on his heels. No. To hit and run, and run as quickly as he hits, will be his policy, for a time, at least."

5. Desecration

"**D**OCTOR DE GRANDIN—GENTLEMEN!**" DONALD Tanis burst into the breakfast room as de Grandin, Renouard and I were completing our morning meal next day. "Sonia—my wife—she's gone!"

"Eh? What is it you tell me?" de Grandin asked. "Gone?"

"Yes, sir. She rides every morning, you see, and today she left for a canter in the park at six o'clock, as usual. I didn't feel up to going out this morning, and lay abed rather late. I was just going down to breakfast when they told me her horse had come back to the stable—alone."

"Oh, perhaps she had a tumble in the park," I suggested soothingly. "Have you looked—"

"I've looked everywhere," he broke in. "Soldiers' Park's not very large, and if she'd been in it I'd have found her long ago. After what happened last night, I'm afraid—"

"*Morbleu, mon pauvre,* you fear with reason," de Grandin cut him short. "Come, let us go. We must seek her—we must find her, right away, at once; without delay, for—"

"If ye plaze, sor, Sergeant Costello's askin' for Doctor de Grandin," announced Nora McGinnis, appearing at the breakfast room door. "He's got a furrin gentleman wid him," she amplified as de Grandin gave an exclamation of impatience at the interruption, "an' says as how he's most partic'lar to talk wid ye a minit."

Father Pophosepholos, shepherd of the little flock of Greeks, Lithuanians and Russians composing the congregation of St. Basil's Church, paused at the doorway beside the big Irish policeman with uplifted hand as he invoked divine blessing on the inmates of the room, then advanced with smiling countenance to take the slim white fingers de Grandin extended. The aged *papa* and the little Frenchman were firmest friends, though one lived in a thought-world of the Middle-Ages, while the other's thoughts were modern as the latest model airplane.

"My son," the old man greeted, "the powers of evil were abroad last night. The greatest treasure in the world was ravished from my keeping, and I come to you for help."

"A treasure, *mon père?*" de Grandin asked.

Father Pophosepholos rose from his chair, and we forgot the cheap, worn stuff of his purple cassock, his broken shoes, even the pinchbeck gold and imitation amethyst of his pectoral cross as he stood in patriarchal majesty with upraised hands and back-thrown head. "The most precious body and blood of our blessed Lord," he answered sonorously. "Last night, between the sunset and the dawn, they broke into the church and bore away the holy Eucharist." For a moment he paused, then in all reverence echoed the Magdalen's despairing cry: "They have taken away my Lord, and I know not where they have laid Him!"

"*Ha,* do you say it?" The momentary annoyance de Grandin had evinced at the old priest's intrusion vanished as he gazed at the cleric with a level stare of fierce intensity. "Tell me of the sacrilege. All—tell me all. Right away; at once, immediately. I am all attention!"

Father Pophosepholos resumed his seat and the sudden fire which animated him died down. Once more he was a tired old man, the threadbare shepherd of a half-starved flock. "I saw you smile when I mentioned a treasure being stolen from *me*," he told de Grandin gently. "You were justified, my son, for St. Basil's is a poor church, and I am poorer still. Only the faith which is in me sustains me through the struggle. We ask no help from the public, and receive none; the rich Latins look on us with pity, the Anglicans sometimes give us slight assistance; the Protestant heretics scarcely know that we exist. We are a joke to them, and, because we're poor, they sometimes play mischievous pranks on us—their boys stone our windows, and once or twice when parties of their young people have come slumming they have disturbed our services with their thoughtless laughter or ill-bred talking during service. Our liturgy is only meaningless mummery to them, you see.

"But this was no childish mischief, not even the vandalism of irreverent young hoodlums!" his face flushed above its frame of gray beard. "This was deliberately planned and maliciously executed blasphemy and sacrilege!

"Our rubric makes no provision for low mass, like the Latins'," he explained, "and daily celebration of the Eucharist is not enjoined; so, since our ceremony of consecration is a lengthy one, we customarily celebrate only once or twice a week, and the pre-sanctified elements are reserved in a tabernacle on the altar.

"This morning as I entered the sanctuary I found everything in disorder. The veils had been torn from the table, thrown upon the floor and fouled with filth, the ikon of the Virgin had been ripped from the reredos and the tabernacle violated. They had carried off the elements together with the chalice and paten, and in their place had thrust into the tabernacle the putrefying carcass of a cat!" Tears welled in the old man's eyes as he told of the sacrilege.

Costello's face went brick-red with an angry flush, for the insult put upon the consecrated elements stung every fiber of his nature. "Bad cess to 'em!" he muttered. "May they have th' curse o' Cromwell!"

"They took my chasuble and cope, my alb, my miter and my stole," the priest continued, "and from the sacristy they took the deacon's vestments—"

"*Grand Dieu*, I damn perceive their game!" the little Frenchman almost shouted. "At first I thought this might be but an act of wantonness performed by wicked boys. I have seen such things. Also, the chalice and the paten might have some little value to a thief; but this is no mere case of thievery mixed with sacrilege. *Non*. The stealing of the vestments is conclusive proof.

"Tell me, *mon père*," he interrupted himself with seeming irrelevance, "it is true, is it not, that only the celebrant and the deacon are necessary for the office of consecration? No subdeacon is required?"

The old priest nodded wonderingly.

"And these elements were already consecrated?"

"They were already consecrated," the clergyman returned. "Presanctified, we call it when they are reserved for future services."

"Thank God, no little one then stands in peril," de Grandin answered.

"*Mon père*, it gives me greatest joy to say I'll aid in tracking down these miscreants. Monsieur Tanis, unless I am more greatly mistaken than I think, there is direct connection between your lady's disappearance and this act of sacrilege. Yes, I am sure of it!" He nodded several times with increasing vigor.

"But, my dear fellow," I expostulated, "what possible connection can there be between—"

"*Chut!*" he cut me short. "This is the doing of that villain Konstantin! Assuredly. The wife he has again abducted, though he has not attempted to go near the husband. For why? *Pardieu*, because by leaving Monsieur Donald free he still permits the wife one little, tiny, ray of hope. With vilest subtlety he holds her back from the black brink of despair and suicide that he may force her to compliance to his will by threats against the man she loves. *Sacré nom d'un artichaut*, I shall say yes! Certainly; of course."

"You—you mean he'll make Sonia go with him—leave me—by threats against my life?" young Tanis faltered.

"*Précisément.* That and more, I fear, Monsieur," de Grandin answered somberly.

"But what worse can he do than that? You—you don't think he'll kill her, do you?" the husband cried.

The little Frenchman rose and paced the study a moment in thoughtful silence. At last: "Courage, *mon brave*," he bade, putting a kindly hand on Tanis' shoulder. "You and Madame Sonia have faced perils—even the perils of the grave—before. Take heart! I shall not hide from you that your present case is as desperate as any you have faced before; but if my guess is right, as heaven knows I hope it is not, your lady stands in no immediate bodily peril. If that were all we had to fear we might afford to rest more easily; as it is—"

"As it is," Renouard cut in, "let us go with all celerity to St. Basil's church and look to see what we can find. The trail grows cold, *mon Jules*, but—"

"But we shall find and follow it," de Grandin interrupted. "*Parbleu*, we'll follow it though it may lead to the fire-doors of hell's own furnaces, and then—"

The sharp, insistent ringing of the telephone broke through his fervid prophecy.

"This is Miss Wilkinson, supervisor at Casualty Hospital, Doctor Trowbridge," a professionally precise feminine voice informed me. "If Detective Sergeant Costello is at your office, we've a message for him. Officer Hornsby is here, about to go on the table, and insists we put a message through to Sergeant Costello at once. We've already called him at headquarters, and they told us—"

"Just a minute," I bade. "It's for you, Sergeant," I told Costello, handing him the instrument.

"Yes," Costello called into the mouthpiece. "Yes; uh-huh. *What?* Glory be to God!"

He swung on us with flushing face and blazing eyes. "'Twas Hornsby," he announced. "He wuz doin' relief traffic duty out at Auburndale an' Gloucester Streets, an' a car run 'im down half an hour ago. There wuz no witnesses to th' accident, an' Hornsby couldn't git th' license number, but just before they struck 'im he seen a felly ridin' in th' car.

"You'll be rememberin' Hornsby wuz in th' raidin' party that captured this here Doctor Sun?" he asked de Grandin.

The Frenchman nodded.

"Well, sor, Hornsby's got th' camera eye. He don't forget a face once he's seen it, even for a second, an' he tells me Doctor Sun wuz ridin' in th' car that bowled 'im over. They run 'im down deliberate, sor, an' Sun Ah Poy was ridin' wid a long, tall, black-faced felly wid slantin' eyebrows an' a pan like th' pictures ye see o' Satan in th' chur-rches, sor!"

"And what was this one doing with his pan?" Renouard demanded. "Is it that—"

"Pan," Costello shouted, raising his voice as many people do when seeking to make clear their meaning to a foreigner, "'twas his pan I'm speaking of. Not a pan; his pan—his mush—his map—his puss, ye know.

"*Pas possible!* The miscreant held a pan of mush for his cat to eat, and a map, also, while his motor car ran down the gendarme?"

"Oh, go sit in a tree—*no!*" Costello roared. "It's his face I'm afther tellin' ye of. Hornsby said he had a face—a face, git me; a face is a pan an' a pan's a face—like th' divil's, an' he wuz ridin' in th' same car wid this here now Doctor Sun Ah Poy that's made his getaway from th' asylum! Savvy?"

"Oh, *mais oui*," the Frenchman grinned. "I apprehend. It is another of the so droll American idioms which you employ. *Oui-da*; I perceive him."

"'Tis plain as anny pikestaff they meant to do 'im in deliberately," Costello went on, "an' they like to made good, too. Th' pore felly's collarbone is broke, an' so is several ribs; but glory be to heaven, they wuz goin' so fast they bumped 'im clean out o' th' road an' onto th' sidewalk, an' they kep' on goin' like th' hammers o' hell widout waitin' to see how much they'd hurt 'im."

"You hear, my friends?" de Grandin cried, leaping to his feet, eyes flashing, diminutive, wheat-blond mustache twitching with excitement like the whiskers of an angry tomcat. "You heard the message of this gloriously devoted officer of the law who sends intelligence to Costello even as he waits to go upon the operating-table? What does it mean? I ask. No, I demand what does it mean?

"Sun Ah Poy rides in a car which maims and injures the police, and with him rides another with a face like Satan's. *Mordieu, mes amis*, we shall have hunting worthy of our utmost skill, I think.

"*Sun Ah Poy and Konstantin have met and combined against us!* Come, my friends, let us take their challenge.

"Come, Renouard, my old one, this is more than mere police work. The enemy laughs at our face, he makes the thumb-nose at us and at all for which we stand. Forward to the battle, *brave comrade. Pour la France!*"

6. Allies Unawares

FOUR OF US—DE GRANDIN, Renouard, Donald Tanis and I—sat before my study fire and stared gloomily into the flames. All day the other three, accompanied by Costello, had combed the city and environs, but neither sign nor clue, trail nor trace of the missing woman could they find.

"By heaven," Tanis cried, striking his forehead with his hand in impotent fury, "it looks as if the fellow were the devil himself!"

"Not so bad a guess, *mon brave*," de Grandin nodded gloomily. "Certain it is he is on friendly terms with the dark powers, and, as usual, Satan is most kindly to his own."

"*Ah bah, mon Jules*," Renouard rejoined, "you do but make a bad matter so much worse with your mumblings of Satan and his cohorts. Is it not sufficient that two poor ladies of this town are placed in deadly peril without your prating of diabolical opponents and—"

"*Two* ladies?" Tanis interrupted wonderingly. "Why, has he abducted some one else—"

"*Bien non*," Renouard's quick explanation came. "It is of another that I speak, *Monsieur*. This Konstantin, who has in some way met with Sun Ah Poy and made a treaty of alliance with him, has taken your poor lady for revenge, even as he sought to do when first we met him, but Sun Ah Poy has also reasons to desire similar vengeance of his own, and all too well we know how far his insane jealousy and lust will lead him. Regard me, if you please: As I have previously told you, I came across the world in search of Sun Ah Poy, and took him bloody-handed in commission of a crime of violence. Clear from Cambodia I trailed him, for there he met, and having met, desired a white girl-dancer in the mighty temple shrine at Angkor. Just who she was we do not know for certain, but strongly circumstantial evidence would indicate she was the daughter of a missionary gentleman named Crownshield, an American, who had been murdered by the natives at the instigation of the heathen priests and whose widowed mother had been spirited away and lodged within the temple until she knew the time of woman and her child was born. Then, we suppose, the mother, too, was done to death, and the little white girl reared as a *bayadère*, or temple-dancer.

"The years went on, and to Cambodia came a young countryman of yours, a citizen of Harrisonville, who met and loved this nameless mystery of a temple *coryphée*, known only as Thi-bah, the dancing-woman of the temple, and she returned his passion, for in Cambodia as elsewhere, like cries aloud to like, and this milk-skinned, violet-eyed inmate of a heathen shrine knew herself not akin to her brown-faced fellow members of the temple's *corps du ballet*.

"*Enfin*, they did elope and hasten to the young man's home in this city, and on their trail, blood-lustful as a tiger in the hunt, there followed Sun Ah Poy, determined to retake the girl whom he had purchased from the priests; if possible to slay the man on whom her favor rested, also. *Parbleu*, and as the shadow follows the body when the sun is low, Renouard did dog the footsteps of this Sun Ah Poy. Yes.

"*Tiens*, almost the wicked one succeeded in his plans for vengeance, but with the aid of Jules de Grandin, who is a clever fellow, for all his stupid looks and silly ways, I captured him and saved the little lady, now a happy wife and an American citizeness by marriage and adoption.

"How I then fared, how this miscreant of a Sun Ah Poy made apes and monkeys of the law and lodged himself all safely in a madhouse, I have already related. How he escaped and all but gave me my quietus you know from personal, first-hand experience. Certainly.

"Now, consider: Somewhere in the vicinage there lurk these two near-mad men with twin maggots of jealousy and vengeance gnawing at their brains. Your so unfortunate lady is already in their power—Konstantin has scored a point in his game of passion and revenge. But I know Sun Ah Poy. A merchant prince he was in former days, the son of generations of merchant princes, and Chinese merchant princes in the bargain.

"Such being so, I know all well that Sun Ah Poy has not united forces with this Konstantin unless he is assured of compensation. My death? *Pouf*, a bagatelle! Me he can kill—at least, he can attempt my life—whenever he desires, and do it all unaided. Last night we saw how great his resource is and how casually he tossed a stink-bomb through the window by way of telling me he was at liberty once more. No, no, my friend; he has not joined with Konstantin merely to be assured that Renouard goes home in one of those elaborate containers for the dead your undertakers sell. On the contrary. He seeks to regain the custody of her who flouted his advances and ran off with another man. Thus far his purpose coincides with Konstantin's. They both desire women whom other men have won. One has succeeded in his quest, at least for the time being; the other still must make his purpose good. Already they have run down a *gendarme* who stood in their way—thus far they work in concert. Beyond a doubt they will continue to be allies till their plans are consummated. Yes."

The clatter of the front-door knocker silenced him, and I rose to answer the alarm, knowing Nora McGinnis had long since gone to bed.

"Is there a feller named Renyard here?" demanded a hoarse voice as I swung back the door and beheld a most untidy taximan in the act of assaulting the knocker again.

"There's a gentleman named Renouard stopping here," I answered coldly. "What—"

"A'right, tell 'im to come out an' git his friend, then. He's out in me cab, drunk as a hard-boiled owl, an' won't stir a foot till this here Renyard feller comes fer 'im. Tell 'im to make it snappy, will yuh, buddy. This here Chinaman's so potted I'm scared he's goin' to—"

"A Chinaman?" I cut in sharply. "What sort of Chinaman?"

"A dam' skinny one, an' a mean one, too. Orderin' me about like I wuz a servant or sumpin', an'—"

"Renouard—de Grandin!" I called over my shoulder. "Come here, quickly, please! There's a Chinaman out there in that cab—'a skinny Chinaman,' the driver calls him—and he wants Renouard to come out to him. D'ye suppose—"

"*Sacré nom d'un porc*, I damn do!" de Grandin answered. To the taximan he ordered:

"Bring in your passenger at once, my friend. We can not come out to him; but—"

"Say, feller, I ain't takin' no more orders from a Frog than I am from a Chink, git me?" the cabman interposed truculently. "You'll come out an' git this here drunk, an' like it, or else—"

"*Précisément*; or else?" de Grandin shot back sharply, and the porchlight's rays gleamed on the wicked-looking barrel of his small but deadly automatic pistol. "Will you obey me, or must I shoot?"

The taximan obeyed, though slowly, with many a backward, fearful glance, as though he did not know what instant the Frenchman's pistol might spit death. From the cab he helped a delicate, bent form muffled to the ears in a dark overcoat, and assisted it slowly up the steps. "Here he is," he muttered angrily, as he transferred his tottering charge to Renouard's waiting hands.

The shrouded form reeled weakly at each step as de Grandin and Renouard assisted it down the hall and guided it to an armchair by the fire. For a moment silence reigned within the study, the visitant crouching motionless in his seat and wheezing asthmatically at intervals. At length de Grandin crossed the room, took the wide brim of the black-felt hat which obscured the man's face in both his hands and wrenched the headgear off.

"Ah?" he ejaculated as the light struck upon the caller's face. "A-a-ah? I thought as much!"

Renouard breathed quickly, almost with a snort, as he beheld the livid countenance turned toward him. "Sun Ah Poy, thou species of a stinking camel, what filthy joke is this you play?" he asked suspiciously.

The Chinaman smiled with a sort of ghastly parody of mirth. His face seemed composed entirely of parchment-like skin stretched drum-tight above the bony processes; his little, deep-set eyes were terrible to look at as empty sockets in a skull; his lips, paper-thin and bloodless, were retracted from a set of broken and discolored teeth. The countenance was as lifeless and revolting as the mummy of Rameses in the British Museum, and differed from the dead man's principally in that it was instinct with conscious evil and lacked the majesty and repose of death.

"Does this look like a jest?" he asked in a low, faltering voice, and with a twisted, claw-like hand laid back a fold of his fur overcoat. The silken Chinese blouse within was stained with fresh, warm blood, and the gory spot grew larger with each pulsation of his heart.

"*Morbleu*, it seems you have collided with just retribution!" de Grandin commented dryly. "Is it that you are come to us for treatment, by any happy chance?"

"Partly," the other answered as another horrifying counterfeit of mirth writhed across his livid mouth. "Doctor Jules de Grandin is a surgeon and a man of honor; the oath of Aesculapius and the obligation of his craft will not allow him to refuse aid to a wounded man who comes to him for succor, whoever that man may be."

"*Eh bien*, you have me there," de Grandin countered, "but I am under no compulsion to keep your presence here a secret. While I am working on your wound the police will be coming with all haste to take you back in custody. You realize that, of course?"

We cut away his shirt and singlet, for undressing him would have been too hazardous. To the left, between the fifth and sixth ribs, a little in front of the mid-axillary line, there gaped a long incised wound, obviously the result of a knife-thrust. Extensive hemorrhage had already taken place, and the patient was weakening quickly from loss of blood. "A gauze pack and styptic collodion," de Grandin whispered softly, "and then perhaps ten minims of adrenalin; it's all that we can do I fear. The state will save electric current by this evening's work, my friend; he'll never live to occupy the chair of execution."

The treatment finished, we propped the patient up with pillows. "Doctor Sun," de Grandin announced professionally, "it is my duty to inform you that death is very near. I greatly doubt that you will live till morning."

"I realize that," the other answered weakly, "nor am I sorry it is so. This wound has brought me back my sanity, and I am once again the man I was before I suffered madness. All I have done while I was mentally deranged comes back to me like memories of a disagreeable dream, and when I think of what I was, and what I have become, I am content that Sun Ah Poy should die.

"But before I go I must discharge my debt—pay you my fee," he added with another smile, and this time, I thought, there was more of gentleness than irony in the grimace. "My time is short and I must leave some details out, but such facts as you desire shall be yours," he added.

"This morning I met Konstantin the Russian as I fled the police, and we agreed to join forces to combat you. He seemed to be a man beset, like me, by the police, and gladly did I welcome him as ally." He paused a moment, and a quick spasm of pain flickered in his face, but he fought it down. "In the East we learn early of some things the Western world will never learn," he gasped. "The lore of China is filled with stories of some beings whose existence you deride. Yet they are real, though happily they become more rare each day. Konstantin is one of them; not wholly man, nor yet entirely demon, but a dreadful hybrid of the two. Not till he'd taken me to his lair did I discover this—he is a servant of the Evil One.

"It cost my life to come and tell you, but *he must be exterminated*. My life for his; the bargain is a trade by which the world will profit. What matters Sun Ah Poy beside the safety of humanity? Konstantin is virtually immortal, but he *can* be killed. Unless you hunt him out and slay him—"

"We know all this," de Grandin interrupted; "at least, I have suspected it. Tell us while you have time where we may find him, and I assure you we shall do to him according to his sins—"

"Old Shepherd's Inn, near Chestertown—the old, deserted place padlocked three years ago for violation of the Prohibition law," the Chinaman broke in. "You'll find him there at night, and with him—go there before the moon has set; by day he is abroad, and with him goes his captive, held fast in bonds of fear, but when the moon has climbed the heavens—" He broke off with a sigh of pain, and little beads of perspiration shone upon his brow. The man was going fast; the pauses between his words were longer, and his voice was scarcely louder than a whisper.

"Renouard"—he rolled his head toward the Inspector—"in the old days you called me friend. Can you forget the things I did in madness and say good-bye to the man you used to know—will you take my hand, Renouard? I can not hold it out to you—I am too weak, but—"

"Assuredly, I shall do more, *mon vieux*," Renouard broke in. "*Je vous salue!*" He drew himself erect and raised his right hand in stiff and formal military greeting. Jules de Grandin followed suit.

Then, in turn, they took the dying man's hand in theirs and shook it solemnly.

"Shades—of—honorable—ancestors, comes—now—Sun—Ah—Poy to be among—you!" the Oriental gasped, and as he finished speaking a rattle sounded in his throat and from the corners of his mouth there trickled thin twin streams of blood. His jaw relaxed, his eyes were set and glazed, his breast fluttered once or twice, then all was done.

"Quicker than I thought," de Grandin commented as he lifted the spare, twisted body from the chair and laid it on the couch, then draped a rug over it. "The moment I perceived his wound I knew the pleural wall was punctured, and it was but a matter of moments before internal hemorrhage set in and killed him, but my calculations erred. I would have said half an hour; he has taken only eighteen minutes to die. We must notify the coroner," he added practically. "This news will bring great happiness to the police, and rejoice the newspapers most exceedingly, as well."

"I wonder how he got that wound?" I asked.

"You wonder?" he gave me an astonished glance. "Last night we saw how Konstantin can throw a knife—Renouard's shoulder is still sore in testimony of his skill. The wonder is he got away at all. I wish he had not died so soon; I should have liked to ask him how he did it."

7. Though This Be Damnation

SHEPHERD'S INN WAS LIMNED against the back-drop of wind-driven snow like the gigantic carcass of a stranded leviathan. Remote from human habitation or activity, it stood in the midst of its overgrown grounds, skeletal remains of small summer-houses where in other days Bacchus had dallied drunkenly with Aphrodite stood starkly here and there among the rank-grown evergreens and frost-blasted weeds; flanking the building on the left was a row of frontless wooden sheds where young bloods of the nineties had stabled horse and buggy while reveling in the bar or numerous private dining-rooms upstairs; a row of hitching-posts for tethering the teams of more transient guests stood ranked before the porch. The lower windows were heavily barred by rusted iron rods without and stopped by stout wooden shutters within. Even creepers seemed to have felt the blight which rested on the place, for there was no patch of ivy green upon the brickwork which extended upward to the limit of the lower story.

Beneath a wide-boughed pine we paused for council. "Sergeant," de Grandin ordered, "you and Friend Trowbridge will enter at the rear—I have here the key which fits the door. Keep watchful eyes as you advance, and have your guns held ready, for you may meet with desperate resistance. I would advise that one of you precede the other, and that the first man hold the flashlight, and hold it well out from his body. Thus, if you're seen by Konstantin and he fires or flings a knife at the light, you will suffer injury only to your hand or arm. Meanwhile, the one behind will keep sharp watch and fire at any sound or movement in the dark—a shotgun is most pleasantly effective at any range which can be had within a house.

"Should you come on him unawares, shoot first and parley afterward. This is a foul thing we face tonight, my friends—one does not parley with a rattle-snake, neither does one waste time with a viper such as this. *Non*, by no means. And as you hope for pardon of your sins, shoot him but once; no matter what transpires, you are not to fire a second shot. Remember.

"Renouard and I shall enter from the front and work our way toward you. You shall know when we are come by the fact that our flashlight will be blue— the light in that I give you will be red, so you may shoot at any but a blue light, and we shall blaze away whenever anything but red is shown. You understand?"

"Perfectly, sor," the Irishman returned.

We stumbled through the snow until we reached the rear door and Costello knelt to fit the key into the lock while I stood guard above him with my gun.

"You or me, sor?" he inquired as the lock unlatched, and even in the excite-ment of the moment I noted that its mechanism worked without a squeak.

"Eh?" I answered.

"Which of us carries th' light?"

"Oh. Perhaps I'd better. You're probably a better shot than I."

"O.K. Lead th' way, sor, an' watch your shtep. I'll be right behint ye."

Cautiously we crept through the service hall, darting the red rays of our flash to left and right, through the long-vacant dining-room, finally into the lobby at the front. As yet we saw no sign of Konstantin nor did we hear a sound betokening the presence of de Grandin or Renouard.

The foyer was paved with flagstones set in cement sills, and every now and then these turned beneath our feet, all but precipitating us upon our faces. The air was heavy and dank with that queer, unwholesome smell of earth one associates with graves and tombs; the painted woodwork was dust-grimed and dirty and here and there wallpaper had peeled off in leprous strips, exposing patches of the corpse-gray plaster underneath. From the cen-ter of the hall, slightly to the rear, there rose a wide grand staircase of wood. A sweep of my flashlight toward this brought an exclamation of surprise from both of us.

The central flight of stairs which led to the landing whence the side-flights branched to left and right, was composed of three steps and terminated in a platform some six feet wide by four feet deep. On this had been placed some sort of packing-case or table—it was impossible to determine which at the quick glance we gave it, and over this was draped a cover of some dark material which hung down nearly to the floor. Upon this darker covering there lay a strip of linen cloth and upright at the center of the case was fixed some sort of picture or framed object, while at either end there stood what I first took to be candelabra, each with three tall black candles set into its sockets. "Why," I began in a whisper, it looks like an—"

"Whist, Doctor Trowbridge, sor, there's some one comin'!" Costello breathed in my ear. "Shall I let 'em have it?" I heard the sharp click of his gunlock in the dark.

"There's a door behind us," I whispered back. "Suppose we take cover behind it and watch to see what happens? If it's our man and he comes in here, he'll have to pass us, and we can jump out and nab him; if it's de Grandin and Renouard, we'll hail them and let them know there's no one in the rear of the house. What d'ye say?"

"A'right," he acquiesced. "Let's go."

We stepped back carefully, and I heard Costello fumbling with the door. "O.K., sor, it's open," he whispered. "Watch your shtep goin' over th' sill; it's a bit high."

I followed him slowly, feeling my way with cautious feet, felt his big bulk brush past me as he moved to close the door; then:

"Howly Moses!" he muttered. "It's a trap we're in, sor! It were a snap-lock on th' door. Who th' devil'd 'a' thought o' that?"

He was right. As the door swung to there came a faint, sharp click of a spring lock, and though we strained and wrenched at the handle, the strong oak panels refused to budge.

The room in which we were imprisoned was little larger than a closet, windowless and walled with tongue-and-groove planks in which a line of coat hooks had been screwed. Obviously at one time it had functioned as a sort of cloak room. For some reason the management had fancied decorations in the door, and some five feet from the floor twin designs of interlacing hearts had been bored through the panels with an auger. I blessed the unknown artist who had made the perforations, for they not only supplied our dungeon generously with air but made it possible for us to see all quarters of the lobby without betraying our proximity.

"Don't be talkin', sor," Costello warned. "There's some one comin'!"

The door across the lobby opened slowly, and through it, bearing a sacristan's taper, came a cowled and surpliced figure, an ecclesiastical-looking figure which stepped with solemn pace to the foot of the staircase, sank low in genuflection, then mounted to the landing and lit the candles on the right, retreated, genuflected again, then lit companion candles at the left.

As the wicks took fire and spread a little patch of flickering luminance amid the dark, my first impression was confirmed. The box-like object on the stairs was an altar, clothed and vested in accordance, with the rubric of the Orthodox

Greek Church; at each end burned a trinity of sable candles which gave off an unpleasant smell, and in the center stood a gilt-framed ikon.

Now the light fell full upon the sacristan's face and with a start I recognized Dimitri, the burly Russian Renouard had felled the night we first met Konstantin and Sonia.

The leering altar-wait retired, backed reverently from the parodied sanctuary, returned to the room whence he had entered, and in a moment we heard the sound of chanting mingled with the sharp, metallic clicking of a censer's chains.

Again Dimitri entered, this time swinging a smoking incense-pot, and close behind him, vested as a Russian priest, walked a tall, impressive figure. Above his sacerdotal garb his face stood out sharply in the candles' lambent light, smooth-shaven, long-jawed, swarthy of complexion. His coal-black eyes were deep-set under curiously arched brows; his lusterless black hair was parted in the middle and brushed abruptly backward, leaving a down-pointing triangle in the center of his high and narrow forehead which indicated the commencement of a line which was continued in the prominent bowed nose and sharp, out-jutting chin. It was a striking face, a proud face, a face of great distinction, but a face so cruel and evil it reminded me at once of every pictured image of the devil which I had ever seen. Held high between his upraised hands the evil-looking man bore carefully a large chalice of silver-gilt with a paten fitted over it for cover.

The floating cloud of incense stung my nostrils. I sniffed and fought away a strong impulse to sneeze. And all the while my memory sought to classify that strong and pungent odor. Suddenly I knew. On a vacation trip to Egypt I had spent an evening at an Arab camp out in the desert and watched them build their fires of camel-dung. That was it, the strong smell of ammonia, the faintly sickening odor of the carbonizing fumet!

Chanting slowly in a deep, melodious voice, his attendant chiming in with the responses, the mock-priest marched to the altar and placed the sacred vessels on the fair cloth where the candle-rays struck answering gleams from their cheap gilding. Then with a deep obeisance he retreated, turned, and strode toward the doorway whence he came.

Three paces from the portal he came to pause and struck his hands together in resounding claps, once, twice, three times; and though I had no intimation what I was about to see, I felt my heart beat faster and a curious weakness spread through all my limbs as I waited breathlessly.

Into the faint light of the lobby, vague and nebulous as a phantom-form half seen, half apprehended, stepped Sonia. Slowly, with an almost regal dignity she moved. She was enfolded from white throat to insteps in a long and clinging cloak of heavily embroidered linen which one beautiful, slim hand clutched tight round her at the breast. Something familiar yet queerly strange about the garment struck me as she paused. I'd seen its like somewhere, but never on a woman—the candlelight struck full upon it, and I knew. It was a Greek priest's white-linen over-vestment, an alb, for worked upon it in threads of gold and threads of silver and threads of iridescent color were double-barred Lorraine crosses and three mystic Grecian letters.

"Are you prepared?" the pseudo-priest demanded as he bent his lusterless black eyes upon the girl's pale face.

"I am prepared," she answered slowly. "Though this be damnation to my soul and everlasting corruption to my body, I am prepared, if only you will promise me that he shall go unharmed!"

"Think well," the man admonished, "this rite may be performed only with the aid of a woman pure in heart—a woman in whom there can be found no taint or stain of sin—who gives herself willingly and without reserve, to act the part I call on you to play. Are *you* such an one?"

"I am such an one," she answered steadily, though a ripple of heart-breaking horror ran across her blenching lips, even as they formed the words.

"And you make the offer willingly, without reserve?" he taunted. "You know what it requires? What the consequences to your flesh and soul must be?" With a quick motion he fixed his fingers in her short, blond hair and bent her head back till he gazed directly down into her upturned eyes. "*Willingly?*" he grated. "Without reserve?"

"Willingly," she answered with a choking sob. "Yes, willingly, ten thousand times ten thousand times I offer up my soul and body without a single reservation, if you will promise—"

"Then let us be about it!" he broke in with a low, almost soundless laugh.

Dimitri, who had crouched before the altar, descended with his censer and bowed before the girl till his forehead touched the floor. Then he arose and wrapped the loose ends of his stole about him and passed the censer to the other man, while from a fold of his vestments he drew a strange metal plate shaped like an angel with five-fold outspread wings, and this he waved above her head while she moved slowly toward the altar and the other man walked backward, facing her and censing her with reeking fumes at every step.

A gleam of golden slippers shone beneath her cloak as she approached the lowest of the altar steps, but as she halted for a moment she kicked them quickly off and mounted barefoot to the sanctuary, where she paused a breathless second and blessed herself, but in reverse, commencing at a point below her breast and making the sign of the cross upside-down.

Then on her knees she fell, placing both hands upon the altar-edge and dropping her head between them, and groveled there in utter self-abasement while in a low but steady voice she repeated words which sent the chills of horror through me.

I had not looked inside a Greek book for more than thirty years, but enough of early learning still remained for me to translate what she sang so softly in a firm, sweet voice:

My soul doth magnify the Lord,
And my spirit hath rejoiced
In God my Savior,
For He hath regarded the lowliness
Of His handmaiden . . .

The canticle was finished. She rose and dropped the linen cloak behind her and stretched her naked body on the altar, where she lay beneath the candles' softly glowing light like some exquisite piece of carven Carrara marble, still, lifeless, cold.

Chalice and paten were raised and placed upon the living altar-cloth, their hard, metallic weight denting the soft breasts and exquisite torso, their silver-gilt reflecting little halos of brightness on the milk-white skin. The vested man's voice rose and fell in what seemed to me an endless chant, his kneeling deacon's heavy guttural intoning the response. On, endlessly on, went the deep chant of celebration, pausing a breathless moment now and then as the order of the service directed that the celebrant should kiss the consecrated place of sacrifice, then hot and avid lips pressed shrinking, wincing flesh.

Now the rite was ended. The priest raised high the chalice with its hallowed contents and turned his back upon the living altar with a scream of cachinnating laughter. "Lucifer, Lord of the World and Prince Supreme of all the Powers of the Air, I hold thy adversary in my hands!" he cried. "To Thee the Victory, Mighty Master, Puissant God of Hell—behold I sacrifice to Thee the Nazarene! His blood be on our heads and on our children's—"

"*Eh bien, Monsieur*, I know not of your offspring, but blood assuredly shall be on your head, and that right quickly!" said Jules de Grandin, appearing suddenly in the darkness at the altar-side. A stab of lurid flame, a sharp report, and Konstantin fell forward on his face, a growing smear of blood-stain on his forehead.

A second shot roared answer to the first, and the crouching man in deacon's robes threw up both hands wildly, as though to hold himself by empty air, then leaned slowly to the left, slid down the altar steps and lay upon the floor, a blotch of moveless shadow in the candlelight.

Inspector Renouard appeared from the altar's farther side, his smoking service revolver in his hand, a smile of satisfaction on his face. "*Tiens*, my aim is true as yours, *mon* Jules," he announced matter-of-factly. "Shall I give the woman one as well?"

"By no means, no," de Grandin answered quickly. "Give her rather the charity of covering for her all-charming nudity, my friend. Quick, spread the robe over her."

Renouard obeyed, and as he dropped the desecrated alb on the still body I saw a look of wonder come into his face. "She is unconscious," he breathed. "She faints, my Jules; will you revive her?"

"All in good time," the other answered. "First let us look at this." He stirred the prostrate Konstantin with the toe of his boot.

How it happened I could not understand, for de Grandin's bullet had surely pierced his frontal bone, inflicting an instantly-fatal wound, but the prone man stirred weakly and whimpered like a child in pain.

"Have mercy!" he implored. "I suffer. Give me a second shot to end my misery. Quick, for pity's sake; I am in agony!"

De Grandin smiled unpleasantly. "So the lieutenant of the firing-party thought," he answered. "So the corporal who administered *le coup de grâce* believed, my friend. Them you could fool; you can not make a monkey out of Jules de Grandin. No; by no means. Lie here and die, my excellent adorer of the Devil, but do not take too long in doing it, for we fire the building within the quarter-hour, and if you have not finished dying by that time, *tiens*"—he raised his shoulders in a shrug—"the fault is yours, not ours. No."

"Hi, there, Doctor de Grandin, sor; don't be after settin' fire to this bloody devils' roost wid me an Doctor Trowbridge cooped up in here!" Costello roared.

"*Morbleu*," the little Frenchman laughed as he unlocked our prison, "upon occasion I have roasted both of you, my friends, but luckily I did not do it actually tonight. Come, let us hasten. We have work to do."

Within the suite which Konstantin had occupied in the deserted house we found sufficient blankets to wrap Sonia against the outside cold, and having thus prepared her for the homeward trip, we set fire to the ancient house in a dozen different spots and hastened toward my waiting car.

Red, mounting flames illuminated our homeward way, but we made no halt to watch our handiwork, for Sonia was moaning in delirium, and her hands and face were hot and dry as though she suffered from typhoid.

"To bed with her," de Grandin ordered when we reached my house. "We shall administer hyoscine and later give her strychinia and brandy; meanwhile we must inform her husband that the missing one is found and safe. Yes; he will be pleased to hear us say so, I damn think."

8. The Tangled Skein Unraveled

JULES DE GRANDIN, SMELLING most agreeably of *Giboulées de Mas* toilet water and dusting-powder, extremely dapper-looking in his dinner clothes and matching black-pearl stud and cuff-links, decanted a fluid ounce or so of Napoleon brandy from the silver-mounted pinch bottle standing handily upon the tabouret beside his easy-chair, passed the wide-mouthed goblet beneath his nose, sniffing the ruby liquor's aroma with obvious approval, then sipped a thimbleful with evident appreciation.

"Attend me," he commanded, fixing small bright eyes in turn on Donald Tanis and his wife, Detective Sergeant Costello, Renouard and me. "When dear Madame Sonia told us of her strange adventures with this Konstantin, I was amazed, no less. It is not given every woman to live through such excitement and retain her faculties, much less to sail at last into the harbor of a happy love, as she has done. Her father's fate also intrigued me. I'd heard of his strange suicide and how he did denounce the Bolshevik spy, so I was well prepared to join with Monsieur Tanis and tell her that she was mistaken when she declared the man who kidnapped her was Konstantin. I knew the details of his apprehension and his trial; also I knew he fell before the firing-squad.

"Ah, but Jules de Grandin has the open mind. To things which others call impossible he gives consideration. So when I heard the tale of Konstantin's execution at Vincennes, and heard how he had been at pains to learn if they would give him the mercy-shot, and when I further heard how he did not die at once, although eight rifle-balls had pierced his breast; I thought, and thought right deeply. Here were the facts—" he checked them off upon his outspread fingers:

"Konstantin was Russian; Konstantin had been shot by eight skilled riflemen—four rifles in the firing-squad of twelve were charged with blanks—he had not died at once, so a mercy-shot was given, and this seemed to kill him to death. So far, so ordinary. But ah, there were extraordinary factors in the case, as well. *Oui-da*. Of course. Before he suffered execution Konstantin had said some things which showed he might have hope of returning once again to wreak grave mischief on those he hated. Also, Madame Sonia had deposed it had been he who kidnapped her. She was unlikely to have been mistaken. Women do not make mistakes in matters of that kind. No. Assuredly not. Also, we must remember, Konstantin was Russian. That is of great importance.

"Russia is a mixture, a potpourri of mutual conflicting elements. Neither European nor Asiatic, neither wholly civilized nor savage, modern on the surface, she is unchanging as the changeless East in which her taproots lie. Always she has harbored evil things which were incalculably old when the first deep stones of Egypt's mighty pyramids were laid.

"Now, together with the werewolf and the vampire, the warlock and the witch, the Russian knows another demon-thing called *callicantzaros*, who is a being neither wholly man nor devil, but an odd and horrifying mixture of the two. Some call them foster-children of the Devil, stepsons of Satan; some say they are the progeny of evil, sin-soaked women and the incubi who are their paramours. They are imbued with semi-immortality, also; for though they may be killed like other men, they must be slain with a single fatal blow; a second stroke, although it would at once kill ordinary humankind, restores their lives—and their power for wickedness.

"So much for the means of killing a *callicantzaros*—and the means to be avoided. To continue:

"Every so often, preferably once each year about the twenty-fifth of February, the olden feast of St. Walburga, or at the celebration of St. Peter's Chains on August 1, he must perform the sacrilege known as the Black Mass or Mass to Lucifer, and hold thereby Satanic favor and renew his immortality.

"Now this Black Mass must be performed with certain rules and ceremonies, and these must be adhered to to the letter. The altar is the body of an unclothed woman, and she must lend herself with willingness to the dreadful part she plays. If she be tricked or made to play the part by force, the rite is null and void. Moreover, she must be without a taint or spot of wickedness, a virtuous woman, pure in heart—to find a one like that for such a service is no small task, you will agree.

"When we consider this we see why Konstantin desired Madame Sonia for wife. She was a Russian like himself, and Russian women are servient to their men. Also, by beatings and mistreatment he soon could break what little independence she possessed, and force her to his will. Thus he would be assured of the 'altar' for his Devil's Mass.

"But when he had procured the 'altar' the work was but begun. The one who celebrated this unclean rite must do so fully vested as a priest, and he must wear the sacred garments which have been duly consecrated. Furthermore he must use the consecrated elements at the service, and also the sacred vessels.

"If the Host can be stolen from a Latin church or the presanctified elements from an altar of the Greek communion, it is necessary only that the ritual be fulfilled, the benediction said, and then defilement of the elements be made in insult of the powers of Heaven and to the satisfaction of the Evil One. But if the Eucharist is unobtainable, then it is necessary to have a duly ordained priest, one who is qualified to cause the mystery of transubstantiation to take place, to say the office. If this form be resorted to, there is a further awful rite to be performed. A little baby, most usually a boy, who has not been baptized, but whose baby lips are too young and pure for speech and whose soft feet have never made a step, must be taken, and as the celebrant pronounces 'Hoc est enim corpus meum,' he cuts the helpless infant's throat and drains the gushing lifeblood into the chalice, thus mingling it with the transmuted wine.

"It was with knowledge of these facts that I heard Father Pophosepholos report his loss, and when he said the elements were stolen I did rejoice most greatly, for then I knew no helpless little one would have to die upon the altar of the Devil's Mass.

"And so, with Madame Sonia gone, with the elements and vestments stolen from St. Basil's Church and with my dark suspicions of this Konstantin's true character, I damn knew what was planned, but how to find this server of the Devil, this stepson of Satan, in time to stop the sacrilege? Ah, that was the question! Assuredly.

"And then came Sun Ah Poy. A bad man he had been, a very damn-bad man, as Friend Renouard can testify; but China is an old, old land and her sons are steeped in ancient lore. For generations more than we can count they've known the demon *Ch'ing Shih* and his ghostly brethren, who approximate the vampires of the West, and greatly do they fear him. They hate and loathe him, too, and there lay our salvation; for wicked as he was, Doctor Sun would have no dealings with this cursed Konstantin, but came to warn us and to tell us where he might be found, although his coming cost his life.

"And so we went and saw and were in time to stop the last obscenity of all—the defilement of the consecrated Eucharist in honor of the Devil. Yes. Of course."

"But, Doctor de Grandin, I was the altar at that mass," Sonia Tanis wailed, "and I *did* offer myself for the Devil's service! Is there hope for such as I? Will Heaven ever pardon me? For even though I loathed the thing I did, I *did* it, and"—she faced us with defiant, blazing eyes—"I'd do it again for—"

"*Précisément, Madame*," de Grandin interrupted. "'For—' That 'for' is your salvation; because you did the thing you did for love of him you married to save him from assassination. 'Love conquers all,' the Latin poet tells us. So in this case. Between your sin—if sin it were to act the part you did to save your husband's life—and its reward, we place the shield of your abundant love. Be assured, *chère Madame*, you have no need to fear, for kindly Heaven understands, and understanding is forgiveness."

"But," the girl persisted, her long, white fingers knit together in an agony of terror, her eyes wide-set with fear, "Donald would never have consented to my buying his safety at such a price, he—"

"*Madame*," the little Frenchman fairly thundered, "I am Jules de Grandin. I do not make mistakes. When I say something, it is so. I have assured you of your pardon; will you dispute with me?"

"Oh, Sonia," the husband soothed, "it's finished, now, there is no more—"

"*Hélas*, the man speaks truth, Friend Trowbridge," de Grandin wailed. "It is finished—there is no more! How true, my friend; how sadly true.

"The bottle, it is empty!"

The Devil's Bride

I. "Alice, Where Are You?"

FIVE OF US SAT on the twin divans flanking the fireplace where the eucalyptus logs burned brightly on their polished-brass andirons, throwing kaleidoscopic patterns of highlights and shadows on the ivory-enameled woodwork and the rug-strewn floor of the "Ancestors' Room" at Twelvetrees.

Old David Hume, who dug Twelvetrees' foundations three centuries ago, had planned that room as shrine and temple to his *lar familiaris*, and to it each succeeding generation of the house had added some memento of itself. The wide bay window at the east was fashioned from the carved poop of a Spanish galleon captured by a buccaneering member of the family and brought home to the quiet Jersey village where he rested while he planned new forays on the Antilles. The tiles about the fireplace, which told the story of the fall of man in blue-and-white Dutch delft, were a record of successful trading by another long dead Hume who flourished in the days when *Nieuw Amsterdam* claimed all the land between the Hudson and the Delaware, and held it from the Swedes till Britain with her lust for empire took it for herself and from it shaped the none too loyal colony of New Jersey. The carpets on the floor, the books and *bric-à-brac* on the shelves, each object of *vertu* within the glass-doored cabinets, had something to relate of Hume adventures on sea or land whether as pirates, patriots, traders or explorers, sworn enemies of law or duly constituted bailiffs of authority.

Adventure ran like ichor in the Hume veins, from David, founder of the family, who came none knew whence with his strange, dark bride and settled on the rising ground beside the Jersey meadows, to Ronald, last male of the line, who went down to flames and glory when his plane was cut out from its squadron and fell blazing like a meteor to the shell-scarred earth at Neuve Chapelle. His *croix de guerre*, posthumously awarded, lay in the cabinet beside the sword the Continental Congress had presented to his great-great-grandsire in lieu of long arrearage of salary.

Across the fire from us, between her mother and her fiancé, sat Alice, final remnant of the line, her half-humorous, half-troubled glance straying to each of us in turn as she finished speaking. She was a slender wisp of girlhood, with a mass of chestnut hair with deep, shadow-laden waves which clustered in curling tendrils at the nape of her neck, a pale, clear complexion, the ivory tones of which were enhanced by the crimson of her wide sensitive mouth and the long, silken lashes and purple depths of the slightly slanting eyes which gave her face a piquant, oriental flavor.

"You say the message is repeated constantly, Mademoiselle?" asked Jules de Grandin, my diminutive French friend, as he cast a fleeting look of unqualified approval at the slim satin slipper and silk-sheathed leg the girl displayed as she sat with one foot doubled under her.

"Yes, it's most provoking when you're trying to get some inkling of the future, especially at such a time as this, to have the silly thing keep saying—"

"Alice, dear," Mrs. Hume remonstrated, "I wish you wouldn't trifle with such silly nonsense, particularly now, when—" She broke off with what would unquestionably have been a sniff in anyone less certainly patrician than Arabella Hume, and glanced reprovingly at her daughter.

De Grandin tweaked the needle-pointed tips of his little blond mustache and grinned the gamin grin which endeared him to dowager and debutante alike. "It is mysterious, as you have said, *Mademoiselle*," he agreed, "but are you sure you did not guide the board—"

"Of course I am," the girl broke in. "Just wait: I'll show you." Placing her coffee cup upon the Indian mahogany tabouret, she leaped petulantly from the couch and hurried from the room, returning in a moment with a ouija board and table.

"Now watch," she ordered, putting the contrivance on the couch beside her. "John, you and Doctor Trowbridge and Doctor de Grandin put your hands on the table, and I'll put mine between them, so you can feel the slightest tightening of my muscles. That way you'll be sure I'm not guiding the thing, even unintentionally. Ready?"

Feeling decidedly sheepish, I rose and joined them, resting my finger tips on the little three legged table. Young Davisson's hand was next mine, de Grandin's next to his, and between all rested Alice's slender, cream-white fingers. Mrs. Hume viewed the spectacle with silent disapproval.

For a moment we bowed above the ouija board, waiting tensely for some motion of the table. Gradually a feeling of numbness crept through my hands and wrists as I held them in the strained and unfamiliar pose. Then, with a sharp and jerky start the table moved, first right, then left, then in an ever-widening circle till it swung sharply toward the upper left-hand corner of the board, pausing momentarily at the A, then traveling swiftly to the L, thence with constant acceleration back to I. Quickly the message was spelled out; a pause, and then once more the three-word sentence was repeated:

ALICE COME HOME

"There!" the girl exclaimed, a catch, half fright, half annoyance, in her voice. "It spelled those very words three times today. I couldn't get it to say anything else!"

"Rot. All silly nonsense," John Davisson declared, lifting his hands from the table and gazing almost resentfully at his charming fiancée. "You may believe you didn't move the thing, dear, but you must have, for—"

"Doctor de Grandin, Doctor Trowbridge," the girl appealed, "you held my hands just now. You'd have known if I'd made even the slightest move to guide the table, wouldn't you?" We nodded silent agreement, and she hurried on:

"That's just what's puzzling me. Why should a girl who's going to be married tomorrow be telling herself, subconsciously or otherwise, to 'come home'? If the board had spelt 'Go home,' perhaps it would have made sense, for we're going to our own place when we come back from our wedding trip; but why the constant repetition of 'Come home,' I'd like to know. Do you suppose—"

The raucous hooting of an automobile horn broke through her question and a moment later half a dozen girls accompanied by as many youths stormed into the big hall.

"Ready, old fruit?" called Irma Sherwood, who was to be the maid of honor. "We'd better be stepping on the gas; the church is all lit up and Doctor Cuthbert's got the organ all tuned and humming." She threw a dazzling smile at us and added, "This business of getting Alice decently married is more trouble than running a man down for myself, Doctor Trowbridge. One more rehearsal of these nuptials and I'll be a candidate for a sanitarium."

St. Chrysostan's was all alight when we arrived at the pentice and paused beside the baptismal font awaiting the remainder of the bridal party; for, as it ever is with lovers, John and Alice had lagged behind the rest to exchange a few banalities of the kind relished only by idiots, little children and those engaged to wed.

"Sorry to delay the show, friends and fellow citizens," Alice apologized, as she leaped from Davisson's roadster and tossed her raccoon coat aside. "The fact is, John and I had something of importance to discuss, and"—she raised both hands to readjust her hat—" and so we lingered by the way to—"

"Alice!" Mrs. Hume's voice betokened shocked propriety and hopeless protest at the antics of her daughter's graceless generation. "You're *surely* not going to wear that—that thing in church?" Her indignant glance indicated the object of her wrath. "Why, it's hardly decent," she continued, then paused, as though vocabulary failed her while she pointed mutely to the silver girdle which was clasped about her daughter's slender waist.

"Of course, I shall, old dear," the girl replied. "The last time one of us was married she wore it, and the one before wore it, too. Hume women always wear this girdle when they're married. It brings 'em luck and insures big fam—"

"*Alice!*" the sharp, exasperated interruption cut her short. "If you have to be indelicate, at least you might remember where we are."

"All right, Mater, have it your own way, but the girdle gets worn, just the same," the girl retorted, pirouetting slowly, so that the wide belt's polished bosses caught flashes from the chandelier and flung them back in gleaming, lance-like rays.

"*Mon Dieu, Mademoiselle*, what is it that you wear? May I see it, may I examine it?" de Grandin demanded excitedly, bending forward to obtain a closer view of the shining corselet.

"Of course," the girl replied. "Just a moment, till I get it off." She fumbled at a fastening in front, undid a latch of some sort and put the gleaming girdle in his hand.

It was a beautiful example of barbaric jewelry, a belt, perhaps a corset would be the better term, composed of two curved plates of hammered silver so formed as to encircle the wearer's abdomen from front to hips, joined together at the back by a wide band of flexible brown leather of exquisitely soft texture. In front the stomach-plates were locked together by four rings with a long silver pin which went through them like a loose rivet, with a little ball at the top fastened by a chain of cold-forged silver links. The metal was heavily bossed and rather crudely set with a number of big red and yellow stones. From each plate depended seven silver chains, each terminating in a heart-shaped ornament carved from the same kind of stones with which the belt was jeweled, and these clanked and jingled musically as the little Frenchman held the thing up to the light and gazed at it with a look of mingled fascination and repulsion. "*Grand Dieu!*" he exclaimed softly. "It is! I can not be mistaken; it is assuredly one of them, but—"

Alice bent smilingly across his shoulder. "Nobody knows quite what it is or where it comes from," she explained, "but there's a tradition in the family that David Hume's mysterious bride brought it with her as a part of her marriage portion. For years every daughter of the house wore it to be married, and it's been known as 'the luck of the Humes' for goodness knows how long. The legend is that the girl who wears it will keep her beauty and her husband's love and have an easy time in child—"

"Alice!" Once more her mother intervened.

"All right, Mother, I won't say it," her daughter laughed, "but even nice girls know you don't find babies in a cabbage-head nowadays." Then, to de Grandin:

"I'm the first Hume girl in three generations, and the last of the family in the bargain; so I'm going to wear the thing for whatever luck there is in it, no matter what anybody says."

The answering smile de Grandin gave her was rather forced. "You do not know whence it comes, nor what its history is?" he asked.

"No, we don't," Mrs. Hume returned, before her daughter could reply, "and I'm heartily sorry Alice found the thing. I almost wish I'd sold it when I had the chance."

"Eh?" he turned upon her almost sharply. "How is that, *Madame?*"

"A foreign gentleman called the other day and said he understood we had this thing among our curios and that it might be for sale. He was very polite, but quite insistent that I let him see it. When I told him it was not for sale he seemed greatly disappointed and begged me to reconsider. He even offered to allow me to set whatever price I cared to, and assured me there would be no quibble over it, even though we asked a hundred times the belt's intrinsic worth. I fancy he was an agent with *carte blanche* from some wealthy collector, he seemed so utterly indifferent where money was concerned."

"And did he, by any chance, inform you what this belt may be, or whence it came?" de Grandin queried.

"Why, no; he merely described it, and begged to be allowed to see it. One hardly likes to ask such questions from a chance visitor, you know."

"*Précisément.* One understands, *Madame,*" he nodded.

THE PROCESSION WAS QUICKLY marshaled, and attended by her maids, Alice marched serenely up the aisle. As she had no male relative to do the office, the duty of giving her in marriage was delegated to me, both she and her mother declaring that no one more deserved the honor than the one who had assisted her into the world and brought her through the measles, chickenpox and whooping cough.

"'And we'll have Trowbridge somewhere in the first one's name, old dear,'" Alice promised in a whisper as she patted my arm while we halted momentarily at the chancel steps.

"Now, when Doctor Bentley has pronounced the warning 'if no one offers an impediment to the marriage,'" the curate who was acting as master of ceremonies informed us, "you will proceed to the communion rail and—"

Somewhere outside, faint and faraway-seeming, but gaining quickly in intensity, there came a high, thin, whistling sound, piercing, but so high one could scarcely hear it. Rather, it seemed more like a screaming heard inside the head than any outward sound, and strangely, it seemed to circle round the three of us—the bride, the bridegroom and me—and to cut us definitely off from the remainder of the party.

"Queer," I thought. "There was no wind a moment ago, yet—" The thin, high whining closed tighter round us, and involuntarily I put my hands to my ears to shut out the intolerable sharpness of it, when with a sudden crash the painted window just above the altar burst as though a missile struck it, and through the ragged aperture came drifting a billowing yellow haze—a cloud of saffron dust, it seemed to me—which hovered momentarily above the unveiled cross upon the altar, then dissipated slowly, like steam evaporating in winter air.

I felt an odd sensation, almost like a heavy blow delivered to my chest, as I watched the yellow mist disintegrate, then straightened with a start as another sound broke on my hearing.

"Alice! Alice, where are you?" the bridegroom called, and through the bridal party ran a wondering murmur.

"Where's Alice? She was right there a moment ago! Where *is* she? Where's she gone?"

I blinked my eyes and shook my head. It was so. Where the bride had stood, her fingers resting lightly on my arm, a moment before, there was only empty space.

Wonderingly at first, then eagerly, at last with a frenzy bordering on madness, we searched for her. Nowhere, either in the church or vestry room or parish house, was sign or token of the missing bride, nor could we find a trace of her outside the building. Her coat and motor gloves lay in a crumpled heap within the vestibule; the car in which she came to the church still stood beside the curb; an officer whose beat had led him past the door two minutes earlier declared he had seen no one leave the edifice—had seen no one on the block, for that matter. Yet, discuss and argue as we might, search, seek and call, then tell ourselves it was no more than a silly girl's prank, the fact remained: Alice Hume was gone—vanished as utterly as though absorbed in air or swallowed by the earth, and all within less time than the swiftest runner could have crossed the chancel, much less have left the church beneath the gaze of half a score of interested people for whom she was the center of attraction.

"She must have gone home," someone suggested as we paused a moment in our search and gazed into each other's wondering eyes. "Of course, that's it! She's gone back to Twelvetrees!" the others chorused, and by the very warmth of their agreement gave tokens of dissent.

At last the lights were dimmed, the church deserted, and the bridal party, murmuring like frightened children to each other, took up their way toward Twelvetrees, to which, we were agreed, the missing bride had fled.

But as we started on our way, young Davisson, with lover's prescience of evil to his loved one, gave tongue to the question which trembled silently on every lip. "Alice!" he cried out to the unresponsive night, and the tremor in his voice was eloquent of his heart's agony, "Alice, beloved—*where are you?*"

2. Bulala-Gwai

"COMING?" I ASKED AS the sorrowful little motorcade began its pilgrimage to Twelvetrees.

De Grandin shook his head in short negation. "Let them go on," he ordered. "Later, when they have left, we may search the house for Mademoiselle Alice, though I greatly doubt we shall find her. Meanwhile, there is that here which I would investigate. We can work more efficiently when there are no well-meaning nincompoops to harass us with senseless questions. Come." He turned on his heel and led the way back into the church.

"Tell me, Friend Trowbridge," he began as we walked up the aisle, "when that window yonder broke, did you see, or seem to see, a cloud of yellowness drift through the opening?"

"Why, yes, I thought so," I replied. "It looked to me like a puff of muddy fog—smoke, perhaps—but it vanished so quickly that—"

"*Très bien*," he nodded. "That is what I wished to know. None of the others mentioned seeing it and our eyes play strange tricks on us at times. I thought perhaps I might have been mistaken, but your testimony is enough for me."

With a murmuring of excuse, as though apologizing for the sacrilege, he moved the bishop's chair to a point beside the altar, mounted nimbly on its tall, carved back, and examined the stone casing of the broken window intently. From my station outside the communion rail I could hear him swearing softly and excitedly in mingled French and English as he drew a card from his pocket, scraped something from the window-sill upon the card, then carefully descended from his lofty perch.

"Behold, regard, attend me, if you will, Friend Trowbridge," he ordered. "Observe what I have found." As he extended the card toward me I saw a line of light, yellow powder, like pollen from a flower, gathered along one edge.

"*Regardez!*" he commanded sharply, raising the slip of pasteboard level with my face. "Now, if you please, what did I do?"

"Eh?" I asked, puzzled.

"Your hearing functions normally. What is it that I did?"

"Why, you showed me that card, and—"

"Precisely. And—?" He paused with interrogatively arched brows.

"And that's all."

"*Non.* Not at all. By no means, my friend," he denied. "Attend me: First I did, as you have said, present the card to you. Next, when it was fairly level with your nostrils, I did blow on it, oh so gently, so that some of the powder on it was inhaled by you. Next I raised my arms three times above my head, lowered them again, then capered round you like a dancing Indian. Finally, I did tweak you sharply by the nose."

"Tweak me by the nose!" I echoed aghast. "You're crazy!"

"Like the fox, as your slang so drolly expressed it," he returned with a nod. "My friend, it has been exactly one minute and forty seconds by my watch since you did inhale that so tiny bit of dust, and during all that time you were as utterly oblivious to all that happened as though you had been under ether. Yes. When first I saw I suspected. Now I have submitted it to the test and am positive it is so."

"What on earth are you talking about?" I asked.

"*Bulala-Gwai*, no less."

"Bu—*what?*"

He seated himself in the bishop's chair, crossed his knees and regarded me with the fixed, unwinking stare which always reminded me of an earnest tom-cat. "Attend me," he commanded. "My duties as an army medical officer and as a member of *la Sûreté*, have taken me to many places off the customary map of tourists. The Congo Français, by example. It was there that I first met *bula-la-gwai*, which was called by our gendarmes the snuff of death, sometimes *la petite mort*, or little death.

"*Barbe d'un rat vert*, but it is well named, my friend! A traveler journeying through the interior once lay down to rest on his camp bed within his tent. He meant to sleep for thirty minutes only. When he awoke he found that twenty-six hours had gone—likewise all his paraphernalia. Native robbers had inserted a tube beneath his tent flap, blown a minute pinch of their death snuff into the enclosure, then boldly entered and helped themselves to all of his effects. Again, a tiny paper torpedo of the stuff was thrown through the window of a locomotive cab while it stood on a siding. Both engineer and fireman were rendered unconscious for ten hours, during which time the natives denuded the machine of every movable part. So powerful an anesthetic is *bulala-gwai* that so much of it as can be gotten on a penknife's point, if blown into a room fourteen feet square will serve to paralyze every living thing within the place for several minutes.

"The secret of its formula is close-guarded, but I have been assured by witch-men of the Congo that it can be made in two strengths, one to kill at once, the other to stupefy, and it is a fact to which I can testify that it is sometimes used successfully to capture both elephants and lions alive.

"I once went with the local inspector of police to examine premises which had been burglarized with the aid of this so powerful sleeping-powder, and on the window-sill we did behold a minute quantity of it. The inspector scooped it up on a card and called a native gendarme to him, then blew it in the negro's face. The stuff had lost much potency by exposure to the air, but still it was so powerful that the black was totally unconscious for upward of five minutes, and did not move a muscle when the inspector struck him a stinging blow on the cheek and even touched a lighted cigarette against his hand. Not only that, when finally he awakened he did not realize he had been asleep at all, and would not believe us till we showed him the blister where the cigarette had burned him.

"Very good. It is twenty years and more since I beheld this powder from the Devil's snuff-box, but when I saw that yellow cloud come floating through the broken window, and when I realized Mademoiselle Alice had decamped unseen by us before our very eyes, I said to me, 'Jules de Grandin, here, it seems, is evidence of *bulala-gwai*, and nothing else.'

"'You may be right, Jules de Grandin,' I answered me, 'but still you are not sure. Wait until the others have departed with their silly gabble-gabble, then ask Friend Trowbridge if he also saw the yellow cloud. He knows nothing of *bulala-gwai*, but if he saw that fog of yellowness, you may depend upon it there was such a thing.'

"And so I waited, and when you did agree with me, I searched, and having searched I found that which I sought and—forgive me, good friend!—as there was no other laboratory material at hand, I did test the stuff on you, and now I am convinced. Yes, I damn know how they spirited Mademoiselle Alice away while our eyes were open and unseeing. Who it was that stole her, and why he did it—that is for us to discover as quickly as may be."

He felt for his cigarette case and thoughtfully extracted a "Maryland," then, remembering where he was, replaced it. "Let us go," he ordered. "Perhaps the chatterers have become tired of useless searching at Twelvetrees, and we can get some information from Madame Hume."

"But if this *bulala*—this sleeping-powder, whatever its native name is— was used here, it's hardly likely Alice has gone back to Twelvetrees, is it?" I objected. "And what possible information can Mrs. Hume give? She knows as little about it all as you or I."

"One wonders," he replied, as we left the church and climbed into my car. "At any rate, perhaps she can tell us more of that *sacré* girdle which Mademoiselle Alice wore."

"I noticed you seemed surprised when you saw it," I returned. "Did you recognize it?"

"Perhaps," he answered cautiously. "At least, I have seen others not unlike it."

"Indeed? Where?"

"In Kurdistan. It is a Yezidee bridal belt, or something very like it."

"A what?"

"A girdle worn by virgins who—but I forget, you do not know.

"The work of pacifying subject people is one requiring all the white man's ingenuity, my friend, as your countrymen who have seen service in the Philippines will tell you. In 1922 when French authority was flouted in Arabia, I was dispatched there on a secret mission. Eventually my work took me to Deir-er-Zor, Anah, finally to Baghdad and across British Irak to the Kurdish border. There—no matter in what guise—I penetrated Mount Lalesh and the holy city of the Yezidees.

"These Yezidees are a mysterious sect scattered throughout the Orient from Manchuria to the Near East, but strongest in North Arabia, and feared and loathed alike by Christian, Jew, Buddhist, Taoist and Moslem, for they are worshippers of Satan.

"Their sacred mountain, Lalesh, stands north of Baghdad on the Kurdish border near Mosul, and on it is their holy and forbidden city which no stranger is allowed to enter, and there they have a temple, reared on terraces hewn from the living rock, in which they pay homage to the image of a serpent as the beguiler of man from pristine innocence. Beneath the temple are gloomy caverns, and there, at dead of night, they perform strange and bloody rites before an idol fashioned like a peacock, whom they call Malek Taos, the viceroy of Shaitan—the Devil—upon earth.

"According to the dictates of the Khitab Asward, or Black Scripture, their Mir, or pope, has brought to him as often as he may desire the fairest daughters of the sect, and these are his to do with as he chooses. When the young virgin is prepared for the sacrifice she dons a silver girdle, like the one we saw on Mademoiselle Alice tonight. I saw one on Mount Lalesh. Its front is hammered silver, set with semi-precious stones of red and yellow—never blue, for blue is heaven's color, and therefore is accursed among the Yezidees who worship the Arch-Demon. The belt's back is of leather, sometimes from the skin of a lamb untimely taken from its mother, sometimes of a kid's skin, but in exceptional cases, where the woman to be offered is of noble birth and notable lineage, it is made of tanned and carefully prepared human skin—a murdered babe's by preference. Such was the leather of Mademoiselle Alice's girdle. I recognized it instantly. When one has examined a human hide tanned into leather he can not forget its feel and texture, my friend."

"But this is dreadful—unthinkable!" I protested. "Why should Alice wear a girdle made of human skin?"

"That is precisely what we have to ascertain tonight, if possible," he told me. "I do not say Madame Hume can give us any direct information, but she may perchance let drop some hint that will set us on the proper track. No," be added as he saw protest forming on my lips, "I do not intimate she has wilfully withheld anything she knows. But in cases such as this there are no such things as trifles. Some bit of knowledge which she thinks of no importance may easily prove the key to this so irritating mystery. One can but hope."

ANOTHER CAR, A LITTLE roadster of modish lines, opulent with gleaming chromium, drew abreast of us as we halted at the gateway of the Hume house. Its driver was a woman, elegantly dressed, sophisticated, *chic* from the crown of her tightly fitting black felt hat to the tips of her black leather gloves. As she slackened speed and leaned toward us, our headlights' rays struck her face, illuminating it as an actor's features are picked out by the spotlight on a darkened stage. Although a black lace veil was drawn across her chin and cheeks after the manner of a Western desperado's handkerchief mask, so filmy was the tissue that her countenance was alluringly shadowed rather than obscured. A beautiful face it was, but not a lovely one. Skin light and clear as any blond's was complemented by hair as black and bright as polished basalt, black brows circumflexed superciliously over eyes of almost startling blueness. Her small, petulant mouth had full, ardent lips of brilliant red.

There was a slightly amused, faintly scornful smile on her somewhat vixenish mouth, and her small teeth, gleaming like white coral behind the vivid carmine of her lips, seemed sharp as little sabers as she called to us in a rich contralto: "Good evening, gentlemen. If you're looking for someone, you'll save time and trouble by abandoning the search and going home."

The echo of a cynical, disdainful laugh floated back to us as she set speed to her car and vanished in the dark.

Jules de Grandin stared after her, his hand still halfway to the hat he had politely touched when she first addressed us. Astonishingly, he burst into a laugh. "*Tiens*, my friend," he exclaimed when he regained his breath, "it seems there are more locks than one for which we seek the keys tonight."

3. "David Hume Hys Journal"

ARABELLA HUME CAME QUICKLY toward us as we entered the hall. Sorrow and hope—or the entreaty of hope—was in the gaze she turned on us. Also, it seemed to me, there lay deep in her eyes some latent, nameless fear, vague and indefinable as a child's dread of the dark, and as terrifying.

"Oh, Doctor Trowbridge—Doctor de Grandin—have you found out anything? Do you know anything?" she quavered. "It's all so dreadful, so—so impossible! Can you—have you any explanation?"

De Grandin bent stiffly from the hips as he took her hand in his and raised it to his lips. "Courage, *Madame*," he exhorted. "We shall find her, never fear."

"Oh, yes, yes," she answered almost breathlessly, "she will be found. She *must* be found, with you and Doctor Trowbridge looking for her, I know it. Don't you think a mother who has been as close to her child as I have been to Alice since Ronald was killed may have a sixth sense where she is concerned? I have such a sense. I tell you—I *know*—Alice is near."

The little Frenchman regarded her somberly. "I, too, have a feeling she is not far distant," he declared. "It is as if she were near us—in an adjoining room, by example—but a room with sound-proof walls and a cleverly hidden door. It is for you to help us find that door—and the key which will unlock it—Madame Hume."

"I'll do everything I can," she promised.

"Very good. You can tell us, to begin, all that you know, all you have heard, of David Hume, the founder of this family."

Arabella gave him a half-startled, half-disbelieving glance, almost as though he had requested her to state her views of the Einstein hypothesis or some similarly recondite and irrelevant matter. "I really don't know anything about him," she returned somewhat coldly. "He seems to have been a sort of Melchizedek, appearing from nowhere and without any antecedents."

"U'm?" De Grandin stroked his little wheat-blond mustache with affectionate thoughtfulness. "There are then no records—no family records of any kind—which one can consult? No deeds or wills or leases, by example?"

"Only the family Bible, and that—"

"*Eh bien, Madame*, we may do worse than consult the Scriptures in our present difficulty. By all means, lead us to it," he broke in.

The records of ten generations of Humes were spread upon the sheets bound between the Book of Malachi and the Apocrypha. Of succeeding members of the family there was extensive register, their births, their baptisms, their progeny and deaths, as well as matrimonial alliances being catalogued with painstaking detail. Of David Hume the only entry read: "*Dyed in ye hope of gloryous Resurrection aet yrs 81, mos 7, dys 20, ye 29th Sept. MDCLVII.*"

"*Nom d'un bouc*, and is that all?" De Grandin tugged so viciously at the waxed ends of his mustache that I felt sure the hairs would be wrenched loose from his lip. "Satan bake the fellow for a pusillanimous rogue! Even though he had small pride of ancestry, he should have considered future generations. He should have had a thought for my convenience, *pardieu!*"

He closed the great, cedar-bound book with a resounding bang and thrust it angrily back into the case. But as he shoved the heavy volume from him a hammered brass corner reinforcing the cover caught against the shelf edge, wrenching the tome from his hands, and the Bible fell crashing to the floor.

"Oh, *mille pardons!*" he cried contritely, stooping to retrieve the fallen book. "I did lose my temper, *Madame*, and—*Dieu de Dieu*, what have we here?"

The impact of the fall had split the brittle, age-worn cedar slabs with which the Bible had been bound, and where the wood had buckled gable-wise the glazed-leather inner binding had cracked in a long, vertical fissure, and from this opening protruded a sheaf of folded paper. Even as we leaned forward to inspect it we saw that it was covered with fine, crabbed writing in all but totally faded ink.

Bearing the manuscript to the reading-table de Grandin switched on all the lights in the electrolier and bent over the faded, time-obliterated sheets. For a moment he knit his brows in concentration; then:

"Ah-ha," he exclaimed exultantly, "ah-ha-ha, my friends, we have at last flushed old Monsieur David's secret from its covert! Come close and look, if you will be so good."

He spread the sheets upon the polished table top and tapped the uppermost with the tip of a small, well-manicured forefinger. "You see?" he asked.

Although the passage of three hundred years had dimmed the ink with which the old scribe wrote, enough remained to let us read across the yellowed paper's top: "*David Hume hys Journal*" and below: "*Inscrybed at hys house at Twel-vetrees in ye colonie of New—*"

The rest had faded out, but enough was there to tell us that some secret archive of the family had been brought to light and that the scrivener had been that mysterious ancestor of whom no more was known than that he once lived at Twelvetrees.

"May one trespass on your hospitality for pen and paper, Madame?" de Grandin asked, his little, round blue eyes shining with suppressed excitement, the twin needles of his waxed mustache points twitching like the whiskers of an agitated tomcat. "This writing is so faint it would greatly tax one to attempt reading it aloud, and by tomorrow it may be fainter with exposure to the air; but if you will give leave that I transcribe it while I yet may read, I will endeavor to prepare a copy and read you the results of my work when it is done."

Arabella Hume, scarcely less excited than we, nodded hasty assent, and de Grandin shut himself in the Ancestors' Room with pen and paper and a tray of cigarettes to perform his task.

Twice while we waited in the hall we saw the butler tiptoe into the closed room in answer to the little Frenchman's summons. His first trip was accompanied by a bowl of ice, a glass and a decanter of brandy. "He'll drink himself into a stupor," Arabella told me when the second consignment of liquor was borne in.

"Not he," I assured her with a laugh. "Alcohol's only a febrifuge with him. He drinks it like water when he's working intensively, and it never seems to affect him."

"Oh," she answered somewhat doubtfully. "Well, I hope he'll manage to stay sober till he's finished."

"Wait and see," I told her. "If he's unsteady on his feet, I'll—"

De Grandin's entrance cut my promise short. His face was flushed, his little round blue eyes were shining as though with unshed tears, and his mustache fairly bristling with excitement and elation; but of alcoholic intoxication there was no slightest sign.

"*Voyez*," he ordered, flourishing a sheaf of rustling papers. "Although the writing was so faded that I did perforce miss much of the story of Monsieur the Old One, enough remained to give us information of the great importance. But yes. Your closest attention, if you please."

Seating himself on the table edge and swinging one small, patent leather shod foot in rhythm with his reading, he began:

. . . and now my case was truly worser than before, for though my Moslem captors had been followers of Mahound, these that had taken me from them were worshippers of Satan's self, and nightly bowed the knee to Beelzebub, whom they worshipped in the image of a peacock highte Melek Taos, whose favor they are wont to invoke with every sort of wickedness. For their black scriptures teach that God is good and merciful, and slow to take offense, while Shaitan, as they name the Devil, is ever near and ever watchful to do hurt to mankind, wherefore he must be propitiated by all who would not feel his malice. And so they work all manner of evil, accounting that as virtue which would be deemed most villainous by us, and confessing and repenting of good acts as though they were the deadliest of sins.

Their chief priest is yclept the Mir, and of all their wicked tribe he is the wickedest, scrupling not at murder and finding great delight in such vile acts as caused the Lord aforetimes to rain down fire and brimstone on the evil cities of the plain.

Once as I stood without their temple gate by night I did espy a great procession entering with the light of torches and with every sound of minstrels and mirth, but in the middle of the revelers there walked a group of maidens, and these did weep continually. And when I asked the meaning of this sight they told me that these girls, the very flower of the tribe, had been selected by the Mir for his delight and for the lust and cruelty of those who acted as his counsellors, for such is their religion that the pontifex may choose from out their womanhood as many as he pleases, and do unto them even according to the dictates of his evil will, nor may any say him nay. And as I looked upon these woeful women I beheld that each was clasped about the middle by a stomacher of cunningly wrought silver, and this, they told me, was the girdle of a bride, for their women don such girdles when they are ready to engage in wedlock, or when they tread the path of sorrow which leads them to the Mir and degradation. For he who gives his daughter voluntarily to be devoured by the Mir acquires merit in the eyes of Satan, and to lie as paramour to the Devil's viceroy on earth is accounted honorable for any woman, yea, even greater than to enter into matrimony.

The little Frenchman laid his paper down and turned his quick, bird-like glance upon us. "Is it now clear?" he asked. "This old Monsieur David was undoubtlessly sold as slave unto the Yezidees by Moslems who had in some way captured him. It is, of Sheik-Adi, the sacred city of the Satanists, he writes, and his reference to the silver girdles of the brides is most illuminating. N'est-ce-pas? Consider what he has to say a little later."

Shuffling through the pile of manuscript, he selected a fresh sheet and resumed:

Yet she, who was the daughter of this man of blood and sin, was fair and good as any Christian maid. Moreover, her heart was inclined toward me, and many a kind act she did for me, the Christian slave, who sadly lacked for kindness in that evil mountain city. And so, as it has ever been 'twixt man and maid, we loved, and loving knew that we could not be happy till our fates joined forever. And so it was arranged that we should fly to freedom in the south, where I could take her to wife, for she had agreed to renounce Satan and all his ways to follow in the pathway of the true religion.

Now, in the falling of the year, when crops were gathered and the husbandry was through, these people were wont to gather in their temple of the peacock and make a feast wherewith they praised the power of evil, and on the altar would be offered beasts, birds and women devoted to the service of the arch-fiend. And thus did Kudejah and I arrange the manner of our flight:

When all within the temple was prepared and we could hear the sound of drums and trumpets offering praise unto the Devil, we slipped quickly down the mountain pass, she closely veiled like any Moslem woman, I disguised as a man of Kurdistan, and with us were two mules well laden with gold and jewels of precious stones which she had filched from the treasury of the Mir her sire. Nor did we loiter on the way, but hastened ever till we came to the border of the land of evil and were safe among the Moslems, who treated us right kindly, believing us co-religionists who were fleeing from the worshippers of Satan. And so we came at last to Busra, and thence by ship to Muskat, from whence we sailed again and finally came once more to England.

But ere we breathed the English air again we had been wed with Christian rite; and Kudejah had dropped her heathen name and taken that of Mary, which had also been my mother's. And sure a sweeter bride or truer wife has no man ever had, e'en though she saw the light of day beneath the shadow of the Devil's temple. Yet, though she had accepted Christ and put behind her Lucifer and all his works, when we did stand before the parson to be wed my Mary wore about her the great silver belt which had been fashioned for her marriage when she dwelt on Satan's mountain, and this we have unto this day, as a marriage portion for the women of our house.

Most crafty are those devil men from whom we fled, and well were we aware of it, and so we came to this new land, where I did leave my olden name behind and take the name of Hume, that those who might come seeking us might the better be befooled; and yet, though leagues of ocean toss between us and the worshippers of Satan, a thought still plagues us as a naughty dream may vex a frightened child. The office of high priest to Melek Taos is hereditary in the family of the Mir. The eldest son ascends the altar to perform the rites of blood the moment that his sire has breathed his last, and if there be no son, then must the eldest daughter of the line be wedded unto Satan with formal ceremony and silver girdle, and serve as priestess in her father's stead until a son is born, whereupon she is led forth with all solemnity and put to death with horrid torment, for her sufferings are a libation unto Beelzebub. And thereupon a regency of under-priests must serve the King of Evil till the son is grown to man's estate.

Wherefore, O ye who may come after me in this the family I have founded, I do adjure ye to make choice of death rather than submit unto the demands of the worshippers of Satan, for in the years to come it well may happen that the Mir his line may be exhausted, and then those crafty men of magic who do dwell on Mount Lalesh may seek ye out and summon ye to serve the altar of the Devil. And so I warn ye, if the time should come when ye receive a message from ye know not where, bidding ye simply to come home, that this shall be the sign, and straightway shall ye flee with utmost haste or if ye can not flee then take your life with your own hand, for better far is it to face an outraged God with the bloodstains of self-murder on your hands than to stand before the Seat of Judgment with your soul foredoomed for that ye were a priest and server of the Arch-Fiend in your days on earth.

I have—

"Well?" I prompted as the silence lengthened. "What else?"

"There is no 'else,' my friend," he answered. "As I told you, the ink with which *Monsieur l'Ancêtre* wrote was faded as an old belle's charms; the remainder of his message is but the shadow of a shadow, an angel out of Paradise could not decipher it."

We sat in silence for a moment, and it was Arabella Hume who framed our common thought in words: "He said, 'if the time should come when ye receive a message from ye know not where, bidding ye simply to come home, this shall be the sign'—the message Alice got on the ouija board today—you remember? You saw it repeated yourselves before we went to church!"

De Grandin bent a fixed, unwinking stare on her. "*Madame*," he asked, "can you not give us some description of the stranger who desired that you let him see the wedding girdle of Madame David? Was he, according to your guess, a Levantin?"

Mrs. Hume considered him a moment thoughtfully. Then: "No-o, I shouldn't think so," she replied. "He seemed more like a Spaniard, possibly Italian, though it's hard to say more than that he was dark and very clean-looking and spoke English with that perfect lack of accent which showed it was not his mother tongue. You know—each word sharply defined, as though it might be the result of a mental translation."

"Perfectly," de Grandin nodded. "I should say—"

"Well, *I* should say it's all a lot of nonsense," I broke in. "It may be true old David Hume was sold as a slave to these Devil-Worshippers, and that he ran off with the high priest's daughter—and all the money he could get his hands on. But you know how superstitious people were in those days. The chances are he was filled full of fantastic stories by the Yezidees, and believed everything he heard and more that he imagined. I'd say his conscience was troubling him toward the last; perhaps his mind was failing, too. Look how carefully he hid what he'd written in the cover of the family Bible. Is that the action of a normal man, especially if he seriously intended future generations to profit by his warning?"

Arabella glanced at each of us in turn, finally gave vent to a sigh of relief and put her hand on mine. "Thank you, Samuel," she said. "I knew there was some explanation for it all; but Alice's strange disappearance and all this has so upset me that I'm hardly normal." To de Grandin she added:

"I'm sure Doctor Trowbridge's explanation is the right one. Old David must have been weak-minded when he wrote that senseless warning. He was eighty-one when he died, and you know how old people are inclined to imagine things. Like children, really."

A stubborn, argumentative expression crossed de Grandin's face, but gave place instantly to one of his quick elfin grins. "Perhaps I have put too much trust in the vaporings of a senile old man's broken mind," he admitted. "Nevertheless, the fact remains that Mademoiselle Alice is not here, and the task remains for us to find her. Come, Friend Trowbridge, there is little we can do here and much we can do elsewhere. Let us go, if we have *Madame's* permission to retire." He bowed with Continental grace to Arabella.

"Oh, yes; and thank you so much for what you've done already," Mrs. Hume returned. "I'm half inclined to think this is some madcap prank of Alice's, but"—her expression of false confidence gave way a moment, unmasking the panic fear which gnawed at her heart—"if we hear nothing by morning, I think we'd better summon the police, don't you?"

"By all means," he agreed, taking her hand in his and bending ceremoniously above it ere he turned to accompany me from the house.

"THANK YOU, MY FRIEND," he murmured as we began our homeward drive. "Your interruption was most timely and served to divert poor *Madame's* mind from the awful horror I saw gathering round us."

"Eh?" I returned. "You don't mean to tell me you actually believe that balderdash you read us?"

He turned on me in blank amazement. "And was your avowal of disbelief in Monsieur David's tale not simulated?" he asked.

"Good Lord," I answered in disgust, "d'ye mean to say you swallowed that old dotard's story—all that nonsense about an hereditary priesthood of the Devil-Worshippers, and the possibility of—See here, don't you remember he said if the Mir's male line became extinct the eldest daughter had to serve, and that she must be married to the Devil? That might be possible—mystically speaking—but he specifically said she shall thereafter act as high priestess until a son is born. I know the legend of Robert the Devil, and it was probably implicitly believed in David Hume's day, for the Devil was a very real person then, but we've rather graduated from that sort of mediaevalism nowadays. How can a woman be married to the Devil, and bear him a son?"

There was more of sneer than smile in the mirthless grin he turned on me. "Have you been to India?" he demanded.

"India? Of course not, but what's that got to do with—"

"Then perhaps it is that you do not know of the *deva-dasis*, or wives of Siva. In that benighted land a father thinks he does acquire merit by giving up his daughter to be wedded to the god, and wedded to him she truly is, with all the formal pomp accompanying the espousal of a princess. Thereafter she is accounted honorable as consort of the great God of Destruction—but though her wedded lord is but a thing of carven stone she does not lack for offspring. No, *pardieu*, she is more often than not a mother before her thirteenth birthday, and several times a mother when her twentieth year is reached—if she survives that long.

"Consider the analogy here. From what I have beheld with my own two eyes—and my sight is very keen—and from what I have been told by witnesses who had no need to lie or even stretch the truth, I know that Monsieur David's narrative is based on fact, and very ugly fact at that."

"But what about his hiding his 'warning' in the cover of the Bible?" I persisted. "Surely—"

"Three centuries have passed since he penned those words," de Grandin interrupted, "and in that time much may be forgotten. That David told his children where they might look for guidance if the need for guidance rose I make no doubt. But in the course of time his admonition was forgotten, or—"

He broke off musingly, and I had to prompt him:

"Yes? Or—"

"Or the story of some secret warning has been handed down to each generation," he replied. "Did not it strike you more than once that Madame Hume was not entirely honest—pardon, I should say frank—with us? The fear of something which she could or would not mention was plainly in her eyes when we came from the church, and earlier in the evening her efforts to direct the conversation from that obscure message which her daughter had from the ouija board were far more resolute than they would have been had she had nothing but a distaste for superstitious practice to excuse them. Also, when we did ask for information relative to Monsieur David she suddenly turned cold to us, and had I not persisted would undoubtlessly have turned us from examination of the family Bible. Moreover—"

Again he paused and again I prompted him.

"Jules de Grandin is experienced," he assured me solemnly. "As a member of *la Sûreté* he has had much to do with questioned documents. He knows ink, he knows paper, he can scent a forgery or an attempt at alteration as far as he can recognize the symptoms of coryza. Yes."

"Yes? What then?"

"This, *cordieu!* I played the dolt, the simple, guileless fool, tonight, my friend, but this I say with half an eye as I made transcription of old David's story: Someone—I know not who—*some one has essayed to blot that writing out with acid ink eradicator*. Had the writing been in modern metallic ink the effort would have been successful, but *Monsieur l'Ancêtre* wrote with the old vegetable ink of his time, and so the acid did not quite efface it. It is that to which I owed my ability to read the journal. But believe me, good friend, it was a man—or woman—and not time, which dimmed the writing on those pages and rendered illegible much which old David wrote to warn his descendants, and which would have greatly simplified our problems."

"But who could have done it—and why?" I asked.

He raised his narrow shoulders in an irritable shrug. "Ask the good God—or perhaps the Devil—as to that," he told me. "They know the answer; not I."

4. By Whose Hand?

THREATENING LITTLE FLURRIES OF snow had been skirmishing down from the cloud-veiled sky all evening; before we were halfway to my house the storm attacked in force, great feathery flakes following each other in smothering profusion, obscuring traffic lights, clinging to the windshield; clogging our wheels. Midnight was well past as we stamped up my front steps, brushed our feet on the doormat and paused a moment at the vestibule while I fumbled for my latch-key. As I swung back the door the office phone began a shrill, hysterical cachinnation which seemed to rise in terrified crescendo as I ran down the hall.

"Hullo?" I challenged gruffly.

"Doctor Trowbridge?" the high-pitched voice across the wire called.

"Yes; what—"

"This is Wilbur, sir, Mrs. Hume's butler, you know."

"Oh? Well, what's—"

"It's the missis, sir; she's—I'm afraid you'll be too late, sir; but please hurry. I just found her, an' she's—" His voice trailed off in a wheeze of asthmatic excitement, and I could hear him gasping in a futile effort to regain his speech.

"Oh, all right; do what you can for her till we get there; we'll be right over," I called back. Attempting to ascertain the nature of the illness by questioning the inarticulate domestic would be only a waste of time, I saw, and obviously time was precious.

"Come on," I bade de Grandin. "Something's happened to Arabella Hume; Wilbur is so frightened he's gasping like a newly landed fish and can't give any information; so it may be anything from a broken arm to a stroke of apoplexy, but—"

"But certainly, by all means, of course," the Frenchman agreed enthusiastically. Next to solving a perplexing bit of crime he dearly loved a medical emergency. With deftness which combined uncanny speed with almost super-human accuracy of selection he bundled bandages and styptics, stimulants and sedatives, a sphygmomanometer and a kit of first-aid instruments into a bag, then: "Let us go," he urged. "All is ready."

Wilbur was pacing back and forth on the veranda when we arrived some half an hour later. His face was blue with cold, and his teeth chattered so he could scarcely form the hurried greeting which he gave us.

"Gawd, gentlemen," he told us tremblingly. "I thought you'd never get here!"

"*Eh bien*, so did we," de Grandin answered. "*Madame* your mistress, where is she, if you please?"

"Upstairs, sir, in her dressing-room. I found her like she is just before I called you. I'd finished lockin' up the house an' was going to my room by way of the back stairs when I heard the sound o' something heavy falling up the hall toward the front o' the house, an' ran to see if I was wanted. She didn't answer when I knocked—indeed, it seemed so *hawful* quiet in 'er room that it fair gave me the creeps, sir. So I made bold to knock again; then, when she didn't hanswer, to look in, an'—"

"Lead on, *mon vieux*," de Grandin interrupted. "The circumstances of your discovery can wait, at present. It is Madame Hume that we would see."

The butler was a step or two ahead of us as we climbed the stairs, but as we approached Mrs. Hume's door his footsteps lagged. By the time we stood before the portal he had dropped back to de Grandin's elbow, and made no motion either to rap upon the panels or to turn the knob for us.

"Lead on," de Grandin repeated. "We would see her at once, if you please."

"There's nothing you can do, of course," the servant answered, "but in a case like this it's best to have a doctor, so—"

The little Frenchman's temper broke beneath the strain. "Damn yes!" he snapped, "but save your conversation till a later time, my friend. I do not care for it at present."

Without more ado he turned the latch and swung the door back, stepping quickly past the butler into Arabella's boudoir, but coming to a halt on the threshold.

Close behind him, I stepped forward, but stopped with a gasp at what I saw.

Suspended by a heavy silken curtain cord looped twice about her neck, Arabella Hume hung from the iron curtain rod bridging the archway between her chamber and her dressing-room. A satin-upholstered boudoir-chair lay overturned on its back beneath her and a little to one side, her flaccid feet in their satin evening slippers swung a scant four inches from the floor, her hands draped limply at her sides, and her head was sharply bent forward to the left. Her lips were slightly parted and between them showed a quarter-inch of tongue, like the pale-pink pistil of a blossom protruding from the leaves. Her eyes were partly opened, and already covered with the shining gelatin-film of death, but not at all protuberant.

"Good heavens!" I exclaimed.

"My Gawd, sir, ain't it *hawful?*" whispered Wilbur.

"*Nom de Dieu de nom de Dieu; c'est une affaire du diable!*" said Jules de Grandin.

To Wilbur: "You say you first discovered her thus when you called Doctor Trowbridge?" he demanded.

"Ye-es, sir."

"Then why in the name of ten million small blue devils did you not cut her down? The chances are she was already dead, but—"

"You daren't cut a 'angin' person down till the coroner's looked at 'im, dast you, sir?" the servant replied.

"*Ohé; sacré nom d'un petit bomhomme!*" De Grandin wrenched savagely at the ends of his mustache. "This chimney-corner law; this smug wisdom of ignorance—it will drive me mad. Had you cut the cord by which she hung when you first saw her, it is possible there would have been no need to call the coroner at all, great stupid-head!" he stormed.

Abruptly he put his anger by as one might lay off a garment. "No matter," he resumed, "the mischief is now done. We must to work. Wilbur, bring me a decanter full—*full*, remember—of brandy."

"Yes, sir," the servant answered. "Thank you, sir."

"And, Wilbur—"

"Yes, sir?"

"Take a drink—or two—yourself before you serve me."

"Thank *you*, sir!" The butler departed on his errand with alacrity.

"Quick, my friend," the Frenchman ordered, "we must examine her before he returns."

Snipping through the silken strangling cord with a pair of surgeon's scissors he eased the body down in his arms and bore it to the couch, then with infinite care loosened the ligature about the throat and slipped the noose over her head. "*Morbleu*," he murmured as he laid the cord upon the table, "who taught her to form a hangman's knot, one wonders?"

I took the curtain cord in my hand and looked at it. He was right. The loop which had been round Arabella's neck was no ordinary slipknot, but a carefully fashioned hangman's halter, several turns of end being taken round the cord above the noose, thus insuring greater freedom for the loop to tighten around the throat.

"It may be so," I heard him whisper to himself, "but I damn doubt it."

"What's that?" I asked.

He bent above the body, examining the throat first with his naked eye, then through a small but powerful lens which he drew from his waistcoat pocket.

"Consider," he replied, rising from his task to regard me with a fixed, unwinking stare. "Wilbur tells us that he heard a piece of furniture overturned. That would be the chair on which this poor one stood. Immediately afterward he ran to her room and knocked. Receiving no response, he knocked again; then, when no answer was forthcoming, he entered. With due allowance made for everything, not more than five minutes could have elapsed. Yet she was dead. I do not like it."

"She might not have been dead when he first saw her," I returned. "You know how quickly unconsciousness follows strangulation. She might have been unconscious and Wilbur assumed she was dead; then because of his fool notion that it was unlawful to cut a hanging body down, he left her strangling here while he ran to 'phone us and waited for us on the porch."

The little Frenchman nodded shortly. "How is death caused in hanging?" he demanded.

"Why—er—by strangulation—asphyxia—or fracture of the cervical vertebrae and rupture of the spinal cord."

"*Précisément.* If Madame Hume had choked to death from yonder bar is it not nearly certain that not only her poor tongue, but her eyes, as well, would have been forced forward by pressure on the constricted blood vessels?"

"I suppose so, but—"

"The devil take all buts. See here—"

Drawing me forward he thrust his lens into my hand and pointed to the dead woman's throat. "Look carefully," he ordered. "You will observe the double track made by the wide silk noose with which poor Madame Hume was hanged."

"Yes," I nodded as my eye followed the parallel anemic band marked by the curtain cord. "I see it."

"Very good. Now look more closely—see, hold the glass so—and tell me if you see a third—a so narrow and deeper mark, a spiral track traced in slightly purple bruise beneath the wide, white marks made by the curtain cord?"

"By heaven!" I started as his slender finger pointed to the darker, deeper depression. "It's pretty faint, but still perceptible. I wonder what that means?"

"Murder, *pardieu!*" he spat the accusation viciously. "Hanged poor Madame Arabella undoubtlessly was, but *hanged after she was dead.*

"This so narrow, purple mark, I know him. Ha, do I not, *cordieu?* In the native states of India I have seen him more than once, and never can it be mistaken for other than itself. No. It is the mark of the *roomal* of the *Thags*, the strangling-cord of those who serve Bhowanee the Black Goddess. Scarcely thicker than a harp-string it is, yet deadly as a serpent's fang. See, those evil ones loop it quickly round their victim's neck, draw it tight with crossed ends, then with their knuckles knead sharply at the base of the skull where the atlas lies and, *pouf!* It is done. Yes. Certainly.

"You want more proof?" He rose and faced me with flashing eyes, his little, milk-white teeth bare beneath the line of his mustache. "Then look—" Abruptly he took Arabella's cheeks between his palms and drew her head forward, then rocked it sharply from side to side.

The evidence was indisputable. Such limber, limp flaccidity meant but one thing. The woman's neck was broken.

"But the drop," I persisted. "She might have broken her neck when she kicked the chair from under her, and—"

"Ah bah!" he countered hotly. "That chair-seat is a scant half-meter high, her feet swung at least four inches from the floor; she could not possibly have dropped a greater length than sixteen inches. Her weight was negligible—I lifted her a moment since—not more than ninety-five or ninety-eight pounds, at most. A drop so short for such a light woman could not possibly have broken the spine. Besides, this fracture is high, not lower than the atlas or the axis; the ligature about her neck encompassed the second cervical vertebra. The two things do not match. *Non*, my friend, this is no suicide, but murder cleverly dressed to simulate it."

"Your brandy, sir." Wilbur halted at the door, keeping his eyes averted resolutely from the quiet form upon the couch.

"*Merci bien*," de Grandin answered. "Put it down, *mon vieux*; then, call *Monsieur* the Coroner and tell him we await him. If the other servants have not yet been appraised of *Madame's* death it will do no harm to let them wait till morning."

"Poor Arabella!" I murmured, staring with tear-dimmed eyes at the pathetic little body underneath the coverlet. "Who could have wanted to kill her?"

"*Eh bien*, who could have wanted to steal Mademoiselle Alice away? Who wanted to obtain the Devil-Worshippers' marriage belt? Who sent the strange veiled lady following after us to tell us that our quest was vain?" he answered, bitter mockery in his tones.

"Good heavens, you mean—"

"Precisely, exactly; quite so. I mean no more and certainly no less, my friend. This is assuredly the Devil's business, and right well have his servants done it. Certainly."

JOHN MARTIN, COUNTY CORONER and leading mortician of the city, and Jules de Grandin were firm friends. At the little Frenchman's earnest entreaty he drove Parnell, the coroner's physician, to perform an autopsy which corroborated every assumption de Grandin had made. Death was due to coma induced by rupture of the myelon, not to strangulation, the post-mortem revealed. Moreover, though Parnell rebelled at the suggestion, Robert Hartley, chief bio-chemist at Mercy Hospital, was called in to make a decimetric test of Arabella's liver. Carefully, de Grandin, Martin and I watching him, he macerated a bit of the organ, mixed it with lampblack and strained it through a porcelain filter. While Parnell sulked in a corner of the laboratory the rest of us watched breathlessly as the serous liquid settled in the glass dish beneath the filter. It was clear.

"Well, that's that," said Hartley.

"*Mais oui, c'est démontré*," de Grandin nodded.

"Umpf!" Parnell grunted in disgust.

The ruddy-faced, gray-haired coroner looked interrogatively from one to the other. "Just what's been proved, gentlemen?" he asked.

"Absence of glycogen." Hartley answered.

"Murder, *parbleu!*" de Grandin added.

"Nothing—nothing at all." Parnell assured him.

"But—" the coroner began more bewildered than ever.

"*Monsieur*," de Grandin cut him short, "glycogen, or liver-sugar represents the stored up energy of muscular strength in the machines we call our bodies. When it is plentiful we are strong, active, hearty—what you call filled with pep. As it is depleted we become weakened. When it is gone we are exhausted. Yes.

"Undoubtlessly a woman being strangled would make a tremendous last muscular effort to fight off her assailant. Such an effort, lasting but a little minute, would burn this muscle-power we call glycogen from her liver. Her reservoir of strength would be drained.

"Am I not right?" he turned for confirmation to Hartley, who nodded slow agreement.

"Very well, then. Now, the experiment Doctor Hartley has just performed shows us conclusively that glycogen was practically absent from Madame Hume's liver. Had it been present in even small quantities the filtered liquid would have been cloudy. Yes. But it was clear, or very nearly so, as you did observe with your own two eyes. What then?

"Simply this, *mordieu*: She fought—frenziedly, though futilely—for her life before the vile miscreant who killed her drew his *roomal* tight about her throat and with his diabolically skillful knuckles broke her neck. It was the tightening strangle-cord which prevented outcry, though the chair we found overturned was undoubtlessly turned over in the struggle, not kicked aside by her after she had adjusted the hangman's noose about her neck. No; by no means. Had she been self-hanged there would be ample store of glycogen found in her liver; as it is—" he paused, raising shoulders, elbows, and eyebrows in a shrug of matchless eloquence.

"I—see," said Mr. Martin slowly.

But the jury did not. Doctor Parnell's lukewarm reception of de Grandin's theory, Hartley's refusal to testify to anything save that there was a lack of glycogen found in the liver, and the cleverness with which the stage had been set to give plausibility to suspicion of suicide combined to forge a chain of circumstantial evidence which all the little Frenchman's fiery oratory could not break. Suicide—dead by her own hand while of unsound mind—was the consensus of the jury.

5. The Missing Child

Headlines screamed across the country: "Mother Slays Self as Cops Hunt Vanished Child"—"Broken Heart Makes Mother Seek Death"—"Love-Crazed Woman Suicides as Daughter Disappears"—these were among the more conservative statements which faced Americans from Maine to Oregon as they sat at breakfast, and for a time reporters from the metropolitan dailies were as thick in our town as hungry flies around an abattoir. At length the hue and cry died down, and Arabella's death and Alice's strange disappearance gave way on the front page to the latest tales of scandal in municipal administration.

Jules de Grandin shut himself in the study, emerging only at mealtime or after office hours for a chat with me, smoked innumerable vile-smelling French cigarettes, used the telephone a great deal and posted many letters; but as far as I could see, his efforts to find Alice or run down her mother's murderers were nil.

"I should think you'd feel better if you went out a bit," I told him at breakfast one day. "I know finding Alice is a hopeless task, and as for Arabella's murderer—I'm beginning to think she committed suicide, after all, but—"

He looked up from the copy of the *Morning Journal* he had been perusing and fixed me with a straight, unwinking stare. "The police are co-operating," he answered shortly. "Not a railway station or bus terminal lacks watchers, and no private cars or taxis leave the city limits without submitting to a secret but thorough inspection. What more can we do?"

"Why, you might direct the search personally, or check up such few clues as they may find—" I began, nettled by his loss of interest in the case, but he cut me short with a quick motion of his hand.

"My friend," he told me with one of his Puckish grins, "attend me. When I was a little lad I had a dog, a silly energetic little fellow, all barks and jumps and wagging tail. He dearly loved a cat. *Morbleu*, the very sight of Madame Puss would put him in a frenzy! How he would rush at her, how he would show his teeth and growl and put on the fierce face! Then, when she had retired to the safety of a pear tree, how he would stand beneath her refuge and twitch his tail and bark! *Cordieu*, sometimes I would think he must surely burst with barking!

"And she, the scornful pussy, did she object? *Mille fois non*. Safe in her sanctuary she would eye him languidly, and let him bark. At last, when he had barked himself into exhaustion, he would withdraw to think upon the evils of times, and Madame Puss would leisurely descend the tree and trot away to safety.

"I would often say to him: 'My Toto, you are a great stupid-head. Why do you do it? Why do you not depart a little distance from the tree and lie *perdu*? Then Madame Puss may think that you have lost all interest and come down;

then *pouf!* you have her at your mercy.' But no, that foolish little dog, he would not listen to advice, and so, though he expended great energy and made a most impressive noise, he never caught a cat.

"Friend Trowbridge, I am not a foolish little dog. By no means. It is not I who do such things. Here in the house I stay, with strict instructions that I be not called should any want me on the telephone; I am not ever seen abroad. For all of the display I make, I might be dead or gone away. But I am neither. Always and ever I sit here all watchful, and frequently I do call the gendarmes to find if they have discovered that for which we seek. I know—I see all that takes place. If any makes a move, I know it. But those we seek do not know I know. No, they think Jules de Grandin is asleep or drunk, or perhaps gone away. It is best so, I assure you. Anon, emboldened by my seeming lethargy, they will emerge from out their hiding-place; then—" His smile became unpleasant as he clenched one slender, strong hand with a gesture suggestive of crushing something soft within it. "Then, *pardieu*, they shall learn that Jules de Grandin is not a fool, nor can they make the long nose at him with impunity!" He helped himself to a second portion of broiled mackerel from the hot-water dish and resumed his perusal of the *Journal*. Suddenly:

"*Ohé, misère, calamité, c'est désastrieux!*" he cried. "Read here my friend, if you please. Read it and tell me that I am mistaken!"

Hands shaking with eagerness, he passed the paper to me, indicating a rather inconspicuous item in the lower left-hand corner of the third page.

CHILD VANISHES FROM BAPTIST HOME

Shortly after one o'clock this morning Mrs. Maude Gordon, 47, a matron in the Harrisonville Baptist Home, was awakened by sounds of crying from the ward in which the younger children of the orphanage were quartered. Going quickly to the room the woman found some of the older children sitting up in bed and crying bitterly. Upon demanding what was wrong she was told that a man had just been in the place, flashed a flashlight in several of the children's faces, then picked Charles Eastman, eight months, from his crib which stood near the open window, and made off with him.

The matron at once gave the alarm, and a thorough search of the premises was made, but no trace of the missing child or his abductor could be found. The gates of the orphanage were shut and locked, and the lodge-keeper, who was awakened by the searching party, declared it would have been impossible for anyone to pass in or out without his knowledge, as his were the only keys to the gates beside those in the main office of the home, and the keys were in their accustomed place on his bureau in his bedroom when the alarm reached him. The home's extensive grounds are surrounded by a twelve-foot brick wall, with an overhang on either side, and climbing it either from the outside or from within would be almost impossible without extension ladders.

The Eastman child's parents are dead and his only living relative so far as known is an uncle, lately released from the penitentiary. Police are checking up on this man's movements during the night, as it is thought he may have stolen the child to satisfy a grudge he had against the mother, now dead, whose testimony helped convict him on a charge of burglary five years ago.

"Well?" I asked as I laid the paper down. "Is that what you read?"

"*Hélas*, yes. It is too true!"

"Why, what d'ye mean—" I began, but he cut in hurriedly.

"Perhaps I do mistake, my friend. Although I have lived in your so splendid country for upward of five years, there is still much which is strange to me. Is it that the sect you call the Baptists do not believe in infant baptism—that only those of riper years are given baptism by them?"

"Yes, that's so," I answered. "They hold that—"

"No matter what they hold, if that be so," he interrupted. "That this little one had not been accorded baptism is enough—*parbleu*, it is much. Come, my friend, the time for concealing is past. Let us hasten, let us rush; let us fly!"

"Rush?" I echoed, bewildered. "Where?"

"To that orphan home of the so little unbaptized Baptists, of course," he answered almost furiously. "Come, let us go right away, immediately, at once."

MAINTAINED BY LIBERAL ENDOWMENTS and not greatly taxed by superfluity of inmates, the Baptist Home for Children lay on a pleasant elevation some five miles out of Harrisonville. Its spacious grounds, which were equipped with every possible device for fostering organized play among its little guests were, as the newspaper accounts described, surrounded by a brick wall of formidable height with projecting overhangs flanging T-wise, from the top. Moreover, in an excess of caution, the builder had studded the wall's crest with a fringe of broken bottle-glass set in cement, and anyone endeavoring to cross the barrier must be prepared not only with scaling ladders so long as to be awkward to carry, but with a gangway or heavy pad to lay across the shark-tooth points of glass with which the wall was armored. De Grandin made a rapid reconnaissance of the position, twisting viciously at his mustache meanwhile. "Ah, *hélas*, the poor one!" he murmured as his inspection was completed. "Before, I had some hope; now I fear the worst."

"Eh?" I returned. "What now?"

"Plenty, *pardieu*—a very damn great plenty!" he answered bitterly. "Come, let us interview the *concierge*. He is our only hope, I fear."

I glanced at him in wonder as we neared the pretty little cottage in which the gatekeeper maintained his home and office.

"No, sir," the man replied to de Grandin's question, "I'm sure no one could 'a' come through that gate last night. It's usually locked for th' night at ten o'clock, though I mostly sit up listenin' to th' radio, a little later, an' if anything real important comes up, I'm on hand to open th' gates. Last night there wasn't a soul, man or woman, 'ceptin' th' grocery deliveryman, come in here after six o'clock—very quiet day it was, 'count th' cold weather, I guess. I wuz up a little later than usual, too, but turned in 'bout 'leven o'clock, I should judge. I'd made th' rounds o' th' grounds with Bruno a little after seven, an' believe me, I'm here to tell you no one could 'a' been hidin' anywhere without his knowin' it. No sir!

"Here, Bruno!" be raised his voice and snapped his fingers authoritatively, and a ponderous mastiff, seemingly big enough to drag down an elephant, ambled in and favored us with a display of awe-inspiring teeth as his black lips curled back in a snarl.

"Bruno slept right beside my bed, sir," the gatekeeper went on, "an th' winder wuz open; so if anyone had so much as stopped by th' gate to monkey with it, he'd 'a' heard 'em, an'—well, it wouldn't 'a' been so good for 'em, I'm tellin' you. I recollec' once when a pettin' party across th' road from th' gate, Bruno got kind o' suspicious-like an' first thing any of us knew he'd bolted through th' winder an made for 'em—like to tore th' shirt off th' feller 'fore I woke up an called 'im off."

De Grandin nodded shortly. "And may one examine your room for one little minute, *Monsieur?*" he asked courteously, "We shall touch nothing, of course, and request that you be with us at all times."

"We-ell—I don't—oh, all right," the watchman responded as the Frenchman's hand strayed meaningfully toward his wallet. "Come on."

The small neat room in which the gatekeeper slept had a single wide window opening obliquely toward the gate and giving a view both of the portal and a considerable stretch of road in each direction, for the gatehouse was built into, and formed an integral part of the wall surrounding the grounds. From window-sill to earth was a distance of perhaps six feet, possibly a trifle less.

"And your keys were where, if you please?" de Grandin asked as he surveyed the chamber.

"Right on the bureau there, where I put 'em before I went to bed last night, an' they wuz in th' same place this mornin' when they called me from th' office, too. Guess they'd better 'a' been there, too. Anyone tryin' to sneak in an' pinch 'em would 'a' had old Bruno to deal with, even if I hadn't wakened, which I would of, 'count of I'm such a light sleeper. You have to be, in a job like this."

"Perfectly," the Frenchman nodded understandingly as he walked to the window, removed the immaculate white-linen handkerchief from his sleeve and flicked it lightly across the sill. "Thank you, *Monsieur*, we need not trouble you further, I think," he continued, taking a bill from his folder and laying it casually on the bureau before turning to leave the room.

At the gateway he paused a moment, examining the lock. It was a heavy snap-latch of modern workmanship, strong enough to defy the best efforts of a crew of journeymen safe-blowers.

"*C'est très simple*," he murmured to himself as we left the gate and entered my car. "Behold, Friend Trowbridge."

Withdrawing the white handkerchief from his cuff he held it toward me. Across its virgin surface there lay, where he had brushed it on the watchman's window-sill, a smear of yellow powder.

"*Bulala-gwai*," he told me in a weary, almost toneless voice.

"What, that devil-dust—"

"*Précisément*, my friend, that devil-dust. Was it not simple? To his window they did creep, most doubtlessly on shoes with rubber soles, which would make no noise upon the frozen ground. *Pouf!* the sleeping-powder is tossed into his room, and he and his great mastiff are at once unconscious. They remove his keys; it is a so easy task. The gate is unlocked, opened; then made fast with a retaining wedge, and the keys replaced upon his bureau. The little one is stolen, the gate closed behind the kidnappers, and the spring-latch locks itself. When the alarm is broadcast *Monsieur le Concierge* can swear in all good conscience that no one has gone through the gate and that his keys are in their proper place. But certainly; of course they were. By damn, but they are clever, those ones!"

"Whom do you mean? Who'd want to steal a little baby from an orphan's home?"

"A little *unbaptized* baby—and a boy," he interjected.

"All right, a little unbaptized boy."

"I would give my tongue to the cat to answer that," he told me solemnly. "That they are the ones who spirited Mademoiselle Alice away from before our very eyes we can not doubt. The technique of their latest crime has labeled them; but why *they*, whose faith is a bastardized descendant of the old religion of Zoroaster—a sort of disreputable twelfth cousin of the Parsees—should want to do this—*non*, it does not match, my friend. Jules de Grandin is much puzzled." He shook his head and pulled, so savagely at his mustache that I feared he would do himself permanent injury.

"What in heaven's name—" I began. And:

"In heaven's name, *ha!* Yes, we shall have much to do in heaven's name, my friend," he cut in. "For a certainty we are aligned against a crew who ply their arts in hell's name."

6. The Veiled Lady Again

H ARRISONVILLE'S NEWEST CITIZENS, GROSS weight sixteen pounds, twelve ounces, delayed their advent past all expectations that night, but with their overdue arrival came trying complications, and for close upon three hours two nurses, a badly worried young house physician and I fought manfully to bring mother and her twins back across death's doorstep. It was well past midnight when I climbed my front steps, dog-tired, with hands that trembled from exhaustion and eyes still smarting from the glare of surgery lamps. "Half a gill of brandy, then bed—and no morning office hours tomorrow," I promised myself as I tiptoed down the hall.

I poured the spirit out into a graduate and was in the act of draining it when the sudden furious clamor of the night bell arrested my upraised hand. Acquired instinct will not be denied. Scarcely aware of what I did, I put the brandy down untasted and stumbled, rather than walked, to the front door to answer the alarm.

"Doctor—Doctor, let me in—hide me. Quick, don't let them see us talking!" the fear-sharpened feminine whisper cut through the darkened vestibule and a woman's form lurched drunkenly forward into my arms. She was breathing in short, labored gasps, like a hunted creature.

"Quick—quick"—again that scarcely audible murmur, more pregnant with terror than a scream—"shut the door—lock it—bolt it—stand back out of the light! Please!"

I retreated a step or two, my visitor still clinging to me like a drowning woman to her rescuer. As we passed beneath the ceiling-light I took glance at her, I was vaguely conscious of her charm, of her beauty, of her perfume, so delicate that it was but the faint, seductive shadow of a scent. A tightly fitting hat of black was set on her head, and draped from this, from eartip to eartip, was stretched a black-mesh veil, its upper edge just clearing the tip of her nose but covering mouth, cheeks and chin, leaving the eyes and brow uncovered. Through its diaphanous gauze I could see the gleam of carmined lips and tiny, pearl-like teeth, seemingly sharp as little sabers as the small, childish mouth writhed back from them in panic terror.

"Why—why"—I stammered—"it's the lady we saw when we—"

"Perfectly; it is *Mademoiselle l'Inconnue*, the lady of the veil," de Grandin finished as he descended the last three steps at a run, and in a lavender dressing-gown and purple kidskin slippers, a violet muffler draped round his throat, stepped nimbly forward to assist me with my lovely burden.

"What is it, *Mademoiselle?*" he asked, half leading, half carrying her toward the consulting-room; "have you perhaps come again to tell us that our search is vain?"

"No, no-o!" the woman moaned, leaning still more heavily upon us. "Help me, oh, help me, please! I'm wounded; they—he—oh, I'll tell you everything!"

"Excellent!" de Grandin nodded as he flung back the door and switched on the electric lights. "First let us see your hurt, then—*mon Dieu*, Friend Trowbridge, she had swooned!"

Even as he spoke the woman buckled weakly at the knees, and like a lovely doll from which the sawdust has been let, crumpled forward toward the floor.

I freed one hand from her arm, intent on helping place her on the table, and stared at it with an exclamation of dismay. The fingers were dyed to the knuckles with blood, and on the girl's dark motor coat an ugly dull-red stain was sopping-wet and growing every moment.

"*Très bien*, so!" de Grandin murmured, placing his hands beneath her arms and heaving her up the examination table. "She will be better here, for—*Dieu des chiens*, my friend, observe!"

As the heavy outdoor wrap the woman wore fell open we saw that it, a pair of modish patent leather pumps, her motor gloves and veil-draped hat were her sole wardrobe. From veil-swathed chin to blue-veiled instep she was as nude as on the day she came into the world.

No wound showed on her ivory shoulders or creamy breast, but on her chest, immediately above the gently swelling breasts, was a medallion-shaped outline or cicatrix inside which was crudely tattooed this design:

"Good heavens?" I exclaimed. "What is it?"

"*Précisément*, what is it—and what are these?" the little Frenchman countered, ripping aside the flimsy veil and exposing the girl's pale face. On each cheek, so deeply sunk into the flesh below the malar points that they could only be the result of branding, were two small cruciform scars, perhaps three-quarters of an inch in height by half an inch in width, describing the device of a passion cross turned upside-down.

"Why, of all ungodly things—" I began, and:

"*Ha*, ungodly do you say, *mon vieux? Pardieu*, you call it by its proper name!" said Jules de Grandin. "An insult to *le bon Dieu* was intended, for this poor one wears upon her body—"

"I c-couldn't stand it!" moaned the girl upon the table. "Not that—not that! He looked at me and smiled and put his baby hand against my cheek! He was the image of my dear little—no, *no*, I tell you! You mustn't! O-o-oh, *no*!"

For a moment she sobbed brokenly, then: "Oh, *mea culpa, mea maxima culpa!* Remember not our offenses nor the offenses of our forefathers—spare us, good Lord—I will, I tell you! Yes I'll go to him and tell, if—Doctor de Grandin"—her voice sank to a sibilant whisper and she half rose from the table, glaring about with glazed, unseeing eyes—"Doctor de Grandin, watch for the chalk-signs of the Devil—follow the pointing tridents; they'll lead you to the place when— oh, *mea culpa, mea maxima culpa!* Have pity, Jesu!"

"Delirium," I diagnosed. "Quick, de Grandin, she's running a pretty high temperature. Help me turn her; the wound seems in her back."

It was. Puncturing the soft flesh a little to the left of the right shoulder, glancing along the scapula, then striking outward to the shoulder tip was a gunshot wound, superficial, but undoubtedly painful, and productive of extensive hemorrhage.

With probe and cotton and mercurochrome we sterilized the wound, then made a gauze compress liberally sprinkled with Senn's mixture and made it fast with cross-bandages of adhesive tape. Three-quarters of a grain of morphine injected in her arm provided a defense against recurring pain and sank her in a deep and peaceful sleep.

"I think she'd best be taken to a hospital," I told him when our work was finished. "We've given all the first aid that we can, and she'll be better tended there—we've no facilities for bed-rest here, or—"

"Agreed," he broke in. "To City Hospital, by all means. They have a prison ward there."

"But we can't put her there," I objected. "She's guilty of no crime, and besides, she's in no condition to go out alone for several days. She'll be there when we want her without the need of bars to keep her in."

"Not bars to keep her in," he told me. "Bars *to keep them out*, my friend."

"Them? Who—"

"The good God knows *who*, I only suspect *what*," he answered. "Come, let us take her there without delay."

"CAN'T BE DONE, SON," Doctor Donovan told de Grandin when we arrived at City Hospital with our patient. "The prison ward's exclusively reserved for gents and ladies on special leave from the hoosegow, or those with some specific charge pending against 'em. You'd not care to place a charge against the lady, would you?"

De Grandin considered him a moment. "Murder is still a relatively serious offense, even in America," he returned thoughtfully. "Can not she be held as a material witness?"

"To whose murder?" asked the practical Donovan.

"The little Eastman boy's—he who was stolen from the Baptist Home last night," the Frenchman replied.

"Hold on, feller, be your age," the other cautioned. "Who says the little lad's been murdered? The police can't even find him alive, and till they find his body there's no *corpus delicti* to support a murder charge."

Once more the Frenchman gazed somberly at him: "Whether you know it or not, my friend," he answered seriously, "that little one is dead. Dead as mutton, and died most unpleasantly—like the sinless little lamb he was. Yes.

"Maybe you've got some inside dope on the case?" Donovan suggested hopefully.

"No—only reason and intuition, but they—"

"They won't go here," the other cut in. "We can't put this girl in the prison ward without a warrant of some sort, de Grandin: it's against the rules and as much as my job's worth to do it. There might be all sorts of legal complications: suits for false imprisonment, and that sort of thing. But see here, she came fumbling at your door mumbling all sorts of nonsense and clearly out of her head, didn't she?"

The Frenchman nodded.

"All right, then, we'll say she was batty, loony, balmy in the bean, as they say in classic Siamese. That'll give us an excuse for locking her up in H-3, the psychopathic ward. We've got stronger bars on those windows than we have in the prison ward. Plenty o' room there, too: no one but some souses sleeping off D.T.'s and the effects of prohibition whoopee. I'll move 'em over to make room for—by the way, what's your little playmate's name, anyhow?"

"We do not know," returned de Grandin. "She is *une inconnue*."

"Hell, I can't spell that," Donovan assured him. "We'll have to write her down unknown. All right?"

"Quite," the little Frenchman answered with a smile. "And now you will receive her?"

"Sure thing," the other promised.

"Hey, Jim!" he hailed an orderly lounging in the corridor, "bring the agony cart. Got another customer for H-3. She's unconscious."

"O.K., Chief," the man responded, trundling forward a wheeled stretcher.

Frightened, pitiful moans of voyagers in the borderland of horror sifted through the latticed doors of the cells facing the corridors of H-3 as we followed the stretcher down the hall. Here a gin-crazed woman sobbed and screamed in mortal terror at the phantoms of alcoholic delirium; there a sodden creature, barely eighteen, but with the marks of acute nephritis already on her face, choked and regurgitated in the throes of deathly nausea. "Three rousing cheers for the noble experiment," Doctor Donovan remarked, an ugly sneer gathering at the corners of his mouth. "I wish to God those dam' prohibitionists had to drink a few swigs of the kind of poison they've flooded the country with! If I had my way—"

"Jasus!" screamed a blear-eyed Irishwoman whose cell we passed. "Lord ha' mercy on us: 'Tis she!" For a moment she clung to the wicket of her door like a monkey to the bars of its cage, staring horror-struck at the still form upon the stretcher.

"Take it easy, Annie," Donovan comforted. "She won't hurt you."

"Won't hur-rt me, is it?" the woman croaked. "Won't har-rm me, wid th' Divil's silf mar-rchin' down th' hall beside her! Can't you see th' horns an' tail an' the flashin', fiery eyes of 'im as he walks beside her, Doctor darlin'? Oh, Lord ha' mercy; bless an' save us, Howly Mither!" She signed herself with the cross, and stared with horror-dazed, affrighted eyes at the girl on the litter till our pitiful procession turned the bend that shut us from her sight.

7. The Mutter of a Distant Drum

IT WAS A WINDY night of scudding clouds which had brought a further fall of snow, and our progress was considerably impeded as we drove home from the hospital. I was nearly numb with cold and on the verge of collapse with fatigue when we finally stabled the car and let ourselves in the back door. "Now for that dose of brandy and bed," I promised myself as we crossed the kitchen.

"Yes, by blue," de Grandin agreed vigorously, "you speak wisdom, my friend. Me. I shall be greatly pleased to join you in both."

By the door of the consulting-room I halted. "Queer," I muttered. "I'd have sworn we turned the lights off when we left, but—"

"S-s-sh!" De Grandin's sibilant warning cut me short as he edged in front of me and drew the small but vicious automatic pistol, which he always carried, from its holster underneath his left armpit. "Stand back, Friend Trowbridge, for I, Jules de Grandin, will deal with them!" He dashed the door wide open with a single well-directed kick, then dodged nimbly back, taking shelter behind the jamb and leveling his pistol menacingly. "Attention, hands up—I have you covered!" he called sharply.

From the examination table, where he had evidently been asleep, an under-sized individual bounced rather than rose, landing cat-like on both feet and glaring ferociously at the door where de Grandin had taken cover.

"Assassin!" he shouted, clenching his fists and advancing half a pace toward us.

"*Morbleu*, he has found us!" de Grandin almost shrieked. "It is the *apache*, the murderer, the robber of defenseless little ones and women! Have a care, monster"—he leaped into the zone of light shed by the desk lamp and brandished his pistol—"stand where you are, if you would go on living your most evil life!"

Disdainful of the pistol as though it were a pointed finger the other advanced, knees bent in an animal-crouch, hands half closed, as though preparing for a death grip on de Grandin's throat. A single pace away he halted and flung wide his arms. "*Embrasse-moi!*" he cried; and in another moment they were locked together in a fond embrace like sweethearts reunited after parting.

"Oh, Georges, *mon* Georges, you are the curing sight for tired eyes: You are truly heaven-sent!" de Grandin cried when he had in some measure regained his breath. "Between the sight of your so unlovely face and fifty thousand francs placed in my hand, I should assuredly have chosen you, *mon petit singe!*" To me he added:

"Assuredly you recall Monsieur Renouard. Friend Trowbridge? Georges Jean Jacques Joseph Marie Renouard, *Inspecteur du Service de la Sûreté Generale?*"

"Of course," I answered, shaking hands with the visitor. "Glad to see you again, Inspector." The little colonial administrator had been my guest some years before, and he, de Grandin and I had shared a number of remarkable adventures. "We were just about to take a drink," I added, and the caller's bright eyes lit up with appreciation. "Won't you join us?"

"*Parbleu*," Renouard assured me. "I do most dearly love your language, Monsieur Trowbridge, and most of all I love the words that you just said!"

Our liquor poured, we sat and faced each other, each waiting for the other to begin the conversation. At length:

"I called an hour or so ago," Renouard commenced, "and was admitted by your so excellent maid. She said that you were out, but bade me wait; then off she went to bed—nor do I think that she did count the silver first. She knows me. Yes. *Bien alors*, I waited, and fell asleep while doing so."

I looked at him with interest. Though shorter by some inches than the average American, Renouard could not be properly called under-sized. Rather, he was a giant in miniature. His very lack of height gave the impression of material equilibrium and tremendous physical force. Instinctively one felt that the thews of his arms were massive as those of a gladiator and that his torso was sheathed in muscles like that of a professional wrestler. A mop of iron-gray hair was brushed back in an uprearing pompadour from his wide, low brow, and a curling white mustache adorned his upper lip, while from his chin depended a white beard cut square across the bottom in the style beloved of your true Frenchman. But most impressive of all was his cold, pale face—a face with the pallor of a statue—from which there burned a pair of big, deep-set eyes beneath circumflexes of intensely black and bushy brows.

"*Eh bien, mon Georges*," de Grandin asked. "What storm wind blows you hither? You were ever the fisher in troubled water."

Renouard gulped down his brandy, stroked his mustache and tugged his beard, then drew forth a Russian leather case from which he extracted a

Maryland cigarette. "Women, *parbleu!* One sometimes wonders why the good God made them." He snapped an English lighter into flame and with painstaking precision set his puissant cigarette aglow, then folded his big white hands demurely in his lap and glanced inquiringly at us with his bright dark eyes as though we held the answer to his riddle.

"*Tiens*, my friend." de Grandin laughed. "Had he not done so it is extremely probable that you and I would not be here indulging in this pleasant conversation. But women bring you here and why?"

Renouard expelled a double stream of acrid smoke from his nostrils, emitting a snort of annoyance at the same time. "One hardly knows the words to tell it," he replied.

"The trouble starts in Egypt. During the war, and afterward until the end of martial law in 1923, Egypt, apart from the Continental system of *maisons de tolerance*, was outwardly at least as moral as London. But since the strong clean hand of Britain has been loosed there has been a constantly increasing influx of white slaves to the country. Today hardly a ship arrives in Alexandria without its quota of this human freight. The trade is old, as old as Nineveh and Tyre, and to suppress it altogether is a hopeless undertaking, but to regulate it, ah, that is something different.

"We were not greatly exercised when the numbers of unfortunate girls going from Marseilles increased in Egypt, but when respectable young girls— *mais oui*, girls of more than mere bourgeois respectability, even daughters of *le beau monde*, were sucked beneath the surface, later to be boiled up as inmates of those infamous Blue Houses of the East—then we did begin to take sharp notice.

"They sent for me. 'Renouard,' they said, 'investigate and tell us what is which.'

"*Très bon*, I did commence. The dossiers of half a dozen girls I took, and from the ground upward I did build their cases. Name of a little blue man!" He leaned forward, speaking a low, impressive tone scarce above a whisper: "There was devilment, literally, I mean, my friends, in that business. By example:

"Each one of these young girls was of an independent turn: She reveled in the new emancipation of her sex. Oh, but yes! So much she relished this new freedom that the ancient inhibitions were considered out of date. The good God, the gentle Christ Child, the Blessed Mother—*ah bah*, they were outmoded: she must follow after newer—or older—gods.

"*Eh bien*, exceedingly strange gods they were, too. In Berlin, Paris, London and New York there is a sect which preaches for its gospel 'Do What Thou Wilt; This Shall Be the Whole of the Law.' And as the little boy who eats too many bonbons inevitably achieves a belly-ache, so do the followers of this unbridled license reap destruction ultimately. But certainly.

"Each one of these young girls I find she has enlisted in this strange, new army of the freed. She has attended meetings where they made strange prayers to stranger gods, and—eventually she ends a cast-off plaything, eaten with drugs and surfeited with life, in the little, infamous Blue Houses of the East. Yes.

"I found them all. Some were dying, some were better dead, some had still a little way to tread the dreary path of hell-in-life, but all—*all*, my friends—were marked with this device upon their breasts. See, I have seen him so often I can draw him from memory." Taking a black-oilcloth bound notebook from his pocket he tore out a leaf and scribbled a design upon it.

De Grandin and I stared at each other in blank amazement as he passed the sheet to us.

"Good Lord!" I ejaculated. "It's exactly like—"

"*Précisément; la même chose*—it is the same that Mademoiselle of the Veil displayed," de Grandin agreed. With shining eyes he turned to face Renouard. "Proceed, my friend," he begged. "When you have done we have a tale to tell."

"Ah, but I am far from done," the Inspector replied. "*Bien non*. I did investigate some more, and I found much. I discovered, by example, that the society to which these most unhappy girls belonged was regularly organized, having grand and subordinate lodgers, like Freemasons, with a central body in control of all. Moreover, I did find that at all times and at all places where this strange sect met, there was a Russian in command, or very near the head. Does that mean anything to you? No?

"Very well, then, consider this: Last year the Union of the Militant Godless, financed by the Soviet government, closed four thousand churches in Russia by direct action. Furthermore, still well supplied with funds, they succeeded in doing much missionary work abroad. They promoted all sorts of atheistic societies, principally among young people. In America on the one hand they gave much help to such societies as 'The Lost Souls' among college students, and on the other they greatly aided fanatical religious sects which aim at the abolition of innocent amusement—in the name of Christ. Associations for making the Sabbath Day unpleasant by closing of the cinemas, the shops and all places of recreation, have received large grants of money from the known agents of this Godless Union. Moreover, we know for certain that much of the legislation fostered by these bodies has been directly proposed by Russian agents posing as staunch upholders of fundamental religion. You see? On the one side atheism is promoted among the young, on the other religion's own ministers are whipped on by flattery or outright bribery to do such things as will make the churches hateful to all liberal-minded people. The scheme is beautifully simple, and it has worked well.

"Again: In England only half a year ago a clergyman was unfrocked for having baptized a dog, saying he would make it a good member of the Established

Church. We looked this man's antecedents up and found that he was friendly with some Russians who posed as *émigrés*—refugees from the Bolshevik oppression. Now this man, who has no fortune and no visible means of support, is active every day in preaching radical atheism, and in weaning his former parishioners from their faith. He lives, and lives well. Who provides for him? One wonders.

"Defections in the clergy of all churches have been numerous of late, and in every instance one or more Russians are found on friendly terms with the apostate man of God.

"*Non*, hear me a little further," he went on as de Grandin was about to speak. "The forces of disorder, and of downright evil, are dressing their ranks and massing their shock troops for attack. Far in the East there is the mutter of a distant drum, and from the fastnesses of other lands the war-drum's beat is answered. Consider:

"In the Congo there is renewed activity by the Leopard Men, those strange and diabolical societies whose members disguise themselves as leopards, then seek and kill their prey by night. The authorities are taking most repressive measures, but still the Leopard Societies flourish more than ever, and the blacks are fast becoming unruly. There will be difficulties.

"In Paris, London and Berlin again and yet again churches are despoiled of sacred plate and blessed vestments, the host is stolen from the altar, and every kind of sacrilege is done. A single instance of this sort of thing, or even several, might be coincidence, but when the outrages are perpetrated systematically, not once, but scores of times, and always at about the same time, though in widely separated places, coincidences become statistics. There can no longer be a doubt; the black mass is being celebrated regularly in all the greater cities of the world; yet we do not think mere insult to God is all that is intended. No, there is some central, underlying motive for this sudden and widespread revival of satanism. One wonders what.

"And here another puzzle rises: In Arabia, north of Irak, in the Kurdish mountains, is the headquarters of a strange people called the Yezidees. About them we know little, save that they have served the Devil as their god time out of mind. Had they been strong numerically, they would have been a problem, for they are brave and fierce, and much given to killing, but they are few in number and their Moslem neighbors ring them round so thoroughly that they have been forced back upon themselves and seldom do they trouble those who do not trouble them. But"—he paused impressively—"on Mount Lalesh, where their great temple stands, strange things have been brewing lately. What it is we do not clearly know, but their members have been gathering from all parts of the East, from as far as Mongolia, in some instances, to celebrate some sort of mystic ceremony. Not only that, but strangers—Europeans, Africans, white, black and yellow men, who have no business being there, have been observed en route to Kurdistan, like pilgrims journeying to Mecca. Less than a month ago a party of brigands waylaid some travelers near Aleppo. Our gendarmes rescued them—they were a party of Americans and Englishmen, with several Spaniards as well and *all were headed for Kurdistan and Mount Lalesh.* Again one wonders why.

"Our secret agents have been powerless to penetrate the mystery. We only know that many Russians have been sent to enter the forbidden city of the Yezidees; that the Yezidees, who once were poor, are now supplied with large amounts of ready cash; and that their bearing toward their neighbors has suddenly become arrogant.

"Wild rumors are circulated: There is talk of a revival of the cult of the Assassins, who made life terrible for the Crusaders and the Mussulmans alike. There are whispers of a prophetess to come from some strange land, a prophetess who will raise the standard of the Devil and lead his followers against the Crescent and Cross. Just what it is we do not surely know, but those of us who know the East can perceive that it means war. The signs are unmistakable; a revolution is fomenting. Some sort of unholy *jihad* will be declared, but where the blow will fall, or when, we can not even guess. India? Indo-China? Arabia? Perhaps in all at once. Who knows? London is preparing, so is Paris, and Madrid is massing troops in Africa—but who can fight a figure carved in smoke? We must know at whom to strike before we can take action, *n'est-ce-pas?*

"But this much I can surely tell: One single man, a so-mysterious man whose face I have not seen, but whose trail is marked as plainly as a snake's track in the dust, is always found at hand where the strings of these far-separated things are joined and knotted in a cord. He was a prime mover in the societies to which those wretched girls belonged; he was among those friendly with the unfrocked English clergyman; he was almost, but not quite, apprehended in connection with the rifling of the sanctuary of a church in Cologne; he has been seen in Kurdistan. Across France, England, Arabia and Egypt have I trailed him, always just a little bit too late. Now he is in America. Yes, *parbleu*, he is in this very city!

"*C'est tout!* I must find him, and finding him, I must achieve a method to destroy him, even if I have to stoop to murder. The snake may wiggle, even though his head has been decapitated, but God knows he can no longer bite when it is done. So do I."

Jules de Grandin leaned across the desk and possessed himself of Renouard's cigarette case, extracted from it a vile-smelling Maryland and lit it with a smile, "I know the answers to your problems—or some of them, at least—my friend," he asserted. "This very night there came to us—to this very house—a deserter from the ranks of the accursed, and though she raved in wild delirium, she did let fall enough to tell us how to find this man you seek, and when we find him—" The hard, cold light, which always reminded me of winter sunshine glinting on a frozen stream, came into his eyes, and his thin lips tightened in an ugly line. "When we have found him," he continued, "we shall know what to do. Name of an umbrella, we damn shall!

"The piecemeal information which you have fits admirably with what we already know and better yet with that which we suspect. Listen to me carefully—"

The sudden jangle of the telephone broke in.

"Doctor Trowbridge?" called a deep bass voice as I snatched up the instrument and growled a gruff "hullo?"

"Yes."

"Costello—Detective Sergeant Costello speakin'. Can you an' Doctor de Grandin be ready in five minutes to go wid me? I'd not be afther askin' ye to leave yer beds so early if it warn't important, sor, but—"

"That's all right, Sergeant, we haven't been to bed as yet." I told him. "We're pretty well done in, but if this is important—"

"Important, is it? Glory be to God, if th' foulest murther that iver disgraced th' Shtate o' Jersey ain't important, then I can't think what is. 'Tis out to th' Convent o' th' Sacred Heart, by Rupleyville, sor, an'—I'll take it kindly if ye'll go along wid me, sor. Th' pore ladies out there'll be needin' a docthor's services, I'm thinkin', an' St. Joseph knows I'm afther needin' all th' expert help that Doctor de Grandin can give me, too."

"All right, we'll be waiting for you," I replied as I put the monophone back in its hooks and turned to notify de Grandin and Renouard of our engagement.

8. "In Hoc Signo—"

THE QUERULOUS CRESCENDO OF a squad car's siren sounded outside our door almost as I finished speaking, and we trooped down the front steps to join the big Irish policeman and two other plainclothes officers occupying the tonneau of the department vehicle. "Sure, Inspector Renouard," Costello greeted heartily as he shook hands, "'tis glad I am to see ye this mornin'. There's nothin' to do in this case but wor-rk like th' devil an trust in God, an' th' more o' us there's here to do it, th' better our chances are. Jump in, gentlemen." To the uniformed chauffeur he ordered: "Shtep on it, Casey."

Casey stepped. The powerful Cadillac leaped forward like a mettlesome horse beneath the flailings of a lash, and the cold, sharp air of early winter morning was whipped into our faces with breathtaking force as we sped along the deserted road at nearly eighty miles an hour.

"What is it? What has happened?" de Grandin cupped his hands and shouted as we roared past the sleeping houses of the quiet suburb. Costello raised his gloved hand to his mouth, then shook his head. No voice was capable of bellowing above the screeching of the rushing wind.

Almost before we realized it we were drawn up before the tall graystone walls of the convent, and Costello was jerking vigorously at the bell-pull beside the gate. "From headquarters, Ma'am," he announced tersely, touching his hat as the portress drew back the little wicket in the door and gazed at us inquiringly.

Something more than ordinary silence seemed to brood above the big bare building as we followed our conductress down the clean-swept corridor to the public reception parlor: rather, it seemed to me, the air was charged with a sort of concentrated, apprehensive emanation of sheer terror. Once, when professional obligations required my attendance at an execution, I had felt some such eerie sensation of concentrated horror and anticipation as the other witnesses and I sat mute within the execution chamber, staring alternately with fright-filled eyes at the grim electric chair and the narrow door through which we knew the condemned man would soon emerge.

As we reached the reception room and seated ourselves on the hard, uncomfortable chairs, I suddenly realized the cause of the curiously anxious feeling which possessed me. From every quarter of the building—seemingly from floors and walls and ceilings—there came the almost mute but still perceptible soft sibilation of a whispered chorus. Whisper, whisper, *whisper*; the faint, half audible susurration persisted without halt or break, endless and untiring as the lisping of the tide upon the sands. It worried me, it beat upon my ears like water wearing on a stone: unless it stopped, I told myself, I would surely shout aloud with all my might for no other reason than to drown its everlasting monotonous reiteration.

The tap of light soled shoes and the gentle rustle of a skirt brought relief from the oppressive monotone, and the Mother Superior of the nunnery stood before us. Costello bowed with awkward grace as he stepped forward. De Grandin and Renouard were frigidly polite in salutation; for Frenchmen, especially those connected with official life, have not forgotten the rift between the orders and the Government of France existing since the disestablishment of 1903.

"We're from headquarters, Mother," Costello introduced: "We came as quickly as we could. Where is it—she—the body, if ye please?"

Mother Mary Margaret regarded him with eyes which seemed to have wept so much that not a tear was left, and her firm lips trembled as she answered: "In the garden, officer. It's irregular for men to enter there, but this is an emergency to which the rules must yield. The portress was making her rounds a little before matins when she heard somebody moving in the garden and looked out. No one was visible, but something looked strange to her, so she went out to investigate.

She came to me at once, and I called your office on the 'phone immediately. Then we rang the bell and summoned all the sisters to the chapel. I told them what I thought they ought to know and then dismissed them. They are in their cells now, reciting the rosary for the repose of her soul."

Costello nodded shortly and turned to us, his hard-shaven chin set truculently. "Come on, gentlemen; let's git goin'," he told us. "Will ye lead us to th' gate?" he added to the Mother Superior.

The convent gardens stretched across a plot of level ground for several hundred feet behind the building. Tall evergreens were marshaled in twin rows about its borders, and neatly trimmed privet hedges marked its graveled paths. At the far end, by a wall of ivy-covered masonry some twelve feet high, was placed a Calvary, a crucifix, nine or ten feet high, set in a cairn, which overlooked the whole enclosure. It was toward this Costello led us, his blue-black jaw set bellicosely.

De Grandin swore savagely in mingled French and English as the light, powdery snow rose above the tops of his patent leather evening pumps and chilled his silk-shod feet. Renouard looked round with quick, appraising glances. I watched Costello's face, noting how the savage scowl deepened as he walked.

I think we recognized it simultaneously.

Renouard gave a short half-scream, half-groan.

"*Sacré nom de sacré nom de sacré nom!*" de Grandin swore.

"Jasus!" said Costello.

I felt a sinking in the middle of my stomach and had to grasp Costello's arm to keep from falling with the sudden vertigo of overpowering nausea. The lifeless figure on the crucifix was not a thing of plaster or of painted wood, it was human—flesh and blood!

Nailed fast with railway spikes through outstretched hands and slim crossed feet, she hung upon the cross, her slender, naked body white as carven ivory. Her head inclined toward her left shoulder and her long, black hair hung loosed across the full white breasts which were drawn up firmly by the outspread arms. Upon her head had been rudely thrust an improvised crown of thorns—a chaplet of barbed wire cut from some farmer's fence—and from the punctures that it made, small streams of coral drops ran down. Thin trickles of blood oozed from the torn wounds in her hands and feet, but these had frozen on the flesh, heightening the resemblance to a tinted simulacrum. Her mouth was slightly opened and her chin hung low upon her breast, and from the tongue which lay against her lower lip a single drop of ruby blood, congealed by cold even as it fell, was pendent like a ruddy jewel against the flesh.

Upon her chest, above her breasts, glowed the tattooed mark which we had seen when she appealed to us for help a scant four hours earlier.

Above the lovely, thorn-crowned head where the replica of Pontius Pilate's inscription had been set, another legend was displayed, an insulting, mocking challenge from the murderers: "*In Hoc Signo*—in this sign," and then a grim, derisive picture of a leering devil's face:

"Ah, *la pauvre!*" de Grandin murmured. "Poor Mademoiselle of the Veil, were not all the bars and bolts of the hospital enough to keep you from them after all? I should have stayed with you, then they would not—" He broke off, staring meditatively at the figure racked upon the cross, his little, round blue eyes hardening as water hardens with a sudden frost.

IN HOC SIGNO

Renouard tugged at his square-cut beard, and tears welled unashamed in his bright, dark eyes.

Costello looked a moment at the pendent figure on the crucifix, then, doffing his hat, fell to his knees, signed himself reverently and began a hasty, mumbled prayer for the dying.

De Grandin neither wept nor prayed, but his little eyes were hard and cold as eyes of polished agate inlaid in the sockets of a statue's face, and round his small and thin-lipped mouth, beneath the pointed tips of his trim, waxed mustache, there gathered such a snarling grin of murderous hate as I had never seen. "Hear me, my friends," he ordered. "Hear me, you who hang so dead and lovely on the cross; hear me, all ye that dwell in heaven with the blessed saints," and in his eyes and on his face was the terrifying look of the born killer; "when I have found the one who did this thing, it had been better far for him had he been stillborn, for I shall surely give him that which he deserves. Yes, though he take refuge underneath the very throne of God Himself, I swear it upon this!" He laid his hand against the nail-pierced feet of the dead girl as one who takes a ritual oath upon a sacred relic.

It was grisly business getting her from the cross, but at last the spikes were drawn and the task completed. While Costello and Renouard examined every inch of trodden snow about the violated Calvary, de Grandin and I bore the body to the convent mortuary chapel, composed the stiffened limbs as best we could, then notified the coroner.

"This must by no means reach the press, *Monsieur*," de Grandin told the coroner when be arrived. "Promise you will keep it secret, at least until I give the word."

"H'm, I can't do that very well," Coroner Martin demurred. "There's the inquest, you know; it's my sworn duty to hold one."

"Ah, but yes; but if I tell you that our chances of capturing the miscreants who have done this thing depend upon our secrecy, then you will surely withhold publicity?" de Grandin persisted. "Can you not, by example, summon your jury, show them the body, swear them in, and then adjourn the public hearing pending further evidence?"

Mr. Martin lowered his handsome gray head in silent thought. "You'll testify the cause of death was shock and exposure to the cold?" he asked at length.

"Name of a small asparagus tree, I will testify to anything!" answered Jules de Grandin.

"Very well, then, We'll hush the matter up. I won't call Mother Mary Margaret at all, and Costello can tell us merely that he found her, nude in the convent garden. Just how he found her is a thing we'll not investigate too closely. She disappeared from City Hospital psychopathic ward—the inference is she wandered off and died of exposure. It will be quite feasible to keep the jury from seeing the wounds in her hands and feet; I'll hold the official viewing in one of the reposing-rooms of my funeral home and have the body covered with a robe from the neck down. How's that?"

"*Monsieur*," de Grandin drew himself up stiffly and raised his hand in formal military salute, "permit me to inform you that you are a great man!

"*Allons*, speed, quickness, hurry, we must go!" he ordered when the pitiful body had been taken away and Costello and Renouard returned from their inspection of the garden.

"Where are we rushin' to now, sor?" the big detective asked.

"To City Hospital, *pardieu!* I would know exactly how it comes that one whose custody was given to that institution last night should thus be taken from her bed beneath their very noses and murderously done to death in this so foul manner."

"SAY, DE GRANDIN, WAS that gal you and Trowbridge brought here last night any kin to the late Harry Houdini?" Doctor Donovan greeted as we entered his office at City Hospital.

De Grandin favored him with a long, hard stare. "What is it that you ask?" he demanded.

"Was she a professional disappearing artist, or something of the kind? We saw her locked up so tight that five men and ten little boys couldn't have got her out, but she's gone, skipped, flown the coop; and not a soul saw her when she blew, either."

"Perfectly, we are well aware she is no longer with you," de Grandin answered. "The question is how comes it that you, who were especially warned to watch her carefully, permitted her to go."

"Humph, I wish I knew the answer to that one myself," Donovan returned. "I turned in a few minutes after you and Trowbridge went, and didn't hear anything further till an hour or so ago when Dawkins, the night orderly in H-3, came pounding on my door with some wild story of her being gone. I threw a shoe at him and told him to get the devil away and let me sleep, but he kept after me till I finally got up in self-defense.

"Darned if he wasn't right, too. Her room was empty as a bass drum, and she was nowhere to be found, though we searched the ward with a fine-tooth comb. No one had seen her go—at least, no one will admit it, though I think someone's doing a piece of monumental lying."

"U'm?" de Grandin murmured non-committally. "Suppose we go and see."

The orderly, Dawkins, and Miss Hosskins, the night supervisor of the ward, met us as we passed the barred door. "No, sir," the man replied to de Grandin's quick questions. "I didn't see or hear—gee whiz! I wonder if that could 'a' had anything to do with it—no, o' course it couldn't!"

"Eh?" de Grandin returned sharply. "Tell us the facts, *Monsieur*. We shall draw our own conclusions, if you please."

"Well sir," the man grinned sheepishly, "it was somewhere about five o'clock, possibly a bit later, an' I was sort o' noddin' in my chair down by th' lower end o' th' corridor when all of a sudden I heard a funny-soundin' kind o' noise—sort o' like a high wind blowin', or—let's see—well, you might compare it to the hum of a monster bee, only it was more of a whistle than a buzz, though there was a sort o' buzzin' sound to it, too.

"Well, as I was sayin', I'd been noddin', an' this sudden queer noise woke me up. I started to get up an' see what it was all about, but it didn't come again, so I just sat back an'—"

"And went to sleep, eh?" Donovan cut in. "I thought you'd been lying, you swine. Fine chance we have of keeping these nuts in—with you orderlies snoring all over the place!"

"Monsieur Donovan, if you please!" Renouard broke in with lifted hand. To Dawkins: "You say this was a high, shrill sound, *mon vieux*; very high and very shrill?"

"Yes, sir, it was. Not real loud, sir, but so *awful!* shrill it hurt my ears to listen to it. It seemed almost as though it made me sort o' unconscious, though I don't suppose—"

"*Tiens*, but I do," Renouard broke in. "I think I understand."

Turning to us he added seriously: "I have heard of him. Our agents in Kurdistan described him. It is a sound—a very high, shrill sound—produced by blowing on some sort of reed by those followers of Satan from Mount Lalesh. He who hears it becomes first deafened, then temporarily paralyzed. According to our agents' testimony, it is a refinement of the wailing of the Chinese screaming boys; that high, thin, piercing wail which so disorganizes the hearers' nervous system that his marksmanship, is impaired, and often he is rendered all but helpless in a fight."

De Grandin nodded. "We know, my friend," he agreed. "The night Mademoiselle Alice disappeared we heard him—Friend Trowbridge and I—but that time they used their devil-dust as well, to make assurance doubly sure. It is possible that their store of *bulala-gwai* is low, or entirely exhausted, and so they now rely upon the stupefying sound to help them at their work.

"*Mademoiselle*," he bowed to Miss Hosskins, "did you, too, by any chance, hear the strange sound?"

"I—I can't say I did," the nurse answered with embarrassment. "The fact is, sir, I was very tired, too, and was rather relying on Dawkins being awake to call me if anything were needed, so—" she paused, a flush suffusing her face.

"Quite so," de Grandin nodded. "But—"

"But I *did* wake up with a dreadful headache—almost as though something sharp had been thrust in my ears—just before Dawkins reported that the patient in forty-seven was missing," she added.

Again de Grandin nodded, "I fear there is nothing more to learn," he returned wearily. "Come, let us go."

"Doctor, Doctor darlin', they wuz here last night, like I told ye they'd be!" the drunken Irishwoman called to Donovan as we went past her door.

"Now, Annie," Donovan advised, "you just lie back and take it easy, and we'll have you in shape to go out and get soused again in a couple o' days."

"Annie th' divil, me name's Bridget O'Shay, an' well ye know it, bad cess to ye!" the woman stormed. "An' as fer shlapin' in this place again, I'd sooner shlape in hell, for 'tis haunted be divils th' house is!

"Last night, Doctor, I heard th' banshee keenin' outside me windy, an' 'Bridget O'Shay,' says I to mesilf, 'th' fairy-wife's come for ye!' an' I lays down on th' floor wid both fingers in me ears to shtop th' sound o' her callin'.

"But presently there comes a throop o' divils mar-rchin' up th' corridor, th' one in front a-playin' on some sort o' divil's pipes which I couldn't hear a-tall, a-tall, fer havin' me fingers shtuck in me ears; an' walkin' clost behint him there wuz two others wans, an' they all wuz walkin' like they knew where they wuz goin'.

"I watched 'em till they tur-rned th' bend an' then I took me finger from wan ear, but quick enough I shtuffed it back, fer there wuz th' horriblest screamin' noise in all th' place as would 'a' deafened me entirely if I hadn't shtopped me ears agin.

"Prisently they come again, th' foremost wan still playin' on 'is pipes o' hell, an' wan o' 'em carryin' sumpin acrost 'is shoulders all wrapped up in a blanket, whilst th' other wuz a-lookin' round from right to left, an' 'is eyes wuz like peat-fires bur-rnin' in a cave, sor, so they wuz. I ducked me head as he wint past, for well I knowed they'd murder me if I wuz seen, and I know what it wuz, too. 'Twas Satan on earth come fer that woman ye brung in here last night, an' well I know she'll not be seen agin!"

"Gosh, that *was* some case of jimjams you had last night!" Donovan laughed. "Better see Father O'Connell and take the pledge again, Annie, or they'll be putting you in the bughouse for keeps one of these days. It's true the girl's wandered off, but we don't think anything has happened to her. We don't know where she is, even."

"*Eh bien*, my friend," de Grandin contradicted as we left the psychopathic ward, "you are most badly mistaken. We know quite definitely where the poor one is."

"Eh? The devil!" Donovan returned. "Where is she?"

"Upon a slab in Coroner Martin's morgue."

"For Pete's sake! Tell me about it; how'd it happen; I'm interested—"

"The papers will contain a story of her death," de Grandin answered as he suppressed a yawn. "I, too, am interested greatly—in five eggs with ham to match, ten cups of coffee and twelve hours' sleep. *Adieu, Monsieur.*"

9. Thoughts in the Dark

I WAS TOO NEAR THE boundary line of exhaustion to do more than dally with the excellent breakfast which Nora McGinnis, my super-efficient household factotum, set before us, but Renouard, with the hardihood of an old campaigner, wolfed huge portions of cereal, fried sausages and eggs and hot buttered toast, washing them down with innumerable cups of well-creamed coffee, while de Grandin, ever ready to eat, drink or seek adventure, stowed away an amazing cargo of food.

"*Très bon*, now let us sleep," he suggested when the last evidence of food had vanished from the table. "*Parbleu*, me, I could sleep for thirty days unceasingly, and as for food, the thought of it disgusts me!

"Madame Nora," he raised his voice and turned toward the kitchen, "would it be too much to ask that you have roast duckling and apple tart for dinner, and that you serve it not later than five this evening? We have much to do, and we should prefer not to do it on an empty stomach."

"No office hours today, Nora," I advised as I rose, swaying with sleepiness, "and no telephone calls for any of us, either, please. Tell anyone who cannot wait to get in touch with Doctor Phillips."

How long I slept I do not know, but the early dark of midwinter evening had fallen when I sat suddenly bolt-upright in my bed, my nerves still vibrating like telephone wires in a heavy wind. Gradually, insistently, insidiously, a voice had seemed commanding me to rise, don my clothes and leave the house. Where I should go was not explained, but that I go at once was so insistently commanded that I half rose from the bed, reluctance, fear and something close akin to horror dragging me back, but that not-to-be-ignored command impelling my obedience. Then, while I wrestled with the power which seemed dominating me, a sudden memory broke into my dream, a memory of other dreams of long ago, when I woke trembling in the darkened nursery, crying out in fright, then the stalwart bulk of a big body bending over me, hands firm yet tender patting my cheek reassuringly, and the mingled comforting smell of starched linen. Russian leather and good tobacco coming through the darkness while my father's soothing voice bade me not to be afraid, for he was with me.

The second dream dispelled the first, but I was still a-tremble with the tension of the summons to arise when I struggled back to consciousness and looked about the room.

Half an hour later, bathed, shaved and much refreshed, I faced de Grandin and Renouard across the dinner table.

"*Par l'amour d'un bouc*, my friends," de Grandin told us, "this afternoon has been most trying. Me, I have dreamed most unpleasant dreams—dreams which I do not like at all—and which I hope will not soon be repeated."

"*Comment cela?*" Renouard inquired.

"By blue, I dreamed that I received direct command to rise and dress and leave the house—and what is more, I should have done so had I not awakened!"

"Great Scott," I interjected, "so did I!"

"Eh, is it so?"

Renouard regarded each of us in turn with bright, dark eyes, shrewd and knowing as a monkey's. "This is of interest," he declared, tugging at his square-cut beard. "From what we know, it would seem that the societies to which the unfortunate young ladies who first did bring me in this case are mixed in some mysterious manner with the Yezidees of Kurdistan, *n'est-ce-pas?*"

De Grandin nodded, watching him attentively.

"Very well, then. As I told you heretofore, I do not know those Yezidees intimately. My information concerning them is hearsay, but it comes from sources of the greatest accuracy. Yes. Now, I am told, stretching over Asia, beginning in Manchuria and leading thence across Tibet, westward into Persia, and finally clear to Kurdistan, there is a chain of seven towered temples of the Yezidees, erected to the glorifying of the Devil. The chiefest of these shrines stands upon Mount Lalesh, but the others are, as the electricians say, 'hooked up in series.' No, underneath the domes of each one of these temples there sits at all times a priest of Satan, perpetually sending off his thought-rays—his mental emanations. Oh, do not laugh, my friends, I beg, for it is so! As priests or nuns professed to the service of God offer up perpetual adoration and prayers of intercession, so do these servants of the archfiend continually give forth the praise and prayer of evil. Unceasingly they broadcast wicked influences, and while I would not go so far as to assert that they can sway humanity to sin, some things I know.

"I said I did not know the Yezidees, but that is only partly so. Of them I have heard much, and some things connected with them I have seen. For instance: When I was in Damascus, seeking out some answer to the riddle of the six women, I met a certain Moslem who had gone to Kurdistan and while there incurred the enmity of the Yezidee priests. What he had done was not entirely clear, although I think that he had in some way profaned their idols. However that may be, Damascus is a long and tiresome journey from the confines of Lalesh, where Satan's followers hold their sway, but—

"Attend me"—he leaned forward till the candle-light struck odd reflections from his deep-set eyes—"this man came to me one day and said he had received command to go out into the desert. Whence the command came he did not know, but in the night he dreamed, and every night thereafter he had dreamed, always the same thing, that he arise and go into the desert. 'Was it a voice commanding?' I did ask, and, 'No,' he said, 'it was rather like a sound unheard but felt—like that strange ringing in his ears we sometimes have when we have taken too much quinine for the fever.'

"I sent him to a doctor and the learned medical fool gave him some pills and told him to forget it. *Ha*, forget that never-ending order to arise and leave, which ate into his brain as a maggot eats in cheese? As well he might have told one burning in the fire to dismiss all thought of torment from his mind!

"There finally came a time when the poor fellow could no longer battle with the psychic promptings of the priests of Satan. One night he left the house and wandered off. Some few days later the desert patrol found his burnoose and boots, or what was left of them. The jackals, perhaps with the aid of desert bandits, had disposed of all the rest.

"Now we tread close upon these evil-doers' heels. I have followed them across the ocean. You, my Jules, and you, Monsieur Trowbridge, have stumbled on their path, and all of us would bring them to account for their misdoings. What then?

"What, indeed, but that one of them, who is an adept at the black magic of their craft, has thrown himself into a state of concentration, and sent forth dire commands to us—such subtle, silent orders as the serpent gives the fascinated bird? You, my Jules, have it. So have you, Monsieur Trowbridge, for both of you are somewhat psychic. Me, I am the hard, tough-headed old policeman, practical, seeing little farther than my nose, and then seeing only what I do behold, no more. Their thought-commands, which are a species of hypnotism, will probably not reach me, or, if they do, will not affect my conduct.

"Your greatest danger is while you sleep, for then it is the sentry of your conscious mind will cease to go his guardian rounds, and the gateway to your inner consciousness will be wide open. I therefore think it wise that we shall share one room hereafter. Renouard is watchful; long years of practicing to sleep with one hand on his weapon and one eye open for attack have schooled him for such work. You cannot move without my knowing, and when I hear you move I wake you. And when I wake you their chain is broken. Do you agree?"

The thought occurred to Jules de Grandin and me at once.

"Alice—" I began, and:

"Yes, *parbleu*, Mademoiselle Alice!" cried de Grandin. "That message which she had, that constant but not understood command: 'Alice, come home!' It was undoubtlessly so given her. Remember, a day or so before she first received a spy of theirs, pretending to be seeking curios for some collector, came to the house, and saw the marriage girdle of the Yezidees. That was what he wanted, to assure himself that the Alice Hume their spies had run to earth was indeed the one they sought, the descendant of that high priest's daughter of the ancient days, she who had run off with the Christian Englishman. Yes, *par la barbe d'un chat*, no wonder that she could write nothing else upon her ouija board that day: no wonder she puzzled why she had that thought-impression of command to go. Already they had planted in her mind the order to abandon home and love and God and to join herself to their unholy ranks!

"By blue, my Georges, you have solved two problems for us. It was you who told us of the meaning of that shrilling cry which Friend Trowbridge and I did hear the night on which she disappeared and which made the hospital *attachés* unable to repel invasion of their ward; now you have thrown more light upon the subject, and we know it was that Mademoiselle Alice had that thought-command to leave before she could suspect that such things were.

"I think it would be wise if we consulted—"

"Detective Sergeant Costello," Nora McGinnis announced from the dining-room door.

"Ah, my friend, come in," de Grandin cried. "You are in time to share a new discovery we have made."

Costello had no answering smile for the little Frenchman's greeting. His eyes were set in something like a stare of horror, and his big, hard-shaven chin trembled slightly as he answered:

"An' ye're in time to share a discovery wid me, sor, if ye'll be good enough to shtep into th' surgery a moment."

Agog with interest we followed him into the surgery, watched him extract a paper parcel from his overcoat pocket and tear off the outer wrappings, disclosing a packet of oiled silk beneath.

"What is it? What have you found?" de Grandin questioned eagerly.

"This," the Irishman returned. "Look here!" He tore the silken folds apart and dumped their contents on the instrument table. A pair of little hands, crudely severed at the wrists, lay on the table's porcelain top.

10. Wordless Answers

DE GRANDIN WAS THE first to recover from the shock. The double background of long practice as a surgeon and years of service with the secret police had inured him to such sights as would break the nerve of one merely a doctor or policeman. Added to this was an insatiable curiosity which drove him to examine everything he saw, be it beautiful or hideous. With a touch as delicate as though he had been handling some frail work of woven glass he took one of the little hands between his thumb and forefinger, held it up to the surgery light and gazed at it with narrowed eyes and faintly pursed lips. Looking at him, one would have said he was about to whistle.

"A child's?" I asked, shrinking from too close examination of the ghastly relic.

"A girl's," he answered thoughtfully. "Young, scarcely more than adolescent, I should say, and probably not well to do, though having inclination toward the niceties of life. Observe the nails."

He turned the small hand over, and presented it palm-downward for my scrutiny. "You will observe," he added, "that they are nicely varnished and cut and filed to a point, though the shaping is not uniform, which tells us that the treatment was self-done, and not the work of a professional manicurist. Again, they are most scrupulously clean, which is an indication of the owner's character, but the cuticle is inexpertly trimmed; another proof of self attention. Finally"—he turned the hand palm-up and tapped the balls of the fingers lightly—"though the digits are white and clean they are slightly calloused at the sides and the finger tips and the nail region are inlaid with the faintest lines of ineradicable soil—occupational discoloration which no amount of soap and scrubbing-brush will quite remove. Only acid bleacher or pumice stone would erase them, and these she either did not know of, or realized that their continued use would irritate the friction-skin. *Enfin*, we have here the very pretty hands of a young working girl possessing wholesome self-respect, but forced to earn her daily bread by daily toil. A factory operative, possibly, surely not a laundress or charwoman. There is too much work-soil for the first, too little for the second."

Again he held the hand up to the light. "I am convinced that this was severed while she was alive," he declared. "See it is practically free of blood; had death occurred some time before the severance, the blood would not have been sufficiently liquid to drain off—though the operation might have been made a short time after death," he added thoughtfully.

"Have you anything to add, my friend?" he asked Costello.

"No, sor. All we know is we found th' hands," the Irishman replied. "They wuz found layin' side by side, wid th' fingers touchin', like they might 'a' been clasped in prayer, but had fallen apart like, *just outside th' wall o' convent garden, sor.*"

"*Nom d'un miracle du bon Dieu!*" exclaimed de Grandin, with that near-blasphemous intimacy he affected for the Deity. "I had some other things in mind tonight but this must take precedence. Come, let us go, rush, hasten, fly to where you found them, then lay our course from there until she shall be found!"

THE CONVENT OF THE Sacred Heart stood on an elevation from which it overlooked surrounding territory, and in the hollow to the east lay the little settlement of Rupleyville, a neat but unpretentious place comprised for the most part of homes of thrifty Italians who had been graduated from section gangs upon the Lackawanna's right of way to small truck-farming, huckstering or fruit-stand keeping. A general store, a bakery, a little church erected to Saint Rocco, and a shop in which two glass globes filled with colored water and the sign *Farmacia Italiana* proclaiming its owner's calling were the principal edifices of the place.

To the latter de Grandin led us, and introduced himself in a flood of voluble Italian. The little wrinkled pharmacist regarded him attentively, then replied torrentially waving his hands and elevating shoulders and eyebrows till I felt sure both would be separated from their respective sub-structures. At length:

"*Perfetto; eccellente!*" de Grandin cried, raising his hat ceremoniously. "Many thanks, *Signor*. We go at once." To us: "Come, my friends; I think that we are on the trail at last."

"What did you find out, sor?" Costello asked as the little Frenchman led us hurriedly down the single street the hamlet boasted.

"Ah, but of course, I did forget you do not speak Italian," de Grandin answered contritely. "When we had looked upon the spot where you did find the little hands, I told me, 'It are useless to stand here staring at the earth. Either the poor one from whom those hands were cut are living or dead. In any event, she are not here. If she are alive, she might have wandered off though not far, for the bleeding from her severed wrists would be too extensive. If she are dead, she could not have moved herself, yet, since she are not here, some one must have moved her. Jules de Grandin, let us inquire.'

"And so I led the way to this small village, and first of all I see the pharmacist's shop. 'Very good,' I tell me, 'the druggist are somewhat of a doctor; injured persons frequently appeal to him for help. Perhaps he will know something.' And so I interrogate him.

"He knew nothing of a person suffering grievous hurt, but he informed me that a most respectable old woman living near had come to him some time ago in greatest haste and implored that he would sell her opium, as well as something which would staunch the flow of blood. The woman was not suffering an injury. The inference is then that she sought the remedies for someone else. *N'est-ce-pas?* Of course. Very well, it is to her house that we go all quickly."

We halted at the small gate of a cottage garden. The paling fence was innocent of paint, but neatly whitewashed, as were the rough plank sidewalls of the house. An oil-lamp burned dimly in the single room the cottage boasted, and by its feeble light we saw an old woman, very wrinkled, but very clean, bending over a low bed which lay in shadow.

De Grandin knocked imperatively on the whitewashed door, then, as no answer was forthcoming, pushed back the panels and stepped across the threshold.

The room was nearly bare of furniture, the bed, a small table and two rough unpainted chairs completing its equipment. The little kerosene lamp, a cheap alarm clock and two gayly colored pictures of religious scenes were the sole attempts at ornament. The aged woman, scrupulously neat in smooth black gown and cheap jet brooch, straightened on her knees beside the bed as we came in and raised a finger to her wrinkled lips. "Quiet pleez," she murmured. "She iss a-sleepa. I have give"—she sought the English word, then raised her shoulders in a shrug of impotence and finished in Italian—"I give *oppio*."

De Grandin doffed his hat and bowed politely, then whispered quickly in Italian. The woman listened, nodded once or twice, then rose slowly and beckoned us to follow her across the room. "*Signori*," she informed us in a whisper. "I am a poor woman, me; but I have the means to live a little. At night—what you call him? *si*, scrub—I scrub floors in the bank at the city. Sometimes I come home by the bus at morning, sometimes I walk for save the money. Last night—this morning—I walk.

"I pass the *convento* just when the dark is turning into light today, and I go for walk downhill to her I hear somebody groan—*o-oh, a-ah!* like that. I go for see who are in trouble, and find this *povera* lying in the snow.

"*Dio Santo*, what you think? Some devil he have cut her arms off close by the hand! She is bleeding fast.

"I call to her, she try for answer, but no can. What you think some more? That devil have cut out her tongue and blood run out her mouth when she try to speak!

"I go for look some more. *Santissima Madonna*, her eyes have been put out! Oh, I tell you, *Signori*, it is, the sight of sadness that I see!

"I think at first I run for help; then I think. 'No, while I am gone she may die from bleeding. I take her with me.' So I do.

"I am very strong, me. All my life, in old country, in new country, I worka verree hard. Yes, sure. So I put her on my back—so!—and make the run—not walk, run—all way downhill to my house here. Then I put clothes upon her where her hands should be and put her in my bed; then I run all the way by the *farmacia* for medicine. The drug man not like for sell me *oppio*, but I beg him on my knee and tell him it is for save a life. Then he give it to me. I come back with a run and make soup of it and from it feed her with a spoon. At first she spit it out again, but after time she swallow it, and now she not feel no more pain. She is asleep, and when she wake I give her more until her hurt all better. I not know who she is, *Signori*, but I not like for see her suffer. She iss so young, so pretty, so—what you say?—niza? Yes. Sure."

De Grandin twisted his mustache and looked at her appreciatively. At length: "*Madame*, you are truly one of God's good noblewomen," he declared, and raised her gnarled and work-worn fingers to his lips as though they had been the white jeweled fingers of a countess.

"Now, quick, my friends," he called to us. "She must have careful nursing and a bed and rest and the best medical attendance. Call for an ambulance from the pharmacy, my sergeant. We shall await you here."

Swiftly, speaking softly in Italian, he explained the need of expert nursing to the woman, adding that only in a hospital could we hope to revive the patient sufficiently to enable her to tell us something of her assailants.

"But no!" the woman told him. "That can not be, *Signor*. They have cut off her hands, they have cut out her tongue, they have put out her eyes. She can not speak or write or recognize the ones who did it, even though you made them arrest and brought them to her. Me, I think maybe it was the Mafia did this, though they not do like this before. They kill, yes; but cut a woman up like this, no. Sicilians verree bad men, but not bad like that, I think."

"*Ma mere*," de Grandin answered, "though all you say is true, nevertheless I shall find a way for her to talk and tell us who has done this thing, and how we best may find him. How I shall do it I cannot tell, but that I shall succeed I am assured. I am Jules de Grandin, and I do not fail. Most of my life has been devoted to the healing of the sick and tracking down the wicked. I may not heal her hurts, for only God's good self can grow new hands and replace her ruined eyes and tongue, but vengeance I can take on those who outraged her and all humanity when they did this shameful thing, and may Satan roast me on a spit and serve me hot in my own gravy with damned, detestable turnips as a garnish if I do not so, I swear it. She shall talk to me in hell's despite.

"*Mais oui*, you must accept it," he insisted as he tendered her a bill and the woman made a gesture of refusal. "Think of your ruined gown, your soiled bed-clothing, and the trouble you have been to. It is your due, not a reward, my old one."

She took the money reluctantly, but thankfully, and he turned impatiently to me. "Stand by, my friend," he ordered; "we must go with her when they have come, for every moment is of preciousness. Me, I do not greatly like the looks of things; the brutal way in which her hands were amputated, the exposure to the cold, the well-meaning but unhygienic measures of assistance which the kindly one has taken. Infection may set in, and we must make her talk before it is too late."

"Make her talk?" I echoed in amazement. "You're raving, man! How can she talk without a tongue, or—?"

"*Ah bah!*" he interrupted. "Keep the eyes on Jules de Grandin, good Friend Trowbridge. The Devil and his servants may be clever, but he is cleverer. Yes, by damn much more so!"

The clanging ambulance arrived in a few minutes, for the call Costello sent was urgent, and a bored young intern, collegiate raccoon coat slipped on over his whites entered the cottage, the stretcher-bearers close behind him. "Hear you got a pretty bad case here—" he began, then straightened as he saw de Grandin. "Oh, I didn't know *you* were in charge here, Doctor," he finished.

The little Frenchman, whose uncanny skill at surgery had made his name a by-word in the local clinics, smiled amiably. "Quickly, *mon brave*," he ordered. "It is imperative that we should get her hence as rapidly as possible. I desire to converse with her."

"O.K., sir," the youngster answered. "What's wrong?" He drew out his report card and poised a pencil over it.

De Grandin nodded to the litter-bearers to begin their task as he replied: "Both hands amputated by transverse cuts incising the *pronator quadratus*; the tongue clipped across the apex, both eyes blinded by transverse knife cuts across the cornea and striking through the anterior chamber and crystalline lens."

"You—she's had all that done to her, an' you're going to *converse* with her?" the boy asked incredulously. "Don't you mean—"

"I mean precisely what I say, *mon vieux*," de Grandin told him positively. "I shall ask her certain questions, and she shall answer me. Come, make haste, or it may be too late."

A T THE HOSPITAL, DE Grandin, aided by a wondering nurse and intern, removed the old Italian woman's make-shift bandages from the girl's severed wrists, applied a strong anodyne liniment of aconite, opium and chloroform, and wound fresh wrappings on the stumps with the speed and skill of one who served a long and strenuous apprenticeship in trench dressing-stations and field hospitals.

Some time elapsed before the strong narcotic soup administered by the old Italian lost its effect, but at length the patient showed slight signs of consciousness.

"Ma fille," de Grandin said, leaning forward till his lips were almost against the maimed girl's bandaged face, "you are in great trouble. You are temporarily deprived of speech and sight, but it is necessary that you tell us what you can, that we may apprehend those who did this thing to you. At present you are in Mercy Hospital, and here you will be given every care.

"Attend me carefully, if you please. I shall ask you questions. You shall answer me by spelling. Thus"—he seated himself at the foot of the bed and placed his hand lightly on the blanket where her feet lay—"for a you will move your foot once, for b twice, and so on through the alphabet. You understand?"

A pause, then a slight movement underneath the bedclothes, twenty-five twitches of the foot, then five, finally nineteen: "Y-e-s."

"Très bon, let us start." Drawing a notebook from his pocket he rested it upon his knee, then poised a stylographic pen above it. "Leave us, if you will, my friends," he ordered. "We shall be better if alone.

"Now, ma pauvre?" he turned toward the mutilated girl, ready to begin his interrogatory.

Something like an hour later he emerged from the sickroom, tears gleaming in his eyes and a taut, hard look about his mouth. "It is finished—done—completed," he announced, sinking wearily into a chair and in defiance of every house rule drawing out an evil-smelling French cigarette and setting it alight.

"What's finished?" I demanded.

"Everything; all!" he answered. "My questioning and the poor one; both together. Name of a miracle, I spoke truth when I told her that blond lie and said her loss of sight and speech was temporary, for now she sees and sings in God's own Paradise. The shock and loss of blood she suffered were too much— she is gone."

He drew a handkerchief from his cuff and wiped his eyes, then: "But not until she told me all did she depart," he added fiercely. "Give me a little time to put my notes in order, and I shall read them to you."

Three-quarters of an hour later he and I, Costello and Renouard were closeted in the superintendent's office.

"Her name was Veronica Brady," he began, referring to his transcript of the notes he had taken in the dead girl's room, "and she lived beneath the hill the other side the convent. She was an operative in the Hammel factory, and was due at work at slightly after seven. In order to arrive in time she had to take an early bus, and as the snow was deep, she set out early to meet the vehicle on the highway. As she was toiling up the hill this morning, she was attracted by a group of people skirting the convent wall, a woman and three men. The woman was enveloped in some sort of long garment—it seemed to her like a blanket draped round her—and seemed struggling weakly and pleading with the men, two of whom pushed and drove her onward, like a beast to slaughter, while the third one walked ahead and seemed to take no notice of the others.

"They reached the convent wall, and one of the men climbed upon another's shoulders, seized the woman and dragged her up, then leaped the wall. The second man mounted on the third one's shoulders, reached the wall-crest, then leaned down and assisted his companion up. As the last one paused a moment on the summit of the wall, preparatory to leaping over into the garden, he spied Mademoiselle Veronica, jumped down and seized her, then called to his companions. They bade him bring her, and he dragged her to the wall and forced her up to the villain waiting at the top. Thereafter they drew her to the garden, gagged her with handkerchiefs and ripped her stockings off, binding her hands and feet with them. Then, while she sat propped against the wall, she witnessed the whole vile scene. The base miscreants removed the effigy of Christ from the crucifix and broke it into pieces; then with railway spikes they nailed the woman upon the cross, and thrust a crown of barbed wire on her head and set an inscription over her. This done, they stood away and cursed her with all manner of vile oaths and pelted her with snowballs while she hung and died in torment.

"At length the coming of the dawn warned them their time was short, and so they gave attention to their second victim explaining that the one whom they had crucified had paid the penalty of talking, they then informed poor Mademoiselle Veronica that they would save her from such fate by making it impossible that she should betray them. And then they took the bindings from her wrists and ankles, made her resume her stockings and walk with them until they reached the wall. Across the wall they carried her; then in the snow outside they bade her kneel and clasp her hands in prayer while she looked her last upon the world.

"The poor child thought they meant to kill her. How little could she estimate their vileness! For, as she folded her hands in supplication, *zic!* a sudden knife-stroke hit her wrists, and scarcely realizing what she did, she found herself looking down at two small, clasped hands, while from her wrists there spurted streams of blood. The blow was quick and the knife sharp; she scarcely felt the stroke, she told me, for it was more like a heavy blow with a fist or club than a severing cut which deprived her of her hands.

"But before she realized what had befallen her she felt her throat seized by rough hands, and she was choked until her tongue protruded. A sudden searing pain, as though a glowing iron had been thrust into her mouth, was followed by a blaze of flashing light; then—darkness—utter, impenetrable darkness, such as she had never known before, fell on her, and in the snow she writhed in agony of mind and body. Shut off from every trace of light and with her own blood choking back the screams for help she tried to give, in her ears was echoed the laughter of her tormenters.

"The next she knew she was lifted from the snow and borne on someone's shoulders to a house, bandages were wound about her wrists and eyes, and anon a biting, bitter mixture was poured into her tortured mouth. Then merciful oblivion until she woke to find herself in Mercy Hospital with Jules de Grandin questioning her.

"Ah, it was pitiful to make her tell this story with her feet, my friends, and very pitiful it was to see her die, but far rather would I have done so than know that she must live, a maimed and blinded creature.

"Ha, but I have not done. No. She told me of the men who did this sacré, dastard thing. Their leader was a monstrous-looking creature, a person with an old and wrinkled face, not ugly, not even wicked, but rather sad and thoughtful, and in his wrinkled face there burned a pair of ageless eyes, all but void of expression, and his body was the lithe, well-formed body of a youth. His voice, too, was gentle, like his eyes, but gentle with the terrible gentleness of the hissing serpent. And though he dressed like us, upon his head was set a scarlet turban ornamented with a great greenish-yellow stone which shone and flickered, even in the half-light of the morning, like the evil eye of a ferocious tiger.

"His companions were similar in dress, although the turbans on their heads were black. One was tall, the other taller. Both were swarthy of complexion, and both were bearded."

"By their complexions and their beards, and especially by their noses, she thought them Jewish. The poor one erred most terribly and slandered a most great and noble race. We know them for what they truly were, my friends, Kurdish hellions, Yezidee followers and worshippers of Satan's unclean self!"

He finished his recital and lit another cigarette. "The net of evidence is woven," he declared. "Our task is now to cast it over them."

"Ye're right there, sor, dead right," Costello agreed. "But how're we goin' to do it?"

De Grandin looked at him a moment, then started, as one who suddenly recalls a duty unperformed. "By blue," he cried, "we must at once to Monsieur the Coroner's; we must secure those photographs before it is too late!"

11. The Strayed Sheep

"Hullo, Doctor de Grandin," Coroner Martin greeted as we entered the private office of his luxurious funeral home, "there's been a young man from Morgan's Photonews Agency hanging around here waiting for you for the last hour or so. Said you wanted him to take some pictures, but couldn't say what. It might be all right, then again, it mightn't, and he may be on a snooping expedition—you never can tell with those fellows—so I, told him to wait. He's back in the recreation room with my boys now, smoking his head off and cussing you out."

The quick smile with which de Grandin answered was more a mechanical facial contortion than an evidence of mirth. "Quite yes," he agreed. "I greatly desire that you let us take some photographs of *Mademoiselle l'Inconnue*—the nameless lady whose body you took in charge at the convent this morning. We must discover her identity, if possible. Is all prepared according to your promise?"

Professional pride was evident as Mr. Martin answered, "Come and see her, if you will."

She lay upon a bedstead in one of the secluded "slumber rooms"—apartments dedicated to repose of the dead awaiting casketing and burial—a soft silk comforter draped over her, her head upon a snowy pillow, and I had to look a second time to make sure it was she. With a skill which put the best of Egypt's famed practitioners to shame, the clever-handed mortician had eradicated every trace of violent death from the frail body of the girl, had totally obliterated the nail-marks from her slender hands and erased the cruel wounds of the barbed wire from her brow. Even the deeply burned cross-brands on her cheeks had been effaced, and on her calm, smooth countenance there was a look of peace which simulated natural sleep. The lips, ingeniously tinted, were slightly parted, as though she breathed in light, half-waking slumber, and so perfect was the illusion of life that I could have sworn I saw her bosom flutter with faint respiration.

"Marvellous, *parfait, magnifique!*" de Grandin pronounced, gazing admiringly at the body with the approval one artist may accord another's work. "If you will now permit the young man to come hither, we shall take the pictures; then we need trouble you no more."

The young news photographer set up his camera at de Grandin's orders, taking several profile views of the dead girl. Finally he raised the instrument till its lens looked directly down upon the calm, still face, and snapped a final picture.

Next day the photographs were broadcast to the papers with the caption: "Who Knows Her? Mystery woman, found wandering in the streets of Harrisonville, N.J., was taken to the psychopathic ward of City Hospital, but managed to escape. Next morning she was found dead from exposure in a garden in the suburbs. Authorities are seeking for some clue to her identity, and anyone who recognizes her is asked to notify Sergeant J. Costello, Detective Bureau, Harrisonville Police Dept. (Photo by Morgan's Photonews, Inc.)"

W E WAITED SEVERAL DAYS, but no response came in. It seemed that we had drawn a blank.

At last, when we had about abandoned hope, the telephone called me from the dinner table, and Costello's heavy voice advised: "There's a young felly down to headquarters, sor, that says he thinks he recognizes that there now unknown gur-rl. Says he saw her picture in th' *Springfield Echo*. Will I take 'im over to th' coroner's?"

"Might as well," I answered. "Ask Mr. Martin to let him look at the body; then, if he still thinks he knows her, bring him over and Doctor de Grandin and I will talk with him."

"Right, sor," Costello promised. "I'll not be botherin' ye wid anny false alar-rms."

I went back to dessert, Renouard and Jules de Grandin.

S OME THREE-QUARTERS OF AN hour later while we sipped our postprandial coffee and liqueurs in the drawing-room, the doorbell shrilled and Nora ushered in Costello and a serious-faced young man. "Shake hands wid Mr. Kimble, gentlemen," the sergeant introduced. "He knows her, a'right. Identified her positively. He'll be claimin' th' remains in th' mornin', if ye've no objections."

De Grandin shook hands cordially enough, but his welcome was restrained. "You can tell whence the poor young lady came, and what her name was, perhaps, *Monsieur?*" he asked, when the visitors had been made comfortable with cognac and cigars.

Young Mr. Kimble flushed beneath the little Frenchman's direct, unwinking stare. He was tall, stoop-shouldered, hatchet-faced, bespectacled. Such animation as he had seemed concentrated in his rather large and deep-set hazel eyes. Except for them he was utterly commonplace, a man of neutral coloring, totally undistinguished, doomed by his very nature to the self-effacement consequent upon unconquerable diffidence. "A clerk or bookkeeper," I classified him mentally, "possibly a junior accountant or senior routine worker of some sort." Beside the debonair de Grandin, the fiery and intense Renouard and the brawny, competent Costello, he was like a sparrow in the company of tanagers.

Now, however, whatever remnant of emotion remained in his drab, repressed personality welled up as he replied: "Yes sir, I can tell you; her name was Abigail Kimble. She was my sister."

"U'm," de Grandin murmured thoughtfully, drawing at his cigar. Then, as the other remained silent:

"You can suggest, perhaps, how it came she was found in the unfortunate condition which led to her incarceration in the hospital, and later to her so deplorable demise?" Beneath the shadow of his brows he watched the young man with a cat-stare of unwinking vigilance, alert to note the slightest sign betokening that the visitor had greater knowledge of the case than the meager information in the newspaper supplied.

Young Kimble shook his head. "I'm afraid not," he replied. "I hadn't seen her for two years; didn't have the slightest idea where she was." He paused for a moment, fumbling nervously with his cigar; then: "Whatever I may say will be regarded confidentially?" he asked.

"But certainly," de Grandin answered.

The young man tossed his cigar into the fire and leaned forward, elbows on knees, fingers interlaced. "She was my sister," he repeated huskily. "We were born and reared in Springfield. Our father was—" He paused again and hunted for a word, then: "A tyrant, a good church-member and according to his lights a Christian, so righteous that he couldn't be religious, so pious that he couldn't find it in him to be kind or merciful. You know the breed. We weren't allowed to play cards or dance, or even go to parties, he was afraid we might play 'kissing games.' We had family prayers each night and morning, and on Sunday weren't allowed to play—my sister's dolls and my toys were put away each Saturday and not allowed outside the closet till Monday morning. Once when he caught me reading *Moby Dick*—I was a lad of fifteen, too, then—he snatched it from me and threw it in the fire. He'd 'tolerate no novel-reading in a Christian home,' he told me.

"I stood for it; I reckon it was in me from my Puritan ancestors, but Abigail was different. Our grandfather had married an Irish girl—worked her to death and broke her heart with pious devilishness before she was twenty-five—and Abigail took after her. Looked like her, too, they said. Father used to pray with her, pray that she'd be able to 'tear the sinful image of the Scarlet Woman' from her heart and give herself to Jesus. Then he'd beat her for her soul's salvation, praying all the time."

A bitter smile lit up his somber features, and something, some deep-rooted though almost eradicated spirit of revolt, flickered in his eyes a moment. "You can imagine what effect such treatment would have on a high-spirited girl," he added. "When Abby was seventeen she ran away.

"My father cursed her, literally. Stood in the doorway of our home and raised his hands to heaven while he called God's curse upon a wilful, disobedient child."

Again the bitter, twisted smile flickered across his face. "I think his God heard him," he concluded.

"But, *Monsieur*, are we to understand you did not again behold your so unfortunate sister until—" de Grandin paused with upraised brows.

"Oh, yes, I saw her," the young man answered caustically. "She ran away, as I said, but in her case the road of the transgressor was hard. She'd been brought up to call a leg a limb and to think the doctors brought babies in their satchels. She learned the truth before a year had gone.

"I got a note from her one day, telling me she was at a farmhouse outside town and that she was expecting a baby. I was working then and making fairly good money for a youngster, keeping books in a hardware store, but my father took my wages every Saturday night, and I was allowed only a dollar a week from them. I had to put that on the collection plate on Sunday.

"When Abby's letter came I was almost frantic. I hadn't a nickel I could use, and if I went to my father he would quote something from the Bible about the wages of sin being death, I knew.

"But if you're driven far enough you can usually manage to make plans. I did. I deliberately quit my job at Hoeschler's. Picked a fight with the head bookkeeper, and made 'em discharge me.

"Then I told my father, and though I was almost twenty-one years old, he beat me till I thought I'd drop beneath the torture. But it was all part of my plan, so I gritted my teeth and bore it.

"I got the promise of another job before I quit the first one, so I went to work at the new place immediately; but I fooled the old man. My new salary was twenty dollars a week, twice as much as I'd received before, but I told him I had to take a cut in pay, and that they gave me only ten. I steamed the pay envelope open and took out ten dollars, then resealed it and handed it to him with the remaining ten each Saturday. He never knew the difference.

"As quickly as I could I went to see my sister, told her not to worry, and engaged a doctor. I paid him forty dollars on account and signed notes for the balance. Everything was fixed for Abigail to have the proper care.

"He was a pretty little fellow, her baby; pretty and sweet and innocent as though he hadn't been a"—he halted, gagging on the ugly word, then ended lamely—"as if his mother had been married.

"Living was cheaper in those days, and Abby and the baby made out nicely at the farm for 'most two years. I'd had two raises in pay, and turned the increase over to her, and she managed to pick up some spare change at odd work, too, so everything went pretty well—" He stopped again, and the knuckles of his knitted hands showed white and bony as the fingers laced together with increased pressure.

"Yes my friend, until—" de Grandin prompted softly.

"Till she was taken sick," young Kimble finished. "It was influenza. We'd been pretty hard hit up Springfield way that spring, and Abigail was taken pretty bad. Pneumonia developed, and the doctor didn't hold out much hope to her. Her conscience was troubling her for running out on the old man and on account of the baby, too, I guess. Anyhow, she asked to see a minister.

"He was a young man, just out of the Methodist seminary, with a mouth full of Scriptural quotations and a nose that itched to get in other people's business. When she'd confessed her sin he prayed with her a while, then came hot-foot to the city and spilled the story to my father. Told him erring was human, but forgiveness divine, and that he had a chance to bring the lost sheep back into the fold—typical preacher's cant, you know.

"I was of age, then, but still living home. The old man came to me and taxed me with my perfidy in helping Abby in her life of shameful sin, and—what was worse!—holding back some of my salary from him. Then he began to pray, likening himself to Abraham and me to Isaac, and asking God to give strength to his arm that he might purge me of all sin, and tried to thrash me.

"I said tried, gentlemen. The hardware store I worked in had carried a line of buggy-whips, but the coming of the motor car had made them a back number. We hadn't had a call for one in years, and several of the men had brought the old things home as souvenirs. I had one. My father hit me, striking me in the mouth with his clenched fist and bruising my lips till they bled. Then I let him have it. All the abuse I'd suffered from that sanctimonious old devil since my birth seemed crying out for redress right then, and, by God, it got it! I lashed him with that whip till it broke in my hands, then I beat him with the stock till he cried for mercy. When I say 'cried', I mean just that. He howled and bellowed like a beaten boy, and the tears ran down his face as he begged me to stop flogging him.

"Then I left his house and never entered it again, not even when they held his funeral from it.

"But that didn't help my sister. The old man knew where she was living, and as soon as his bruises were healed he went out there, saw the landlady and told her he was the baby's grandfather and had come to take it home. My sister was too sick to be consulted, so the woman let him take the boy. He took him to an orphanage, and the child died within a month. Diphtheria immunization costs money, and the folks who ran that home—it was proof of a lack of faith in Providence to vaccinate the children for diphtheria, they said; but when you herd two hundred children in a place and one of 'em comes down with the disease, there's bound to be some duplication. Little Arthur died and they were going to bury him in Potter's Field, but I heard of it and claimed the body and gave it decent burial.

"My sister lay half-way between life and death for weeks. Finally she was well enough to ask for her son, and they told her he had gone off with his grandfather. She was almost wild with fear of what the old man might do to the child, but still too weak to travel, and the nervous strain she labored under set her back still further. It was nearly midsummer when she finally went to town.

"She went right to the house and demanded that he give her back her child—told him she'd never asked him for a cent and never would, and every penny that he'd paid out for the little boy would be refunded to him.

"He'd learned his lesson from me, but my sister was a mere woman, weak from a recent illness; no need to guard his tongue while he talked with her. And so he called her every vile name imaginable and that her hope of heaven was gone, for she was living with a parent's curse upon her. Finally he told her that her child was dead and buried in a pauper's grave. He knew that was a lie, but he couldn't forego the joy of hurting her by it.

"She came to me, half crazed with grief, and I did what I could to soothe her. I told her that the old man lied, and knew he lied, and that little Arthur had been buried in Graceland, with a tombstone set above his grave. Then, of course, she wanted to go see the place."

Tears were falling from the young man's eyes as he concluded: "I never shall forget that afternoon, the last time that I ever saw my little sister living. It was nearly dark when we reached the grave, and she had to kneel to make out the inscription on the stone. Then she went down like a mother bending by a crib, and whispered to the grass above her baby's face. 'Good-night little son; good-night and happy dreams, I'll see you early in the morning.' Then realization seemed to come to her. 'Oh, God,' she cried, 'there won't be any morning! Oh, my baby; my little baby boy! They took you from me and killed you, little son—they and their God!'

"And then beside her baby's grave she rose and held her hands up to the sky and cursed the father who begot her and who had done this thing to her; she cursed his church and his religion, cursed his God and all His works, and swore allegiance to the Devil! I'm not a religious man, gentleman. I had too big an overdose of it when I was a child, and I've never been in church since I left my father's house; but that wild defiance of hers and her oath of fealty to everything we'd been taught to hate and fear fairly gave me the creeps.

"I never saw her from that night to this. I gave her a hundred dollars, and she took the evening train to Boston, where I understand she got mixed up with all sorts of radical movements. The last I heard of her before I saw her picture in the paper yesterday was when she wrote me from New York saying she'd met a Russian gentleman who was preaching a new religion; one she could subscribe to and accept. I didn't quite understand what it was all about, but I gathered it was some sort of New Thought cult, or something of the kind. Anyway, 'Do What Thou Wilt. This Shall Be the Whole of the Law,' was its gospel, as she wrote it to me."

De Grandin leaned forward, his little round blue eyes alight with interest and excitement. "Have you, by any chance, a picture of your little nephew, *Monsieur!*" he asked.

"Why, yes, I think so," young Kimble answered. "Here's a snapshot I took of him and Abigail out at the farm the winter before her illness. He was about eight or nine months old then." From an inner pocket he drew a leather wallet and from it took a worn and faded photograph.

"*Morbleu*, I damn knew it; of course, that is the explanation!" de Grandin cried as he looked at the picture. "Await me, my friends, I shall return at once!" he shouted, leaping from his seat and rushing from the room.

In a moment he was back, another picture in his hand. "Compare," he ordered sharply; "put them together, and tell me what it is you see."

Mystified but eager, Renouard, Costello and young Kimble leaned over my shoulder as I laid the photographs side by side upon the coffee table. The picture to the right was the one Kimble furnished us. It showed a woman, younger than the one we knew, and with the light of happiness upon her face, but indisputably the beautiful veiled lady whose tragic death had followed her visit to us. In her arms nestled a pretty, dimpled little boy with dark curling hair clustering in tendrils round his baby ears, and eyes which fairly shone with life and merriment.

The picture to the left was one de Grandin had obtained from the Baptist Home of the little Eastman boy who vanished. Though slightly younger, his resemblance to the other child was startling. Line for line and feature for feature, each was almost the perfect duplicate of the other.

De Grandin tweaked his mustache as he returned the snapshot to young Kimble. "Thank you, *Monsieur*," he said. "Your story has affected us profoundly. Tomorrow, if you will make formal claim to your sister's body, no obstacle to its release will be offered by the coroner, I promise you." Behind the visitor's back he made violent motions to Costello, indicative to our wish to be alone.

The Irishman was quick to take the hint, and in a few minutes had departed with young Mr. Kimble. Half an hour later he rejoined us, a frown of deep perplexity upon his brow.

"I'll bite, Doctor de Grandin, sor," he confessed. "What's it all about?"

12. The Trail of the Serpent

"BUT IT IS OBVIOUS," the little Frenchman answered. "Do not you see it, Renouard, Trowbridge?" he turned his bright bird-like gaze on us.

"I'm afraid not," I replied. "Just what connection there is between the children's resemblance and—"

"Ah, *bah!*" he interrupted. "It is elementary. Consider, if you please. This poor Mademoiselle Abigail, she was hopelessly involved with the Satanists, is it not so?"

"Yes," I agreed. "From what her brother told us, there's not much doubt that the sect with which she was connected is the same one Renouard told us about, but—"

"But be roasted on the grates of hell! Can you think no farther back than the hinder side of your own neck, great stupid one? What did she say when she came rushing to this house at dead of night and begged us for protection? Think, remember, if you can."

"Why, she was raving incoherently; it's rather hard to say that anything she told us was important, but—"

"*Dites*—more of your *sacré* buts! Attend me: She came to us immediately after the small Baptist one had been abducted, and she did declare: 'He was the image of my dear little—' Her statement split upon that word, but in the light of what we now know, the rest is obvious. The little Eastman child resembled her dead baby; she could not bear to see him slaughtered, and cried out in horror at the act. When they persisted in this fiendishness she threatened them with us—with me, to be exact—and ran away to tell us how they might be found. They shot at her and wounded her, but she won through to us, and though she raved in wild delirium, she told enough to put us on the trail. But certainly. Did she not say, 'Watch for the chalk-signs of the Devil—follow the pointed trident? But yes."

He turned to Sergeant Costello and demanded: "And have your men been vigilant, *mon vieux*? Do they keep watch for childish scrawls on house or fence or sidewalk, as I bade?"

Costello eyed him wonderingly. "Sure, they are," he answered. "Th' whole force has its orders to look out for 'em though th' saints know that ye're after wantin' wid 'em when ye find 'em."

"Very good," de Grandin nodded. "Attend me, I have known such things before. You, too, Renouard. Only a word was needed to put me on the trail. That word was furnished by the poor young woman whom they crucified.

"In Europe, when the Satanists would gather for their wicked rites they send some secret message to their members, but never do they tell the place of the meeting. No, the message might be intercepted and the police come. What then?

"Upon the walls of houses, on sidewalks, or on fences they draw a crude design of Satan, a foolish childish thing which will escape notice as scrawling of naughty little boys, but each of these drawings differs from the others, for whereas one will have the Devil's pitchfork pointing one way, another will point in a different direction. The variation will not be noticed by one who does not know the significance of the scrawls, but to those who know for what they look the pointing tridents are plain as markers on a motor highway. One need but follow the direction of the pointing tridents from picture to picture in order to be finally led right to the door of Satan's temple. Yes; of course. It is so."

"Indubitably," Renouard accorded, with a vehement nod.

"But what's th' little Eastman boy to do wid it?" Costello asked.

"Everything, *parbleu*," de Grandin and Renouard replied in sober chorus.

"It was undoubtlessly for the Black Mass—the Mass of Saint Secaire—the little one was stolen. Satan is the *singe de Dieu*—the impudent imitator of God and in his service is performed a vile parody of the celebration of the mass. The celebrant is, when possible, an unfrocked priest, but if such a one can not be found to do the office, any follower of the Devil may serve.

"In the latter case a wafer already consecrated must be stolen from the monstrance of the church or impiously borne from communion in the mouth of a mock-communicant. Then, robed as a priest, the buffoon who officiates ascends the Devil's altar and mouths the words prescribed in the missal, but reverses all the ritual gestures, kneeling backward to the altar, signing himself with the cross upside down and with his left hand reciting such prayers as he pleases backward. At the end he holds aloft the sacred Host, but instead of veneration the wretched congregation shrieks out insults, and the elements are then thrown to the ground and trampled underfoot.

"*Ha*, but if a renegade priest can be persuaded to officiate, there is the foulest blasphemy of all, for he still has the words of power and the right to consecrate the elements, and so he says the mass from start to finish. For greater blasphemy the altar is the naked body of a woman, and when the rubric compels the celebrant to kiss the sanctuary, his lips are pressed against the human faircloth. The holy bread is consecrated, likewise the wine, but with the wine there is mingled the lifeblood of a little unbaptized baby boy. The celebrant, the deacon and subdeacon partake of this unholy drink, then share it with the congregation, and also they accept the wafer, but instead of swallowing it in reverence they spit it forth with grimaces of disgust and every foul insult.

"You apprehend? The Mass of Saint Secaire was duly celebrated on the night poor Mademoiselle Abigail came knocking at our door, and the little Eastman boy had been the victim. You noticed that she wore no clothing, save her outdoor wraps? Was that mere eccentricity? No, *parbleu*, it was evidence no less. Evidence that she quit the nest of devils as she was and came forthwith to us with information which should lead to their undoing. She had undoubtlessly served as altar cloth that night, my friends, and did not tarry for an instant when she fled—not even long enough to clothe herself. The little victim of that night so much resembled her dead babe that the frozen heart within her was softened all at once, and she became once more a woman with a woman's tender pity, instead of the cold instrument of evil which her pious devil of a father had made her. Certainly. The strayed sheep had come back into the fold."

He tore the end from a blue packet of French cigarettes, set one of the vile-smelling things in his eight-inch amber holder, and thoughtfully ignited it "Renouard, *mon vieux*," he said, "I have thought deeply on what you told us. I was reluctant at the first to credit what the evidence disclosed, but now I am convinced. When the small Eastman boy was stolen I could not fit the rough joints of the puzzle to each other. Consider—" He spread his fingers fanwise and checked the items off on them:

"Mademoiselle Alice disappears, and I find evidence that *bulala-gwai* was used. 'What are the meaning of this?' I ask me. 'This snuff-of-sleep, he is much used by savage Africans, but why should he be here? It are a puzzle.'

"Next we find proof that Mademoiselle Alice is the lineal descendant—presumably the last one—of that Devil's priest of olden days whose daughter married David Hume. We also see that a spy of the Yezidees has proved her identity to his own satisfaction before she is abducted. The puzzle is more mystifying.

"Then we do find poor, Madame Hume all dead. The outward evidence says 'suicide,' but I find the hidden proof of murder. Murder by the *roomal* of the *Thags* of India. *Que diable?* The *Thags* are worshippers of Kali, the Black Goddess, who is a sort of female devil, a disreputable half-sister of the Evil One, and in her honor they commit all sorts of murders. But what, I ask to know, are *they* doing here? Already we have Yezidees of Kurdistan, witch-doctors from Central Africa, now *Thags* from India injected in this single case. *Mon Dieu*; I suffer *mal de tête* from thinking, but nowhere can I find one grain of logic in it. *Non*, not anywhere, *cordieu!*

"Anon the little Eastman baby disappears. He is a Baptist; therefore, unbaptized. Time was, I know, when such as he were wanted for the mass of wickedness, but how can he be wanted by the Yezidees? They have no dealings with the Mass of Saint Secaire, the aping of a Christian rite is not a part of their dark ceremonies; yet here we have *bulala-gwai* again, and *bulala-gwai* was also used when the Yezidees—presumably—stole Mademoiselle Alice from before our very eyes.

"'Have the Yezidees, whose cult is rooted in obscure antiquity, and dates back far beyond the Christian Era, combined the rites of medieval Satanists?' I ask. It are not likely, yet what is one to think?

"Then comes this poor young woman and in her delirium lets fall some words which, in the light of what we know tonight, most definitely connect the stolen baby—the baby stolen even as Mademoiselle Alice was—with the sacrifice of the Mass of Saint Secaire.

"Now I think of you and what you tell us. How you have found unfortunate young women, all branded on the breast like Mademoiselle Abigail, all of them once members of the sect of Satanists, each chapter of which unclean cult is led or inspired by one from Russia. And you tell us of this League of Godlessness which is a poisonous fungus spreading through the world from that cellar of unclean abominations we call Russia.

"'Pains of a most dyspeptic bullfrog.' I inform me, 'I see a little, so small light!' And by that light I read the answer to my riddle. It is this: As business men may take a dozen old and bankrupt enterprises possessed of nothing but old and well-known names, and weld them into one big and modern corporation which functions under a new management, so have these foes of all religion seized on the little, so weak remnants of diabolism and welded them together in a formidable whole. In Africa, you say, the cannibal Leopard Men are on the rampage. The emissaries of Moscow are working with them—have they not brought back the secret of *bulala-gwai* to aid them in their work? In Kurdistan the Yezidees, an obscure sect, scarce able to maintain itself because it is ringed round by Moslems, is suddenly revived, shows new activity. Russia, which prays the world for charity to feed its starving people, can always find capital to stimulate its machinations in other lands. The Arabian gendarmerie find European pilgrims en route to Mount Lalesh, the stronghold of the Yezidees; such things were never known before, but—

"'*Ha*, another link in this so odious chain!' I tell me. 'In Europe and in America the cult of Satanism, almost dead as witchcraft, is suddenly revived in all its awful detail. That it is growing rapidly is proved by the number of renegade clergymen of all faiths, a number never paralleled before in such short time. From all sides comes evidence of its activities; from London, Paris and Berlin we hear of violated churches; little children—*always boys*—are stolen in increasing numbers and are not held to ransom; they merely disappear. The connection is most obvious. Now we have proof that this vile cult is active in America—right here in Harrisonville, *parbleu*."

"My friends, upon the crumbling ruins of the ancient Yezidee religion and the time-obliterated relics of witchcraft and demonism of the Middle Ages, this Union of the Godless are rearing a monstrous structure designed to crush out all religion with its weight. The trail of the serpent lies across the earth; already his folds are tightening round the world. We must annihilate him, or he will surely strangle us. Yes. Certainly."

"But Alice—" I began. "What connection has she with all this—"

"Much—all—everything!" he cut in sharply. "Do you not recall what the secret agents of France have said, that in the East there is talk of a white prophetess who shall raise the Devil's standard and lead his followers on to victory against the Crescent and the Cross? That prophetess is Alice Hume! Consolidated with the demonology of the West, the Devil-Worship of the East will take new force. She has been sought—she has been found, *cordieu!*—and anon she will be taken to some place appointed for her marriage to the Devil; then, with the fanaticism of the Yezidees and the fervor of the atheistic converts as a motivating force, with the promise of the Devil's own begotten son to come eventually as a result of this marriage, with the gold of Soviet Russia and the contributions of wealthy ones who revel in the freedom to do wickedness this new religion gives, they will advance in open warfare. The time to act is now. If we can rescue Mademoiselle Alice and exterminate the leaders of this movement, we may succeed in stemming the tide of hell's rebellion. Failing that"— he spread his hands and raised his shoulders in a shrug of resignation.

"All right," I countered, "how do we go about it? Alice has been gone two weeks—ten days to be exact—and we haven't the slightest clue to her location. She may be here in Harrisonville, she may have gone to Kurdistan, for all we know. Why aren't we looking for her?"

He gazed at me a moment, then: "I do not lance an abscess till conditions warrant it," he answered. "Neither do we vent our efforts, fruitlessly in this case. Mademoiselle Alice is the focal point of all these vile activities. Where she is, there are the leaders of the Satanists, and—where they are, there is she.

"From what Mademoiselle Abigail told us, we may assume there will be other celebrations of the Mass of Wickedness—when we find one of these and raid it, our chances of finding Alice are most excellent. Costello's men are on the lookout, they will inform us when the signs are out; until that time we jeopardize our chances of success by any move we make. I feel—I know—the enemy is concentrated here, but if we go to search for him he will decamp, and instead of the city which we know so well, we shall have to look for him only God knows where. *Alors*, our best activity is inactivity."

"But," I persisted, "what makes you think they're still in the city? Common sense would have warned them to get out before this, you'd think, and—"

"*Non*: You mistake," he told me bluntly. "The safest hiding-place is here. Here they logically should not be, hence this is the last place in which we should be thought to look for them. Again, temporarily at least, this is their headquarters in America. To carry out such schemes as they plan requires money, and much money can be had from converts to their cult. Wealthy men, who might fear to follow nothing but the dictates of their unconscionable consciences, will be attracted by the freedom which their creed permits, and will join them willingly—and willingly contribute to their treasury. It is in hope of further converts that they linger here, as well as to await the blowing over of the search for Alice. When the hue and cry has somewhat abated, when some later outrage claims the public interest, they can slip out all unnoticed. Until that time they are far safer in the shadows of police headquarters than if they took to hasty flight, and—"

BR-r-r-ring! The telephone's sharp warning shut him off.

"Costello? Yes, just a moment," I answered, passing the instrument to the sergeant.

"Yeah, sure—eh? Glory be to God!" Costello said, responding to the message from across the wire. To us: "Come on, gentlemen; it's time to get our feet against the pavement," he admonished. "Two hours ago some murderin' hoodlums beat up a nursemaid wheelin' a baby home from a visit wid its grandmother, an' run off wid it. An' the boys have found th' chalk-marks on th' sidewalks. It looks—"

"*Non d'un chou-fleur*, it looks like action!" de Grandin cried exultantly. "Come, Friend Trowbridge; come, my Renouard, let us go at once, right away, immediately!"

Renouard and he hurried up the stairs while I went to the garage for the car. Two minutes later they joined us, each with a pair of pistols belted to his waist. In addition to the firearms, de Grandin wore a long curve-bladed Gurkha knife, a wicked, razor-bladed weapon capable of lopping off a hand as easily as a carving-knife takes off the wing of a roast fowl.

Costello was fuming with impatience. "Shtep on it, Doctor Trowbridge, sor,' he ordered. "Th' first pitcher wuz at Twenty-Eighth an' Hopkins Streets; if ye'll take us there we'll be after follyin' th' trail I've tellyphoned to have a raidin' party meet us there in fifteen minutes."

"But it is grand, it is immense; it is magnificent, my friend!" de Grandin told Renouard as we slipped through the darkened streets.

"It is superb!" Renouard assured de Grandin.

"Bedad, here's where Ireland declares war on Kur-r-distan!" Costello told them both.

13. Inside the Lines

A LARGE, BLACK AND VERY shiny limousine was parked at the curb near the intersection of Twenty-Eighth and Hopkins Streets, and toward it Costello led the way when we halted at the corner. The vehicle had all the earmarks of hailing from some high-class mortician's garage, and this impression was heightened by a bronze plate displayed behind the windshield with the legend *Funeral Car* in neat block letters. But there was nothing funeral—except perhaps potentially—about the eight passengers occupying the tonneau. I recognized Officers Hornsby, Gilligan and Schultz, each with a canvas web-belt decorated with a service revolver and nightstick buckled outside his blouse, and with a vicious-looking sub-machine gun resting across his knees. Five others, similarly belted, but equipped with fire axes, boat-hooks and slings of tear-bombs, huddled out of sight of casual passers-by on the seats of the car. "Camouflage," Costello told us with a grin, pointing to the funeral sign; then: "All set, Hornsby? Got ever'thing, axes, hooks, tear-bombs, an—"

"All jake, sir. Got th' works," the other interrupted. "Where's th' party?"

The sergeant beckoned the patrolman loitering at the corner. "Where is it?" he demanded.

"Right here, sir," the man returned, pointing to a childish scrawl on the cement sidewalk.

We examined it by the light of the street lamp. Unless warned of its sinister connotation, no one would have given the drawing a second glance, so obviously was it the mark of mischievous but not exceptionally talented children. A crudely sketched figure with pot-belly, triangular head and stiffly jointed limbs was outlined on the sidewalk in white chalk of the sort every schoolboy pilfers from the classroom. Only a pair of parentheses sprouting from the temples and a pointed beard and mustache indicated the faintest resemblance to the popular conception of the Devil, and the implement the creature held in its unskillfully drawn hand might have been anything from a fishing-pole to a pitchfork. Nevertheless, there was one fact which struck us all. Instead of brandishing the weapon overhead, the figure pointed it definitely toward Twenty-Ninth Street. De Grandin's slender nostrils twitched like those of a hunting dog scenting the quarry as he bent above the drawing. "We have the trail before us," he whispered. "Come, let us follow it. *Allons!*"

"Come on, youse guys; folly us, but don't come too close unless we signal." Costello ordered the men waiting in the limousine.

Down Hopkins Street, shabby, down-at-the-heel thoroughfare that it was, we walked with all the appearance of nonchalance we could master, paused at Twenty-Ninth Street and looked about. No second guiding figure met our eye.

"*Dame!*" de Grandin swore. "*C'est singulier.* Can we have—*ah, regardez-vous, mes amis!*" The tiny fountain pen searchlight he had swung in an ever widening circle had picked out a second figure, scarcely four inches high, scribbled on the red-brick front of a vacant house. The trident in the demon's hand directed us down Twenty-Ninth Street toward the river.

A moment only we stopped to study it, and all of us were impressed at once with one outstanding fact; crudely drawn as it was, the second picture was a duplicate in miniature of the first, the same technique, if such a word could be applied to such a scrawl, was evident in every wavering line and faulty curve of the small picture. "*Morbleu*," de Grandin murmured, "he was used to making these, the one who laid this trail. This is no first attempt."

"*Mais non*," Renouard agreed.

"Looks that way," I acquiesced.

"Sure," said Costello. "Let's get goin'."

Block after block we followed the little sprawling figures of the Devil scrawled on sidewalk, wall or fence, and always the pointing tridents led us toward the poorer, unkempt sections of the city. At length, when we had left all residential buildings and entered a neighborhood of run-down factories and storehouses, de Grandin raised his hand to indicate a halt.

"We would better wait our reinforcements," he cautioned; "there is too great an opportunity for an ambuscade in this deserted quarter, and—*ah, par la barbe d'un poisson rouge!*" he cried. "We are in time, I think. Observe him, if you please."

Fifty or a hundred yards beyond us a figure moved furtively. He was a shadow of a man, sliding noiselessly and without undue movement, though with surprising speed, through the little patch of luminance cast by a flickering gas street-lamp. Also he seemed supremely alert, perceptive and receptive with the sensitiveness of a wild animal of the jungle stalking wary prey. The slightest movement of another in the semi-darkness near him would have needed to be more shadow-silent than his own to escape him.

"This," remarked Renouard, "will bear investigating. Let me do it, my Jules, I am accustomed to this sort of hunting." With less noise than a swimmer dropping into a darkened stream he disappeared in the shadow of a black-walled warehouse, to emerge a moment later halfway down the block where a street lamp stained the darkness with its feeble light. Then he melted into the shadow once again.

We followed, silently as possible, lessening the distance between Renouard and ourselves as quickly as we could, but making every effort at concealment.

Renouard and the shadow-man came together at the dead-end of a cross-street where the oil-stained waters of the river lapped the rotting piles.

"Hands up, my friend!" Renouard commanded, emerging from the darkness behind his quarry with the suddenness of a magic-lantern view thrown on a screen. "I have you under cover; if you move, your prayers had best be said!" He advanced a pace, pressing the muzzle of his heavy pistol almost into the other's neck, and reached forward with his free hand to feel, with a trained policeman's skill, for hidden weapons.

The result was surprising, though not especially pleasing. Like an inflated ball bounced against the floor, Renouard rose in the air, flew over the other's shoulder and landed with a groan of suddenly expelled breath against the cobblestones, flat upon his back. More, the man whose skill at jujitsu accomplished his defeat straightened like a coiled steel spring suddenly released, drew an impressively large automatic pistol and aimed it at the supine Frenchman. "Say *your* prayers, if you know any, you"—he began, but Costello intervened.

Lithe and agile as a tiger, for all his ponderous bulk, the Irishman cleared the space between them with a single leap and swung his club in a devastating arc. The man sagged at the knees and sank face forward to the street, his pistol sliding from his unnerved hand and lying harmless in the dust beside him.

"That's that," remarked the sergeant. "Now, let's have a look at this felly."

He was a big man, more lightly built, but quite as tall as the doughty Costello, and as the latter turned him over, we saw that though his hair was iron-gray, his face was young, and deeply tanned. A tiny, dark mustache of the kind made popular by Charlie Chaplin and British subalterns during the war adorned his upper lip. His clothes were well cut and of good material, his boots neatly polished, and his hands, one of which was ungloved, well cared for—obviously a person with substantial claims to gentility, though probably one lacking in the virtue of good citizenship, I thought.

Costello bent to loose the buttons of the man's dark overcoat, but de Grandin interposed a quick objection. "*Mais non, mon sergent*," he reproved, "our time is short. Place manacles upon his hands and give him into custody. We can attend to him at leisure, at present we have more important pots upon the fire."

"Right ye are, sor," the Irishman agreed with a grin, locking a pair of handcuffs on the stunned man's wrists. He raised his hand in signal, and as the limousine slid noiselessly alongside: "Keep an eye on this bur-r-d, Hornsby," he ordered. "We'll be wantin' to give 'im th' wor-rks at headquarters—afther we git through wid this job, y' understand."

Officer Hornsby nodded assent, and we returned to our queer game of hare and hounds.

I T MIGHT HAVE BEEN a half-hour later when we came to our goal. It was a mean building in a mean street. The upper floors were obviously designed for manufacturing, for half a dozen signs proclaimed that desirable lofts might be rented from as many agents. "ALTERATIONS MADE TO SUIT TENANT FOR A TERM OF YEARS." The ground floor had once been occupied by an emporium dispensing spirituous, malt and vinous liquors, and that the late management had regarded the law of the land with more optimism than respect was evident from the impressive padlock on the door and the bold announcement that the place was "CLOSED BY ORDER OF U.S. DISTRICT COURT."

Beside the door of what had been the family entrance in days gone by was a sketch of Satan, his trident pointing upward—the first of the long series of guiding sketches to hold the spear in such position. Undoubtedly the meeting place was somewhere in the upper portion of the empty seeming building, but when we sought an entrance every door was closed and firmly barred. All, indeed, were furnished with stout locks on the outside. The evidence of vacancy was plain and not to be disputed, whatever the Satanic scrawl might otherwise imply.

"Looks like we're up agin a blank wall, sor," Costello told de Grandin. "This place is empty as a bass drum—probably ain't had a tenant since th' prohibition men got sore 'cause someone cut off their protection money an' slapped a padlock on th' joint."

De Grandin shook his head in positive negation. "The more it seems deserted the more I am convinced we are arrived at the right place," he answered. "These locks, do they look old?"

"H'm," the sergeant played his searchlight on the nearest lock and scratched his head reflectively. "No, sor, I can't say they do," he admitted. "If they'd been here for a year—an' th' joint's been shut almost that long—they ought to show more weather-stain, but what's that got to do wid—"

"Ah, bah," de Grandin interrupted, "to be slow of perception is the policeman's prerogative, but you abuse the privilege, my friend! What better means of camouflage than this could they desire? The old locks are removed and new ones substituted. Each person who is bidden to the rendezvous is furnished with a key; he follows where the pointing spears of Satan lead, opens the lock and enters. Voilà tout!"

"Wallah me eye," the Irishman objected. "Who's goin' to lock up afther 'im? If—"

A sudden scuffle in the dark, a half-uttered, half-suppressed cry, and the sound of flesh, colliding violently with flesh cut him off.

"Here's a bird I found layin' low acrost th' street, sir," Officer Hornsby reported, emerging from the darkness which surrounded us, forcing an undersized individual before him. One of his hands was firmly twisted in the prisoner's collar, the other was clamped across his mouth, preventing outcry.

"I left th' gang in th' car up by th' entrance to th' alley," he continued, "an' come gum-shoein' down to see if I wuz needed, an' this gink must 'a' seen me buttons, for he made a pass at me an' missed, then started to let out a squawk, but I choked 'im off. Looks like he wuz planted as a lookout for th' gang, an—"

"Ah?" de Grandin interrupted. "I think the answer to your question is here, my sergeant." To Hornsby: "You say that he attempted an assault?"

"I'll tell th' cock-eyed world," the officer replied. "Here's what he tried to ease into me." From beneath his blouse he drew a short, curve-bladed dagger, some eight inches in length, its wicked keen-edged blade terminating in a vicious vulture's-beak hook. "I'd 'a' made a handsome-lookin' corpse wid that between me ribs," he added grimly.

De Grandin gazed upon the weapon, then the captive. "The dagger is from Kurdistan," he declared. "This one"—he turned his back contemptuously on the prisoner—"I think that he is Russian, a renegade Hebrew from the Black Sea country. I know his kind, willing to sell his ancient, honorable birthright and the god of his fathers for political preferment. What further did he do, if anything?"

"Well, sir, he kind of overreached his self when he drove at me wid th' knife—I reckon I must 'a' seen it comin', or *felt* it, kind of. Anyhow, he missed me, an' I cracked 'im on the wrist wid me nightstick, an' he dropped his sticker an' started to yell. Not on account o' the pain, sir—it warn't that sort o' yell—but more as if he wuz tryin' to give th' tip-off to 'is pals. Then I claps me hand acrost 'is trap an' lets 'im have me knuckles. He flings sumpin—looked like a bunch o' keys, as near as I could make out—away an'—well, here we are, sir.

"What'll I do wid 'im, Sergeant?" He turned inquiringly to Costello.

"Put th' joolry on 'im an' slap 'im in th' wagon wid the other guy," the sergeant answered.

"I got you," Hornsby replied, saluting and twisting his hand more tightly in the prisoner's collar. "Come on, bozo," he shook the captive by way of emphasis, "you an' me's goin' bye-bye."

"And now, my sergeant, for the strategy," de Grandin announced. "Renouard, Friend Trowbridge and I shall go ahead. Too many entering at once would surely advertise our coming. The doors are locked and that one threw away the keys. He had been well instructed. To search for them would take up too much time, and time is what we cannot well afford to waste. Therefore you will await us here, and when I blow my whistle you will raid the place. And oh, my friend, do not delay your coming when, I signal! Upon your speed may rest a little life. You understand?"

"Perfectly, sor," Costello answered. "But how're ye goin' to crack th' crib—git in th' joint, I mean?"

De Grandin grinned his elfish grin. "Is it not beautiful?" he asked, drawing something from the inside pocket of his sheepskin reefer. It was a long instrument of tempered steel, flattened at one end to a thin but exceedingly tough blade.

The Irishman took it in his hand and swung it to and fro, testing its weight and balance. "Bedad, Doctor de Grandin, sor," he said admiringly, "what an elegant burglar was spoilt when you decided to go straight!"

De Grandin motioned to Renouard and me, and crept along the base of the house wall. Arrived at a soiled window, he inserted the thin edge of his burglar tool between the upper and lower casings and probed and twisted it experimentally. The window had been latched, but a little play had been left between the sashes. Still, it took us but a moment to determine that the casings, though loose, were securely fastened.

"*Allons*," de Grandin murmured, and we crept to another window. This, too, defied his efforts, as did the next two which we tested, but success awaited us at our fifth trial. Persistence was rewarded, and the questing blade probed and pushed with gentle persuasion till the rusty latch snapped back and we were able to push up the sash.

Inside the storehouse all was darker than a cellar, but by the darting ray of de Grandin's flashlight we finally descried a flight of dusty stairs spiraling upward to a lightless void. We crept up these, found ourselves in a wide and totally empty loft, then, after casting about for a moment, found a second flight of stairs and proceeded to mount them.

"The trail is warm—*pardieu*, it is hot!" he murmured. "Come, my friends, forward, and for your lives, no noise!"

The stairway terminated in a little walled-off space, once used as a business office by the manufactory which had occupied the loft's main space, no doubt. Now it was hung with draperies of deep-red velours realistically embroidered with the figure of a strutting peacock some six or eight feet high. "Melek Taos—the Peacock Spirit of Evil. Satan's viceroy upon earth," de Grandin told us in a whisper as we gazed upon the image which his flashing searchlight showed. "Now do you stand close beside me and have your weapons ready, if you please. We may have need of them."

Across the little intervening space he tiptoed, put aside the ruddy curtains and tapped timidly on the door thus disclosed. Silence answered his summons, but as he repeated the hail with soft insistence the door swung inward a few inches and a hooded figure peered cautiously through the opening.

"Who comes?" the sentinel whispered. "And why have ye not the mystic knock?"

"The knock, you say?" de Grandin answered almost soundlessly. "*Morbleu*, I damn think that we have one—do you care for it?" Swiftly he swung the steel tool with which he had forced the window and caught the hooded porter fairly on the cranium.

"Assist me, if you please," he ordered in a whisper, catching the man as he toppled forward and easing him to the floor. "So. Off with his robe, while I insure his future harmlessness."

With the waist-cord from the porter's costume he bound the man's hands and ankles, then rose, donned the red cassock and tiptoed through the door.

"Ss-s-st!" His low, sharp hiss came through the dark, and we followed him into the tiny anteroom. A row of pegs was ranged around the wall, and from them hung hooded gowns of dark-red cloth, similar to that worn by the senti-nel. Obedient to de Grandin's signaled order, Renouard and I arrayed ourselves in gowns, pulled the hoods well forward to obscure our features, and, hands clasped before us and demurely hidden in our flowing sleeves, crept silently across the vestibule, paused a moment at the swinging curtains muffling the door, then, with bowed heads, stepped forward in de Grandin's wake.

We were in the chapel of the Devil-Worshippers.

14. The Serpent's Lair

HANGINGS OF DARK-RED STUFF draped loosely from the ceiling of the hall, obscuring doors and windows, their folds undulating eerily, like fluttering cerements of unclean phantoms. Candles like votive lights flickered in cups of red glass at intervals round the walls, their tiny, lambent flames diluting rather than dispelling the darkness which hovered like vapor in the air. Only in one spot was there light. At the farther end of the draped room was an altar shaped in imitation of the Gothic sanctuary of a church, and round this blazed a mass of tall black candles which splashed a luminous pool on the deep red drugget covering the floor and altar-steps. Above the altar was set a crucifix, reversed, so that the thorn-crowned head was down, the nail-pierced feet above, and back of this a reredos of scarlet cloth was hung, the image of a strutting peacock appliquéd on it in flashing sequins. On the table of the altar lay a long cushion of red velvet, tufted like a mattress. Two ranks of backless benches had been set transversely in the hall, a wide center aisle between them, smaller aisles to right and left, and on these the congregation sat in strained expectancy, each member muffled in a hooded gown so that it was impossible to distinguish the features, or even the sex, of a given individual.

A faint odor of incense permeated the close atmosphere; not sweet incense, such as churches use, but something with a bitter, pungent tang to it, and—it seemed to me—more than a hint of the subtle, maddening aroma of burnt cannabis, the *bhang* with which fanatics of the East intoxicate themselves before they run amok. But through the odor of the incense was another smell, the heavy smell of paraffin, as though some careless person had let fall an open tank of it, soaking the thick floor-covering before the error could be rectified.

Somewhere unseen to us, perhaps behind the faintly fluttering draperies on the walls, an organ was playing very softly as Renouard, de Grandin and I stole quickly through the curtained doorway of the anteroom and, unobserved, took places on the rearmost bench.

Here and there a member of the congregation gave vent to a soft sigh of suppressed anticipation and excitement, once or twice peaked cowls were bent together as their wearers talked in breathless whispers; but for the most part the assemblage sat erect in stony silence, motionless, yet eager as a flock of hooded vultures waiting for the kill which is to furnish them their feast.

An unseen gong chimed softly as we took our seats, its soft resonant tones penetrating the dark room like a sudden shaft of daylight let into a long-closed cellar, and the congregation rose as one, standing with hands clasped before them and heads demurely bowed. A curtain by the altar was pushed back, and through the opening three figures glided. The first was tall and gaunt, with a Slavic type of face, wild, fantastic dyes and thick, fair hair; the second was young, still in his early twenties, with the lithe, free carriage, fiery glance and swarthy complexion of the nomadic races of southeastern Europe or western Asia. The third was a small, frail, aged man—that is, he seemed so at first glance. A second look left doubt both of his frailty and age. His face was old, long, thin and deeply etched with wrinkles, hard-shaven like an actor's or a priest's and in it burned a pair of big sad eyes—eyes like Lucifer's as he broods upon the high estate from which he fell. His mouth was tight-lipped, but very red, drooping at the corners, the mouth of an ascetic turned voluptuary. His body, in odd contrast to his face, seemed curiously youthful, erect and vigorous in carriage, a strange and somehow terrifying contrast, it seemed to me. All three were robed in gowns of scarlet fashioned like monks' habits, with hooded capes pendant at the back and knotted cords of black about the waist. On the breast of each was emblazoned an inverted passion cross in black; each had a tonsure shaven on his head; each wore red-leather sandals on his feet.

A gentle rustling sounded as the trio stepped into the circle of light before the altar, a soughing of soft sighs as the audience gave vent to its pent-up emotion.

The old-young man moved quickly toward the altar, his two attendants at his elbows, sank to one knee before it in humble genuflection; then, like soldiers at command to wheel, they turned to face the congregation. The two attendants folded hands before them, bringing the loose cuffs of their sleeves together; the other advanced a pace, raised his left hand as though in benediction and murmured: "*Gloria tibi, Lucifero!*"

"*Gloria tibi, Lucifero!*" intoned the congregation in a low-voiced chant.

"Praise we now our Lord the Peacock, Melek Taos, Angel Peacock of our Lord the Prince of Darkness!" came the chanted invocation of the red priest.

"Hail and glory, laud and honor, O our Lord, great Melek Taos!" responded the auditors.

"Let us not forget the Serpent, who aforetime in the Garden undertook the Master's bidding and from bondage to the Tyrant freed our parents, Eve and Adam!" the red priest admonished.

"Hail thee, Serpent, who aforetime in the Garden men call Eden, from the bondage of the Tyrant freed our parents Eve and Adam!" cried the congregation, a wave of fervor running through them like fire among the withered grass in autumn.

The red priest and his acolytes wheeled sharply to the left and marched beyond the limits of the lighted semicircle made by the altar candles, and suddenly the hidden organ, which had been playing a sort of soft improvisation, changed its tune. Now it sang a slow andante strain, rising and falling with persistent, pulsating quavers like the almost tuneless airs which Eastern fakirs play upon their pipes when the serpents rise to "dance" upon their tails.

And as the tremulous melody burst forth the curtains parted once again and a girl ran out into the zone of candlelight. For a moment she poised on tiptoe, and a gasp of savage and incredulous delight came from the company. Very lovely she was, violet-eyed, daffodil-haired; with a body white as petals of narcissi dancing in the wind. Her costume gleamed and glittered in the flickering candlelight, encasing her slim frame from hips to armpits like a coiled green hawser. It was a fifteen-foot live boa constrictor!

As she moved lithely through the figures of her slow, gliding dance to the sensuous accompaniment of the organ, the great reptile loosed its hold upon her torso and waved its hideous, wedge-shaped head back and forth in perfect time. Its glistening, scaly head caressed her cheek, its lambent forked tongue shot forth to meet her red, voluptuous mouth.

Gradually the wailing minor of the organ began to quicken. The girl spun round and round upon her toes, and with that odd trick which we have of noting useless trifles at such times, I saw that the nails of her feet had been varnished to a gleaming pink, like the nails of a hand, and as she danced they cast back twinkling coral-toned reflections of the candles' flames. The great snake seemed to waken. Silently, swiftly, its sleek body extended, flowing like a stream of molten green metal about the girl, slithering from her bare white breast to her bare white feet, then knotting once again about her hips and waist like a gleaming girdle of death. Round and round she whirled like a lovely animated top, her grisly partner holding her in firm embrace. Finally, as the music slowed once more, she fell exhausted to the carpet, and the snake again entwined itself about her body, its devilish head raised above her heaving shoulders, its beady eyes and flickering tongue shooting silent challenge to the world to take her from it.

The music still whined on with insistent monotone, and the girl rose slowly to her knees, bowed to the altar till her forehead touched the floor and signed herself with the cross—in reverse, beginning at her breast and ending at her brow. Then, tottering wearily beneath the burden of the great snake's weight, she staggered through the opening between the swaying curtains.

The organ's wailing ceased, and from the shadow shrouded rear of the hall there came the low intoning of a chant. The music was Gregorian, but the words were indistinguishable. Then came the high, sweet chiming of a sacring bell, and all the audience fell down upon their knees, heads bowed, hands clasped, as a solemn, robed procession filed up the aisle.

First marched the crucifer, arrayed in scarlet cassock and white surplice and what a crucifix he bore! The rood was in reverse, the *corpus* hung head-downward, and at the staff-head perched the image of a strutting peacock, its silver overlaid with bright enamel, simulating the natural gaudy colors of the bird. Next came two men in crimson cassocks, each with a tall black candle flickering in his hand, and then a man who bore a staff of silver bells, which chimed and tinkled musically. Two other surpliced acolytes came next, walking slowly backward and swinging censers which belched forth clouds of pungent smoke. Finally the red priest, now clothed in full canonicals, chasuble, alb and amice, while at his elbows walked his two attendants in the dalmatic and tuni-cle of deacon and subdeacon.

Two by two behind the men there came a column of girls garbed in a sort of conventual habit—long, loose-cuffed sleeves, full skirts reaching to the ankle, high, cope-like collars—all of brilliant scarlet embroidered with bright orange figures which waved like flickering flames as the garments swayed. The gowns were belted at the waist, but open at the throat, leaving chest and bust uncov-ered and disclosing on each breast the same symbol we had seen on Abigail Kimble's white flesh. Upon their heads they wore tall caps of stiff red linen, shaped somewhat like a bishop's miter and surmounted by the silver image of a peacock. As they walked sedately in the wake of the red priest their bare white feet showed with startling contrast to the deep red of their habits and the dark tones of the carpet.

A brazen pot of glowing charcoal was swung from a long rod borne by the first two women, while the next two carried cushions of red plush on which there lay some instruments of gleaming metal. The final members of the column were armed with scarlet staves which they held together at the tips, forming a sort of open arbor over a slight figure swathed in veils which marched with slow and faltering steps.

"*Morbleu*," de Grandin whispered in my ear, "*une proselyte!* Can such things be?"

His surmise was correct. Before the altar the procession halted, spread out fanwise, with the veiled girl in their midst. The women set their fire-pot on the altar steps—and blew upon the embers with a bellows till they glowed with sud-den life. Then into the red nest of coals they put the shining instruments and stood back, waiting, a sort of awful eagerness upon their faces.

"Do what thou wilt; this shall be the whole of the law!" the red priest chanted.

"Love is the law; love free and unbound," the congregation intoned.

"Do what thou wilt shall be the law," the Priest repeated; "therefore be ye goodly, dress ye in all fine raiment, eat rich foods and drink sweet wines, even wines that foam. Also take thy fill of love, when and with whom ye will. Do what thou wilt; this is the law."

The women gathered round the kneeling convert, screening her from view, as the red priest called:

"Is not this better than the death-in-life of slaves who serve the Slave-God and go oppressed with consciousness of sin, vainly striving after tedious virtues? *There is no sin*—do what thou wilt; that is the law."

The red-robed women started back and left the space before the altar open. In the candle-lighted clearing, the altar-lights, reflected in the jewels which glimmered in her braided hair, knelt the convert, stripped of her enshrouding veils, clad only in her own white beauty. The red priest turned, took something from the glowing fire-pot—

A short, half-strangled exclamation broke from the kneeling girl as she half started to her feet, but three watchful red-robed women sprang upon her, seized her wrist and head, and held her rigid while the priest pressed the glowing branding-iron tight against her breast, then with a deftness which denoted practice, took a second tool and forced it first against one cheek, and then the other.

The branded girl groaned and writhed within her guardians' grasp, but they held her firmly till the ordeal was finished, then raised her, half fainting to her feet, and put a crimson robe on her, a yellow sash about her waist and a crimson miter on her head.

"Scarlet Women of the Apocalypse, behold your sister—Scarlet Woman, you have put behind your consciousness of right and wrong, look on the others of your sisterhood!" the red priest cried. "Show them the sign, that all may know that which ye truly are!"

Now pride, perhaps the consciousness that all connection with religious teaching had been cut, seemed to revive the almost swooning girl. Though tears still glinted on her eyelids from the torment she had undergone, a wild bold recklessness shone in her handsome face as she stood forth before the other wearers of the brand and pridefully, like a queen, drew back her ruddy robe, displaying the indelible signs of evil stamped upon her flesh. Her chin was raised, her eyes glowed through their tears with haughty pride as she revealed the symbols of her covenant with hell.

The little silver bells burst forth into a peal of admonition. Priest and people dropped upon their knees as the curtains by the altar were drawn back and another figure stepped into the zone of candlelight.

Slowly, listlessly, almost like one walking in a dream she stepped. A long and sleeveless smock of yellow satin, thickset with red figures of dancing demons, hung loosely from her shoulders. A sort of uraeus fashioned like a peacock was set crown-like on her head, rings set with fiery gems glowed on every toe and finger, great ruby pendants dangled from her ears. She seemed a very Queen in Babylon as she proceeded to the altar between the ranks of groveling priests and women and sank to her knees, then rose and signed herself with the cross, beginning at the breast and ending at the brow.

A whispered ripple which became a wave ran rapidly from lip to lip: "It's she; the Queen, the Prophetess, the Bride-Elect! She has graced us with her presence!"

De Grandin murmured something in my ear, but I did not hear him. My other senses seemed paralyzed as my gaze held with unbelieving horror to the woman standing at the altar. The Queen—the Devil's Bride-Elect—was Alice Hume.

15. The Mass of St. Secaire

PREPARATIONS FOR THE SACRILEGIOUS sacrament had been carefully rehearsed. For a long moment Alice stood erect before the altar, head bowed, hands clasped beneath her chin; then parting her hands and raising them palm-forward to the level of her temples, she dropped as though forced downward by invincible pressure, and we heard the softly thudding impact as she flung herself prostrate and beat her brow and palms against the crimson altar-carpet in utter self abasement.

"Is all prepared?" the red priest called as, flanked by deacon and subdeacon, he paused before the altar steps.

"Not yet; we make the sanctuary ready!" two of the scarlet-robed women returned in chorus as they stepped forward, bent and raised Alice Hume between them. Quickly, like skilled tiring women working at their trade, they lifted off her yellow robe with its decorations of gyrating devils, drew the glinting ruby rings from her toes and fingers, unhooked the flashing pendants from the holes bored through her ears. Then they unloosed her hair, and as the cloven tide of silken tresses rippled down, took her by the hands and led her slowly up the stairway to the altar. There one of them crouched to the floor, forming herself into a living stepping-stone, while, assisted by the other, Alice trod upon her back, mounted to the altar and laid her white form supine on the long, red cushion. Then, ankles crossed and hands with upturned palms laid flaccidly beside her, she closed her eyes and lay as still as any carven statue. They put the sacred vessels on her breast, the golden chalice thick-inlaid with gems, the heavy, hand-chased paten with its freight of small, red wafers, and the yellow plate shone brightly in the candlelight, its reflection casting halos of pale gold upon the ivory flesh.

The red priest mounted quickly to the altar, genuflected with his back to it, and called out: "*Introibo ad altare Dei*—I will go up into the altar of God."

Rapidly the rite proceeded. The fifty-second Psalm—*quid gloriaris*—was said, but blasphemously garbled, God's name deleted and the Devil's substituted, so that it read: "Why boastest thou thyself, thou tyrant, that thou canst do mischief, whereas the evilness of Satan endureth yet daily?"

Then came confession, and, as *oremus te Domine* was intoned the priest bowed and kissed the living altar as provided by the rubric. Again repeating *Dominus vobiscum*, he pressed a burning kiss upon the shrinking flesh.

The subdeacon took a massive black-bound book and bore it to the deacon, who swung the censer over it; then, while the other held it up before him, he read aloud:

"In the beginning God created seven spirits as a man lighteth one lamp from another, and of these Lucifer, whose true name is forbidden to pronounce, was chiefest. But he, offended by the way in which God treated His creations, rebelled against the Tyrant, but by treachery was overthrown.

"Therefore was he expelled from heaven, but seized dominion of the earth and air, which he retaineth to this day. And those who worship him and do him honor will have the joys of life all multiplied to them, and at the last shall dwell with him in that eternal place which is his own, where they shall have dominion over hosts of demons pledged to do their will.

"Choose ye, therefore, man; choose ye whether ye will have the things of earth added to an endless authority in hell, or whether ye will submit to the will of the Tyrant of the Skies, have sorrow upon earth and everlasting slavery in the world to come."

The deacon and subdeacon put the book aside, crossing themselves in reverse, and the call came mockingly: "May our sins be multiplied through the words contained in this Gospel."

The red priest raised the paten high above the living altar, intoning: "*Suscipe sancte Pater hanc immaculatum hostiam—*"

De Grandin fumbled underneath his robe. "Renouard, my friend," he whispered, "do you go tell the good Costello to come quickly. These cursed curtains round the walls, I fear they will shut in my whistle's sound, and we must have aid at once. Quickly, my friend, a life depends on it!"

Renouard slipped from his place and crept toward the door, put back the curtain with a stealthy hand, and started back dismayed. Across the doorway we had entered a barrier was drawn, an iron guard-door intended to hold back flames should the building catch afire.

What had occurred was obvious. Recovered from the blow de Grandin dealt him the seneschal had struggled from his bonds and barred the portal, then—could it be possible that he had gone, unseen behind the screen of curtains hanging from the walls and warned the others of our presence?

De Grandin and Renouard reached for their firearms, fumbling with the unfamiliar folds of their disguises. . . .

Before a weapon could be drawn we were assaulted from behind, our elbows pinioned to our sides, lengths of coiling cords wound tightly around our bodies. In less than half a minute we were helpless, firmly bound and set once more in our places on the bench. Silently and swiftly as a serpent twines its coils about a luckless rabbit our assailants did their work, and only they and we, apparently, knew what occurred. Certainly the hellish ritual at the altar never faltered, nor did a member of the congregation turn round to see what passed behind.

Two women of the Scarlet Sisterhood had crept back of the curtains by the altar. Now they emerged, bearing between them a little, struggling boy, a naked, chubby little fellow who fought and kicked and offered such resistance as his puny strength allowed and called out to his "Daddy" and his "Mamma" to save him from his captors.

Down on the altar steps they flung the little boy; one woman seized his little, dimpled hands, the other took his feet, extending his small body to its greatest length. The deacon and subdeacon had stepped forward. . . .

I shut my eyes and bowed my head, but my ears I could not stop, and so I heard the red priest chant: "*Hic est enim calix sanguins mea*—this is the chalice of my blood—" I smelled the perfume of the incense, strong, acrid, sweet yet bitterly revolting, mounting to my brain like some accursed Oriental drug; I heard the wail which slowly grew in volume, yet which had a curiously muffled quality about it, the wail which ended in a little strangling, suffocated bleat!

I knew! Though not a Catholic, I had attended mass with Catholic friends too often not to know. The priest had said the sacred words of intention, and in a church the deacon would pour wine, the subdeacon water in the chalice. But this was not a church; this was a temple dedicated to the Devil, and mingled with the red wine was not water. . . . A bitter memory of my childhood hurried back across the years: They'd given me a lamb when I was five years old, all summer I had made a pet of it. I 'loved' the gentle, woolly thing. The autumn came, and with it came the time for slaughter . . . that agonizing, strangling bleat! That blood-choken cry of utter anguish!

Another sound cut in. The red priest once again was chanting, this time in a language which I could not understand, a ringing, sonorous tongue, yet with something wrong about it. Syllables which should have been noble in their cadences were clipped and twisted in their endings.

And now another voice—an abominably guttural voice with a note of hellish chuckling laughter in it—was answering the priest, still in that unknown tongue. It rose and fell, gurgled and chuckled obscenely, and though its volume was not great it seemed to fill the place as rumbling thunder fills the summer sky. Sweat broke out on my forehead. Luckily for me I had been seated by my captors; otherwise I should have fallen where I stood. As surely as I knew my heart was hammering against my ribs, I knew the voice of incarnate evil was speaking in that curtained room—with my own ears I heard the Devil answering his votary!

Two red-robed priestesses advanced, one from either side of the altar. Each bore an ewer of heavy hammered brass, and even in the candles' changing light

I saw the figures on the vessels were of revolting nastiness, beasts, men and women in attitudes of unspeakable obscenity. The deacon and subdeacon took the vessels from the women's hands and knelt before the priest, who dropped upon his knees with outspread hands and upturned face a moment, then rose and took the chalice from the human altar's gently heaving breast and held it out before him as a third red nun came forward, bearing in her outstretched hands a queer, teapot-like silver vessel.

I say a teapot, for that is what it most resembled when I saw it first. Actually, it was a pitcher made of silver, very brightly polished, shaped to represent a strutting peacock with fanned-out tail and erected crest, its neck outstretched. The bird's beak formed the spout of the strange pitcher, and a funnel-shaped opening in the back between the wings permitted liquids to be poured into it.

The contents of the chalice, augmented and diluted by ruby liquors from the ewers which the women brought, were poured into the peacock-pitcher—a quart or so, I estimated—and the red priest flung the chalice awy contemptuously and raised the new container high above his head, so that its polished sides and ruby eyes flung back the altar candles' lights in myriad darting rays.

"Vile, detestable wretches—miscreants!" de Grandin whispered hoarsely. "They mingle blood of innocents, my friends; the wine which represents *le precieux sang de Dieu* and the lifeblood of that little baby boy whose throat they cut and drained a moment hence! *Parbleu*, they shall pay through the nose for this if Jules de Grandin—"

The red priest's deep voice boomed an invitation: "Ye who do truly and earnestly repent you of all your good deeds, and intend to lead a new life of wickedness, draw nigh and take this unholy sacrament to your souls' damnation, devoutly kneeling!"

The congregation rose and ranged themselves upon their knees in a semi-circle round the altar. From each to each the red priest strode, thrusting the peacock's hollow beak into each opened mouth, decanting mingled wine and blood.

"You see?" de Grandin's almost soundless whisper came to me. "They study to give insult to the end. They make the cross-sign in reverse, the crucifix they have turned upside-down; when they administer their sacrament of hell they give the wine before the wafer, mocking both the Anglican and Latin rites. *Saligauds!*"

The ceremony proceeded to "*ite missa est*," when the celebrant suddenly seized a handful of red, triangular wafers from the paten and flung them broadcast out upon the floor. Pandemonium best describes the scene that followed. Those who have seen a group of urchins scrambling for coins tossed by some prankish tourist can vision how that audience of gowned and hooded worshippers of Satan clawed and fought for fragments of the host, groveled on the floor, snatching, scratching, grasping for the smallest morsel of the wafer, which, when obtained, they popped into their mouths and chewed with noisy mastication, then spat forth with exclamations of disgust and cries of foul insult.

As the guards who stood behind us joined the swinish scramble for the desecrated host, de Grandin suddenly lurched forward, hunched his shoulders, then straightened like a coiling spring released from tension. Supple as an eel— and as muscular—he needed but the opportunity to wriggle from the ligatures which lashed his elbows to his sides.

"Quick, my friends, the haste!" he whispered, drawing his sharp Gurkha knife and slashing at our bonds. "We must—"

"*Les gendarmes*—the police!"

The fire-door leading to the anteroom banged back as the hooded warder rushed into the hall, screaming his warnings. He turned, slammed the door behind him, then drew a heavy chain across it, snapping a padlock through its links. "They come—*les gendarmes!*" he repeated hysterically.

The red priest barked a sharp command, and like sailors trained to spring to quarters when the bugles sound alarm, some half-dozen Satanists rushed to the walls, upset the guttering votive lamps, then scuttled toward the altar. Their companions already had disappeared behind the curtains hanging round the shrine.

"*Qui est*—" Renouard began, but de Grandin cut him short.

"Quickly, for your lives!" he cried, seizing us by the elbows and forcing us before him.

Now we understood the heavy, sickening smell of kerosene which hovered in the room. From top to hem the shrouding curtains at the walls were soaked in it, requiring but the touch of fire to burst into inextinguishable flame. Already they were blazing fiercely where the upset lamps had lighted them, and the heavy, suffocating smoke of burning oil was spreading like mephitic vapor through the room. In a moment the place would be a raging hell of fire.

Beyond the heavy fire-door we heard Costello's peremptory hail: "Open up here; open in th' law's name, or we'll break th' door!" Then the thunder of nightsticks on the steel-sheathed panels, finally the trap-drum staccato of machine-gun bullets rattling on the metal barricade.

Too late to look for help that way, we knew. The door was latched and bolted, and barred with a locked chain, and a geyser of live flame was spurting upward round it, for the wooden walls were now ablaze, outlining the fireproof door in a frame of death.

Now the oil-soaked carpet had begun to burn; red tongues of flame and curling snakes of smoke were darting hungrily about our feet.

"On!" cried de Grandin. "It is the only way! They must have planned this method of defense in case of raid; surely they have left a rathole for their own escape!"

His guess seemed right, for only round the altar were the flames held back, though even there they were beginning to make progress.

Sleeves held before our faces for such poor protection as they gave, we stumbled toward the altar through the choking smoke. A big, cowled man rose out of nowhere in my path, and aimed a blow at me. Scarce knowing what I did I struck at him, felt the sharp point of my hunting knife sink into the soft flesh of his axilla, felt the warm blood spurt upon my hand as his artery was severed, and—rushed on. I was no longer Samuel Trowbridge, staid, middle-aged practitioner of medicine, I was not even a man, I was a snarling, elemental beast, alive to only one desire, to save myself at any cost; to butcher anything that barred my path.

We lurched and stumbled up the stairway leading to the altar, for there the smoke was somewhat thinner, the flames a trifle less intense. "*Succès*," de Grandin cried, "the way lies here, my friends—this is the exit from their *sacré* burrow! Follow on; I can already see—

"*Qui diable?*" He started back his pistol flashing in the firelight.

Behind the altar, looming dimly through the swirling smoke, a man's shape bulked. One glance identified him. It was the big, young, white-haired man Costello had knocked unconscious to save Renouard an hour or so before.

In his arms he held the fainting form of Alice Hume.

16. Framed

"HANDS UP!" DE GRANDIN barked. "Elevate your hands or—"

"Don't be an utter ass," the other advised tartly. "Can't you see my hands are full?" Displaying no more respect for the Frenchman's pistol than if it had been a pointed finger, he turned on his heel, then flung across his shoulder as a sort of afterthought, "if you want to save your hides a scorching you'd best be coming this way. There's a stairway here—at least, there was fifteen minutes ago."

"*Fanons d'un corbeau*, he is cool, this one!" de Grandin muttered with grudging admiration, treading close upon the stranger's heels.

Sandwiched between our building and the next was a narrow, spiral stairway, a type of covered fire escape long since declared illegal by the city. Down this the stranger led us, de Grandin close behind him, his pistol ready, his flashlight playing steadily on the other's back. "One false step and I fire," he warned as we descended the dark staircase.

"Oh be quiet," snapped our guide. "One false step and I'll break my silly neck! Don't talk so much, you make me nervous."

Two paces ahead of us, he paused at the stairway's bottom, kicked a metal firedoor open, then drew aside to let us pass. We found ourselves in a narrow alleyway, darker than a moonless midnight, but with a single feeble spot of light diluting the blackness at its farther end, where the weak rays of a flickering gas street lamp battled with the gloom.

"Now what?" the little Frenchman asked. "Why do we stand here like a flock of silly sheep afraid to enter through a gate? Why—"

"S-s-st!" our guide's sharp hiss shut him off. "I think they're waiting for us out there, they—ha? I knew it!"

The faintly glowing reflection of the street lamp's light was shut off momentarily as a man's form bulked in the alley exit.

De Grandin tapped me on the arm. "Elle est nue—she has no protection from the chill," he whispered with a nod toward Alice. "Will you not put your robe upon her? I shall require mine for disguise a little longer, or—"

"All right," I answered, slipping off my scarlet cassock and draping it about the girl's nude loveliness while the man who held her in his arms assisted me with quick, deft hands.

"Dimitri—Franz?" a voice called cautiously from the alley entrance. "Are you there? Have you brought the Bride?"

For a moment we were silent, then: "Yes," our companion answered thickly, as though he spoke with something in his mouth, "she's here, but—"

His answer broke abruptly, and I felt rather than saw him shift the girl's weight to his left arm as he fumbled under his coat with his right hand.

"But what?" the hail came sharply. "Is she injured? You know the penalty if harm comes to her. Come here!"

"Here, take her," the stranger whispered, thrusting Alice into my arms. To de Grandin: "How about that pistol you've been so jolly anxious to shoot off, got it ready?"

"Certainement. Et puis?" the Frenchman answered.

"All right; look lively—this way!"

Silently as shadows the three of them, de Grandin, the stranger and Renouard, crept down the alley, leaving me to follow with the fainting girl as best I could.

Just inside the entrance to the passageway the stranger, spoke again: "The Bride is safe, but—" Once more his thick speech halted; then, "Franz is hurt; he can not walk well, and—"

"Then kill him, and be quick!" the sharp command came back. "None must fall into their hands alive. Quick; shoot him, and bring the Bride, the car is waiting!"

A muffled shot sounded, followed by a groan, then: "Bring the Prophetess at once!" came the angry command. "What are you waiting for—"

"Only for you, old thing!" With a booming shout of mingled exultation and hilarity, the strange man leaped suddenly from the shadow of the alley's mouth, seized his interrogator in his arms and dragged him back to the shelter of the passageway's arched entrance.

"Hold him, Frenchy!" he commanded. "Don't let him get away; he's—"

A spurting dart of flame stabbed through the darkness and a sharp report was followed by the viscious *whin-n-ng!* of a ricocheting bullet which glanced from the vaulted roof and whined past me in the dark.

I crouched to the cement pavement, involuntarily putting myself between the firing and the girl in my arms. A second report sounded, like an echo of the first, followed by a screaming cry which ended in a choking groan, then the sound of running feet.

"That's one who'll never slit another throat," the stranger remarked casually.

I waited for a moment, then, as there seemed no further danger to my unconscious charge, rose and joined the others. "What happened?" I asked.

"Oh, as we were escaping from the fire up there this poor fellow came to help us, and this other one shot him," the unknown man replied coolly. "Rankest piece of cold-blooded murder I ever saw. Positively revoltin'. Eh, Frenchy?"

"But certainly," de Grandin agreed. "He shot the noble fellow down *à froid.* Oh, yes; I saw it with my own two eyes."

"I, too," Renouard supplemented.

"Are you crazy?" I demanded. "I saw one of you grapple with this man, then when the other shot at you, you returned his fire, and—"

A kick which nearly broke my tibia was delivered to my shin. "*Ah bah,* how could you see, my friend?" de Grandin asked me almost angrily. "You were back there with Mademoiselle Alice, and the night is dark. I tell you this so estimable, noble fellow would have aided us, had not this vile miscreant assassinated him. He would have killed us, too—all three of us—had not *Monsieur*—er— this gentleman, gallantly gone forth and pulled him down with his bare hands at peril of his life. Yes, of course. That is how it was. See, here is the weapon with which the wicked murder was committed."

"Right-o, and ain't it unfortunate that it's a German gun?" the stranger added. "They'll never be able to trace it by its serial number, now. However, we're all eyewitnesses, to the crime, and any ballistics expert will be able to match the bullet and the gun. So—"

"But you fired that shot!" I accused.

"I?" his tone was pregnant with injured innocence. "Why, I didn't have a weapon—"

"*Mais certainement,*" de Grandin, chimed in eagerly, "the sergeant took his weapon from him when they had their so unfortunate misunderstanding in the street." In a fierce whisper he added: "Learn to hold your tongue in matters not concerning you, my friend. *Regardez!*" He turned his flashlight full upon the prisoner's face.

It was the red priest.

The bellowing halloo of a fire engine's siren sounded from the other street, followed by the furious clanging of a gong. "Come," de Grandin ordered. "The fire brigade has come to fight the flames, and we must find Costello. I hope the noble fellow came to no harm as he tried to rescue us."

"Glory be, Doctor de Grandin, sor!" Costello cried as we rounded the corner and returned to the street from which we had entered the temple an hour or so earlier. "We waited for ye till we figgered ye'd been unable to signal, then went in to git ye; but th' murtherin' divils had barred th' door an' set th' place afire—be gob, I thought ye'd 'a' been cremated before this?"

"Not I," de Grandin answered with a chuckle. "It is far from so, I do assure you. But see, we have not come back empty-handed. Here, safe in good friend Trowbridge's arms, is she whom we did seek, and here"—he pointed to the red priest who struggled futilely in the big stranger's grasp—"here is one I wish you to lock up immediately. The charge is murder. Renouard and I, as well as this gentleman, will testify against him."

"Howly Moses! Who the divil let *you* out?" the sergeant demanded, as he caught sight of our strange ally. "I thought they put the bracelets on ye, an'—"

"They did," the other interrupted with a grin, "but I didn't think such jewelry was becoming to my special brand of homeliness, so I slipped 'em off and went to take a walk—"

"Oh, ye did, eh? Well, young felly, me lad, ye can be afther walkin' right, straight back, or—"

"But no!" de Grandin cut in quickly. "I shall be responsible for him, my sergeant. He is a noble fellow. It was he who guided us from the burning building, and at the great peril of his life seized this wicked one and wrenched his pistol from him when he would have killed us. Oh, yes: I can most confidently vouch for him.

"Come to Doctor Trowbridge's when you have put that so wicked man all safely in the jail," he added as we made off toward my car. "We shall have much to tell you."

"But it was the only way, *mon vieux*," de Grandin patiently explained as we drove homeward. "Their strategy was perfect—or almost so. But for good luck and this so admirable young man, we should have lost them altogether. Consider: When they set fire to that old building it burned like tinder; even now the fire brigade fights in vain to save it. With it will be utterly destroyed all evidences of their vile crimes, the paraphernalia of their secret worship—even the bones of their little victims.

"When their leader fell into our hands we had no single shred of evidence to hold him; he had simply to deny all we said, and the authorities must let him go, for where was proof of what he did? Nowhere, *parbleu*—it was burned up! Of course. But circumstances so fell out that we killed one of his companions. *Voilà*, our chance had come! We had been wooden-heads not to have grasped it. So we conspire to forswear his life. As the good Costello would express it, we have put the frame around him. It is illegal, I admit, yet it is justice. You yourself know he did slay a little baby boy, yet you know we can not prove he did it; for none of us beheld the little corpse, and it is now but a pile of ashes mixed with other ashes. How many more like it there may be we do not surely know, but from what poor Mademoiselle Abigail told us, we know of one, at least.

"And must they die all unavenged? Must we stand by and see that spawn of hell, that devil's priest go free because as the lawyers say, the *corpus deliciti* of his crimes can not be established for want of the small corpses? *Non, cordieu*, I say it shall not be! While he may not suffer legally for the murders which he did, the law has seized him—and *pardieu*, the law will punish him for a crime he did not do. It may not be the law, my friend; but it is justice. Surely, you agree?"

"I suppose so," I replied, "but somehow it doesn't seem—"

"Of course it does," he broke in smilingly, as though a simple matter had been settled. "Our next great task is to revive Mademoiselle Alice, make her as comfortable as may be, then notify her grieving fiancé that she is found. *Parbleu*, it will be like a tonic to see that young man's face when we inform him we have found her!"

17. "Hiji"

ALICE WAS REGAINING CONSCIOUSNESS as de Grandin and I carried her upstairs and laid her on the guest-room bed. More accurately, she was no longer in a state of actual swoon, for her eyes were open, but her whole being seemed submerged in a state of lethargy so profound that she was scarcely able to move her eyes and gaze incuriously about the room.

"Mademoiselle," de Grandin, whispered soothingly, "you are with friends. Nothing can harm you now. No one may order you to do that which you do not wish to do. You are safe."

"Safe," the girl repeated. It was not a query, not an assertion; merely a repetition, parrotwise, of de Grandin's final word.

She gazed at us with fixed, unquestioning eyes, like a newborn infant, or an imbecile. Her face was blank as an unwritten sheet.

The little Frenchman gave her a quick, sharp glance, half surprised, half speculative. "But certainly," he answered. "You know us, do you not? We are your friends, Doctor Trowbridge, Doctor de Grandin."

"Doctor Trowbridge, Doctor de Grandin." Again that odd, phonographic repetition, incurious, disinterested, mechanical, meaningless.

She lay before us on the bed, still as she had lain upon the devil's altar, only the gentle motion of her breast and the half-light in her eyes telling us she was alive at all.

The Frenchman put his hand out and brushed the hair back from her cheeks, exposing her ears. Both lobes had been bored to receive the golden loops of the earrings she had worn, and the holes pierced through the flesh were large enough to accommodate moderately thick knitting needles; yet the surrounding tissue was not inflamed, nor, save for a slight redness, was there any sign of granulation round the wounds. "Electrocautery," he told me softly. "They are modern in their methods, those ones, at any rate. Observe here, also, if you please—"

Following his tracing forefinger with my eyes, I saw a row of small, deep-pitted punctures in the white skin of her forearms. "Good heavens!" I exclaimed. "Morphine? Why, there are dozens of incisions! They must have given her enough to—"

He raised his hand for silence, gazing intently at the girl's expressionless, immobile face.

"*Mademoiselle*," he ordered sharply, "on the table yonder you will find matches. Rise, go to them, take one and light it; then hold your finger in the flame while you count three. When that is done, you may come back to bed. *Allez!*"

She turned her oddly lifeless gaze on him as he pronounced his orders. Somehow, it seemed to me, reflected in her eyes his commands were like writing appearing supernaturally, a spirit-message on a medium's blank slate. Recorded, somehow, in her intelligence—or, rather, perceptivity—they in nowise altered the paper-blankness of her face.

Docilely, mechanically and unquestioningly, like one who walks in sleep, she rose from the bed, paced slowly across the room, took up the tray of matches and struck one.

"Hold!" de Grandin cried abruptly as she thrust her finger in the flame, but the order came a thought too late.

"One," she counted deliberately as the cruel fire licked her ivory hand, then obedient to his latest order, removed her finger, already beginning to glow angry-red with exposure to the flame, blew out the match, turned slowly, and retraced her steps. Not a word or inarticulate expression, not even by involuntary wincing, did she betray rebellion at his orders or consciousness of the sharp pain she must have felt.

"No, my friend," he turned to me, as though answering an unspoken question, "it was not morphine—then. But it must be so now. Quick, prepare and give a hypodermic of three-quarters of a grain as soon as is convenient. In that way she will sleep, and not be able to respond to orders such as mine—or worse."

Wonderingly I mixed the opiate and administered it, and de Grandin prepared a soothing unguent to bandage her burned finger. "It was heroic treatment," he apologized as he wound the surgical gauze deftly round her hand, "but something drastic was required to substantiate my theory. Otherwise I could not have rested."

"How do you mean?" I asked curiously.

"Tell me, my friend," he answered irrelevantly, fixing me with his level, unwinking stare, "have not you a feeling—have not you felt that Mademoiselle Alice, whatever might have been her provocation, was at least in some way partly guilty with those murderers who killed the little helpless babes in Satan's worship? Have not you—"

"Yes!" I interrupted. "I *did* feel so, although I hesitated to express it. You see, I've known her all her life, and was very fond of her, but—well, it seemed to me that though she were in fear of death, or even torture, the calm way in which she accepted everything, even the murder of that helpless child—confound it, that got under my skin! When we think how poor Abigail Kimble sacrificed her life rather than endure the sight of such a heartless crime, I can't help but compare the way Alice has taken everything, and—"

"*Précisément*," he broke in with a laugh. "I, too, felt so, and so I did experiment to prove that we were wrong. Mademoiselle Abigail—the good God rest her soul!—was herself, in full possession of her faculties, while Mademoiselle Alice was the victim of *scopolamine apomophia*."

"*Scopolamine apomophia?*" I repeated blankly.

"*Mais certainement*; I am sure of it."

"Isn't that the so-called 'truth serum'?"

"*Précisément*."

"But I thought that had been discredited as a medical imposture—"

"For the purpose for which it was originally advertised, yes." he agreed. "Originally it was claimed that it could lead a criminal to confess his crimes when questioned by the officers, and in that it failed, but only because of its mechanical limitations.

"*Scopolamine apomophia* has a tendency to so throw the nervous system out of gear that it greatly lessens what we call the inhibitions, tearing down the warning signs which nature puts along the road of action. Subjected to its action, the criminal's caution, that cunning which warns him to refrain from talking lest he betray himself, is greatly lessened, for his volition is practically nullified. But that is not enough. No. Under *scopolamine apomophia*, if the injection be strong enough, he will repeat what is said to him, but that is not 'confession' as the law demands it. It is but parroting the accusation of the officers. So it has been discredited for judicial use.

"But for the purpose which those evil ones desired it was perfect. With a large dose of *scopolamine apomophia* injected in her veins, Mademoiselle Alice became their unresisting tool. She had no will nor wish nor consciousness except as they desired. Her mind was but a waxen record on which they wrote directions, and as the record reproduces words when placed upon the phonograph, so she reacted blindly to their orders.

"*Par exemple*: They dose her with the serum of *scopolamine apomophia*. They say to her, 'You will array yourself in such a way, and when the word is given you will stand thus before the altar, you will abase yourself in this wise, you will cross yourself so. Then you will permit the women to disrobe you until you stand all nude before the people, but you will not feel embarrassed. No. You will thereon mount the altar and lay yourself upon it as it were a bed and stay there till we bid you rise.'

"And as they have commanded, so she does. Did you not note the similarity of her walk and general bearing when she crossed the room a moment hence and when she stood before the altar of the devil?"

"Yes," I agreed, "I did."

"*Très bon*. I thought as much. Therefore, when I saw those marks upon her arms and recognized them as the trail of hypodermic needles, I said to me: 'Jules de Grandin, it are highly probably that *scopolamine apomophia* has been used on her.' And I replied, 'It are wholly likely, Jules de Grandin.'

"Very well, then. Let us experiment. It has been some time since she was dosed with this medicine which steals her volition, yet her look and bearing and the senseless manner she repeats our words back at us reminds me greatly of one whom I had seen in Paris when the gendarmes had administered *scopolamine apomophia* to him.

"*Bien alors*, I did bid her rise and hurt herself. Only a person whose instinct of self-preservation has been blocked would go and put his hand in living flame merely because another told him to, *n'est-ce-pas*?

"Yet she did do it, and without protest. As calmly as though I requested that she eat a bonbon, she rose and crossed the room and thrust her so sweet finger into searing flame. *La pauvre!* I did hate myself to see her do it, yet I knew that unless she did I must inevitably hate her. The case is proved, good Friend Trowbridge. We have no need to feel resentful toward her. The one we saw bow down before the devil's altar, the one we saw take part in their vile rites, was not our Mademoiselle Alice. No, by no means, it was but her poor image, the flesh which she is clothed in. The real girl whom we sought, and whom we brought away with us, was absent, for her personality, her consciousness and volition were stolen by those evil men exactly as they stole the little boys they slew upon the altar of the devil."

I nodded, much relieved. His argument was convincing, and I was eager to be convinced.

"Now we have sunk her in a sleep of morphine, she will rest easily," he finished. "Later we shall see how she progresses, and if conditions warrant it, tomorrow young John Davisson shall once more hold his *amoureuse* against his heart. Yes. That will be a happy day for me.

"Shall we rejoin the others? We have much to talk about; and that Renouard, how well I know him! The bottle will be empty if we do not hasten!"

"SO I HANGED THE blighters out of hand," the stranger was telling Renouard as de Grandin and I rejoined them in the study.

"Admirable. Superb. I approve," Renouard returned, then rose and bowed with jack-knife formality to the stranger, de Grandin and me in turn. "Jules, Doctor Trowbridge," he announced, "permit that I make you acquaint with Monsieur le Baron Ingraham, late of His Majesty's *gendarmerie* in Sierra Leone—Monsieur le Baron, Doctor Jules de Grandin, Doctor Trowbridge. I am Inspector Renouard of the *Service-Sûreté*."

Smilingly the stranger acknowledged the introductions, adding: "It ain't quite as bad as the Inspector makes it out, gentlemen. My pater happened to leave me a baronetcy—with no money to support the title—but you'd hardly call me a baron, I fear. As to the *gendarmerie*, I was captain in the Sierra Leone Frontier Police, but—"

"Exactly, precisely, quite so," Renouard interjected. "It is as I said. Monsieur le Baron's experiences strangely parallel my own. Tell them, if you please Monsieur le Bar—?"

"Give over!" cried the other sharply. "I can't have you Monsieur le Baroning me all over the place, you know—it gives me the hump! My sponsors in baptism named me Haddingway Ingraham Jameson Ingraham—H-I-J-I, you know—and I'm known in the service as 'Hiji.' Why not compromise on that— we're all policemen here, I take it?"

"All but Doctor Trowbridge, who has both the courage and the wit to qualify," de Grandin answered. "Now, Monsieur Hiji, you were about to tell Inspector Renouard—" He paused with upraised eyebrows.

The big Englishman produced a small, black pipe and a tin of Three Nuns, slowly tamped tobacco in the briar and eyed us quizzically. He was even bigger than I'd thought at first, and despite his prematurely whitened hair, much younger than I'd estimated. Thirty-one or -two at most, I guessed. "How strong is your credulity?" he asked at length.

"*Parbleu*, it is marvelous, magnificent," declared de Grandin. "We can believe that which we know is false, if you can prove it to us!"

"It'll take a lot of believing," Ingraham answered, "but it's all true, just the same.

"A year or so ago, about the time Inspector Renouard was beginning to investigate the missing girls, queer rumors began trickling back to Freetown from the Reserved Forest Areas. We've always had leopard societies in the back country—gangs of cannibals who disguise themselves as leopards and go out stalking victims for their ritual feasts—of course, but this seemed something rather new. Someone was stirring up the natives to a *poro*—an oath-bound resistance to government. The victims of the latest leopard outrages were men who failed to subscribe to the rebellion. Several village headmen and sub-chiefs had been popped into the pot by the leopard men, and the whole area was getting in an awful state of funk.

"Nobody wants to go up in the Reserved Forests, so they sent me. 'Let good old Hiji do it; Hiji's the lad for this show!' they said; so I took a dozen Houssa policemen, two Lewis guns and ten pounds or so of quinine and set out.

"Ten days back in the brush we ran across the leopards' spoor. We'd stopped at a Mendi village and I sent word forward for the headman to come out. He didn't come.

"That wasn't so good. If I waited too long for him outside the place I'd lose face; if I went in to him after summoning him to come to me; he would have 'put shame on me.' Finally I compromised by going in alone.

"The chief lolled before his hut with his warriors and women around him, and it didn't take more than half an eye to see he'd placed no seat for me.

"'I see you, Chief,' I told him, swaggering, forward with the best assurance I could summon. I also saw that he was wearing a string of brummagem beads about his neck, as were most of his warriors, and wondered at it, for no license had been issued to a trader recently, and we'd had no reports of white men in the section for several years.

"'I see you, white man,' he replied, but made no move to rise or offer me a seat.

"'Why do you thus put shame upon the King-Emperor's representative?' I demanded.

"'We want no dealings with the Emperor-King, or any of his men,' the fellow answered. 'The land is ours, the English have no right here; we will have no more of him.' The patter rattled off his tongue as glibly as though he had been a soap-box orator preaching communism in Hyde Park.

"This was rank sedition, not at all the sort of thing to be countenanced, you know, so I went right for the blighter. 'Get up from there, you unholy rotter,' I ordered, 'and tell your people you have spoken with a crooked tongue, or—'

"It was a lucky thing for me I'm handy with my feet. A spear came driving at me, missing me by less than half an inch, and another followed it, whistling past my head so close I felt the wind of it.

"Fortunately, my men were hiding just outside, and Bendingo, my half-caste Arab sergeant, was a willing worker with the Enfield. He shot the foremost spearman through the head before the fellow had a chance to throw a second weapon, and the other men began to shoot before you could say, 'knife.' It was a gory business, and we'd rather killed half the poor beggars before they finally called it quits.

"The chief was most apologetic when the fracas ended, of course, and swore he had been misled by white men who spoke with crooked tongues.

"This was interesting. It seemed, from what the beggar told me, there had been several white men wandering at large through the area distributing what would be equivalent to radical literature at home—preaching armed and violent rebellion to government and all that sort of thing. Furthermore, they'd told the natives the brummagem beads they gave 'em would act as 'medicine' against the white man's bullets, and that no one need fear to raid a mission station or refuse to pay the hut-tax, for England had been overthrown and only a handful of Colonial administrators remained—no army to come to their rescue if the natives were to rise and wipe 'em out.

"This was bad enough, but worse was coming. It appeared these playful little trouble-makers were preaching miscegenation. This was something new. The natives had never regarded themselves as inferior beings, for it's strictly against regulations to say or do anything tending to do more than make 'em respect the whites as agents of the government, but they'd never—save in the rarest instances—attempted to take white women. Oh, yes they killed 'em sometimes, often with torture, but that was simply part of the game—no chivalry, you know. But these white agitators were deliberately urging the Timni, Mendis and Sulima to raid settlements and mission stations and spare the women that they might be carried off as prizes.

"That was plenty. Right there the power of the British rule had to be shown, so I rounded up all the villagers who hadn't taken to the woods, told 'em they'd been misled by lying white men whom I'd hang as soon as caught, then strung the chief up to the nearest oil-palm. His neck muscles were inordinately strong and he died in circumstances of considerable elaboration and discomfort, but the object lesson was worth while. There'd be no more defiance of a government agent by *that* gang.

"We were balked at every turn. Most of our native informers had been killed and eaten, and the other blacks were sullen. Not a word could we get from 'em regarding leopard depredations, and they shut up like a lot of clams when we asked about the white trouble-makers.

"We'd never have gotten anywhere if it hadn't been for Old Man Anderson. He was a Wesleyan missionary who ran a little chapel and clinic 'way up by the French border. His wife and daughter helped him. He might have loved his God; he certainly had a strange love for his womenfolk to bring 'em into that stinkin' hellhole.

"It was a month after our brush with the Mendi when we crashed through the jungle to Anderson's. The place was newly raided, burned and leveled to the ground, ashes still warm. What was left of the old man we found by the burned chapel—all except his head. They'd taken that away for a souvenir. We found the bodies of several of his converts, too. They'd been flayed, their skins stripped off as you'd turn off a glove. His wife and daughter were nowhere to be found.

"They hadn't taken any special pains to cover up their tracks, and we followed at a forced march. We came upon 'em three days later.

"The blighters had eaten 'emselves loggy, and drunk enough trade-gin to float the *Berengaria*, so they didn't offer much resistance when we charged. I'd always thought a man who slaughtered unresisting enemies was a rotten beast, but the memory of old Anderson's dismembered body and those pink, skinless corpses made me revise my notion. We came upon 'em unawares, opened with the Lewis guns from both sides of the village and didn't sound cease firin' till the dead lay round like logwood corded in a lumber camp. Then, and not till then, we went in.

"We found old Mrs. Anderson dead, but still warm. She'd—I think you can imagine what she'd been through, gentlemen.

"We found the daughter, too. Not quite dead.

"In the four days since her capture she'd been abused by more than a hundred men, black and white, and was barely breathing when we came on her. She—"

"White and black, *Monsieur?*" de Grandin interrupted.

"Right-o. The raiding party had been led by whites. Five of 'em. Stripped off their clothes and put on native ornaments, carried native weapons, and led the blacks in their hellish work. Indeed, I don't believe the poor black beggars would have gone out against the 'Jesus Papa' if those white hellions hadn't set 'em up to it.

"They'd regarded Rebekah Anderson as good as dead, and made no secret of their work: The leader was a Russian, so were two of his assistants. A fourth was Polish and the last some sort of Asiatic—a Turk, the poor child thought.

"They'd come up through Liberia, penetrated the Protectorate and set the natives up to devilment, finally organizing the raid on Anderson's. Now their work was done, and they were on their way.

"She heard the leader say he was going to America, for in Harrisonville, New Jersey, the agents of his society had found a woman whom they sought and who would lead some sort of movement against organized religion. The poor kid didn't understand it all—no more did I—but she heard it, and remembered.

"The white men had left the night before, striking east into French Guinea on their way to the coast, and leaving her as a plaything for the natives.

"Before the poor child died she told me the Russian in command had been a man with a slender, almost boyish body, but with the wrinkled face of an old man. She'd seen him stripped for action, you know, and was struck by the strange contrast of his face and body.

"One other thing she told me: When they got to America they intended holding meetings of their damned society, and the road to their rendezvous would be directed by pictures of the Devil with his pitchfork pointing the way the person seeking it should take. She didn't understand, of course, but—I had all the clues I wanted, and as soon as we got back to Freetown I got a leave of absence to hunt that foul murderer down and bring him to justice."

The young man paused a moment to relight his pipe, and there was something far from pleasant in his lean and sun-burned face as he continued: "Rebekah Anderson went to her grave like an old Sumerian queen. I impounded every man who'd had a hand in the raid and put 'em to work diggin' a grave for her, then a big, circular trench around it. Then I hanged 'em and dumped their carcasses into the trench to act as guard of honor for the girl they'd killed. You couldn't bribe a native to go near the place, now.

"I was followin' the little pictures of the Devil when Renouard set on me. I mistook him for one of 'em of course, and—well, it's a lucky thing for all of us Costello bashed me when he did."

De Grandin's little, round blue eyes were alight with excitement and appreciation. "And how did you escape, *Monsieur?*" he asked.

The Englishman laughed shortly. "Got a pair of handcuffs?" he demanded.

"I have," supplied Renouard.

"Lock 'em on me."

The manacles clicked round his wrists and he turned to us with a grin. "Absolutely no deception, gentlemen, nothing concealed in the hands, nothing up the sleeves," he announced in a droning sing-song, then, as easily as though slipping them through his shirt sleeves, drew his hands through the iron bracelets. "Just a matter of small bones and limber muscles," he added with another smile. "Being double-jointed helps some, too. It was no trick at all to slip the darbies off when the constables joined Costello for the raid. I put the irons on the other person—locked 'em on his ankles—so the boys would find 'em when they came back to the motor."

"But—" Renouard began, only to pause with the next word half uttered. From upstairs came a quavering little frightened cry, like the tremulous call of a screech-owl or of a child in mortal terror.

"No noise!" de Grandin warned as he leaped from his seat and bounded up the stairway three steps at a time, Renouard and Ingraham close behind him.

We raced on tiptoe down the upper hall and paused a second by the bed-room door; then de Grandin kicked it open.

Alice crouched upon the bed, half raised upon one elbow, her other arm bent guardingly across her face. The red robe we had put upon her when we fled the Devil's temple had fallen back, revealing her white throat and whiter breast, her loosened hair fell across her shoulders.

Close by the open window, like a beast about to spring, crouched a man. Despite his changed apparel, his heavy coat and tall, peaked cap of astrakhan, we recognized him in a breath. Those big, sad eyes fixed on the horror-stricken girl, that old and wrinkle-bitten face, could be none other's than the red priest's. His slender, almost womanish hands were clenched to talons, every muscle of his little, spare frame was taut—stretched harp-string tight for the leap he poised to make. Yet there was no malignancy—hardly any interest—in his old, close-wrinkled face. Rather, it seemed to me, he looked at her a gaze of brooding speculation.

"*Parbleu, Monsieur du Diable*, you honor us too much; this call was wholly unexpected!" de Grandin said, as he stepped quickly forward.

Quick as he was, the other man was quicker. One glance—one murderous glance which seemed to focus all the hate and fury of a thwarted soul—he cast upon the Frenchman, then leaped back through the window.

Crash! de Grandin's pistol-shot seemed like a clap of thunder in the room as he fired at the retreating form, and a second shot sped through the window as the intruder landed on the snow below and staggered toward the street.

"Winged him, by Jove!" the Englishman cried exultantly. "Nice shooting, Frenchy!"

"Nice be damned and roasted on the grates of hell—" de Grandin answered furiously. "Is he not free?"

They charged downstairs, leaving me to comfort Alice, and I heard their voices as they searched the yard. Ten minutes later they returned, breathing heavily from their efforts, but empty-handed.

"Slipped through us like an eel!" the Englishman exclaimed. "Must have had a motor waiting at the curb, and—"

"*Sacré nom d'un nom d'un nom!*" de Grandin stormed. "What are they thinking of, those stupid-heads? Is not he charged with murder? Yes, *pardieu*, yet they let him roam about at will, and—it is monstrous; it is vile; it is not to be endured!"

Snatching up the telephone he called police headquarters, then: "What means this, Sergeant?" he demanded when Costello answered. "We sit here like four *sacré* fools and think ourselves secure, and that one—that so vile murderer—comes breaking in the house and—what? *Pas possible!*"

"It is, sor," we heard Costello's answer as de Grandin held the receiver from his ear. "That bur-rd ye handed me is in 'is cell this minute, an' furthermore, he's been there every second since we locked 'im up!"

18. Reunion

LOOKING VERY CHARMING AND demure in a suit of Jules de Grandin's lavender pajamas and his violet silk dressing-gown, Alice Hume lay upon the chaise-lounge in the bedroom, toying with a grapefruit and poached egg. "If you'd send for Mother, please," she told us. "I'd feel so much better. You see"— her voice shook slightly and a look of horror flickered in her eyes—"you see there are some things I want to tell her—some advice I'd like to get—before you let John see me, and—why, what's the matter?" She put the breakfast tray upon the tabouret and looked at us in quick concern. "Mother—there's nothing wrong, is there? She's not ill? Oh—"

"My child," de Grandin answered softly, "your dear mother never will again be ill. You shall see her, certainly; but not until God's great tomorrow dawns. She is—"

"Not—*dead?*" the word was formed rather than spoken, by the girl's pale lips.

The little Frenchman nodded slowly.

"When? How?"

"The night you—you went away, *ma pauvre*. It was murder."

"Murder?" slowly, unbelievingly, she repeated. "But that *can't* be! Who'd want to murder my poor mother?"

De Grandin's voice was level, almost toneless. "The same unconscionable knaves who stole you from the marriage altar," he returned. "They either feared she knew too much of family history—knew something of the origin of David Hume—or else they wished all earthly ties you had with home and kindred to be severed. At any rate, they killed her. They did it subtly, in such a manner that it was thought suicide, but it was murder, none the less."

"O-oh!" The girl's faint moan was pitiful, hopeless. "Then I'm all alone, all, all alone—I've no one in the world to—"

"You have your *fiancé*, the good young Monsieur Jean," the Frenchman told her softly. "You also have Friend Trowbridge, as good and staunch a friend as ever was, then there is Jules de Grandin. We shall not fail you in your need, my small one."

For a moment she regarded us distractedly, then suddenly put forth her hands, one to Jules de Grandin, one to me. "Oh, good, kind friends," she whispered. "Please help me, if you can. God knows I am in need of help, if ever woman was, for I'm as foul a murderess as ever suffered death. I was accessory to those little children's murders—I was—oh—what was it that the lepers used to cry? 'Unclean'? Oh, God, I am unclean, unclean—not fit to breathe the air with decent men! Not fit to marry John! How could *I* bring children into the world? I who have been accessory to the murder of those little innocents?" She clenched her little hands to fists and beat them on her breast, her tear-filled eyes turned upward as though petitioning pardon for unpardonable sin. "Unclean, unclean!" she wailed. Her breath came slowly, like that of a dumb animal which resents the senseless persistency of pain.

"What is that you say? A murderess—*you?*" de Grandin shot back shortly.

"Yes—I. I lay there on their altar while they brought those little boys and cut their—oh, I didn't want to do it, I didn't want them to be killed; but I lay there just the same and let them do it—I never raised a finger to prevent it!"

De Grandin took a deep breath. "You are mistaken, *Mademoiselle*," he answered softly. "You were in a drugged condition; the victim of a vicious Oriental drug. In that all-helpless state one sees visions, unpleasant visions, like the figments of a naughty dream. There were no little boys; no murders were committed while you lay thus upon the Devil's altar. It was a seeming, an illusion, staged for the edification of those wicked men and women who made their prayer to Satan. In the olden days, when such things were, they sacrificed small boys upon the altar of the Devil, but this is now; even those who are far gone in sin would halt at such abominations. They were but waxen simulacra, mute, senseless reproductions of small boys, and though they went through all the horrid rite of murder, they let no blood, they did perform no killings. No; certainly not." Jules de Grandin, physician, soldier and policeman, was lying like the gallant gentleman he was, and lying most convincingly.

"But I heard their screams—I heard them call for help, then strangle in their blood!" the girl protested.

"All an illusion, *ma chère*," the little Frenchman answered. "It was a ventriloqual trick. At the conclusion of the ceremony the good Trowbridge and I would have sworn we heard a terrible, thick voice conversing with the priest upon the altar; that also was a juggler's trick, intended to impress the congregation. *Non, ma chere*, your conscience need not trouble you at all; you are no accessory to a murder. As to the rest, it was no fault of yours; you were their prisoner and the helpless slave of wicked drugs; what you did was done with the body, not the soul. There is no reason why you should not wed, I tell you."

She looked at him with tear-dimmed eyes. Though she had mastered her first excess of emotion, her slender fingers clasped and unclasped nervously and she returned his steady gaze with something of the vague, half-believing apprehension of a child. "You're sure?" she asked.

"Sure?" he echoed. "To be sure I am sure, *Mademoiselle*. Remember, if you please, I am Jules de Grandin; I do not make mistakes.

"Come, calm yourself. Monsieur Jean will be here at any moment; then—"

He broke off, closing his eyes and standing in complete silence. Then he put his fingers to his pursed lips and from them plucked a kiss and tossed it upward toward the ceiling. "*Mon dieu*," he murmured rapturously, "*la passion delicieuse*, is it not magnificent?"

"Alice! Alice, beloved—" Young Davisson's voice faltered as he rushed into the room and took the girl into his arms. "When they told me that they'd found you at last, I could hardly believe—I knew they were doing everything but—" Again his speech halted for very pressure of emotion.

"Oh, my dear!" Alice took his face between her palms and looked into his worshipping eyes. "My dear, you've come to me again, but—" She turned from him, and fresh, hot tears lay upon her lashes.

"No buts, *Mademoiselle!*" de Grandin almost shouted. "Remember what I said. Take Love when he comes to you, my little friends; oh, do not make excuses to turn him out of doors—hell waits for those who do so! There is no obstacle to your union, believe me when I say so. Take my advice and have the good *curé* come here this very day, I beg you!"

Both Davisson and Alice looked at him amazed, for he was fairly shaking with emotion. He waved a hand impatiently. "Do not look so, make no account of doubts or fears or feelings of unworthiness!" he almost raged. "Behold me, if you please; an empty shell, a soulless shadow of a man, a being with no aim in life, no home nor fireside to bid him welcome when he has returned from duty! Is that the way to live? *Mille fois non*, I shall say not, but—"

"I let Love pass me by, my friends, and have regretted it but once, and that once all my aimless, empty life. *Écoutez-moi!* In the springtime of our youth we met, sweet Héloise and I, beside the River Loire. I was a student at the Sorbonne, my military service yet to come; she cher Dieu, was an angel out of Paradise!

"Beside the silver stream we played together; we lay beneath the poplar trees, we rowed upon the river; we waded barefoot in the shallows. Yes, and when we finished wading she plucked cherries, red ripe cherries from the trees, and twined their stems about her toes, and gave me her white feet to kiss. I ate the cherries from her feet and kissed her toes, one kiss for every cherry, one cherry for each kiss. And when we said *bonne nuit—mon Dieu*, to kiss and cling and shudder in such ecstasy once more!

"Alas, my several times great grandsire, he whose honored name I bore, had cut and hacked his way through raging Paris on the night of August 24 in

1572—how long his bones have turned to ashes in the family tomb—while her ancestors had worn the white brassard and cross, crying, 'Messe ou mort! A bas les Huguenots!'"

He paused a moment and raised his shoulders in a shrug of resignation. "It might not be," he ended sadly. "Her father would have none of me, my family forbade the thought of marriage. I might have joined her in her faith, but I was filled with scientific nonsense which derided old beliefs; she might have left the teachings of her forebears and accepted my ideas, but twenty generations of belief weigh heavily upon the shoulders of a single fragile girl. To save my soul she forfeited all claim upon my body; if she might not have me for husband she'd have no mortal man, so she professed religion. She joined the silent Carmelites, the Carmelites who never speak except in prayer, and the last fond word I had from her was that she would pray ceaselessly for my salvation.

"Hélas, those little feet so much adored—how many weary steps of needless penance have they taken since that day so long ago! How fruitless life has been to me since my stubbornness closed the door on happiness! Oh, do not wait, my friends! Take the Love the good God gives, and hold it tight against your hearts—it will not come a second time!

"Come, Friend Trowbridge," he commanded me, "let us leave them in their happiness. What have we, who clasped Love's hand in ours long years ago, and saw the purple shadow of his smile grow black with dull futility, to do with them? Nothing, pardieu! Come, let us take a drink."

We poured the ruby brandy into wide-mouthed goblets, for de Grandin liked to scent its rich bouquet before he drank. I studied him covertly as he raised his glass. Somehow, the confession he had made seemed strangely pitiful. I'd known him for five years, nearly always gay, always nonchalant, boastfully self-confident, quick, brave and reckless, ever a favorite with women, always studiously gallant but ever holding himself aloof, though more than one fair charmer had deliberately paid court to him. Suddenly I remembered our adventure of the "Ancient Fires"; he had said something then about a love that had been lost. But now, at last I understood Jules de Grandin—or thought I did.

"To you, my friend," be pledged me. "To you, and friendship, and brave deeds of adventure, and last of all to Death, the last sweet friend who flings the door back from our prison, for—"

The clamoring telephone cut short his toast.

"Mercy Hospital," a crisp feminine voice announced as I picked up the instrument. "Will you and Doctor de Grandin come at once? Detective Sergeant Costello wants to see you just as soon as—oh, wait a minute, they've plugged a phone through from his room."

"Hullo. Doctor Trowbridge, sor," Costello's salutation came across the wire a moment later. "They like to got me, sor—in broad daylight too."

"Eh? What the deuce?" I shot back. "What's the trouble, Sergeant?"

"A chopper, sor."

"A *what?*"

"Machine-gun, sor. Hornsby an' me wuz standin' be th' corner o' Thirty-Fourth an' Tunlaw Streets half an hour back, when a car comes past like th' hammers o' hell, an' they let us have a dose o' bullets as they passed. Pore Hornsby got 'is first off—went down full o' lead as a Christmas puddin' is o' plums, sor-but I'm just messed up' a little. Nawthin' but a bad ar-rm, an' a punctured back, praise th' Lord!"

"Good heavens!" I exclaimed. "Have you any idea who—"

"I have that, sor; I seen 'im plain as I see you—as I would be seein' ye if ye wuz here, I mean, sor, an'—"

"Yes?" I urged as he paused a moment and a swallow sounded audibly across the wire.

"Yes, sor. I seen 'im, an' there's no mistake about it. It were th' felly you an' Doctor de Grandin turned over to me to hold fer murther last night. I seen 'im plain as day; there's no mistakin' that there map o' hisn."

"Good Lord, then he did escape!"

"No, sir; he didn't. He's locked up tight in his cell at headquarters this minute, waitin' arraignment fer murther!"

19. The Lightning-Bolts of Justice

THAT EVENING ALICE SUFFERED from severe headaches and shortly afterward with sharp abdominal pains. Though a careful examination disclosed neither enlarged tonsils nor any evidence of mechanical stoppage, the sensation of a ball rising in her throat plagued her almost ceaselessly; when she attempted to cross the room her knees buckled under her as though they had been the boneless joints of a rag-doll.

Jules de Grandin pursed his lips, shook his head and tweaked the needle-ends of his mustache disconsolately. "*L'hysterie,*" he murmured. "It might have been foreseen. The emotional and moral shock the poor one has been through is enough to shatter any nerves. *Hélas*, I fear the wedding may not be so soon, Friend Trowbridge. The experience of marriage is a trying one to any woman—the readjustment of her mode of life, the blending of her personality with another's—it is a strain. No, she is in no condition to essay it."

Amazingly, he brightened, his small eyes gleaming as with sudden inspiration. "*Parbleu*, I have it!" he exclaimed. "She, Monsieur Jean and you, *mon vieux*, shall take a trip. I would suggest the Riviera, were it not that I desire isolation for you all until—no matter. Your practise is not so pressing that it can not be assumed by your estimable colleague, Doctor Phillips; and Mademoiselle

Alice will most certainly improve more quickly if you accompany her as personal physician. You will go? Say that you will, my friend; a very great much depends on it!"

Reluctantly, I consented, and for six weeks Alice, John Davisson and I toured the Caribbean, saw devastated Martinique, the birthplace of the Empress Josephine, drank Haitian coffee fresh from the plantation, investigated the sights and sounds and, most especially, the smells of Panama and Colon, finally passed some time at the Jockey Club and Sloppy Joe's in Habana. It was a well and sun-tanned Alice who debarked with us and caught the noon train out of Hoboken.

Arrangements for the wedding were perfected while we cruised beneath the Southern Cross. The old Hume house would be done over and serve the bride and groom for home, and in view of Alice's bereavement the formal ceremony had been canceled, a simple service in the chapel of St. Chrysostom's being substituted. Pending the nuptials Alice took up residence at the Hotel Carteret, declaring that she could not think of lodging at my house, warm as was my invitation.

"All has been finished," de Grandin told me jubilantly as he, Renouard and Ingraham accompanied me from the station. "The justice of New Jersey, of which you speak so proudly; she has more than justified herself. Oh yes."

"Eh?" I demanded.

Renouard and Ingraham chuckled.

"They gave it to him," the Englishman explained.

"In the throat—the neck, I should remark," Renouard supplied, wrestling bravely with the idiom.

"The party will be held tomorrow night," de Grandin finished.

"Who—what—whatever are you fellows saying?" I queried. "What party d'ye mean, and—"

"Grigor Bazarov," de Grandin answered with another laugh, "the youthful-bodied one with the aged, evil-face; the wicked one who celebrated the Black Mass. He is to die tomorrow night. Yes, *parbleu*, he dies for murder!"

"But—"

"Patience, *mon vieux*, and I shall tell you all. You do recall how we—Monsieur Hiji, Renouard and I—did apprehend him on the night we rescued Mademoiselle Alice? Of course. Very well.

"You know how we conspired that he should be tried for a murder which he did not perpetrate, because we could not charge him with his many other crimes? Very good. So it was.

"When we had packed you off with Monsieur Jean and his so charming fiancée, your testimony could not serve to save him. No, we had the game all to ourselves, and how nobly we did swear his life away! *Mordieu*, when they heard how artistically we committed perjury, I damn think Ananias and Sapphira hung their heads and curled up like two anchovies for very jealousy! The jury almost wept when we described his shameful crime. It took them only twenty minutes to decide his fate. And so tomorrow night he gives his life in expiation for those little boys he sacrificed upon the Devil's altar and for the dreadful death he brought upon poor Abigail.

"Me, I am clever, my friend. I have drawn upon the wires of political influence, and we shall all have seats within the death house when he goes to meet the lightning bolt of Jersey justice. Yes, certainly, of course."

"You mean we're to witness the execution?"

"*Mais oui; et puis.* Did I not swear he should pay through the nose when he slew that little helpless lad upon the Devil's altar? But certainly. And now, by damn, he shall learn that Jules de Grandin does not swear untruly—unless he wishes to. Unquestionably."

DEFTLY, LIKE MEN ACCUSTOMED to their task, the state policemen patted all our pockets. The pistols my companions wore were passed unquestioned, for only cameras were taboo within the execution chamber.

"All right, you can go in," the sergeant told us when the troopers had completed their examination, and we filed down a dimly lighted corridor behind the prison guard.

The death room was as bright as any clinic's surgery, immaculate white tile reflecting brilliant incandescent bulbs' hard rays. Behind a barricade of white-enameled wood on benches which reminded me of pews, sat several young men whose journalistic calling was engraved indelibly upon their faces, and despite their efforts to appear at ease it took no second glance to see their nerves were taut to the snapping-point; for even seasoned journalists react to death—and here was death, stark and grim as anything to be found in the dissecting rooms.

"The chair," a heavy piece of oaken furniture, stood near the farther wall, raised one low step above the tiled floor of the chamber, a brilliant light suspended from the ceiling just above it, casting its pitiless spotlight upon the center of the tragic stage. The warden and a doctor, stethoscope swung round his neck as though it were a badge of office, stood near the chair, conversing in low tones; the lank cadaverous electrician whose duty was to send the lethal current through the condemned man's body, stood in a tiny alcove like a doorless telephone booth slightly behind and to the left of the chair. A screen obscured a doorway leading from the room, but as we took our seats in front I caught a fleeting glimpse of a white-enameled wheeled bier, a white sheet lying neatly folded on it. Beyond, I knew, the surgeon and the autopsy table were in readiness when the prison doctor had announced his verdict.

The big young Englishman went pale beneath his tropic tan as he surveyed the place; Renouard's square jaw set suddenly beneath his bristling square-cut beard; de Grandin's small, bright eyes roved quickly round the room, taking stock of the few articles of furniture; then, involuntarily his hand flew upward to tease the tightly waxed hairs of his mustache to a sharper point. These three, veterans of police routine, all more than once participants in executions, were fidgeting beneath the strain of waiting. As for me—if I came through without the aid of smelling-salts, I felt I should be lucky.

A light tap sounded on the varnished door communicating with the death cells. A soft, half-timid sort of tap it was, such as that a person unaccustomed to commercial life might give before attempting to enter an office.

The tap was not repeated. Silently, on well-oiled hinges, the door swung back, and a quartet halted on the threshold. To right and left were prison guards; between them stood the Red Priest arrayed in open shirt and loose black trousers, list slippers on his feet. As he came to a halt I saw that the right leg of the trousers had been slit up to the knee and flapped grotesquely round his ankle. The guards beside him held his elbows lightly, and another guard brought up the rear.

Pale, calm, erect, the condemned man betrayed no agitation, save by a sudden violent quivering of the eyelids, this perhaps, being due to the sudden flood of light in which he found himself. His great, sad eyes roved quickly round the room, not timorously, but curiously, finally coming to rest upon de Grandin. Then for an instant a flash showed in them, a lambent flash which died as quickly as it came.

Quickly the short march to the chair began. Abreast of us, the prisoner wrenched from his escorts, cleared the space between de Grandin and himself in one long leap, bent forward and spat into the little Frenchman's face.

Without a word or cry of protest the prison guards leaped on him, pinioned his elbows to his sides and rushed him at a staggering run across the short space to the chair.

De Grandin drew a linen kerchief from his cuff and calmly wiped the spittle from his cheek. "*Eh bien*," he murmured, "it seems the snake can spit, though justice has withdrawn his fangs, *n'est-ce-pas?*"

The prison warders knew their work. Straps were buckled round the prisoner's wrists, his ankles, waist. A leather helmet like a football player's was clamped upon his head, almost totally obscuring his pale, deep-wrinkled face.

There was no clergyman attending. Grigor Bazarov was faithful to his compact with the Devil, even unto death. His pale lips moved: "God is tyranny and misery. God is evil. To me, then, Lucifer!" he murmured in a singsong chant.

The prison doctor stood before the chair, notebook in hand, pencil poised. The prisoner was breathing quickly, his shoulders fluttering with forced respiration. A deep, inhaling gulp, a quick, exhaling gasp—the shoulders slanted forward.

So did the doctor's pencil, as though he wrote. The thin-faced executioner, his quiet eyes upon the doctor's hands, reached upward. There was a crunching of levers, a sudden whir, a whine, and the criminal's body started forward, lurching upward as though he sought to rise and burst from the restraining straps. As much as we could see of his pale face grew crimson, like the face of one who holds his breath too long. The bony, claw-like hands were taut upon the chair arms, like those of a patient in the dentist's chair when the drill bites deeply.

A long, eternal moment of this posture, then the sound of grating metal as the switches were withdrawn, and the straining body in the chair sank limply back, as though in muscular reaction to fatigue.

Once more the doctor's pencil tilted forward, again the whirring whine. Again the body started up, tense, strained, all but bursting through the broad, strong straps which bound it to the chair. The right hand writhed and turned, thumb and forefinger meeting tip to tip, as though to take a pinch of snuff. Then absolute flaccidity as the current was shut off.

The prison doctor put his book aside and stepped up to the chair. For something like a minute the main tube of his questing stethoscope explored the reddened chest exposed as he put back the prisoner's open shirt, then: "I pronounce this man dead."

"*Mon dieu*," exclaimed Renouard.

"For God's sake!" Ingraham muttered thickly.

I remained silent as the white-garbed orderlies took the limp form from the chair, wrapped it quickly in a sheet and trundled it away on the wheeled bier to the waiting autopsy table.

"I say," suggested Ingraham shakily, "suppose he ain't quite dead? It didn't seem to me—"

"*Tiens*, he will be thoroughly defunct when the surgeon's work is done," de Grandin told him calmly. "It was most interesting, was it not?"

His small eyes hardened as he saw the sick look on our faces. "Ah bah, you have the sympathy for him?" he asked almost accusingly. "For why? Were they not more merciful to him than he was to those helpless little boys he killed, those little boys whose throats he slit—or that poor woman whom he crucified? I damn think yes!"

20. The Wolf-Master

"TIENS, MY FRIENDS, I damn think there is devilment afoot!" de Grandin told us as we were indulging in a final cup of coffee in the breakfast room some mornings later.

"But no!" Renouard expostulated

"But yes!" his confrere insisted.

"Read it, my friend," he commanded, passing a folded copy of *The Journal* across the table to me. To Ingraham and Renouard he ordered: "Listen; listen and become astonished!"

Magnate's Menagerie on Rampage
Beasts on Karmany Estate Break Cages and Pursue Intruder—Animals' Disappearance a Mystery.

I read aloud at his request.

Early this morning keepers at the private zoo maintained by Winthrop Karmany, well known retired Wall Street operator, at his palatial estate near Raritan, were aroused by a disturbance among the animals. Karmany is said to have the finest, as well as what is probably the largest, collection of Siberian white wolves in captivity, and it was among these beasts the disturbance occurred.

John Noles, 45, and Edgar Black, 30, caretakers on the Karmany estate, hastily left their quarters to ascertain the cause of the noise which they heard coming from the wolves' dens about 3:30 A.M. Running through the dark to the dens, they were in time to see what they took to be a man enveloped in a long, dark cloak, running at great speed toward the brick wall surrounding the animals' enclosure. They also noticed several wolves in hot pursuit of the intruder. Both declare that though the wolves had been howling and baying noisily a few minutes before, they ran without so much as a growl as they pursued the mysterious visitor.

Arriving at the den the men were amazed to find the cage doors swinging open, their heavy locks evidently forced with a crowbar, and all but three of the savage animals at large.

The strange intruder, with the wolves in close pursuit, was seen by Noles and Black to vault the surrounding wall, but all had disappeared in the darkness when the keepers reached the barrier. Citizens in the vicinity of the Karmany estate are warned to be on the lookout for the beasts, for though they had been in confinement several years and consequently have lost much of their native savagery, it is feared that unless they are speedily recaptured or voluntarily find their way back to their dens, they may revert to their original ferocity when they become hungry. Livestock may suffer from their depredations, and if they keep together and hunt in a pack even human beings are in danger, for all the beasts are unusually large and would make dangerous antagonists.

This morning at daylight a posse of farmers, headed by members of the state constabulary, was combing the woods and fields in search of the missing animals, but though every spot where wolves might be likely to congregate was visited, no trace of them was found. No one can be found who admits seeing any sign of the runaway wolves, nor have any losses of domestic animals been reported to the authorities.

The manner in which the wolf pack seems to have vanished completely, as well as the identity of the man in black seen by the two keepers, and the reason which may have actuated him in visiting the Karmany menagerie are puzzling both the keepers and authorities. It has been intimated that the breaking of the cages may have been the vagary of a disordered mind. Certain insane persons have an almost uncontrollable aversion to the sight of caged animals, and it is suggested an escaped lunatic may have blundered into the Karmany zoo as he fled from confinement. If this is so it is quite possible that, seeing the confined beasts, he was suddenly seized with an insane desire to liberate them, and consequently forced the locks of their cages. The released animals seem to have been ungrateful, however, for both Noles and Black declare the mysterious man was obviously running for his life while the wolves pursued him in silent and ferocious determination. However, since no trace of the body has been found, nor any report of a man badly mauled by wolves made in the locality, it is supposed the unidentified man managed to escape. Meanwhile, the whereabouts of the wolf pack is causing much concern about the countryside.

Karmany is at present occupying his southern place at Winter Haven, Fla., and all attempts to reach him have been unsuccessful at the time this issue goes to press.

"H'm, it's possible," I murmured as I put the paper down.

"Absolutely," Ingraham agreed.

"Of course; certainly," de Grandin nodded, then, abruptly: "What is?"

"Why—er—a lunatic *might* have done it," I returned. "Cases of zoophilia—"

"And of zoöfiddlesticks!" the little Frenchman interrupted. "This was no insanatic's vagary, my friends; this business was well planned beforehand, though why it should be so we can not say. Still—"

'I don't care if he is at breakfast, I've got to see him!' a hysterically shrill voice came stridently from the hallway, and John Davisson strode into the breakfast room, pushing the protesting Nora McGinnis from his path. "Doctor de Grandin—Doctor Trowbridge—*she's gone!*" he sobbed as he half fell across the threshold.

"*Mon Dieu*, so soon?" de Grandin cried. "How was it, *mon pauvre?*"

Davisson stared glassy-eyed from one of us to the other, his face working spasmodically, his hands clenched till it seemed the bones must surely crush.

"He stole her—he and his damned wolves!"

"Wolves? I say!" barked Ingraham.

"*Grand Dieu*—wolves!" Renouard exclaimed.

"*A-a-ah*—wolves? I begin to see the outlines of the scheme," de Grandin answered calmly. "I might have feared as much.

"Begin at the beginning, if you please, *Monsieur*, and tell us everything that happened. Do not leave out an incident, however trivial it may seem; in cases such as this there are no trifles. Begin, commence; we listen."

Young Davisson exhaled a deep, half-sobbing breath and turned his pale face from de Grandin to Renouard, then back again.

"We—Alice and I—went riding this morning as we always do," he answered. "The horses were brought round at half-past six, and we rode out the Albemarle Pike toward Boonesburg. We must have gone about ten miles when we turned off the highway into a dirt road. It's easier on the horses, and the riders, too, you know.

"We'd ridden on a mile or so, through quite a grove of pines, when it began to snow and the wind rose so sharply it cut through our jackets as if they had been summerweight. I'd just turned round to lead the way to town when I heard Alice scream. She'd ridden fifty feet or so ahead of me, so she was that much behind when we turned.

"I wheeled my horse around, and there, converging on her from both sides of the road, were half a dozen great white wolves!

"I couldn't believe my eyes at first. The brutes were larger than any I'd ever seen, and though they didn't growl or make the slightest sound I could see their awful purpose in their gleaming eyes and flashing fangs. They hemmed my poor girl in on every side, and as I turned to ride to her, they gathered closer, crouching till their bellies almost touched the ground, and seemed to stop waiting for some signal from the leader of the pack.

"I drove the spurs into my mare and laid the whip on her with all my might, but she balked and shied and reared, and all my urging couldn't force her on a foot.

"Then, apparently from nowhere, two more white beasts came charging through the woods and leaped at my mount's head. The poor brute gave a screaming whinny and bolted.

"I tugged at the bridle and sawed at her mouth, but I might have been a baby for all effect my efforts had. Twice I tried to roll out of the saddle, but she was fairly flying, and try as I would I didn't seem able to disengage myself. We'd reached the Pike and, traveled half a mile or so toward town before I finally brought her to a halt.

"Then I turned back, but at the entrance to the lane she balked again, and nothing I could do would make her leave the highway. I dismounted and hurried down the lane on foot, but it was snowing pretty hard by then, and I couldn't even be sure when I'd reached the place where Alice was attacked. At any rate, I couldn't find a trace of her or of her horse."

He paused a moment breathlessly, and de Grandin prompted softly: "And this 'he' to whom you referred when you first came in, *Monsieur?*"

"Grigor Bazarov!" the young man answered, and his features quivered in a nervous tic. "I recognized him instantly!

"As I rushed down that lane at break-neck speed on my ungovernable horse I saw—distinctly, gentlemen—a human figure standing back among the pines. It was Grigor Bazarov, and he stood between the trees, waving his hands like a conductor leading an orchestra. Without a spoken syllable *he was directing that pack of wolves.* He set them after Alice and ordered them to stop when they'd surrounded her. He set them on me, and made them leap at my horse's head without actually fleshing their teeth in her and without attempting to drag me from the saddle—which they could easily have done. Then, when he'd worked his plan and made my mare bolt, he called them back into the woods. It was Alice he was after, and he took her as easily as a shepherd cuts a wether from the flock with trained sheep-dogs!"

"How is this?" de Grandin questioned sharply. "You say it was Grigor Bazarov. How could you tell? You never saw him."

"No, but I've heard you tell of him, and Alice had described him, too. I recognized those great, sad eyes of his, and his mummy-wrinkled face. I tell you—"

"But Bazarov is dead," I interrupted. "We saw him die last week—all of us. They electrocuted him in the penitentiary at Trenton, and—"

"And while he was all safely lodged in jail he broke into this house and all but made away with Mademoiselle Alice," de Grandin cut in sharply. "You saw him with your own two eyes, my Trowbridge. So did Renouard and Monsieur Hiji. Again, while still in jail he murdered the poor Hornsby, and all but killed the good Costello. The evidence is undisputed, and—"

"I know, but he's dead, now!" I insisted.

"There is a way to tell," de Grandin answered. "Come, let us go."

"Go? Where?"

"To the cemetery, of course. I would look in the grave of this one who can be in jail and in your house at the same time, and kill a gendarme in the street while safely under lock and key. Come, we waste our time, my friends."

We drove to the county court house, and de Grandin was closeted with the Recorder Glassford in his chambers a few minutes. "*Très bon,*" he told us as he reappeared. "I have the order for the exhumation. Let us make haste."

T HE EARLY MORNING SNOW had stopped, but a thin veneer of leaden clouds obscured the sky, and the winter sun shone through them with a pale, half-hearted glow as we wheeled along the highway toward the graveyard. Only people of the poorer class buried their dead in Willow Hills; only funeral directors of the less exclusive sort sold lots or grave-space there. Bazarov's unmarked grave was in the least expensive section of the poverty-stricken burying-ground, one short step higher than the Potter's Field.

The superintendent and two overalled workmen waited at the graveside, for de Grandin had telephoned the cemetery office as soon as he obtained the order for the exhumation. Glancing perfunctorily at the little Frenchman's papers, the superintendent nodded to the Polish laborers. "Git goin'," he commanded tersely, "an' make it snappy."

It was dismal work watching them heave lumps of frosty clay from the grave. The earth was frozen almost stony-hard, and the picks struck on it with a hard, metallic sound. At length, however, the dull, reverberant thud of steel on wood warned us that the task was drawing to a close. A pair of strong web straps were lowered, made fast to the rough box enclosing the casket, and at a word from the superintendent the men strained at the thongs, dragging their weird burden to the surface. A pair of pick-handles were laid across the open grave and the rough box rested on them. Callously, as one who does such duties every day, the superintendent wrenched the box-lid off, and the laborers laid it by the grave. Inside lay the casket, a cheap affair of chestnut covered with shoddy broadcloth, the tinny, imitation-silver nameplate on its lid already showing a dull, brown-blue discoloration.

Snap! The fastenings which secured the casket lid were thrown back; the superintendent lifted the panel and tossed it to the frozen ground.

Head resting on the sateen rayon pillow, hands folded on his breast, Grigor Bazarov lay before us and gave us stare for stare. The mortuarian who attended him had lacked the skill or inclination to do a thorough job, and despite the intense cold of the weather putrefaction had made progress. The dead man's mouth was slightly open, a quarter-inch or so of purple, blood-gorged tongue protruding from his lips as though in low derision; the lids were partly raised from his great eyes, and though these had the sightless glaze of death, it seemed to me some subtle mockery lay in them.

I shuddered at the sight despite myself, but I could not forbear the gibe: "Well, is he dead?" I asked de Grandin.

"*Comme un mouton,*"—he answered, in nowise disconcerted.

"Restore him to his bed, if you will be so good, *Monsieur,*" he added to the superintendent, "and should you care to smoke—" A flash of green showed momentarily as a treasury note changed hands, and the cemetery overseer grinned.

"Thanks," he acknowledged. "Next time you want to look at one of 'em, don't forget we're always willing to oblige."

"Yes, he is dead," the Frenchman murmured thoughtfully as we walked slowly toward the cemetery gate, "dead like a herring, yet—"

"Dead or not," John Davisson broke in, and his words were syncopated by the chattering of his teeth, "dead or not, sir, the man we just saw in that coffin was the man I saw beside the lane this morning. No one could fail to recognize that face!"

21. White Horror

"HERE'S A SPECIAL DELIVERY letter for Misther Davisson, come whilst yez wuz out, sor," Nora McGinnis announced as we entered the house. "Will ye be afther havin' the' tur-key or th' roast fer dinner tonight, an' shall I make th' salad wid tomatoes or asparagus?"

"Turkey, by all means, he is a noble bird," de Grandin answered for me, and tomatoes with the salad, if you please, *ma petite*."

The big Irishwoman favored him with an affectionate smile as she retired kitchenward, and young Davisson slit the envelope of the missive she had handed him.

For a moment he perused it with wide-set, unbelieving eyes, then handed it to me, his features quivering once again with nervous tic.

John Darling:

    When you get this I shall be on my way to fulfil the destiny prepared for me from the beginning of the world. Do not seek to follow me, nor think of me, save as you might think kindly of one who died, for I am dead to you. I have forever given up all thought of marriage to you or any man, and I release you from your engagement. Your ring will be delivered to you, and that you may some day put it on the finger of a girl who can return the love you give is the hope of

ALICE.

"*I can't—I won't believe* she means it!" the young man cried. "Why, Alice and I have known each other since we were little kids; we've been in love since she first put her hair up, and—"

"*Tiens*, my friend," de Grandin interrupted as he gazed at the message, "have you by chance spent some time out in the country?"

"Eh?" answered Davisson, amazed at the irrelevant question.

"Your hearing is quite excellent, I think. Will you not answer me?"

"Why—er—yes, of course, I've been in the country—pent practically all my summers on a farm when I was a lad, but—"

"*Très bon*," the little Frenchman laughed. "Consider: Did not you see the wicked Bazarov urge on his wolves to take possession of your sweetheart? But certainly. And did he not forbear to harm you, being satisfied to drive you from the scene while he kidnapped Mademoiselle Alice? Of course. And could he not easily have had his wolf-pack drag you from your horse and slay you? You have said as much yourself. Very well, then; recall your rural recollections, if you will:

"You have observed the farmer as he takes his cattle to the butcher. Does he take the trouble to place his cow in leading strings? By no means. He puts the little, so weak calf, all destined to be veal upon the table in a little while, into a wagon, and drives away to market. And she, the poor, distracted mother-beast, she trots along behind, asking nothing but to keep her little baby-calf in sight. Lead her? *Parbleu*, ropes of iron could not drag her from behind the tumbril in which her offspring rides to execution! Is it not likely so in this case also? I damn think yes.

"This never-to-be-sufficiently-anathematized stealer of women holds poor Mademoiselle Alice in his clutch. He spares her *fiancé*. Perhaps he spares him only as the cruel, playful pussy-cat forbears to kill the mouse outright; at any rate, he spares him. For why? *Pardieu*, because by leaving Monsieur Jean free he still allows poor Mademoiselle Alice one little, tiny ray of hope; with such vile subtlety as only his base wickedness can plan, he holds her back from black despair and suicide that he may force her to his will by threats against the man she loves. *Sacré nom d'un artichaut*, I shall say yes! Certainly, of course."

"You mean—he'll make her go with him—leave me—by threats against my life?" young Davisson faltered.

"*Précisément, mon vieux*. He has no need to drug her now with *scopolamine apomophia*; he holds her in a stronger thrall. Yes, it is entirely likely."

He folded the girl's note between his slim, white hands, regarding it idly for a moment; then, excitedly: "Tell me, Monsieur Jean, did Mademoiselle Alice, by any chance, know something of telegraphy?"

"Eh? Why, yes. When we were kids we had a craze for it—had wires strung between our houses with senders and receivers at each end, and used to rouse each other at all sorts of hours to tap a message—"

"*Hourra*, the Evil One is circumvented! *Regardez-vous*."

Holding the letter to the study desk-lamp, he tapped its bottom margin with his finger. Invisible except against the light, a series of light stratches, as though from a pin-point or dry pen, showed on the paper:

·−−−/−−−/−·/·/···// −−/··/·−··/·−·/

"You can read him?" he asked anxiously "Me, I understand the international, but this is in American Morse, and—"

"Of course I can," young Davisson broke in. "'Jones' Mill,' it says. Good Lord, why didn't I think of that?"

"Ah? And this mill of Monsieur Jones—"

"Is an old ruin several miles from Boonesburg. No one's occupied it since I can remember, but it can't be more than three miles from the place where we met the wolves, and—"

"*Eh bien*, if that be so, why do we sit here like five sculptured figures on the Arc de Triomphe? Come, let us go at once, my friends. Trowbridge, Renouard, Friend Hiji, and you, Friend Jean, prepare yourselves for service in the cold. Me, I shall telephone the good Costello for the necessary implements.

"*Oui-da, Messieurs les Loups*, I think that we shall give you the party of surprise—we shall feed you that which will make your bellies ache most villainously!"

IT WAS SOMETHING LIKE a half-hour later when the police car halted at the door. "It's kind o' irreg'lar, sor," Sergeant Costello announced as he lugged several heavy satchels up the steps with the aid of two patrolmen, "but I got permission fer th' loan. Seems like you got a good stand-in down to headquarters."

The valises opened, he drew forth three submachine guns, each with an extra drum of cartridges, and two riot guns, weapons similar to the automatic shotgun, but heavier in construction and firing shells loaded with much heavier shot.

"You and Friend Jean will use the shotguns, Friend Trowbridge," de Grandin told me. "Renouard, Ingraham and I will handle the quick-firers. Come, prepare yourselves at once. Heavy clothing, but no long coats; we shall need leg-room before the evening ends."

I fished a set of ancient hunting-togs out of my wardrobe—thick trousers of stout corduroy, a pair of high lace boots, a heavy sweater and suede jerkin, finally a leather cap with folds that buckled underneath the chin. A few minutes' search unearthed another set for Davisson, and we joined the others in the hallway. De Grandin was resplendent in a leather aviation suit; Renouard had slipped three sweaters on above his waistcoat and bound the bottoms of his trousers tight about his ankles with stout linen twine; Ingraham was arrayed in a suit of corduroys which had seen much better days, though not recently.

"Are we prepared?" de Grandin asked. "*Très bon*. Let us go."

The bitter cold of the afternoon had given way to slightly warmer weather, but before we had traversed half a mile the big, full, yellow moon was totally obscured by clouds, and shortly afterward the air was filled with flying snowflakes and tiny, cutting grains of hail which rattled on the windshield and stung like whips when they blew into our faces.

About three-quarters of a mile from the old mill I had to stop my motor for the road was heavy with new-fallen snow and several ancient trees had blown across the trail, making further progress impossible.

"*Eh bien*, it must be on foot from now on, it seems," de Grandin murmured as he clambered from the car. "Very well; one consents when one must. Let us go; there is no time to lose."

The road wound on, growing narrower and more uneven with each step. Thick ranks of waving, black-boughed pines marched right to the border of the trail on either side, and through their swaying limbs the storm-wind soughed eerily, while the very air seemed colder with a sharper, harder chill, and the wan and ghastly light which sometimes shines on moonless, snow-filled winter nights, seemed filled with creeping, shifting phantom-shapes which stalked us as a wolf-pack stalks a stag.

"*Morbleu*, I so not like this place, me," Renouard declared. "It has an evil smell."

"I think so, too, *mon vieux*," de Grandin answered. "Three times already I have all but fired at nothing. My nerves are not so steady as I thought."

"Oh, keep your tails up," Ingraham comforted. "It's creepy as a Scottish funeral here, but I don't see anything—"

"*Ha*, do you say it? Then look yonder, if you will, and tell me what it is you do not see, my friend," de Grandin interrupted.

Loping silently across the snow, themselves a mere shade darker than the fleecy covering of the ground, came a pack of great, white wolves, green-yellow eyes a-glint with savagery, red tongues lolling from their mouths as they drew nearer through the pines, then suddenly deployed like soldiers at command, and, their cordon formed, sank to the snow and sat there motionless.

"*Cher Dieu*," Renouard said softly. "It is the pack of beasts which made away with Mademoiselle Alice, and—"

A movement stirred within the pack. A brute rose from its haunches, took a tentative step forward, then sank down again, belly to the snow, and lay there panting, its glaring eyes fixed hungrily upon us.

And as the leader moved, so moved the pack. A score of wolves were three feet nearer us, for every member of the deadly circle had advanced in concert with the leader.

I stole a quick glance at de Grandin. His little round blue eyes were glaring fiercely as those of any of the wolves; beneath his little blond mustache his lips were drawn back savagely, showing his small, white, even teeth in a snarl of hate and fury.

Another rippling movement in the wolf-pack, and now the silence crashed, and from the circle there went up such pandemonium of hellish howls as I had never heard; not even in the worst of nightmares. I had a momentary vision of red mouths and gleaming teeth and shaggy, gray-white fur advancing toward me in a whirlwind rush, then:

"Give fire!" de Grandin shouted.

And now the wolf-pack's savage battle-cry was drowned out by another roar as de Grandin, Ingraham and Renouard, back touching back, turned loose the venom of their submachine guns. Young Davisson and I, too, opened fire with our shotguns, not taking aim, but pumping the mechanisms frenziedly and firing point-blank into the faces of the charging wolves.

How long the battle lasted I have no idea, but I remember that at last I felt de Grandin's hand upon my arm and heard him shouting in my ear: "Cease firing, Friend Trowbridge, there is no longer anything to shoot. *Parbleu*, if wolves have souls, I damn think hell is full with them tonight!"

22. The Crimson Clue

HE TURNED ABRUPTLY TO Renouard: "*Allez au feu, mon brave*," he cried, "*pour la partie!*"

We charged across the intervening patch of snow-filled clearing, and more than once de Grandin or Renouard or Ingraham paused in his stride to spray the windows of the tumbledown old house with a stream of lead. But not a shot replied, nor was there any sign of life as we approached the doorless doorway.

"Easy on," Ingraham counseled. "They may be lyin' doggo, waitin' for a chance—"

"But no," de Grandin interrupted. "Had that been so, they surely would not have missed the chance to shoot us to death a moment ago—we were a perfectly defined target against the snow, and they had the advantage of cover. Still, a milligram of caution is worth a double quintal of remorse; so let us step warily.

"Renouard and I will take the lead. Friend Trowbridge, you and Friend Jean walk behind us and flash your searchlights forward, and well above our heads. That way, if we are ambushed, they will shoot high and give us opportunity to return their fire. Friend Hiji, do you bring up the rear and keep your eyes upon the ground which we have traversed. Should you see aught which looks suspicious, shoot first and make investigation afterward, I do not wish that we should die tonight."

Accordingly, in this close formation, we searched the old house from its musty cellar to its drafty attic, but nowhere was there any hint of life or recent occupancy until, as we forced back the sagging door which barred the entrance to the old grain bins, we noted the faint, half-tangible aroma of *narcisse noir*.

"Alice!" John Davisson exclaimed. "She's been here—I recognize the scent!"

"U'm?" de Grandin murmured thoughtfully. "Advance your light a trifle nearer, if you please, Friend Trowbridge."

I played the flashlight on the age-bleached casing of the door. There, fresh against the wood's flat surface were three small pits, arranged triangularly. A second group of holes, similarly spaced, were in the handhewn planking of the door, exactly opposite those which scarred the jamb.

"Screw-holes," de Grandin commented, "and on the outer side. You were correct, Friend Jean; your nose and heart spoke truly. This place has been the prison of your love—here are the marks where they made fast the lock and hasp to hold her prisoner—but *hélas*, the bird is flown; the cage deserted."

Painstakingly as a paleographer might scan a palimpsest, he searched the little, wood-walled cubicle, flashing his search-light's darting ray on each square inch of aged planking. "*Ah-ha?*" he asked of no one in particular as the flashlight struck into a corner, revealing several tiny smears of scarlet on the floor.

"*Morbleu!* Blood?" Renouard exclaimed. "Can it be that—"

De Grandin threw himself full length upon the floor, his little, round blue eyes a scant three inches from the row of crimson stains. "Blood? *Non!*" he answered as he finished his examination. "It is the mark of *pomade pour les levres*, and unless I do mistake—"

"You mean lipstick?" I interrupted. "What in the world—"

"*Zut!*" he cut me short. "You speak too much, my friend." To Davisson:

"See here, Friend Jean, is not some system of design in this? Is it not—"

"Of course it is!" the young man answered sharply. "It's another telegraphic message, like the one she sent us in the letter. Can't you see? 'Dash, dash; dot, dash; dot, dot, dot; dot, dash; dash, dot—' He read the code through quickly.

De Grandin looked at him with upraised brows. "*Exactement*," he nodded, "and that means—"

"M-a-c-a-n-d-r-e-w-s s-i-e—" Davisson spelled the message out, then paused, shook his head in puzzlement, and once again essayed the task.

"I can't get any sense from it," he finally confessed. "That's what it spells, no doubt of it, but what the devil—"

"I say, old chap, go over it once more," asked Ingraham. "I may be blotto, but—"

Crash! The thunderous detonation shook the floor beneath us and a heavy beam came hurtling from the ceiling, followed by a cataract of splintered planks and rubble.

Crash! A second fulmination smashed the wooded wall upon our right and a mass of shattered brick and timber poured into the room.

"*Bombes d'air!*" Renouard cried wildly. "Down—down, my friends; it is the only way to—" His warning ended in a choking grunt as a third explosion ripped the cover off our hiding place and a blinding pompom of live flame flashed in our eyes.

I felt myself hurled bodily against the farther wall, felt the crushing impact as I struck the mortised planks, and then I felt no more.

"TROWBRIDGE, MY FRIEND, MY good, brave comrade; do you survive, have you been killed to death? *Mordieu*, say that you live, my old one!" I heard de Grandin's voice calling from immeasurable distance, and slowly realized he held my head upon his shoulder while with frantic hands he rubbed snow on my brow.

"Oh, I'm all right, I guess," I answered weakly, then sank again in comforting oblivion.

When next I struggled back to consciousness, I found myself on my own surgery table, de Grandin busy with a phial of smelling salts, a glass of aromatic spirit on the table, and a half-filled tumbler of cognac next to it. "Thanks be to God you are yourself once more!" he exclaimed fervently, handed me the water and ammonia and drained the brandy glass himself. "*Pardieu*, my friend, I thought that we should surely lose you!" he continued as he helped me to a chair.

"You had a close squeak no doubt of it," Ingraham agreed.

"What happened?" I demanded weakly.

De Grandin fairly ground his teeth in rage. "They made a foolishness of us," he told me. "While we were busy with their *sacré* wolves they must have been escaping, and the thunder of our guns drowned out the whirring of their motors. Then, when we were all safe and helpless in the house, they circled back and dropped the hand grenades upon us. Luckily for us they had no aerial torpedoes, or we should now be practising upon the harp. As it is—" he raised his shoulders in a shrug.

"B—but, you mean they had a *plane?*" I asked amazed.

"Ha, I shall say as much!" he answered. "Nor did they stop to say a 'by-your-leave' when they obtained it. This very night, an hour or so before we journeyed to that thirty-thousand-times-accursed mill of Monsieur Jones, two men descended suddenly upon the hangars at New Bristol. A splendid new amphibian lay in the bay, all ready to be drawn into her shed. The people at the airport are much surprised to see her suddenly take flight, but—aviators are all crazy, else they would remain on land, and who shall say what form their latest madness takes? It was some little time before the truth was learned. Then it was too late.

"Stretched cold upon the runway of the hangar they found the pilot and his mechanician. Both were shot dead, yet not a shot was heard. The miscreants had used silencers upon their guns, no doubt.

"*Tiens*, at any rate, they had not stopped at murder, and they had made off with the plane, had landed it upon the frozen millpond, then sailed away, almost—but not quite, thank God!—leaving us as dead as we had left their guardian wolves."

"*Hélas*, and we shall never overtake them!" Renouard said mournfully. "It is too obvious. They chose the amphibian plane that they might put to sea and be picked up by some ship which waited; and where they may be gone we can not say. There is no way of telling, for—"

"Hold hard, old thing; I think perhaps there is!" the Englishman broke in. "When Trowbridge toppled over it knocked the thought out of my head, but I've an idea we may trace 'em. I'll pop off to the cable office and send a little tracer out. We ought to get some solid information by tomorrow."

W E WERE STILL AT breakfast the next morning when the young man from the cable office came. "Mr. In-gra-ham here?" he asked.

"Don't say it like that, young feller, me lad, it's Ingraham—'In' as in 'inside,' and 'graham' as in biscuit, you know," returned the Englishman with a grin as he held out his hand for the message.

Hastily he read it to himself, then aloud to us:

No strangers seeking access to the bush through here but French report a hundred turned back from Konakri stop unprecedented number of arrivals at Monrovia stop investigation underway

Symmes
Supt

"*Très Bon*," de Grandin nodded. "Now, if you will have the goodness to translate—" he paused with brows raised interrogatively.

"Nothin' simpler, old thing," the Englishman responded. "You see, it was like this:

"'Way up in the back country of Sierra Leone, so near the boundary line of French Guinea that the French think it's British territory and the British think it's French, an old goop named MacAndrews got permission to go diggin' some twenty years ago. He was a dour old Scotsman, mad as a dingo dog, they say, but a first-rate archeologist. There were some old Roman ruins near the border, and this Johnny had the idea he'd turn up something never in the books if he kept at it long enough. So he built a *pukka* camp and settled down to clear the jungle off; but fever beat his schedule and they planted the old cove in one of his own trenches.

"That ended old Mac's diggin', but his camp's still there. I passed it less than five years ago, and stopped there overnight. The natives say the old man's ghost hangs around the place, and shun it like the plague—haven't even stolen anything."

"Ah?" de Grandin murmured. "And—"

"Oh, quite, old dear. A big 'and'. That's what got the massive intellect workin', don't you know. There's a big natural clearin' near MacAndrews and a pretty fair-sized river. The place is so far inland nobody ever goes there unless he has to, and news—white man's news, I mean is blessed slow gettin' to the coast. Could anything be sweeter for our Russian friends' jamboree?

"Irak is under British rule today, and any nonsense in that neighborhood would bring the police sniffin' round. The Frenchmen in Arabia don't stand much foolishness, so any convocation of the Devil-Worshippers is vetoed in advance so far as that locality's concerned. *But what about MacAndrew's?* They could plant and harvest the finest crop of merry young hell you ever saw out there and no one be the wiser. But they've got to get there. That's the blighted difficulty, me lad. Look here—"

He drew a pencil and notebook from his pocket and blocked out a rough map: "Here's Sierra Leone; here's French Guinea; here's Liberia. Get it? Our people in Freetown have to be convinced there's some good reason why before they'll pass a stranger to the bush country; so do the French. But Liberia—any man, black, white, yellow or mixed, who lands there with real money in his hand can get unlimited concessions to go hunting in the back country, and no questions asked.

"There you are, old bean. When Davisson decoded that message on the floor last night it hit me like a brick. The gal had told us where she was in the letter; now, she takes a chance we'll go to Jones' Mill and starts to write a message on the floor. They've talked before her, and she takes her lipstick and starts to write her destination down—'MacAndrews, Sierra Leone'—but only gets 'MacAndrews' and the first three letters of 'Sierra' down when they come for her and she has to stop. That's the way I've figured it—it's great to have a brain like mine!

"Now, if they've really picked MacAndrews' old camp for their party, there'll be a gatherin' of the clans out there. And the visitors will have to come overland, or enter through Freetown, one of the French ports or Liberia. That's reasonin', old top.

"So I cabled Freetown to see if anyone's been tryin' to bootleg himself through the lines, or if there'd been much sudden immigration through the

French ports. You have the answer. All these coves will have to do is strike cross-country through the bush and—"

"And we shall apprehend them!" Renouard exclaimed delightedly.

"Right-o, dear sir and fellow policeman," the Englishman returned. "I'm bookin' passage for West Africa this mornin', and—"

"Book two," Renouard cut in. "This excavation of Monsieur MacAndrews, it is near the border; me, I shall be present, with a company of Senegalese gendarmes and—"

"And with me, *pardieu!* Am I to have no pleasure?" broke in Jules de Grandin.

"Me, too," John Davisson asserted. "If they've got Alice, I must be there too."

"You might as well book passage for five," I finished. "I've been with you so far, and I'd like to see the finish of this business. Besides, I owe 'em something for that bomb they dropped on me last night."

23. Pursuit

THERE WAS NO SCARCITY of offered labor when we debarked at Monrovia. A shouting, sweating, jostling throng of black boys crowded round us, each member of the crowd urging his own peculiar excellence as a baggage-carrier in no uncertain terms. Foremost—and most vocal—was a young man in long and much soiled nightgown, red slippers and very greasy tarboosh. "Carry luggage, sar? Carry him good; not trust dam' bush nigger!" he asseverated, worming with serpentine agility through the pressing crowd of volunteers and plucking Ingraham's sleeve solicitously.

"Right; carry on, young feller," the Englishman returned, kicking his kit toward the candidate for partnership.

"Hi-yar, this way—grab marster's duffle!" the favored one called out, and from the crowd some half-dozen nondescript individuals sprang forward, shouldered our gear and, led by the man Ingraham had engaged, preceded us at a shuffling jog-trot up the winding street toward the apology for a hotel.

Evidently Ingraham was familiar with conventions, for when we had arrived at our hotel he made no effort to distribute largess among the porters, but beckoned to the head man to remain in our room while the remainder of the gang dispersed themselves in such shade as offered in the street outside, awaiting the emergence of their leader.

The moment the door closed a startling transformation came over our chief porter. The stooping, careless bearing which marked his every movement fell from him like a cloak, his shoulders straightened back, his chin went up, and heels clicked together, he stood erectly at attention before Ingraham. "Sergeant Bendigo reporting, sar," he announced.

"At ease," commanded Ingraham. Then: "Did you go out there?"

"Yes, O Hiji, even as you ordered, so I did. Up to the place where all of the great waters break in little streams I went, and there at the old camp where ghosts and djinn and devils haunt the night I found the tribesmen making *poro*. Also, O Hiji, I think the little leopards are at large again, for in the night I heard their drums, and once *I saw them* dancing round a fire while something— *wah*, an unclean thing, I think—stewed within their pots. Also, I heard the leopard scream, but when I looked I saw no beast, only three black feller walking through a jungle path."

"U'm? Any white men there?" demanded Ingraham.

"Plenty lot, sar. No jolly end. Plenty much white feller, also other feller with dark skin, not white like Englishman or French, not black like bush boy or brown like Leoni, but funny-lookin' feller, some yeller, some brown, some white, but dark and big-nosed, like Jewish trading man. Some, I think, are Hindoos, like I see sometime in Freetown. They come trekking long time through the jungle from Monrovia, ten, twenty, maybe thirty at once, with Liberian bush boys for guide, and—"

"All right, get on with it," Ingraham prompted sharply.

"Then make killing palaver, Hiji," the young man told him earnestly. "Those bush boys come as guides; but *they* not return. They start for home, but something happen—I saw one speared from ambush. I think those white men put bad thoughts in bush men's heads. Very, very bad palaver, sar."

"What's doing up at MacAndrews'?"

"*Hou!* Bush nigger from all parts of the forest work like slaves; all time they dig and chop. Clear off the jungle, dig up old stones where ghosts are buried. I think there will be trouble there."

"No doubt of it," the Englishman concurred. Then: "Tell me, O Sergeant Man, was there among these strangers some one woman of uncommon beauty whom they guarded carefully, as though a prisoner, yet with reverence, as though a queen?"

"Allah!" exclaimed the sergeant, rolling up his eyes ecstatically.

"Never mind the religious exercises. Did you see the woman?"

"*Wah*, a woman, truly, Hiji, but a woman surely such as never was before. Her face is like the moon at evening, her walk like that of the gazelle, and from her lips drips almond-honey. Her voice is like the dripping of the rain in thirsty places, and her eyes—*bismillah*, when she weeps the tears are sapphires. She has the first-bloom of the lotus on her cheek, and—"

"Give over, you've been reading Hafiz or Elinor Glyn, young feller. Who's the leader of this mob?"

"*Wallah!*"—Sergeant Bendigo passed his fingers vertically across his lips and spat upon the floor—"he is called Bazarri, Hiji, and verily he is the twin of

Satan, the stoned and the rejected. A face of which the old and wrinkled monkey well might be ashamed is his, with great sad eyes that never change their look, whatever they behold. *Wah*, in Allah's glorious name I take refuge from the rejected one—"

"All right; all right, take refuge all you please, but get on with your report," Ingraham cut in testily. "You say he has the natives organized?"

"Like the blades of grass that come forth in the early rains, O Hiji. Their spears are numerous as the great trees of the forest, and everywhere they range the woods lest strangers come upon them. They killed two members of the Mendi who came upon them unawares, and I was forced to sleep in trees like any of the monkey people; for to be caught near MacAndrews' is to enter into Paradise—and the cooking-pot."

"Eh? The devil! They're practising cannibalism?"

"Thou sayest."

"Who—"

"The white man of the evil, wrinkled face; he whom they call Bazarri; he has appointed it. Also he gives them much trade gin. I think there will be shooting before long; spears will fly as thick as gnats about the carcass—*hai*, and bullets, too. The little guns which stutter will laugh the laugh of death, and the bayonets will go *bung*, as we drive them home to make those dam' bush feller know our lord the Emperor-King is master still."

"Right you are," the Englishman returned, and there was something far from pleasant at the corners of his mouth as he smiled at Sergeant Bendigo.

"Gentlemen"—he turned to us—"this is my sergeant and my right-hand man. We can accept all that he tells us as the truth.

"Sergeant, these men come from far away to help us hunt this evil man of whom you tell me."

The sergeant drew himself erect again and tendered us a grave salute. His slightly flaring nostrils and smooth, brown skin announced his Negroid heritage, but the thin-lipped mouth, the straight, sleek hair and finely modeled hands and feet were pure Arab, while the gleaming, piercing eyes and quick, cruel smile were equally pure devil. De Grandin knew him for a kindred spirit instantly.

"*Tiens, mon brave*, it is a fine thing you have done, this discovering of their devil's nest," he complimented as he raised his hand in answer to the sergeant's military courtesy. "You think we yet shall come to grips with them?"

Bendigo's eyes shone with anticipation and delight, his white teeth flashed between his back-drawn lips. "May Allah spare me till that day!" He answered. It was a born killer speaking, a man who took as aptly to the deadly risks of police work as ever duckling took to water.

"Very well, Sergeant," Ingraham ordered: "Take the squad and hook it for Freetown as fast as you can; we'll be along in a few days."

Bendigo saluted again, executed a perfect about-face and marched to the door. Once in the hotel corridor he dropped his military bearing and slouched into the sunshine where his confreres waited.

"Stout feller, that," Ingraham remarked. "I sent him a wire to go native and pop up to MacAndrews' and nose round, then follow the trail overland to Monrovia, pickin' up what information he could *en route*. It's a holy certainty nothing happened on the way he didn't see, too."

"But isn't there a chance some of that gang he called to help him with our luggage may give the show away?" I asked. "They didn't seem any too choice a crowd to me."

Ingraham smiled a trifle bleakly. "I hardly think so," he replied. "You see, they're all members of Bendigo's platoon. He brought 'em here to help him carry on."

D E GRANDIN AND RENOUARD went on to Dakar, while Ingraham, John Davisson and I took packet north to Freetown.

Our expedition quickly formed. A hundred frontier policemen with guns and bayonets, five Lewis guns in charge of expert operators, with Ingraham and Bendigo in command, set out in a small wood-burning steamer toward Falaba. We halted overnight at the old fortress town, camping underneath the loop-holed walls, then struck out overland toward the French border.

The rains had not commenced, nor would they for a month or so, and the *Narmattan*, the ceaseless northwest wind blowing up from the Sahara, swept across the land like a steady draft from a boiler room. The heat was bad, the humidity worse; it was like walking through a superheated hothouse as we beat our way along the jungle trails, now marching through comparatively clear forest, now hacking at the trailing undergrowth, or pausing at the mud-bank of some sluggish stream to force a passage while our native porters beat the turbid water with sticks to keep the crocodiles at a respectful distance.

"We're almost there," Ingraham announced one evening as we sat before his tent, imbibing whisky mixed with tepid water, "and I don't like the look of things a bit."

"How's that?" I asked. "It seems extremely quiet to me; we've scarcely seen—"

"That's it! We haven't seen a bloomin' thing, or heard one, either. Normally these woods are crawlin' with natives—Timni or Sulima, even if the beastly Mendi don't show up. This trip we've scarcely seen a one. Not only that, they should be gossipin' on the *lokali*—the jungle telegraph-drum, you know—tellin' the neighbors miles away that we're headin' north by east, but—damn it; I don't *like* it!"

"Oh, you're getting nerves," Davisson told him with a laugh. "I'm going to turn in. Good-night."

Ingraham watched him moodily as he walked across the little clearing to his tent beneath an oil-palm tree. "Silly ass," he muttered. "If he knew this country as I do he'd be singin' a different sort o' chanty. Nerves—good Lord!"

He reached inside his open tunic for tobacco pouch and pipe, but stiffened suddenly, like a pointer coming on a covey of quail. Next instant he was on his feet, the Browning flashing from the holster strapped against his leg, and a savage spurt of flame stabbed through the darkness.

Like a prolongation of the pistol's roar there came a high-pitched, screaming cry, and something big and black and bulky crashed through the palm-tree's fronds, hurtling to the earth right in Davisson's path.

We raced across the clearing, and Ingraham stooped and struck a match. "Nerves, eh?" he asked sarcastically, as the little spot of orange flame disclosed a giant native, smeared with oil and naked save for a narrow belt of leopard hide bound round his waist and another band of spotted fur wound round his temples. On each hand he wore a glove of leopard skin, and fixed to every finger was a long, hooked claw of sharpened iron. One blow from those spiked gloves and anyone sustaining it would have had the flesh ripped from his bones.

"Nerves, eh?" the Englishman repeated. "Jolly good thing for you I had 'em, young feller me lad, and that I saw this beggar crouchin' in the tree—

"The devil! You would, eh?" The inert native, bleeding from a bullet in his thigh, had regained the breath the tumble from the tree knocked from him, raised on his elbow and struck a slashing blow at Ingraham's legs. The Englishman swung his pistol barrel with crushing force upon the native's head; then, as Bendigo and half a dozen Houssas hurried up:

"O Sergeant Man, prepare a harness for this beast and keep him safely till his spirit has returned."

The sergeant saluted, and in a moment the prisoner was securely trussed with cords.

Some twenty minutes later Bendigo stood at Ingraham's tent, a light of pleased anticipation shining in his eyes. "Prisoner's spirit has come back, O Hiji," he reported.

"Good, bring him here.

"I see you, Leopard Man," he opened the examination when they brought the fettered captive to us.

The prisoner eyed him sullenly, but volunteered no answer.

"Who sent you through the woods to do this evil thing?" Ingraham pursued.

"The leopard hates and kills, he does not talk," the man replied.

"*Oko!*" the Englishman returned grimly. "I think this leopard will talk, and be jolly glad to. Sergeant, build a fire!"

Sergeant Bendigo had evidently anticipated this, for dry sticks and kindling were produced with a celerity nothing short of marvelous.

"I hate to do this, Trowbridge," Ingraham told me, "but I've got to get the truth out of this blighter, and get it in a hurry. Go to your tent if you think you can't stand it."

The captive howled and beat his head against the earth and writhed as though he were an eel upon the barbs when they thrust his bare soles into the glowing embers; but not until the stench of burning flesh rose sickeningly upon the still night air did he shake his head from side to side in token of surrender.

"Now, then, who sent you?" Ingraham demanded when the prisoner's blistered feet were thrust into a canvas bucket full of water. "Speak up, and speak the truth, or—" he nodded toward the fire which smoldered menacingly as a Houssa policeman fed it little bits of broken sticks to keep it ready for fresh service.

"You are Hiji," said the prisoner, as though announcing that the sun had ceased to shine and the rivers ceased to flow. "You are He-Who-Comes-When-No-Man-Thinks-Him-Near. They told us you were gone away across the mighty water."

"Who told you this great lie, O fool?"

"Bazarri. He came with other white men through the woods and told us you were fled and that the soldiers of the Emperor-King would trouble us no more. They said the Leopard Men should rule the land again, and no one bid us stop."

"What were you doing here, son of a fish?"

"Last moon Bazarri sent us forth in search of slaves. Much help is needed for this digging which he makes, for he prepares a mighty pit where, in a night and a night, they celebrate the marriage of a mortal woman to the King of all the Devils. My brethren took the prisoners back, but I and as many others as a man has eyes remained behind to—"

"To stage a little private cannibalism, eh?"

"They told us that the soldiers would not come this way again," the prisoner answered in excuse.

Ingraham smiled, but not pleasantly. "That's the explanation, eh?" he murmured to himself. "No wonder we haven't seen or heard anything of the villagers. These damned slavers have taken most of 'em up to MacAndrews' and those they didn't kill or capture are hidin' in the bush." To the prisoner:

"Is this Bizarri a white man with the body of a youth and the wrinkled face of an old monkey?"

"Lord, who can say how you should know this thing?"

"Does he know that I am coming with my soldiers to send him to the land of ghosts?"

"Lord, he does not know. He thinks that you have gone across the great water. If he knew you were here he would have gone against you with his guns, and with the Leopard Men to kill you while you slept."

"The Emperor-King's men never sleep," retorted Ingraham. To Bendigo: "A firing-party for this one, Sergeant. The palaver is over.

"We must break camp at once," he added as eight tarbooshed policemen marched smartly past, their rifles at slant arms. "You heard what he said; they're all set to celebrate that girl's marriage to the Devil in two more nights. We can just make it to MacAndrews' by a forced march."

"Can't you spare this poor fellow's life?" I pleaded. "You've gotten what you want from him, and—"

"No chance," he told me shortly. "The penalty for membership in these Leopard Societies is death; so is the punishment for slaving and cannibalism. If it ever got about that we'd caught one of the 'Little Leopards' red-handed and let him off, government authority would get an awful black eye."

He buttoned his blouse, put on his helmet and marched across the clearing. "Detail halt; front rank, kneel; ready; take aim—fire!" his orders rang in sharp staccato, and the prisoner toppled over, eight rifle bullets in his breast.

Calmly as though it were a bit of everyday routine, Sergeant Bendigo advanced, drew his pistol and fired a bullet in the prone man's ear. The head, still bound in its fillet of leopard skin, bounced upward with the impact of the shot, then fell back flaccidly. The job was done.

"Dig a grave and pile some rocks on it, then cover it with ashes from the fire," Ingraham ordered. To me he added:

"Can't afford to have hyenas unearthin' him or vultures wheelin' round, you know. It would give the show away. If any of his little playmates found him and saw the bullet marks they might make tracks for MacAndrews—and we want to get there first."

We broke camp in half an hour, pushed onward through the night and marched until our legs were merely so much aching muscles the next day. Six hours' rest then again the endless, hurrying march.

Twice we saw evidence of the Leopards' visits, deserted villages where blackened rings marked the site of burned huts, red stains upon the earth, vultures disputing over ghastly scraps of flesh and bone.

As we passed through the second village the scouts brought back a woman, a slender frightened girl of fifteen or so, with a face which might have been a Gorgon's and a figure fit to make a Broadway entrepreneur discharge his entire chorus in disgust.

"Thou art my father and my mother," she greeted Ingraham conventionally.

"Where are thy people?" he demanded.

"In the land of ghosts, lord," she replied. "A day and a day ago there came to us the servants of Bazarri, men of the Little Leopards, with iron claws upon their hands and white men's guns. They said to us: 'The Emperor-King is overthrown; no longer shall his soldiers bring the law to you. Come with us and serve Bazarri, who is the servant of the Great King of All Devils, and we shall make you rich.'

"'This is bad palaver, and when Hiji comes he will hang you to a tree,' my father told them.

"'Hiji is gone across the great water, and will never come here more,' they told my father. Then they killed many of my people, and some they took as slaves to serve Bazarri where the King of Devils makes a marriage with a mortal woman. Lord, hadst thou been here three days ago my father had not died."

"Maiden," Ingraham answered, "go tell thy people to come again into their village and build the huts the evil men burned down. Behold, I and my soldiers travel swiftly to give punishment to these evil men. Some I shall hang and some my men will shoot; but surely I shall slay them all. Those who defy the Emperor-King's commands have not long lives."

THE SUDDEN TROPIC DARK had long since fallen, and it was almost midnight by the hands on Ingraham's luminous watch dial when we reached the edge of a large clearing with a sharply rising hill upon its farther side. From behind this elevation shone a ruddy light, as though a dozen wooden houses burned at once.

"Quiet, thirty lashes for the one who makes a sound," said Ingraham as we halted at the forest edge. "Get those Lewis guns ready; fix bayonets.

"Sergeant, take two men and go forward. If anyone accosts you, shoot him down immediately. We'll charge the moment we hear a shot."

Twenty minutes, half an hour, three-quarters, passed. Still no warning shot, no sign of Sergeant Bendigo or his associates.

"By the Lord Harry, I'm half a mind to chance it!" Ingraham muttered. "They may have done Bendigo in, and—"

"No, sar, Bendigo is here," a whisper answered him, and a form rose suddenly before us. "Bendigo has drunk the broth of serpent's flesh, he can move through the dark and not be seen."

"I'll say he can," the Englishman agreed. "What's doing?"

"No end dam' swanky palaver over there," returned the sergeant. "Many people sit around like elders at the council and watch while others make some show before them. I think we better go there pretty soon."

"So do I," returned his officer.

"Attention, charge bayonets; no shooting till I give the word. Quick step, march!"

We passed across the intervening clearing, mounted the steep slope of grassy bank, and halted at the ridge. Before us, like a stage, was such a sight as I had never dreamed of, even in my wildest flights of fancy.

24. The Devil's Bride

"GREAT GUNS!" INGRAHAM EXCLAIMED as we threw ourselves upon our stomachs and wriggled to the crown of the hill. "Old MacAndrews knew a thing or two, dotty as he was! Look at that masonry—perfect as it was when Augustus Caesar ruled the world! The old Scotsman would have had the laugh on all of 'em, if he'd only lived."

What I had thought a long, steep-sided natural hill was really the nearer of two parallel earthen ramparts, and between these, roughly oval in form, a deep excavation had been made, disclosing tier on tier of ancient stone benches rising terrace-like about an amphitheater. Behind these were retaining walls of mortised stone—obviously the well-preserved remains of a Roman circus.

The arena between the curving ranks of benches was paved with shining sand, washed and rewashed until it shone with almost dazzling whiteness, and the whole enclosure was aglow with ruddy light, for stretching in an oval round the sanded floor was set a line of oil-palms, each blazing furiously, throwing tongues of orange flame high in the air and making every object in the excavation visible as though illumined by the midday sun.

The leaping, crackling flames disclosed the tenants of the benches, row after row of red-robed figures, hoods drawn well forward on their faces, hands hidden in the loose sleeves of their gown, but every one intent upon the spectacle below, heads bent, each line of their voluminously robed bodies instinct with eagerness and gloating, half-restrained anticipation.

The circus proper was some hundred yards in length by half as many wide. Almost beneath us crouched a group of black musicians who, even as we looked, began a thumping monody on their double-headed drums, beating a sort of slow adagio with one hand, a fierce, staccato syncopation with the other. The double-timed insistence of it mounted to my head like some accursed drug. Despite myself I felt my hands and feet twitching to the rhythm of those drums, a sort of tingling racing up my spine. The red-robed figures on the benches were responding, too, heads swaying, hands no longer hidden in their sleeves, but striking together softly, as if in acclamation of the drummers' skill.

At the arena's farther end, where the double line of benches broke, was hung a long red curtain blazoned with the silver image of the strutting peacock, and from behind the folds of the thick drapery we saw that some activity was toward, for the carmine cloth would swing in rippling folds from time to time as though invisible hands were clutching it.

"Now, I wonder what the deuce—" Ingraham began, but stopped abruptly as the curtain slowly parted and into the firelight marched a figure. From neck to heels he was enveloped in a robe of shimmering scarlet silk, thick-sewn with glistening gems worked in the image of a peacock. Upon his head he wore a beehive-shaped turban of red silk set off with a great medallion of emeralds.

One look identified him. Though we had seen him suffer death in the electric chair and later looked upon him lying in his casket, there was no doubt in either of our minds. The Oriental potentate who paced the shining sands before us was Grigor Bazarov, the Red Priest who officiated at the Mass of St. Secaire.

Beside him, to his right and left, and slightly to the rear, marched the men who acted as deacon and subdeacon when he served the altar of the Devil, but now they were arrayed in costumes almost as gorgeous as their chief's, turbans of mixed red and black upon their heads, brooches of red stones adorning them, curved swords flashing in jeweled scabbards at their waists.

Attended by his satellites the Red Priest made the circuit of the colosseum, and as he passed, the red-robed figures on the benches arose and did him reverence.

Now he and his attendants took station before the squatting drummers, and as he raised his hand in signal the curtains at the arena's farther end were parted once again and from them came a woman, tall, fair-haired, purple-eyed, enveloped in a loose-draped cloak of gleaming cloth of gold. A moment she paused breathlessly upon the margin of the shining sand, and as she waited two tall black women, stark naked, save for gold bands about their wrists and ankles, stepped quickly forward from the curtain's shrouding folds, grasped the golden cloak which clothed her and lifted it away, so that she stood revealed nude as her two serving-maids, her white and lissom body gleaming in sharp contrast to their black forms as an ivory figurine might shine beside two statuettes of ebony.

A single quick glance told us she was crazed with aphrodisiacs and the never-pausing rhythm of the drums. With a wild, abandoned gesture she threw back her mop of yellow hair, tossed her arms above her head and, bending nearly double, raced across the sands until she paused a moment by the drummers, her body stretched as though upon a rack as she rose on tiptoe and reached her hands up to the moonless sky.

Then the dance. As thin as nearly fleshless bones could make her, her figure still was slight, rather than emaciated, and as she bent and twisted, writhed and whirled, then stood stock-still and rolled her narrow hips and straight, flat abdomen, I felt the hot blood mounting in my cheeks and the pulses beating in my temples in time with the insistent throbbing of the drums. Pose after pose instinct with lecherous promise melted into still more lustful postures as patterns change their forms upon the lens of a kaleidoscope.

Now a vocal chorus seconded the music of the tom-toms:

Ho, hol, hola,
Ho, hol, hola;
Tou bonia berbe Azid!

The Red Priest and the congregation repeated the lines endlessly, striking their hands together at the ending of each stanza.

"Good God!" Ingraham muttered in my ear. "D'ye get it Trowbridge?"

"No," I whispered back. "What is it?"

"'*Tou bonia berbe Azid*' means 'thou has become a lamb of the Devil!' It's the invocation which precedes a human sacrifice!"

"B-but—" I faltered, only to have the words die upon my tongue, for the Red Priest stepped forward, unsheathing the scimitar from the jeweled scabbard at his waist. He tendered it to her, blade foremost, and I winced involuntarily as I saw her take the steel in her bare hand and saw the blood spurt like a ruby dye between her fingers as the razor-edge bit through the soft flesh to the bone.

But in her wild delirium she was insensible to pain. The curved sword whirled like darting lightning round her head, circling and flashing in the burning palm-trees' light till it made a silver halo for her golden hair. Then—

It all occurred so quickly that I scarcely knew what happened till the act was done. The wildly whirling blade reversed its course, struck inward suddenly and passed across her slender throat, its super-fine edge propelled so fiercely by her maddened hand that she was virtually decapitated.

The rhythm of the drums increased, the flying fingers of the drummers increased, the flying fingers of the drummers beating a continuous roar which filled the sultry night like thunder, and the red-robed congregation rose like one individual, bellowing wild approval at the suicide. The dancer tripped and stumbled in her corybantic measure, a spate of ruby lifeblood cataracting down her snowy bosom; wheeled round upon her toes a turn or two, then toppled to the sand, her hands and feet and body twitching with a tremor like the jerking of a victim of St. Vitus dance. She raised herself upon her elbows and tried to call aloud, but the gushing blood drowned out her voice. Then she fell forward on her face and lay prostrate in the sand, her dying heart still pumping spurts of blood from her severed veins and arteries.

The sharp, involuntary twitching of the victim ceased, and with it stopped the gleeful rumble of the drums. The Red Priest raised his hand as if in invocation. "That the Bride of Lucifer may tread across warm blood!" he told the congregation in a booming voice, then pointed to the crimson pool which dyed the snowy sand before the trailing scarlet curtain.

The two black women who had taken off her cloak approached the quivering body of the self-slain girl, lifted it—one by the shoulders, the other by the feet—and bore it back behind the scarlet curtain, their progress followed by a trail of ruddy drops which trickled from the dead girl's severed throat at every step they took.

Majestically the Red Priest drew his scarlet mantle round him, waved to the drummers to precede him, then followed by his acolytes, passed through the long red curtains in the wake of the victim and the bearers of the dead.

A whispering buzz, a sort of oestrus of anticipation, ran through the red-robed congregation as the archpriest vanished, but the clanging, brazen booming of a bell cut the sibilation short.

Clang!

A file of naked blacks marched out in the arena, each carrying a sort of tray slung from a strap about his shoulders, odd, gourd-like pendants hanging from the board. Each held a short stave with a leather-padded head in either hand, and with a start of horror I recognized the things—trust a physician of forty years' experience to know a human thigh-bone when he sees it!

Clang!

The black men squatted on the glittering, firelit sand, and without a signal of any sort that we could see, began to hammer on the little tables resting on their knees. The things were crude marimbas, primitive xylophones with hollow gourds hung under them for resonators, and, incredible as it seemed, produced a music strangely like the reeding of an organ. A long, resounding chord, so cleverly sustained that it simulated the great swelling of a bank of pipes; then, slowly, majestically, there boomed forth within that ancient Roman amphitheater the Bridal Chorus from *Lohengrin*.

Clang!

Unseen hands put back the scarlet curtain which had screened the Red Priest's exit. There, reared against the amphitheater's granite-wall, was a cathedral altar, ablaze with glittering candles. Arranged behind the altar like a reredos, was a giant figure, an archangelic figure with great, outspread wings, but with the lone, bearded face of a leering demon, goat's horns protruding from its brow. The crucifix upon the altar was reversed, and beneath its down-turned head stretched the scarlet mattress which I knew would later hold a human altar-cloth. To right and left were small side altars, like sanctuaries raised to saints in Christian churches. That to the right bore the hideous figure of a man in ancient costume with the head of a rhinoceros. I had seen its counterpart in a museum; it was the figure of the Evil One of Olden Egypt, Set, the slayer of Osiris. Upon the left was raised an altar to an obscene idol carved of some black stone, a female figure, gnarled and knotted and articulated in a manner suggesting horrible deformity. From the shoulder-sockets three arms sprang out to right and left, a sort of pointed cap adorned the head, and about the pendulous breasts serpents twined and writhed, while a girdle of gleaming skulls, carved of white bone, encircled the waist. Otherwise it was nude, with a nakedness which seemed obscene even to me, a medical practitioner for whom the human body held no secrets. Kali, "the Six-Armed One of Horrid Form," goddess of the murderous Thags of India, I knew the thing to be.

Clang!

The bell beat out its twelfth and final stroke, and from an opening in the wall directly under us a slow procession came. First walked the crucifer, the *corpus* of his cross head-downward, a peacock's effigy perched atop the rood; then, two by two, ten acolytes with swinging censers, the fumes of which swirled slowly through the air in writhing clouds of heady, maddening perfume. Next marched a robed and surpliced man who swung a tinkling sacring bell, and then, beneath a canopy of scarlet silk embossed with gold, the Red Priest came, arrayed in full ecclesiastical regalia. Close in his footsteps marched his servers, vested as deacon and subdeacon, and after them a double file of women votaries arrayed in red, long veils of crimson net upon their heads, hands crossed demurely on their bosoms.

Slowly the procession passed between the rows of blazing palm-trees, deployed before the altar and formed in crescent shape, the Red Priest and his acolytes in the center.

A moment's pause in the marimba music; then the Red Priest raised his hand, palm forward, as if in salutation, and chanted solemnly:

To the Gods of Egypt who are Devils,
To the Gods of Babylon in Nether Darkness,
To all the Gods of all Forgotten Peoples,
Who rest not, but lust eternally — Hail!

Turning to the rhinoceros-headed monster on the right he bowed respectfully and called:

Hail Thee who are Doubly Evil,
Who comest forth from Ati,
Who proceedest from the Lake of Nefer,
Who comest from the Courts of Sechet — Hail!

To the left he turned and invoked the female horror:

Hail, Kali, Daughter of Himavat,
Hail, Thou about whose waist hang human skulls,
Hail, Devi of Horrid Form,
Malign Image of Destructiveness,
Eater-up of all that it good,
Disseminator of all which is wicked — Hail!

Finally, looking straight before him, he raised both hands above his head and fairly screamed:

And Thou, Great Barran-Sathanas,
Azid, Beelzebub, Lucifer, Asmodeum,
Or whatever name Thou wishest to be known by,
Lucifer, Mighty Lord of Earth,
Prince of the Powers of the Air;
We give Thee praise and adoration,
Now and ever, Mighty Master,
Hail, all hail, Great Lucifer. Hail, all hail!

"All hail!" responded the red congregation.

Slowly the Red Priest mounted to the sanctuary. A red nun tore away her habit, rending scarlet silk and cloth as though in very ecstasy of haste, and, nude and gleaming white, climbed quickly up and laid herself upon the scarlet cushion. They set the chalice and the paten on her branded breast and the Red Priest genuflected low before the living altar, then turned and, kneeling with his back presented to the sanctuary, crossed himself in reverse with his left hand and, rising once again, his left hand raised, bestowed a mimic blessing on the congregation.

A long and death-still silence followed, a silence so intense that we could hear the hissing of the resin as the palm-trees burned, and when a soldier moved uneasily beside me in the grass the rasping of his tunic buttons on the earth came shrilly to my ears.

"Now, what the deuce—" Ingraham began, but checked himself and craned his neck to catch a glimpse of what was toward in the arena under us; for, as one man, the red-robed congregation had turned to face the tunnel entrance leading to the amphitheater opposite the altar, and a sigh that sounded like the rustling of the autumn wind among the leaves made the circuit of the benches.

I could not see the entrance, for the steep sides of the excavation hid it from my view, but in a moment I descried a double row of iridescent peacocks strutting forward, their shining tails erected, their glistening wings lowered till the quills cut little furrows in the sand. Slowly, pridefully, as though they were aware of their magnificence, the jeweled birds marched across the hippodrome, and in their wake—

"For God's sake!" exclaimed Ingraham.

"Good heavens!" I ejaculated.

"Alice!" John Davisson's low cry was freighted with stark horror and despairing recognition.

It was Alice; unquestionably it was she; but how completely metamorphosed! A diadem of beaten gold, thickset with flashing jewels, was clasped about her head. Above the circlet, where dark hair and white skin met at the temples, there *grew a pair of horns!* They grew, there was no doubt of it, for even at that distance I could see the skin fold forward round the bony base of the protuberances; no skilful make-up artist could have glued them to her flesh in such a way. Incredible—impossible—as I knew it was, it could not be denied. A pair of curving goat-horns *grew* from the girl's head and reared upward exactly like the horns on carved or painted figures of the Devil!

A collar of gold workmanship, so wide its outer edges rested on her shoulders, was round her neck, and below the gleaming gorget her white flesh shone like ivory; for back, abdomen and bosom were unclothed and the nipples of her high-set, virgin breasts were stained a brilliant red with henna. About her waist was locked the silver marriage girdle of the Yezidees, the girdle she had worn so laughingly that winter evening long ago when we assembled at St. Chrysostom's to rehearse her wedding to John Davisson. Below the girdle—possibly supported by it—hung a skirt of iridescent sequins, so long that it barely cleared her ankles, so tight that it gave her only four or five scant inches for each pace, so that she walked with slow, painstaking care lest the fetter of the garment's hem should trip her as she stepped. The skirt trailed backward in a point a foot or so behind her, leaving a little track in the soft sand, as though a serpent had crawled there and, curiously, giving an oddly serpentine appearance from the rear.

Bizarre and sinister as her costume was, the transformation of her face was more so. The slow, half-scornful, half-mocking smile upon her painted mouth, the beckoning, alluring glance which looked out from between her kohl-stained eyelids, the whole provocative expression of her countenance was strange to Alice Hume. This was no woman we had ever known, this horned, barbaric figure from the painted walls of Asur; it was some wanton, cruel she-devil who held possession of the body we had known as hers.

And so she trod across the shining sand on naked, milk-white feet, the serpent-track left by her trailing gown winding behind her like an accusation. And as she walked she waved her jewel-encrusted hands before her, weaving fantastic arabesques in empty air as Eastern fakirs do when they would lay a charm on the beholder.

> *Hail, Bride of Night,*
> *Hail, horned Bride of Mighty Lucifer;*
> *Hail, thou who comest from the depths of far Abaddon;*
> *Hail and thrice hail to her who passes over*
> *blood and fire*
> *That she may greet her Bridegroom! Hail, all hail!*

cried the Red Priest, and as he finished speaking, from each side the altar rushed a line of red-veiled women, each bearing in her hands a pair of wooden pincers between the prongs of which there glowed and smoldered a small square of super-heated stone. That the rocks were red-hot could not be denied, for we could see the curling smoke and even little licking tongues of flame as the wooden tongs took fire from them.

The women laid their fiery burdens down upon the sand, making an incandescent path of glowing stepping-stones some ten feet long, leading directly to the altar's lowest step.

And now the strange, barbaric figure with its horn-crowned head had reached the ruddy stain upon the sand where the dancing suicide had bled her life away, and now her snowy feet were stained a horrid scarlet, but never did she pause in her slithering step. Now she reached the path of burning stones, and now her tender feet were pressed against them, but she neither hastened or retreated in her march—to blood and fire alike she seemed indifferent.

Now she reached the altar's bottom step and paused a moment, not in doubt or fear, but rather seeming to debate the easiest way to mount the step's low lift and yet not trip against the binding hobble of her skirt's tight hem.

At length, when one or two false trials had been made she managed to get up the step by turning side-wise and raising her nearer foot with slow care, transferring her weight to it, then mounting with a sudden hopping jump.

Three steps she had negotiated in this slow, awkward fashion, when:

"For God's sake, aren't you going to do anything?" John Davisson hissed in Ingraham's ear. "She's almost up—are you going to let 'em go through with—"

"Sergeant," Ingraham turned to Bendigo, ignoring John completely, "are the guns in place?"

"Yas, sar, everything dam' top-hole," the sergeant answered with a grin.

"Very well, then, a hundred yards will be about the proper range. Ready—"

The order died upon his lips, and he and I and all of us sat forward, staring in hang-jawed amazement.

From the tunnel leading to the ancient dungeons at the back of the arena, a slender figure came, paused a moment at the altar steps, then mounted them in three quick strides.

It was Jules de Grandin.

He was in spotless khaki, immaculate from linen-covered sun-hat to freshly polished boots; his canvas jacket and abbreviated cotton shorts might just have left the laundress' hands, and from the way he bore his slender silver-headed cane beneath his left elbow one might have thought that he was ready for a promenade instead of risking almost sure and dreadful death.

"*Pardonnez moi. Messieurs—Mesdames*" he bowed politely to the company of priests and women at the altar—"but this wedding, he can not go on. No, he must be stopped—right away; at once."

The look upon the Red Priest's face was almost comical. His big, sad eyes were opened till it seemed that they were lidless, and a corpse-gray pallor overspread his wrinkled countenance.

"Who dares forbid the banns?" he asked, recovering his aplomb with difficulty.

"*Parbleu,*" the little Frenchman answered with a smile, "the British Empire and the French Republic for two formidable objectors; and last, although by no means least, *Monsieur*, no less a one than Jules de Grandin."

"Audacious fool!" the Red Priest almost howled.

"But certainly," de Grandin bowed, as though acknowledging a compliment, "*l'audace, encore de l'audace, toujours de l'audace*; it is I."

The Devil's Bride had reached the topmost step while this colloquy was toward. Absorbed in working herself up to the altar, she had not realized the visitor's identity. Now, standing at the altar, she recognized de Grandin, and her pose of evil provocation dropped from her as if it were a cast-off garment.

"Doctor—Doctor de Grandin!" she gasped unbelievingly, and with a futile, piteous gesture she clasped her hands across her naked bosom as though to draw a cloak around herself.

"*Précisément, ma pauvre*, and I am here to take you home," the little Frenchman answered, and though he looked at her and smiled, his little sharp blue eyes were alert to note the smallest movement of the men about the altar.

The Red Priest's voice broke in on them. "Wretched meddler, do you imagine that your God can save you now?" he asked.

"He has been known to work much greater miracles," de Grandin answered mildly. "Meantime, if you will kindly stand aside—"

The Red Priest interrupted in a low-pitched, deadly voice: "Before tomorrow's sun has risen we'll crucify you on that altar, as—"

"As you did crucify the poor young woman in America?" de Grandin broke in coldly. "I do not think you will, my friend."

"No? Dimitri, Kasimir—seize this cursed dog!"

The deacon and subdeacon, who had been edging closer all the while, leaped forward at their master's bidding, but the deacon halted suddenly, as though colliding with an unseen barrier, and the savage snarl upon his gipsy features gave way to a puzzled look—a look of almost comic pained surprise. Then we saw spreading on his face a widening smear of red—red blood which ran into his eyes and dripped down on his parted lips before he tumbled headlong to the crimson carpet spread before the altar.

The other man had raised his hands, intent on bringing them down on de Grandin's shoulders with a crushing blow. Now, suddenly, the raised hands shook and quivered in the air, then clutched spasmodically at nothing, while a look of agony spread across his face. He hiccupped once and toppled forward, a spate of ruby blood pouring from his mouth and drowning out his death cry.

"And still you would deny me one poor miracle, *Monsieur?*" de Grandin asked the Red Priest in a level, almost toneless voice.

Indeed, it seemed miraculous. Two men had died—from gunshot wounds, by all appearances—yet we had heard no shot. But:

"Nice work, Frenchy!" Ingraham whispered approvingly. "They have some sharpshooters with silencers on their guns up there," he told me. "I saw the flashes when those two coves got it in the neck. Slick work, eh, what? He'll have those fellers groggy in a minute, and—"

The Red Priest launched himself directly at de Grandin with a roar of bestial fury. The little Frenchman sidestepped neatly, grasped the silver handle of his cane where it projected from his left elbow, and drew the gleaming sword blade from the stick.

"Ah-ha?" he chuckled, "*Ah-ha-ha, Monsieur Diablotin*, you did not bargain for this, *hein?*" he swung the needlelike rapier before him in a flashing circle, then, swiftly as a cobra strikes, thrust forward, "That one for the poor girl whom you crucified!" he cried, and the Red Priest staggered back a step, his hand raised to his face. The Frenchman's blade had pierced his left eyeball.

"And take this for the poor one whom you blinded!" de Grandin told him as he thrust a second time, driving the rapier point full in the other eye.

The Red Priest tottered drunkenly, his hands before his blinded eyes, but de Grandin knew no mercy. "And you may have this for the honest gendarme whom you shot," he added, lashing the blind man's wrinkled cheeks with the flat of his blade, "and last of all, take this for those so helpless little lads who died upon your cursed altar!" He sank backward on one foot, then straightened suddenly forward, stiffening his sword-arm and plunging his point directly in the Red Priest's opened mouth.

A scream of agonizing pain rang out with almost deafening shrillness, and the blind man partly turned, as though upon an unseen pivot, clawed with horrid impotence at the wire-fine blade of the little Frenchman's rapier, then sank slowly to the altar, his death-scream stifled to a sickening gurgle as his throat filled up with blood.

"*Fini!*" de Grandin cried, then:

"If you are ready, *Mademoiselle*, we shall depart," he bowed to Alice, and:

"*Holè—la corde!*" he cried abruptly, raising his hand in signal to some one overhead.

Like a great serpent, a thick hemp hawser twisted down against the amphi-theater's wall, and in the fading light shed from the burning trees we saw the gleam of blue coats and red fezzes where the native gendarmes stood above the excavation, their rifles at the "ready."

De Grandin flung an arm around Alice, took a quick turn of the rope around his other arm, and nodded vigorously. Like the flying fairies in a pantomime they rose up in the air, past the high altar, past the horned and pinioned image of the Devil, past the stone wall of the colosseum, upward, to the excavation's lip, where ready hands stretched out to drag them back to safety.

Now the red congregation was in tumult. While de Grandin parleyed with the Red Priest, even while he slew him with his sword, they had sat fixed in stupor, but as they saw the Frenchman and the girl hauled up to safety, a howl like the war-cry of the gathered demons of the pit rose from their throats—a cry of burning rage and thwarted lust and bitter, mordant disappointment. "Kill him!—after him!—crucify him!—burn him!" came the shouted admonition, and more than one cowled member of the mob drew out a pistol and fired it at the light patch, which de Grandin's spotless costume made against the shadow.

"Fire!" roared Ingraham to his soldiers, and the crashing detonation of a rifle volley echoed through the night, and after it came the deadly clack-clack-clatter of the Lewis guns.

And from the farther side of the arena the French troops opened fire, their rifles blazing death, their Maxims spraying steady streams of bullets at the massed forms on the benches.

Suddenly there came a fearful detonation, accompanied by a blinding flare of flame. From somewhere on the French side a *bombe de main*—a hand gre-nade—was thrown, and like a bolt of lightning it burst against the stone wall shoring up the terraced seats about the colosseum.

The result was cataclysmic. The Roman architects who designed the place had built for permanency, but close upon two thousand years had passed since they had laid those stones, and centuries of pressing earth and trickling subsoil waters had crumbled the cement. When the Satanists turned back the earth they had not stopped to reinforce the masonry or shore up the raw edges of their cutting. Accordingly, the fierce explosion of the bursting bomb precipitated broken stone and sand and rubble into the ancient hippodrome, and instantly a landslide followed. Like sand that trickles in an open pit the broken stone and earth rushed down, engulfing the arena.

"Back—go back!" Ingraham cried, and we raced to safety with the earth falling from beneath our very feet.

It was over in a moment. Only a thin, expiring wisp of smoke emerging through a cleft in the slowly settling earth told where the palm-trees had been blazing furiously a few minutes before. Beneath a hundred thousand tons of sand and crumbling clay and broken stone was buried once again the ancient Roman ruin, and with it every one of those who traveled round the world to see a mortal woman wedded to the Devil.

"By gosh, I think that little Frog was right when he said '*fini*,'" Ingraham exclaimed as he lined his Houssas up.

"*Hamdullah*, trouble comes, O Hiji!" Sergeant Bendigo announced. "Leopard fellers heard our shooting and come to see about it, Allah curse their noseless fathers!"

"By Jove, you're right!" Ingraham cried. "Form square—machine-guns to the front. At two hundred yards—fire!" The volley blazed and crackled from the line of leveled rifles and the shrewish chatter of the Lewis guns mingled with the wild, inhuman screams of the attackers.

On they came, their naked, ebon bodies one shade darker than the moonless tropic night, their belts and caps of leopard skin showing golden in the gloom. Man after man went down before the hail of lead, but on they came; closer, closer, closer!

Now something whistled through the air with a wicked, whirring sound, and the man beside me stumbled back, a five-foot killing spear protruding from his breast. "All things are with Allah, the Merciful, the Compassionate!" he choked, and the blood from his punctured lung made a horrid gurgling noise, like water running down a partly occluded drain.

Now they were upon us, and we could see the camwood stains upon their faces and the markings on their wicker shields and the gleaming strings of human toe and finger bones which hung around their necks. We were outnumbered ten to one, and though the Houssas held their line with perfect discipline, we knew that it was but a matter of a quarter-hour at most before the last of us went down beneath the avalanche of pressing bodies and stabbing spears.

"*Basonette au cannon—Chargez!*" the order rang out sharply on our left, followed by the shrilling of a whistle from the right, and a half a hundred blue-clothed Senegalese gendarmes hurled themselves upon the left flank of our enemies, while as many more crashed upon the foemen from the right, bayonets flashing in the gun-fire, black faces mad with killing-lust and shining with the sweat of fierce exertion.

Now there was a different *timbre* in the Human Leopards' cries. Turned from hunters into quarry, like their bestial prototypes they stood at bay; but the lean, implacable Senegalese were at their backs, their eighteen-inch bayonets stabbing mercilessly, and Ingraham's Houssas barred their path in front.

At last a Leopard Man threw down his spear, and in a moment all were empty-handed. "*Faire halte!*" Renouard commanded, jamming his pistol back into its holster and shouldering his way between the ranks of cringing-captives.

"*Monsieur le Capitaine*," he saluted Ingraham with due formality, "I greatly deprecate the circumstances which have forced us to invade your territory, and herewith tender our apologies, but—"

"Apology's accepted, sweet old soul!" the Englishman cut in, clapping an arm about the Frenchman's shoulders and shaking him affectionately. "But I'd like to have your counsel in an important matter."

"*Mais certainement*," Renouard returned politely. "The matter for discussion is—" he paused expectantly.

"Do we hang or shoot these blighters?" Ingraham rejoined, nodding toward the group of prisoners.

25. The Summing Up

RENOUARD AND INGRAHAM STAYED behind to gather up loose ends—the "loose ends" being such members of the Leopard Men as had escaped the wholesale execution—for they were determined to exterminate the frightful cult. De Grandin and I, accompanied by a dozen Senegalese gendarmes, took Alice overland to Dakar, and Renouard dispatched a messenger before us to advise the hospital that we would need a private room for several days.

Since the night de Grandin rescued her, the girl had lain in a half-stupor, and when she showed signs of returning consciousness the little Frenchman promptly gave her opiates. "It is better that she wake when all is finished and regard the whole occurrence as a naughty dream," he told me.

"But how the deuce did they graft those devilish horns on her?" I wondered. "There is no doubt about it; the things are growing, but—"

"All in good time," he soothed. "When we arrive at Dakar we shall see, my friend."

We did. The morning after our arrival we took her to the operating room, and while she lay in anesthesia, de Grandin deftly laid the temporal skin aside, making a perfect star-shaped incision.

"Name of a little blue man, behold my friend!" he ordered, bending across the operating table and pointing at the open wound with his scapel tip. "They were clever, those ones, *n'est-ce-pas?*"

The lower ends of the small horns had been skilfully riveted to thin disks of gold and these had been inserted underneath the skin, which had then been sewn in place, so that the golden disks, held firmly between skin and tissue, had acted as anchors for the horns, which thus appeared to grow upon the young girl's head.

"Clever?" I echoed. "It's diabolical."

"*Eh bien*, they are frequently the same, my friend."

He sewed the slit skin daintily with an invisible subcutaneous stitch, matching the cut edges so perfectly that only the thinnest hair-line of red showed where he worked.

"*Voilà*," he announced. "This fellow Jules de Grandin puzzles me, my friend. When he acts the physician I am sure he is a better doctor than policeman, but when he is pursuing evil-doers I think he is better gendarme than physician. The devil take the fellow; I shall never make him out!"

THE LITTLE FREIGHTER WALLOWED in the rising swells, her twin propellers churning the blue water into buttermilk. Far astern the coast of Africa lay like the faintest wisp of smoke against the sky. Ahead lay France. De Grandin lit another cigarette and turned his quick, bird-like look from Renouard to me, then to the deck chairs where Davisson and Alice lay side by side, their fingers clasped, the light that never was on land or sea within their eyes.

"*Non*, my friends," he told us, "it is most simple when you understand it. How could the evil fellow leave his cell at the *poste de police*, invade Friend Trowbridge's house and all but murder *Mademoiselle*? How could he be lodged all safely in his cell, yet be abroad to kill poor Hornsby and all but kill the good Costello? How could he die in the electric chair, and lie all dead within his coffin, yet send his wolves to kidnap Mademoiselle Alice! You ask me!

"*Ah-ha*, the answer is he did not! What do you think from that, *hein?*"

"Oh, for heaven's sake, stop talking rot and tell us how it was—if you really know," I shot back crossly.

He grinned delightedly. "Perfectly, my friend. *Écoutez-moi, s'il vous plaite.* When these so trying questions first began to puzzle me I drew my bow at venture. 'If *la Sûreté* can not tell me of him I am shipwrecked—no, how do you call him? sunk?'—I tell me. But I have great faith. A man so wicked as Bazarov, and an European as well, has surely run afoul of the law in France, I think, and if he has done so the *Sûreté* most certainly has his *dossier*. And so I get his photograph and fingerprints from the governor of the prison and forward them to Paris. My answer waited for me at police headquarters at Dakar. It is this:

"Some five and forty years ago there lived in Mohilef a family named Bazarov. They had twin sons, Grigor and Vladimir. They were Roman Catholics.

"To be a Roman Catholic in Imperial Russia was much like being a Negro in the least enlightened of your Southern states today, my friends. Their political disabilities were burdensome, even in that land of dreadful despotism, and they walked in daily fear of molestation by the police, as well, since by the very fact of their adherence to the Church of Rome they were more than suspected of sympathy with Poland's aspirations for independence. The Poles, you will recall, are predominantly Roman Catholic in religion.

"Very well. The brothers Bazarov grew up, and in accordance with their parents' fondest wish, were sent to Italy to study for the church. In time they came back to their native land, duly ordained as fathers in the Roman Church, and sent to minister to their co-religionists in Russia. The good God knows there was a need of fathers in that land of orphans.

"Now in Russia they had a law which made the person having knowledge— even, indirect—of conspiracy to change the form of government, with or without violence, punishable by penal sentence for six years if he failed to transmit information to the police. A harmless literary club was formed in Mohilef and the brothers Bazarov attended several meetings, as a number of the members were of the Roman faith.

"When the police learned of this club, they pounced upon the members and though there was not evidence enough to convict a weasel of chicken-killing, the poor wretches were found guilty, just the same, and sentenced to Siberia. The two young priests were caught in the police net, too, and charged with treasonably withholding information—because it was assumed they must have heard some treasonable news when they sat to hear confessions! *Enfin*, they were confined within the fortress-prison of St. Peter and St. Paul.

"They were immured in dungeons far below the level of the river, dungeons into which the water poured in time of inundation, so that the rats crawled on their shoulders to save themselves from drowning. What horrid tortures they were subject to within that earthly hell we can not surely say; but this we know: When they emerged from four years' suffering inside those prison walls, they came forth old and wrinkled men; moreover, they, who had received the rites of holy ordination, were atheists, haters of God and all his works, and sworn to sow the seed of atheism wherever they might go.

"We find them, then, as members of a group of anarchists in Paris, and there they were arrested, and much of their sad story written in the archives of the *Sûreté*.

"Another thing: As not infrequently happens among Russians, these brethren were possessed of an uncanny power over animals. Wild, savage dogs would fawn on them, the very lions and tigers in the zoo would follow them as far as the limits of their cages would permit, and seemed to greet them with all signs of friendship.

"You comprehend?"

"Why—you mean that while Grigor was under arrest his brother Vladimir impersonated him and broke into my house, then went out gunning for Costello—" I began, but he interrupted with a laugh.

"Oh, Trowbridge, great philosopher, how readily you see the light when someone sets the lamp aglow!" he cried. "Yes, you are right. It was no supernatural ability which enabled him to leave his prison cell at will—even to make a mock of Death's imprisonment. Grigor was locked in prison—executed—but Vladimir, his twin and double, remained at large to carry on their work. But now he, too, is dead. I killed him when we rescued Mademoiselle Alice."

"One other thing, my Jules," Renouard demanded. "When they prepared to wed *Mademoiselle* to Satan, they made her walk all barefoot upon those burning stones. Was not that magic of a sort?"

De Grandin tweaked the needle-points of his mustache. "A juggler's trick," he answered. "That fire-walking, he is widely practised in some places, and always most successfully. The stones they use are porous as a sponge. They heat to incandescence quickly, but just as quickly they give off their heat. When they were laid upon the moistened sand these stones were cool enough to hold within your ungloved hand in thirty seconds. Some time was spent in mummery before they bade *Mademoiselle* to walk on them. By the time she stepped upon them they were cold as any money-lender's heart."

THE SHIP'S BELL BEAT out eight quick strokes. De Grandin dropped down from his seat upon the rail and tweaked the waxed tips of his mustache until they stood out like twin needles from each side of his small and thin-lipped mouth. "Come, if you please," he ordered us.

"Where?" asked Alice.

"To the chart room, of course. The land has disappeared"—he waved his hand toward the horizon where rolling blue water met a calm blue sea—"and we are now upon the high sea."

"Well?" demanded John.

"Well? Name of a little green pig with most deplorably bad manners! I shall say it is well. Do not you know that masters of ships on the high seas are empowered by the law to solemnize the rite of marriage?"

Something of the old Alice we had known in other days looked from the tired and careworn face above the collar of her traveling-coat as she replied: "I'm game." Then, eyes dropped demurely, and a slight flush in her cheeks, she added softly: "If John still wants me."

"DEARLY BELOVED, WE ARE gathered together here in the sight of God, and in the face of this company, to join together this man and this woman in holy matrimony," read the captain from the Book of Common Prayer . . . "If any man can show just cause why they may not lawfully be joined together, let him now speak, or else forever after hold his peace."

"Yes, *pardieu*, let him speak—and meet his death at Jules de Grandin's hands!" the little Frenchman murmured, thrusting one hand beneath his jacket where his automatic pistol rested in its shoulder holster.

"AND NOW, WITH DUE solemnity, let us consign this *sacré* thing unto the ocean, and may the sea never give up its dead!" de Grandin announced when John and Alice Davisson, Renouard and I came from the captain's sanctum, the tang of champagne still upon our lips. He raised his hand and a silvery object glittered in the last rays of the setting sun, flashed briefly through the air, then sank without a trace beneath the blue sea water. It was the marriage girdle of the Yezidees.

"Oh," Alice cried, "you've thrown away 'the luck of the Humes'!"

"Precisely so, *cherie*," he answered with a smile. "There are no longer any Humes, only Davissons. *Le bon Dieu* grant there may be many of them."

WE HAVE JUST RETURNED from the christening of Alice's twin boys, Renouard de Grandin and Trowbridge Ingraham Davisson. The little villains howled right lustily when Doctor Bentley put the water on their heads, and:

"*Grand Dieu des porcs*, the Evil One dies hard in those small sinners!" said Jules de Grandin.

Ingraham, engrossed with ministerial duties in West Africa, was unable to be present, but the silver mugs he sent the youngsters are big enough to hold their milk for years to come.

As I write this, Renouard, de Grandin and Costello are very drunk in my consulting-room. I can hear Costello and Renouard laugh with that high-pitched cachinnation which only those far gone in liquor use at some droll anecdote which Jules de Grandin tells.

I think that I shall join them. Surely, there is one more drink left in the bottle.

The Dark Angel

I

"TIENS, MY FRIEND," JULES de Grandin selected an Hoyo de Monterey from the humidor and set it alight with gusto, "say what you will, there is no combination more satisfying to the soul and body than that of the processes of digestion and slow poisoning by nicotine. No." He regarded the gleaming tip of his diminutive patent-leather evening pump with marked satisfaction, and wafted a smoke-wreath slowly toward the ceiling. "To make our happiness complete," he added, "needs only the presence of—"

"Detective Sergeant Costello, if ye please, sor," interrupted Nora McGinnis, my household factotum, appearing at the drawing-room door with the unexpected suddenness of a specter taking shape from nothingness.

"Eh, do you say so, *petite?*" the little Frenchman answered with a chuckle. "Bid him enter, by all means."

The big, red-headed plainclothes man advanced in Nora's wake, a smile of real affection for the Frenchman on his face. Behind him marched an equally big man, ruddy-faced, white-haired, with that look of handsome distinction so many commonplace Irishmen acquire at middle life.

"Shake hands wid me friend, Chief O'Toole, o' th' Norfolk Downs force, gentlemen," Costello bade with a nod toward his companion. "Timmie, this is Doctor de Grandin I've been tellin' ye about, an' Doctor Trowbridge."

"Pleased to meet yez, gentlemen," Chief O'Toole acknowledged with a smile and bone-crushing grip for each of us. "Jerry's been tellin' me ye might be willin' to give me a lift wid th' damndest—beg pardon—th' most puzzlin' case I've ever had th' evil luck to run agin."

De Grandin transferred his cigar to his left hand and tweaked the needle points of his tightly waxed blond mustache with his right. "If the good Sergeant

Costello vouches for the case, *mon chef*, I make no doubt that it will intrigue me," he answered. "Tell us of it, if you please."

"Well, sor," Chief O'Toole lowered himself ponderously into a chair and regarded the gray uniform cap be had removed with a stare which seemed to indicate he sought inspiration from its silklined depths, "well, sor, it's this way. Over to Norfolk Downs we've been havin' one hell o'—one most distressful time o' it, an' none o' us seems able to say what it's all about." He paused, twisting the cap between his large, white hands and examining its peaked visor as though he'd never seen the thing before.

"U'm?" de Grandin shot a quick glance at the visitor. "This is of interest, but not instructive. If you will amplify your statement—"

"Beg pardon, sor, maybe I could help," Costello interrupted. "Timmie—Chief O'Toole—an' me's been friends for twenty year an' more. We wuz harness bulls together an' got our detectives' badges at th' same time. When they started that swell real estate development over to Norfolk Downs, they put in a paid police force, an' offered th' job o' chief to Timmie. He's a good officer, sor, as none knows better than I, but keepin' burglars in their place an' nabbin' speeders is more in his line than handlin' this sort o' trouble. There's been some mighty queer doin's at Norfolk Downs o' late, an' th' whole community's terrified. Not only that; they're sayin' Timmie's not competent, an' one more killin' like they've had an' he'll be warmin' some employment office bench. He wuz over to me house this evenin' to talk things over, an' th' minute I heard about it I says to meself, 'Here's a case fer Doctor de Grandin, or I'm a Dutchman.' So here we are, sor."

O'Toole took up the explanation. "If ye're askin' me about it, I'll say th' Divil's in it, sor," he told de Grandin solemnly.

"The Devil?" de Grandin eyed him narrowly. "You mean that Satan has a hand in it, or do you use an idiom?"

"No, sor, I mean exactly what I said," the chief replied. "'Twas a matter o' three months or so ago—th' night afther Christmas—when Mike Scarsci got his'n. Everybody in th' Downs knew Mike, and no one knew much good o' him. Some said he wuz a bootlegger, and some a runner fer a joint down Windsor way—th' kind o' place where ye git what ye pay fer an' no questions asked, an' if ye feel th' want o' womanly sympathy, there's a young an' pretty hostess to give ye what ye crave. However that might be, sor, we used to see Mike sliding round th' place, whispering to th' respectable folks who might not be so good when they thought no one wuz lookin', an' I'd 'a' run him out o' town, only I didn't dast offend his customers. So I wuz content to keep a eye on him, just until he pulled off sumpin I could rightly pinch him fer.

"Well, that night we heard him drive up th' Edgemere Road in that big, expensive roadster o' his, an' seen him turn th' corner like he wuz headed fer one o' th' big houses on th' hill. I didn't see it meself, sor, but one o' me men, name o' Gibbons, wuz near by when it happened. He seen th' car go round th' bend an' disappear behind some rhododendron bushes, an' all of a sudden he heard somebody give a yell as if th' Divil's self wuz on 'im, an' then two shots come close together. Next moment wuz a flash o' fire so bright it blinded him, an'—that wuz all.

"But when he came a-runnin' to th' place where Scarsci's car wuz stalled, he found Mike wid his gun still in his hand, an' th' front mashed out o' his head— leastwise, most of it wuz gone, but enough remained to show *th' footprint of a monster goat stamped on 'im*, sor. Furthermore, there wuz th' smell o' brimstone in th' air."

De Grandin raised the narrow black brows which showed such marked con-trast to his wheat-blond hair. "*Eh bien, mon chef*," he murmured. "This devil of yours would seem to be a most discriminating demon; at least in Monsieur Scarsci's case. Am I to understand that you give credence to the story?"

A tinge of red showed in O'Toole's broad face. "Ye are, sor," he returned. "I wuz brought up amongst goats, sor; I'd know their tracks when I seen 'em, even if me eyes were tight shut; an' I recognized th' print on Scarsci's forehead. Besides—" he paused a moment, swallowing uneasily, and a dogged, stubborn look came in his eyes. "Besides, I seen th' thing meself, sor." O'Toole breathed quickly, pantingly, as one who shifts a burden from his chest.

"We all thought it mighty queer how Mike got kilt," he went on, "but th' coroner said he must 'a' run into a tree or sumpin—though th' saints knows there wuz no tree there—so we had to let it pass. But widin another week, sor, Old Man Withers wuz found layin' dead furninst th' gate o' his house, an' he died th' same way Mike did—wid th' top mashed out o' his head an' th' mark o' th' beast on his brow. There warn't no possibility o' *his* runnin' into no tree— not even a tree as wuzn't there, sor—for there he wuz, spread-eagled on th' sidewalk wid his mouth wide open, an' his eyes a-starin' at th' sky, an' there wuz blood an' brains oozin' from a hole in his head big enough to put yer fist into.

"There wuz plenty said th' old man wuz a bad lot; it's certain he never let a nickel get away once he got his hands on it, an' many a one as borrowed money from him lived to regret it; but that's not here nor there. Th' fact is he wuz dead, an' th' jury had to bring it in a homicide, though, o' course, they couldn' blame no one specifically.

"Then, last o' all, wuz Mr. Roscoe. A harmless, inoffensive sort o' cuss he wuz, sor; quiet-spoken an' gentleman-like as any that ye'd meet. He had some money an' didn't need to work, but he wuz a sort o' nut on atheism, an' ran some kind o' paper pokin' fun at th' churches fer his own amusement.

"'Twas about midnight ten days ago, when th' thing got *him*. I'd finished up me work at th' Borough Hall, an' wuz headin' fer home when I passed th' bus station. Mr. Roscoe gits off'n th' last bus from Bloomfield, an' we walks along together. As we wuz walkin' past St. Michael's church we seen th' light which burns before th' altar, an', 'O'Toole,' says Mr. Roscoe, ''tis a shame that they should waste th' price o' oil to keep that thing a-goin' when there's so much misery an' sufferin' in th' world. If I could have me way,' says he, 'I'd raise th' divil wid—'

"An' then it wuz upon us, sor. Taller than me by a good foot, it wuz, an' all covered wid scales, like a serpent. Two horns wuz growin' from its head, an' its eyes wuz flashin' fire. I couldn't rightly say it had a tail, fer there wuz small chance to look at it; but may I never stir from this here chair if it didn't have a pair o' big, black wings—an' it flew right at us.

"Mr. Roscoe give a funny sort o' cry an' put his cane up to defend hisself. I wuz yankin' at me gun, but me fingers wuz all stiff wid cold, an' th' holster wouldn't seem to come unsnapped.

"Th' next I knew, somethin' give a awful, screamin' laugh, an' then there wuz a flash o' fire right in me face, an' I'm a-coughin' an' a-chokin' wid th' fumes o' sulfur in me nose, an' I when gits so I can see again, there's no one there a-tall but Mr. Roscoe, an' he stretched out beside me on th' sidewalk wid his skull mashed in an' th' Divil's mark upon his brow. Dead he were, so dead as yesterday's newspaper.

"I'd made shift to snatch me gun out whilst th' fire wuz still blindin' me, an' had fired an' where I thought th' thing must be, but all I ever found to show that I'd hit sumpin wuz this thing—" From his blouse pocket he withdrew an envelope, and from it took a small, dark object.

De Grandin took it from him, examined it a moment, then passed it on to me. It was a portion of a quill, clipped across the shaft some three or four inches from the tip, the barbs a brilliant black which shone with iridescent luster in the lamplight. Somewhat heavier than any feather I had ever felt, it was, and harder, too, for when I ran my thumb across its edge it rasped my skin almost like the teeth of a fine saw. Indeed, the thing was more like the scale from some gigantic reptile, cut in foliations to simulate a quill, than any feather I had ever seen.

"I never saw a quill like this, before," I told O'Toole, and:

"Here's hopin' that ye never do again, sor," he responded earnestly, "fer, as sure as ye're a-settin' on that chair, that there's a feather from a Divil's Angel's wing!"

"BEGGIN' YER PARDON, SOR," Nora McGinnis once more appeared abruptly at the door, "there's a young man wid a special delivery letter fer Doctor de Grandin. Will ye be afther lookin' at it now, sor, or will it wait?"

"Bring it in at once, if you will be so good," the Frenchman answered. "All special letters merit quick attention."

Bowing mute apology to us, he slit the envelope and glanced quickly through the brief typewritten missive. "*Parbleu,* 'tis very strange!" he exclaimed as he finished reading. "You came to me regarding these so strange events, *mon chef,* and on your heels comes this. Attend me, if you please:

My dear Doctor de Grandin:

I have heard of your ability to arrive at explanations of cases which apparently possess a supernatural aspect, and am writing you to ask if you will take the Borough of Norfolk Downs as client in a case which will undoubtedly command the limit of your talents.

Our police force admit their helplessness, special investigators hired from the best detective agencies have failed to give us any satisfaction. Our people are terrified and the entire community lives in a feeling of constant insecurity.

In view of this I am authorized to offer you a retainer of one thousand dollars immediately upon your acceptance of the case, and an additional fee of fifty dollars a day, plus reasonable expenses, provided you arrive at a solution of the mystery which is not only causing our citizens much anxiety but has already reached the newspapers in a garbled form and is causing much unfavorable publicity for Norfolk Downs as a residential center.

Your promptness in replying will be appreciated by

Yours faithfully,
ROLLAND WILCOX,
Mayor of Norfolk Downs.

"An' will ye take th' case, sor?" O'Toole asked eagerly.

"Sure, Doctor de Grandin, sor, ye'll be doin' me a favor, an' Timmie, too, if ye'll say yes," Costello added.

"Assuredly," de Grandin answered with a vigorous nod. "Tomorrow afternoon the good Doctor Trowbridge and I shall wait upon *Monsieur le Maire* and say to him: '*Voilà, Monsieur,* here we are. Where is the thousand dollars, and where the mystery that you would have us solve? But yes; certainly.'"

2

THE WEALTHY REALTORS AND expensive architects who mapped out Norfolk Downs had done their work artistically. Houses of approved English architecture, Elizabethan, Tudor, Jacobean, with here and there an example of the Georgian or Regency periods, set well back in tastefully planted grounds along wide, tree-bordered roads which trailed gracefully in curves and avoided every hint of the perpendicularity of city streets. Commercial buildings were restricted to such few shops as were essential to the convenience of the community—a grocery, drug store, delicatessen and motor service station—and these were confined to a circumscribed zone and effectually disguised as private dwellings, their show windows fashioned as oriels, neatly sodded yards, set with flower beds and planted with evergreens, before them.

Mayor Wilcox occupied a villa in Edgemere Road, a great, rambling house of the half-timbered English style with Romantic chimneys, stuccoed walls and many low, broad windows. A snug, well-kept formal garden, fenced in by neatly trimmed hedges of box and privet, was in front; at the side was a pergola and rose garden where marble statues, fountains and a lily-pond stood in incongruous contrast to the Elizabethan house and Victorian front-garden.

"I understand you've had some of the details of the case already from O'Toole, Doctor de Grandin," Mayor Wilcox said when we had been escorted to his study at the rear of the villa's wide central hall.

The Frenchman inclined his head. "Quite so," he answered. I was most solemnly assured you were suffering from diabolic visitation, *Monsieur le Maire*."

Wilcox laughed shortly, mirthlessly. "I'm not so sure he's wrong," he answered.

"*Eh*, you have some reason to believe—" de Grandin started, then broke off questioningly.

The mayor looked from one of us to the other with a sort of shamefaced expression. "It's really very odd," he returned at length. "Folloilott rather inclines to the diabolical theory, too, but he's so mediæval-minded, anyway, that—"

"And this Monsieur Fol—this Monsieur with the funny name, who is he, if you please?"

"Our rector—the priest in charge of St. Michael and All Angels'; queer sort of chap; modern and all that, you know, but believes in all sorts of supernatural nonsense, and—"

"One little moment, if you please," de Grandin interrupted. "Let us hear the reasons for the good man's assumptions, if you will. Me, I know the by-ways of ghostland as I know my own pocket, and I solemnly assure you there is no such thing as the supernatural. There is undoubtedly the superphysical; there is also that class of natural phenomena which we do not understand; but the supernatural? *Non*, it is not so."

Mayor Wilcox, who was bald to the ears and affected a pointed beard and curling mustache which gave him a Shakespearian appearance, glanced sharply at the Frenchman, as though in doubt of his sincerity, then, as he met the earnest gaze of the small, blue eyes, responded with a shrug:

"It was the Michael which started him. Our church, you know, is largely constructed from bits of ruined abbeys brought from England. The font is sixteenth century, the altar even earlier, and some of the carvings date back to pre-Tudor times. The name-saint, the Archangel Michael, is represented by a particularly fine bit of work showing the Champion of Heaven overcoming the Fiend and binding him in chains. It was in first-rate shape despite its age when we received it, and every precaution was taken when we set it over the church porch. But just before the first of these mysterious killings took place the stone fetter which bound the Devil became broken in some way. Folloilott was the first to notice it, and directed my attention to the missing links. He seemed in a dreadful state of funk when he told us the bits of missing stone were nowhere to be found.

"'Well, we'll have a stone-cutter over and have new ones carved,' I told him, but it seemed that wouldn't do at all. Unless the identical links which were missing could be found and reset right away, something terrible would descend on the community, he assured me. I'd have laughed at him, but he was so earnest about it anyone could see he was sincere.

"'I tell you, Wilcox,' he said, 'those links are symbolical. The Archfiend is unchained upon the earth, and dreadful things will come to us unless we can confine him in those sacred fetters right away!' You have to know Folloilott to understand the impressive way he said it. Why, I almost believed it, myself, he was so serious about it all.

"Well, the upshot of it all was we searched the churchyard and all the ground around, but couldn't find a single trace of those stone links. Next night the boot—the Scarsci man was killed in the way O'Toole told you, and since that time we've had two other inexplicable murders.

"No one can offer any explanation, and the detectives we hired were as much at sea as any of us. What do you think of it, sir?"

"U'm," de Grandin took his narrow chin between a thoughtful thumb and finger and pinched it till the dimple in its tip deepened to a cleft. "I think we should do well to see this statue of St. Michael and also the so estimable clergyman with the unpronounceable name. Can this be done at once?"

Wilcox consulted his watch. "Yes," he answered. "Folloilott says evensong about this time every day, rain, shine or measles. We'll be in time to see him if we step over to the church right away."

WINTER WAS DYING HARD. The late afternoon was bitter for so late in March. A leaden sky, piled high with asphalt-colored clouds, held a menace of snow, and along the walks curled yellow leaves from the wayside trees scuttered, and paused and scuttered on again as though they fled in hobbled fear from the wind that came hallooing from the north.

Chimes were playing softly in the square bell-tower of the church as we approached, their vibrant notes scarce audible against the wind's wild shouting:

Abide with me: fast falls the eventide;
The darkness deepens; Lord, with me abide . . .

A look of almost ineffable sadness swept across de Grandin's features, swift as the passing of a thought. "Have her ever in Thy gracious keeping, Lord!" he murmured, and signed the cross before his face, so quickly one might have thought him stroking his mustache.

"There's Folloilott, now!" Wilcox exclaimed. "I say, Mr. Folloilott, here—"

A tall young man in shovel hat and Inverness coat strode quickly across the patch of lawn separating the church from the brick-and-sandstone rectory. If he heard the mayor's greeting above the wind he gave no sign as he thrust the nail-studded door of the vestry aside and entered the sacred edifice.

"Humph, he's a sacerdotal fool!" our companion exclaimed half angrily. "You might as well try to get a number on a broken telephone as attract his attention when he's about his parish duties."

"U'm?" de Grandin murmured. "The one-tracked mind, as you call him in American, *hein*? And this St. Michael of whom you spoke, where is he, if you please?"

"There," Wilcox answered, pointing his blackthorn stick to a sculptured group set in the wall above the pentice.

The group, cut in high relief upon a plinth of stone, represented the Arch-angel, accoutered in cuirass and greaves, erect above the fallen demon, one foot upon his adversary's throat, his lance poised for a thrust in his right hand, the left holding a chain which was made fast to manacles latched around the fiend's wrists. The whole thing, rather crudely carved, had an appearance of immense age, and even from our point of view, some forty feet away, we could see that several links of the chain, as well as the bracelets binding the Devil's hands, had weathered and chipped away.

"And *Monsieur l'Abbé* insists this has connection with these so strange deaths?" the Frenchman asked musingly.

"He affects to believe so; yes," Wilcox answered, impatience in his voice.

"*Eh bien*, in former times men have believed in stranger things," de Grandin returned. "Come, let us go in; I would observe him more closely, if you please."

Like too many churches, St. Michael and All Angels' did not boast impressive congregations at ordinary services. A verger in a black-serge robe, three or four elderly and patently virgin ladies in expensive but frumpish costumes and a young and slender girl almost nun-like in her subdued gray coat and hat were the sole attendants besides ourselves.

The organ prelude finished as we found seats in a forward pew, and the Reverend Mr. Folloilott entered from the vestry, genuflected to the altar and began to intone the service. Rather to my surprise, he chose the long, or Nicene

Creed, in preference to the shorter one usually recited at the evening service, and at the words, "and was incarnate by the Holy Ghost," his genuflection was so profound that it was almost a prostration.

Immediately following the collect for peace he descended from the chancel to the body of the church and began the office of general supplication.

It was chilly to the point of frostiness in the church, but perspiration streaked the cleric's face as in a voice vibrant with intense emotion he cantillated the entreaty:

O holy, blessed and glorious Trinity, three persons and one God; have mercy upon us miserable sinners. . . .

From our seats in the transept we were almost abreast of the priest as he knelt at the litany desk, and I caught de Grandin studying him covertly while the interminable office was recited. Mr. Folloilott's face was cameo-sharp in profile, pale, but not with poor health; lean rather than thin, with a high, narrow brow, deep-set, almost piercingly clear eyes of gray, high-bridged, prominent nose and long, pointed chin. The mouth was large, but thin-lipped, and the hair which grew well forward at the temples intensely black. A rather strong, intelligent face, I thought, but one marked by asceticism, the face of one who might be either unflinching martyr or relentless inquisitor, as occasion might direct.

"No use trying to see him now," Wilcox told us when benediction was pronounced and the congregation rose from their knees after a respectful interval. "He'll be about his private devotions for the next half-hour, and—ah, by George, I have it! I'm having another friend for dinner tonight: What d'ye say we have Folloilott and Janet in as well? You'll have all the chance you want to talk with him."

"Excellent," de Grandin acquiesced. "And who is Janet, may one ask? Madame Fol—the reverend gentleman's wife?"

"Lord, no!" the mayor responded. "Folloilott's a dedicated celibate. Janet's his ward."

"Ah?" the Frenchman answered with a barely perceptible rising inflection. I drove my elbow in his ribs lest he say more. The frank expressions of de Grandin's thoughts were not always acceptable to American ears, as I well knew from certain contretemps in which he had involved me in the past.

3

EIGHT OF US GATHERED at the Jacobean oak table in Mr. Wilcox's dining-room that evening: the mayor and his wife, a slender, dark young man of scholarly appearance with refined, Semitic features, George, Wilcox's son, recently admitted to the bar and his father's partner in practise, the Reverend Basil Folloilott and his ward, Janet Payne, de Grandin and I. The meal was good, though simple: clear soup, fried sole, a saddle of Canada hare, salad and an ice; white wine with the fish, claret with the roast.

De Grandin studied each of the guests with his quick, stock-taking glance, but Janet excited my curiosity most of all. She was slight and unmistakably attractive, but despite her smooth and fresh-colored complexion she somehow conveyed an impression of colorlessness. Her long, fair hair was simply arranged in a figure 8 knot at the nape of her neck; her large, blue, heavy-lidded eyes seemed to convey nothing but disinterested weariness. Her lips were a thought too full for beauty, but she had a sweet, rather pathetic smile, and she smiled often, but talked rarely. "H'm," I wondered professionally, "is she anemic, or recovering from an illness?"

The sound of Wilcox's voice broke through my revery: "I saw Withers' executors today, Mr. Silverstein," he told the young Jewish gentleman, "and I don't think there's much doubt that they'll renew the loan."

To us he added in explanation, "Mr. Silverstein is Rabbi of the Congregation Beth Israel. Withers held a mortgage on their temple and was pressing them for payment in full when he was—when he died. The executors seem more leniently inclined."

A sharp kick on my shin made me wince with pain, but before I could cry out, de Grandin's hand was pressing mine and his eyes beckoning my attention to the clergyman across the table. The reverend, gentleman's face had gone an almost sickly gray, and an expression of something like consternation was on his features.

I was about to ask if I could be of service when our hostess rose, and with her Janet went into the drawing-room. Evidently the custom of leaving the gentlemen at table with their cigars still obtained in Wilcox's house. For just an instant as she passed the girl's glance rested on young Wilcox, and in it was tenderness and such yearning that I almost cried aloud, for it was like the look of a pauper's child before a toyshop window at Christmas time.

De Grandin noted the look, too. "Tiens, Monsieur l'Abbé," he said genially as he lighted his cigar, "unless I greatly miss my guess, you shall soon celebrate a most joyous ceremony."

The clergyman looked puzzled. "How do you meam?" he asked.

"Why, when Mademoiselle Jeannette marries with Monsieur Georges, to be sure, you will most certainly perform the cere—"

The other cut him off. "Janet has no place for earthly love in her life," he answered. "Hers is one of those devoted souls which long for sweet communion with the Heavenly Bridegroom. As soon as she has come of age she will become a postulate in the order of the Resurrection. All plans are made; it is her life's vocation. She has been trained to look for nothing else since she was a little girl."

De Grandin shot a doubtful, questioning glance at me, and I nodded confirmation. St. Chrystosom's, where I had served as vestryman for nearly thirty years was "moderate," being neither Methodistically "low" nor ritualistically "high," but in a vague way I knew the ritualistic branch of the Episcopal Church supported monastic and conventual orders with discipline and rules as strict as any sponsored by the Greek and Latin churches, especially women's orders, where the members took their vows for life and lived as closely cloistered as mediæval nuns.

An awkward pause ensued. De Grandin tweaked the points of his mustache and seemed meditating a reply, and knowing him as I did, my teeth were on edge with apprehension, but Wilcox saved the situation. "I was telling Doctor de Grandin your theory of the strange deaths—how the breaking of the fetter in St. Michael's hand might be responsible," he told the clergyman.

Young Rabbi Silverstein looked puzzled. "Surely, you're not serious, Mr. Folloilott?" he asked. "You can't mean you believe there's some connection between a graven image and these murders. Why, it's—"

Folloilott rose, his face drawn and working with half-suppressed emotion. "To one of *your* religion, sir," he answered cuttingly, "the statue of the Archangel Michael may be a 'graven image'; to *us* it is a holy thing, endued with heavenly powers. As for these 'murders,' as you call them, I am convinced no earthly agency has anything to do with them; no human hand struck the blows which rid the world of those moral lepers. They are unquestionably the visitations of an outraged Heaven upon contemners of Divine authority. The call to repentance has gone forth, even as it did in the days of the Patriarch Noah. Heaven is outraged at the iniquity of man, and the Dark Angel of Death is abroad; you may almost hear the beating of his dreadful sable wings. There is no one as when the first-born was slain of old, to sprinkle blood upon the lintels of our doors that he may spare us and pass on. Repentance is the only way to safety. No mortal man can stay his flight, no mortal date impede him in his awful errand!"

"*Tiens*, there you do make the great mistake, *Monsieur*," de Grandin answered with one of his quick, elfin grins. "I dare do so. The law forbids such killings, and be he angel or devil, he who has committed them must answer to the law. Furthermore, which is of more immediate importance, he must answer to Jules de Grandin. Certainly; of course."

"*You?*" the tall cleric looked down at the little Frenchman incredulously.

"Even as you say, *Monsieur l'Abbé.*"

For a moment they faced each other across the table, Folloilott's piercing gaze seeking to beat down de Grandin's level stare, and failing as the wind may fail to move a firmly planted rock. At length:

"You take grave risks lightly, sir," the clergyman admonished.

"It is a habit of long standing, *Monsieur*," de Grandin answered in a tone-less, level voice, his little, round blue eyes set in a fixed, unwinking stare against the other's burning gaze.

THE CLERGYMAN EXCUSED HIMSELF a short while afterward, and we were left alone before the fire.

"I think your rector needs a rest," I told the mayor. "His nerves are all unstrung from overwork, I'd say. Once or twice I fancied he was on the verge of a breakdown this evening."

"He *did* look rather seedy," Wilcox admitted. "Guess we'll have to send him off to Switzerland again this summer. He's a great mountain-climber, you know; quite a hunter, too. Some years ago he went exploring in the Andes and brought back some rare specimens. They say he's one of the few men who ever succeeded in bringing down a condor in full flight."

De Grandin glanced up sharply. "A condor, did you say, *Monsieur*—one of those great Andean vultures?" he demanded.

"Yes," Wilcox answered. "He risked his life to do it; but he shot one down from an eminence of several thousand feet. Got two of 'em, in fact, but one was lost. The other's stuffed and mounted in the museum at Harrisonville."

"A condor?" murmured Jules de Grandin musingly. "He shot a condor, this one, and—"

Furious knocking at the door, followed by the tread of heavy boots in the tiled passage cut him short. "Doctor de Grandin, sor," Chief O'Toole burst into the dining-room, amazement and something strangely like terror in his florid face, "there's another one been kilt. We just got th' word!"

"*Mille tonnerres*—another? Beneath our very noses?" The Frenchman leaped from his seat as a bounced ball rises in the air, and fairly rushed toward the coat closet where his outdoor wraps were hung. "Come, Friend Trowbridge, rush, hasten; fly!" he bade me. To O'Toole:

"Lead on, *mon chef*, we follow close behind!"

"'Tis Misther Bostwick, this time, sor," the chief confided as we walked along the frosty street. "Not five minutes ago I took a call at headquarters, an', 'Is this th' chief o' police?' a lady asks, all scared and trembly-like.

"'It is,' says I, 'an' what can I be doin' fer ye, Miss?'

"'Come over to Misther Bostwick's, if yez please,' she tells me. 'Sumpin terrible has happened!'

"So over to Misther Bostwick's house I goes, an' she warn't exaggeratin' none, sor, I'll say that fer her. Th' place is a holy wreck, an' pore Bostwick's a-settin' there in his livin'-room wid th' back mashed out o' his head an' th' mark o' th' Divil on his brow."

De Grandin took a few steps in thoughtful silence; then: "And what was Monsieur Bostwick's besetting sin, *mon chef?*" he asked.

"*Eh?*"

"What was it this one did which might offend a straight-laced moralist?"

O'Toole returned a short, hard laugh. "How'd ye guess it, sor?" he asked.

"Name of an old and thoroughly decaying cheese—I ask *you*, not you me!" the Frenchman almost shouted.

"Well, sor, Norfolk Downs ain't like some places; we don't go pokin' too much into th' private life o' th' citizens as pays our salaries, an'—"

"*À bas* the explanations and apologies! What was it this one did, I ask to know!"

"Well, sor, if ye must know, they do say as how he wuz uncommon fond o' th' ladies. Time afther time I seen th' pretty ladies shteppin' out o' their cars before his door, an' late o' nights th' light wuz goin' in his house. Yet he were a bachelor, sor, an' his bootlegger's bill must 'a' been tremenjous, judgin' be th' empty bottles that wuz carted from his place. I've heard tell as how some o' his little playmates had husbands o' their own, too, but as 'twas all done quiet an' orderly-like, I never interfered, an'—"

"No matter, one understands," de Grandin cut him short. "Are we arrived?"

4

W E WERE. ABLAZE WITH lights, the big, brick house in which Theodore Bostwick had lived his gay and not particularly righteous life stood before us, a uniformed policeman at the door, another waiting in the hall. Crouched on a settle by the fire, shaking with sobs and plainly in an agony of fear, a very pretty little lady in a very pretty pajama ensemble raised a tear-stained face to us.

"Oh, don't—please don't let them give my name to the papers!" she besought as de Grandin paused before her.

"Softly, *Mademoiselle*," he soothed, tactfully ignoring the platinum-and-diamond band encircling the third finger of her left hand. "We do but seek the facts. Where were you when it happened, if you please?"

"I—I'd come downstairs to get some ice," the little woman answered, dabbing at her eyes with a wisp of rose-colored cambric. "Ted—Mr. Bostwick, wanted some ice for the cocktails, and I said I'd come down and get it from the Frigidaire, and—" She paused and shivered as though a chill had laid its icy finger on her, despite the superheated room.

"Yes, *Mademoiselle*, and—" de Grandin prompted softly.

"I heard Ted call out once—I couldn't understand him, and called back, 'What?' and then there was a dreadful clatter in the big room upstairs, as if everything were being smashed, and I was frightened.

"I waited for a moment, then went upstairs, and—oh, it was dreadful!"

"*Précisément*, one understands as much; but what was it you saw?"

"You'll see it for yourself, when you go up. Ted was sitting there—looking straight at me—and everything around him was all broken. I took one look at him and turned to run, but on the steps I must have fainted, for I fell, and when I came to I was lying at the bottom of the stairs, and—"

"What did you do next?" he asked as she paused again.

"I—I fainted."

"*Morbleu*, again?"

"Yes, again!" something half stubborn, half hysterical was in her answer. "I was going to the telephone to call the officers when I chanced to glance up, and there—" Once more her voice trailed off to nothingness, and the color drained from her pink cheeks, leaving them ghastly-white beneath the rouge.

The little Frenchman looked at her, compassion in his gaze. "What was it that you saw, *ma pauvre?*" he asked gently.

"A—a face, sir. It looked at me through the window for just an instant, but I'll not forget it if I live to be a hundred. There was nothing above it, nothing below it—it seemed to hang there, like the head of a decapitated man suspended in the air—and it *glared* at me. It was long—twice as big as any face I've ever seen—and a sort of awful grayish color—like the underside of a toad!—and great tusks protruded from its mouth. The eyes were green and glowing with some dreadful light, and there were horns growing from the forehead. I tell you there *were!*" She paused a moment while she fought for breath; then, very softly: "It was the Devil!"

"*Eh bien, Mademoiselle*, this is of interest, certainly. And then, if you please—"

"Then I fainted again. I don't know how long I lay on the floor, but as soon as I came to I called police headquarters."

De Grandin turned to Chief O'Toole. "You came at once?" he asked.

"Yes, sor."

"Who came with you?"

"Kelley an' Shea, sor."

"*Très bien.* You searched the place inside and out? What of the doors and windows?"

"Locked, sor; locked tight as wax. Th' little lady here let us in, afther askin' who we wuz, an' we heard her throw th' lock an' draw th' inside bolt an' chain-fastener. Th' back door wuz tight locked, an' every windy in th' place but one wuz closed an' latched. Th' big windy in th' livin'-roorn upstairs wuz shut, but not latched, sor."

"Very good. And that window there—the one through which *Mademoiselle* declares she saw the face—what of it?"

"It's more'n ten foot from th' ground, sor, an' fixed—th' frame's set fast in th' jamb, so's it can't be opened a-tall."

"Very good. Let us ascend and see what we shall see above."

T HE UPSTAIRS LIVING-ROOM OF Bostwick's house was a blaze of light, for Chief O'Toole and his aides had turned on every available bulb when they made their preliminary search.

"Ah?" de Grandin murmured softly as we paused upon the threshold "A-ah?"

Facing us through the doorway which gave upon the upper hall, his chin sunk on his breast, hands clenched into rigid fists upon the arms of his chair, a man sat staring endlessly at nothing with sightless, film-glazed eyes. He had been in early middle life—forty-five, perhaps, possibly fifty years old—with profuse hair and a vandyke beard in which the brown was thickly flecked with gray. In life his face must have been florid, but now it shone under the glowing electric bulbs with the ash-gray pallor which belongs only to death, his parted lips almost as blanched as his cheeks, little gouts of perspiration, glistening like beads of oil, dewing his high, white forehead.

The room behind him was a welter of confusion. Chairs were overturned, even broken, the contents of the center table—bits of expensive bric-à-brac and objects of *vertu*—were strewn upon the rich Turkey carpet, the pieces of an almost priceless K'angshi vase lay scattered in one corner.

De Grandin advanced and slowly surveyed the corpse, walking round it, observing it from every side. A little to the left and above the right ear a deep, wedge-shaped depression showed in the skull, blood, a little ruptured brain-substance and serous cerebrospinal fluid escaping from the wound. The Frenchman looked at me with elevated brows and nodded questioningly. I nodded back. Death must have been instantaneous.

"D'ye see it, sor?" O'Toole demanded in an awed whisper, pointing to the dead man's forehead.

There was no denying it. Impressed upon the flesh, as though stamped there with almost crushing force, was the bifurcated imprint of a *giant goat's hoof*.

"They must 'a' had th' divil of a fight," O'Toole opined as he surveyed the devastated room.

De Grandin looked about him carefully. "It seems so," he agreed, "but why the Evil One should vent his wrath upon the poor man's chattels when he had killed the owner gives one to wonder, n'est-ce-pas?"

"An'—an' d'ye notice th' *shmell*, sor?" O'Toole added diffidently.

De Grandin's narrow nostrils contracted and expanded nervously as he sniffed the air. I, too, inhaled, and down the back of my neck and through my checks ran tiny ripples of horror-chills. There was no mistaking it—trust one who'd served a term as city health officer to know! Faint, but clearly perceptible, there was the pungent, acrid *scent of burning sulfur* in the room.

De Grandin's small blue eyes were very round and almost totally expressionless as he looked from O'Toole to me and back again. At length: "*Oui-da,*" he agreed, "*c'est le soufre, vraiment.* No matter, we have other things to do than inhale silly scents."

"But, sor—" O'Toole began.

"But be grilled upon the grates of hell, *mon vieux.* What make you of this?" he pointed to a splash of blood, roughly circular in shape, and some four or five inches in diameter, which disfigured the carpet almost underneath the window.

"Huh? Why that's where he bled, sor," the Irishman replied, after a moment's study of the ruddy spot.

"*Exactement,* my friend—where he bled. Now, consider this—" Wheeling, he led us back to the seated body, and pointed in turn to the dead man's collar and the back of the chair. Scarcely a bloodstain showed on them.

"I don't think I quite git ye, sor," the chief admitted after a long scrutiny.

"*Ah hah,* my friend, are you then blind?" the Frenchman asked him almost angrily. "Consider: One window was open, or unlatched, at least; and by that window we find blood. It is almost the only blood we find. But Monsieur Bostwick is seated in his chair, almost as though awaiting visitors. Is that the way a man would be if he had died in fight?"

"Well, sor"—O'Toole put up a hand to scratch his head—"he *might* 'a' staggered to that chair an' died there, afther he'd been struck—"

"Name of a blue rat, my friend, how can you say so?" de Grandin interrupted. "The blow which killed this poor one caused instant death. Doctor Trowbridge will bear me out in that. No human man could live three seconds following such a blow. Besides, if the man had staggered across the room, there would be blood upon the floor if he leant forward as he crawled toward the chair, or blood upon his collar if he stood upright; yet we see none save in this single spot. That is the spot where he bled, my friend. He was undoubtlessly struck dead close by the window, then carried to that chair and placed there with both feet flat upon the floor, and hands composed upon the arms, and then the one who killed him smashed the furniture to bits. The testimony of the room can be interpreted no other way."

The Irishman glanced round the room, then at the dead man. "Howly Mither," he exclaimed at length, "I'm damned if I don't think th' dominie is right, sor. It *were* th' Divil as done this thing. No mortal man could fly up to that windy an' kill th' pore felly in that way!" He paused to bless himself, then: "Let's be goin', sor. There's no good comin' from our stayin' here!"

De Grandin nodded in agreement. Then, as we reached the lower hall: "We shall not need the pretty lady's testimony, Chief. I believe her story absolutely—she was too frightened to be lying—and nothing she can tell us will throw light upon the case. Meantime, if you will have a strict watch kept, and see that no one comes or goes, except the undertaker's men when they come for the body, I shall be greatly in your debt."

To the trembling, half-hysterical girl he announced: "You are free to go at will, *petite*, and were I you, I should not long remain here; one never knows who may come, and having come, depart and retail gossip."

"You mean I may go—now?" she asked in incredulous delight.

"Perfectly, my little cabbage, to go and sin—with more discretion in the future."

5

Pale daylight had scarcely dawned when de Grandin nudged and kicked me into wakefulness. "Have you forgotten that we inspect Monsieur Bostwick's house today?" he asked reproachfully. "Come, my friend, rush, hasten, make the hurry; we have much to do and I would be about it while there are not too many to observe our actions."

Our hasty toilets made and a call put through to ask O'Toole to meet us, we hurried to the house of death, and while we waited for the chief, de Grandin made a careful circuit of the place. "This is undoubtlessly the window where the little lady with the fragile morals saw the evil face look through," he mused, pausing under the big chimney which reared itself along the southern wall.

"Yes," I agreed, "and it's directly underneath the window of the room where Bostwick's body was found, too; the window Chief O'Toole said was closed but unlocked."

"Excellent," he clapped his hands, as though applauding at a play. "I shall make something of you yet, Friend Trowbridge. You have right, now—*ah? Que diable?*"

He broke off sharply, crouched suddenly upon the frozen lawn and crept forward quickly, as though intent upon taking something by surprise. "You see?" he asked in a tense whisper.

A tiny coppice of dwarf spruce was planted in the angle of the chimney and the house-wall, and as he pointed I saw that one or two small branches were freshly broken, the tender wood showing white and pallid through the ruptured bark.

Following him, I saw him part the lower boughs, examine the frosty ground with his nose almost thrust into it, then saw him straighten like a coiled spring suddenly released from tension. "Behold!" he bade me, seizing my wrist and dragging me forward. Upon the hard earth showed a tiny stain, a dull, brown-colored stain, no larger than a split bean, but unmistakable. Blood!

"How—" I began, but:

"And look at this—ten thousand small blue devils!—look at this, my friend, and tell me what it is you see!" he ordered sharply. Nearer the house, where the chimney's warmth had kept the frost from hardening the earth to any great extent, there showed two prints—footprints—but such footprints!

One was obviously human, a long and slimly aristocratic foot, shod with a moccasin or some sort of soft shoe, for there was no well-defined impression of a built-up heel. But close beside it, so placed it must have been left by the same person, was the clear-cut, unmistakable impression of a hoof—*a cloven hoof*—as though an ox or giant goat had stamped there.

"Well!" I exclaimed, then paused for very want of words in which to frame my reeling thoughts.

"*Non*," he denied emphatically. "It is most unwell, Friend Trowbridge. It is diabolical, no less. *Tout la même*"—he raised his narrow shoulders in a shrug—"I shall not be dissuaded. Though Satan's self has done these things, I'll not desist until I have him clapped in jail, my friend. Consider, has not the mayor of Norfolk Downs retained me for that purpose? Come, let us go. I see the good O'Toole approaching, and he will surely be made ill if he should see this thing."

Once more we searched the house as carefully as a jeweler might search a gem for hidden flaws, but nowhere was there any clue to help us. At length: "We must look at the roof," de Grandin said. "It may be we shall find some little, so small thing to aid us there; the good God knows we have not found it here."

"Arra, Doctor de Grandin, sor, 'tain't Christmastime fer nigh another year," O'Toole objected.

"Eh, what is it that you tell me—*noël?*" the Frenchman answered sharply.

"Why, sor, ye must be afther thinkin' it wuz Santy Claus as did in Misther Bostwick, instead o'—instead o' Satan." He looked quickly round, as though he feared some hidden listener, then signed himself furtively with the cross.

De Grandin grinned acknowledgment of the sally, but led the way uncompromisingly to the attic from which a trapdoor let upon the steep, tiled roof. Pausing for a moment to survey the serrated rows of semi-cylindrical tiles with which the housetop was covered, he threw a leg over the ridgepole and began slowly working his way toward the chimney. Early as it was, several small boys loitering in the street, the policeman on guard outside the house and a dog of highly doubtful ancestry were on hand to witness his aerial performance, and as he reached the chimney and clung to it, both arms encircling the tall terra-cotta pot with which the flue was capped, we caught a flash of black and saw the Reverend Basil Folloilott pause in a rapid walk and gaze up wonderingly.

De Grandin hugged the chimney some three minutes, crooked his knee across the angle of the roof and leant as far downward as was possible, examining the glazed, round tiles, then slowly hitched himself back to the trap-door where O'Toole and I were waiting.

"Find anythin', sor?" the chief inquired good-humoredly.

"Enough to justify the risk of breaking the most valuable neck which I possess," the Frenchman answered with a smile. "*Parbleu*, enough to give one food for speculation, too, I am inclined to think!"

"What wuz it?"

The Frenchman opened his hand, and in the palm of his gray glove we saw a slim, dark object resting, a little wisp of horsehair, I supposed.

"What—" O'Toole began, but:

"No whats, my friend, no whys, not even any wherefores, if you please," the other cut him short. "Me, I shall cogitate upon this matter—this and some others. Anon I may announce the goal to which my thoughts have led. Meantime I am too well aware that it is villainously cold up here and I am most tremendously in need of food."

BREAKFAST WAS LAID IN the pleasant room adjoining Wilcox's kitchen when we returned, and de Grandin did full justice to the meal. He was commencing his fifth cup of well-creamed coffee when a maid announced the Reverend Basil Folloilott.

Despite the coldness of the day, the clergyman's pale face was even paler than its usual wont as he came into the breakfast room, still a little short of breath from rapid walking. "Dreadful news of Mr. Bostwick," he announced as he greeted us reservedly. "The poor unfortunate, cut off in deadly sin—if only he had seen the light in time—"

"Who says he was cut off in sin, *Monsieur?*" de Grandin broke in suddenly.

"I do," the clergyman's pale lips snapped shut upon the words. "I *know* he was. Time after time, night after night, I saw his paramours arriving at his door as I watched from my study window, and I went to him with messages of peace— redemption and release through hearty and unfeigned repentance. But he—"

"*Eh bien, Monsieur*, one can guess without great difficulty what he said to you," the Frenchman answered with a laugh.

"One can," the cleric answered hotly. "He told me to go to the devil—me, the messenger of holiness. There was no hope for such as he. He led a life of sin; in sin he died, and God can find no pity for a wretch like him. The Lord Himself—"

"It seems I have read somewhere of a lady whose behavior was not all a lady's conduct ought to be, yet who was counted of some worth in later days," de Grandin interrupted softly.

An ugly sneer gathered at the corners of Folloilott's mouth. "Indeed?" he asked sarcastically. "She was a countrywoman of yours, no doubt, Monsieur de Grandin?"

"No-o," the Frenchman answered slowly, while a malicious twinkle flickered in his eyes. "She was from Magdala—the Scriptures call her Mary Magdalene, and somewhere I have heard the Blessed Master did not bar her out of Paradise, although her life had been at least as bad as that of Monsieur Bostwick."

"I say, de Grandin, you seem to take delight in getting a rise out of Folloilott," Wilcox accused when the clergyman had taken a hasty and offended leave.

The almost boorish manner of the preacher puzzled me. "Perhaps the man's a pious hypocrite," I hazarded, but:

"*Mais non*," denied the Frenchman. "Pious he is, I freely grant—but a hypocrite? No, it is not so. He is in deadly earnest, that one. How much his deadliness exceeds his earnestness I should not care to guess, but—" He lapsed into a moody silence.

"What d'ye mean?" I urged. "Are you implying that—"

"*Ah bah*, I did but let my wits go wool-gathering—there is a black dog running through my brain, Friend Trowbridge," he apologized. "Forget what I have said; I was conversing through the hat, as you so drolly say."

6

DE GRANDIN WAS BUSY all that day, making a hasty trip to the city, returning for luncheon, then dashing off to consult Chief O'Toole till nearly dinner time.

He kept the table in an uproar with his witty sallies throughout the meal, and when dessert was served young George Wilcox pulled a long face. "I'd rather sit right here and talk with you than go out tonight, Doctor de Grandin," he declared, "but—"

"Ah-ha; ah-ha-ha—I see him!" laughed de Grandin. "I too was young upon a time, my friend. I know the ecstasy of the little hand's soft pressure, the holy magic which can be found within the loved one's glance. Go to her with speed, *mon vieux*; you were not half a man if you delayed your tryst to talk with such a silly one as Jules de Grandin. Hold her hand gently, *mon brave*, it is a fragile thing, I make no doubt."

The boy retreated with a sheepish grin and heightened color.

"I wish George wouldn't see her," Mrs. Wilcox sighed plaintively. "They're terribly in love, of course, but Mr. Folloilott won't hear of it—he's mapped the poor girl's life for her, you know, and next May she starts on her novitiate at Carlinville. I suppose he knows best, he's such a thoroughly *good* man, but—" She broke off with another sigh, as though she felt herself a heretic for questioning the rector's wisdom.

We played bridge after dinner, but de Grandin's mind was not upon the game. He lost consistently, and shortly after ten o'clock excused himself on the plea he had a busy day before him, paid his losses and furtively beckoned me to join him in our room.

"Friend Trowbridge," he informed me earnestly, "we must do something for those children. It is an outrage two young hearts should thus be pried apart. You saw the look she gave him yesternight at table—a look in which her very heart beat for release against the fetters of her eyes. You saw the look on young *Monsieur's* face this evening. Our business is to help them to each other."

"Our business is to find out who's perpetrating these murders—if it's not the Devil himself, as O'Toole and Folloilott seem to think," I broke in roughly. "This boy-and-girl affair's just puppy love. They may think their hearts are broken, but—"

"*Zut*, who says it?" he cried sharply. "I tell you, good Friend Trowbridge, a man's heart breaks but once, and then it is forever. *Misère de Dieu*, do I not know it? As for these killings, my friend, I am the wiser, though not sadder, man to-night. Attend me: At Harrisonville I had the tiny flecks of hard-dried liquid which we found outside Monsieur Bostwick's window analyzed. They were, as I suspected, blood—human blood. Also, while he was absent on some parish duty, I did feloniously and most unlawfully insert myself into the reverend gentleman's study, and made a careful search. Behold what I have found—" From the pocket of his dinner coat he took several small, twisted things, grayish, curved objects which looked for all the world like sections of a hard, gray doughnut.

"What the deuce—" I began, but he stopped me with a grin.

"Chains, my friend—chains of the devil, no less. The mystery of the holy Michael's tether for the Devil is explained. I would not go so far as to declare that the good cleric broke that carven chain, then spread the story of impending doom about; but unquestionably he had possession of the missing links, even while he helped search for them in places where he knew that they were not. What do you make of that?"

"Why—" I looked at him in openmouthed amazement. "Why—"

"Exactly, precisely; quite so. It is our task to find out why, and unless I am more mistaken than I think I am, we shall know something ere we see another morning."

Yawning, he stripped off his jacket and waistcoat, pulled his pajama coat on above his shirt, and proceeded to snap on every available bulb in the room. Once more he yawned prodigiously, went to the window and unbarred it, flinging wide the casement and spreading wide his arms in a tremendous stretch. I yawned in sympathy as he stood there with jaws agape, the personification of a man who can withstand the urge to sleep no longer.

A moment he stood thus, then, snapping off the light, leaped quickly in the bed and pulled the comforter about his neck.

"Good Lord, you're not going to sleep *that* way, are you?" I asked, amazed.

"*Pardieu*, I shall not sleep at all, my friend!" he answered in a whisper. "And you will please have the goodness not to shout. Climb into bed if you desire, and pull the blankets over you, but do not sleep; we shall have need of wakefulness before the night is done, I damn think."

Despite his admonition, I dropped off. The respite from the cares of my practise and the dull evening at cards combined to wear down my will to stay awake. How long I slept I do not know, but something—that odd sixth sense which rouses sleeping cats, dogs and physicians—brought me full-conscious from the fairyland of dreams. No time was needed to orient myself; my eyes turned unbidden to the window which de Grandin had left open.

The steady southwest wind had chased the clouds before it, and the moonlight fell as bright, almost, as midday on the planted lawn outside. Bars of the silvery luminance struck through the open casement and lay along the floor, as bright and unobscured as—stay, there was a shadow blotting out the moonlight, something was moving very slowly, soundlessly, outside the window.

I strained my eyes to pierce the intervening gloom, then sat bolt-upright, horror gripping at my throat, chill, grisly fear dragging at my scalp.

Across the eighteen-inch-wide sill it came, as quiet as a creeping snake; a great, black thing, the moonlight glinting evilly on the polished scales which overlaid its form. From its shoulders, right and left, spread great, black wings, gleaming with a sort of horrid, half-dulled luster, and as they grasped the window-sill I caught a glimpse of long, curved talons, pitiless as those of any vulture, but larger and more cruel by far than those of any bird.

But awful as the dread form was, the countenance was more so. A ghastly sort of white it was, not white as snow or polished bone is white, not white as death's pale visage may be white, but a leprous, unclean white, the sort of pallor which can not be dissociated from disease, corruption and decay. Through the pale mask of horror looked two brilliant glaring eyes, like corpse-lights shining through the sockets of a fleshless skull and from the forehead reared a pair of curving, pointed horns. A dreadful memory rushed across the years, a memory of childish fear which had lain dormant but undead for nearly half a century. With my own eyes I saw in living form the figure of Apollyon out of *Pilgrim's Progress!*

I tried to cry aloud, to warn de Grandin of the visitant's approach, but only a dull, croaking sound, scarce louder than a sigh, escaped my palsied lips.

Low as the utterance was, it seemed to carry to the creeping horror. With a wild, demoniac laugh it launched itself upon the bed where my little friend lay sleeping, and in an instant I heard the sickening impact of a blow—another blow—and then a high, cracked voice crying: "Accursed of God, go now and tell your master who keeps watch and ward upon the earth!"

Weapon I had none, but at the bedside stood a table with a chromium carafe of chilled spring water, and this I hurled with all my might straight at the awful face.

A second marrow-freezing cry went up, and then a flash of blinding light—bright as a summer storm's forked lightning on a dark night—flared in my eyes, and I choked and gasped as strangling fumes of burning sulfur filled my mouth and nostrils.

"De Grandin, oh, de Grandin!" I wailed, leaping from the bed and blundering against furniture as I sought the light. Too well I knew that Jules de Grandin could not hear my voice, already I had seen the effects of such flailing blows as I had heard; the little Frenchman lay upon his bed, his head crushed in, his gallant spirit gone for ever from his slender, gallant body.

"*Tiens*, my friend, you battled him right manfully. I dare assert his belly is most villainously sore where you hit it with the bottle," de Grandin's voice came to me from the farther end of the room, and as my light-burned eyes regained their sight, I saw him crawl forth from behind an overstuffed armchair.

My first impulse was to rush upon him and clasp him in my arms; then sudden hot resentment rose within me. "You were there all the time," I accused. "Suppose it had struck me instead of—"

"Of the pillow which I so artistically arranged within the bed to simulate myself?" he interrupted with an impish grin. "In such a case I should have brought this into play." He waved the heavy French army revolver which he held in his right hand. "I could have dropped him at any time, but I desired to see what he was about. It was a gallant show, *n'est-ce-pas?*"

"But—but was it *really* human?" I demanded, shuddering at the dreadful memory of the thing. "D'ye suppose a bullet *could* have reached it? I could have sworn—"

"Assuredly you could," he acquiesced and chuckled. "So can the good O'Toole, and so can our most reverend friend, the *abbé* with the funny name, but—"

A thunderous knocking at the door broke through his words. "Doctor de Grandin, is everything all right?" Mayor Wilcox called anxiously. "I thought I heard a noise in your room, and—nothing's happened, has it?"

"Not yet," the Frenchman answered coolly. "Nothing of any consequence, *Monsieur le Maire*; but something of importance happens shortly, or Jules de Grandin will eat turnips for next Christmas dinner."

"That's good," Mayor Wilcox answered. "At first I thought it might be George stumbling over something as he came in, but—"

"*Ha? Petit Monsieur Georges*—he is still out?" the Frenchman interrupted shrilly.

"Yes, but—"

"*Grand Dieu des porcs, grand Dieu des coqs; grand Dieu des artichauts*—come, Friend Trowbridge, for your life, for his life, for their lives; we must hasten, rush, fly to warn them of the horror which stalks by night! Oh, make haste, my friend; make haste, I beg of you!"

Wondering, I got into my hat and overcoat while de Grandin thrust the heavy pistol in his outer pocket and beat his hands together as he urged me feverishly to hurry.

"Tell me, *Monsieur*," he asked the mayor, "where does Monsieur Georges make the assignation with his sweetheart? Not at the rectory, I hope?"

"That's the worst of it," Wilcox answered. "Folloilott's forbidden him the house, so Janet slips out and meets him somewhere and they drive around; I shouldn't be surprised if they were parked along the roadside somewhere; but only Heaven knows where. With all this reckless driving and bootlegging and hijacking going on, I'm in a perfect jitter every night till he gets home, and—"

"Name of a mannerless small blue pig, our task is ten times harder!" the Frenchman interrupted. "Come, Friend Trowbridge, we must search the secret paths, seek out the cars secluded by the roadside and warn them of their peril. *Pardieu*, I should have warned him of it ere he left the house!"

7

THERE WAS SOMETHING VAGUELY sinister in the night as we set out; a chill not wholly due to the shrewd wind which blew in from the meadows was biting at my nerves as we walked quickly down the winding, darkened road. Some half a dozen blocks beyond the house we came on a parked car, but when de Grandin flashed his searchlight toward it the angry question of a strange young man informed us we had failed to find the pair we sought. Nevertheless:

"The thing responsible for the deaths which have terrorized the town is out tonight, my friends," the little Frenchman warned. "We ourselves have seen it but a moment since, and—"

"Then you stay here and see it by yourself, old chap!" the young man bade, as he disengaged himself from the clinging arms of his companion, shot his self-starter and set his car in motion.

Three other amorous couples took to flight as we gave warning, and de Grandin was close upon hysteria when the darting shaft of luminance from his flashlight at last picked out the dark-blue body of young Wilcox's modish roadster. As we crept softly forward we heard a woman's voice, rich, deep contralto, husky with emotion:

"My darling, more to me than this world and the next, it must—it *has* to be—good-bye. There is no way I can avoid it, no other way, my dear. It's fate—the will of God—whatever we may choose to call it, dear; but it has to be. If it were anyone else, it might be different, but you know him; you know how much he hates the world and how much such things mean to him. And if it were only that he wanted me to do it, I might defy him—though I never did before. Love might make me brave enough to do it—but it's more than that. I'm vowed and dedicated, dear; long, long ago I took an oath upon my naked knees to do this thing, and I can not—I dare not break it. Oh, my dearest one, why—why—did I have to meet you before they had me safely in the sisterhood? I might have been happy, for you can't miss the sunshine if you've always been blind, but now—" She paused, and in a faint glow of the dashboard light we saw her take his face between her hands, draw his head to her and kiss him on the lips.

"*Monsieur—Mademoiselle—*" the Frenchman started, but never finished speaking.

Out of the blackness of surrounding night, its body but a bare shade lighter than the gloom, dreadful, fleshless head and horrid eyes agleam, emerged the phantom-thing we'd seen a half-hour earlier in our bedroom. The night wind whistled with a kind of hellish glee between the sable pinions of the thing's extended wings, and the gleam of phosphorescence in its hollow, orbless eye-holes was like the staring of a basilisk. I stood immobile, rooted in my tracks, and watched destruction bearing down upon the hapless lovers.

Not so de Grandin. "*Sa-ha, Monsieur l'Assistant du Diable*, it seems we meet again—unhappily for you!" he announced in a deadly, quiet voice, and as he spoke the detonation of his pistol split the quiet night as summer thunder rends a lowering rain-cloud. *Crash—crash!* the pistol roared again; the phantom-thing paused, irresolute as though a will of hidden steel had suddenly been reared in its path, and as it halted momentarily, the Frenchman fired again, coolly, deliberately, taking careful aim before he squeezed the trigger of his heavy weapon.

A sort of crackling, like the scuttering of dry, dead leaves along the autumn roads, sounded as the fearsome thing bent slowly back, tottered uncertainly a moment, then fell to earth with a sharp, metallic rattle and lay there motionless, its wide, black wings outspread, its scale-clad arms outflung, its legs grotesquely twisted under it.

"*Tiens.* I did not shoot too soon, it seems," de Grandin told young Wilcox cheerfully as he neared the roadster and smiled upon the startled lovers. "Had I delayed a second longer I damn think that the papers would have told the story of another murder in the morning."

I walked up to the supine monster, a sort of grisly terror tugging at my nerves, even though my reason reassured me it was dead.

The eyeholes in the skull-like face still glared malevolently, but a closer look convinced me that nothing more uncanny than luminous paint was responsible for their sullen gleam.

Half timidly, half curiously, I bent and touched the thing. The face was but a mask of some plaster-like substance, and this was cracked and broken just above the eyes, and through the fissure where de Grandin's ball had gone there came a little stream of blood, dyeing the gray-white surface of the plaster mask a sickening rusty-red. About the body and the limbs was drawn a tightly-fitting suit of tough, black knitted fabric, similar to the costume of an acrobat, and to the cloth was sewn row after row of overlapping metal scales. One foot was clothed in what looked like a heavy stocking of the same material as the suit, while to the other was affixed two plinths of solid rubber—evidently the halves of a split rubber heel. Here was the explanation of the cloven footprint we had seen impressed upon the earth by Bostwick's house.

Still grasped within the thing's right hand there lay the handle of the oddest-looking hammer I had ever seen—heavy as a blacksmith's sledge, but fashioned like an anvil, one end a sharp and pointed cone, the other flat, but fitted with a sort of die shaped like the hoof of a gigantic goat. "That's it!" I murmured, as if I would convince myself. "That's what was used to stamp the Devil's mark upon the victims' faces. First smash the skull with the pointed end, and then reverse the weapon and stamp the victim with the Devil's brand!"

Again I bent to touch the ghastly head, and at my touch the mask rolled sidewise, then, shattered as it had been by de Grandin's bullet, split in two parts, laying bare the face beneath.

"De—de Grandin!" I croaked hoarsely, "it—it's—"

"Of course it is," he supplied as my lips refused to frame the name. "I have known for some time it was the reverend gentleman—who else could it have been?"

He turned his shoulder toward me and called across it: "Leave him as he lies, my friend; he will make interesting material for the coroner."

"But—but don't you even want to *look*?" I expostulated, horrified by his indifference.

"For why?" he answered. "I saw him when he tried to batter out my brains. That look was quite enough, my friend; let the others gaze on him and marvel; let us return to Monsieur Wilcox's house with these ones; there is something I would say to them anon."

8

DE GRANDIN CALLED O'TOOLE and told him briefly what had happened, then having notified him where the body lay, hung up the telephone and turned a level stare upon young Wilcox and the girl.

"My friends," he told them sternly "you are two fools—two mutton-headed, senseless fools. How dare you trifle with the love the good God gives you? Would you despise His priceless gift? *Ah bah*, I had thought better of you!"

"But, Doctor de Grandin," Janet Payne's reply was like a wail, "I can't do otherwise; I'm vowed and dedicated to a life of penance and renunciation. He made me take an oath, and—"

"*A-ah?*" the Frenchman's voice cut through her explanation. "He made you, *hein?* Very good; tell us of it, if you will be so kind."

"I was a little girl when he first took me," she answered, her voice growing calmer as she spoke. "My parents and I were traveling in Ecuador when we came down with fever. We were miles from any city and medical help could not be had. Mr. Folloilott came along while we were lying at the point of death in a native's hut, and nursed us tenderly. He risked his death from fever every moment he was with us, but showed no sign of fear. Mother died the day he came, and Father realized he had not long to live; so when the kind clergyman offered to take me as his ward, he gladly consented and signed a document Mr. Folloilott prepared. Then he died.

"It was a long, long time before I was strong enough to travel, but finally my strength came back, and we got through to the coast. Mr. Folloilott had the paper Father signed validated at the consul's office, then brought me back to this country. I never knew if I had any relatives or not. I know my guardian never looked for them.

"For a long time, till I was nearly twelve years old, he never let me leave the house alone. I never had a playmate, and Mr. Folloilott acted as my tutor. I spoke French and Spanish fluently and could read the hardest Greek and Latin texts at sight before I was eleven, and had gone through calculus when I was twelve. The Book of Common Prayer and the Hymnal were my text-books, and I could repeat every hymn from *New Every Morning Is the Love* to *There is a Blessed Home Beyond this Land of Woe* by heart."

"*Mon Dieu!*" exclaimed de Grandin pityingly.

"When I had reached thirteen he sent me to a sisters' school," the girl continued. "I boarded there and didn't leave during vacation; so I was much more advanced than any of the other pupils, and when I was fifteen they sent me home—back to Mr. Folloilott, I mean.

"Of course, coming back to the lonely rectory with no company but my guardian was hard after school, and I was homesick for the convent. He noticed it, and one day asked me if I shouldn't like to go back to Carlinville to stay. I told him that I would, and—"

She paused a moment and a thoughtful pucker gathered between her brows, as though an idea had struck her for the first time. "Why"—she exclaimed—"why, it was no better than a trick, and—"

"*Eh bien*, we do digress, *Mademoiselle*," the Frenchman interrupted with a smile. "The evidence first, if you please, the verdict afterward. You told the reverend gentleman you should like to return to the good sisters, and—"

"And then he took me to the church," she answered, "and led me to the chancel, where he made me stop and turn my stockings down so that I knelt on my bare knees, while he held a Bible out to me, and made me put my hands on it and swear that I would dedicate myself to holy poverty, chastity and obedience, and as soon as I had reached eighteen, would go to Carlinville and enter as a postulant, progressing to the novitiate and finally making my profession as a nun.

"It was shortly after that Mr. Folloilott received the call to Norfolk Downs and I met George, and—" her voice trailed off, and once again sobs choked her words.

De Grandin tweaked the ends of his mustache and smiled a trifle grimly. "I wish I had not shot him dead so quickly," he muttered to himself; then, to the girl:

"A promise such as that is no promise at all, *Mademoiselle*. As you yourself have said, it was a trick, and a most despicable one, at that. Now listen to my testimony, *Mademoiselle*:

"When Monsieur Wilcox called me to this place to look into these so strange murders, I was most greatly puzzled. The evidence of Chief O'Toole all pointed to some superphysical agency at work, and as I'd had much practise as a phantom-fighter, it was for me to say what tactics I should use, for what may rout a ghostly enemy is often useless when opposed to human foes, while what will kill a human being dead is useless as a pointed finger when directed at a spirit. You apprehend? Very good.

"So when I learned that *Monsieur* your guardian with the funny name I can not say had laid the onus of these killings on a piece of broken sculpture, I was most greatly interested. Stranger things had happened in the past; things quite as strange will doubtless happen in the future. The theory that the Devil was unloosed seemed tenable but for one little single thing: Everyone this Devil killed was some one of an evil life. 'This is the very devil of a Devil, Jules de Grandin,' I tell me. 'Most times the Evil One attacks the good; this time the Evil One has singled out the evil for attack. It does not hang together; it has the smell of fish upon it. *Oui-da*, but of course.'

"Accordingly, I made the careful study of your guardian. He is a very pious man; that much one sees while both his eyes are closed. *Ha*, but piety and goodness are not of necessity the same. By no means. Gilles de Retz, the greatest monster ever clothed in flesh, he was a *pious* man, but far from being good. Cotton Mather, who hanged poor, inoffensive women on the gallows tree, he was a pious man; so was Torquemada, who fouled the pure air of heaven with the burnings of the luckless Jews in Spain. They all were pious—too pious to be truly good, *parbleu!*

"The evening when I met your guardian at dinner, I studied him some more. I hear Monsieur Wilcox tell the young rabbi that the debt upon his temple is extended. How does *Monsieur* your guardian take that statement? It makes him ill, by blue! Furthermore, he has upon his face the look of one who finds too late that he had made a great and terrible mistake. The loan would have been called had not the money-lender died. Now, for the first time, the clergyman finds the hated Jews have profited by the Shylock's death—and he looks as if he were about to die! 'Jules de Grandin, this are strange,' I tell me. 'You must keep the eye on this one, Jules de Grandin.' And, 'Jules de Grandin, I shall do so,' I reply to me.

"Meanwhile he has been at great pains to tell us all once more that these killings are the work of righteous Heaven. Is it more superstition—or something else—which makes him tell me this? One wonders.

"When he had gone I learn that he has been a hunter and a mountain-climber, that he has shot a condor down in flight. '*Ah-ha*,' I say to me, 'what doss this mean, if anything?'

"The police chief has shown to me a feather clipped by his bullet from the dreadful being which commits these murders. I have looked at it and recognized it. Although it has been metallized by a process of electro-plating, I have recognized it instantly. It is the feather of a condor. *U'm-m.* Once more one wonders, *Mademoiselle.*

"And while we sit and talk before the fire, there come the tidings of another killing. Monsieur Bostwick has been slain.

"We go at once and find him in his chair, dead like a mutton, and very peaceful in his pose; yet all his goods and chattels have been smashed to bits. The blow which killed him had done so instantly, and there is blood to mark the spot where he fell—yet he sits in his chair. I look around and come to a conclusion. The smashing of the furniture is but a piece of window-dressing to cover up the manner of the killing.

"But who can enter in a house where all the windows, save a single one upon the second floor, are latched, strike down a man, then vanish in thin air? I ask to know. Moreover, what was it that was seen to look into a window ten feet from the ground? I can not answer, but the next day I find that which helps me toward conclusions.

"There is blood upon the ground by Monsieur Bostwick's house; a little, tiny drop, it is, but I take it that it fell from off the murderer's weapon. There are also footprints—most extraordinary footprints—in the soft earth by the house. 'The murderer have stood here,' I inform me.

"'Quite so,' I agree with me, 'but where was he before he stood there?'

"So up upon the roof I go, and there I find a strand of horsehair. I think: *Monsieur* your guardian is a skilled mountain-climber; he had been to South America. In that land the *vaqueros*, or herdsmen, use lariats of plaited horsehair in their work; they find them lighter and stronger than hemp. That I remember. I remember something else: A skilled mountaineer might have lassoed the chimney of that house, have drawn himself up to the roof, then lowered himself to the open window of the second-story room. He might have struck down Monsieur Bostwick from the window, then smashed the furniture to make it seem a struggle had been had. That done, he might have closed the window after him, lowered himself to the ground by his lariat, and made off while no one was the wiser. To disengage the lasso from the chimney would have been an easy task, I know, for I have seen it done when jutting rocks, instead of chimneys, held the mountain-climbers' ropes.

"As he slid down his rope he looked into the window of the hall, and when his evil mask was seen, they said it was the Devil. Yes, it were entirely possible.

"Now, while I stood upon the roof seeking that little strand of horsehair upon which hung my theory, who passed but your good guardian? He sees me there, and realizes I am hot upon the explanation of the crime. Anon he comes to Monsieur Wilcox's house—perhaps to talk with me and find out what I know—and I exert myself to be most disagreeable. I wish to sting him into overt action.

"*Parbleu*, I have not long to wait! This very night he comes into my room and would have served me as he did the others, but I am not beneath his hammer when it falls, and good Friend Trowbridge knocks the wind from him with a carafe.

"And then, too late, I learn that you and Monsieur Georges have the assignation. All well I know how that one will attack you if he finds you. To such a one the greatest insult is the thwarting of his will. And so I rush to warn you. The rest you know."

"The man was mad!" I exclaimed.

"Of course," replied the Frenchman "He was fanatically ascetic, and you can not make the long nose at Dame Nature with impunity, my friend. As your Monsieur John Hay has said:

. . . he who Nature scorns and mocks
By Nature is mocked and scorned.

"He brought his madness on himself, and—"

"But that sulfurous, blinding fire we saw—O'Toole saw it, too. What was that?"

"Have you never attended a banquet, my friend?" he asked with a grin.

"A banquet—whatever are you talking about?"

"About a banquet, *parbleu*—and about the photographs they take of such festivities. Do you not recall the magnesium flares the photographers set off to take their indoor pictures?"

"You—you mean it was only flashlight powder?" I stammered.

"Only that, my friend; nothing more fantastic, I assure you. Blazing in the dark, it blinded those who saw it; they smelled the acrid, pungent smoke, and imagination did the rest. *Voilà*; we have the 'fires of hell' of which the good O'Toole did tell us."

Young Wilcox turned to Janet. "You see, dear," he urged, "that promise was extracted from you by a trick. It can't be binding, and I love you so much—"

De Grandin interrupted. "There is another vow that you must take, my child," he told the girl solemnly.

"A—a vow?" she faltered. "Why, I thought—I was beginning to think—"

"Then think of this: Can you repeat: 'I Janet, take thee, Georges, to my wedded husband?"

A blush suffused her face, but: "I'll take that vow, if George still wants me," she replied.

"Wants you? *Par la barbe d'un cochon vert*, of a surety he wants you!" the Frenchman almost shouted. "And me, *pardieu*, I greatly want a drink of brandy!"

The Heart of Siva

"Is there a doctor in the house?" Sharp-toned, almost breathless, the query cut through the sussuration of comment following the second divertissement offered by the Issatakko Ballet Russe. The gay, chattering buzz-buzz of conversation which characterizes every audience during the entr'acte was hushed to a barely audible, curious murmur which rippled from lip to lip: "What is it? What's happened? Is it a—"

"Here, *Monsieur le Directeur!*" Jules de Grandin announced, rising in his chair and seizing me by the shoulder. "Here are two of us; we come at once.

"Your pardon, *Mesdames, Messieurs,*" he added to our neighbors as, regardless, of the toes he trampled and the shins he kicked, he forced his way to the aisle, dragging me behind him, and made swiftly for the passageway leading backstage from the rear of the lower tier of boxes.

"And now, *Monsieur*, what is it, if you please?" he asked as the iron-sheathed fire-door clanged shut behind us and we found ourselves in the dim-lit, mysterious space behind the wings.

"One of our girls, Mam'selle Niki," the perspiring manager half gulped, half gasped, mopping a dew of glistening, oily moisture from the top of his pink and hairless head with a crumpled white-silk handkerchief. "She was due to go on in the next number—Flora, who shares her room, had already come down and was waiting, but Niki didn't answer the bell, and when we sent for her we found she hadn't even begun to change. She's had a seizure of some sort, I'm afraid. If you'll come with me, please, gentlemen—"

He turned toward a winding spiral of iron stairs, his bald head gleaming in the subdued rays of a cage-protected electric light, the breath wheezing with oily sibilance between fat lips.

De Grandin and I followed as best we could, picking our path between masses of scenery, across coiling, serpent-like electric cables, winding our way up the twisting stairs, and finally coming to pause before a narrow metal door on which our guide knocked sharply. No answer being received, he thrust the portal open and stood aside to let us enter.

The cubicle into which we stepped was reminiscent in shape, size and general appearance of a cell in one of our more modern jails. Cement walls dressed with rough-cast plaster bore penciled sketches of girls' heads, with occasional more intimate details of anatomy, accompanied here and there by snatches of decidedly un-Tennysonian verse. A cluster of electric lights set in the ceiling gave brilliant illumination to a narrow, unpainted table with two make-up boxes on it.

Crumpled on the floor before the second make-up box lay a girl. As nearly as I could determine at first glance, she was clothed in a sleazy rayon kimono figured with atrocious caricatures of green flamingos feeding from a purple pool. For the rest, bracelets, bell-hung anklets and breast-boxes of imitation silver set with glass jewels and ear- and nose-rings of pinchbeck seemed to complete her costume. Her slim, bare body was smeared with umber grease-paint in simulation of a Hindoo woman's sunburnt skin, and a small, red caste mark set between her eyes completed the illusion, but where the coarse-haired wig of black had slipped from her forehead there showed a thin line of pallid scalp and a straying tendril of fine, light hair, proclaiming her a natural blond.

Flaccid as a cast-off rag doll she lay, one arm grotesquely doubled underneath her, the other, laden with its loops of imitation jewelry, extended toward us, slender, dark-stained fingers with strawberry-tinted nails clutched into a little, rounded fist on which the cheap rings glittered fulgently.

De Grandin crossed the little room in two quick strides, dropped to one knee and took the girl's thin wrist between a practised thumb and finger. A moment he knelt thus, then, putting out his hand, raised her left eyelid.

"*Ah-ha*," the nasal, non-committal ejaculation which held no hint of laughter, yet somehow conveyed an implication of grim humor that told me he had found something; something wholly unexpected.

He bent again to look at her clenched hand, gently prizing the stiff fingers open, and from his waistcoat pocket produced a small lens, fitted with a collapsible tube, like a jeweler's loop, set it in his eye and raised the little, brown-stained hand, regarding it intently. His elbows moved, but since his back was to me I could not tell what he was doing as he bent still closer to the inert form. At length:

"*Monsieur*, this poor one doubtless has a *doublure*—an understudy?" he asked the manager.

"Why, yes, but—"

"*Très bon*; you would be advised to call her to the stage. *Mademoiselle* will not be able to appear again tonight—or ever. *Elle est morte*."

"You—you don't mean she's—"

"Perfectly, *Monsieur*; she is dead."

"But what are we to do?—this will ruin us!" Tears of terror and self-pity welled up in the manager's rather prominent blue eyes. "This mustn't reach the papers, sir! That threat—that note—"

"*Ah-ha!*" again that nasal, enigmatic sound, half query, half challenge. "There was a note, *hein?* What did it say?"

A look of panic swept across the manager's broad face. "Note?" he repeated. "Oh, no, Doctor, you misunderstood; I was referring to a promissory note which falls due on the first. If this death becomes public we shan't be able to meet it!"

"U'm?"

"Poor Niki," the manager hurried on, obviously intent on changing the subject as quickly as might be. "She seemed so well just a few minutes ago. She must have had a seizure of some sort."

"Seizure is the word, *Monsieur*," de Grandin agreed grimly, fixing the other with a level stare. Then:

"*Allez*; get on, begin your show. Me, I have work to do!" He fairly pushed the other from the room; then, to me:

"'Phone for the coroner, Friend Trowbridge," he commanded. "Bid him come quickly for this poor one's body, if you please. Do you await him here, and ask him to withhold the autopsy until he hears from me. I shall be in the rear of the auditorium, awaiting you when you have done with him."

"Couldn't you determine the cause of death?" I asked curiously as he turned to leave.

"Truly, my friend; only too well."

"Why, then, can't you sign the death certificate and save Mr. Martin the bother—"

"*Mais non*, the law forbids it. This so unfortunate young woman was murdered."

"Murdered?"

"*Précisément*; most foully done to death, or I misread the signs."

I FOUND HIM LOUNGING AT the rear of the theater, with the studied boredom of a seasoned boulevardier when, the girl's body entrusted to Coroner Martin's custody, I quit my lonely vigil with the dead.

The third presentment of the Issatakko Ballet was in progress, depicting one of those never-ending conflicts between gods and men with which the elder religions teem. Seated beneath the outstretched branches of a tree was a young ascetic, thighs doubled under him; feet, soles up, resting on his crossed calves. His head sunk low upon his breast, hands lying flat; palms up, upon his knees, he sat stone still in silent contemplation whereby he sought to acquire mastery of the secrets of the universe and share the power of the gods.

Far away, faint as the whisper of a lilting summer zephyr, a wind arose, stirring the foliage of the tree under which the youthful yogi sat, scattering a gay cascade of ruby-tinted blossoms over him. The crouching figure sat immobile.

Now the wind lifted and the great trees bowed their heads in terror as the Storm King drove his chariot across the sky. Black clouds piled menacingly, bank on bank, obscuring every shaft of light which shot down through the forest, and spears of vivid lightning stabbed the darkness while the thunder roared a fierce, continuous cannonade. Still the yogi sat in moveless contemplation.

Then suddenly a blaze of light effaced the gathering shadows and upon a dais we saw the seated form of Siva, the Destroyer. Cross-legged sat the god, feet doubled under him; the lithe body, gleaming like burnished bronze, bare from soles to brow, save where great bands of gold encircled ankles, waist and wrists, and where a heavy collar of dull gold, thick-set with carven coral, rested round the neck. Upon the head was reared a coronet of seven leaping flames, and between the eyes was set the caste-mark of the followers of Siva. Plainly, it was a girl who impersonated the dread third person of the Indian Trimutri, but by ingenious use of lights and draperies perspective was so altered that a second girl behind the first was totally invisible, save where her arms were thrust to right and left beneath the other's, giving a perfect illusion of a human form with four pectoral limbs. Each hand of the four arms was held identically, thumbs and forefingers pressed daintily together, as though about to lift a pinch of snuff. For a moment the six-limbed form sat motionless; then as the orchestra began a soft andante, the arms began to move, rippling bonelessly from shoulder down to wrist, supple as twining serpents, fascinating as the movements of a reptile when it would put a spell upon its prey.

Some moments this endured; then, as though summoned by the eery beckoning of those reptilian hands, a bevy of girls drew near, the light reflected from the brooding deity's throne shining on their rings and belts and tinkling silver anklets. These were, I knew, the Apsaras or Houris from the Hindoo paradise, and as they neared the throne of Siva and groveled to the earth before the squatting god, their mission was made clear; for with a final gesture of its fourfold hands the deity commanded that they exercise their wiles upon the brooding yogi who took no note of storm or hurricane or the threatening bolts of lightning sent to drive him from his meditation.

The figure of the god dissolved in darkness, and with subdued gurgles off laughter the Houris formed themselves into a ring and danced about the seated mystic entreating him with every artifice of Eastern love to look upon their charm and forget his contemplation in the pleasures of the flesh. Still no response from the brooding, seated figure.

Now, covered with chagrin at failing to arouse the young man's passion, the Apsaras drew off, their arms across their faces to hide the tears of shame which started to their eyes; and suddenly the music changed. No longer was it light and gay and frolicsome, a fitting tune for little, silver-bangled feet to dance to; it was a sort of sensuous largo, a creeping, reptant, slowly moving thing instinct with subtle menace as the sinuous turnings of a snake, redolent with the sort of awful blasphemy which might attend the unclean secret worship of some band of obscene ophiolatrists.

By a clever bit of stage mechanics a shadow-spot was thrown upon the scene. That is, as a shaft of light might strike upon a darkened stage, picking out the figure of the actor upon which it rested there was now centered a spot of shadow in the midst of light, and in this, slowly, with a sinuousness which raised the hair upon my head with the age-old, atavistic fear of all warm-blooded creatures for the snake, there danced—or rather writhed—a figure.

She was not nude. Had she been so, the lewd obscenity of her would have been less repulsive. Instead she wore a skin-tight costume of fine net transparent as air across the front; save where patches of black, green, or yellow-blue sequins were sewn upon it at breast and waist and thigh. Across the back, from waist to heels, the net was set with gleaming snake-scales, and a trailing train of the material swept upon the floor behind her. Upon each great and little toe of her feet there gleamed an emerald-studded ring, so that each step she took was like the forward-darting of a green-eyed snake, while on her arms were flesh-tight sleeves of shining scales and on her hands were mittens fashioned like the wedge-shaped heads of cobras-de-capello. Upon her head, obscuring hair and face, save for her vivid, scarlet-painted mouth, was drawn a hood of flashing emerald scales.

She was the daughter of Kadru, the snake-goddess, sent from the realm of Takshaka, the serpent-king, to do the work at which the Apsaras failed.

And well she did it!

Each movement was enticement and repulsion rolled in one; the fascinating glinting of her scales was beauty wed to horrifying menace. The slow, mesmeric movement of her hands beckoned with inducement which combined the promise of god-forbidden joys with the pledge of sure destruction. I understood, as I watched breathlessly, how it was that mankind held the serpent in a detestation bordering on loathing, yet in the days before the old gods lost their right to worship, reared altars to the snake and paid him honor with blood-sacrifice.

The young ascetic raised his eyes as the serpent-daughter circled round and round his seat of meditation. At first stark horror shone upon his face; then, slowly, came a look of wondering curiosity; at length a fascinated ecstasy of longing and desire. Her scale-clad hands danced forth to touch his cheeks, her hooded head bent toward him, and straight into his eyes she looked, red mouth provocatively parted, low laughter which was half a hiss inviting him to—*what*?

The strain was past endurance. With a wild cry of renunciation the youth sprang up, all thought of contemplation cast aside. He had looked into the eyes of the snake-woman, and looking, cast off his hope of Nirvana in favor of the promise she held out to him.

Her laughter, hard and clear as any note of silver clapper striking on a silver bell, sank lower, softened to a sibilating hiss; her scale-sheathed arms went round his quivering shoulders; her gleaming, supple body seemed to melt and merge with his, her hooded head sank forward; her flaming, blood-red mouth found his and sucked his soul away. He stiffened like a nerveless body shocked with electricity, held taut as a violin string stretched until the breaking-point is reached; then suddenly, as though the breath she drew forth from his lips were all that held him upright, he wilted. Like a candle in a superheated room, like a doll from which the sawdust has been let, like a toy balloon when punctured with a pin he wilted, dropping flaccid and lifeless in the serpent-witch's cruel embrace. And as she let his limp form sink down to the moss beneath the tree the daughter of the snake-king bent above him and laughed a low and hissing laugh, a laugh of sated cruelty and triumph blended into one, but a laugh which split and broke upon a sob as she gazed down on what had been a man.

Then the purple curtains clashed together and the lights went up. The final act of Issatakko's Ballet Russe was done.

For a long moment silence reigned within the auditorium. A program dropped, and its rustle sounded like the scuttering of frost-dried leaves across a country churchyard in midwinter. A woman tittered half hysterically, and checked herself abruptly, as though she'd been at vespers, or at a funeral service. Then, wave on crashing wave, like breakers surging on a boulder-studded shore, applause broke forth, and for fully five minutes the theater rang with the impact of wildly clapping hands.

De Grandin struck his hands together gently, but there was no enthusiasm in his gaze as the curtains swung apart, revealing the entire Issatakko troupe lined up in acknowledgment of the ovation. Rather, it seemed to me, his eyes roved questingly about the auditorium, seeking something other than a farewell glimpse of the performers whom the audience applauded to the echo. At length:

"Do you observe them, too, my friend?" he asked, nudging me in the side with the sharp angle of a bent elbow as he nodded toward the center aisle.

I followed the direction of his nod with my glance. A party of three dark men, immaculate in faultless evening dress, correct in every detail, even to the waxen-leaved gardenias in their lapels, was walking toward the exit. The foremost man was rather under middle height and surprizingly broad across the shoulders. His arms were long, hanging nearly to his knees, and there was something simian in his rolling gait. Although his face was dark as any negro's, there was nothing negroid in his features or the straight black hair plastered smoothly to his head. Behind him walked a slightly taller man, lighter in skin, slenderer in build, and as he turned his face toward me a moment I caught a fleeting glimpse of his eyes, odd, opaque-looking eyes devoid of either luster or expression. The third man of the party was younger, thin to the point of emaciation, hairless as a mummy, despite his youth. Without quite knowing why, I was unpleasantly impressed by them.

"Now, by the nightcaps of the seven Ephesian Sleepers, one wonders," de Grandin muttered to himself.

"Wonders what?" I asked.

"Where the fourth one went, *parbleu!*" he answered. "Five minutes—maybe six—ago, another one, almost the counterpart of that *sacré singe* who leads, left his seat and the theater. I should greatly like to know—"

"They seem men of refinement," I cut in. "Possibly they're from New York's negro colony and—"

"And perhaps they come from hell, with the taint of brimstone on their breath, which is more likely," he retorted. "Those are no negro-men, my friend; no, they are Asiatics, and Hindoos in the bargain."

"Well?" I countered, hardly knowing whether to be more exasperated than amused. "What of it?"

"*Exactement*—what?" he answered. "Come, let us go and see."

Instead of leaving by the front, he led me down the farther aisle, fumbled for a moment at the leaves of a fire-door, finally let us out into the alley leading to the stage entrance. Hastening down this narrow, tunnel-like passage he came to an angle of the wall, halted momentarily, then:

"*Ah-ha? Ah-ha-ha?*" he exclaimed sharply. "Behold, observe, my friend! I feared as much!"

Lying in a heap, her clothing disarranged, her straw-braid hat some distance from her, was a girl, motionless as an artist's lay-figure cast aside when its usefulness is done.

De Grandin dropped beside her, pressed an ear against her breast, then rising quickly stripped off his dinner coat and folded it into a pad over which he laid the girl face-down, the folded garment forming a pillow under the lower part of her chest. Kneeling across her, he pressed his hands firmly on each side of her back beneath the scapulæ, bearing steadily while he counted slowly: "*Un—deux—trois*," swinging back, releasing the pressure, then leaning forward, applying it again.

"Whatever are you doing?" I demanded. That he was applying the Schäfer method of resuscitation was obvious, but why he did it was a mystery to me. In nearly half a century of practise I had yet to see such treatment for a case of fainting.

"*Parbleu*, I build a house, I go to take a ride on horseback, I attend a dinner at the Foreign Office, what else?" he answered with elaborate sarcasm, continuing to exert alternating pressures on the prone girl's costal region.

A low moan and a gasp told us that the patient was responding to his treatment, and he leaped up nimbly, raised her to a sitting posture with her back against the wall, then bent down smiling.

"You are here, outside the theater, *Mademoiselle*," he told her, anticipating the question with which nine fainting patients out of ten announce return to consciousness. "Will you tell us, if you please, exactly what occurred to you before you swooned?"

The girl raised both hands to her neck, caressing her throat gently with her finger tips. "I—I scarcely know what happened," she replied. "I had to get home early, so I went out before the finale, and was dressed and ready when the curtain was rung down. Just as I left the theater something seemed to—to fall on me; it seemed as though a great, soft hand had closed around my throat and two big fingers pressed beneath my ears. Then I fainted, and—"

"*Précisément*, Mademoiselle, and can you tell us if you cried for help?"

"Why, no; you see, it took me so by surprise that I just sort of gasped and—"

"Thank you, that explains it," he broke in. "I wondered how you had survived; now I understand. When you gasped in sudden terror you filled your lungs with air. Thereafter, right away, immediately, you fainted, and the muscles of your neck were utterly relaxed. Squeeze as he would, he could not quite succeed in strangling you, for your flaccid flesh offered no resistance to the pressure of his *roomal*, and the air you had inspired was enough to aerate your blood and support life until we came upon you. But it was a near thing, *cordieu*—one little minute longer, and you would have been—*pouf!*" He put his gathered thumb and fingers to his lips, and wafted a kiss upward toward the summer sky.

"But I don't understand—"

"Nor need you, *Mademoiselle*. You were set upon, you were almost done to death; but by the mercy of a kindly heaven and the prompt advent of Jules de Grandin, you were saved. May we not have the pleasure of securing a conveyance for you?"

He bowed to her with courtly Continental grace, assisting her to rise.

"And may one ask your name?" he added as we reached the avenue and I held up my stick to hail a cruising taxicab.

She turned a long, appraising look on us, taking careful stock of my bald pate fringed with whitening hair, my professional beard and conservatively cut dinner clothes, then, with brightening eyes, took in de Grandin's English-tailored suit, his trimly waxed wheat-blond mustache and sleek blond hair. With a smile which answered that which the little Frenchman turned toward her she answered, "Certainly, I'm billed as Mam'selle Toni on the program, but my real name's Helen Fisk."

"Now, what?" I asked as the taxi drove away.

"First of all to see *Monsieur le Directeur*; perhaps to pull his nose; at any rate to talk to him like an uncle freshly come from Holland," he returned, leading the way back to the theater.

Monsieur Serge Orloff, managing director of Issatakko's Ballet Russe whose real name must have been quite different from the one he bore in public, sat in sweaty and uncomfortable loneliness in the little cubicle which served him for an office. "Ah, gentlemen," he greeted as we entered, "I'm sure I'm very much obliged to you for what you did this evening. I suppose there'll be some charge for your—ah—professional assistance?" He drew a Russia leather wallet from the inside pocket of his evening coat and fingered it suggestively.

"*Monsieur*," de Grandin told him bluntly, "I think you are a liar."

"Wha—*what?*" the other stammered. "What's that?"

"Precisely, exactly; quite so," the Frenchman answered. "That note of which you spoke when first we met. It was no note of promise, and you know it very well; you also know we know it. It was a threat—a warning of some kind, and you must let us see it. Right away, at once."

"But my dear sir—"

"To blazing hell with your dear sirs—the note, *Monsieur*." He thrust his hand out truculently.

Orloff looked at him consideringly a moment, then with a racial shrug opened his wallet and gave the Frenchman a slip of folded paper.

"U'm?" de Grandin scanned the missive rapidly while I looked across his shoulder:

Manager, Issatakko Ballet:
    Impious man, be warned that your spectacle, *La Mort d'un Yogin*, is an insult to the gods it parodies. If you would save the sacrilegious women who take part in it, and yourself, from the vengeance of the Great Destroyer, you will discontinue it at once. Death, sure and inescapable, shall be the lot of all who further this vile insult to divinity. Be warned in time and do not further brave the vengeance of the gods of India.
                                        (Signed) The Slaves of Siva.

"What does it mean, 'the Great Destroyer'?" I asked.

"Siva," he replied, almost petulantly. "He is the third person of the Hindoo triad. Brahma, the Creator, is the first, Vishnu, the Preserver, second, and Siva, the Destroyer, the last and greatest of them all." Then, to the manager:

"This thing, when did you get it, if you please, *Monsieur?*"

"About a month ago, sir. We opened in Bridgeport, Connecticut, you know; and this note was slipped under my office door the morning following the first try-out performance."

"U'm? And has any effort been made to enforce the threat—before tonight?"

"Tonight? You don't mean Niki was a victim of—"

"Niki and Toni, too, *Monsieur*. The first was killed outright by a very clever piece of villainy; the second would have died by the strangling-handkerchief— the *roomal* of the *thags*—had I not smelt the fish and hastened to her aid, before I surely knew that she had been attacked."

"Oh, this is terrible!" Orloff fairly wailed. "I dare not let this news leak out. Oh, what *shall* I do?"

"First, *Monsieur*, you would be advised to secure police protection for your troupe. Have them—and yourself as well, well guarded while entering, leaving or within the theater—"

"But I can't do that. That would involve publicity, and—"

"Very well," the Frenchman bowed with frigid politeness. "Do as you please, *Monsieur*. I leave to hold a session at the city mortuary and"—there was no humor in the smile he turned upon the manager—"unless you act on my advice, I greatly fear that I shall see you there ere long."

"COLORED MEN? WHY, YES, sir: there's been one of 'em buying tickets to every performance since we opened," the ticket-seller, who boasted the proud title of assistant treasurer of the Issatakko Ballet, told de Grandin as we stopped before his wicket in the lobby. "Funny thing, too; one of 'em, not always the same feller, stops here every afternoon and buys four tickets for the evening show. I don't know who he gets 'em for, but he's here each afternoon, as regular as clockwork. Always gets the best seats in the house, too."

Nodding courteous acknowledgment of the information, de Grandin sought the ticket-taker. It appeared, from what the latter had to say, that "four dinges come every evenin', an' one of 'em always runs out sort o' early, with th' other three leavin' when the show lets out."

"*Eh bien*, my friend," de Grandin told me as we set out for the city morgue, "it would seem there is a definite connection between the advent of those dark-skinned gentlemen, the note of warning which so disturbed Monsieur Orloff, and the death of that unfortunate young woman in her dressing-room tonight. *N'est-ce-pas?*"

CORONER MARTIN GREETED US cordially as we entered his funeral home, which also housed the city's autopsy room. "No, there's been no post-mortem yet," he answered de Grandin's anxious question. "Fact is, Doctor Parnell, the coroner's physician, is out of town on six weeks' vacation, and as he has no official substitute, I—"

"Ah, *parbleu*, our problem then is solved!" the Frenchman broke in delight-edly. "Appoint me in his place, Monsieur, and I shall perform the autopsy at once, immediately. Yes; of course."

The coroner regarded him thoughtfully. They were firm friends, the tall, gray-haired mortician and the dapper little Frenchman, and each held the other's professional attainments in high regard. "By George, I'll do it!" Mr. Martin agreed. "It's a bit irregular, for I suppose you're not strictly 'a physician and surgeon regularly resident in the county,' but I think my authority permits me to make such interim appointments as I choose. Have you any theory of the death?"

"Decidedly, Monsieur. This so unfortunate young woman was murdered."

"Murdered? Why, there's no trace of violence, or—"

"That is where you do mistake; observe, if you please." Crossing the brightly lighted, white-tiled room, de Grandin moved the sheet shrouding the still form upon the operating-table and pointed to the inner corner of the left eye. "You see?" he asked.

Bending forward, we descried the tiniest spot of black. It might have been a bead of mascara displaced from her elaborately made-up lashes; perhaps an accumulation of dust.

"Blood," de Grandin told us solemnly. "I noticed it when first I viewed the body, and I said to me, 'Jules de Grandin, why is it that this poor one bleeds from the eye? Has she fallen, sustained a fracture of the skull, with consequent concussion of the brain?'

"'It are not likely,' I reply to me, 'for had she done so she would have bled also from the nose; perhaps the ear, as well.'

"Then I remember of a body which I once examined in France. A very cunning murder had been done that time, but physicians of the Ministry of Justice discovered him. Yes, of course. This is how it had been done:

"Above the eye there is a little cul-de-sac, a pouch, roofed off by the so thin bone of the supraorbital plate, upon which rests the brain. A long, thin instrument of steel, like, by example, the pins with which the pretty ladies used to fasten on their hats, could be thrust in there, curved above the eye, and easily pierce the thin bone of the supraorbital plate. *Voilà*, the instrument punctures the frontal lobe, a hemorrhage results and a synthetic apoplexy takes place. Death follows. You see? *Mais, c'est très simple.*

"And, my friends"—he turned his level, unwinking cat-stare on each of us in turn—"the murderer in that other case was an Asiatic—a Hindoo. The technique in that case was like that in the case before us; I damn suspect the nationality of the murderers is similar, too. Come, let us see if Jules de Grandin is mistaken."

With the uncanny speed and certainty which characterized all his surgery he set to work with bistoury and saw and chisel, laid the scalp and lifted off the skull-vault. "Observe him, gentlemen," he ordered, pointing with his knife-blade to the dissected frontal lobe. "Here is the blood-clot which caused death, and here"—he directed our attention to the neatly sawed skull—"you will observe the small hole in the roof of the orbit, the hole by which the instrument of death penetrated the brain. Is it not all plain?"

I had to look a second time before I could discern the hole, but at length I saw it. There was no doubt of it, the roof of the supraorbital plate had been pierced, and death had followed the resultant brain-hemorrhage.

"Good heavens, this is fiendish!" exclaimed the coroner.

"Perfectly," agreed de Grandin placidly.

"And you suspect the murderer?"

"I am certain that he is one of four whom I did see tonight, but which one I can not surely say. Moreover, *hélas*, knowing and proving are two very different things. Our next task is to match our knowledge with our evidence, and—"

The buzzer of the operating-room telephone broke through his words, and with a murmured apology Mr. Martin crossed the room and took up the receiver.

"What, at the Hotel Winfield?" he demanded sharply. "Yes, I have it—O-r-l-o-f-f. Right. Send Jack and Tommy over with the ambulance."

"What is it, Monsieur Martin?" de Grandin asked, and as the coroner turned from the 'phone I felt my pulses beating faster.

"Oh," answered Mr. Martin wearily, "it's another case for us. Mr. Orloff, the manager of the Issatakko Ballet, has just been found dead in his room at the Hotel Winfield."

"*Nom d'un nom d'un nom d'un nom!* So soon?" cried Jules de Grandin. I warned the silly, avaricious fool of his danger, but he valued gold above life and would not have police protection, and—"

"Quick, *Monsieur*," he besought Martin, "bid them hold the ambulance. Friend Trowbridge and I must accompany them; we must see that body—observe the way it lies and all surrounding circumstances—before it has been moved."

Stripping off rubber gloves and apron he thrust his arms into his dinner jacket, seized me by the elbow and fairly dragged me up the stairs to the garage where the ambulance was waiting, engine purring.

"You're sure one of those men we saw in the theater tonight killed that girl?" I asked as we dashed through the midnight street, our howling siren sounding strident warning.

"But certainly," he answered. "We have the similarity of technique in the stabbing through the eye, we have the threatening note to Monsieur Orloff, we have the circumstance of attempted garroting of Mademoiselle Hélène, last of all—this." From an envelope he produced a strand of crisp, black hair. "I found it bedded under the fingernail of the dead girl when I examined her remains in the theater," he explained. "She put up some resistance, but her assailant was too powerful."

"But this is curly hair," I objected. "Those men all had perfectly straight hair, and—"

"On their heads, yes," he conceded. "But this is hair from a beard, my friend. What then? The fourth man, the one who left the theater before the others, wore a beard. That it was he who attempted to garrote Mademoiselle Hélène in the alley I am certain; that he also killed poor Mademoiselle Niki in her dressing-room I am convinced, but—"

"How can you prove it?"

"*Ha*, there is the pinch of the too-tight shoe!" he agreed ruefully. "*Tout la même*, if it can be proved, Jules de Grandin is the man to do it. He is one devilish clever fellow, that de Grandin."

SPRAWLED SUPINELY ACROSS HIS bed, eyes staring sightlessly at the ceiling, mouth slightly agape, tongue protruding, lay the little, fat manager of the Issatakko Ballet. It needed no second glance to tell that he was dead, and it required only a second look to tell the manner of his dying; for round his throat, just above the line of his stiffly starched dress collar, was a livid, anemic depression no wider than a lead pencil, but so deep it almost pierced the skin. Habituated to viewing both the processes and results of violent death, de Grandin crossed the room with a rapid stride, took the dead man's head between his palms and slowly raised it. It was as though the head were joined to the body by a cord rather than a column of bone and muscle; for there was no resistance to the little Frenchman's slender hands as the dead chin nodded upward.

"*Parbleu*, again?" de Grandin muttered.

"What?" I asked.

"It is the strangler's mark, my friend," he answered, fingering the dead man's broken neck with delicately probing fingers. "Nothing but a *thag's* garrote leaves a mark like this and breaks the neck in this manner. One trained in the murder-school of Kalika has done this thing, and—ah? A-a-ah? *Que diable?*"

Bending forward suddenly he raised the manager's clenched hand. Protruding from between the first and second finger was a wisp of black, curling hair.

"*Parbleu*, he sheds his hair as an old hen drops feathers at the moulting-season, that one," the Frenchman muttered grimly. "And, *sang du diable*, I shall drag him to his death by those selfsame hairs, or may I eat fried turnips for my Christmas dinner!"

"Whatever are you vaporing about?" I demanded.

"This, *mordieu!*" he answered sharply. "Even as the poor young Mademoiselle Niki, this unfortunate man grappled unavailingly with his assailant. In his case, as in hers, the murderer leant close to do his work, and in each instance his victim grasped him by the beard, yet could not hold him. But they managed to pluck away a hair and hold it in their hands as death came to them. The inference is clear, unmistakable. The same man did both murders."

"Well?"

"By damn it, no! It is not well at all, my friend. It is quite entirely otherwise. Attend me: This *sacré* killer, this strangler, this stabber-in-the-eye, he is emboldened by success. He thinks because he has been able to do these things that he can continue on his road of wickedness. 'These crimes I make are unexplained,' he says to him. 'These Western fools are frightened, but they know not what it is they fear. *Voilà*, I continue in the future as in the past, killing when and where I please, and no one shall suspect me or call me to account.'

"Say you so, *Monsieur l'Assassin?* Be happy while you may; Jules de Grandin has his nose upon your trail!"

"But no, Monsieur, not by no means; there it is you make the grand mistake!" de Grandin assured Mr. Masakowski, the new manager of the Issatakko Ballet, next morning. "Your decision to abandon this enterprise will prove financially disastrous; it will stamp you as a weakling; it will also greatly inconvenience me."

Masakowski, a lean, hawk-nosed man with the earmarks of Southeastern Europe written large upon him, regarded the little Frenchman with a look in which fear and cupidity were almost evenly blended. "I'd like to carry on the show," he admitted. "The house is a sell-out and we're turning 'em away for the next three nights, but—well, you know what happened last night. Orloff's dead; murdered, I've heard it said, and Niki died mighty strangely in her dressing-room, too. Now Julia and Riccarda are reported absent. I called their house when they were half an hour late, and the landlady said they didn't even come home last night. Something darn funny about that." He broke off, drumming on the cigarette-burned edge of his desk with long, nervous fingers.

De Grandin tweaked the needle-ends of his tiny, blond mustache. "You tell me two young ladies of the chorus are missing?" he asked.

"Not from the chorus; they were principals," Masakowski returned. "You remember the last episode, 'The Death of a Yogi'? Where, after thunder and lightning and tempest fail to rouse the ascetic from his contemplation Siva appears and summons the snake-queen to put her spell on him? Julia and

Riccarda take the part of Siva. It's no cinch for two people to be as perfectly synchronized in movement as those girls are—the illusion they give of a single body with four arms is perfect, and took a lot of rehearsing. With them out of the show we'll have a tough time getting on, and we can't cut out that number—it's the hit of the piece."

"And have you no understudies for them?"

Masakowski ran a thin, artistically long hand through thick, artistically long hair. "That's just the trouble," he almost wailed. "Toni's understudied Julia, and we've another girl who can fill in with the second pair of arms—but they won't act. They say there's a jinx on the part and absolutely refuse to go on. And I can't rehearse another pair of girls in time for the evening show, so—"

"Mademoiselle Toni?" de Grandin interrupted. "She is here, perhaps?"

"Yes, she's here, all right, but—"

"*Très bon.* Me, I shall see her, talk with her, persuade her. I have the influence with that young lady."

"Yeah?" The manager was unimpressed. "Get her to take that part tonight and I'll give you and your friend season passes to any seats in the house

"Agreed, by blue!" the little Frenchman answered with a smile, and led the way backstage where electricians, performers and stage hands discussed the tragedy of the preceding night in the quaint jargon of their kind.

"Holà Mademoiselle; comment allez-vous?" de Grandin hailed Miss Fisk with a smile.

"Oh, good morning," the girl returned. "Awful about Monsoor Orloff, ain't it?"

"Deplorable," agreed the Frenchman, "but if the so superb performance should cease on that account, the calamity would be complete. It rests entirely on your charming shoulders, *Mademoiselle*."

"Huh?" She eyed him with quick suspicion; then, satisfied that he was serious: "How d'ye mean?"

He motioned her away from her companions before replying, then whispered, "*Monsieur* the Manager tells me you will not consent to do the dance of Siva—"

"I'll tell the cock-eyed world I won't!" she broke in vehemently. "Some one's hung the Indian sign on that job, and I ain't askin' for nothin' bul-lieve you me. First Félicie and Daphné take a powder on us; then this morning, right after Monsoor Orloff dies, Riccarda, and Julia turn up missing. Now they want me to take it on. Not much!"

"*Mille pardons, Mademoiselle*," de Grandin answered in bewilderment, "what is it that you say concerning Mesdemoiselles Daphné and Félicie? They took a remedy? No, I do not comprehend."

A little, gurgling laugh forced itself between the girl's pretty, brightly painted lips. Then, with sudden seriousness, she explained: "A month ago, when the show was having its tryout up in Bridgeport, Old Orloff got some sort o' note that scared him speechless. None of us knew just what it was, but he was like a feller with the finger on him—tore his hair—or went through the motions, rather, seeing he was bald as a skinned onion, and swore some enemy was out to wreck the show.

"Well, anyhow, he was more scared than a cat at a dog show for the next four days; then, when nothin' happened, he kind o' cooled down. But you should 'a' seen him when Daphné and Félicie quit us without notice. You'd 'a' thought—"

"Quit? How?" he cut in.

"How? Just quit, that's all. They left the theater Sat'day night and never showed up again. None o' us have heard a word from either of 'em. Unless"—she halted, and a shiver, as though from sudden chill, ran through her scantily clad, exquisite form—"unless that statue—" Again that odd, half-frightened halt in speech, again a shudder of repulsion.

"The statue, *Mademoiselle?*" de Grandin prompted as she made no move to finish.

"Sure, that's another dam' funny thing about this business, Doctor. We'd just struck this burg—city, I mean—when an express van backs up to the theater with that statue all crated up, and addressed to Monsoor Orloff. There was an anomonous note with it, too."

"An anomonous—" de Grandin began questioningly, then: "Ah, *mais oui,* one apprehends. And this 'anomonous' message, *Mademoiselle*; it said what, if you remember?"

"It sounded kind o' nutty to me; sumpin about some sculptor havin' seen the show in Bridgeport and fallen ravishin'ly in love with the Dance o' Siva, or some such nonsense, and how he'd set up day and night chiselin' out a representation o' the divine pantomime, or sumpin, and wouldn't Monsoor Orloff please accept this token of an anomonous admirer and well-wisher, or sumpin like that.

"Old Orloff—Monsoor Orloff, I mean—was pleased as Punch with it and had it set up in the lobby. It's out there now, I guess, but I don't know. The thing always gave me the creeps—it looks so much like Daphné, and every time I went past it, it seemed like she was somewhere tryin' to tell me sumpin, and couldn't, so I just quit lookin' at it.

"Now Julia and Riccarda have vanished into thin air, as the feller says, just like Daphné and Félicie, and I should take Daphné's place? I—guess—not! My mother didn't raise any half-wit children."

De Grandin gave his small mustache a soft, affectionate pat, then twisted its twin needle-points with such sudden savagery that I feared he'd tear them loose from his face. "*Mademoiselle*," he asked abruptly, "you are Irish, are you not?"

"Yes, of course; but what's that got to do with it?"

"Much; everything, perhaps. Your people see much farther through the mysteries of life—and death—than most. Will you await us here? We would examine this statue which affects you so unpleasantly."

THE STATUE OF SIVA stood upon a three-foot onyx pedestal in the theater's main lobby, and represented a slender, graceful four-armed female figure seated cross-legged, feet drawn up so far that they rested instep-down upon the bent thighs, soles upward. A pair of arms which grew naturally from the shoulders were bent at obtuse angles, thumbs and fingers daintily joined, as though holding a pinch of powder. Immediately below these arms there sprang from the axillæ a second pair of limbs, which extended outward to right and left, the right hand clasping what appeared to be a wand tipped by an acorn, the left hand cupped, a twisting flame of fire rising from its hollowed palm. Upon its head was set a seven-spindled crown. The head was slightly bent, eyes closed, a look of brooding calm upon the small, regular features. The whole thing was executed in some smooth, black, gleaming substance—whether lacquered bronze, ebony or stained and varnished plaster I could not say—and the workmanship was exquisitely fine, even the tiny lines in the palms of the hands and soles of the feet and the scarcely perceptible serrations in the lips being represented with a faithfulness exactly reproducing nature. Save for a gem-studded collar, armlets, bracelets and anklets, the form was nude, but the gently swelling breasts were so slim and youth-like as almost to suggest a being of a neuter gender, a form endowed with grace, charm and beauty, yet sexless as an angel of the Apocalypse.

De Grandin walked slowly round the sculptured figure, examining it critically. "By blue," he murmured, "he was no jerry-workman, the one who made this thing. But no, his technique, it is—*cordieu*, my friend, I think it too perfect!"

Vaguely, I understood his criticism. No connoisseur of art, I was yet aware of some subtle difference between the life-sized effigy before us and other works of sculpture. Other statues I had seen suggested life, action or emotion, expressing their themes through representation rather than through reproduction. This thing was no simulacrum of humanity, it was humanity's own self, complete to the tiniest, faintest anatomical detail, and differed from other statuary as a bald and literal photograph differs from a portrait done in oils. Something not to be defined, something which impressed no physical sense, yet which impressed me sharply, repulsed me as I looked upon the statue.

"*Morbleu!*" the little Frenchman's sharp ejaculation brought me back from the thoughtful mood into which I'd lapsed. "*Les mouches*, my friend, do you see them?"

"Eh?" I asked. "*Mouches*—flies? Where?"

"There, *cordieu!*" he answered in a low, hard whisper. "See, regard, observe them, if you will." His slender, well-manicured forefinger pointed dramatically to several tiny inert forms lying on the polished plinth on which the statue sat. They were a half-dozen common houseflies, still and dead, some turned back-down, some lying on their sides.

"Well?" I asked wonderingly.

"Well be baked and roasted on the grates of hell!" he answered shortly. "Your nose, my friend, can you use it? What is it that you smell?" Seizing me by the neck he thrust my face forward so violently that I thought he'd bruise my nose against the statue's polished, ebon surface. "Smell, smell—smell it, *mordieu!*" he commanded angrily.

Obediently I contracted my nostrils in a sniff, then wrenched loose from his grip. "Why, it smells like—like formalin," I muttered.

"'Smells like formalin'?" he mimicked. "*Grand Dieu des porcs*, it *is* formalin, great stupid-head! What does it here?"

"Why—" I began, but:

"*Parbleu*, yes; you have said it—why?" he interrupted. "Why and double why, my friend. That is the problem we are set to solve."

Drawing a letter from his jacket he emptied the envelope, swept the defunct insects into it and placed it tenderly in his waistcoat pocket. "Now for Mademoiselle Hélène," he announced, leading the way backstage once more.

"*Mademoiselle*," he whispered when the girl, obedient to his beckoning finger, joined us in a secluded corner, "you must go on tonight. You and Mademoiselle Dorothée must impersonate the Great God Siva at tonight's performance. I—"

"Says you," the girl broke in. "Listen, I'm not takin' any chances with that part. Last night some darn fool was whistlin' in his dressing-room, and you know how unlucky for the show that is—I know it; didn't I like to get choked to death as I was leavin' the theater? This morning, on my way here, I ran head-on into a cross-eyed man, and a black-cat an' two kittens crossed my path just as I turned into the alley to the stage door. Think I'm goin' to take on that hoodoo part with all them signs against me? Not much! Four girls who did that Siva dance before have disappeared. How do I know what's happened to 'em? Who knows—"

"I do!" de Grandin's interruption was sharp as cutting steel. "I can say what their fate was—they were murdered!"

"My Gawd!" Amazement, incredulity, but, strangely, little fear, showed in the girl's startled face.

"Perfectly, Mademoiselle. Mademoiselle Niki and Monsieur Orloff, they were murdered too, if not by the same hand, undoubtlessly by the same gang.

"Attend me—" His voice was low, scarcely above a whisper, but freighted with such authority that the girl forbore to interrupt, though we saw curiosity pressing at her lips like water at a straining dam when the freshets swell the streams in springtime. "I have every reason to believe these deaths and disappearances were due to a campaign of murder and intimidation subtly planned and craftily carried out by a quartet of the shrewdest criminals which the world has ever seen," he continued. "I tell you this because I think you can be trusted.

"Furthermore, *Mademoiselle*, because I think you have the courage of your splendid Irish race I ask that you will do this dance tonight; perhaps tomorrow night, and several nights thereafter. The miscreants who murdered Mesdemoiselles Niki, Félicie and Daphné, who killed Monsieur Orloff and also doubtless did away with Julia and Riccarda, will unquestionably attempt your life if you perform this dance. For your protection you have only Jules de Grandin and *le bon Dieu*; yet it is only by luring them to attack you that we may hope to apprehend them and make them pay the penalty for their misdeeds. I do not minimize the danger, though Heaven, especially when it has Jules de Grandin as ally, is mighty to protect the innocent. Will you accept the risk? Will you help us in our aim to fulfil justice?"

For a long moment Helen Fisk looked at him as though he were a total stranger. Then, gradually, a look of hard determination came into her face, a stiffening in her softly molded chin, a hardening in her eyes of Irish blue. "I'll do it," she agreed. "Gawd knows my teeth'll be chatterin' so's I can't say my Hail Marys, but I'll take it on. If it's the only way to get the scum that did in Félicie and Daphné, I'm game to try, but I'll be so scared—"

"Not you; I know your kind; you will laugh at danger—" de Grandin told her but:

"Yeh, I'll laugh at it, all right—from the teeth out!" Miss Fisk cut in.

"*N'importe*; that you do laugh at all is all that matters," he assured her. "*Mademoiselle, je vous salue!*" He bent his sleek, blond head, and a quick flush mounted Helen Fisk's cheeks as for the first time in her life she felt a man's lips on her fingers.

H E WAS BUSY IN the laboratory most of the afternoon, and when he finally emerged he wore a faintly puzzled look upon his face. "It was formalin, beyond a doubt." he announced, "but why? It are most puzzling."

"What is?" I asked.

"The manner of those flies' demise. I have examined their so small corpses, and all are filled with formaldehyde. Something lured them to that *sacré* effigy of Siva, and there they met their death—died before one could pronounce the so droll name of that Monsieur Jacques Robinson—and died by formalin poisoning. The statue, too, as you can testify, gave off the perfume of formaldehyde, but why should it be so?"

"Hanged if I know," I answered. "It's really a most remarkable piece of work, that statue. Some one with an uncanny gift for sculpture must have seen that dance and have been so inspired by it that he made the thing and gave it to poor Orloff, but—"

"Quite yes, that is the story we have heard," he acquiesced, "but has it not the smell of fish upon it? Artists, I know, are not wont to hide their light beneath a bushel-basket. But no. Rather, they will seek for recognition till it wearies you. Why, then, should a man with talent such as this one had seek anonymity? Such modesty rings counterfeit, my friend."

"Well," I temporized, "vanity takes strange forms, you know, sometimes—"

"Vanity, ha! *Tu parles, mon ami!*" With a sudden dramatic gesture he struck both hands against his temples. "Oh, Jules de Grandin, thou great stupid-head, how near they came to giving you the little fish of April, even as they did to poor, dead Orloff! But no, you are astute, shrewd, clever, *mon brave*, they shall not make the monkey out of you!

"*Au 'voir*, my friend," he flung across his shoulder as he hurried from the room, "I have important duties to perform. Be sure you're at the theater on time. A spectacle not upon the program will be shown tonight, unless I greatly miss my guess!"

TRYING TO LOOK AS unself-conscious as possible—and succeeding very poorly—Detective Sergeant Jeremiah Costello, star sleuth of the Harrison-ville police force and bosom friend of Jules de Grandin, strolled back and forth across the theater lobby, his obviously seldom-used dinner clothes occasioning him more than a little embarrassment. Here and there amid the fashionable audience hurrying toward the ticket-taker's gate I descried other plainclothes men, all equally uncomfortable in formal clothes, but all alert, keen-eyed, watchful of every face among the crowd. The effigy of Siva, I noted, had been taken from the lobby.

Backstage, uniformed men mounted guard at every vantage-point. It would have been impossible for anyone not known to have gone ten feet toward dressing-rooms or wings without being challenged. Outside in the alley by the stage door a patrolman supplemented the guardianship of the regular watchman, and a limousine was parked across the alleyway, a uniformed policeman in the tonneau, another perched alertly in the cab beside the chauffeur.

The show began as usual, spectacle followed spectacle, each in turn being hailed with tumultuous applause. When "The Death of a Yogi" was presented we watched breathless as Helen Fisk and her partner did the sitting dance of Siva and the daughter of Kadru lured the young ascetic's soul from out his body with her venomed Judas-kiss.

"Well, so far everything's all right," I congratulated as the purple curtains drew together before the stage, but de Grandin cut my optimistic statement short.

"Will you observe them, my friend?" he whispered jubilantly, driving his sharp elbow into my ribs. "*Parbleu*, do they not look as sad as the stones in the road?"

Up the center aisle, with anger, something like chagrin upon their swarthy faces, came the same trio we had noted on the previous occasion. With them, whispering excitedly to the slender, light-hued man, was a short, thick-set, bearded ruffian, impeccable in evening dress, but plainly out of place in Occidental clothes. He was black as any negro out of Africa, but his straight, black hair and curling beard, parted in the center, and the wild, fanatic rolling of his bloodshot eyes labeled him an Asiatic, and one habituated to the use of opium or hashish, I guessed.

"A little while ago he rose and left the others," de Grandin whispered with a chuckle. "When he went out he looked for all the world like Madame Puss intent on dining on canary-bird; when he returned, *parbleu*, he made me think of a small dog who creeps back to his master with his tail between his legs. The *gendarmes* we had set on watch had spoiled his fun completely!"

CONVOYED BY POLICEMEN, THE members of the Issatakko troupe left the theater, their guardians staying with them till their doors were safely locked. "Now, I'm afther thinkin' we can go to bed, sors?" Costello asked as he reported all the actors had been safely taken home.

"There is a guard at Mademoiselle Hélène's house?" de Grandin asked.

"There is that, sor," the sergeant answered. "I've got a felly on patrol in th' street, an another in th' alley at th' back. I'm thinkin' it'll be a dam' smart man as gits into that young lady's house tonight widout a invitation."

The little Frenchman nodded thoughtfully; then: "Suppose we go and see that all is well before we take a good-night drink," he suggested. "It was I who urged her to perform that dance tonight; I would not have my conscience tell me I had failed to give protection to her in case she suffered injury."

The street in which Helen Fisk lodged was flanked by double rows of narrow, tall brick houses, flat-fronted, monotonous, uniform as a company of grenadiers. As I drew my car to a halt beneath the lamp post which stood before the lodging-house, a uniformed policeman suddenly materialized from the darkness, glanced inquiringly at de Grandin and me, then saluted smartly as he recognized Costello.

"Everything O.K., O'Donnell?" the sergeant asked.

"Yes, sir; quiet as a graveyard at midnight, so far," the officer replied. "I ain't even seen a—"

A sudden burst of light, dazzling as a very flare, followed by the sharp, staccato *rat-tat-tat* of machine-gun fire cut short his words.

"Glory be to God!" Costello cried. "What th' hell—"

Dragging at the pistol in his shoulder-holster, he hastened down the street toward the intersecting roadway whence the disturbance came, followed full-tilt by Officer O'Donnell. A moment later another form emerged from the shadow of the house and the street lamp glittered momentarily on brass buttons and silver shield as the patrolman who had mounted guard at the rear hurried past to join Costello and O'Donnell in the chase.

"*Par la barbe d'un poisson vert*," began de Grandin; then:

"Up, my friend; up quickly; I fear it is a ruse to draw away the guards; we must act quickly!" Fairly dragging me by a reluctant elbow, he rushed up the short flight of brownstone steps leading to the rooming-house door, pressed upon the panels with an impatient hand and stepped quickly into the dimly lighted hall.

"You see?" he asked in a fierce whisper. "The door is unlocked—open! How comes it?" For a brief instant he bent to examine the fastenings; then:

"Observe him, my friend," he commanded. Looking where he pointed I descried a thin wedge of wood, like a match-stick sharpened to a point, thrust into the Yale lock, making it impossible for the latch to fly into position when the catch had been released. "*Diablerie!*" he muttered. "Costello and the others, they have gone in chase of the wild goose. Come, we must find Mademoiselle Hélène right away, at once."

"I heard her say she lived on the third floor," I whispered, "but whether front or back I don't—"

"No matter," he cut in. "We shall find her—*prie Dieu* we find her first! Up, my friend; mount the front stairs, while I go up the back. We shall meet at the top floor, and should you see another coming down, detain him at all costs. We can not take the chances, now."

He scuttled down the hall and let himself through the swing-door which communicated with the kitchen, waving encouragement and haste to me as he disappeared.

Walking as softly as I could, I crept up the stairs leading to the second floor, began ascending the narrow, spiral flight which gave access to the top story, at last, rather out of breath, paused at the entrance to the long and narrow hallway which bisected the third floor of the house.

Although there were two fixtures set into the wall, only a single electric bulb was burning, and by its rather feeble glow I discerned narrow, white-enameled doors opening to right and left upon the corridor, like staterooms on the passage in a steamship cabin. The place was utterly untenanted, not even a mouse disputing my possession. A moment I paused, waiting for de Grandin; then, as no sign of him appeared, I took a tentative step or two toward the rear of the house, ears attuned for his step upon the stairs.

A faint, light *click*, like the slipping of a well-oiled lock, sounded at my back, and as I turned something whistled past my face, a sharp *pop!* sounded, and the electric bulb burst with a little spurt of fire. Next moment the hallway was drowned in devastating, smothering darkness.

Half terrified, I paused a moment in my tracks; then, fumbling for my matchcase, I struck a light and held the little torch above my head.

"Oh!" I exclaimed involuntarily, shrinking back a step. Creeping stealthily on hands and knees, like in obscene and monstrously overgrown spider, was a man, a small, scrawny, dark-visaged man, silent as a snake in his sinister progress. As the matchlight shone momentarily on him it glinted eerily on the blade of a short curved dagger clenched between his teeth. Brief as my inspection was, I recognized him as one of the quartet of Hindoos we had seen in the theater.

For a moment I stood frozen, aghast; then, marshaling my courage, I challenged sharply: "Halt—stand where you are, or I'll shoot!" Reaching in my waistcoat pocket, I clicked the cover of my glasses-case, hoping desperately that it simulated the sound of a revolver being cocked.

A low, soft laugh, sinister as the hissing of a serpent, answered me, and the fellow rose to his feet, raising his hands level with his ears and grinning at me maliciously. "Will the *sahib* shoot me, then?" he asked, letting the knife fall from between his teeth. "Is there no mercy in your head for me, *bazur?*" The words were humble, abject, but the tone was gravid with biting irony.

"Turn around," I ordered gruffly. "Now, march, and no tricks, or—*ugh!*"

So near my ears I heard its whistling descent, so close to my face I felt its rough, hairy strands brush my nose-tip, something whirled snake-like through the darkness, looped about my neck and jerked sharply back, squeezing the life-breath from my throat, forcing my tongue and eyes forward with the sudden ferocity of its strangling grip. The throttling knot drew tight and tighter round my trachea; bone-hard, merciless knuckles kneaded swiftly, savagely at my spine where it joined the skull, seeking to break my neck. I tried to cry for help, but nothing but a stifled gurgle sounded from my swelling lips. Burned out, the match fell from my numbing fingers, and darkness blotted out the sneering face in front of me. Tiny sparks danced and flashed before my eyes; a roaring like the down-pour of a dozen Niagaras pounded in my ears. "This is how poor Orloff died!" I thought, fighting vainly to escape the strangling coil about my neck.

A sudden shaft of sharp, white light stabbed through the darkness, illuminating the Hindoo's face before me for a fleeting moment. In the flash I saw the grinning mouth square open like an old Greek horror-mask, saw the swift shadow of a slim, white hand—and something else!—pass like a darting ray of light across the dusky throat an inch or so below the chin, saw the welling spate of blood which gushed across the writhing tongue and gleaming teeth. Then came a horrid, choking gurgle, as of something drowning, and the light blinked out. But:

"Spawn of the sewer—species of a stinking camel—take that to hell, and say I gave it to you!" de Grandin's whisper sounded in my ear, and the strangling-cord loosed its biting grip as the man behind me gave a grunt of surprised pain and fell forward, almost oversetting me.

I turned about, clutching at the wall for support, and beheld my late assailant rolling on the floor, mouthing and slobbering horribly as be hugged both hands to his abdomen. "*Ai-i-i-i!*" his scream of mortal agony no thicker than the squeaking of a frightened mouse, and even that died in an anguished wheeze. From crotch to sternum he was slit as cleanly as a butcher slits a slaughtered hog for gutting.

I leaned against the wall, weak with retching nausea at the spectacle de Grandin's pocket torch disclosed.

"It is a good cut, that," the little Frenchman announced softly as he tiptoed across the hall, fumbled a moment and switched on the electric light. "Me, I rather favor it for autopsy work, although the general preference is for the vertical incision beginning at the—"

"Oh—*don't!*" I pleaded, near to swooning at the sight the lighted hall-lamp brought to view. Face downward on the floor lay the fellow I had apprehended, the ever-widening pool of blood which soaked into the carpet telling of his severed throat. Only the tremulous, spasmodic twitching of his clawing fingers told me that he still retained some little spark of life. Hunched on one shoulder, the cord with which he sought to strangle me still gripped in his hand, lay the other Hindoo, blood gushing from the foot-long incision which ran vertically up his abdomen. Jules de Grandin stood at ease, regarding his handiwork with every evidence of scientific satisfaction, a long, curved-bladed kurkri knife, whetted to a razor-edge, dangling by a thong from his right hand.

"*Eh bien, mon vieux*, you look as *triste* as hell upon a rainy Sunday afternoon!" he told me. "Is it that you have never seen the cover stripped from off the human entrails—you, a medical practitioner, a surgeon, an anatomist? *Ah bah*, for shame, my friend; you stand there quaking like a student making his first trip to the dissecting-room!"

"But," I gasped, still faint with stomach-sickness, "this is too—"

"Wrong again, my old one," he corrected with a grin. "Not two, but three. When I left you down below I crept all softly up the stairs until I readied the turn between this story and the one beneath. *Ah ha*, and what did I see there? What but a *sacré* son of Mother India going on all fours like a sly-boots up the stairs ahead of me! Oh, very silently he went; so silently he made no sound at all. He had to be seen to be believed, that one!

"What to do? I had my pistol, and I had my very useful knife, as well. Should I shoot I could not miss him, but what if there were others? The noise would surely put them on their guard, and I desired to surprise them. Accordingly, I chose the knife. I crept a little faster and reached my silent friend before he guessed that I was there at all. Then, very gently, I inserted my knife-tip between his second and third cervical vertebrae. *Voilà.* He died with exemplary expedition and with no unnecessary noise. 'Very good,' I tell me. 'So far, so perfect.'

"Then, still silently, I continued on my upward way. I came into the hall, and what did I behold? I ask to know. You, *cordieu*, standing at the stairhead, as innocent as any unborn lamb, while, crouched behind an angle of the wall, immediately in front of me, a thief-faced rascal was watching you. But ah—even as I saw this, I saw another thing. A door opened very softly in the hall behind you, a bearded ruffian—the same one we had seen in the theater—peered forth, raised up a little stick of wood and flung it quickly at the light. He broke the bulb, and you were left in darkness!

"I heard you stumble in the dark, I saw you light a match, and by its light I saw you parley with the miscreant with the knife. *Tiens*, I also saw the other one advance upon you from the rear, drop his strangling-cord about your throat and begin the pleasant process of choking you to death. 'This thing has ceased to be a joke,' I tell me; 'it are time that Jules de Grandin put a stop to it.'"

"You saved my life; no doubt of it," I told him. "I'm very grateful—"

"*Chut*, it was a pleasure," he cut in, looking complacently at the stiffening bodies on the floor before us.

"Come," he commanded. "We must find Mademoiselle Hélène. She was not in the room from which the bearded man attacked you, for that door had not been forced, and I particularly warned her to bar her door tonight. These other doors have not been opened, for the two who came before me up the stairs had no chance to get in mischief ere I found them. Therefore, it follows that—ah, *que diable?*"

He broke off, pointing to the lower margin of the door beside which we stood. Where the door and sill came together a tiny hole, scarcely large enough to let a man insert his finger, had been gouged, and a little pile of fresh sawdust lay about the hole.

"Well—" I began, but:

"Not at all; by no means, it is very dam' unwell, I suspect!" he interrupted. "One does not surely know, of course, but—"

He rose and beat upon the panels. "*Mademoiselle*, Mademoiselle Hélène?" he called softly. "Are you there? Answer, if you are, but on no account get off the bed."

"Who is it?" Helen Fisk's voice responded. "Doctor de Grandin? Is anything wrong?"

"We hope not, but we fear the worst," he answered. "Stay where you are, for your life, *Mademoiselle*, and do not be alarmed when we break in the door—"

"I'll let you in," the girl replied, and we heard a rustling of the bed-linen. And:

"No! *Pour l'amour de Dieu*, do not set foot to floor, I beg!" he shouted. "We come!"

Retreating to the far side of the hall he charged full-tilt against the bedroom door, driving his shoulder against the white-enameled panels, bursting the flimsy lock and half running, half stumbling into the pitch-dark room.

"Stand back, Friend Trowbridge—remain upon your bed, *Mademoiselle!*" he warned, pausing at the threshold and darting his flashlight quickly about the apartment. "Death lies in wait upon the floor, and—*ah?* So!"

Like a pouncing cat he leaped across the cheap rag rug with which the room was carpeted, his searchlight playing steadily upon a tiny, cord-like black coil beneath a chintz-upholstered chair. With a slanting, chopping motion he brought his big, curved knife-blade down once, twice, and yet again, dividing the tiny snake into half a dozen fragments with the slicing blows. "*Ha*, little brother to the Devil, you are quick, but I am quicker; you are venomous, but so am I, *pardieu!*" he cried. "Go back to hell, from whence you came, and tell those other snakes I sent you there to keep them company—they, too, have felt this knife tonight!"

"What is it?" cried Miss Fisk and I in chorus.

He danced across the room, turned on the light; then, with the air of a gallant assisting a fine lady from her coach, put out his hand and helped the girl down from the bed.

"Do not approach too near, my beautiful," he warned. "Those tiny, tender feet of yours might take a wound from him, dead though he be."

"What *is* it?" Straight and slim as a boy in her close-cropped hair and Shantung silk pajamas, Helen Fisk looked with more curiosity than fear at the dismembered little serpent underneath the chair.

"A krait, *parbleu*," he answered. "*Bungarus coerulens*, the zoölogists call him, and he is not a customer to trifle with, by any means. Nor, *cordieu*, had you stepped from off your bed and had he sunk those little, so small fangs into your foot or ankle, '*Dirige, Domine in conspectu tuo viam meum*' the good priests would have sung for you, *ma chère*, for death follows his bite in from six to eight minutes. Little cousin to the cobra that he is, his bite is far more deadly than that of his disreputable big kinsman."

"Gawd, you took a chance with it!" the girl exclaimed admiringly.

"Not very much," he admitted, stroking his mustache complacently. "He can strike only his own length, and my knife was a good two inches longer than his body."

"But how'd he come to get in my room?" she asked, bewildered. "D'ye s'pose there's any more of 'em here?"

"No to your second question, *Mademoiselle*—through a hole bored in your door to your first," he answered, smiling. "Those sons of sin cut a little, so small opening in the door, sent their silent messenger of death into your room, and were about to decamp when—we detained them, Friend Trowbridge and I." To me he added:

"That accounts for that fellow's knife, *mon ami*; it was with that he bored the hole in Mademoiselle Hélène's door, and he was doubtless about to take departure when your step upon the stair arrested him and he remained to assist his partner of the strangling-cord in finishing you, if help were needed."

"What's that?" the girl demanded. "You mean the guy who almost killed me at the theater was *here*, and attacked Doctor Trowbridge?"

"*Was* here is correct, *Mademoiselle*."

"Where's he at now?"

"*Eh bien*, who can say? I do not think the life he led was very good; his chances of salvation, I should say, were of the slimmest."

"You—you mean you *kilt* him?"

"Perfectly, *Mademoiselle*. Both him and his two assistants."

"Gee, but you're *wonderful!*" Before we realized what she was about, Helen Fisk had laid a hand upon each of his cheeks, drawn his face close to hers and kissed him on the mouth.

"*Pardieu*, my lovely one," de Grandin chuckled, "you do greatly tempt me to make murder my vocation. For a reward such as that—"

The thumping thunder of heavy boots upon the stairs cut short his speech.

"Doctor de Grandin; Doctor de Grandin, are ye there, sor?" demanded Sergeant Jeremiah Costello as, one of the policemen in his wake, he dashed headlong up the stairs.

"Yes, *morbleu*, here am I," de Grandin answered tartly, "and never was I less entranced at sight of your so ugly *tête de roux*, thou breaker-up of romance! What is it now?"

"Someone's been givin' us th' runaround," the sergeant panted. "Some son-of-a-gun—howly Mither, are they dead, sor?" he broke off as he saw the corpses on the floor.

"Like a herring," de Grandin returned nonchalantly. "You were saying—?"

"Well, sor, it looks like some one stood us up. When we seen that there now flash o' light an' heard th' shots a-poppin', we made sure it wuz a gang war broke out agin; so down to th' corner we hotfooted it, like three dam' fools, an' what d'ye think we found?"

The little Frenchman grinned, a thought maliciously. "*Pétards*—how do you call him?—firecrackers?" he replied.

"Good Lord, how'd ye guess it, sor?"

"*Ah hah*, the trick is ancient, *mon vieux*; so old and threadbare that even you should be immune to it. However, it worked, and if I and Doctor Trowbridge had not been on hand to circumvent their wickedness our poor young lady here would now have been a lovely corpse, and, what is more, I should have missed an evening's pleasure. As it is—"

"What's goin' on here, I'd like to know?" an irate landlady, mountainous in righteous wrath and a canton flannel nightrobe, mounted the third-floor stairs. "What's th' meanin' o' this breakin' in a decent woman's house at midnight, an'—"

"Arrah, woman, hold your whist!" Costello interrupted. "'Tis meself an' Doctor de Grandin an' Doctor Trowbridge yonder as kilt them three murtherin' haythins that come into yer place to stab ye all whilst ye wuz sleepin'—an! ye've got th' brassbound nerve to ask us what we're doin' here!"

"Ye mean ye *kilt* somebody in my house—in *my* house, givin' th' place a bad name an' ruinin' me business?" the landlady demanded shrilly. "I'll have th' law on ye fer this, so help me—'

"Ye'll be feelin' me take me hand off'n th' side o' yer face if ye don't shut up an' quit interferin' wid a officer o' th' law in th' performance o' his dooty!" Costello told her sharply. "Go on, go lay down somewheres an' give yer tongue a rest till we've finished wid this business. We need no wimmin to tell us how to do our wor-rk, so we don't."

The majesty of the law vindicated and the landlady effectually squelched, the sergeant turned once more to de Grandin. "We seen a felly runnin' down th' street when we got to th' corner, sor," he reported, "an' whilst we didn't have nothin' agin him, exactly, I thought it best to run 'im in on general principles. Fellies runnin' loose at midnight when some one's made a monkey out o' th' police force will bear investigatin', I'm after thinkin', sor."

"*Exactement*," the Frenchman nodded in agreement. "What sort of person is your prisoner?"

"Why, I should say he's kin to them—to these pore fellies that ye kilt," Costello answered. "Dark like them, he is, an' kind o' slim, an' snooty as a sparry full o' worms; talkin' about his rights, an' how he'll have me broke, an' bein' sarcastical as th' very divil an' all."

"*Comment?* I know his kind. What answer did you give to his abuse?" The anticipatory gleam kindling in the little Frenchman's small, blue eyes burst into sudden flame of merriment as Costello answered simply:

"Bedad, I sloughed 'im in th' jaw, sor!"

N EITHER OF US WAS much surprised to recognize Costello's prisoner as the slender, patrician Hindoo we had seen in the theater in company with the men de Grandin had disposed of. With a badly swelling eye, dress clothes sadly disarranged and a pair of handcuffs on his wrists, the fellow was put to it to maintain his air of lofty hauteur, but sustain it he did, glancing now and again at Costello with venomous hatred mingled with fear, at de Grandin and me with unaffected scorn.

"Where are you taking me?" he asked in faultless, Oxonian English. "I refuse to answer questions or to go with you until I see my lawyer."

"Easy on, laddie buck," Costello cautioned. "Ye'll go where we bid ye, an' no questions asked, or I'll know th' reason why. As for answerin' what we ask, I'm afther thinkin' ye'll talk a-plenty, an' be glad to. Come on!"

T HE LIGHT BURNED BRIGHTLY in Coroner Martin's operating-room, cast-ing back reflections from the white-tiled walls, the terrazzo floor and the gleaming porcelain of the embalming-tables. Shrouded with a sheet, a bulky object occupied the center of the room, and toward it de Grandin walked like a demonstrator of anatomy about to address his class.

"*Messieurs*," he began, "I have here Exhibit A, as they say in the court-room—the statue of the Great God Siva, taken from the lobby of the Issatakko theater this afternoon.

"Trowbridge, *mon vieux*, you will recall the deceased flies we found upon the statue's pedestal? *Bon*. Me, I have analyzed their corpses and found them dead from formaldehyde poisoning. Very good.

"Doctor Trowbridge," again he turned to me, for all the world like counsel examining a witness, "can you recall an odor which we descried about that statue when we looked at it?"

"Why, yes," I answered. "It was formalin. I thought it odd, but—"

"We have no great concern with buts," he cut in quickly. "Behold—"

With a sweep of his hand he tore the sheet from the statue and pointed dramatically to the glistening, dark-hued composition of which the thing was made. "A month or so ago two young women of the Issatakko Ballet Russe dis-appeared," he told us. "They impersonated the god Siva in the spectacle of the Yogi's Death. No one has seen them since; no one knows where they are gone, or where they are at present.

"*Ha*, is it so? No, *tête-bleu*, it is not! They are here, my friends—behold them!"

Snatching up a heavy wooden maul he dealt the statue a sudden vicious blow, repeated it; rained stroke on stroke upon it.

"Look out, you'll break it, man!" I cried, shocked by his act of vandalism.

"*Bon Dieu*, but I intend to!" he panted, striking savagely again at the image's arm. A black, shining flake, four inches long by two in width, detached itself from the bent arm of Siva, fell to the hard-tiled floor with a tinkling, metallic sound, and in the opening thus made there showed, dull, livid, but glistening strangely in the strong light of the operating-room, an arm of human *flesh!*

The gruesome work went on. Flake after flake of shining, black veneer was chipped away and slowly, horribly, there came to view the naked body of a woman.

"Behold, my friends," de Grandin ordered, his voice a sibilant, knife-sharp whisper, "behold the core—*the heart of Siva!*"

As disclosure followed on disclosure I felt a tightening in my throat, an odd, cold, prickling sensation in my scalp and at the back of my neck. A four-inch-long incision had been made in the girl's thigh, thus opening the great femoral artery. The hemorrhage must have been terrific, death following almost instantly. Thereafter the body was seated with folded legs in the attitude assumed by Siva in the ballet, fine steel wires were wound about the limbs to hold them in position where necessary, and the body pumped full of dilute formaldehyde, thus preserving it and imparting a lasting rigidity. A second pair of arms, severed from their owner's body close to the trunk, had been similarly embalmed and sewn into the armpits of the seated girl, thus supplying the four pectoral limbs required for the sitting dance, and, the monstrous effigy finally molded out of human flesh, the whole was coated with a shell of quick-hardening varnish composed of silicate and gypsum, colored black with bitumen.

"Had not the varnish cracked a little and some of the formalin which was lodged between it and the flesh leaked out, we never should have known," de Grandin told us as he finished peeling off the coating from the statue's "heart" of human flesh. "But so intent on lasting preservation was the miscreant that he oversaturated the tissues with the formalin. *Alors*, a little of it found its way through the little, so small crack in the plaster coating, the busybody little flies must come exploring, must stick their noses into it—must die.

"I see them lying dead. 'Have not they chosen a most queer place to die?' I ask me. 'Other flies buzz at will about this theater lobby, other little flies walk with impunity upon the statue's head, its hands, its feet; but those who settle here upon its base, *parbleu*, they die all suddenly.'

"And then I smell the odor of formaldehyde. '*Que diable?*' I ask me. 'Formaldehyde, what is it doing here? In the medical dissecting-room, yes; in the preparation room of embalmers, again yes; in the lobby of a theater, in the statue of the Great God Siva—*mille nons*, it is not right or proper!'

"I look upon this statue. It are too perfect. It are not a work of art, it are, rather, an exact copy—no, a counterfeit—of life. 'Business of the monkey has been made by some one, I damn think,' I tell me. But yet I am not sure. And so I take those most unfortunate flies' small corpses and subject them to analysis. All are dead of formalin. Now I am nearly almost certain.

"And so I go to make examination of that statue once again. I take with me a little hammer and a chisel. While no one looks, I chip a bit of it away. *Ha*, what is it that I see? Flesh, *cordieu*; woman's flesh—dead woman's flesh!

"*Ah ha, ah-ha-ha*, I apprehend it all, now. I know where those two missing girls have gone—one is the body, one is the missing arms of Siva!

"I lay my trap tonight. Once more the dance of Siva is performed, but now the police are on guard; the dancers cannot be molested. Nevertheless, I know in my own head that an attempt will be made to do them harm, and so I go to watch.

"It are even as I think. This man here draws the red herring across the trail; he fools Costello and the others to run down to the corner while his powder-squibs go *pop-pop-pop!* While they are there his helpers find an entrance to Mademoiselle Hélène's house and would have slain her with a snake if Doctor Trowbridge and I had not been there.

"*Ha*, but we are there, and I kill them all, I kill their snake, I kick their so carefully laid plans upside down, as the cow knocks over the filled milk-bucket. Yes, certainly. Their plans are nicely made but in them they have overlooked one thing.

"That thing is Jules de Grandin!"

"You lie!" the prisoner cried, almost in a scream. "You didn't kill them; you're lying!"

"You say so?" de Grandin asked sarcastically. "Monsieur Martin, will you have your young men bring what waits without to us?"

Coroner Martin stepped to the door and beckoned silently.

Without a word three of his assistants came single-file through the door, each trundling a wheeled bier freighted with a sheeted form. As they passed him, de Grandin snatched the sheets away, disclosing the bodies of the Hindoos he had killed in the rooming-house.

"And now, *Monsieur*," he asked in a gentle voice, bowing with mock courtesy to the prisoner, "do you still have doubts of my veracity?"

The fellow stared at the three corpses in horror. His eyes seemed starting from his head as, in a choking voice, he croaked:

"Yes, yes, I did it; I killed them as you said, the wantons, defilers of the gods. I executed them for blasphemy, and I'd have killed that other pate-faced harlot, too, if you had not been here, you—" he glared insanely at de Grandin for a moment, then raised his manacled hands to his face.

"*Sang de Dieu*, but I say you shall not!" the little Frenchman shouted, leaping on the man as a cat might pounce upon a mouse, wrestling with him violently a moment, then springing back triumphantly, a little, jet-black pill displayed between his thumb and fingertip.

"Could he have swallowed this he would have died at once," he told us. "As it is, we shall have the pleasure of seeing him decently and legally put to death for the vile, unconscionable murderer of women that he is.

"Meantime—" His little, round blue eyes swept us one by one, finally came to rest upon Costello. "*Mon sergent*, I am most vilely and unsupportably dry," he complained. "You are well acquainted with the best speakeasies which the city boasts. Will not you, of your charity, take me where I can relieve this torment of a thirst?"

The Bleeding Mummy

OUTSIDE, THE MIDWINTER WIND hurled wave after wave of a sleet-bar-rage against the window-panes, keening a ferocious war-chant the while. Within, the glow of sawn railway ties burning on the brass fire-dogs blended pleasantly with the shaded lamplight. Jules de Grandin put aside the copy of *l'Illustration* he had been perusing since dinnertime, stretched his slender, wom-anishly small feet toward the fire and regarded the gleaming tips of his patent leather pumps with every evidence of satisfaction. "*Tiens*, Friend Trowbridge," he remarked lazily as he watched the leaping firelight quicken in reflection on his polished shoes, "this is most entirely pleasant. Me, not for anything would I leave the house on such a night. He is a fool who quits his cheerful fire to—"

The sharp, peremptory clatter of the front door knocker battered through his words, and before I could hoist myself from my chair the summons was repeated, louder, more insistently.

"I say, Doctor Trowbridge, will you come over to Larson's? I'm afraid some-thing's happened to him—I hate to drag you out on such a night, but I think he really needs a doctor, and—" Young Professor Ellis half staggered into the hall as the driving wind thrust him almost bodily across the doorstep.

"I ran over to see him a few minutes ago," he added as I slammed the door against the storm, "and as I went up his front path I noticed a light burning in an upper window, though the rest of the house was dark. I knocked, but got no answer, then went into the yard to call to him, when all of a sudden I heard him give the most God-awful yell, followed by a shriek of laughter, and as I looked up at his window he seemed to be struggling with something, though there was no one else in the room. I rang his bell a dozen times and pounded on the door, but not another sound came from the house. At first I thought of notifying the police; then I remembered you lived just round the corner, so I came here, instead. If Larson's been taken ill, you can help; if we need the police, there's always time to call 'em, so—"

"*Eh bien*, my friends, why do we stand here talking while the poor Professor Larson is in need of help?" demanded Jules de Grandin from the study door. "Have you no professional pride, Friend Trowbridge? Why do we linger here?"

"Why, you've only finished saying you wouldn't budge from the house tonight," I retorted accusingly. "Do you mean—"

"But certainly I do," he interrupted. "Only two kinds of people can not change their minds, my friend, the foolish and the dead. Jules de Grandin is neither. Come, let us go."

"No use getting out the car," I murmured as we donned our overcoats. "This sleet would make driving impossible."

"Very well, then, let us walk; but let us be about it swiftly," he responded, fairly pushing me through the door and out into the raging night. Heads bent against the howling storm, we set out for Professor Larson's house.

"I DIDN'T EXACTLY HAVE AN engagement with Larson," Professor Ellis admitted as we trudged along the street. "Fact is, I expect he'd about as soon have seen the devil as me, but—have you heard about his latest mummy?" he broke off.

"His what?" I answered sharply.

"His mummy. He brought it in from Africa last week, and he's been talking about it ever since. This evening he was going to remove the wrappings, so I just ambled over to his house on the off chance he'd let me stick around.

"Larson's a queer chap. Good man in anthropology, and all that, of course, but a lone wolf when it comes to work. He found this mummy by accident in a cleverly hidden tomb near Naga-ed-dêr, and that country was given up as thoroughly worked out thirty years ago, you know. Funny thing about it, too. While they were excavating the sepulcher two of his workmen were bitten by tomb spiders and died in convulsions. That's unusual, for the Egyptian tomb spider's not particularly venomous, though he's an ugly-looking brute. They'd just about cleared the shaft of rubble and started working toward the funerary chamber when all Larson's *fellaheen* ran out on him, too; but he's a stubborn devil, and he and Foster stuck it out, with the help of such men as they could hire in the neighborhood.

"They had the devil of a time getting the mummy down the Nile, too. Half the crew of their *dehabeeyah* came down with some mysterious fever, and several of 'em died, and the rest deserted; and just as they were ready to sail from Alexandria, Foster, who was Larson's assistant, came down with fever and died within three days. Larson hung on like grim death, though, and brought the mummy through—smuggled it right past the Egyptian customs men disguised as a crate of Smyrna sponges."

"But see here," I interrupted, "both you and Professor Larson are members of the Harrisonville Museum staff. How does it happen he's able to treat this mummy as his personal property? Why didn't he take it to the museum instead of his house?"

Ellis gave a short laugh. "Don't know Larson very well, do you?" he asked. "Didn't I say he's a lone wolf? This expedition to Naga-ed-dêr was a fifty-fifty affair; the Museum paid half the shot, and Larson just about beggared himself to make up the difference. He had a theory there were some valuable Fifth Dynasty relics to be found at Naga, and everybody laughed at him. When he'd justified his theory he was like a spoiled kid with a stick of candy, and wouldn't share his find with anyone; when I suggested he let me help him unwrap the thing he told me to take a running jump in the lake. I hadn't an idea, really, he'd let me in when I called on him tonight, but when I heard him yelling and laughing and saw him jumping around like a chestnut on a griddle, I thought maybe he'd gone off his rocker, and ran to get you as quickly as I could. Here we are. We'll probably be told to go to hell for our trouble, but he *might* need help."

As he finished speaking, Ellis sounded a thunderous knock on Larson's door. Only the skirling of the wind around the angle of the house and the flapping of an unsecured window-blind responded.

"*Pardieu*, either he is gravely ill or most abominably deaf, that one!" declared de Grandin, sinking his chin in the fur collar of his coat and grasping at his hat as the storm-wind all but wrenched it from his head.

Ellis turned to us in indecision. "D'ye think—" he began, but:

"Think what you please, my friends, and freeze your feet while doing," the little Frenchman interrupted testily. "Me, I go into that house right away, immediately, this minute." Trying the door and nearest window, and finding both securely fastened, he dashed his gloved band through the pane without more ado, undid the latch and raised the sash. "Do you follow, or remain behind to perish miserably with cold?" he called as he flung a leg across the sill.

D E GRANDIN IN THE lead, we felt our way across the darkened drawing-room, across the hall, and up the winding staircase. Every room inside the house, save one, was black as ancient Egypt during the plague of darkness, but a thin stream of light trickling out into the hall from beneath Professor Larson's study door led our footsteps toward his sanctum as a lighthouse guides a ship to port upon a starless night. "Larson!" Ellis called softly, rapping on the study door. "Larson, are you there?"

No answer came, and he seized the door-knob, giving it a tentative twist. The handle turned in his grasp, but the door held firm, for the lock had been shot from the inside.

"One side, if you will be so kind, *Monsieur*," requested Jules de Grandin, drawing as far back as the width of the hall permitted, then dashing himself forward like a football player battering toward the goal. The flimsy door fell before his rush, and the darkened hall was flooded with a freshet of dazzling light. For a moment we paused on the threshold, blinking owlishly; then:

"Good heavens!" I exclaimed.

"For Gawd's sake!" came Ellis' rejoinder.

"*Eh bien*, I rather think it is the devil's," Jules de Grandin murmured.

The room before us was a chaos of confusion, as though its contents had been stirred with a monster spoon in the hands of a maliciously mischievous giant. Furniture was overturned; some of the chair covers had been ripped open, as though a ruthless, hurrying searcher had cut the upholstery in search of hidden valuables; pictures hung crazily upon the walls.

In the middle of the study, beneath the glare of a cluster of electric lights, stood a heavy oaken table, and on it lay a mummy-case stripped of its cover, a slender, China-tea-colored form swathed in crisscrossed linen bandages, reclining on the table by the case.

Close to the baseboard of the wall beneath the window crouched a grotesque, unhuman thing, resembling a farmer's cast-off scarecrow or a hopelessly outmoded tailor's dummy. We had to look a second time and strain our unbelieving eyes before we recognized Professor Larson in the crumpled form.

Stepping daintily as a cat on a shower-splashed pavement, de Grandin crossed the room and sank to one knee beside the huddled form, drawing his right glove off as he knelt.

"Is—is he—" Ellis whispered hoarsely, halting at the word of which laymen seem to have a superstitious fear.

"Dead?" de Grandin supplied. "*Mais oui, Monsieur*; like a herring. But he has not been so long. No; I should hazard a guess that he was still living when we left the house to come here."

"But—isn't there something we can do? There must be something—" Ellis asked tremulously.

"But certainly; we can call the coroner," de Grandin answered. "Meanwhile, we might examine this." He nodded toward the mummy lying on the table.

Ellis' humane concern for his dead colleague dropped from him like a worn-out garment as he turned toward the ancient relic, the man eclipsed completely by the anthropologist. "Beautiful—superb!" he murmured ecstatically as he gazed at the unlovely thing. "See, there's no face-mask or funerary statue, either on the mummy or the case. Fifth Dynasty work, as sure as you're alive, and the case is—I say, do you see it?" he broke off, pointing excitedly at the open cedar coffin.

"See it? But certainly," de Grandin answered sharply. "But what is it you find extraordinary, if one may ask?"

"Why, don't you see? There's not a line of writing on that mummy-case! The Egyptians always wrote the titles and biographies of the dead upon their coffins, but this one is just bare, virgin wood. See"—he leant over and tapped the thin, hard shell of cedar—"there's never been a bit of paint or varnish on it! No wonder Larson kept it to himself. Why, there's never been a thing like this discovered since Egyptology became a science!"

De Grandin's glance had wandered from the coffin to the mummy. Now he brushed past Ellis with his quick, cat-like step and bent above the bandaged form. "The *égyptologie* I do not know so well," he admitted, "but medicine I know perfectly. What do you make of this, *hein?*" His slender forefinger rested for a moment on the linen bands encircling the desiccated figure's left pectoral region.

I started at the words. There was no doubt about it. The left breast, even beneath the mummy-bands, was considerably lower than the right, and faintly, but perceptibly, through the tightly bound linen there showed the faintest trace of brown-red stain. There was no mistaking it. Every surgeon, soldier and embalmer knows that telltale stain at sight.

Professor Ellis' eyes opened till they were nearly as wide as de Grandin's. "Blood!" he exclaimed in a muted voice. "Good Lord!" Then:

"But it can't be blood; it simply can't, you know. Mummies were eviscerated and pickled in natron before desiccation; there's no possibility of any blood being left in the body—"

"Oh, no?" the Frenchman's interruption was charged with sarcasm. "Nevertheless, *Monsieur*, de Grandin is too old a fox to be instructed in the art of sucking eggs. Friend Trowbridge"—he turned to me—"how long have you been dealing pills to those afflicted with bellyache?"

"Why," I answered wonderingly, "about forty years, but—"

"No buts, my friend. Can you, or can you not recognize a blood-stain when you see it?"

"Of course, but—"

"What, then, is this, if you will kindly tell us?"

"Why, blood, of course; anyone can tell that—"

"*Précisément*—it is blood, Monsieur Ellis. The good and most reliable Doctor Trowbridge corroborates me. Now, let us examine the coffin of this so remarkable mummy which, despite your pickling in natron and your desiccation, can still shed blood." With a wave of his hand he indicated the case of plain, unvarnished cedar-wood.

"By George, this is unusual, too!" Ellis cried, bending above the coffin. "D'ye see?"

"What?" I queried, for his eyes were shining with excitement as he gazed into the violated casket.

"Why, the way the thing's fastened. Most mummy-case lids are held in place by four little flanges—two on each side—which sink into mortises cut in the lower section and held in place by hardwood dowels. This has eight, three on each side and one at each end. H'm, they must have wanted to make sure whoever was put in there couldn't break loose. And—great Scott, will you look there!" Excitedly he pointed to the bottom of the case.

Once more I looked my wonderment. The abnormalities which struck his practised eye were quite invisible to me.

"See how they've lined the case with spices? I've opened several hundred mummy-cases, but I never saw *that* before."

As he had said, the entire bottom of the coffin was strewn with loose spices to a depth of four inches or so. The aromatics had crumbled to a fine powder, but the mingled clove and cinnamon, aloes and thyme gave off a pungent, almost suffocating aroma as we bent above the bathtub-like coffin.

De Grandin's small blue eyes were very round and bright as he glanced quickly from me to Ellis, then back again. "I damn think this explains it," he announced. "Unless I am much more mistaken than I think I am, this body never was a mummy, at least not such a mummy as the old embalmers customarily produced. Will you assist me?" He bowed invitingly to Ellis, placing his hands beneath the mummy's shoulders at the same time.

"Take the feet, if you please, *Monsieur*," he bade, "and lift it gently—gently, if you please—it must be put exactly where it was until the coroner has viewed the room."

They raised the bandaged form six inches or so above the table, then set it down again, and astonishment was written on their faces as they finished.

"What is it?" I asked, completely mystified by their glances of mutual understanding.

"It weighs—" began de Grandin, and:

"Sixty pounds, at least!" completed Ellis.

"Well?"

"Well, be everlastingly consigned to Satan's lowest subcellar!" rejoined the little Frenchman sharply. "It is not well at all, my friend; it is completely otherwise. You know your physiology; you know that sixty percent or more of us is water, simply H2O, such as is found in rivers, and on the tables of Americans in lieu of decent wine. Mummification is dehydration—the watery contents of the body is removed and nothing left but bone and desiccated flesh, a scant forty per cent of the body's weight in life. This body is a small one; in life it could have weighed scarcely a hundred pounds; yet—"

"Why, then, it must have been only partly mummified," I interrupted, but he cut in with:

"Or not at all, my friend. I damn think that we shall find some interesting disclosures when these wrappings are removed. A bleeding mummy, and a mummy which weighs more than half its lifetime weight—yes, the probabilities of a surprise are great, or I am more mistaken than I think.

"Meantime," he turned toward the door, "there is the routine of the law to be complied with. The coroner must be told of Monsieur Larson's death, and there is no need for us to burn these lights while we are waiting."

Bowing politely to us to precede him, he switched off the study lights before closing the door and followed us to the lower hall where the telephone was located.

"I simply can't imagine how it happened," Professor Ellis murmured, striding nervously across his late colleague's drawing-room while we waited the advent of the coroner. "Larson seemed in the pink of condition this afternoon, and—good Lord, what's that?"

The sound of a terrific struggle, like that of two men locked in a death-grip, echoed through the quiet house.

Thump—thump—thump! Heavy, pounding footsteps banged upon the floor above our heads; then crash! came a smashing impact, as of overturning furniture, a momentary pause, a strident scream and the sudden crescendo of a wild, discordant laugh. Then silence once again.

"Good heavens!" I exclaimed, panic grasping at my throat. "Why, it's directly overhead—in the study, where we left the mummy and—"

"Impossible!" Professor Ellis contradicted. "Nobody could have gotten past us to that room, and—"

"Impossible or not, Friend Trowbridge speaks the truth, by damn!" the little Frenchman shouted, springing from his chair and racing toward the stairs. "*En avant, mes enfants*—follow me!"

Three steps at a stride he mounted headlong up the stairway, paused a moment at the closed door of the study while he whipped a pistol from his pocket, then his weapon swinging in a circle before him, advanced with a quick leap, snapped on the lights and:

"Hands up!" he shouted warningly. "A single offer of resistance and you breakfast with the devil in the morning—*grand Dieu*, my friends, behold!"

Save that one or two chairs had been overset, the room was just as we had left it. Upon the table lay the supine, bandaged mummy, its spice-filled case uncovered by its side; the thing which had been Larson crouched shoulders-to-the-wall, as though stricken in an attempt to turn a somersault; the window-blind flapped cracklingly in the chilling winter wind.

"The window—it's open!" cried Professor Ellis. "It was closed when we were here, but—"

"*Dieu de Dieu de Dieu de Dieu*—does not one know it?" de Grandin interrupted angrily, striding toward the open casement. "*Parbleu*, the way in which you pounce upon the obvious is greatly trying to my nerves, Friend Ellis, and— ah? A-a-a-ah? One sees, one perceives, one understands—almost!"

Abreast of him, we gazed across the sill, and obedient to the mute command of his pointing finger, looked at the snow-encrusted roof of the first floor bay-window which joined the house-wall something like two feet below the study window. Gouged in the dead-white veneer of snow were four long, parallel streaks, exposing the slate beneath. "U'm," he murmured, lowering the sash and turning toward the door, "the mystery is in part explained, my friends.

"That window, it would be the logical place for a burglar to force entry," he added as we trooped down the stairs. "The roof of the bay-window has but very little slope, and stands directly underneath the window of Professor Larson's study. One bent on burglary could hardly fail to note its possibilities as an aid to crime, and the fact that we had light going only in the downstairs room was notice to the world that the upper story was untenanted. So—"

"Quite so, but there wasn't any burglar there," Ellis interrupted practically.

De Grandin favored him with such a stare as a teacher might bestow on a more than ordinarily dull pupil. "One quite agrees, *mon ami*," he replied. "However, if you will have the exceeding goodness to restrain your curiosity—and conversation—for a time, it may be we shall find that which we seek."

The dark, hunched-up object showed with startling vividness against the background of the snow-powdered lawn as we descended from the porch. De Grandin knelt beside it and struck a match to aid in his inspection. It was a ragged, unkempt figure, unwashed, unshaven; a typical low-class sneak-thief who had varied his customary sorry trade with an excursion into the higher profession of housebreaking with disastrous results to himself. He crouched as he had fallen from the bay-window's sloping roof, one arm twisted underneath him, his head bent oddly to one side, his battered, age-discolored hat mashed in at the crown and driven comically down upon his head till his ears were bent beneath it. Little lodes of sleety snow had lodged within the wrinkles of his ragged coat, and tiny threads of icicles had formed on his mustache.

The man was dead, no doubt of it. No one, not even the most accomplished contortionist, could twist his neck at that sharp angle. And the manner of his death was obvious. Frightened at sight of the mummy, the poor fellow had endeavored to effect a hasty exit by the open window, had slipped upon the sleet-glazed roof of the bay-window and fallen to the ground, striking head-first and skidding forward with his full weight on his twisted neck.

I voiced my conclusions hastily, but de Grandin shook a puzzled head. "One understands the manner of his death," he answered thoughtfully. "But the reason, that is something else again. We can well think that such a creature would have a paralyzing fear when he beheld the mummy stretched upon the table, but that does not explain the antics he went through before he fell or jumped back through the window he had forced. We heard him thrash about; we heard him kick the furniture; we heard him scream with mirthless laughter. For why? Frightened men may scream, they sometimes even laugh hysterically, but what was there for him to wrestle with?"

"That's just what Larson did!" Professor Ellis put in hastily. "Don't you remember—"

"*Exactement*," the Frenchman answered with a puzzled frown. "Professor Larson cries aloud and fights with nothing; this luckless burglar breaks into the very room where Monsieur Larson died so strange a death, and he, too, wrestles with the empty air and falls to death while laughing hideously. There is something very devilish here, my friends."

WHEN WE HAD GONE back in the house young Ellis looked at us with something very near to panic in his eyes. "You say that we must leave that mummy as it is until the coroner has seen it?" he demanded.

"Your understanding is correct, my friend," de Grandin answered.

"All right, we'll leave the dam' thing there, but just as soon as Mr. Martin has finished with it, I think we'd better take it out and burn it."

"Eh, what is it that you say? Burn it, *Monsieur*?" de Grandin asked.

"Just that. It's what the Egyptologists call an 'unlucky' mummy, and the sooner we get rid of it the healthier it'll be for all of us, I'm thinking. See here"— he glanced quickly upward, as though fearing a renewed outbreak in the room above, then turned again to us—"do you recall the series of fatalities following Tutankhamen's exhumation?"

De Grandin made no answer, but the fixed, unwinking stare he leveled on the speaker, and the nervous way his trimly waxed mustache quivered at the corners of his mouth betrayed his interest.

Ellis hurried on: "Call it nonsense if you will—and you probably will—but the fact is there seems something in this talk of the ancient gods of Egypt having power to curse those disturbing the mummies of people dying in apostasy. You know, I assume, that there are certain mummies known as 'unlucky'—unlucky for those who find them, or have anything to do with them? Tutankhamen is probably the latest, as well as the most outstanding example of this class. He was a heretic in his day, and had offended the 'old ones' or their priests, which amounted to the same thing. So, when he died, they buried him with elaborate ceremonies, but set no image of Amen-Ra at the bow of the boat which carried him across the lake of the dead, and the plaques of Tem, Seb, Nephthys, Osiris and Isis were not prepared to go with him into the tomb. Tutankhamen, notwithstanding his belated efforts at reconciliation with the priesthood, was little better than an atheist according to contemporary Egyptian belief, and the wrath of the gods went into the tomb with him. It was not their wish that his name be preserved to posterity or that any of his relics be brought to light again.

"Now, think what happened: When Lord Carnarvon located the tomb, he had four associates. Carnarvon and three of his helpers are dead today. Colonel Herbert and Doctor Evelyn-White were among the first to go into Tut's tomb. Both died within a year. Sir Archibald Douglas was engaged to make an X-ray—he died almost before the plates could be developed. Six out of seven French journalists who went into the tomb shortly after it was opened died in less than a year, and almost every workman engaged in the excavations died before he had a chance to spend his pay. Some of these men died one way, some another, but the point is: they all died.

"Not only that; even minor articles taken from the tomb seem to exercise a malign influence. There is absolute proof that attendants in the Cairo Museum whose duties keep them near the Tutankhamen relics sicken and die for no apparent reason. D'ye wonder they call him an 'unlucky' mummy?"

"Very good, Monsieur, what then?" de Grandin prompted as the other lapsed into a moody silence.

"Just this: That mummy-case upstairs is bare of painting as the palm of your hand, and the orthodox Egyptians of the Fifth Dynasty would no more have thought of putting a body away without suitable biographical and religious writings on the coffin than the average American family today would think of holding a funeral without religious services of some sort. Further than that, the evidence points to that body's never having been embalmed at all—apparently it was merely wrapped and put into a coffin with a layer of spices around it. Embalming had religious significance in ancient Egypt. If the flesh corrupted, the spirit could not return at the end of the prescribed cycle and reanimate it, and to be buried unembalmed was tantamount to a denial of immortality. This body had only the poorest makeshift attempt at preservation. It looks as though this person, whoever he was, died outside the religious pale, doesn't it?"

"You make out a strong case, Monsieur," de Grandin nodded, "but—"

"All right, then look at the thing's history so far: Larson's workmen died while working in the tomb. How? By tomb-spider bite!

"Bosh! A tomb-spider is hardly more poisonous than our own garden spiders. I know; I've been bitten by the things, and suffered less inconvenience than when a scorpion stung me in Yucatan.

"Then, on the passage down the Nile most of the boat crew sickened, and some of 'em died, with a strange fever; yet they were hardy devils, used to the climate and in all probability immune to anything in the way of illness the country could produce. Then Foster, Larson's assistant, pegged out just as they were setting sail from Egypt. Looks as though some evil influence were working, doesn't it?

"Now, tonight: Larson was all ready to unwrap the mummy, but never got past taking it from the box. He's dead—'dead like a herring,' as you put it—and only God knows how he died. Right while we're waiting for the coroner to come, this poor devil of a burglar breaks into the house, *fights with some unseen thing*, just as Larson did, and dies. Say what you will"—his voice rose almost to a scream—"there's an aura of terrible misfortune round that mummy, and death is waiting for whoever ventures near it!"

De Grandin patted the waxed ends of his diminutive mustache affectionately. "What you say may all be true, *Monsieur*," he conceded, "but the fact remains that both Doctor Trowbridge and I have been near the mummy; yet we were never better in our lives—though I could do nicely with a gulp or so of brandy at this time. Not only that, Professor Larson spent nearly his entire fortune and a considerable portion of the Museum's funds in finding this so remarkable cadaver. It would be larceny, no less, for us to burn it as you suggest."

"All right," Ellis answered with a note of finality in his voice. "Have it your own way. As soon as the coroner's through with me I'm going home. I wouldn't go near that cursed mummy again for a fortune."

"HULLO, DOCTOR DE GRANDIN," Coroner Martin greeted, stamping his feet and shaking the snow from his coat. "Bad business, this, isn't it? Any idea as to the cause of death?"

"The one outside unquestionably died from a broken neck," the Frenchman answered. "As for Professor Larson's—"

"Eh, the one outside?" Mr. Martin interrupted. "Are there *two* of 'em?"

"Humph, we're lucky there aren't five," Ellis cut in bitterly. "They have been dying so fast we can't keep track of 'em since Larson started to unwrap that—"

"One moment, if you please, *Monsieur*," de Grandin interrupted as he raised a deprecating hand. "Monsieur the Coroner is a busy man and has his duties to perform. When they have been completed I make no doubt he will be glad to listen to your interesting theories. At present"—he bowed politely to the coroner—"will you come with us, *Monsieur*?" he asked.

"Count me out," said Ellis. "I'll wait down here, and I want to warn you that—"

We never heard the warning he had for us; for, de Grandin in the lead, we mounted the stairs to the study where Professor Larson and the mummy lay.

"H'm," Mr. Martin, who in addition to being coroner was also the city's leading funeral director, surveyed the room with a quick, practised glance, "this looks almost as if—" he strode across the room toward Larson's hunched-up body and extended one hand, but:

"*Grand Dieu des cochons*—stand back, *Monsieur!*" de Grandin's shouted admonition halted Mr. Martin in mid-stride. "Back, *Monsieur*; back, Friend Trowbridge—for your lives!" Snatching me by the elbow and Mr. Martin by the skirt of his coat, he fairly dragged us from the room.

"What on earth—" I began as we reached the hall, but he pushed us toward the stairway.

"Do not stand and parley!" he commanded shortly. "Out—out into the friendly cold, while there is still time, my friends! *Pardieu*, I see it now—Monsieur Ellis has right; that mummy—"

"Oh—*oh—o-o-o-oh!*" The sudden cry came to us from the floor below, followed by the sound of scuffling, as though Ellis and another were struggling madly. Then came an awful, marrow-freezing laugh, shrill, mirthless, sardonic.

"*Sang du diable*—it has him!" de Grandin shouted, as he rushed madly toward the stair, leaped to the balustrade and shot downward like a meteor.

Coroner Martin and I followed sedately, and found the Frenchman standing mute and breathless at the entrance of the drawing-room, his thin, red lips pursed as though emitting a soundless whistle. Professor Larson's parlor was furnished in the formal, stilted style so popular in the late years of the last century, light chairs and couches of gilded wood upholstered in apple-green satin, a glass-doored cabinet for bric-à-brac, a pair of delicate spindle-legged tables adorned with bits of Dresden china. The furniture had been tossed about the room, the light-gray velvet rug turned up, the china-cabinet smashed and flung upon its side. In the midst of the confusion Ellis lay, his hands clenched at his sides, his knees drawn up, his lips retracted in a grim, sardonic grin.

"Good God!" Coroner Martin viewed the poor, tensed body with staring eyes. "This is dreadful—"

"*Cordieu*, it will be more so if we linger here!" de Grandin cried. "Outside, my friends. Do not wait to take your coats or hats—come out at once! I tell you death is lurking in each shadow of this cursed place!"

He herded us before him from the house, and bade us stand a moment, hatless and coatless, in the chilling wind. "I say," I protested through chattering teeth, "this is carrying a joke too far, de Grandin. There's no need to—"

"Joke?" he echoed sharply. "Do you consider it a joke that Professor Larson died the way he did tonight; that the misguided burglar perished in the same way; that even now the poor young Ellis lies all stiff and dead inside that cursed hellhole of a house? Your sense of humor is peculiar, my friend."

"What was it?" Coroner Martin asked practically. "Was there some infection in the house that made Professor Ellis scream like that before he died, or was it—"

"Tell me, *Monsieur*," de Grandin interrupted, "have you facilities for fumigation at your mortuary?"

"Of course," the coroner returned wonderingly. "We've apparatus for making both formaldehyde and cyanogen gas, depending on the class of fumigation required, but—"

"Very good. Be so good as to hasten to your place of business and return as quickly as may be with *materiel* for cyanogen fumigation. I shall await you here. Make haste, *Monsieur*, this matter is of utmost urgency, I assure you."

W HILE MR. MARTIN WAS obtaining the apparatus for fumigation, de Grandin and I hastened to my house, procured fresh outdoor clothing and retraced our steps. Though I made several attempts to discover what he had found at Larson's, his only answers were impatient shrugs and half-articulate exclamations, and I finally gave over the attempt, knowing he would explain in detail when he thought it proper. Hands deep in pockets, heads drawn well down into our collars, we waited for the coroner's return.

With the deftness of long practise Mr. Martin's assistants set the tanks of mercuric cyanide in place at the front and back doors of the Larson house, ran rubber hose from them to the keyholes and lighted spirit lamps beneath them. When Mr. Martin suggested that the bodies be removed before fumigation began, de Grandin shook his head decidedly. "It would be death—or most unnecessary risk of death, at best—to permit your men to enter till the gas has had at least a day to work within the house," he answered.

"But those bodies should be cared for," the coroner contended, speaking from the professional knowledge of one who had practised mortuary science for more than twenty years.

"They will undergo no putrefactive changes worthy of account," the Frenchman answered. "The gas will act to some extent as a preservative, and the risk to be avoided is worth the trouble."

As Coroner Martin was about to counter, he continued: "Demonstration outweighs explanation ten to one, my friend. Permit that I should have my way, and by this time tomorrow night you will be convinced of the good foundation for my seeming stubbornness."

S HORTLY AFTER EIGHT O'CLOCK the following evening we met once more at Larson's house, and as calmly as though such crazy actions were an everyday affair with him, de Grandin smashed window after window with his walking-stick, and bade us wait outside for upward of a quarter-hour. At last:

"I think that it is safe to enter now," he said. "The gas should be dispelled. Come, let us go in."

We tiptoed down the hall to the drawing-room where Professor Ellis lay, and de Grandin turned on every available light before entering the room. Beside the young man's rigid body he went to his knees, and seemed to be examining the floor with minutest care. "Whatever are you doing—" I began, when:

"*Triomphe*, I have found him!" he announced. "Come and see."

We crossed the room and stared in wonder at the tiny object which he held between the thumb and finger of his gloved right hand. It was a tiny, ball-like thing, scarcely larger than a dried bean, a little, hairy spider with a black body striped about the abdomen with lines of vivid vermilion. "You observe him?" he asked simply. "Was I not wise to order our retreat last night?"

"What is the thing?" I demanded. "It's harmless-looking enough, but—"

"*Eh bien*, there is a very great but there, my friend," he retorted with a mirthless smile. "You saw what had been Monsieur Larson; you looked upon the poor, new-dead young Ellis? This—this little, seemingly so harmless thing it was which killed them. It is a *katipo*, or *latrodectus Nasselti*, the deadliest spider in the world. Even the cobra's bite is but a sweetheart's kiss beside the sting of this so small, deadly thing. Those bit by him are seized immediately with convulsions— they beat the air, they stumble and they whirl, at length they give vent to a dreadful scream which simulates a laugh. And then they fall and die.

"Does not that make it clear? The wholly irrational antics performed by Professor Larson ere he died could be explained in no sane manner. They puzzled me. I was not willing to accept Professor Ellis' theory that the mummy was 'unlucky,' although, as the good God knows, it proved so for him. However, that Professor Larson was entirely dead could not be doubted, nor could one readily assign a reason for his death. *Tiens*, in such a case the coroner must be called, and so we telephoned for Monsieur Martin.

"Meantime, as we sat waiting in this room, a poor, half-starving devil of a man decided he would break into the house and steal whatever he could find. He mounted the bay-window's roof, and, guided by his evil star, set foot inside the chamber where the mummy and Professor Larson lay. We heard him trample on the floor; we heard him give that dreadful, laughing scream; we searched for him, and found him dead upon the lawn.

"Very good. In due time Monsieur Martin comes; we lead him to the place where Monsieur Larson is, and as we go into the room I chance to look into the spices strewn about the bottom of that mummy-case. *Ha*—what is it that I see? *Parbleu*, I see a movement! Spices do not move, my friend, except they be blown on by the wind, and there is no wind in that room. Moreover, spices are not jettyblack with bands of red about their bellies. *Non, pardieu*, but certain spiders are. I see him and I know him. In the Eastern Islands, in Java, in

Australia, I have seen him, and I have also seen his deadly work. He is the *latrodectus Nasselti*, called *katipo* by the natives, and his bite is almost instant and most painful death. More, those bitten by him dance about insanely in a sort of frantic seizure; they laugh—but not with happiness!—they scream with mirthless laughter; then they die. I did not wish to dance and laugh and die, my friends; I did not wish that you should do so, either. There was no time for talk or explanation; our only safety lay in flight, for they are tropic things, those spiders, and once we were outside the cold would kill them. I was about to call a warning to Monsieur Ellis, too; but I was, *hélas*, too late.

"Beyond a doubt one of the spiders had fastened on his clothing while he bent over to inspect that mummy-case. The insect clung to him when he left the room, and while he waited downstairs for us it crawled until it came in contact with his naked skin; then, angered, it may be, by some movement which he made, it bit him and he died.

"When I saw him lying here upon the floor I took incontinently to flight. Jules de Grandin is no coward, but who could say how many of those cursed spiders had crawled from the mummy-case and found hiding-places in the shadows—even in our clothing, as in the case of Monsieur Ellis? To stay here was to court a quick and highly disagreeable death; accordingly I rushed you out into the storm and asked Monsieur Martin to provide fumigation for the house forthwith. Now, since the cyanogen gas has killed every living thing inside this house, it is safe for us to enter.

"The bodies may safely be taken away by your assistants at any time, *Monsieur*," he finished with a bow to Mr. Martin.

"EH BIEN, WERE HE but here, we could set poor Monsieur Ellis' mind at rest concerning many things," de Grandin murmured as we drove toward my house. "He could not understand how Professor Larson's servants died by spider-bite, since the Egyptian tomb-spider is known to be innocuous, or nearly so. The answer now is obvious. In some way which we do not understand, a number of those poisonous black spiders found their way into that mummy-case. They are terrestrial in their habits, living in the earth and going forth by night. Light irritates them, and when the workmen brought their torches into the tomb they showed their annoyance by biting them. Death, accompanied by convulsions, followed, and because the small black spiders were invisible in the shadows, the harmless tomb-spiders received the blame. Some few of the black spiders came overseas with Professor Larson; when he pried the lid from that mummy-case—perhaps when he thrust his hand into the scattered spices to lift the mummy out—they fastened on him, bit him; killed him. You apprehend?"

"H'm, it sounds logical enough," I answered thoughtfully, "but have you any idea how those spices came in that coffin? Poor Ellis seemed to think we'd hit on something extraordinary when he saw them; but he's gone now and—great Scott, de Grandin, d'ye suppose those old Egyptian priests could have planted spider eggs among the spices, hoping they would hatch eventually, so that whoever molested the body in years to come would stand a chance of being bitten and killed?"

For a moment he drummed soundlessly with gloved fingers on the silver head of his stick. At length: "My friend, you interest me," he declared solemnly. "I do not know that what you say is probable, but the manner of that mummy's preparation is unusual. I think we owe it as a debt to poor, dead Ellis to look into the matter thoroughly."

"Look into it? How—"

"Tomorrow we shall unwrap the body," he responded as casually as though unshrouding centuries-old dead Egyptians were an everyday activity with us. "If we can find some explanation hidden in the mummy-clothes, well and good. If we do not—*eh bien*, the dead have spoken before; why not again?"

"The—dead—have—spoken?" I echoed slowly, incredulously. "What in the world—"

"Not in this world, precisely," he interrupted with the shadow of a smile, "but there are those who look behind the veil which separates us from the ones we call the dead, my friend. We shall try other methods first. Those failing—" he recommenced his drumming on the handle of his cane, humming softly:

Sacré de nom,
Ron, ron et ron;
La vie est brêve,
La nuit est longue—

Next evening we unwrapped the mummy.

It was an oddly assorted group which gathered in the basement of Harrisonville Museum to denude the ancient dead of its cerements. Hodgson, the assistant curator of the department of archeology, a slender little man in gold-bowed, rimless spectacles, bald to the ears and much addicted to the habit of buttoning and unbuttoning his primly untidy double-breasted jacket, stood by in a state of twittering nervousness as de Grandin set to work.

"Who sups with the devil needs a long spoon," the little Frenchman quoted with a smile as he drew a pair of heavy rubber gloves on his hands before taking up his scissors and snipping one of the criss-crossed linen bands with which the body was tightly wrapped. "I do not greatly fear that any of those small black imps of hell survived Monsieur Martin's gas," he added, laying back a fold of yellowed linen, "but it is well to be prepared. The cemeteries are full to overflowing with those who have thought otherwise."

Yard after endless yard of linen he reeled off, coming at length to a strong, seamless shroud drawn sackwise over the body and tied at the feet with a stout cord. The cloth of which the sack was made seemed stronger and heavier than the bandages, and was thickly coated with wax or some ceraceous substance, the whole being, apparently, airtight and watertight.

"Why, bless my soul, I never saw anything like *this* before," stammered Doctor Hodgson, leaning forward across de Grandin's shoulder to stare curiously at the inner shroud.

"So much we gathered from Monsieur Ellis before—when he first viewed this body," de Grandin answered dryly, and Professor Hodgson retreated with an odd little squeaking exclamation, for all the world like that of an intimidated mouse.

"*Sale lâche!*" the Frenchman whispered softly, his contempt of Hodgson's cowardice written plainly on his face. Then, as he cut the binding string away and began twitching the waxed shroud upward from the mummy's shoulders:

"Ah ha? Ah-ha-ha—*que diable?*"

The body brought to view beneath the blue-white glare of the electric bulbs was not technically a mummy; though the aromatic spices and the sterile, arid atmosphere of Egypt had combined to keep it in a state of most unusual preservation. The feet, first parts to be exposed, were small and beautifully formed, with long, straight toes and narrow heels, the digits and soles, as well as the whole plantar region, stained brilliant red. There was surprizingly little desiccation, and though the terminal tendons of the *brevis digitorum* showed prominently through the skin, the effect was by no means revolting; I had seen equal prominence of flexor muscles in living feet where the patient had suffered considerable emaciation.

The ankles were sharp and shapely, the legs straight and well turned, with the leanness of youth, rather than the wasted look of death; the hips were narrow, the waist slender and the gentle swelling bosoms high and sharp. Making allowance for the early age at which women of the Orient mature, I should have said the girl died somewhere in her middle teens; certainly well under twenty.

"Ah?" de Grandin murmured as the waxed sack slid over the body's shoulders. "I think that here we have the explanation of those stains, Friend Trowbridge, n'est-ce-pas?"

I looked and gulped back an exclamation of horrified amazement. The slim, tapering arms had been folded on the breast, in accordance with the Egyptian custom, but the humerus of the left arm had been cruelly crushed, a compound comminutive fracture having resulted, so that a quarter-inch or more of splintered bone thrust through the skin above and below the deltoid attachment. Not only this: the same blow which had crushed the arm had smashed the bony structure of the chest, the third and fourth left ribs being snapped in two, and through the smooth skin underneath the breast a prong of jagged bone protruded. A hemorrhage of considerable extent had followed, and the long-dried blood lay upon the body from left breast to hip in a dull, brown-red veneer. Waxed though the mummy-sack had been, the welling blood had found its way through some break in the coating, had soaked the tightly knotted outer bandages, and borne mute testimony of an ancient tragedy.

The finely cut features were those of a woman in her early youth. Semitic in their cast, they had a delicacy of line and contour which bespoke patrician breeding. The nose was small, slightly aquiline, high-bridged, with narrow nostrils. The lips were thin and sensitive, and where they had retracted in the process of partial desiccation, showed small, sharp teeth of startling whiteness. The hair was black and lustrous, cut short off at the ears, like the modern Dutch bob affected by young women, parted in the middle and bound about the brows with a circlet of hammered gold set with small studs of lapis lazuli. For the rest, a triple-stranded necklace of gold and blue enamel, armlets of the same design and a narrow golden girdle fashioned like a snake composed the dead girl's costume. Originally a full, plaited skirt of sheer white linen had been appended to the girdle, but the fragile fabric had not withstood the years of waiting in the grave, and only one or two thin wisps of it remained.

"*La pauvre!*" exclaimed the Frenchman, gazing sadly at the broken little body. "I think, my friends, that we see here a demonstration of that ancient saying that the blood of innocents can not be concealed. Unless I am more wrong than I admit, this is a case of murder, and—"

"But it might as well have been an accident," I cut in. "I've seen such injuries in motor-wrecks, and this poor child might have been the victim of a chariot smashup."

"I do not think so," he returned. "This case has all the marks of ritual murder, my friend. Observe the—"

"I think we'd better wrap the body up again," Hodgson broke in hastily. "We've gone as far as we can tonight, and—well, I'm rather tired, gentlemen, and if you don't mind, we'll call the session off." He coughed apologetically, but there was the mild determination of weak men who have authority to make their wishes law in his manner as he spoke.

"You mean that you're afraid of something that might happen?" de Grandin countered bluntly. "You fear the ancient gods may take offense at our remaining here to speculate on the manner of this poor one's death?"

"Well," Hodgson took his glasses off and wiped them nervously, "of course, I don't believe those stories that they tell of these 'unlucky' mummies, but—you're bound to admit there have been some unexplained fatalities connected with this case. Besides—well, frankly, gentlemen, this body's less a mummy than a corpse, and I've a terrible aversion to being around the dead, unless they've been mummified."

De Grandin smiled sarcastically. "The old-time fears die hard," he assented. "Nevertheless, *Monsieur*, we shall respect your sensibilities. You have been most kind, and we would not try your nerves still further. Tomorrow, if you do not mind, we shall pursue our researches. It may be possible that we shall discover something hitherto unknown about the rites and ceremonies of those old ones who ruled the world when Rome had scarce been thought of."

"Yes, yes; of course," Hodgson coughed as he edged near the door. "I'm sure I shall be happy to give you a pass to the Museum tomorrow—only"—he added as an afterthought—"I must ask that you refrain from mutilating the body in any way. It belongs to the Museum, you know, and I simply can not give permission for an autopsy."

"*Morbleu*, but you are the shrewd guesser, *Monsieur*," de Grandin answered with a laugh. "I think you must have read intention in my eyes. Very well; we consent. There shall be no post-mortem of the body made. *Bon soir, Monsieur.*"

"I'M SORRY, DOCTOR DE Grandin," Hodgson greeted us the next morning, "but I'm afraid you'll not be able to pursue any further investigations with the mummy—the body, I mean—we unwrapped last night."

The little Frenchman stiffened in both body and manner. "You mean that you have altered your decision, *Monsieur?*" he asked with cold politeness.

"Not at all. I mean the body's disintegrated with exposure to the air, and only a few wisps of hair, the skull and some unarticulated bones remain. While they weren't quite airtight, the bandages and the wax-coated shroud seem to have been able to keep the flesh intact, but exposure to our damp atmosphere has reduced them to a heap of bone and dust."

"U'm," the Frenchman answered. "That is unfortunate, but not irreparable. I think our chance of finding out the cause and manner of the poor young lady's death is not yet gone. Would you be good enough to lend us the ornaments, some of the mummy-cloth and several of the bones, *Monsieur?* We guarantee their safe return."

"Well," Hodgson hesitated momentarily, "it's not quite regular, but if you're sure you will return them—"

"*Monsieur*," de Grandin's voice broke sharply through the curator's apologetic half-refusal, "I am Jules de Grandin; I am not accustomed to having my good faith assailed. No matter, the experiment which I have in mind will not take long, and you are welcome to accompany us. Thus you need never have the relics out of sight at any time. Will that assure you of their safe return?"

Hodgson undid the buttons of his jacket, then did them up again. "Oh, don't think I was doubting your *bona fides*," he returned, "but this body cost the

Museum a considerable sum, and was the indirect cause of our losing two valuable members of the staff. I'm personally responsible for it, and—"

"No matter," de Grandin interrupted, "if you will come with us I can assure you that the articles will be within your sight at all times, and you may have them back again this morning."

Accordingly, Hodgson superintending fussily, we selected the gold and lapis lazuli diadem, the broken humerus, one of the fractured ribs and several lengths of mummy-cloth which bore the dull-red blood stains, and thrust them into a traveling-bag. De Grandin paused to call a number on the 'phone, talked for a moment in a muted tone, then directed me to an address in Scotland Road.

HALF AN HOUR'S DRIVE through the brisk winter air brought us to a substantial brownstone-fronted residence in the decaying but still eminently respectable neighborhood. Lace curtains hung at the tall windows of the first floor and the windows of the basement dining-room were neatly draped with scrim. Beside the carefully polished bell-pull a brass plate with the legend, *Creighton, Clairvoyant*, was set. A neat maid in black and white uniform responded to de Grandin's ring and led us to a drawing-room rather overfurnished with heavy pieces of the style popular in the middle nineties. "Mrs. Creighton will be down immediately, sir; she's expecting you," she told him as she left the room.

My experience with those who claim ability to "look beyond the veil" was limited, but I had always imagined that they set their stages more effectively than this. The carpet, patterned with impossible roses large as cabbages, the heavy and not especially comfortable golden oak chairs upholstered in green plush, the stereotyped oil paintings of the Grand Canal, of Capri by moonlight and Vesuvius in action, were pragmatic as a plate of prunes, and might have been duplicated, item by item, in the "parlor" of half a hundred non-fashionable but respectable boarding-houses. Even the faint aroma of cooking food which wafted up to us from the downstairs kitchen had a reassuring and worldly tang which seemed entirely out of harmony with the ghostly calling of our hostess.

Madame Creighton fitted her surroundings perfectly. She was short, stout and matronly, and her high-necked white linen blouse and plain blue skirts were far more typical of the busy middle-class housewife than of the self-admitted medium. Her eyes, brown and bright, shone pleasantly behind the lenses of neat, rimless spectacles; her hair, already shot with gray, was drawn tightly back from her forehead and twisted in a commonplace knot above her occiput. Even her hands were plump, short-fingered, slightly workworn and wholly commonplace. Nowhere was there any indication of the "psychic" in her dress, face, form or manner.

"You brought the things?" she asked de Grandin when introductions were completed.

Nodding, he placed the relics on the oaken table beside which she was seated. "These were discovered—" he began, but she raised her hand in warning.

"Please don't tell me anything about them," she requested. "I'd rather my controls did all that, for one never can be sure how much information secured while one is conscious may be carried over into the subconscious while the trance is on, you know."

Opening a drawer in the table she took out a hinged double slate and a box of thin, white chalk.

"Will you hold this, Doctor Trowbridge?" she asked, handing me the slate. "Take it in both hands, please, and hold it in your lap. Please don't move it or attempt to speak to me until I tell you."

Awkwardly I took the blank-faced slate and balanced it on my knees while Mrs. Creighton drew a small crystal ball from a little green-felt bag, placed it on the table between the broken arm-bone and the fractured rib, then, with a snap of the switch, set an electric light in a gooseneck fixture standing on the table aglow. The luminance from the glowing bulb shone directly on the crystal sphere, causing it to glow as though with inward fire.

For a little time—two minutes, perhaps—she gazed intently at the glass ball; then her eyes closed and her head, resting easily against the crocheted doily on the back of her rocking-chair, moved a little sidewise as her neck muscles relaxed. For a moment she rested thus, her regular breathing only slightly audible.

Suddenly, astonishingly, I heard a movement of the chalk between the slates. I had not moved or tilted them, there was no chance the little pencil could have rolled, yet unquestionably the thing was moving. Now, I distinctly *felt* it as it traveled slowly back and forth across the tightly folded leaves of the slate, gradually increasing its speed till it seemed like a panic-stricken prisoned thing rushing wildly round its dungeon in search of escape.

I had a momentary wild, unreasoning desire to fling that haunted slate away from me and rush out of that stuffy room, but pride held me in my chair, pride made me grip those slates as a drowning man might grip a rope; pride kept my gaze resolutely on Mrs. Creighton and off of the uncanny thing which balanced on my knees.

I could hear de Grandin breathing quickly, hear Hodgson moving restlessly in his chair, clearing his throat and (I knew this without looking) buttoning and unbuttoning his coat.

Mrs. Creighton's sleep became troubled. Her head rolled slowly, fretfully from side to side, and her breathing became stertorous; once or twice she gave vent to a feeble moan; finally the groaning, choking cry of a sleeper in a nightmare. Her smooth, plump hands clenched nervously and doubled into fists, her arms and legs twitched tremblingly; at length she straightened stiffly in her chair, rigid as though shocked by a galvanic battery, and from her parted lips there came a muffled, strangling cry of horror. Little flecks of foam formed at the corners of her mouth, she arched her body upward, then sank back with a low, despairing whimper, and her firm chin sagged down toward her breast—I knew the symptoms! No medical practitioner can fail to recognize those signs.

"*Madame!*" de Grandin cried, rising from his chair and rushing to her side. "You are unwell—you suffer?"

She struggled to a sitting posture, her brown eyes bulging as though a savage hand were on her throat, her face contorted with some dreadful fear. For a moment she sat thus; then, with a shake of her head, she straightened, smoothed her hair, and asked matter-of-factly: "Did I say anything?"

"No, *Madame*, you said nothing articulate, but you seemed in pain, so I awakened you."

"Oh, that's too bad," she answered with a smile. "They tell me I often act that way when in a trance, but I never remember anything when I wake up, and I never seem any the worse because of anything I dream while I'm unconscious. If you had only waited we might have had a message on the slate."

"We have!" I interrupted. "I heard the pencil writing like mad, and nearly threw the thing away!"

"Oh, I'm so glad," responded Mrs. Creighton. "Bring it over, and we'll see what it says."

The slate was covered with fine writing, the minute characters, distinct as script etched on a copper plate, running from margin to margin, spaces between the lines so narrow as to be hardly recognizable.

For a moment we studied the calligraphy in puzzled silence; then.

"*Mort de ma vie*, we have triumphed over Death and Time, my friends!" de Grandin cried excitedly. "*Attendez, si'l vous plait.*" Opening the slates before him like a book he read:

Revered and awful judges of the world, ye awful ones who sit upon the parapets of hell, I answer guilty to the charge ye bring against me. Aye, Atoua, who now stands on the brink of deathless death, whose body waits the crushing stones of doom, whose spirit, robbed for ever of the hope of fleshly tegument, must wander in Amenti till the end of time has come, confesses that the fault was hers, and hers alone.

Behold me, awesome judges of the living and the dead, am I not a woman, and a woman shaped for love? Are not my members beautiful to see, my lips like apricots and pomegranates, my eyes like milk and beryl, my breasts like ivory set with coral? Yea, mighty ones, I am a woman, and a woman formed for joy.

Was it my fault or my volition that I was pledged to serve the great All-Mother, Isis, or ever I had left the shelter of my mother's flesh? Did I abjure the blissful agony of love and seek a life of sterile chastity, or was the promise spoken for me by another's lips?

I gave all that a woman has to give, and gave it freely, knowing that the pains of death and after death the torment of the gods awaited me, nor do I deem the price too great to pay.

Ye frown? Ye shake your dreadful heads upon which rest the crowns of Amun and of Kneph, of Seb and Tem, of Suti and Osiris' mighty self? Ye say that I speak sacrilege? Then hear me yet awhile: She who stands in chains before ye, shorn of reverence as a priestess of Great Mother Isis, shorn of all honor as a woman, tells ye these things to your teeth, knowing that ye can not do her greater hurt than that she stands already judged to undergo. Your reign and that of those ye serve draws near its end. A little while ye yet may strut and preen yourselves and mouth the judgments of your gods, but in the days that wait your very names shall be forgot, save when some stranger delves into your tombs and drags your violated bodies forth for men to make a show of. Aye, and the very gods ye serve shall be forgotten—they shall sink so low that none shall call their names, not even as a curse, and in their ruined temples none shall do them reverence, and no living thing be found, save only the white-bellied lizard and the fearful jackal.

And who shall do this thing? An offspring of the Hebrews! Yea, from the people ye despise a child shall spring, and great shall be His glory. He shall put down your gods beneath his feet and spoil them of all glory and respect; they shall become but shadow-gods of a forgotten past.

My name ye've stricken from the roll of priestesses, no writing shall be graven on my tomb, and I shall be forgotten for all time by gods and men. So reads your judgment. I give ye, then, the lie. Upon a day far in the future strange men from a land across the sea shall open wide my tomb and take my body from it, nor shall my flesh taste of corruption until those strangers look upon my face and see my broken bones, and seeing, wonder how I died. *And I shall tell them.* Yea, by Osiris' self I swear that though I have been dead for centuries, I shall relate the manner of my judgment and my death, and they shall know my name and weep for me, and on your heads they shall heap curses for this thing ye do to me.

Pile now your stones of doom upon my breast, break my bones and still the fevered beating of my heart. I go to death, but not from out the memory of men as ye shall go. I have spoken.

Below the writing was a little scrawl of drawing, as crudely executed as a child's rough chalk-sketch on a wall; yet as we looked at it we seemed to see the outline of a woman held upon the ground by kneeling slaves while a man above her poised a heavy rock to crush her exposed breast and another stood in readiness to aid the executioner:

"*Cordieu!*" de Grandin exclaimed as we gazed upon the drawing. "I shall say she told the truth, my friends. She was a priestess of the goddess Isis, and as such was sworn to lifelong chastity, with awful death by torture as the penalty for violation of her vow. Undoubtlessly she loved not wisely, but too well, as women have been wont to love since time began, and upon discovery she was sentenced to the death decreed for those who did forget their obligations to the goddess. Her chest was broken in with stones, and without benefit of mummification her mutilated body was put in a casket void of any writing which might give a clue to her identity. Without a single invocation to the gods who held the fate of her poor spirit in their hands, they buried her. But did she triumph? Who says otherwise? We know her name, Atoua, we know the reason and the manner of her death. But those old priests who judged her and decreed her doom—who knows their names, yes, *parbleu*, who knows or cares a single, solitary damn where their vile mummies lie? They are assuredly gone into oblivion, while she—*tiens*, at least she is a personality to us, and we are very much alive."

"Excuse me, gentlemen, if you're quite finished with these relics, I'll take them, now," Professor Hodgson interrupted. "This little séance has been interesting, but you must admit nothing sufficiently authentic to be incorporated in our archives has been developed here. I fear we shall have to label these bones and ornaments as belonging to an unidentified body found by Doctor Larson at Naga-ed-dêr. Now, if you don't mind I shall get—"

"Get anywhere you wish, *Monsieur*, and get there quickly," de Grandin broke in furiously. "You have presided over relics of the dead so long your brain is clogged with mummy-dust. As for your heart—*mort d'un rat mort*, I do not think you have one!

"As for me," he added with a sudden smile, "I return at once to Doctor Trowbridge's. This poor young lady's tragic fate affects me deeply, and unless some urgent business interferes, I plan to drown my sorrow—*morbleu*, I shall do more. Within the hour I shall be most happily intoxicated!"

The Door to Yesterday

DINNER WOULD BE READY in fifteen minutes, and we were to have lobster Cardinal, a thing Jules de Grandin loved with a passion second only to his fervor for *La Marseillaise*. Now he was engaged in the rite of cocktail-mixing, intent upon his work as any alchemist brewing an esoteric philtre. "Now for the vermouth," he announced, decanting a potion of amber liquid into the tall silver shaker half filled with gin and fine-shaved ice with all the care of a pharmacist compounding a prescription. "One drop too little and the cocktail she is spoiled; one little so small drop too much, and she is wholly ruined. Ah—so; she is now precisely perfect, and ready for the shaking!" Slowly, rhythmically, he began to churn the shaker up and down, gradually increasing the speed in time with the bit of bawdy ballad which he hummed:

> *Ma fille, pour pénitence,*
> *Ron, ron, ron, petit patapon,*
> *Ma fille, pour pénitence,*
> *Nous nous embrasserons—*

"Captain Chenevert; Misther Gordon Goodlowe!" announced Nora McGinnis, my household factotum, from the study doorway, annoyance at having strangers call when dinner was about to be served showing on her broad Irish face.

On the heels of her announcement came the callers: Captain Chenevert; a big, deep-chested young man attired in that startling combination of light and dark blues in which the State of New Jersey garbs its gendarmerie; Mr. Goodlowe, a dapper, slender little man with neatly cropped white hair and short-clipped white mustache, immaculate in black mohair jacket and trousers, his small paunch trimly buttoned underneath a waistcoat of spotless linen.

"Sorry to interrupt you, gentlemen," Captain Chenevert apologized, "but there have been some things happening at Mr. Goodlowe's place which no one can explain, and one of my men got talking with a member of your local force—Detective Sergeant Costello—who said that Doctor de Grandin could get to the bottom of the trouble if anybody could."

"Eh, you say the good Costello sent you?" de Grandin asked, giving the cocktail mixer a final vigorous shake. "He should know better. Me, I am graduated from the *Sûreté*; I no longer take an interest in criminal investigation."

"We understood as much," the captain answered. "That's why we're here. If it had been a matter of ordinary crime-detection, or an extraordinary one, I think that we could handle it; but it's something more than that, sir." He paused and grinned rather sheepishly; then: "This may sound nutty to you, but I'm more than half convinced there's something supernatural about the case."

"Ah?" De Grandin put the cocktail shaker by. "U'm?" He flung a leg across the table-corner and, half sitting, half standing, regarded the visitors in turn with a fixed, unwinking stare. "*Ah-ha?* This is of interest," he admitted, breaking open a blue packet of Maryland cigarettes and setting one of the malodorous things aglow. "Proceed, if you please, gentlemen. Like the ass of Monsieur Balaam, I am all ears."

Mr. Goodlowe answered: "Last year my brother, Colonel Clarke Clay Goodlowe, sold his seat on the stock exchange and retired from active business," he began. "For some years he had contemplated returning to Kentucky, but when he finally gave up active trading in the market he found that he'd become acclimated to the North—reckon the poor fellow just couldn't bear to get more than an hour or two away from Wall Street, as a matter of fact—so he built himself a home near Keyport. He moved there with his daughter Nancy, my niece, last April, and died before he'd been there quite a month."

De Grandin's slender, jet-black eyebrows rose a fraction of an inch nearer the line of his honey-colored hair. "Very good, *Messieurs*," he answered querulously. "Men have died before—men have been dying regularly since Mother Eve and Father Adam partook of the forbidden fruit. What is there so extraordinary in this especial death?"

"I didn't see my brother's body—" Mr. Goodlowe began.

"But I did!" Captain Chenevert broke in. "Every bone from skull to metatarsus was broken, and the whole form was so hammered out of shape that identification was almost impossible."

"Ah?" de Grandin's small blue eyes flickered with renewing interest. "And then—"

Mr. Goodlowe took up the narrative: "My niece was almost prostrated by the tragedy, and as I was in England at the time it was impossible for me to join her right away. Accordingly, Major Derringer, a rather distant kinsman, and his wife came up from Lexington to attend the funeral and make such preliminary arrangements as were necessary until I could come home.

"The day following the funeral, Major Derringer was found on the identical spot where my brother's body was discovered—dead."

"Crushed and mauled almost out of resemblance to anything human," Captain Chenevert supplied.

"Mrs. Derringer was taken severely ill as a result of her husband's dreadful death," Mr. Goodlowe added. "She was put to bed with special nurses in attendance day and night, and while the night nurse was out of the room for a moment she rose and slipped through the window, wandered across the lawn in her nightclothes, and—"

The thing was like an antiphon. De Grandin looked inquiringly at Captain Chenevert as Mr. Goodlowe paused, and the trooper nodded grimly.

"The same," he snapped. "Same place, same dreadful mutilation—everything the same, except—"

"Yes, *parbleu*, except—" de Grandin prompted sharply as the young policeman paused.

"Except that Mrs. Derringer had bled profusely where compound fractures of her ribs had forced the bones through her sides, and on the tiled floor of the loggia near the spot where she was found was *the trail of a great snake marked in blood*."

"Good heavens!" I exclaimed.

"By damn-it," murmured Jules de Grandin, "this is truly such a case as I delight in, *Monsieur le Capitaine*. If you gentlemen will be good enough to join us at dinner, I shall do myself the honor of accompanying you to this so strange house where guests are found all crushed to death and serpents write their autographs in blood. Yes, certainly; of course."

PROSPECT HILL, THE LATE Colonel Goodlowe's house, was a reproduction of an English country seat done in the grand manner. Built upon a rise of ground, heading a little valley in the hills, it was a long, low red-brick mansion flanked by towering oaks and chestnut-trees. Leveled off before the house was a wide terrace paved with tesselated tiles and bordered by a stone balustrade punctuated at regular intervals by wide-mouthed urns of stone in which petunias blossomed riotously. A flight of broad, low steps ran down through succeeding terraced levels of smooth-shaved lawns to a lake where water-lilies bloomed and several swans swam lazily. Across a stretch of greensward to the left was a formal garden where statued nymphs stooped to beds of clustering roses which drenched the air with almost drugging sweetness. Low, colonnaded loggias, like cloisters, branched off from the house at either side, the left connecting with the rose-garden, the right leading to a level square of grass in which was set a little summer-house of red brick and wrought iron.

"One moment, if you please," de Grandin ordered as we clambered from the car before the house. "Show me, if you will be so good, *Monsieur le Capitaine*, exactly where it was they found Madame Derringer and the others. We might as well prepare ourselves by making a survey of the terrain."

We walked across the lawn toward the little summer-house, and Captain Chenevert halted some six feet from the loggia. "I'd say we found 'em here," he answered. "U'm, yes; just about here, judging by the—" He paused a moment, as though to orient himself, then stepped forward to the green-tile paving of the loggia, drawing an electric flashlight from his blouse pocket as he did so.

The long summer twilight had almost faded into night, but by such daylight as remained, aided by the beam of Captain Chenevert's torch, we could descry, very faintly, a sinuating, weaving trail against the gray-green of the tiles. I recognized it instantly. There is no boy brought up in the country districts before the coming of the motor-car had caused earth roads to give way to hard-surfaced highways who can not tell a snake-track when he sees it in the dust!

But never had I seen a track like this. In form it was a duplicate of trails which I had seen a thousand times, but in size—it might have been the mark left by a motor-lorry's wheel. Involuntarily I shuddered as I beheld the grisly thing, and Captain Chenevert's hand stole instinctively to the walnut stock of the revolver which dangled in its holster from his belt. Gordon Goodlowe, scion of a dozen generations of a family who chose death in preference to dishonor, held himself in check by almost superhuman force. Jules de Grandin showed no more emotion than if he were in a museum viewing some not-especially interesting relic of the past.

"U'm?" he murmured softly to himself, studying the dull, reddish-brown tracing with pursed lips and narrowed eyes. "He must have been the *bisaïeul* of the serpents, this one." He raised his narrow shoulders in a shrug, and:

"Come, let us go in," he suggested. "Perhaps there is more to see inside."

Mr. Goodlowe cleared his throat angrily, but Captain Chenevert laid a quick hand on his elbow. "S-s-sh!" he cautioned softly. "Let him handle this his own way. He knows what he's about."

AN AGED, BUT BY no means decrepit colored butler met us at the door. In one hand he held an old fashioned candle-lamp, in the other a saucer containing grains of wheat.

"What the devil?" Mr. Goodlowe snapped. "Has the electric power gone off again, Julius?"

"Yes, sir," said the colored man, his words, despite the native softness of his voice, having a peculiar intonation revealing that his mother tongue was not the English of the South. "The current has been gone since six o'clock this afternoon, and the telephone has been out of order for some time, as well."

"Dam' poor service!" muttered Goodlowe, but:

"How long's it been since your light and telephone died before?" sharply queried Captain Chenevert.

I saw the Negro shiver, as though he felt a sudden draft of gelid air. "Not since Madame Derringer—" he began, but the captain shut him off.

"That's what I thought," he answered; then, to de Grandin, in a whisper:

"Something dam' funny about this, sir. Their electric light all died the night Mrs. Derringer was—er—died, and the telephone went dead at the same time. Same thing happened on both previous occasions, too. D'ye mind if I pop over to the barracks and put in a trouble call? I've got my motorcycle parked out in the yard."

De Grandin had been studying the butler with that intent, unwinking stare of his, but now turned to the trooper with a nod. "By all means," he replied. "Go there, and go quickly, my friend. Also return as quickly as may be with one of your patrol cars, if you please. Park it at the entrance of the grounds, and approach on foot. It may be we shall be in need of help, and I would have it that our reinforcements come unannounced, if possible."

"O.K.," the other answered, and turned upon his heel.

"How's Miss Nancy, Julius?" Mr. Goodlowe asked. "Feeling any better?"

"No, sir, I'm afraid she's not," the butler replied, and again it seemed to me that he shivered like a man uncomfortable with cold, or in mortal terror.

Jules de Grandin's gaze had scarcely left the Negro since he saw him first. Now, abruptly, he addressed him in a sudden flow of queer, outlandish words, vaguely reminiscent of French, but differing from it in tone and inflection, no less than in pronunciation, as the argot of the slums differs from the language of polite society.

The Negro started violently as de Grandin spoke to him, glanced shame-facedly at the plate of wheat he held, then, keeping his eyes averted, answered in the same outlandish tongue. Throughout the dialogue was constantly repeated a queer, harsh-sounding word: "*loogaroo*," though what it meant I had no faintest notion. At length:

"*Bon*," de Grandin told the butler; then, to Mr. Goodlowe and me: "He says that *Mademoiselle* your niece is feeling most unwell, *Monsieur*, and that he thinks it would be well if we prescribed for her. He and his wife have attempted to assist her, but she has fallen into a profound stupor from which they can not rouse her, and it was while attempting to summon a physician from Keyport that he discovered the telephone had gone out of order. Have we your permission to attend *Mademoiselle*?"

"Yes, of course," Mr. Goodlowe answered, and, as we followed the butler up the wide, balustraded stairway:

"Dam' West Indian niggers—I can't think why Clarke had 'em around. I'll be gettin' rid of 'em in short order, as soon as I can get some of our servants up here from the South. Why the devil couldn't he have told *me* about Nancy?"

"Perhaps because he had no opportunity," de Grandin answered with a mildness wholly strange to him. "I surmised that he came from Haiti or Martinique by his accent and by—no matter. Accordingly, I addressed him in his native *patois*, and he responded. I must apologize for breaking in upon your conversation, but there were certain things I wished to know, and deemed it best to ask him quickly, before he fully understood the nature of my mission here."

"Humph," responded Mr. Goodlowe. "Did you find out what you wanted?"

"Perfectly, *Monsieur*. Forgive me if I do not tell you what it is. At present I have no more than the vaguest of vague suspicions, and I should not care to make myself a laughing-stock by parading crazy theories unbacked by any facts."

Plainly, Mr. Goodlowe was unimpressed with Jules de Grandin as an investigator, and it was equally plain that he had in mind setting forth his dissatisfaction in no uncertain terms, but our advent at his niece's bedroom door cut off all further conversation.

"Miss Nancy—oh, Miss Nancy!" the butler called in a soft, affectionate tone, striking lightly on the panels with his knuckles.

No answer was forthcoming, and, waiting a moment, the old Negro opened the door and held his candle high, standing aside to permit us to pass.

In the faint, yellow light of half a dozen candles flickering in wall-sconces we descried a girl lying still as death upon the tufted mattress of a high, four-poster bed. Her eyes were closed, her hands were folded lightly on her breast, and on her skin was the ghastly, whitish-yellow pallor of the moribund or newly dead. Small gouts of perspiration lay like tiny beads of limpid oil upon her forehead; a little ridge of glistening globules of moisture had formed upon her upper lip.

"My God, she's dead!" cried Mr. Goodlowe, but:

"Not dead, but sleeping—though not naturally," de Grandin answered. "See, her breast is moving, though her respirations are most faint. Attend her, Friend Trowbridge."

Placing his finger-tip against her left radial artery, he consulted the dial of the diminutive gold watch strapped against the under side of his left wrist, motioning me to take her right-hand pulse.

"Great heavens!" I exclaimed as I felt the feeble throbbing in her wrist. "Why, her heart's beating a hundred and twenty, and—"

"I make it a hundred and twenty-six," he interrupted. "What diagnosis would you make from the other signs, my friend?"

"Well," I considered, lifting the girl's eyelids and holding a candle to her face, we have pallor of the body surface, subnormal temperature, rapid pulse and weak respiration, together with dilated pupils—acute coma induced by anemia of the brain, I'd say."

"Consequent on cardiac insufficiency?" he added.

"That's my guess."

"Perfectly. Mine also," he agreed.

"A little brandy ought to help," I hazarded, but:

"Undoubtlessly," he acquiesced, "but we shall not administer it.

"*Monsieur*," he turned to Mr. Goodlowe, "will you be good enough to leave us? We must take measures for *Mademoiselle's* recovery, and"—he raised his brows and shoulders in a shrug—"it would be better if you left us with the patient."

Obediently, our host turned from the room, and as the door swung to upon him:

"*Dépêchez, mon vieux!*" de Grandin told the butler, who at his signaled order, had remained in the room. "Cords, if you please; make haste!"

Lengths of linen were snatched down from the windows, quickly twisted into bandages, then bound about the girl's wrists and ankles, finally knotted to the uprights of the bed. Last of all, several bands were passed completely around her body and the bed, binding her as fast upon the mattress as ever criminal was lashed upon the rack.

"Whatever are you doing?" I asked him angrily as he knotted a final cincture. "This is positively inhuman, man."

"I fear it is," he admitted; then, turning to the butler:

"Summon your wife to stand guard, *mon brave*, and bid her call us instantly if *Mademoiselle* awakes and struggles to be free. You understand?"

"*Parfaitement, M'sieu*," returned the other.

"What the deuce does it mean?" I demanded as we descended the stairs. "First you interrogate that servant in some outlandish gibberish; then you lash that poor, sick girl to her bed, as though she were a violent maniac—that's the damnedest treatment for anemic coma I ever saw! Now—"

"*Cordieu*, my friend, unless I am much more mistaken than I think, that is the damnedest anemic coma that I ever saw, as well!" he broke in. "Anon I shall explain, but—ah, here is the good Monsieur Goodlowe; there are things which he can tell us, too." We entered the library where Mr. Goodlowe paced furiously before the fireless fireplace, a long cigar, unlighted, in his mouth.

"There you are!" he barked as we entered the room. "How's Nancy?"

De Grandin shook his head despondently. "She is not so good, *Monsieur*," he answered sadly. "We have done what we could for her at present, and the butler's wife sits watching by her bed; meanwhile, we should like to ask you several things, if you will kindly answer."

"Well?" Goodlowe challenged.

"How comes it that *Monsieur* your brother had servants from the French West Indies in his service, rather than Negroes from his native state?"

"I don't see that has any bearing on the case," our host objected, "but if you're bound to have the family pedigree—"

"Oh, yes, that would he most helpful," de Grandin assured him with a smile.

The other eyed him narrowly, seeking to determine whether he spoke ironically, and at length:

"Like most Kentuckians, our family came from Virginia," he returned. "Greene Clarke, our maternal great-grandfather, was a ship-owner in Norfolk, trading principally with the West Indies—it was easier to import sugar from Saint Domingue, as they called it then, than to bring it through the Gulf from Louisiana; so he did a thriving trade with the islands. Eventually, he acquired considerable land holdings in Haiti, and put a younger brother in charge as overseer. The place was overrun and burned when the Blacks revolted, but our great-granduncle escaped and later, when Christophe set up stable government, the family re-acquired the lands and farmed them until the Civil War. The Virginia branch of the family always kept up interest in the West Indian trade, and Clarke, in his younger days, spent considerable time in both Haiti and Martinique. It was on one of his sojourns in Port au Prince that he acquired Julius and Marie as household servants. They came with him to the States and were in his service more than forty years. They'll not be here much longer, though. I don't like West Indian niggers' impudent ways, and I'm going to give 'em the boot as soon as I can get a couple of our servants up here."

De Grandin nodded thoughtfully; then:

"You have no record of your ancestor's activities in Haiti before the Blacks' revolt?" he asked.

"No," Mr. Goodlowe answered shortly.

"Ah? A pity, *Monsieur*. Perhaps we might find in that some explanation of the so strange deaths which seem to curse this house. However—but let it pass for the present; we must seek our explanation elsewhere, it would seem."

He busied himself lighting a cigarette, then turned once more to Mr. Goodlowe. "Captain Chenevert should be here shortly," he announced. "It might be well if you accompany him when he leaves, *Monsieur*. Unless I misread the signs, the malign genius which presides over this most unfortunate house is ready for another manifestation, and you are in all probability the intended victim. We may foil it and learn something which will enable us to thwart it permanently in your absence; if you remain—*eh bien*, who can say what may occur?"

Mr. Goodlowe eyed him coldly. "You're suggesting that I run away?" he asked.

"Ah, no; by no means, *Monsieur*, merely that you make a temporary retreat while Friend Trowbridge and I fight a rear-guard engagement. You can not help us by your presence. Indeed, your being here may prove a great embarrassment."

"I'm sorry, sir," our host returned, "but I can't agree to any such arrangement. I've called you in to solve this case at Captain Chenevert's suggestion, and against my own best judgment. If I'm to pay you, I must at least demand that you put me in possession of all facts you know—or think you know. Thus far your methods have been more those of the fortune-telling charlatan than the detective, and I must say I'm not impressed with them. Either you will handle the case under my direction, or I will write you a check for services to date and call another into consultation."

De Grandin's little, round blue eyes flashed ominously, with a light like winter ice reflecting January moonlight. His thin lips drew away from his small, white teeth in a smile which held no mirth, but he controlled his fiery temper by an almost superhuman effort. "This case intrigues one, Monsieur Goodlowe," he answered stiffly. "It is not on your account that I hesitate to leave it; but rather out of love for mastering a mystery. Be so good as to listen attentively, if you please:

"To begin, when first I saw your butler I thought I recognized in him the earmarks of the Haitien. Also, I noted that he bore a saucer filled with wheat when he responded to our knock. Now, in Haiti, as I know from personal experience, the natives have a superstition that when an unclean spirit comes to haunt a place, protection can be had if they will scatter grains of rice or wheat before the door. The visitant must pause to count the scattered grain, they think, and accordingly daylight will surprise him before the tale is told. The *Quashee*, or Haitien blacks, refer indifferently to various unpleasant members of the spirit world as 'loogaroo,' which is, of course, a corruption of *loup-garou*, or werewolf.

"Very well. I drew my bow at random and addressed your man in Haitien *patois*, and instantly he answered me. He told me much, for one who bears himself addressed in the language of his childhood in a strange land will throw away reserve and give full vent to his emotions. He told me, by example, that he was in the act of scattering grain about the house, and especially upon the stairs and in the passage leading to Mademoiselle Nancy's room, because he was convinced that the *loogaroo* which had already made 'way with three members of your family was planning a fresh outrage. For why? Because, by blue, on each occasion previously the electric light inside the house had died for no apparent reason, and all outside connections by telephone had similarly died. Captain Chenevert, who had made investigation of the deaths, noted this coincidence, also, and remarked upon it. He is now gone to report the failure of your light and telephone to the proper parties.

"But something else, of even greater interest, your butler disclosed. The day before her father's death, the day Monsieur Derringer died so strangely, and immediately preceding Madame Derringer's so tragic death, Mademoiselle Nancy exhibited just such signs of illness as she showed today—dullness, listlessness, headache; finally a heavy stupor almost simulating death, from which no one could rouse her. Never before—and he has known her all her life—had she shown signs of such an illness. Indeed, she was always a most healthy young lady, not subject to the customary feminine ills of headache, biliousness or stomach-sickness. *Alors*, he was of opinion that these sinking-fits of hers were connected in some manner with the advent of the *loogaroo*.

"I must admit I think he reasoned wisely. When Doctor Trowbridge and I examined her, your niece showed every sign of anemic coma; this in a lady who has always been most healthy, is deserving of remark; especially since she shows no evidence of cardiac deficiency intervening these strange seizures. You comprehend?"

"I comprehend you've let yourself be fooled by the bestial superstitions of an ignorant savage!" Mr. Goodlowe burst out disgustedly. "If this is a sample of the way you solve your cases, sir, I think we'd better call it quits and—"

"*M'sieu, M'sieu l'Médecin, dépêchez-vous—Ma'mselle est—*" the urgent whisper cut him short as an elderly Negress, deeply wrinkled but still possessing the fine figure and graceful carriage of the West Indian black, appeared at the library door.

"We come—at once, immediately, right away!" de Grandin answered, turning unceremoniously from Mr. Goodlowe and hastening up the stairs.

"Detain him without, my friend," he whispered with a nod toward Goodlowe as we reached the sickroom door. "Should he find her bound, he may ask questions, even become violent, and I shall be too busy to stop my work and slay him."

Accordingly, I blocked the bedroom door as best I could while the little Frenchman and the Negress hastened to the bed.

Nancy Goodlowe was stirring, but not conscious. Rather, her movements were the writhings of delirium, and, like a patient in delirium, she seemed endowed with supernatural strength; for the strong bandages which bound her wrists had been thrown off, and the surcingle of cotton which held her to the bed was burst asunder.

"*Morbleu*, what in Satan's name is this—" began de Grandin, then, abruptly: "But, *gloire de Dieu*, what is *that?*"

He brushed past the bed, leant out the window and pointed toward the patch of smooth-shaven lawn before the loggia red-brick-and-iron summer-house. What seemed to be a jet of vapor rising from a broken steam-pipe was whirling like a dust-swirl above the grass plot, rotating still more swiftly;

at length concrescing and solidifying. An optical illusion it doubtless was, but I could have sworn the gyrating haze took form and substance as I gazed and became, beneath my very eyes, the image of *a great white snake*.

"Here, damn you, what d'ye mean by this?" Mr. Goodlowe burst past me into the girl's bedroom and snatched furiously at the cotton bindings which half restrained his niece upon the bed. "By gad, sir, I'll teach you to treat gentlewomen this way!" he stormed; then, surprisingly:

"Ah?"

Raising furious eyes to de Grandin as the little Frenchman peered out the window, he had caught sight of the ghastly, whirling wreath of vapor on the lawn.

The thing by now had definitely assumed a serpent's form. And it was a moving serpent; a serpent which circumvoluted in a giant ring, rearing and swaying its ugly, wedge-shaped head from side to side; a serpent which made loops and figure-eights upon the moonlit lawn, and described great, flowing triangles which melted into squares and hexagons and undulating, coiling mounds, an ever-changing, never-hastening, never-resting figure of activity.

"Ah?" Mr. Goodlowe repeated, horror and blank incredulity in the querying monosyllable.

We saw his face. The eyes were staring, glassy, void of all expression as the eyes of one new-dead; his jaw hung down and his mouth was open, round and expressionless as the entrance to a small, empty cave. His breath sounded stertorously, like a snore. For a moment he stood thus; then, hands held before him like a sleep-walker, or a person playing blind man's bluff, he turned, shambled down the hall and began a slow and halting descent of the stairs.

"*Loogaroo — loogaroo — Ayida Oueddo!*" gibbered the Negro servant, her horror-glazed eyes rolling in a very œstrus of fear as she gazed alternately at the whirling thing upon the lawn, the struggling girl upon the bed, and Jules de Grandin.

"Silence!" cried the Frenchman; then, clearing the space between the window and the bed at a single leap; "Mademoiselle Nancy, awake!" he ordered, seizing the girl's shoulders and shaking her furiously from side to side as a terrier might shake a rat.

For a moment they struggled thus, seemingly engaged in a wrestling bout, but finally the girl's dark eyes opened and she looked him in the face.

De Grandin's little, round blue eyes seemed starting from his head, the veins along his temple swelled and throbbed as he leant abruptly forward till his nose and that of Nancy Goodlowe nearly touched. "Attend me—carefully!" he commanded in a voice which sounded like a hiss. "You will go back to sleep, a simple, restful, natural sleep, and both your waking and subconscious minds shall be at rest. You will awake when daylight comes, and not before. I, Jules de

Grandin, order it. You comprehend? Sleep—sleep—*sleep!*" he finished in a low and crooning voice, swaying the girl's shoulders to and fro, as one might rock a restless child.

Slowly she sank back on her pillow, composed herself as quietly as a tired little girl might do, and in a moment seemed to fall asleep, all traces of the delirium which had held her in its grip a moment since departed.

"Oh!" Involuntarily the exclamation broke from me. The writhing, twisting serpent on the lawn had vanished, and I could not rightly say whether what remained was a wraith of whirling vapor or a spot of bright moonlight which seemed to move as the shadow of some wind-blown bough swept over it.

"Come, my friend," de Grandin ordered sharply, snatching at my elbow as he dashed from the room. "We must find him."

Mr. Goodlowe had left the house and crossed the intervening lawn by the time we reached the door. As we came up with him he stood a few feet from the place where we had seen the great white snake, staring about him with puzzled, wide, lack-luster eyes.

"Wha—what am I doing here?" he faltered as the Frenchman caught him by the shoulder and administered a gentle shake.

"Do not you remember, *Monsieur?*" de Grandin asked. "Do you not recall the thing you saw out here—the thing which beckoned you to come, and whose summons you obeyed?"

Goodlowe looked vaguely from one of us to the other. "I—I seem to have some recollection of some one—something—which called me out," he answered in a sleepy, faltering voice, "but who it was or what it was I can't remember."

"No?" de Grandin returned curiously. "*Eh bien*, perhaps it is as well, or better. You are tired, *Monsieur*. I think you would do better if you slept, as we should, also. Tomorrow we shall talk about this case at length."

Docile as a sleepy child, our fiery-tempered host permitted us to lead him to the house and assist him into bed.

De Grandin made a final tour of inspection, noted the light, natural sleep in which Nancy Goodlowe lay, then followed Julius to the room assigned us. Clad in lavender pajamas, mauve dressing-gown and purple kid slippers, he sat beside the window, gazing moodily out upon the moonlit lawn, lighting one vile-smelling French cigarette from the glowing stump of another, muttering unintelligibly to himself from time to time, like one who makes a mental calculation of a puzzling problem in arithmetic.

"For goodness' sake, aren't you ever coming to bed?" I asked crossly. "I'm sleepy, and—"

"Then go to sleep, by all means," he shot back sharply. "Sleep, animal; rest yourself in swinish ease. Me, I am a sentient human being; I have thoughts to think and plans to make. When I have done, then I shall rest. Until that time you will oblige me by not obtruding yourself upon my meditations."

"Oh, all right," I answered, turning on my side and taking him at his word.

Gordon Goodlowe was in a chastened mood next morning. While he had no clear recollections of the previous evening's events, there was a haunting fear at the back of his mind, a sort of nameless terror which dogged his footsteps, yet evaded his memory as fancied images half seen from the tail of the eye dissolve into nothingness when we turn about and seek to see them by direct glance.

Miss Goodlowe remained in bed, apparently suffering from no specific illness, but in a greatly weakened state. "I think she'll be all right, with rest and a restricted diet," I ventured as de Grandin and I left her room, but:

"*Non*, my friend, you have wrong," the little Frenchman told me with a vigorous shake of his head. "Tonight, unless I much mistake my diagnosis, she will have another seizure, and—"

"You'll hypnotize her again?" I interjected.

"By blue, not by any means!" he broke in. "Me, this evening I shall be a spectator at the show, though not, perhaps, an idle one. No, on second thought I am decided I shall be quite active. Yes, certainly."

When Captain Chenevert arrived with assurances that "trouble-shooters" of the electric and telephone companies could find no mechanical reason for the failure of service in the Goodlowe house, and when, by trial, we found both electric light and telephone in perfect working order, de Grandin showed no surprise. Rather, he seemed to take the mystery of alternating failure and function in the service as confirmation of some theory he had formed.

Shortly after noon, accompanied by Julius, the butler, he made a hurried trip in Captain Chenevert's police car, returning before dinner time with a covered tin pail filled with something which splashed as he bore it to the kitchen and put it near the stove, where it would remain warm, but not become really hot.

I passed a rather dismal day. Mr. Goodlowe was in such a state of nervous fear that he seemed incapable of carrying on a conversation; Miss Goodlowe lay quietly in bed, refusing food, and answering questions with a gentle patience which reminded me of a convalescent child; de Grandin bustled about importantly. Now in conference with Captain Chenevert, now with Julius, now delving into some old family records which he found in the library. By dinner time I was in a state where I would have welcomed a game of cribbage as a pastime.

Our host excused himself shortly after dinner, and the young police captain, de Grandin and I were left alone with cigars and liqueurs on the terrace. "You're sure you've got some dope on it?" Chenevert asked suddenly, flinging his cigar away with nervous petulance, then selecting another from the humidor and lighting it with quick, spasmodic puffs.

"None but the feeble-minded are sure, of that I am indubitably sure," de Grandin answered, "but I think I have at least sufficient evidence to support an hypothesis.

"This house, I found by inquiries which I made in the city, was largely built of second-hand materials; the owner wished that weathered bricks be used, and considerable search was necessary to procure materials of a proper age and quality. The brick and iron work of which that little summer-house is built, by example, came from a demolished structure on the outskirts of Newark, a house once used to restrain the criminally insane. You apprehend the significance of that?"

The young trooper regarded him quizzically a moment, as though seeking to determine whether he were serious. At length: "No. I can't say I do," he confessed.

De Grandin turned interrogatively to me. "Do you, by any happy chance, see a connection in it?" he demanded.

"No," I answered. "I can't see it makes any difference whether the brick and iron came from an insane asylum or a chicken-coop."

He nodded, a trifle sadly. "One should have anticipated some such answer from you," he replied. Then: "Attend me, carefully, both of you," he ordered. "We must begin with the premise that, though it is incapable of being seen or weighed or measured, a thought is a thing, no less than is a pound of butter, a flitch of bacon or a dozen sacerdotal candles. You follow me? *Bien. Bien*, whether you do or not.

"A madhouse is far from being a pleasant place. There human wreckage— the mentally dead whose bodies unfortunately survive them—is brought to be disposed of, imprisoned, cabined, cribbed, confined. Often, those we call 'criminally insane' are very criminal, indeed, though not medically insane. Their madness consists in their having given themselves, body, soul and spirit, to abysmal and unutterable evilness. Very well. From such there emanates—we do not know quite how, though psychical experiment has proved it to be a fact— an active, potent force of evil, and inanimate things, like stone and wood, brick and iron, are capable of absorbing it. Oh, yes.

"I have seen spirit-manifestations evoked from a chip taken from a rafter in a house where great wickedness had been indulged in; I have seen dreams of old, dead, evil days evoked in sensitive subjects doing no more than sleep in the room where some bit of torture-paraphernalia from he prisons of the Spanish Inquisition in Toledo had been placed all unbeknown to them. Yes. There, then, is our starting-point.

"What then? Last night three people saw a most remarkable manifestation on that lawn yonder. I saw it; the Negro butler's wife beheld it; even Doctor

Trowbridge, who most certainly can not be called a psychic, saw it. *Voilà*; that thing was no figment of the fancy, it was there. Of course. Whether Monsieur Goodlowe saw it, in the same sense that we beheld it we can not say. He has no recollection of it. But certainly he saw something—something which caused him to leave his house and walk across the grass plot exactly as did his brother, his kinsman and his female relative, presumably. Had I not been quick, I think we should have seen another tragedy, there, before our very eyes."

"I say," I interrupted, "just what was it you did last night, de Grandin? I have to admit, however much my better judgment tells me it was an optical illusion, that I saw—or thought I saw—a great snake materialize on the lawn; then, when you hypnotized Miss Goodlowe, the thing seemed to fade away. Did she have any connection with—"

"*Ah bah*," he broke in with a nod. "Has the lens any connection with the burning of the concentrated sunlight? By damn-it, I think yes!"

"How—" I began, but:

"You have seen the working of the *verre ardent*—the how do you call him— burning-glass? Yes?"

"Of course," Chenevert and I replied in chorus.

"Very good!" He nodded solemnly. "Very, exceedingly good. All about us, invisible, impalpable, but all about us none the less, are spiritual forces, some good, some evil, all emanations of generations of men who have lived and strug- gled, loved, hated and died long years agone. But this great force is, in the main, so widespread, so lacking in cohesion, that it can not manifest itself physically, except upon the rarest of occasions. At times it can make itself faintly felt, as sunshine can impart a coat of tan to the skin, but to inflict a quick and powerful burn the sunlight must be bound together in a single intense beam by the aid of the burning-lens. Just so with these spiritual forces, whether they be good or naughty. They are here already, as sunlight is abundant on a sunny day, but it needs the services of a medium to bring these forces into focus so they can become physically apparent. Yes; assuredly.

"Now, not all mediums reside in the stuffy back rooms of darkened houses, eking out precarious livelihoods by the contributions of the credulous who desire to consult the spirits of departed relatives. *Hélas*, no. There are many unconscious mediums who all innocently give force and potency to some evil spirit-entity which but for them would be unable to manifest itself at all. Such mediums are most often neurotic young women. They seem ideally fitted to supply the psychoplasm needed by the spirit for materialization, whether that manifestation be for the harmless purpose of ringing a tambourine, tooting a toy trumpet or—committing bloody murder.

"This, of course, I knew already. Also, I knew that on previous occa- sions when members of the Goodlowe family had been so tragically killed,

Mademoiselle Nancy had suffered from strange seizures such as that she had last night. 'It are a wicked thing—a spirit or an elemental—draining the physical energy from her in the form of psychoplasm with which to make itself material,' I tell me. Accordingly, when I see that serpent forming out of nothingness, I turn at once to Mademoiselle Nancy as its source of power.

"She is unconscious, but her subconscious mind is active; she seeks to burst the bonds I put upon her, to what end? One wonders. But one thing I can do if only I can succeed in making her conscious for one little so small minute. I can hypnotize her—put her in a natural sleep in which the unconscious giving off of physio-psychical power will be halted. And so. I wake her, though I have great trouble doing it. I wake her and then I bid her sleep once more. She sleeps, and the building up of that so evil white snake-thing comes abruptly to a halt. Voilà. Très bien."

"What's next?" Chenevert demanded.

"First, a further test of that which summoned Monsieur Goodlowe from the house last night," the little Frenchman answered. "I have taken means which will, I think, insure its harmlessness; but I am curious to see how it goes about its work. That done, we shall destroy the summer-house from which the evil emanation seems to come, and that accomplished, we shall seek for causes of these so strange deaths and for the source of the curse which seems to overhang this family. Logicians reason a posteriori, we shall seek to visualize in the same manner, from ultimate effect to primal cause. You understand?"

Captain Chenevert shook his head, but held his peace.

"I'm hanged if I do," I declared.

"Very well, you shall, in time," he promised with a smile, "but you shall not be hanged. You are too good a friend to lose by hanging, dear old silly Trowbridge of my heart."

IT MUST HAVE BEEN near midnight when the Negro butler ran out on the terrace to summon us. "Ma'mselle is restless, M'sieu l'Médecin," he announced. "My wife is with her, but—"

"Very good," de Grandin cried. "Is all in readiness?"

"Oui, M'sieu."

"Bon. Let us go." He hastened toward the house, and:

"Look upon the lawn my friends," he bade Chenevert and me. "What is it that you see, if anything?"

We turned toward the plot of grass before the summer-house, and I felt a prickling of my scalp and, despite midsummer heat, a sudden chill ran down my neck and back. A jet of whitish vapor was rising from the grass, and as we looked, it began to weave and wind and twist, simulating the contortions of a rearing serpent.

"Good God!" cried Captain Chenevert, reaching for his pistol, but:

"Desist!" de Grandin warned. "I have that ready which will prove more efficacious than your shot, *mon capitaine*, and I do not wish that you should make unnecessary noise. It is better that we do our work in silence. Await me here, but on no account go near it!"

In a moment he and Julius returned, each armed with what looked like those large tin atomizers used to spray insecticide on rose bushes.

They charged across the strip of lawn, their tin weapons held before them as soldiers might hold automatic rifles, deployed while still some distance from the whirling mist, then turned and faced each other, de Grandin running in a circle from left to right, the Negro circling toward him from right to left. Each aimed his atomizer at the earth and we heard the *swish-swish* of the things as they worked the plungers furiously. Although I could not tell what the "guns" held, it seemed to me they sprayed some dark-hued liquid on the grass.

"*Fini!*" the little Frenchman cried as he and Julius completed their circuit. "Now—ha? Ah-ha-ha?" He seemed to freeze and stiffen in his tracks as he looked toward the house.

Chenevert and I turned, too and I heard the captain give a muffled exclamation, even as I caught my breath in surprise. Walking with an undulating, swaying motion which was almost like that of a dance, came Nancy Goodlowe. Her flimsy night-dress fluttered lightly in the faint night breeze. In the moonlight, falling fine as dusted silver powder through the windbreak of Lombardy poplars, she was so wraith-like and ephemeral as to seem a phantom of the imagination. Her arms were raised before her, and bent sharply at the elbows, and again at the wrists, so that her hands thrust forward, for all the world like twin snake-heads, poised to strike. Abruptly she came to a halt, half turned toward the house from which she had come, as though awaiting the advent of a delayed companion, then, apparently reassured, began describing a wide circle on the lawn in a gliding, side-stepping dance. I saw her face distinctly as a moonbeam flashed upon it, a tense drawn face, devoid of all expression as a countenance carved of wood, eyes wide, staring and expressionless, mouth retracted so that a hard, white line of teeth showed behind the soft red line of lips.

And now the drawn, sardonically smiling lips were moving, and a soft contralto chant rose upon the midnight stillness. The words I could not understand. Vaguely, they reminded me of French; yet they were not truly French, resembling that language only as the jargon of a Yorkshireman or the *patois* of our canebrake Negroes simulated the English of an educated Londoner. One word, or phrase, alone I understood: "*Ayida Oueddo—Ayida Oueddo!*" intermixed with connectives of unintelligible gibberish which meant nothing to me.

"Quick, my friends, seize him, lay hands on him, hold him where he is!" de Grandin's whispered order cut through Nancy Goodlowe's chanting invocation, as he motioned us to turn around.

As we swung round we beheld Gordon Goodlowe. Like a wanderer in a dream he came, the night air stirring through his tousled hair, his eyes fast-set and staring with a look of blank, half-conscious horror. His mouth was partly opened, and from the corners there drooled two little streams of spittle. He was like a paralytic moving numbly in a state of quarter-consciousness, a condemned man marching to the gallows in an anesthesia of dread, volition gone from out his limbs and muscles working only through some reflex process entirely divorced from conscious guidance.

"Do not address him, only hold him fast!" de Grandin ordered sharply. "On no account permit him to overstep the line we drew; the other may not come to him; see you that he goes not to it!"

Obediently, Chenevert and I seized Goodlowe by the elbows and stopped him in his stride. He did not struggle with us, nor, indeed, did he seem aware we held him, but we could feel the dead-weight of his body as he leaned toward the twisting, writhing thing inside the circle which de Grandin and Black Julius had marked upon the lawn.

The mist had now solidified. It had become a great, white snake which turned and slid its folds like melting quicksilver, one upon another, rearing up its dreadful head, opening its fang-barbed mouth and hissing with a low, continuous sibilation like the sound of steam escaping from a broken pipe.

I shrank away as the awful thing drew itself into a knot and drove its scale-armored head forward in a sudden lunge toward us, but terror gave way to astonishment as I saw the driving battering-ram of scale and muscle stopped in midair, as though it had collided with an invisible, but impenetrable, barrier. Time and again the monster struck at us, hissing with a sort of venomous fury as each drive fell futilely against the unseen wall which seemed to stand between ourselves and it. Then—

From the little red-brick summerhouse there came a sudden spurt of flame. Unseen by us, de Grandin and the butler had drenched the place with gasoline until the very bricks reeked with it. Now, as they poured a fresh supply of petrol out, they set a match to it, and the orange flames leaped upward hungrily.

A startling change came over the imprisoned reptile. No longer did it seek to strike at Chenevert and Goodlowe and me; rather, its efforts seemed directed to regaining the protection of the blazing summer-house. But the invisible barrier which had held it back from us restrained its efforts to retreat. It struck and struck again, helplessly, at the empty air, then begin to twist and writhe in a new fashion, contorting on itself, swaying its head, shuddering its coils, as though in insupportable agony. And as the lapping tongues of flame leaped higher, the thing began to shrink and shrivel, as though the fire which burnt the roof and cracked the bricks and bent the iron grilles of the little house with its fierce heat, were consuming it.

It was a fearsome sight. To see a twenty-foot snake burned alive—consumed to crisping ashes—would have been enough to horrify us almost past endurance, but to see that mighty, writhing mass of bone and scale and iron-hard muscle cremated by a fire which blazed a half a hundred feet away—so far away that we could scarcely feel the least faint breath of heat—that was adding stark impossibility to nauseating horror.

"*Fini—triomphe—achevé—parfait!*" de Grandin cried triumphantly as he and Julius capered round the blazing summer-house like savages dancing round some sacrificial bonfire. "You were strong and cunning, *Monsieur le Revenant*, but Jules de Grandin, he was stronger and more cunning. *Ha*, but he tricked you cleverly, that one; he made a mock of all your wicked, vengeful plans; he caught you in a trap where you thought no trap was; he snared you in a snare from which there was no exit; he burned you in the fire and made you into nothing—he has consumed you utterly and finally!" Abruptly he ceased his frenzied dance and insane chant of triumph, and:

"See to *Mademoiselle, mon brave*," he ordered Julius. "I think that she will rest the clock around when your wife has put her in her bed. Tomorrow we shall see the last act of this tragedy and then—*eh bien*, the curtain always falls upon the finished play, *n'est-ce-pas?*"

CANDLES BURNED WITH A soft, faintly shifting light in the tall seven-cupped candelabrum which graced the center of the polished mahogany table in the Goodlowe drawing-room. Full to repletion at the end of an exceptionally good dinner, Jules de Grandin was at once affable and talkative. "What was it you and Julius sprayed on the lawn last night?" I had asked as Gordon Goodlowe, his niece, Captain Chenevert and I found seats in the parlor and Julius, quiet-footed as a cat brought in coffee and liqueurs before setting the candles alight and drawing the gold-mesh curtains at the tall French windows.

The little Frenchman's small blue eyes twinkled roguishly as he turned his gaze on me and brushed a wholly imaginary fleck of dust from the sleeve of his immaculate white-linen mess-jacket. "Chicken blood," he answered with an elfin grin.

"*What?*" Chenevert and I demanded in incredulous chorus.

"*Précisément*, your hearing is quite altogether perfect, my friends!" he answered. "Chicken blood—*sang des poulets*, you comprehend?"

"But—" I began, when he checked me with an upraised hand.

"Did you ever stop to think why there are statues of the blessed saints upon the altars of the Catholic church?" he asked.

"Why there are—what the deuce are you driving at?" I demanded.

He drained his cup of brandied coffee almost at a gulp, and patted the needle-sharp ends of his diminutive wheat-blond mustache with affectionate concern. "The old schoolmen knew nothing of what we call 'the new psychology' today," he answered with a chuckle, "but they had as good a working knowledge of it as any of our present-day professors. Consider: In the laboratory we employ rotating mirrors to induce a state of quick hypnosis when we would make experiments; before that we were wont to use gazing-crystals, for very long ago it was found that the person concentrating his attention on a small, bright object was an excellent candidate for hypnotism. Very good, but that is not all. If one stares fixedly at anything, whatever be its size, he soon detects a feeling of detachment stealing over him—I have seen soldiers standing at attention become unconscious and fall fainting to the ground because they focused their gaze upon some object before them, and held it there too long.

"Very well, then. The olden fathers of the Church discovered, not by psychological formulæ, but empirically, that an image placed upon a shrine gave the kneeling worshipper something on which to concentrate his gaze and induced a state of mild semi-hypnosis which made it possible to exclude extrinsic thoughts. It enabled the worshipper, in fine, to coordinate his thought with the wording of his prayer—made the act of praying less like indulging in a conversation with himself. You apprehend? Good. The underlying psychology of the thing the fathers did not know, but they proved by successful experiment that the images fulfilled this important office.

"Similarly: In darkest Africa, where the Voodoo rites of the West Indies had their birth, worshippers of the unclean gods typified by the snake discovered that the blood of fowls, especially chickens, was a potent talisman against their deities, which might otherwise burst the boundaries of control. Every Voodoo rite, whatever its nature, is accompanied by the sacrifice of a fowl, preferably a rooster, and this blood is scattered in a circle *between the worshippers and the altar of their gods*. Why this is we do not know; we only know it is. But upon some ancient day, so long ago that no one knows its date, it was undoubtlessly discovered that the serpent-god of the Voodoo men could be controlled by spreading warm chicken blood across his path. This was a secret which the Haitien Blacks brought with them out of Africa.

"Very good. When Mademoiselle Nancy struggled on her bed the night we came, and we beheld something taking shape upon the lawn, something with a serpent's form, which drew Monsieur Goodlowe from the house by some subtle fascination, what was it that Julius' wife cried out? '*Ayida Oueddo!*'

"Now that, my friends, is the designation of the wife and consort of *Damballah Oueddo*, the great serpent-god of the Voodoo men. She is a sort of Juno in their pantheon, second in power only to her dreadful husband, who in turn, of course, is their Jove.

"*Alors*, her involuntary cry gave me to think. I felt my way, step by careful step, like a blind man tap-tapping with his stick down some unfamiliar street. If that which we saw materialize on the lawn were indeed the form of *Ayida Oueddo*, then the charms used by the Haitien Voodoo men should prove effective here. It is the logic, *n'est-ce-pas?*

"Accordingly, I procured a plentiful supply of chickens' blood from one who deals in poultry, and had it ready for emergency last night. The 'reason why' I can not tell you; I only know that I applied such knowledge as I had to conditions as I found them. I took the chance; I gambled and I won. *Voilà tout*."

"But why'd you burn the summer-house?" Chenevert demanded.

"*Pardieu*, we 'sterilized' it," de Grandin answered. "When we had burned it we put an end to those so evil hauntings which had caused three deaths and nearly caused a fourth. Fire kills all things, my friends: microbes, animals, even wicked spirit manifestations. Tear down a haunted house, and the earth, all soaked in evil emanations of the long-dead wicked, will still give forth its exhalations in the form of what we call 'ghosts' because we lack a better name for them. More: Incorporate one little portion of that haunted place in some new building, and the new structure may prove similarly haunted. But if you burn the place—*pouf!* The hauntings and the haunters cease, and cease forever. The wood or brick or iron of which the haunted house was made acts as a base of operations for the spirit manifestation, but when it is destroyed by fire, or even super-heated, it becomes 'cleansed' in the sense the exorcists use the term, and no longer can it harbor old, unclean and sinful things."

Gordon Goodlowe, no longer skeptical, but frankly interested, put in: "Can you account for the apparition which undoubtedly caused these deaths and almost killed me, Doctor?"

De Grandin pursed his lips as he regarded the glowing end of his cigar intently. "Not altogether," he replied. "Vaguely, as the wearer of a too-tight shoe feels the approach of a storm of rain, I have a feeling that your family's connection with the former French possession of Haiti is involved, but why it should be I do not know.

"However"—he bowed ceremoniously to Nancy Goodlowe—"*Mademoiselle*, your niece has it in her power, I believe, to enlighten us."

"I?" the girl asked incredulously.

"*Précisément, Mademoiselle*. Remember how in each former case you were stricken with a so strange illness, then the serpent-thing appeared. I do not know, of course, but I much suspect that the illnesses were caused by the slow withdrawal of the psycho-physical force which we call psychoplasm in order that it might be absorbed by the evil entity which could not otherwise attain physical force and kill your father and your kinsmen. Therefore, it would seem, you have some—all innocent, I assure you—connection with this so queer business. If that be so, you may remember something which will help us."

"Remember?" the girl burst out. "Why, I've absolutely no recollection of anything. I only know that I've been ill, then lapsed into unconsciousness, and when I woke—"

"Memory is of many kinds, *Mademoiselle*," de Grandin broke in gently. "There are certain ancestral experiences which, though we may have no conscious knowledge of them, are graven deeply on the records of our subconscious memory. Consider: Have you never, in your travels, come upon some old, historic place, and had a sudden feeling of 'Why, I've been here *before*'? Consciously, and in this life, you have not, of course; yet you are greatly puzzled by the so strange familiarity of a scene which you are sure you have never seen before. Yes, of course. The explanation is presumed that some ancestor of yours underwent a deep emotional experience at that place. Incidents historically ancestral have made a deep impression on the family memory, and when proper stimuli are applied, this group memory will work its way up to the surface, as objects, long immersed in water and forgotten, will rise to the top if the pond is sufficiently agitated. You comprehend?"

"I I don't think I do," she answered with a puzzled smile. "Do you mean that something which made a marked impression on my great-great-grandmother, for instance, and of which I'd never heard, might be 'remembered' by me if I were taken to the place where it occurred, or—"

"Precisely, exactly; quite so!" he cut in enthusiastically. "You have it, *Mademoiselle*. In each of us there is some vestige of the past; we are the sum of generations long since dead, even as we are the remote ancestors of generations yet unborn. I do not say that we can do it, but with your consent and assistance, I think it possible that we may probe the past tonight, and learn whence came this curse which has so sorely tried your family. Are you willing?"

"Why, yes, of course, if Uncle Gordon says so."

"You won't hurt her in any, way?" asked Mr. Goodlowe.

"Not in the slightest, *Monsieur*; upon my honor. Be very sure of that."

"All right, then, I'll agree," our host returned.

Nancy Goodlowe seated herself in a big wing chair, hands folded demurely in her lap, head lolling back against the tapestry upholstery. Theretofore I had regarded her as a patient more than a woman—two very different things!—and the realization of her really splendid beauty, her smoldering dark eyes, her strong, white teeth, her alluring bosom and captivating turn of long, lithe limb, struck me suddenly as she lay back in her chair with just enough voluptuousness of attitude to make us realize that she knew she was a woman in a group of men, and as such the center of attraction which was not entirely scientific.

De Grandin took his stand before her, thrust his hand into the left-hand pocket of his cummerbund and drew forth the little gold note-pencil which hung upon the chain to the other end of which was fixed his clinical thermometer. "*Mademoiselle*," he ordered softly, "you will be good enough to look at this—at its very tip, if you please. So? Good. Observe it closely."

Deliberately, as one who beats time to a slow andante tune, he wove the little, gleaming pencil back and forth, describing arabesques and intricate, interlacing figures in the air. Nancy Goodlowe watched him languidly from under long, black eyelashes. Gradually, her attention fixed. We saw her eyes follow every motion of the pencil, finally converge toward each other until it seemed she made some sort of grotesque grimace; then the lids were lowered on her purple eyes, and her head, propped against the chair-back, moved slightly sidewise as the neck muscles relaxed. Her folded hands fell loosely open on her silk-clad knees, and she was, to all appearances, sleeping peacefully. Presently the regular, light heaving of her bosom and the softly sibilated, even breathing, told us she had, indeed, fallen asleep.

The little Frenchman put his pencil in his pocket, crossed the room on tiptoe and stroked her forehead and temples with a quick light touch. "*Mademoiselle*," he whispered, "can you hear me?"

"I can hear you," answered Nancy Goodlowe in a soft and drowsy voice.

"*Bien, ma belle*; you will please project your mental eye upon the screen of memory. Go back, *Mademoiselle*, until you reach the time when first your family crossed the trail of *Ayida Oueddo*, and tell us what it is you see. You hear?"

"I hear."

"You will obey?"

"I will try."

For something like five minutes we sat there, our eyes intent upon the sleeping girl. She rested easily in the big chair, her lips a little parted, her light, even breathing so faint that we could scarcely hear it, but no sign or token did she give that she had seen a thing of which she might tell.

"Ask her if—" Gordon Goodlowe began, but:

"*S-s-s-st!*" de Grandin cut him short. "Be quiet, stupid one, she is—*grand Dieu*, observe!"

As though the room had suddenly become chilled, *Nancy Goodlowe's breath was visible*. Like the steaming vapor seen upon a freezing winter day, a light, halitous cloud, faintly white, tangible as exhaled smoke from a cigarette, was issuing from between the young girl's parted lips.

I felt a sudden shiver coursing down my spine; one of those causeless fits of nervous cold which, occurring independently of outside stimuli, make us say "someone is walking over my grave." Then, definitely, the room grew colder. The humid, midsummer heat gave way to a chilliness which seemed to affect the soul as well as the body; a dull, biting hardness of cold suggestive of the limitless freezing eternities of interstellar space. I heard de Grandin's small, strong teeth click together like a pair of castanets, but his gaze remained intently on the sleeping girl and the gray-white mist which floated from her mouth. "Psychoplasm!" I heard him mutter, half believingly.

The smoke-like cloud hung suspended in the dead-still atmosphere of the room a moment; then gently, as though wafted by a breeze, it eddied slowly toward the farther wall, hung motionless again, and gradually spread out, like the smoke-screen laid by a military airplane, a drifting, gently billowing, but thoroughly opaque curtain, obscuring the wall from ceiling to baseboard.

It is difficult to describe what happened next. Slowly, in the gray-white wreaths of vapor there seemed to generate little points of bluish light, mere tiny specks of phosphorescence scintillant in the still smoke-screen. Gradually, but with ever-quickening tempo, they thickened and multiplied till they floated like a maze of dancing midges, spinning their luminant dance until they seemed to coalesce into little nebulæ of light as large as glowing cigarette-ends, but burning all the while with an intense, blue, eery light. It was as if, in place of the smoke-vapor, the room was cut in twain by a curtain of solid, opaque moonlight.

Gradually the glowing nebulæ changed from their spinning movement to a slow, weaving motion. The luminous curtain was breaking up, forming a definite pattern of highlights and shadows; a picture, as when the acid etches deeply in the copper of a half-tone plate, was taking form before our eyes—we were looking, as through the proscenium of a theater, into another room.

It was a beautiful apartment, regal in its lavishness as though it formed some portion of a royal palace. Walls were spread with Flemish tapestries, chairs and couches were of carven walnut and dull-red mahogany, rare specimens of faience stood on gilt-legged, marble-topped tables. A massive clock, with dial of beaten silver and hands of hammered gold, swung its jeweled pendulum in a case of polished ebony.

Against a chaste white-marble mantelpiece there leaned a woman in a golden gown. She was a charming creature, scarce larger than a child, with small, delicate features of cameo clarity, soft, wavy hair cut rather short and clustering round her neck and ears in a multitude of tiny ringlets. Her eyes were large and dark, her lips full and red; her teeth, as she smiled sadly, were small and white as bits of shell-pearl. There was, too, a peculiar quality to her skin, not dark with sunburn, nor yet with the olive-darkness of the Spaniard or Italian, but rather golden-pink, in perfect complement to the golden tissue of her high-waisted, sleeveless gown. I looked at her in wonder for a moment; then—

"A quadroon!" I classified her, the product of a mixture of two races, a lovely mixed-caste offspring of miscegenation, more beautiful than ninety of each hundred whites, inheriting only the perfection of form and carriage of black ancestors from the Congo.

A door at the farther end of the apartment opened quickly, but soundlessly, and a young man hastened forward. He was in military dress, the uniform of a French officer of a hundred and fifty years ago, but the shoulders of his scarlet-faced white coat were decorated with knots of yarn instead of the more customary epaulets. He paused before the girl, booted heels together, and bowed stiffly from the waist above the pale-gold hand she gave him with the charming precise grace I had so often seen in Jules de Grandin. As he raised her fingers to his lips I saw that like hers, his skin was pale mat gold, and in his dark-brown, wavy hair there was the evidence of African descent.

His lips moved swiftly, but no sound came from them, nor did we hear what she replied. With a start I realized we were witnessing a pantomime, a picture charged with action and swift motion, but silent as the cinematograph before the "movies" became vocal.

What they said we could not tell, but that the young man bore some tidings of importance was evident; that he urged the girl to some course was equally apparent, and that she refused, although with great reluctance and distress, was obvious.

The entrance of the room was darkened momentarily as a third actor strode upon the scene. Clothed in white linen, booted and spurred, a heavy riding-whip in his hand, he fairly swaggered through the choicely furnished room. No quadroon this, no slightest hint of Africa was in his straight, dark hair or sunburned features; this was a member of the dominant, inevitably conquering white race, and, by his features, an American or Englishman. As he drew near the girl and the young officer I realized with a start of quick surprise that the latest comer might have been Gordon Goodlowe at thirty, or perhaps at thirty-five.

He looked with mingled anger and contempt upon the other two a moment, then shot a quick, imperious question at the woman. The girl made answer, wringing her slim hands in a very ecstasy of pleading, but the man turned from her and again addressed the youthful soldier. What answer he received I could not tell, but that it angered him was certain, for without a second's warning he raised his riding-whip and cut the youth across the face with its plaited thong. Blow after blow be rained upon the unresisting boy, and finally, flinging away the scourge, he resorted to his fists, felled the trembling lad to the floor and kicked him as he might have kicked a dog.

I stared in horror at the exhibition of brutality, but even as I looked the picture was obscured, the moving figures faded in a blur of smoky haze, and once again we found ourselves staring at a wall of idly drifting vapor.

Again the little sparkling lights began to dance within the smoke, and now they spun and wove until another scene took form before us. It was a bedroom into which we looked. A tall, four-poster bedstead stood in the foreground, while bureaus and dressing-tables of carved apple-wood were in the corners. Light curtains of some cotton stuff swayed gently at the windows, and across the darkened chamber a shaft of moonlight cut a swath as clear and bright as a spotlight on a darkened stage.

Beside a toilet table stood the girl we'd seen before, more beautiful and winsome in her nightdress of sheer cambric than she had been when clothed in cloth-of-gold. Sadly she regarded her reflection in the oval, gold-framed mirror as she drew a comb of tortoise-shell through her curling, jet-black ringlets; then, as she saw another image in the glass, she straightened in an attitude of panic fear.

Across her creamy shoulders leered the face of the white man who had thrashed the soldier in the scene we had seen before, and now the shadow gave way to the substance as the man himself half walked, half staggered into the room. That he was drunk was evident; that he had drunk until the latent beast was raised in him was also patent as he lurched across the room unsteadily, grasped the trembling girl in his arms and crushed her to him, bruising her protesting lips with kisses which betrayed no trace of love, but were afire with blazing passion.

The girl's slim form bent like a taut bow in his grasp, as she struggled futilely to break away; then, as her groping hands fluttered across the dressing-table's marble top, we saw her slender fingers close upon a slim, thin-bladed dagger, The fine steel, no thicker than a knitting-needle, gleamed in the ray of moonlight as it flashed in an arc, then fleshed itself in the man's back an inch or so beneath the shoulder-blade.

He let her go and fell back with a grimace of mingled rage and pain, a serio-comic expression of surprise spreading on his liquor-flushed and sunburned features. Then like a pouncing beast of prey, he leaped on her.

As a terrier might shake a rat or a savage tomcat maul a luckless mouse, he shook her, swaying her slim shoulders till her head bobbed giddily and her short hair waved flag-like back and forth. Protesting helplessly, she opened her mouth, and the force with which he shook her drove her teeth together on her tongue so that blood gushed from her mouth in a bright spate. Now, not content with shaking, he beat her with his doubled fists, striking her to the floor in a little, huddled heap, then raising her again so that he might once more knock her down.

The brutal beating lasted till I would have put my hand before my eyes to shut the cruel sight out, but quickly as it started it was done. A soundless cry came from the girl's tormenter, and he raised his hand across his shoulder, attempting to assuage the flow of blood; then, half turning as he grasped at empty air, he fell face-forward to the floor. We saw a wide, red stain upon the linen of his shirt as he lay there twitching with convulsive spasms.

The white-gauze curtain at the chamber window fluttered with a sudden movement not caused by the midnight breeze, and a slim, brown hand was thrust across the sill. Between the parted folds of curtain we caught a glimpse of a scarred countenance, the lash-marked face of the young soldier whom we had seen the white man beat. For a moment the face was silhouetted against the background of the night; then the slim hand opened, letting fall some object at the trembling girl's bare feet. It was the dried wing of a tropic vampire-bat.

Once more the scene dissolved in haze, and once again it formed, and now we looked upon a tableau of midnight jungle. Resinous torches, some thrust into the earth, some fastened to the trunks of palm-trees, cast a glow of ruddy light upon the scene. A cloud of heavy smoke ascended from the torches, forming an inky canopy which blotted out the stars. Seated on the ground in a great circle was a vast concourse of blacks, men and women in macabre silhouette against the flickering torchlight, some beating wildly on small, double-headed drums, others, circling in and out in the mazes of a shuffling, grotesque dance. Lewd, lecherous, lascivious, the postures of the dancers melted quickly from one to another, each more instinct with lechery than the one preceding. Some semi-naked, so nude as at the instant of their birth, they danced, and we knew that something devilish was toward, for though we could not catch the tempo of the drums, we felt the tension of the atmosphere.

Now the drummers ceased to hammer on their tom-toms; now the dancers ceased to pose and shuffle in the blood-red glare of torchlight; now the crowd gave back, and through the aisle of panting, crowding bronze-black bodies strode a figure. Her head was bound about with scarlet cloth, and a wisp of silk of the same color was wrapped about her loins, leaving the remainder of her body starkly naked, save for a heavy coating of white pigment. Straight from her shoulders, to right and left, she held her arms, and in each hand was clutched by the feet a cock, one white, the other black. With slow, gliding steps she paced on white-smeared, slim bare feet between the lines of crouching figures who watched her avidly in hot-eyed, slobbering passion.

Before a low and box-shaped altar she came to pause, her arms straight out before her. Her head bent low as an aged, wrinkle-bitten Negress leaped from the shadows and waved a gleaming butcher-knife twice in the lambent torchlight, decapitating a cockerel at each sweep of the steel. The fowls' heads dropped to earth and the painted priestess lifted high the sacrifices, their wings fluttering, their cut necks spurting blood. Slowly she began to wheel and turn beneath the gory shower, then faster, faster, faster, until it seemed that she was spinning like a top. We saw her face a moment as, all dewed with blood, she turned it toward the altar. It was the girl whom we'd seen twice before.

And now the wrinkled crone who had slain the cocks leaped monkey-nimble to the box-like altar, snatched frenziedly at the strong lock and hasp which held the cover down, and flung the lid back from the chest. All eyes, save those of the girl who still spun whirlingly before the sanctuary, were intent upon the box. I watched it, too, wondering what fresh obscenity could be disclosed. Then, with a gasping intake of my breath, I saw.

Slowly, very slowly, there reared from the box the head, the neck, an eight-foot length of body of a great white snake! *Ayida Oueddo*, the White Serpent Goddess, the deity of Voodoo rites! *Ayida Oueddo*, the Goddess of Slaughter— this girl was a vowed priestess of her bloody cult!

The scene obscured once more, then slowly took new form. We stood within a crowded courtroom. Three judges, two in black, one in red, were seated on the dais; flanked by two gendarmes with muskets and fixed bayonets, the golden girl, now clothed in simple white, with a wide straw hat tied underneath her chin with satin ribbons, stood before the court, while the white man she had stabbed stood forward to accuse her.

We saw him hurl his accusation at her, we saw the spectators turn whispering to each other as the evidence was given; we saw her plead in her defense. At last we saw the center judge, the judge all gowned in red, address the girl, and saw her curtsey deeply as she made reply.

We saw the judges' heads, two capped with black, one crowned with red, bow together as they took counsel of each other; then, though we heard no words, we saw the sentence of the court as the red-robed center figure delivered judgment in two syllables:

"À *mort*."

Sentence of death was passed, and she took it smilingly, curtseying low as though to thank the judges for a courtesy bestowed.

We looked upon a public square, so hot beneath the tropic noonday sun that a constant flickering of heat-rays arose from off the kidney stones which formed the pavement. The square was lined with crowding men and women, rich townspeople, wealthy planters and their womenfolk, colored men of every shade from ebony to well-creamed coffee; a battalion of white *infanterie de ligne* in spotless uniforms, a company of mulatto *chasseurs* in their distinctive regalia. In the center, where the sun beat mercilessly, stood a scaffold with an X-shaped frame upon it.

The executioner, a burly, great-paunched brute whose sleeveless shirt disclosed gorilla muscles, was attended by two giant Negroes who looked as though they should have been head-butchers in an abattoir.

A rolling, long tattoo of drums was sounded by the troops' field music as they led her from a house which faced the square, a nun upon her left, a black-frocked priest in shovel hat upon her right, head bowed, lips moving in a ceaseless, mumbled prayer. A youthful *sous-lieutenant*, his boyish mouth hard-set with loathing at the job he had to do, marched before; a squad of sweating gendarmes closed the file.

She was dressed in spotless linen, a straight and simple frock of the fashion which one sees in portraits of Empress Josephine, a wide straw hat bedecked with pink-silk roses and tied coquettishly with wide pink ribbons knotted underneath her chin. Satin shoes laced with narrow ribbons of black velvet round the ankles were upon her little feet, and she held a satin sunshade in her hand.

There was something of *opera bouffe* about it all, this gay parade of wealth and fashion and flashing military uniforms called out to witness one slim girl walk unconcernedly across the public square.

But the thread of comedy snapped quickly as she reached the scaffold's foot. Closing her frivolous parasol, she gave it to the nun, then turned her back upon the executioner while her golden-flecked brown eyes searched the crowd which waited breathless at the margin of the square. At last she found the object which she sought, a tall, broad-shouldered white man in the costume of a planter, who lolled at ease beneath a palm-tree's shade and watched the spectacle through half-closed eyes. Her hand went out, aiming like a pointed weapon, as she hurled a curse at him. We could not hear the words she spoke, but the slow articulation of the syllables enabled us to read her lips:

"As I am crushed this day, so shall you and yours be crushed by my *ouanga*."

Then they stripped the linen garment off her, tore off her hat and little satin shoes, her silken stockings and daintily embroidered lingerie. Stark, utterly birth-naked, they bound her to the planks which formed a six-foot X and broke her fragile bones with a great bar of iron. We could not hear the piteous cries of agony which came each time the executioner beat on her arms and legs with his heavy iron cudgel, we only saw the velvet, gold-hued flesh give way beneath the blows, the slim and sweetly molded limbs go limp and formless as the bones within them broke beneath the flailings of the bar. At last we saw the writhing, childish mouth contort to a scream of final agonized petition: "*Jésus!*" Then the lovely head fell forward between her outstretched arms, and we knew that it was over. Her sufferings were done, and the justice which demanded that the black or mixed-blood who raised hand against a white must die by torment was appeased. The scene once more dissolved in swirling, hazy clouds of mist.

The last scene was the shortest. A maddened mob of shouting, blood-drunk blacks swarmed over the great house where first we saw the girl; they smashed the priceless furniture, hacked and chopped the walls and woodwork in wild,

insensate rage, finally set the place afire. And from every hilltop, every smiling valley, every fruitful farm and bountiful plantation, rose the flames of dev-
astation and the cries of slaughtered women, men and children. The blacks
were in rebellion. Oppression brought its own reward, and those who killed and
maimed and tortured and arrogantly wrought the blood and sweat of others into
gold were killed and maimed and tortured, hounded, harassed, hunted in their
turn. The reign of France upon Saint Domingue was ended, and that centu-
ry-long saturnalia of savagery, that amazing mixture of Congo jungle and Paris
salon called the Republic of Haiti, had begun.

THE CANDLELIGHT BURNED SOFTLY in Pierre's select speakeasy. The *omelette
soufflé* (made with Peychaud bitters) had been washed down with a bottle of
tart *vin blanc*; now, cigars aglow and liqueurs poured, we waited for de Grandin
to begin.

"*Tiens*, but it is simplicity's own self," he informed us. "Does not the whole
thing leap all quickly to the eye? But certainly. Your remote kinsman, Monsieur
Goodlowe, the one you told us first established family holdings in the Island of
Saint Domingue, which now we know as Haiti, undoubtlessly found life weari-
some in the tropics. Women of his race were rare—they were mostly married or
ugly, or both, and, besides, white women pine away and fail beneath the tropic
sun. Not so with the mixed-breeds, however. They, with tropic sunshine in
their veins, flourish like the native vegetation in equatorial lands. Accordingly,
Monsieur l'Ancêtre did as many others did, and took a quarter-blooded beauty
for his wife—without benefit of clergy or of wedding ring. Yes, it has been done
before and since, my friends.

"Now, consider the condition on that island at that time: There were 40,000
whites, of all classes, 24,000 mulattoes and lesser mixed-bloods, whom the law
declared to be free citizens, and over half a million barbarous black slaves. A
very devil of a place. The free mulattoes were the greatest problem. Technically
free as any Frenchman, they yet were scorned and hated by their white co-citi-
zens, many of whom shared paternal ancestors with them. The *affranchis*—free
mulattoes—were imposed upon in every way. They sat apart in church and at
the theater; they were forbidden to wear certain cloths and colors decreed by
fashion; their very regiments of soldiers wore a distinctive uniform. Moreover,
they were made the butt of hatred in the courts. A white man killing a mulatto
might be sentenced to the galleys, or be made to pay a fine. In a very flagrant
case, he might even suffer the inconvenience of being put to death, but even
then his comfort was infringed upon as little as was possible. He was hanged or
shot. At any rate, he died with expedition, and without unnecessary delay. The
mulatto who so far forgot himself as to kill or even to attempt the life of a white,
was prejudged before he entered court, and inevitably perished miserably upon

the torture frame, his bones smashed to splinters by the executioner's iron bar. But no; it was not very pleasant to be a mulatto in Saint Domingue those days.

"Very well, let us start from there. When I beheld those West Indian Negroes in your service, and heard their talk of *loogaroos*, and when I learned an ancestor of yours had settled in Haiti in the olden days, I determined that the whole thing smelled of Voodoo. You know how Julius and I outwitted that white ghost-snake which had killed your relatives; you know my theory of its appearance on your lawn. Very good; we knew how it came there; the *why* was something else. But certainly.

"Mademoiselle Nancy was inextricably mixed up in the case. The evil genius resident in the fiber of the haunted summer-house drew strength and power to work material evil to your family from her. Therefore, having rendered the haunting demon powerless, I decided to have Mademoiselle Nancy act as our spirit-guide and open for us the door to yesterday.

"*Bien*. Accordingly, I asked her to 'remember.' There are many kinds of memory, my friends. Oh, yes. We remember, by example, what happened yesterday, or last year, or when we were very young. Ah-ha, but we remember other things, as well, although we do not know it. Take, for example, the common dream of falling through the air. That is a 'memory,' though the dreamer may never have fallen from a height. Ha, but his remote ancestors who dwelt in trees, they fell, or were in peril of falling, daily. To fall in those days meant injury, and injury meant inability to fight with or escape from an enemy. Therefore, not to fall was the greatest care the race had on its mind. Generations of fearing falls, taking care not to fall, produced a mass memory of the unpleasant results of failing. But naturally. Accordingly, one of today remembers in his dreams the horror of falling from the tree-tops.

"Consider further: Though everyone has dreamed he fell—and often wakened from such dreams with the sweat of terror on his brow—we never have this memory of falling while we are awake. Why so? Because our waking, conscious, modern personality knows no such danger. For that matter, we never have the sense of fleeing from a savage animal while we wake, but when we sleep—*grand Diable*, how often, in a nightmare, do we seek to flee some monstrous beast, and suffer horrors at our inability to run. Another racial memory— that of our remote cave-dwelling ancestors caught fast in a morass while some saber-toothed tiger or cave-bear hunted them for dinner! The answer, then, is that when we resign our waking, workaday consciousness to sleep we open the sealed doors to yesterday and all the different personalities the sum of which we are rise up to plague us. We suffer hunger, thirst or shipwreck which our ancestors survived, though we, as individuals never knew these things at all.

"*Bien tout*. These naughty dreams come to us unannounced. We can not call them up, we can not bid them stay away. But what if we are put to sleep hypnotically, then bidden to remember some specific incident in our long chain of ancestral memory? May not the subconscious mind walk straight to the cabinet in which that memory is filed and bring it to the light?

"That is the question which I asked myself when I considered sending Mademoiselle Nancy back along the trail of memory. It was only an experiment; but it was successful, as you saw.

"Mademoiselle Nancy is a psychic. Like the best of the professional mediums, she possesses that rare substance called psychoplasm in great abundance. Once she was *en rapport* with the olden days she did more than tell us of them, she showed them to us.

"Very well. This young lady of mixed blood whom your ancestor had taken for his light o' love, Monsieur Goodlowe, was also a member of the inner circle of the Voodooists. She was a *mamaloi*, or priestess of the serpent-goddess *Ayida Oueddo*, the consort of the great snake-god *Damballah*.

"Voodoo was a species of Freemasonry from which the whites were barred; many mulattoes and even people with smaller degrees of African blood were active in it. When first we saw her, she was talking with a young mulatto soldier. He had evidently come to summon her to attend a meeting of the Voodooists, and she was unwilling. Perhaps she felt such savage orgies were beneath her; possibly she had put them behind her as a sincere Christian. In any event, she was unwilling to obey the summons and fulfil her duty as a priestess. Then came her master, who was also your ancestor.

"You saw how he abused the messenger of Voodoo. Like all the whites, he hated the dark mysteries of the Voodooists—probably his hatred was akin to that which normal men feel for the snake; one part hate, three parts fear. Most white men thus regarded the secret cult which was, at the end, to knit the slaves and free mulattoes into a single force and sweep the white men from the island.

"Perhaps all would have been well, had not your ancestor become intoxicated that night. But drunk he got, and in his drunken fury he abused her.

"She stabbed him in the back, and perhaps, as much to spite him as for any other reason, determined to act as priestess at the altar of *Ayida Oueddo*. But whatever her decision was, the matter was taken from her hands when the messenger reappeared outside her bedroom window and dropped the bat wing at her feet.

"That bat wing, he was to the Voodooist what the signal of distress is to the Master Mason or the fiery cross is to a member of a Scottish clan. It is a summons which could not be denied. By no means; no, indeed.

"We saw her serve *Ayida Oueddo's* altar, we saw her when she had been apprehended, we saw her led to execution. Ha, and did we not also see her single out your ancestor and hurl her dying curse at him? Did not she say: 'As I am crushed this day, so shall you and yours be crushed by my *ouanga'*? But certainly.

"*Ouanga* in their *patois* is a most elastic term. There is no literal translation for it; vaguely, it means the same as 'medicine' when used by the Red Indian, or 'magic' when spoken of by the Black African, or 'devil-devil' when used by natives of the South Sea islands. Define it accurately we can not; understand it we can. It is the working, as of a charm, through some unknown super-physical agency.

"*Eh bien*, did it not work? I shall say as much. Three of your family died horribly, with their bones crushed, even as were that poor young girl's on that dreadful day of execution so long ago. Only by the mercy of heaven and the cleverness of Jules de Grandin are you alive tonight, and not all crushed to death, *Monsieur*."

"But—" I began.

"But be grilled upon hell's hottest griddle," cut in Jules de Grandin. "I thirst. *Cordieu*, Sahara at its dryest is as the rolling billows of the great Atlantic compared to my poor throat, my friend.

"*Garçon, quatre cognacs—tout vite; s'il vous plaît!*"

A Gamble in Souls

W E CROSSED THE BIG, cement-floored room with its high-set, steel-barred windows and whitewashed walls, and paused before the heavy iron grille stopping the entrance to a narrow, tunnel-like corridor. Our guide cast a sidelong, half-apologetic look in our direction. "Visitors aren't—er—usually permitted past this point," he told us. "This is the 'jumping-off place,' you know, and the fellows in there aren't ordinary convicts, so—"

"Perfectly, *Monsieur*," Jules de Grandin's voice was muted to a whisper in deference to our surroundings, but had lost none of its authoritativeness with lessened volume. "One understands; but you will recall that we are not ordinary visitors. Me, I have credentials from the *Service Sûreté*, and in addition the note from *Monsieur le Gouverneur*, does it not say—"

"Quite so," the warden's secretary assented hastily. Distinguished foreign criminologists with credentials from the French Secret Police and letters of introduction from the governor of the state were not to be barred from the penitentiary's anteroom of death, however irregular their presence might be. "Open the gate, Casey," he ordered the uniformed guardian of the grille, standing aside politely to permit us to precede him.

The death house was L-shaped, the long bar consisting of a one-story corridor some sixteen feet in width, its south wall taken up by a row of ten cells, each separated from its neighbor by a twelve-inch brick wall and from the passageway by steel cage-doors. Through these the inmates looked upon a blank, bleak whitewashed wall of brick, pierced at intervals by small, barred windows set so high that even the pale north light could not strike directly into the cells. Each few feet, almost as immobile as sentries on fixed post, blue-uniformed guards backed against the northern wall, somnolent eyes checking every movement of the men caged in the little cells which lined the south wall. Straight before us at the passage end, terrifying in its very commonplaceness, was a solid metal door, wide enough for three to pass abreast, grained and painted in imitation of golden oak. SILENCE, proclaimed the legend on its lintel. This was the "one-way door" leading to the execution chamber which, with the autopsy room immediately adjoining, formed the foot-bar of the building's L. The air was heavy with the scent peculiar to inefficient plumbing, poor ventilation and the stale smoke of cigarettes. The place seemed shadowed by the vulture-wings of hopelessness.

We paused to gaze upon the threshold, nostrils stinging with the acrid efflu-vium of caged humanity, ears fairly aching with the heaviness of silence which weighed upon the confined air. "Oh, my dear, my darling"—it was a woman's sob-strangled voice which came to us from the gateway of the farthest cell—"I just found out. I—I never knew, my dear, until last night, when he told me. Oh, what shall I do? I—I'll go to the governor—tell him everything! Surely, surely, he'll—"

The man's low-voiced reply cut in: "No use, my dear; there's nothing but your word, you know, and Larry has only to deny it. No use; no use!" He bowed his head against the grating of his cell a moment; then, huskily: "This makes it easier though, Beth dear; it's been the thought that you didn't know, and never could, that hurt, hurt more than my brother's perfidy, even. Oh, my dear, I—"

"I love you, Lonny," came the woman's hoarse avowal. "Will it help you to know that—to hear it from my lips?"

"Help?" A seraphic smile lighted up the tired, lined face behind the bars. "Help? Oh, my darling, when I walk that little way tomorrow night I'll *feel* your love surrounding me; feel the pressure of your hand in mine to give me courage at the end—" He broke off shortly, sobs knotting in his throat, but through his eyes looked such love and adoration that it brought the tears unbidden to my lids and raised a great lump in my throat.

He reached his long, artistically fine hands acros the little space which sep-arated his cell door from the screen of strong steel mesh which guards had set between him and the woman, and she pressed her palm against the wire from her side. A moment they stood thus; then:

"Please, please!" she turned beseechingly to the man in blue who occupied a chair behind her. "Oh, please take the screen away a moment. I—I want so to kiss him good-bye!"

The man looked undecided for a moment, then sudden resolution forming in his immobile face, put forth his hand to move the wire netting.

"Here!" began our guide, but the word was never finished, for quicker than a striking snake, de Grandin's slim, white hand shot out, seized him by the neck immediately below the *medulla oblongata*, exerting sudden steel-tight pressure so that the hail stopped abruptly on a strangled, inarticulate syllable and the man's mouth hung open, round and empty as the entrance to a cave. "*Monsieur*," the little Frenchman promised in an almost soundless whisper, "if you bid him stop I shall most surely kill you." He relaxed the pressure momentarily, and:

"It's against the regulations!" our guide expostulated softly. "He knows he's not allowed to—"

"Nevertheless," de Grandin interrupted, "the screen shall be removed, *Monsieur*. Name of a little blue man, would you deny them one last kiss—when he stands upon death's door-sill? But no!"

The screen had been removed, and, although the steel bars intervened, the man and woman clung and kissed, arms circled round each other, lips and hearts together in a final, long farewell. "Now," gasped the prisoner, releasing the woman's lips from his for an instant, "one long, long kiss, my dearest dear, and then good-bye. I'll close my eyes and stop my ears so I can't hear you leaving, and when I open them again, you'll be gone, but I'll have the memory of your lips on mine when—when—" He faltered, but:

"My dear; my *dear!*" the woman moaned, and stopped his mouth with burning kisses.

"*Parbleu*, it is sacrilege that we should look at them—about face!" whispered Jules de Grandin, and swung himself about so that his back was to the cells. Obedient to his hands upon our elbows, the warden's secretary and I turned, too, and stood thus till the soft tap-tap of the woman's heels informed us she had left the death house.

We followed slowly, but ere we left the place of the condemned I cast a last look at the prisoner. He was seated at the little table which, with a cot and chair, constituted the sole furniture of his cell. He sat with head bowed, elbow on knee, knuckles pressed against his lips, not crying, but staring dry-eyed straight ahead, as though he could already vision the long vistas of eternity into which the state would hurl him the next night.

A long line of men in prison uniform marched through the corridor as we reentered the main building of the penitentiary. Each bore an empty tin cup in one hand, an empty tin plate in the other. They were going to their evening meal.

"Would you care to see 'em eat?" the warden's secretary asked as the files parted at the guard's hoarse "Gangway!" and we walked between the rows of men.

"*Mais non*," de Grandin answered. "Me, I, too, desire to eat tonight, and the spectacle of men eating like caged brutes would of a certainty destroy my appetite. Thank you for showing us about, *Monsieur*, and please, I beg, do not report the guard's infraction of the regulations in taking down that screen. It was a work of mercy, no less, my friend!"

THE MILES CLICKED SWIFTLY off on my speedometer as we drove along the homeward road. De Grandin was for the most part sunk in moody silence, lighting one evil-smelling French cigarette from the glowing stump of another,

occasionally indulging in some half-articulate bit of highly individualized pro-
fanity; once or twice he whipped the handkerchief from his left cuff and wiped
his eyes half-furtively. As we neared the outskirts of Harrisonville he turned to
me, small eyes blazing, thin lips retracted from small even teeth.

"Hell and furies, and ten million small blue devils in the bargain, Friend
Trowbridge," he exclaimed, "why must it be? Is there no way that human justice
can be vindicated without the punishment descending on the innocent no less
than on the guilty? Me, I damn think—" He turned away for a moment, and:

"*Mordieu*, my friend, be careful!" he clutched excitedly at my elbow with
his left hand, while with the other he pointed dramatically toward the figure
which suddenly emerged from the shadowy evergreens bordering the road and
flitted like a wind-blown leaf across the spot of luminance cast by my headlights.

"*Cordieu*, she will not die of senility if she persists in such a way of walking—" he continued, then interrupted himself with a shout as he flung both feet
over the side of the car and rushed down the road to grapple with the woman
whose sudden appearance had almost sent us skidding into the wayside ditch.

Nor was his intervention a split-second too soon; for even as he reached
her side the mysterious woman had run to the center of the highway bridge and
was drawing herself up, preparatory to leaping over the parapet to the rushing
stream which foamed among a bed of jagged rocks some fifty feet below.

"Stop it, *Mademoiselle*! Desist!" he ordered sharply, seizing her shoulders in
his small, strong hands and dragging her back from her perilous perch by main
force.

She fought like a cornered wildcat. "Let me go!" she raged, struggling in the
little Frenchman's embrace, then, finding her efforts to break loose of no avail,
writhed suddenly around and clawed at his cheeks with desperation-strength-
ened fingers. "Let me go; I want to die; I must die; I *will* die, I tell you! Let me
go!"

De Grandin shifted his grip from her shoulders to her wrists and shook
her roughly, as a terrier might shake a rat. "Silence, *Mademoiselle*; be still!" he
ordered curtly. "Cease this business of the monkey at once, or *pardieu*"—he
administered another vigorous shake—"I shall be forced to tie you!"

I added my efforts to his, grasping the struggling woman by the elbows and
forcing her into the twin shafts of light thrown by the car's driving-lamps.

Stooping, the Frenchman retrieved her hat and placed it on her dark head
at a decidedly rakish angle, then regarded her speculatively a moment. "Will
you promise to restrain yourself if we release you, *Mademoiselle?*" he asked after
a few seconds' silent scrutiny.

The girl—she was little more—regarded us sullenly a moment, then burst
into a sharp, cachinnating laugh. "You've just postponed it for a while," she

answered with a shrug of her narrow shoulders. "I'll kill myself as soon as you leave me, anyway. You might as well have saved yourselves the trouble."

"U'm?" de Grandin murmured. "Exactly, precisely, quite so, *Mademoiselle*. I had that very thought in mind, and it is for that reason that we shall not leave you for a little so small moment. Pains of a dyspeptic pig, are we then murderers? But of course not. Tell us where you live, and we shall do ourselves the honor of escorting you there."

She faced us with quivering nostrils and heaving, tumultuous bosom, anger flashing from her eyes, a diatribe of invective seemingly ready to spill from her parted lips. She had a rather pretty, high-bred face unnaturally large, dark eyes, seeming larger because of the violet half-moons under them; death-pale skin contrasting sharply with the little tendrils of dark, curling hair which hung about her cheeks beneath the rim of her wide leghorn hat. There was something vaguely familiar about her features, about the soft, throaty contralto of her voice, about the way she moved her hands to emphasize her words. I drew my brows together in an effort at remembrance, even as de Grandin spoke.

"*Mademoiselle*," he told her with a bow, "you are too beautiful to die, accordingly—ah, *parbleu*, I know you now!

"It is the lady of the prison, my good Trowbridge!" He turned to me, wonder and compassion struggling for the mastery of his face. "But certainly." To her: "Your change of dress deceived me at the first, *ma pauvre*."

He drew away a pace, regarding her intently. "I take back my remark," he admitted slowly. "You have an excellent reason for desiring to be rid of this cruel world of men and man-made justice, *Mademoiselle*, nor am I any stupid, moralistic fool who would deny you such poor consolation as death may bring, but"—he made a deprecating gesture—"this is not the time nor the place nor manner, *Mademoiselle*. It were a shame to break your lovely body on those rocks down there, and—have you thought of this?—there is a poor one's body to be claimed and given decent burial when the debts of justice have been paid. Can not you wait until that has been done, then—"

"Justice?" cried the woman in a shrill, hard voice. "*Justice*? It's the most monstrous miscarriage of justice there ever was! It's murder, I tell you; wilful murder, and—"

"Undoubtlessly," he assented in a soothing voice, "but what is one to do? The law's decree—"

"The law!" she scoffed. "Here's one time where the strength of sin really is the law! Law's supposed to punish the guilty and protect the innocent, isn't it? Why doesn't the law let Lonny go, and take that red-handed murderer who did the killing in his place? Because the law says a wife can't testify against her husband! Because a perjured villain's testimony has sent a blameless man to death—that's why!"

De Grandin turned a fleeting glance on me and made a furtive, hardly noticeable gesture toward the car. "But certainly, *Mademoiselle*," he nodded, "the laws of men are seldom perfect. Will not you come with us? You shall tell us your story in detail, and if there is aught that we can do to aid you, please be assured that we shall do it. At any rate, if you will give consideration to your plan to kill yourself, and having talked with us still think you wish to die, I promise to assist you, even in that. We are physicians, and we have easily available some medicines which will give you swift and painless release, nor need anyone be the wiser. You consent? Good, excellent, *bien*. If you please, *Mademoiselle*." He bowed with courtly, Continental courtesy as he assisted her into my car.

She sat between us, her hands lying motionless and flaccid, palms upward, in her lap. There was something monotonous, flat and toneless, in her deep and rather husky voice as she began her recitation. I had heard women charged with murder testifying in their own defense in just such voices. Emotion played upon too harshly and too long results in a sort of anesthesia, and emphasis becomes impossible.

"My name's Beth Cardener—Elizabeth Cardener," she began without preliminary. "I am the wife of Lawrence Cardener, the sculptor. You know him? No? No matter.

"I am twenty-nine years old and have been married three years. My husband and I have known each other since childhood. Our families had adjoining houses in the city and adjoining country places at Seagirt. My husband and I and his twin brother, Alonzo, played together on the beach and in the ocean in summer and went to school together in the winter, though the boys were two grades above me, being three years older. They looked so much alike that no one but their family and I—who was with them so much that I was almost like a sister—could tell them apart, and Lonny was always getting into trouble for things which Larry did. Sometimes they'd change clothes and one would go to call on the girl with whom the other had an engagement, and no one ever knew the difference. They never fooled me, though; I could usually tell them by a slight difference in their voices, but if I weren't quite sure, there was one infallible clue. Lonny had a little scar behind his left ear. I struck him there with a sand-spade when he was six and I was three. He and Larry had been teasing me, and I flew into a fury. He happened to be nearer, and got the blow. I was terribly frightened after I'd done it, and cried far more than he did. The wound wasn't really serious, but it left a little, white scar, not more than half-an-inch in length, which never disappeared. So, when the boys would try to play a joke on me I'd make them let me turn their ears forward; then I could be certain which was Lonny and which Larry.

"When the war came and the boys were seventeen, both were wild to go, but their father wouldn't let them. Finally Larry ran away and joined the Canadians—they weren't particular in checking up on ages in Canada those days. Before Larry had been gone three weeks his brother joined him, and they were both assigned to the same regiment. Larry was given a lieutenancy shortly after he joined up and Lonny was made a subaltern before they sailed for France.

"Both boys were slightly gassed at the second battle of the Marne and were in recuperation camp until the termination of hostilities. They came back together, in uniform, of course, in '19, and I was in a perfect frenzy of hero-worship. I fell madly in love with both of them. Both loved me, too, and each asked me to marry him. It was hard to choose between them, but Lonny—the one I'd 'marked' with my spade when we were kids—was a little sweeter, a little gentler than his brother, and finally I accepted him. Larry showed no bitterness, and the three of us continued as close, firm friends, even after the engagement, as we'd been before.

"Lonny was determined to become a painter, while Larry had ambitions to become a sculptor, and they went off to Paris for a year of study, together, as always. We were to be married when they returned, and Larry was to be best man. We'd hoped to have a June wedding, but the boys' studies kept them abroad till mid-August, so we decided to postpone it till Thanksgiving Day, and both the boys came down to Seagirt to spend the remainder of the season.

"There was a girl named Charlotte Dey stopping at a neighbor's house, a lovely creature, exquisitely made, with red-gold hair and topaz eyes and skin as white as milk. Larry seemed quite taken with her, and she with him, and Lonny and I began to think that he'd found consolation there. We even wished in that romantic way young lovers have that Larry'd hurry up and pop the question so we could have a double wedding in November.

"You remember I told you our houses stood beside each other? We'd always been so intimate that I'd been like a member of the Cardener family, even before I was engaged to Lonny. We never thought of knocking on each others doors, and if I wanted anything from the Cardeners: or they wanted anything from our house, we were as apt to enter through one of the French windows opening on the verandas as we were to go through the front door.

"One evening, after Lonny and I had said goodnight, I happened to remember that I'd left a book in the Cardener library, and I especially wanted that book early next morning; for it had a recipe for sally lunn in it, and I wanted to get up early and make some as a surprise for Lonny next morning at breakfast. So I just ran across the intervening lawn and up the veranda steps, intent on going through the library window, getting the book and going back to bed without saying anything to anybody. I'd just mounted the steps and started down the porch toward the library when Lonny loomed up in front of me. He'd slipped on his pajamas and beach robe, and had been sitting on a porch rocker. 'Beth!' he exclaimed in a sort of nervous, almost frightened way.

"'Why, yes, it's I,' I answered, putting my hand in his and continuing to walk toward the library window.

"'You mustn't come any farther,' he suddenly told me, dragging me to a stop by the hand which he'd been holding. 'You must go back, Beth!'

"'Why, Lonny!' I exclaimed in amazement. Being told I couldn't go and come at will in the Cardener house was like being slapped in the face.

"'You must go back, please,' he answered in a sort of embarrassed, stubborn way. 'Please, Beth; I can't explain, dear; but please go, quickly!

"There was nothing else to do, so I went. I couldn't speak, and I didnt want him to see me crying and know how much he'd hurt me.

"I didn't go back to my room. Instead I walked across the stretch of lawn behind the house, down to the beach, and sat there on the sand. It was a bright September night, and the full moon made it almost light as day; so I couldn't help seeing what followed. I'd sat there on the beach for fifteen minutes, possibly, when I happened to look back. The boys' rooms opened on the side veranda and to reach the library one had to pass them. Part of the porch was full-roofed, and consequently in shadow; the remainder was roofed with slats, like a pergola, and the moonlight illuminated it almost as brightly as it did the beach and the back lawn. As I glanced back across my shoulder I saw two figures emerge from one of the French windows leading to the boys' rooms; which one I couldn't be sure, but it looked like Lonny's. One was a man in pajamas and beach robe, the other was a woman, clothed only in a light nightdress, kimono and sandals. I sat there in a sort of stupor, too surprised and horrified to move or make a sound, and as I looked the moonlight glinted on the girl's gold hair. It was Charlotte Dey.

"While I sat watching them I saw him take her in his arms and kiss her; then she ran down the steps with a little laugh, calling back across her shoulder, 'See you in the morning, Lonny.'

"'Lonny!' I couldn't believe it. There must be some mistake; the twins were still as like as reflections in a mirror, people were always mistaking them, but— 'See you in the morning, Lonny!' kept dinning in my brain like the surging of the surf at my feet. The world seemed crumbling into dust beneath me, while that endless, laughing refrain kept singing in my ears: 'See you in the morning, Lonny.'

"The man on the porch stood looking after the retreating figure of the girl as she ran across the lawns to the house where she was stopping, then drew a pack of cigarettes and a lighter from the pocket of his robe. As he bent to light the cigarette he turned toward the ocean and saw me sitting on the sand. Next instant he turned and fled, ran headlong to the window of his room, and disappeared in the darkness.

"What I had seen made me sick—actually physically sick. I wanted to run into the house and fling myself across my bed and cry my heart out, but I was too weak to rise, so I just slumped down on the sand, buried my face in my arms and began to cry. I didn't know how long I'd been lying there, praying that my heart actually would break and that I'd never see another sunrise, when I felt a hand upon my shoulder.

"'Why, Beth,' somebody said, 'whatever is the matter?'

"It was one of the boys, which one I couldn't be sure, and he was dressed in corduroy slacks, a sweater and a cap. The bare-head craze hadn't struck the country in those days.

"'Who are you?' I sobbed, for my eyes were full of tears, and I couldn't see very plainly. 'Is it Larry, or—'

"'Larry it is, old thing,' he assured me with a laugh. 'Old Lawrence in the flesh and blood, ready to do his Boy Scout's good daily deed by comforting a lady in distress. I've been taking a little tramp down the beach, looking at the moon and feeling grand and lonesome and romantic, and I come home to find you crying here, as if these sands didn't get enough salt water every day. Where's Lonny?'

"'Lonny   ' I began, but he cut in before I had a chance to finish.

"'Don't tell me you two've quarreled! Why, this was to have been his big night—one of his big nights. The old cuss intimated that he'd be able to bear my absence with true Christian fortitude this evening, as he had some very special spooning to do; so I sought consolation of the Titian-haired Charlotte, only to be told that she, too, had a heavy date. *Ergo*, as we used to say at college, here is Lawrence by his lone, after walking over ten miles of beach and looking over several thousand miles of ocean. Want to go for a swim before you turn in? Go get your bathing-clothes; I'll be with you in a jiff.' He turned to run toward the house, but I called him back.

"'Larry,' I asked, 'you're sure Lonny hinted that he'd like to be alone tonight?'

"'Certain sure; honest true, black and blue, cross my heart and hope to die!' he answered. 'The old duffer almost threw me out bodily, he was so anxious to see me go.'

"'And Charlotte,' I persisted, 'did she say what—with whom—her engagement for this evening was?'

"'Why, no,' he answered. 'I say, see here, old girl, you're not getting green-eyed, are you? Why, you know there's only one woman in the world for Lonny, and—'

"'Is there?' I interrupted grimly.

"'I'll say there is, and you're It, spelled with a capital I, just as Charlotte is the one for me. Have I your blessing when I ask her to be Mrs. Lawrence Cardener tomorrow, Beth? I'd have done it tonight, if she hadn't put me off.'

"I couldn't stand it. Lonny had betrayed us both, made a mockery of the love I'd given him and debauched the girl his brother loved. Before I realized it, I'd sobbed the whole tale out on Larry's shoulder, and before I was through we were holding each other like a pair of lost babes in the wood, and Larry was crying as hard as I.

"He was the first to recover his poise. 'No use crying over a tin of spoiled beans, as we used to say in the army,' he told me. 'He and Charlotte can have each other, if they want. I'm through with her, and him, too, the two-faced, double-crossing swine! Keep your tail up, old girl, don't let him know you know how much he's hurt you; don't let him know you know about it at all; just give him back his ring and let him go his way without an explanation.'

"'Will you take the ring back to him now?' I asked.

"'Surest thing,' he promised, 'but don't ask me to make explanations; I'm digging out tomorrow. Off to Paris the day after. Good-bye, old dear, and—better luck next time.'

"I was up early next morning, too. By sunrise I was back in Harrisonville, breaking every speed regulation on the books on the drive up from Seagirt. By noon I had my application filed for a passport; three days later I sailed for England on the *Vauban*.

"An aunt of mine was married to a London barrister and I stopped with her a while. Lonny wrote me every day, at first, but I sent his letters back unopened. Finally he came to see me, but I wouldn't meet him. He came back twice, but before he could call the third time I packed and rushed off to the country.

"Larry wrote me frequently, and from him I learned that Lonny had joined the Spanish Foreign Legion which was fighting the Riffs, later that he had been discharged and was making quite a name for himself as a painter of Oriental landscapes. He did some quite good portraits, too, and was almost famous when I came back to America after being four years abroad. Lonny tried to see me, but I managed to avoid him, except at parties when there were others about, and finally he stopped annoying me.

"Three years ago I was married to Larry Cardener, but Lonny wasn't our best man. Indeed, we had a very quiet wedding, timed to take place while he was away.

"Larry seemed to have forgotten all his rancor against Lonny, and Lonny was at our house a greal deal. I avoided him at first, but gradually his old sweetness and gentleness won me back, and though I could never quite forget his perfidy to me, somehow, I think that I forgave him."

"He was a changed man, *Madame?*" de Grandin asked softly as the woman halted in her narrative and sat passively, staring sightlessly ahead, hands folded motionless in her lap.

"No," she answered in that oddly uninflected tone, "he was less changed than Larry. A little older, a little more serious, perhaps, but still the same sweet, ingenuous lad I'd known and loved so long ago. Larry had become quite gray—early grayness runs in the Cardener family—while Lonny had only a single gray streak running backward from his forehead where a Riff saber had slashed his scalp. He'd picked up an odd trick, too, of brushing his mustache ever so lightly with his bent forefinger when he was puzzled. He explained this by the fact that most of the officers in the Spanish Legion wore full mustaches, different from the close-cropped ones affected by the British, and that he'd followed the custom, but never got quite used to the extra hair on his face. Now, though he'd gone back to the clipped mustache of his young manhood, the Legion mannerism persisted. I can see him now when he and Larry were having an argument over some point of art technique and Larry got the best of it—he was always cleverer than Lonny—how he'd raise his bent finger and brush first one side of his mustache, then the other."

"U'm," de Grandin commented, and as he did so, unconsciously raised his hand to tweak the needle-pointed ends of his own trimly waxed wheat-blond mustache. "One quite understands, *Madame*. And then?"

"Larry had done well with his art," she answered. "He'd had some fine commissions and executed all successfully, but somehow he seemed changing. For one thing, since prohibition, he'd taken to drinking rather heavily—said he had to do it entertaining business prospects, though that was no excuse for his consuming a bottle of port and half a pint of whisky nearly every evening after dinner—"

"*Quel magnifique!*" de Grandin broke in softly, then: "Pray proceed, *Madame*."

"He was living beyond our means, too. As soon as he began to be successful he discarded the studio at the house and rented a pretentious one downtown. Often he spent the night there, and though I didn't actually know it for a fact, I understood he often gave elaborate parties there at night; parties which cost a lot more than we could afford.

"I never understood it, for Larry didn't take me into his confidence at all, but early this spring he seemed desperately in need of money. He tried to borrow everywhere, but no one would lend to him; finally he went to his father.

"Mr. Cardener was a queer man, easygoing in most ways, but very hard in others. He absolutely refused to lend Larry a cent, but offered to advance him what he needed on his share of his inheritance. He'd made a will in which the boys were co-legatees, each to have one-half the estate, you see. Larry accepted eagerly, then went back for several more advances, until his share was almost dissipated. Then—" she paused, not in a fit of weeping, not even with a sob, but rather as though she had come to an impasse.

"Yes, *Madame*; then?" de Grandin prompted softly.

"Then came the scandal. Mr. Cardener was found dead—murdered—in his library one morning, slashed and cut almost to ribbons with a painter's palette knife. The second man, who answered the door the night before they found him, was a new servant, but he had seen Larry several times and Lonny once. He testified that Lonny came to the house about ten o'clock, quarreled violently with his father, and left in a rage twenty minutes or half an hour later. He identified Lonny positively by the gray streak in his hair, which was otherwise dark brown, and by the fact that he brushed his mustache nervously with the knuckle of his right forefinger, both when he demanded to see his father and when he left. After Lonny'd gone, the servant went to the library, but found the door locked and received no answer to his rapping. He thought Mr. Cardener was in a rage, as he had been on several occasions when Larry had called; so he made no attempt to break into the room. But next morning when they found Mr. Cardener hadn't slept in his bed and the library door was still locked, they broke in, and found him murdered."

"U'm?" de Grandin murmured noncommittally. "And were there further clues, *Madame*?"

"Yes, unfortunately. On the library table, so plainly marked in blood that it could not be mistaken, was the print of Lonny's whole left hand. Not just a fingerprint, but the entire palm and fingers. Also, on the palette knife with which the killing had been done, they found Lonny's fingerprints."

"U'm," repeated Jules de Grandin. "He was at pains to put the noose around his neck, this one."

"So it seemed," agreed our passenger. "Lonny denied being at his father's house that night, or any night within a month, but there was no way be could prove an alibi. He lived alone, having his studio in his house, and his servants, a man and wife, went home every night after dinner. They weren't there the night of the murder, of course. Then there was that handprint and those finger-marks upon the knife."

"*Eh bien, Madame*," de Grandin answered, "that is the hardest nut of all to crack, the deepest river of them all to ford. Human witnesses may lie, human memories may fail, or be woefully inexact, but fingerprints—handprints? No, it is not so. Me, I was too many years associated with the *Service Sûreté* not to learn as much. What laymen commonly deride as circumstantial evidence is the best evidence of them all. I would rather base a case on it than on the testimony of a hundred human witnesses, all of whom might be either honestly mistaken or most unmitigated liars. If you can but explain away—"

"I *can*," the girl broke in with her first show of animation. "Listen: Last year, six months before the murder, three months before Larry made his first request for funds from his father, he began making a collection of casts of famous hands as a hobby. When he told Lonny he wanted to include his among them, Lonny nearly went into hysterics at the idea. But he consented to let Larry take a cast. I don't know much about such things, but isn't it customary to take such impressions directly in plaster of Paris?"

"Plaster of Paris? But certainly," the Frenchman answered with a puzzled frown. "Why is it that you ask?"

"Because Larry took the impression of his brother's hands in gelatin."

"*Grand Dieu des artichauts!*" exclaimed de Grandin. "In *gélatine*? Oh, never-to-be-sufficiently-anathematized treachery! One begins to see the glimmer of a little so small gleam of light in this dark case, *Madame*. Say on. I shake, *parbleu*, I quiver with attention!"

For the first time she looked directly at him, nodding her small head. "At the trial Larry admitted that he'd had advances from his father, but declared he'd gotten them for Lonny. He proved it, too."

"Proved it?" de Grandin echoed. "How do you mean, *Madame?*"

"Just what I say. The canceled checks were shown in court by Mr. Cardener's executor, and every one of them had been endorsed and cashed by Lonny. Lonny swore Larry asked him to cash them for him so that no one could trace the money, because he was afraid of attachment proceedings, but Larry denied this under oath and offered his bank books in substantiation of his claim. None of them showed deposits of any such amounts as he'd had from his father." De Grandin clenched his little hands to fists and beat the knuckles against his temples. "*Mon Dieu*," he moaned, "this case will be the death of me, *Madame*. See if I apprehend you rightly:

"It appeared to those who sat in court"—he checked the items off upon his fingers—"that Monsieur Lawrence, at the risk of incurring paternal displeasure, secured loan after loan on his inheritance, ostensibly for himself, but actually for his brother. He proves he turned his father's loans intact over to Monsieur Alonzo. His brother says he cashed the checks and gave the cash back. This is denied. Furthermore, proof, or rather lack of proof, that the brother ever banked such sums is offered. Sitting as we do behind the scenes, we may suspect that Monsieur Lawrence is indulging in double-dealing; but did we sit out in the theater as did that judge and jury, should we not have been fooled, as well? I think so. What makes you sure that they were wrong and we are right, *Madame*? I do not cast aspersion on your intuition; I merely ask to know."

"I have proof," she answered levelly. "When Lonny had been sentenced and the governor refused to intervene, even to commute his sentence to life imprisonment, it seemed to me that I'd go wild. All these years I'd thought I hated Lonny for what he did that night so long ago; when I finally brought myself to see and talk with him, I thought the hatred had lulled to mere resentment, passive dislike. I was wrong. I never hated Lonny; I'd always loved him, only I loved my foolish, selfish pride more. What if he did—what if he and Charlotte Dey—oh, you understand! Lots of men—most men, I suppose—have affairs before marriage, and their wives and the world think nothing of it. Why should I have set myself up as the exception and demanded greater purity in the man I took to husband than most wives ask—or get? When I realized there was no hope for Lonny, I was nearly frantic, and last night after dinner I begged Larry to try to think of some way we could save him.

"He'd been drinking more than ever lately; last night he was sottish, beastly. 'Why should I try to save the poor fool?' he asked. 'D'ye think I've been to all the trouble to put him where he is just to pull him out?' Then, drunkenly, boastfully, he told me everything.

"It wasn't Lonny whom I'd seen with Charlotte Dey that night at Seagirt. It was Larry. When Lonny said good-night to me and went into the house, he heard Larry and Charlotte in Larry's room, which was next to his. He knocked upon the door and demanded that Larry take her out of there at once, even threatening to tell their father if his order weren't obeyed immediately. Larry tried to argue, but finally agreed, for he seemed frightened when Lonny threatened to tell Mr. Cardener.

"Lonny, furious with his brother and the Dey girl, came out on the veranda to see that Charlotte actually left, and was sitting there when I came up the porch to get the cook-book. He wanted to spare me the humiliation of seeing Larry that way, and demanded that I go back at once. The poor lad was so anxious to help me that his manner was unintentionally rough.

"I'd just been gone a moment when Larry and Charlotte came out. Larry saw me crying on the sand, and the whole scheme came to him like an inspiration. 'Call me Lonny!' he whispered to Charlotte as they said good-night, and the spiteful little minx did it. Then he rushed back to his room, pulled outdoor clothes on over his pajamas and made a circuit of the house, waiting in the shadows till he saw me bow my head upon my arm, then running noiselessly across the lawn and beach till he was beside me and ready to play his little comedy.

"He hated Lonny for taking me away from him, and—you know how the old proverb says those whom we have injured are those whom we hate most?— his hatred seemed to grow and grow as time went on. Finally he evolved this scheme to murder Lonny. After he'd made the gelatine mold of Lonny's hands, he made a rubber casting from it, like a rubber stamp, you know, and then began importuning his father for money. Each time he'd get a check he'd have Lonny cash it for him, then put the money in some secret place. Finally, exactly as he'd planned, his father refused to advance him any more, and they quarreled. Then, knowing that the butler, who had known them both since they were little boys, would be away that night, he stained his hair to imitate Lonny's, called at the house and impersonated his brother. When his father demanded what he meant by the masquerade, he answered calmly that he'd come to kill him, and intended Lonny should be executed for the crime. He stabbed his father with a palette knife he'd stolen from Lonny's studio almost a year before, hacked and slashed the body savagely, and made a careful print of the rubber hand in blood on the library table. Lonny's left-handed, you know, and it was the print of his left hand they found on the table, and the prints of his left fingers which were found marked in blood upon the handle of the knife.

"Now Larry wins either way. Lonny can't take his legacy under his father's will, for he's been convicted of murdering him; therefore, he can't make a will and dispose of his half of the estate. Larry takes Lonny's share as his father's sole surviving next of kin capable of inheriting, and he's already got most of his own through the advances he's received and hidden away. A wife can't testify against her husband in a criminal case; but even if I could repeat what he's confessed to me in court, who'd believe me? He need only deny everything, and I'd not only be ridiculed for inventing such a fantastic story, but publicly branded as my brother-in-law's mistress, as well. Larry told me that last night when I threatened to repeat his story to the governor, and Lonny agreed with him today. Oh, it's dreadful, ghastly, hideous! An innocent man's going to a shameful death for a crime he didn't commit, and a perfidious villain who admits the crime goes scot-free, enjoying his brother's heritage and gloating over his immunity from punishment. There isn't any God, of course; if there were, He'd never let such things occur; but there ought to be a hell, somewhere, where such things can be adjusted."

"*Madame*," de Grandin returned evenly, "do not be deceived. God is not made mock of, even by such scheming, clever rogues as him to whom you're married. Furthermore, it is possible, that we need not wait the flames of hell to furnish an adjustment of this matter."

"But what can you or anyone do?" the girl demanded. "No one will believe me; this story is so utterly bizarre—"

"It is certainly decidedly unusual," de Grandin answered non-committally.

"Oh? You think that I've invented it, too?" she wailed despairingly. "Oh, God, if there is a God, help, *please* help us in our trouble!"

"Quickly, Friend Trowbridge," de Grandin cried. "Assist me with her. She has swooned!"

We drew up at my door even as he spoke, and, the girl's form trailing between us, ascended the steps, let ourselves in and hastened to the consulting-room. The Frenchman eased our light burden down upon the divan while I got sal volatile and aromatic ammonia.

"*Madame*," de Grandin told her when she had recovered consciousness, "you must let us take you home."

"Home?" she echoed almost vaguely, as though the word were strange to her. "I haven't any home. The house where *he* lives isn't home to me, nor is—"

"Nevertheless, *Madame*, it is to that house which you must let us take you. It would be too much to ask that you dissemble affection for one who did so vile a thing, but you can at least pretend to be reconciled to making the best of your helplessness. Please, *Madame*, I beg it of you."

"But why?" She answered wonderingly. "I only promised to delay my suicide till Lonny is—till he doesn't need me any more. Must I endure the added torture of spending my last few hours with *him*? Must my agony be intensified by having him gloat over Lonny's execution?—oh, he'll do it, never doubt that! I know him—"

"Perhaps, *Madame*, it may be that you shall see that which will surprise you before this business is finished," the Frenchman interrupted. "I can not surely promise anything—that would be too cruel—but be assured that I shall do my utmost to establish justice in this case. How? I do not surely know, but I shall try.

"Attend me carefully." He crossed the office, rummaged in the medicine cabinet a moment, then returned with a small phial in his hand. "Do you know what this is?" he asked.

"No," she said wonderingly.

"It is mercuric cyanide, a poison infinitely stronger and more swift in action than potassium cyanide or mercuric chloride, commonly called corrosive sublimate. You could not buy it, the law forbids its sale to laymen, yet here it is. A little so small pinch of this white powder on your tongue and *pouf!* unconsciousness and almost instant death. You want him, *hein?*"

"Oh, yes—yes!" she stretched forth eager hands, like a child begging for a sweetmeat.

"Very good. You shall go home and hide your intentions as ably as you can. You shall be patient under cruelty; you shall make no bungling effort to destroy yourself like that we caught you at tonight. Meanwhile, we shall do what we can for you and Monsieur Lonny. If we fail—*Madame*, this little bottle shall be yours when you demand it of me. Do you agree?"

"Yes," she responded, then, falteringly, as though assenting to her own execution: "I'm ready to go any time you wish to take me."

Gardener's big house was dark when we arrived, but our companion nodded understandingly. "He's probably in the library," she informed us. "It's at the back, and you can't see the lights from here. Thank you so much for what you've done—and what you've promised. Good-night." She alighted nimbly and held her hand out in farewell.

De Grandin raised her fingers to his lips, and: "It may well be that we must see your husband upon business, *Madame*," he whispered. "When is he most likely to be found at home?"

"Why, he'll probably be here till noon tomorrow. He's usually a late riser."

"*Bien, Madame*, it may be that we shall be forced to put him to the incon-venience of rising earlier than usual," he answered enigmatically as he brushed her fingers with his lips again.

"Now, what the devil are you up to?" I demanded reproachfully as we drove away. "You know there's nothing you can do for that poor chap in jail, or for that woman, either. It was cruel to hold out hope, de Grandin. Even your promise of the poison is unethical. You're making yourself an accessory before the fact to homicide by giving her that cyanide, and dragging me into it, too. We'll be lucky if we see the end of this affair without landing in prison."

"I think not," he denied. "I scarcely know how I shall go about it, but I propose a gamble in souls, my friend. Perhaps, with Hussein Obeyid's assistance we may yet win."

"Who the deuce is Hussein Obeyid?"

"Another friend of mine," he answered cryptically. "You have not met him, but you will. Will you be good enough to drive into East Melton Street? I do not know the number, but I shall surely recognize the house when we arrive."

East Melton Street was one of those odd, forgotten backwaters common to all cities where a heterogeneous foreign population has displaced the ancient "quality" who once inhabited the brownstone-fronted houses. Italians, Poles, Hungarians, with a sprinkling of other European miscellany dwelt in Melton Street, each nationality occupying almost definite portions of the thoroughfare, as though their territories had been meted out to them. Far toward the water-end, where rotting piers projected out into the oily waters of the bay and the far from pleasant odors of trash-laden barges were wafted landward on every puff of superheated summer breeze, was the Syrian quarter. Here Greeks, Armenians, Arabians, a scattering of Persians and a horde of indeterminate mixed-breeds of the Levant lived in houses which had once been mansions but were now so sunk in disrepair that the wonder was they had not been condemned long since. Here and there was a house which seemed relatively untenanted, being occupied by no more than ten or a dozen families; but for the most part the places swarmed with patently unwashed humanity, children whose extreme vocality seemed matched only by their total unacquaintance with soap and water sharing steps, windows and iron-slatted fire escapes with slattern women of imposing avoirdupois, arrayed in soiled white nightgowns and unlaced shoes shockingly run over at the heels.

De Grandin called a halt before a house set back in what had been a lawn between a fly-blown restaurant where coatless men played dominoes and consumed great quantities of heavy, deadly-looking food, and a "billiard academy" where rat-faced youths in corset-waisted trousers knocked balls about or perused blatantly colored foreign magazines. The house before which we drew up was so dark I thought it tenantless at first, but as we mounted the low step which stood before its door I caught a subdued gleam of light from its interior. A moment we paused, inhaling the unpleasant perfume of the dark and squalid street while de Grandin pulled vigorously at the brass bellknob set in the stone coping of the doorway.

"It looks as though nobody's home," I hazarded as he rang and rang again, but:

"*Salaam aleikum,*" a soft voice whispered, and the door was opened, not wide, but far enough to permit our entrance, by a diminutive individual in black satin waistcoat, loose, bloomer-like trousers and a red tarboosh several sizes too large for him.

"*Aleikum salaam,*" de Grandin answered, returning the salute the other made. "We should like to see your uncle on important business. Is he to be seen?"

"*Bissahi!*" the other answered in a high-pitched, squeaking voice, and hurried down the darkened hall toward the rear of the house.

"Is your friend his uncle?" I asked curiously, for the fellow was somewhere between sixty-five and seventy years of age, rather well-advanced to possess an uncle, it seemed to me.

The little Frenchman chuckled. "By no means," he assured me. "'Uncle' is a euphemism for 'master' with these people, and used in courtesy to servants."

I was about to request further information when the little old man returned and beckoned us to follow him.

"*Salaam,* Hussein Obeyid," de Grandin greeted as we passed through a curtained doorway, "*es salaat wes salaam aleik!*—Peace be with thee, and the glory!"

A portly, bearded man in flowing robe of striped linen, red tarboosh and red Morocco slippers rose from his seat beside the window, touching forehead, lips and breast with a quick gesture as he crossed the room to take de Grandin's outstretched hand. This, I learned as the Frenchman introduced us formally, was Doctor Hussein Obeyid, "one of the world's ten greatest philosophers," and a very special friend of Jules de Grandin's. Doctor Obeyid was a big man, not only stout, but tall and strongly built, with massive, finely-chiseled features and a curling, square-cut beard of black which gave him somewhat the appearance of an Assyrian andro-sphinx.

The room in which we sat was as remarkable in appearance as its owner. It was thirty feet, at least, in length, being composed of the former front and back "parlors" of the old house, the partitions having been knocked out. Casement windows, glazed with richly painted glass, opened on a small back yard charmingly planted with grass and flowering shrubs; three electric fans kept the air pleasantly in motion. Persian rugs were on the polished floor and the place was dimly lighted by two lamps with pierced brass shades of Turkish fashion. The furniture was an odd conglomeration, lacquered Chinese pieces mingling with Eastern ottomans like enormously overgrown boudoir cushions, with here and there a bit of Indian cane-ware. Upon a stand was an aquarium in which swam several goldfish of the most gorgeous coloring I had ever seen, while near the opened windows stood what looked like an ancient refectory table with bits of chemical apparatus scattered over it. The walls were lined from floor to ceiling with bookcases laden with volumes in unfamiliar bindings and glassed-in cabinets in which was ranged a miscellany of unusual objects—mummified heads, hands and feet, bits of clay inscribed with cuneiform characters, odd weapons and utensils of ancient make, fit to be included in the exhibitions of our best museums. A human skeleton, completely articulated, leered at us from a corner of the room. Such was the rest room and workshop of Doctor Hussein Obeyid, "one of the world's ten greatest philosophers."

De Grandin lost no time in coming to the point. Briefly he narrated Beth Cardener's story, beginning with our first glimpse of her in the penitentiary and ending with our leaving her upon her doorstep. "Once, years ago, my friend," he finished, "on the ancient Djebel Druse—the stronghold of that strange and mystic people who acknowledge neither Turk nor Frenchman as their overlord—I saw you work a miracle. Do you recall? A prisoner had been taken, and—"

"I recall perfectly," our host cut in, his deep voice fairly booming through the room. "Yes, I well remember it. But it is not well to do such things promiscuously, my little one. The Ineffable One has His own plans for our goings and our comings; to gamble in men's souls is not a game which men should play at."

"*Misère de Dieu!*" de Grandin cried, "this is no petty game I ask that you should play, *mon vieux*. Madame Cardener? Her plight is pitiful, I grant; but women's hearts have broken in the past, and they will break till time shall be no more. No, it is not for her I ask this thing, but for the sake of justice. Shall ninety-million-times-damned perfidy vaunt itself in pride at the expense of innocence? 'Vengeance is mine, I will repay, saith the Lord,' truly; but consider: Does He not ever act through human agencies when He performs his miracles? Damn yes. If there were any way this poor one's innocence could be established, even after death, I should not be here; but as it is he is enmeshed in webs of treachery. No sixty-times-accursed 'reasonable' man could be convinced he did not do that murder, and the so puerile Anglo-Saxon law of which the British and Americans prate so boastfully has its hard rules of evidence which for ever bar the truth from being spoken. This monstrous-great injustice must not—can not—be allowed, my friend."

Doctor Obeyid stroked his black beard thoughtfully, "I hesitate to do it," he replied, "but for you, my little birdling, and for justice, I shall try."

"*Triomphe!*" de Grandin cried, rising from his chair and bounding across the room to seize the other in his arms and kiss him on both cheeks. "*Ha*, Satan, thou art stalemated; tomorrow we shall make a monkey of your plans and of the plans of that so evil man who did your work, by damn!" Abruptly he sobered. "You will go with us tomorrow morning?" he demanded.

Doctor Obeyid inclined his head in acquiescence. "Tomorrow morning," he replied.

Then the diminutive, wrinkle-bitten "nephew" who performed the doctor's household tasks appeared with sweet, black coffee and execrable little tarts compounded of pistachio nuts, chopped dates and melted honey, and we drank and ate and smoked long, amber-scented cigarettes until the tower-clock of the nearby Syrian Catholic church beat out the quarter-hour after midnight.

I T WAS SHORTLY AFTER ten o'clock next morning when we called at Cardener's. Doctor Obeyid, looking more imposing, if possible, in a suit of silver-gray corduroy and a wide-brimmed black-felt hat than he had in Eastern robes, towered a full head above de Grandin and six inches over me as he stood between us and beat a soft tattoo on the porch floor with the ferule of his ivory-headed cane. It was a most remarkable piece of personal adornment, that cane. Longer by a half-foot than the usual walking-stick, it was more like the exaggerated staffs borne by gentlemen of the late Georgian period than any modern cane, and its carven ivory top was made to simulate a serpent's head, scales being reproduced with startling fidelity to life, and little beads of some green-colored stone—jade, I thought—being inlaid for the eyes. The wood of the staff was a kind which I could not classify. It was a vague, indefinite color, something between an olive-green and granite-gray, and overlaid with little intersecting lines which might have been in imitation of a reptile's scales or might have been a part of the strange wood's odd grain.

"We should like to see Monsieur Cardener—" began de Grandin, but for once he failed to keep control of the situation.

"Tell him Doctor Obeyid desires to talk with him," broke in our companion, in his deep, commanding voice. "At once, please."

"He's at breakfast now, sir," the servant answered. "If you'll step into the drawing-room and—"

"At once," Hussein Obeyid repeated, not with emphasis, but rather inexorably, as one long used to having his orders obeyed immediately and without question.

"Yes, sir," the butler returned, and led us toward the rear of the house.

Striped awnings kept the late summer sun from the breakfast room's open windows where a double row of scarlet geranium-tops stood nodding in the breeze. At the end of the polished mahogany table in the center of the room a man sat facing us, and it needed no second glance to tell us he was Lawrence Cardener. Line for line and feature for feature, his face was the duplicate of that of the prisoned man whom we had seen the day before. Even the fact that his upper lip was adorned by a close-cropped mustache, while the prisoner was smooth-shaven, and his hair was iron-gray, while the convict's close-clipped hair was brown, did not affect the marked resemblance to any degree.

"What the dev—" he began as the servant ushered us into the room, but Doctor Obeyid cut his protest short.

"We are here to talk about your brother," he announced.

"Ah?" An ugly, sneering smile gathered at the corners of Cardener's mouth. "You are, eh? Well?" He pushed the blue-willow club plate laden with mutton chops and scrambled eggs away from him and picked up a slice of buttered toast. "Get on with it," he ordered. "You wished to talk about my brother—"

"And you," Doctor Obeyid supplied. "It is not too late for you to make amends."

"Amends?" the other echoed, amusement showing in his eyes as he dropped a lump of sugar into his well-creamed coffee and stirred it with his spoon.

"Amends," repeated Obeyid. "You still may go before the governor, and—"

"Oh, so that's it, eh? My precious wife's been talking to you? Poor dear, she's a little touched, you know"—he tapped himself upon the temple significantly—"used to be fearfully stuck on Lonny, in the old days, and—"

"My friend," Obeyid broke in, "it is of your immortal soul that we must talk, not of your wife. Is it possible that you will let another bear the stigma of your guilt? Your soul—"

Cardener laughed shortly. "My soul, is it?" he answered. "Don't bother about *my* soul. If you're so much interested in souls, you'd better skip down to Trenton and talk to Lonny. He's got one now, but he won't have it long. Tonight they're going to—" his voice trailed off to nothingness and his eyes widened as he slowly and deliberately put his spoon down in its saucer. Not fear, but something like a compound of despair and resignation showed in his face as he stared in fascination at Hussein Obeyid.

I turned to glance at our companion, and a startled exclamation leaped involuntarily to my lips. The big Semitic-featured face had undergone a startling transformation. The complexion had altered from swarthy tan to pasty gray, the eyes had started from their sockets, white, globular, expressionless as peeled onions. I had seen such horrible protrusion of the optics in corpses far gone in putrefaction when tissue-gas was bloating features out of human semblance, but never had I seen a thing like this in a living countenance. Doctor Obeyid's lips were moving, but what he said I could not understand. It was a low, monotonous, sing-song chant in some harsh and guttural language, rising and falling alternately with a majesty and power like the surging of a wind-swept sea upon the sands.

How long he chanted I have no idea. It might have been a minute, it might have been an hour, for the clock of eternity seemed stopped as the sonorous voice boomed out the harsh, compelling syllables. But finally it was finished, and I felt de Grandin's hand upon my arm.

"Come away, my friend," he whispered in an awe-struck tone. "The cards are dealt and on the table. The first part of our game of souls is started. *Prie Dieu* that we shall win!"

A LONZO CARDENER WAS SITTING at the little table in his cell, not playing cards, although a pack rested beside the Bible on the clean-scrubbed wood, but merely sitting as though lost in thought, his elbow on his knee, head propped upon his hand. He did not look up as we came abreast of him, but just sat there, staring straight ahead.

"*Monsieur*," de Grandin hailed. "Monsieur Lonny!" The prisoner looked up, but there was no change of expression in his dull and apathetic face. "We are come from her, from Madame Beth," the Frenchman added softly.

The change which overspread the prisoner's face was like a miracle. It was young again, and bright with eagerness, like a lad in love when some one brings him tidings of his sweetheart. "You've come from her?" he asked incredulously. "Tell me, is she well? Is she—"

"She is well, *mon pauvre*, and happier, since she has told her story to us. We came upon her yesternight by chance, and she has told us all. Now, she asks that we should come to you and bid you be of cheer."

Cardener laughed shortly, with harsh mirthlessness. "Rather difficult, that, for a man in my position," he rejoined, "but—"

"My brother," Doctor Obeyid's deep voice, lowered to a whisper, but still powerful as the muted rumbling of an organ's bass, broke in upon his bitter speech, "you must not despair. Are you afraid to die?"

"Die?" A spasm as of pain twitched across the convict's face. "No, sir; I don't think so. I've faced death many times before, and never was afraid of it; but leaving Beth, now, when I've just found her again, is what hurts most. It's impossible, of course, but if I could only see her once again—"

"You shall," Hussein Obeyid promised. "Little brother, be confident. That door through which you go tonight is the entrance to reunion with the one you love. It is the portal to a new and larger life, and beyond it waits your loved one."

Gray-faced horror spread across the prisoner's countenance. "You—you mean she is already dead?" he faltered. "Oh, Beth, my girl; my dear, my dearest dear—"

"She is not dead; she is alive and well, and waiting for you," Obeyid's deep, compelling voice cut in. "Just beyond that door she waits, my little one. Keep up your courage; you shall surely find her there."

"Oh?" Light seemed to dawn upon the prisoner. "You mean that she'll destroy herself to be with me. No—no; she mustn't do it! Suicide's a sin, a deadly sin. I'm going innocent to death; God will judge my innocence, for He knows all, but if she were to kill herself perhaps we should be separated for ever. Tell her that she mustn't do it; tell her that I beg that she will live until her time has come, and that she'll not forget me while she's waiting; for I'll be waiting, too."

"Look at me," commanded Obeyid suddenly, so suddenly that the frantic man forgot his fears and stopped his protestations short to look with wonder-widened eyes at Hussein Obeyid.

The Oriental raised his staff and held it toward the wire screen the guards had placed before the cell. And as he held it out, *it moved.* Before our eyes that staff of carven wood and ivory became a living, moving thing, twining itself about the doctor's wrist, rearing its head and darting forth its bifurcated tongue. "*Bismillah al-rahman al-rahim*—in the name of God, the Merciful, the Compassionate—" murmured Hussein Obeyid, then launched into a low-voiced, vibrant cantillation while the vivified staff writhed and turned its scaly head in cadence to the chant. He did not distort his features as when he cast a spell upon the prisoner's brother; but his face was pale as chiseled marble, and down his high, wide, sloping forehead ran rivulets of sweat as he put the whole force of his soul and mighty body behind the invocation which he chanted.

The look upon the convict's face was mystifying. Twin fires, as of a fever, burned in the depths of his cavernous eyes and his features writhed and twisted as though his soul were racked by the travail of spiritual childbirth. "Beth!" he whispered hoarsely. "Beth!"

I turned apprehensively toward the prison guard who sat immediately behind us. That he had not cried out at the animation of Obeyid's staff and the low-toned invocation of the Oriental ere this surprised me. What I saw surprised me more. The man lounged in his chair, his features dull and disinterested, a look of utter boredom on his face. He saw nothing, heard nothing, noticed nothing!

". . . until tonight, then, little brother," Hussein Obeyid was saying softly. "Remember, and be brave. She will be awaiting you."

"Come," ordered Jules de Grandin, tugging at my sleeve. "The dice are cast. We must wait to read the spots before we can know surely whether we have won."

THEY LED HIM IN to die at twenty minutes after ten. Permission to attend the execution had been difficult to get; but Jules de Grandin with his tireless energy and infinite resource had obtained it. Hussein Obeyid, the little Frenchman and I accepted seats at the far end of the stiffbacked church-like pew reserved for witnesses, and I felt a shiver of sick apprehension ripple down my spine as we took our places. To watch beside the bed of one who dies when medical science has exhausted its resources is heart-breaking, but to sit and watch a life snuffed out, to see a strong and healthy body turned to so much clay within the twinkling of an eye—that is horrifying.

The executioner, a lean, cadaverous man who somehow reminded me of a disillusioned evangelist, stood in a tiny alcove to the left of the electric chair, a heavy piece of oaken furniture raised one low step above the tiled floor of the chamber; the assistant warden and the prison doctor stood between the chair and entrance to the death-room, and although this was no novelty to him, I saw the medic finger nervously at the stethoscope which hung about his neck as though it were a badge of office. A partly folded screen at the farther corner of the room obscured another doorway, but as we took our seats I caught a glimpse of a wheeled stretcher with a cotton sheet lying neatly folded on it. Beyond, I knew, waited the autopsy table and the surgeon's knife when the prison doctor had pronounced the execution a success.

I breathed a strangling, gasping sigh as a single short, imperative tap sounded on the panels of the painted door which led to the death chamber.

Silently, on well-oiled hinges, the door swung back, and Alonzo Cardener stood in readiness to meet the great adventure. His cotton shirt was open at the throat, the right leg of his trousers had been slit up to the knee; as the pitiless white light struck on his head, I saw a little spot was shaved upon his scalp. To right and left were prison guards who held his elbows lightly. Another guard brought up the rear. The chaplain walked before, his Prayer Book open. ". . . *yea, though I walk through the valley of the shadow of death I shall fear no evil, for Thou art with me . . .*"

Cardener's eyes were wide and rapt. The fingers of his right hand closed, not convulsively, but tenderly, as though he took and held another's hand in his. His lips moved slightly, and though no sound came from them, we saw them form a name: "Beth!"

They led him to the chair, but he did not seem to see it; they had to help him up the one low step—his last step in the world—or he would have stumbled on it; for his eyes were gazing down an endless vista where he walked at peace with his beloved, hand in hand.

But as they snapped the heavy straps about his waist and wrists and ankles and set the leather helmet on his head, a sudden change came over him. He struggled fiercely at the bonds which held him in the chair, and although his face was almost hidden by the deadly headgear clamped upon his skull, his lips were unobscured, and from them came a wailing cry of horrified astonishment. "Not me!" he screamed. "Not me—Lonny! I'm—"

Notebook open, and pencil poised, as though to make a memorandum, the prison doctor stood before the chair. Now, as the convict screamed in frenzied fear, the pencil tilted forward, as though the doctor wrote. A sudden, sharp, strange whining sounded, something throbbed and palpitated agonizingly, like stifled heart-beats. The ghastly, pleading cry was checked abruptly as the prisoner's body started up and forward, as though it sought to burst the leathern bonds which held it. The chin and lips went from pale gray to dusky red, like the face of one who holds his breath too long. The hands, fluttering futilely a moment since, were taut and rigid on the chair arms.

A moment—or eternity!—of this, then the grating jar of metal against metal as the switch was thrown and the current was shut off. The straining body dropped back limply in the chair.

Again the doctor's pencil tilted forward, again the whining whir, and the flaccid body started forward, all but bursting through the broad, strong straps which harnessed it into the chair. Then absolute flaccidity as the current was withdrawn again.

The doctor put his book and pencil by and stepped up quickly to the chair. Putting back the prisoner's open shirt—he wore no undershirt—he pressed his stethoscope against the reddened chest exposed to view, listened silently, then, crisp and business-like, announced his verdict:

"I pronounce this man dead."

White-uniformed attendants took the limp form from the chair, wrapped it quickly in a sheet and wheeled it off to the autopsy table.

We signed the roll of witnesses and hurried from the prison, and:

"Drive, my friend, drive as though the fiends of fury rode the wind behind us!" ordered Jules de Grandin. "We must arrive at Madame Cardener's without delay. Right away, immediately; at once!"

Beth Cardener met us at the door, the pallor of her face intensified by the sable hue of the black-velvet pajamas which she wore. "It happened at twenty minutes after ten," she told us as we filed silently into the hall.

De Grandin's small eyes rounded with astonishment as he looked at her. "*Précisément, Madame,*" he acknowledged, "but how is it you know?"

A puzzled look spread on her face as she replied: "Of course, I couldn't sleep—who could, in such circumstances?—and I kept looking at the clock and saying to myself, 'What are they doing to my poor boy now? Is he still in the same world with me?' when I seemed to hear a sort of drumming, whirring noise—something like the deafening vibration you sometimes hear when riding in a motorcar—and then a sudden sharp, agonizing pain shot through me from my head to feet. It was like fire rushing through my veins, burning me to ashes as it ran, and everything went red, then inky-black before my eyes. I felt as if I stifled—no, not that, rather as though every nerve and muscle in my body were suddenly cramping into knots—and at the same time there was a terrible sensation of something from inside me being snatched away in one cruel wrench, as though my heart were dragged out of my breast with a pair of dreadful tongs that burned and seared, even as they tore my quivering body open. If it had lasted, I'd have died, but it left as quickly as it came, and there I was, faint, weak and numb, but suffering no pain, staggering to the window and gasping for breath. As I reached the window I looked up, and a shooting-star fell across the sky. I knew, then; Lonny was no longer in the same world with me. I was lonely, so utterly, devastatingly lonely, that I thought my heart would break. I've never had a child, but if I had one, and it died, I think that I'd feel as I felt the instant that I saw that falling star.

"Then"—she paused, and again that puzzled, wondering look crept into her eyes—"then something, something inside me, like a voice heard in a dream, seemed to say insistently: 'Go to Larry; go to Larry!'

"I didn't want to go; I didn't want to see him or be near him—I loathed the very thought of him, but that strange, compelling voice kept ordering me to go. So I went.

"Larry was sitting in the big chair he always uses in the library. His head had fallen back, and his hands were gripping the arms till the finger-tips bit into the upholstery. His mouth was slightly open and his face was pale as death. I noticed, as I crossed the room, that his feet were well apart, but both flat to the floor. It was"—her voice sank to a husky, frightened whisper—"it was as if *he* were sitting in the death-chair, and had just been executed!"

"U'm, and did you touch him, *Madame?*" de Grandin asked.

"Yes, I did, and his hands were cold—clammy. He was dead. Oh, thank God, he was dead! He murdered his poor brother, just as surely as he killed his father, but he'll never live to boast of it. He died, just as Lonny did, in 'the chair,' only it wasn't human injustice that took his perjured life away; it was the even-handed judgment of just Heaven, and *I'm glad*. I'm glad, do you hear me! I'm glad enough to rush out in the street and tell it to the world; to shout it from the house-tops!"

De Grandin cast a sidelong glance at Hussein Obeyid, who nodded silently. "Perfectly, *Madame*, one understands," the Frenchman answered. "Will you go with us and show us the body? It would be of interest—"

"Yes, yes; I'll show you—I'll be glad, to show you!" she broke in shrilly. "Come; this way, please."

Gray-faced, hang-jawed, pale and flaccid as only the dead can be, Lawrence Cardener sat slumped in the big chair beside the book-strewn-table. I glanced at him and nodded briefly. No use to make a further examination. No doctor, soldier or embalmer need be introduced to death. He knows it at a glance.

But Hussein Obeyid was not so easily assured. Crossing the room, he bent above the corpse, staring straight into the glazed and sightless eyes and murmuring a sort of chanting invocation. "*Bismillah alrahman al-rahman*—in the name of God, the Merciful, the Compassionate; in the name of the One True God—" He drew a little packet from his waistcoat pocket, broke the seal which closed it and dusted a pinch of whitish powder into the palm of his right hand, then rubbed both hands together quickly, as though laving them with soap. In the shadow where he stood we saw his hands begin to glow, as though they had been smeared with phosphorus, but gradually the glow became a quick and flickering faint-blue light which grew and grew in power till it darted wisps of bluish flame from palms and finger-tips.

He grasped his serpent-headed staff between his glowing hands, and instantly the thing became alive, waving slowly to and fro, darting forth its lambent tongue to touch the dead man's eyes and lips and nostrils. He threw the staff upon the floor, and instantly it was a thing of wood and ivory once again.

Now he pressed fire-framed hands upon the corpse's brow, then bent and ran them up and down the length of the slack limbs, finally poising them above the dead man's *omphalos*. The flame which flickered from his hands curved downward like a blue-green waterfall of fire which seemed to be absorbed by the dead body as water would be soaked in thirsty soil.

And now the flaccid, flabby limbs seemed to tighten, to stretch out jerkily, uneasily, as though awaking from a long, uncomfortable sleep. The lolling head began to oscillate upon the neck, the slack jaw closed, the eyes, a moment since glassy with the vacant stare of death, gave signs of unmistakable vitality.

A shrill, sharp cry broke from Beth Cardener. "He's alive," she screamed, horror and heart-sick disappointment in her voice. "O-oh, he's alive!" She turned reproachful, tear-dimmed eyes on Hussein Obeyid. "Why did you revive him?" she asked accusingly. "He might have died, if you hadn't—"

Her voice broke, smothered in a storm of sobs. Thus far the vibrant hatred of the murderer and her exultation over the swift retribution which had overtaken him had kept her nerve from snapping. Now, the realization that the man whose perfidy had betrayed her trust and her lover's life was still alive broke down her resistance, and she fell, half-fainting, on the couch, buried her face in a pillow and gave herself up bodily to retching lamentation.

"*Madame*," de Grandin's voice was sharp, peremptory; "Madame Beth, come here!"

The woman raised her tear-scarred face and looked at him in wonder. "Come here, quickly, if you please, and tell me what it is you see," he ordered again.

She rose, mechanically, like one who walks in sleep, and approached the semiconscious man who slouched in the big chair.

"Behold, observe; *voilà!*" the Frenchman ordered, leaning down and bending Cardener's left ear forward. There, plainly marked and unmistakable, imprinted on the skin above the *retrahens aurem*, was a small white cicatrix, a quarter-inch or so in length.

"Oh?" It was a strangling, gasping cry, such as a patient undergoing unanesthetized edentation might give; wonder was in it, and something like fright, as well.

The little Frenchman raised his hand for silence. "He is coming to, *Madame*," he warned in a soft whisper.

Life, indeed, had come back to the shell above which Doctor Obeyid had chanted. Little by little the dread contours of death had receded, and as the hands lost their rigor and lay, half open, on the chair arms, we saw the fingers flexing and extending in an easier, more lifelike motion.

"*Jodo!*" whispered Cardener, rolling his head listlessly from side to side, like one who seeks to rouse himself from an unpleasant dream.

"*Jodo!*" she repeated in an awed and breathless whisper. "*He* never called me that! Way back, when we were children, Lonny and I gave each other 'intimate names,' and I never told mine to a soul, not my parents, nor my husband. How—"

"Jodo—Beth dear," the half-unconscious man repeated, his fingers searching gropingly for something. "Are you here? I can't see you, dear, but—"

"*Lonny!*" Incredulous, unbelieving joy was in the woman's tones, and:

"Beth, Beth dearest!" Cardener started forward, eyes opening and closing rapidly, as though he had come suddenly from darkness into light. "Beth, they told me you'd be waiting for me—are you really here?"

"Here! Yes, my dear, my very dearest; I am here!" she cried, and sank down to her knees, gathering his head to her bosom and rocking gently back and forth, as though it were a nursing baby. "Oh, my dear, my dear, however did you come?"

"I'm dead?" he queried timidly. "Is this heaven or—"

"Heaven? Yes, if I and all my love can make it so, my darling!" Beth Cardener broke in, and stopped his wondering queries with her kisses.

"Now, what the devil does it mean?" I asked as we drove slowly home after taking Doctor Obeyid to his house in Melton Street.

Jules de Grandin raised his elbows, brows and shoulders in a shrug which seemed to say there are some things even a Frenchman can not understand.

"You know as much as I, my friend," he returned. "You saw it with your own two eyes. What more is there which I can tell you?"

"A lot of things," I countered. "You said yourself that once before you'd seen—"

"Assuredly I had," he acquiesced. "Me, I see many things, but do I know their meaning? Not always. *Par example*: I say to you, 'Friend Trowbridge, I would that you should drive me here or there,' and though you put your foot on certain things and wiggle certain others with your hands, I do not know what you are doing, or why you do it. I only know that the car moves, and that we arrive, at length, where I have wished to go. You comprehend?"

"No, I don't," I answered testily. "I'd like to know how it comes that Lawrence Cardener, who, as we know, was a thorough-going villain if ever there was one, exchanged, or seemed to exchange personalities with the brother whom he sent to death in the electric chair at the very moment of that brother's execution—and how that scar appeared upon his head. His wife vouched for the fact that it wasn't there before."

The little Frenchman twisted the needle-points of his sharply waxed, wheat-blond mutache until I thought that he would surely prick his finger on them. "I can not say," he answered thoughtfully, "because I do not know. The Arabs have a saying that the soul grows on the body like a flower on the stalk. They may be right. Who knows? What is the soul? Who knows, again? Is it that vague, indefinite thing which we call personality? Perhaps.

"Suppose it is; let us assume the flower-analogy again. Let us assume that, as the skilful gardener takes the blossom from the living rose and grafts it on the living dogwood tree, and thereby makes a rose-tree, one skilled in metaphysics can take the soul from out a body at the instant of dissolution and transplant it to another body from which the soul has just decamped, and thereby create a new and different individual, composed of two distinct parts, a soul, or personality, if you please, and a body, neither of which was originally complementary to the other. It sounds strange, insane, but so would talk of total anesthesia or radio have sounded two hundred years ago. As for the scar, that is comparatively simple. You have seen persons under hypnotism lose every drop of blood from one arm or hand, or become completely anemic in one side of the face; you know from medical history, though you may not have seen it, that certain hysterical religious persons develop what are called stigmata—simulations of the bleeding wounds of the Savior or the martyred saints. That is mental in inception, but physical in manifestation, *n'est-ce-pas*? Why, then, could not an outward and physical sign of personality be transferred as easily as the inward and spiritual reality? *Pardieu*, I damn think that it could!"

"But will this 'spiritual graft' endure?" I wondered. "Will this transformation of Larry Cardener into Lonny Cardener last?"

"*Le bon Dieu* knows," he answered. "Me, I most greatly hope so. If it does not, I shall have to make my promise good and give her that mercuric cyanide. Time will tell."

TIME DID. A YEAR had passed, and the final summer hop was being given at the Sedgemoor Country Club. The white walls of the clubhouse shone like an illuminated monument in the dusky blue of the late September night, lights blazed from every window and colored globes decorated the overhanging roofs of the broad verandas which stretched along the front and rear of the building. In the grounds Chinese lanterns gleamed with rose, blue, violet and jade, rivaling the brilliance of the summer stars. Jazz blared from the commodious ballroom and echoed from the big yellow-and-red striped marquee set up by the first green. Jules de Grandin and I sat on the front piazza and rocked comfortably in wide wicker chairs, the ice-cubes in our tall glasses clinking pleasantly.

"*Mordieu*, my friend," the Frenchman exclaimed enthusiastically, "this what do you call him? zhu-leep?—he is divine; magnificent. He is superb; I would I had a tubful of him in which to drown my few remaining sorrows!" He sucked appreciatively at the twin straws, thrust between the feathery mint-stalks, then, abruptly: "*Mort de ma vie*, my friend, look—behold them!" He pointed up excitedly.

From where we sat a little balcony projecting from the upper floor was plainly in our line of vision. As the little Frenchman pointed, I saw a man arrayed in summer dancing-clothes, step out upon the platform and light a cigarette. As he snapped his lighter shut, he raised his left hand and brushed his short, close-cropped mustache with the knuckle of his bent forefinger. He blew a long cone of gray smoke between his lips, and turned to some one in the room behind him. As the light struck on his face, I recognized him. It was Lawrence Cardener, beyond a doubt, but Lawrence Cardener strangely altered. His hair, once iron-gray, was now almost uniformly brown, save where a single streak of white ran, plume-like backward from his forehead.

A woman joined him on the balcony. She was tall, slender, dark; her little, piquant face framed in clusters of curling ringlets. Her lips were red and smiling, her lovely arms and shoulders were exposed by the extreme décolleté of her white-crepe evening gown. I knew her; Beth Cardener, but a different woman from the one whose suicide we had balked twelve months before. This Beth was younger, more girlish in face and carriage, and plainly, she was happy. He turned and offered her his case, then, as she chose a cigarette, extended his lighter. She drew the smoke into her lungs, expelled a fine stream from her mouth, then tossed the cigarette away. As it fell to earth in a gleaming, fiery arc, the man tossed his out after it and put his hands upon her shoulders. Her own white hands, fluttering like homing doves, flew upward, clasped about his neck, and drew his face to hers. Their lips approached and merged in a long, rapturous kiss.

"*Tête bleu, my friend,*" de Grandin cried, "I damn think I can keep my mercuric cyanide; she has no use for it, that one!" He rose, a thought unsteadily, and beckoned me. "Come, let us leave them to each other and their happiness," he ordered. "Me, I very greatly desire several more of those so noble mint zhuleeps. Yes."

The Thing in the Fog

"Tiens, on such a night as this the Devil must congratulate himself!" Jules de Grandin forced his chin still deeper in the upturned collar of his trench-coat, and bent his head against the whorls of chilling mist which eddied upward from the bay in token that autumn was dead and winter come at last.

"Congratulate himself?" I asked in amusement as I felt before me for the curbstone with the ferrule of my stick. "Why?"

"Why? *Pardieu*, because he sits at ease beside the cozy fires of hell, and does not have to feel his way through this eternally-to-be-execrated fog! If we had but the sense—

"*Pardon, Monsieur*, one of us is very clumsy, and I do not think that it is I!" he broke off sharply as a big young man, evidently carrying a heavier cargo of ardent spirits than he could safely manage, lurched against him in the smothering mist, then caromed off at an unsteady angle to lose himself once more in the enshrouding fog.

"Dolt!" the little Frenchman muttered peevishly. "If he can not carry liquor he should abstain from it. Me, I have no patience with these—*grand Dieu*, what is that?"

Somewhere behind us, hidden in the curtains of the thick, gray vapor, there came a muffled exclamation, half of fright, half of anger, the sound of something fighting threshingly with something else, and a growling, snarling noise, as though a savage dog had leapt upon its prey, and, having fleshed its teeth, was worrying it; then: "Help!" The cry was muffled, strangled, but laden with a weight of helpless terror.

"Hold fast, my friend, we come!" de Grandin cried, and, guided by the sounds of struggle, breasted through the fog as if it had been water, brandishing his silver-headed sword-stick before him as a guide and a defense.

A score of quick steps brought us to the conflict. Dim and indistinct as shadows on a moonless night, two forms were struggling on the sidewalk, a large one lying underneath, while over it, snarling savagely, was a thing I took for a police dog which snapped and champed and worried at the other's throat.

"Help!" called the man again, straining futilely to hold the snarling beast away and turning on his side the better to protect his menaced face and neck.

"*Cordieu*, a war-dog!" exclaimed the Frenchman. "Stand aside, Friend Trowbridge, he is savage, this one; mad, perhaps, as well." With a quick, whipping motion he ripped the chilled-steel blade from the barrel of his stick and, point advanced, circled round the struggling man and beast, approaching with a cautious, cat-like step as he sought an opportunity to drive home the sword.

By some uncanny sense the snarling brute divined his purpose, raised its muzzle from its victim's throat and backed away a step or two, regarding de Grandin with a stare of utter hatred. For a moment I caught the smoldering glare of a pair of fire-red eyes, burning through the fogfolds as incandescent charcoal might burn through a cloth, and:

"A dog? *Non, pardieu*, it is—" began the little Frenchman, then checked himself abruptly as he lunged out swiftly with his blade, straight for the glaring, fiery eyes which glowered at him through the mist.

The great beast backed away with no apparent haste, yet quickly enough to avoid the needle-point of Jules de Grandin's blade, and for an instant I beheld a row of gleaming teeth bared savagely beneath the red eyes' glare; then, with a snarling growl which held more defiance than surrender in its throaty rumble, the brute turned lithely, dodged and made off through the fog, disappearing from sight before the clicking of its nails against the pavement had been lost to hearing.

"Look to him, Friend Trowbridge," de Grandin ordered, casting a final glance about us in the mist before he put his sword back in its sheath. "Does he survive, or is he killed to death?"

"He's alive, all right," I answered as I sank to my knees beside the supine man, "but he's been considerably chewed up. Bleeding badly. We'd best get him to the office and patch him up before—"

"Wha—what was it?" our mangled patient asked abruptly, rising on his elbow and staring wildly round him. "Did you kill it—did it get away? D'ye think it had hydrophobia?"

"Easy on, son," I soothed, locking my hands beneath his arms and helping him to rise. "It bit you several times, but you'll be all right as soon as we can stop the bleeding. Here"—I snatched a handkerchief from the breast pocket of my dinner coat and pressed it into his hand—"hold this against the wound while we're walking. No use trying to get a taxi tonight, the driver'd never find his way about. I live only a little way from here and we'll make it nicely if you'll lean on me. So! That's it!"

THE YOUNG MAN LEANED heavily upon my shoulder and almost bore me down, for he weighed a good fourteen stone, as we made our way along the vapor-shrouded street.

"I say, I'm sorry I bumped into you, sir," the youngster apologized as de Grandin took his other arm and eased me somewhat of my burden. "Fact is, I'd taken a trifle too much and was walkin' on a side hill when I passed you." He pressed the already-reddened handkerchief closer to his lacerated neck as he continued with a chuckle: "Maybe it's a good thing I did, at that, for you were within hearing when I called because you'd stopped to cuss me out."

"You may have right, my friend," de Grandin answered with a laugh. "A little drunkenness is not to be deplored, and I doubt not you had reason for your drinking—not that one needs a reason, but—"

A sudden shrill, sharp cry for help cut through his words, followed by another call which stopped half uttered on a strangled, agonizing note; then, in a moment, the muffled echo of a shot, another, and, immediately afterward, the shrilling signal of a police whistle.

"*Tête bleu*, this night is full of action as a pepper-pot is full of spice!" exclaimed de Grandin, turning toward the summons of the whistle. "Can you manage him, Friend Trowbridge? If so I—"

Pounding of heavy boots on the sidewalk straight ahead told us that the officer approached, and a moment later his form, bulking gigantically in the fog, hove into view. "Did anny o' yez see—" he started, then raised his hand in half-formal salute to the vizor of his cap as he recognized de Grandin.

"I don't suppose ye saw a dar-rg come runnin' by this way, sor?" he asked. "I wuz walkin' up th' street a moment since, gettin' ready to report at th' box, when I heard a felly callin' for help, an' what should I see next but th' biggest, ugliest baste of a dar-rg ye iver clapped yer eyes upon, a-worryin' at th' pore lad's throat. I wus close to it as I'm standin' to you, sor, pretty near, an' I shot at it twict, but I'm damned if I didn't miss both times, slick as a whistle—an' me holdin' a pistol expert's medal from th' department, too!"

"U'm?" de Grandin murmured. "And the unfortunate man beset by this great beast your bullets failed to hit, what of him?"

"Glory be to God; I plumb forgot 'im!" the policeman confessed. "Ye see, sor, I wuz that overcome wid shame, as th' felly says, whin I realized I'd missed th' baste that I run afther it, hopin' I'd find it agin an' maybe put a slug into it this time, so—"

"Quite so, one understands," de Grandin interrupted, "but let us give attention to the man; the beast can wait until we find him, and—*mon Dieu!* It is as well you did not stay to give him the first aid, my friend, your efforts would have been without avail. His case demands the coroner's attention."

He did not understate the facts. Stretched on his back, hands clenched to fists, legs slightly spread, one doubled partly under him, a man lay on the sidewalk; across the white expanse of evening shirt his opened coat displayed there spread a ruddy stickiness, while his starched white-linen collar was already sopping with the blood which oozed from his torn and mangled throat. Both external and anterior jugulars had been ripped away by the savagery which had torn the integument of the neck to shreds, and so deeply had the ragged wound gone that a portion of the hyoid bone had been exposed. A spate of blood had driveled from the mouth, staining lips and chin, and the eyes, forced out between the lids, were globular and fixed and staring, though the film of death had hardly yet had time to set upon them.

"Howly Mither!" cried the officer in horror as he looked upon the body. "Sure, it were a hound from th' Divil's own kennels done this, sor!"

"I think that you have right," de Grandin nodded grimly, "Call the department, if you will be so good. I will stand by the body." He took a kerchief from his pocket and opened it, preparatory to veiling the poor, mangled face which stared appealingly up at the fog-bound night, but:

"My God, it's Suffrige!" the young man at my side exclaimed. I left him just before I blundered into you, and—oh, what could have done it?"

"The same thing which almost did as much for you, *Monsieur*," the Frenchman answered in a level, toneless voice. "You had a very narrow escape from being even as your friend, I do assure you."

"You mean that dog—" he stopped, incredulous, eyes fairly starting from his face as he stared in fascination at his friend's remains.

"The dog, yes, let us call it that," de Grandin answered.

"But—but—" the other stammered, then, with an incoherent exclamation which was half sigh, half groaning hiccup, slumped heavily against my shoulder and slid unconscious to the ground.

De Grandin shrugged in irritation. "Now we have two of them to watch," he complained. "Do you recover him as quickly as you can, my friend, while I—" he turned his back to me, dropped his handkerchief upon the dead man's face and bent to make a closer examination of the wounds in the throat.

I took the handkerchief from my overcoat pocket, ran it lightly over the trunk of a leafless tree which stood beside the curb and wrung the moisture from it on the unconscious man's face and forehead. Slowly he recovered, gasped feebly, then, with my assistance, got upon his feet, keeping his back resolutely turned to the grisly thing upon the sidewalk. "Can—you—help—me—to—your—office?" he asked slowly, breathing heavily between the words.

I nodded, and we started toward my house, but twice we had to stop; for once he became sick, and I had to hold him while he retched with nausea, and once he nearly fainted again, leaning heavily against the iron balustrade before a house while he drew great gulps of chilly, fog-soaked air into his lungs.

A T LAST WE REACHED my office, and helping him up to the examination table I set to work. His wounds were more extensive than I had at first supposed. A deep cut, more like the raking of some heavy, blunt-pointed claw than a bite, ran down his face from the right temple almost to the angle of the jaw, and two deep parallel scores showed on his throat above the collar. A little deeper, a little more to one side, and they would have nicked the interior jugular. About his hands were several tears, as though they had suffered more from the beast's teeth than had his face and throat, and as I helped him with his jacket I saw his shirt-front had been slit and a long, raking cut scored down his chest, the animal's claws having ripped through the stiff, starched linen as easily as though it had been muslin.

The problem of treatment puzzled me. I could not cauterize the wounds with silver nitrate, and iodine would be without efficiency if the dog were rabid. Finally I compromised by dressing the chest and facial wounds with potassium permanganate solution and using an electric hot-point on the hands, applying laudanum immediately as an anodyne.

"And now, young fellow," I announced as I completed my work, "I think you could do nicely with a tot of brandy. You were drunk enough when you ran into us, heaven knows, but you're cold sober now, and your nerves have been badly jangled, so—"

"So you would be advised to bring another glass," de Grandin's hail sounded from the surgery door. "My nerves have been on edge these many minutes, and in addition I am suffering from an all-consuming thirst, my friend."

The young man gulped the liquor down in one tremendous swallow, seeing which de Grandin gave a shudder of disgust. Drinking fifty-year-old brandy was a rite with him, and to bolt it as if it had been common bootlegged stuff was grave impropriety, almost sacrilege.

"Doctor, do you think that dog had hydrophobia?" our patient asked half diffidently. "He seemed so savage—"

"Hydrophobia is the illness human beings have when bitten by a rabid dog or other animal, *Monsieur*," de Grandin broke in with a smile. "The beast has rabies, the human victim develops hydrophobia. However, if you wish, we can arrange for you to go to Mercy Hospital early in the morning to take the Pasteur treatment; it is effective and protective if you are infected, quite harmless if you are not."

"Thanks," replied the youth. "I think we'd better, for—"

"*Monsieur*," the Frenchman cut him short again, "is your name Maxwell, by any chance? Since I first saw you I have been puzzled by your face; now I remember, I saw your picture in *le Journal* this morning."

"Yes," said our visitor, "I'm John Maxwell, and, since you saw my picture in the paper, you know that I'm to marry Sarah Leigh on Saturday; so you realize why I'm so anxious to make sure the dog didn't have hydro—rabies, I mean. I don't think Sallie'd want a husband she had to muzzle for fear he'd bite her on the ankle when she came to feed him."

The little Frenchman smiled acknowledgment of the other's pleasantry, but though his lips drew back in the mechanics of a smile, his little, round, blue eyes were fixed and studious.

"Tell me, *Monsieur*," he asked abruptly, "how came this dog to set upon you in the fog tonight?"

Young Maxwell shivered at the recollection. "Hanged if I know," he answered. "Y'see, the boys gave me a farewell bachelor dinner at the Carteret this evening, and there was the usual amount of speech-making and toast-drinking, and by the time we broke up I was pretty well paralyzed—able to find my way about, but not very steadily, as you know. I said good-night to the bunch at the hotel and started out alone, for I wanted to walk the liquor off. You see"—a flush suffused his blond, good-looking face—"Sallie said she'd wait up for me to telephone her—just like old married folks!—and I didn't want to talk to her while I was still thick-tongued. Ray Suffrige, the chap who—the one you saw later, sir—decided he'd walk home, too, and started off in the other direction, and the rest of 'em left in taxis.

"I'd walked about four blocks, and was getting so I could navigate pretty well, when I bumped into you, then brought up against the railing of a house. While I was hanging onto it, trying to get steady on my legs again, all of a sudden, out of nowhere, came that big police-dog and jumped on me. It didn't bark or give any warning till it leaped at me; then it began growling. I flung my hands up, and it fastened on my sleeve, but luckily the cloth was thick enough to keep its teeth from tearing my arm.

"I never saw such a beast. I've had a tussle or two with savage dogs before, and they always jumped away and rushed in again each time I beat 'em off, but this thing stood on its hind legs and fought me, like a man. When it shook its teeth loose from my coat-sleeve it clawed at my face and throat with its fore-paws—that's where I got most of my mauling—and kept snapping at me all the time; never backed away or even sank to all-fours once, sir.

"I was still unsteady on my legs, and the brute was heavy as a man; so it wasn't long before it had me down. Every time it bit at me I managed to get my arms in its way; so it did more damage to my clothes than it did to me with its teeth, but it surely clawed me up to the Queen's taste, and I was beginning to tire when you came running up. It would have done me as it did poor Suffrige in a little while, I'm sure."

He paused a moment, then, with a shaking hand, poured out another drink of brandy and tossed it off at a gulp. "I guess I *must* have been drunk," he admitted with a shamefaced grin, "for I could have sworn the thing *talked* to me as it growled."

"Eh? The Devil!" Jules de Grandin sat forward suddenly, eyes wider and rounder than before, if possible, the needle-points of his tightly waxed wheat-blond mustache twitching like the whiskers of an irritated tomcat. "What is it that you say?"

"Hold on," the other countered, quick blood mounting to his cheeks. "I didn't say it; I said it *seemed* as if its snarls were words."

"*Précisément, exactement*, quite so," returned the Frenchman sharply. "And what was it that he *seemed* to snarl at you, *Monsieur*? Quickly, if you please."

"Well, I was drunk, I admit, but—"

"Ten thousand small blue devils! We bandy words. I have asked you a question; have the courtesy to reply, *Monsieur*."

"Well, it sounded—sort of—as if it kept repeating Sallie's name, like this—" he gave an imitation of a throaty, growling voice: "'Sarah Leigh, Sarah Leigh—you'll never marry Sarah Leigh!'

"Ever hear anything so nutty? I reckon I must have had Sallie in my mind, subconsciously, while I was having what I thought was my death-struggle."

It was very quiet for a moment. John Maxwell looked half sullenly, half defiantly from de Grandin to me. De Grandin sat as though lost in contemplation, his small eyes wide and thoughtful, his hands twisting savagely at the waxed ends of his mustache, the tip of his patent-leather evening shoe beating a devil's tattoo on the white-tiled floor. At length, abruptly:

"Did you notice any smell, any peculiar odor, when we went to Monsieur Maxwell's rescue this evening, Friend Trowbridge?" he demanded.

"Why—" I bent my brows and wagged my head in an effort at remembrance. "Why, no, I didn't—" I stopped, while somewhere from the file-cases of my subconscious memory came a hint of recollection: Soldiers' Park—a damp and drizzling day—the open air dens of the menagerie. "Wait," I ordered, closing both eyes tightly while I bade my memory catalogue the vague, elusive scent; then: "Yes, there was an odor I've noticed at the zoo in Soldiers' Park; it was the smell of the damp fur of a fox, or wolf!"

De Grandin beat his small, white hands together softly, as though applauding at a play. "Capital, perfect!" he announced. "I smelt it too, when first we did approach, but our senses play strange tricks on us at times, and I needed the corroboration of your nose's testimony, if it could be had. Now—" he turned his fixed, unwinking stare upon me as he asked: "Have you ever seen a wolf's eyes—or a dog's—at night?"

"Yes, of course," I answered wonderingly.

"*Très bien*. And they gleamed with a reflected greenness, something like Madame Pussy's, only not so bright, *n'est-ce-pas?*"

"Yes."

"*Très bon*. Did you see the eyes of what attacked Monsieur Maxwell this evening? Did you observe them?"

"I should say I did," I answered, for never would I forget those fiery, glaring orbs. "They were red, red as fire!"

"Oh, excellent Friend Trowbridge; oh, prince of all the recollectors of the world!" de Grandin cried delightedly. "Your memory serves you perfectly, and upholds my observations to the full. Before, I guessed; I said to me, 'Jules de Grandin, you are generally right, but once in many times you may be wrong. See what Friend Trowbridge has to say.' And you, *parbleu*, you said the very thing I needed to confirm me in my diagnosis.

"*Monsieur*," he turned to Maxwell with a smile, "you need not fear that you have hydrophobia. No. You were very near to death, a most unpleasant sort of death, but not to death by hydrophobia. *Morbleu*, that would be an added refinement which we need not take into consideration."

"Whatever are you talking about?" I asked in sheer amazement. "You ask me if I noticed the smell that beast gave off, and if I saw its eyes, then tell Mr. Maxwell he needn't fear he's been inoculated. Of all the hare-brained—"

He turned his shoulder squarely on me and smiled assuringly at Maxwell. "You said that you would call your *amoureuse* tonight, *Monsieur*; have you forgotten?" he reminded, then nodded toward the phone.

The young man picked the instrument up, called a number and waited for a moment; then: "John speaking, honey," he announced as we heard a subdued click sound from the monophone. Another pause, in which the buzzing of indistinguishable words came faintly to us through the quiet room; then Maxwell turned and motioned me to take up the extension 'phone.

"—and please come right away, dear," I heard a woman's voice plead as I clapped the instrument against my ear. "No, I can't tell you over the 'phone, but I must see you right away, Johnny—I must! You're sure you're all right? Nothing happened to you?"

"Well," Maxwell temporized, "I'm in pretty good shape, everything considered. I had a little tussle with a dog, but—"

"A—*dog?*" Stark, incredulous horror sounded in the woman's fluttering voice. "What sort of dog?"

"Oh, just a dog, you know; not very big and not very little, sort o' betwixt and between, and—"

"You're sure it was a *dog?* Did it look like a—a police-dog, for instance?"

"Well, now you mention it, it *did* look something like a police-dog, or collie, or airedale, or something, but—"

"John, dear, don't try to put me off that way. This is terribly, dreadfully important. Please hurry over—no, don't come out at night—yes, come at once, but be sure not to come alone. Have you a sword, or some sort of steel or iron weapon you can carry for defense when you come?"

Young Maxwell's face betrayed bewilderment. "A sword?" he echoed. "What d'ye think I am, dear, a knight of old? No, I haven't a sword to my name, not even a jack-knife, but—I say, there's a gentleman I met tonight who has a bully little sword; may I bring him along?"

"Oh, yes, please do, dear; and if you can get some one else, bring him too. I'm terribly afraid to have you venture out tonight, dearest, but I have to see you right away!"

"All right," the young man answered. "I'll pop right over, honey."

As he replaced the instrument, he turned bewilderedly to me. "Wonder what the deuce got into Sally?" he asked. "She seemed all broken up about something, and I thought she'd faint when I mentioned my set-to with that dog. What's it mean?"

Jules de Grandin stepped through the doorway connecting surgery with consulting-room, where he had gone to listen to the conversation from the desk extension. His little eyes were serious, his small mouth grimly set. "*Monsieur*," he announced gravely, "it means that Mademoiselle Sarah knows more than any of us what this business of the Devil is about. Come, let us go to her without delay."

As we prepared to leave the house he paused and rummaged in the hall coat closet, emerging in a moment, balancing a pair of blackthorn walking-sticks in his hands.

"What—" I began, but he cut me short.

"These may prove useful," he announced, handing one to me, the other to John Maxwell. "If what I damn suspect is so, he will not greatly relish a thwack from one of these upon the head. No, the thorn-bush is especially repugnant to him."

"Humph, I should think it would be particularly repugnant to anyone," I answered, weighing the knotty bludgeon in my hand. "By the way, who is 'he'?"

"Mademoiselle Sarah will tell us that," he answered enigmatically. "Are we ready? *Bon*, let us be upon our way."

THE MIST WHICH HAD obscured the night an hour or so before had thinned to a light haze, and a drizzle of rain was commencing as we set out. The Leigh house was less than half a mile from my place, and we made good time as we marched through the damp, cold darkness.

I had known Joel Leigh only through having shared committee appointments with him in the local Republican organization and at the archdeaconry. He had entered the consular service after being retired from active duty with the Marine Corps following a surgeon's certificate of disability, and at the time of his death two years before had been rated as one of the foremost authorities on Near East commercial conditions. Sarah, his daughter, whom I had never met, was, by all accounts, a charming young woman, equally endowed with brains, beauty and money, and keeping up the family tradition in the big house in Tuscarora Avenue, where she lived with an elderly maiden aunt as duenna.

Leigh's long residence in the East was evidenced in the furnishings of the long, old-fashioned hall, which was like a royal antechamber in miniature. In the softly diffused light from a brass-shaded Turkish lamp we caught gleaming reflections from heavily carved blackwood furniture and the highlights of a marvelously inlaid Indian screen. A carved table flanked by dragon-chairs stood against the wall, the floor was soft as new-mown turf with rugs from China, Turkey and Kurdistan.

"Mis' Sarah's in the library," announced the Negro butler who answered our summons at the door, and led us through the hall to the big, high-ceilinged room where Sarah Leigh was waiting. Books lined the chamber's walls from floor to ceiling on three sides; the fourth wall was devoted to a bulging bay-window which overlooked the garden. Before the fire of cedar logs was drawn a deeply padded divan, while flanking it were great armchairs upholstered in red leather. The light which sifted through the meshes of a brazen lamp-shade disclosed a tabouret of Indian mahogany on which a coffee service stood. Before the fire the mistress of the house stood waiting us. She was rather less than average height, but appeared taller because of her fine carriage. Her mannishly close-cropped hair was dark and inclined toward curliness, but as she moved toward us I saw it showed bronze glints in the lamplight. Her eyes were large, expressive, deep hazel, almost brown. But for the look of cynicism, almost hardness, around her mouth, she would have been something more than merely pretty.

Introductions over, Miss Leigh looked from one of us to the other with something like embarrassment in her eyes. "If—" she began, but de Grandin divined her purpose, and broke in:

"*Mademoiselle*, a short time since, we had the good fortune to rescue *Monsieur* your *fiancé* from a dog which I do not think was any dog at all. That same creature, I might add, destroyed a gentleman who had attended Monsieur Maxwell's dinner within ten minutes of the time we drove it off. Furthermore, Monsieur Maxwell is under the impression that this dog-thing talked to him while it sought to slay him. From what we overheard of your message on the telephone, we think you hold the key to this mystery. You may speak freely in our presence, for I am Jules de Grandin, physician and occultist, and my friend, Doctor Trowbridge, has most commendable discretion."

The young woman smiled, and the transformation in her taut, strained face was startling. "Thank you," she replied; "if you're an occultist you will understand, and neither doubt me nor demand explanations of things I can't explain."

She dropped cross-legged to the hearth rug, as naturally as though she were more used to sitting that way than reclining in a chair, and we caught the gleam of a great square garnet on her forefinger as she extended her hand to Maxwell.

"Hold my hand while I'm talking, John," she bade. "It may be for the last time." Then, as he made a gesture of dissent, abruptly:

"I can not marry you—or anyone," she announced.

Maxwell opened his lips to protest, but no sound came. I stared at her in wonder, trying futilely to reconcile the agitation she had shown when telephoning with her present deadly, apathetic calm.

Jules de Grandin yielded to his curiosity. "Why not, *Mademoiselle?*" he asked. "Who has forbid the banns?"

She shook her head dejectedly and turned a sad-eyed look upon him as she answered: "It's just the continuation of a story which I thought was a closed chapter in my life." For a moment she bent forward, nestling her check against young Maxwell's hand; then:

"It began when Father was attached to the consulate in Smyrna," she continued. "France and Turkey were both playing for advantage, and Father had to find out what they planned, so he had to hire secret agents. The most successful of them was a young Greek named George Athanasakos, who came from Crete. Why he should have taken such employment was more than we could understand; for he was well educated, apparently a gentleman, and always well supplied with money. He told us he took the work because of his hatred of the Turks, and as he was always successful in getting information, Father didn't ask questions.

"When his work was finished he continued to call at our house as a guest, and I—I really didn't love him, I *couldn't* have, it was just infatuation, meeting him so far from home, and the water and that wonderful Smyrna moonlight, and—"

"Perfectly, *Mademoiselle*, one fully understands," de Grandin supplied softly as she paused, breathless; "and then—"

"Maybe you never succumbed to moonlight and water and strange, romantic poetry and music," she half whispered, her eyes grown wider at the recollection, "but I was only seventeen, and he was very handsome, and—and he swept me off my feet. He had the softest, most musical voice I've ever heard, and the things he said sounded like something written by Byron at his best. One moonlit night when we'd been rowing, he begged me to say I loved him, and—and I did. He held me in his arms and kissed my eyes and lips and throat. It was like being hypnotized and conscious at the same time. Then, just before we said good-night he told me to meet him in an old garden on the outskirts of the city where we sometimes rested when we'd been out riding. The rendezvous was made for midnight, and though I thought it queer that he should want to meet me at that time in such a place—well, girls in love don't ask questions, you know. At least, I didn't.

"There was a full moon the next night, and I was fairly breathless with the beauty of it all when I kept the tryst. I thought I'd come too early, for George was nowhere to be seen when I rode up, but as I jumped down from my horse and looked around I saw something moving in the laurels. It was George, and he'd thrown a cape or cloak of some sort of fur across his shoulders. He startled me dreadfully at first; for he looked like some sort of prowling beast with the animal's head hanging half down across his face, like the beaver of an ancient helmet. It seemed to me, too, that his eyes had taken on a sort of sinister greenish tinge, but when he took me in his arms and kissed me I was reassured.

"Then he told me he was the last of a very ancient clan which had been wiped out warring with the Turks, and that it was a tradition of their blood that the woman they married take a solemn oath before the nuptials could be celebrated. Again I didn't ask questions. It all seemed so wonderfully romantic," she added with a pathetic little smile.

"He had another skin cloak in readiness and dropped it over my shoulders, pulling the head well forward above my face, like a hood. Then he built a little fire of dry twigs and threw some incense on it. I knelt above the fire and inhaled the aromatic smoke while he chanted some sort of invocation in a tongue I didn't recognize, but which sounded harsh and terrible—like the snarling of a savage dog.

"What happened next I don't remember clearly, for that incense did things to me. The old garden where I knelt seemed to fade away, and in its place appeared a wild and rocky mountain scene where I seemed walking down a winding road. Other people were walking with me, some before, some behind, some beside me, and all were clothed in cloaks of hairy skin like mine. Suddenly, as we went down the mountainside, I began to notice that my companions were dropping to all-fours, like beasts. But somehow it didn't seem strange to me; for, without realizing it, I was running on my hands and feet, too. Not crawling, you know, but actually running—like a dog. As we neared the mountain's foot we ran faster and faster; by the time we reached a little clearing in the heavy woods which fringed the rocky hill we were going like the wind, and I felt myself panting, my tongue hanging from my mouth.

"In the clearing other beasts were waiting for us. One great, hairy creature came trotting up to me, and I was terribly frightened at first, for I recognized it as a mountain wolf, but it nuzzled me with its black snout and licked me, and somehow it seemed like a caress—I liked it. Then it started off across the unplowed field, and I ran after it, caught up with it, and ran alongside. We came to a pool and the beast stopped to drink, and I bent over the water too, lapping it up with my tongue. Then I saw our images in the still pond, and almost died of fright, for the thing beside me was a mountain wolf, and I was a she-wolf!

"My astonishment quickly passed, however, and somehow I didn't seem to mind having been transformed into a beast; for something deep inside me kept urging me on, on to something—I didn't quite know what.

"When we'd drunk we trotted through a little patch of woodland and suddenly my companion sank to the ground in the underbrush and lay there, red tongue lolling from its mouth, green eyes fixed intently on the narrow, winding path beside which we were resting. I wondered what we waited for, and half rose on my haunches to look, but a low, warning growl from the thing beside me warned that something was approaching. It was a pair of farm laborers, Greek peasants I knew them to be by their dress, and they were talking in low tones and looking fearfully about, as though they feared an ambush. When they came abreast of us the beast beside me sprang—so did I.

"I'll never forget the squeaking scream the nearer man gave as I leaped upon him, or the hopeless, terrified expression in his eyes as he tried to fight me off. But I bore him down, sank my teeth into his throat and began slowly tearing at his flesh. I could feel the blood from his torn throat welling up in my mouth, and its hot saltiness was sweeter than the most delicious wine. The poor wretch's struggles became weaker and weaker, and I felt a sort of fierce elation. Then he ceased to fight, and I shook him several times, as a terrier shakes a rat, and when he didn't move or struggle, I tore at his face and throat and chest till my hairy muzzle was one great smear of blood.

"Then, all at once, it seemed as though a sort of thick, white fog were spreading through the forest, blinding me and shutting out the trees and undergrowth and my companion beasts, even the poor boy whom I had killed, and—there I was kneeling over the embers of the dying fire in the old Smyrna garden, with the clouds of incense dying down to little curly spirals.

"George was standing across the fire from me, laughing, and the first thing I noticed was that *his lips were smeared with blood.*

"Something hot and salty stung my mouth, and I put my hand up to it. When I brought it down the fingers were red with a thick, sticky liquid.

"I think I must have started to scream; for George jumped over the fire and clapped his hand upon my mouth—*ugh*, I could taste the blood more than ever, then!—and whispered, 'Now you are truly mine, Star of the Morning. Together we have ranged the woods in spirit as we shall one day in body, O true mate of a true *vrykolakas!*'

"*Vrykolakas* is a Greek word hard to translate into English. Literally it means 'the restless dead', but it also means a vampire or a werewolf, and the *vrykolakas* are the most dreaded of all the host of demons with which Greek peasant-legends swarm.

"I shook myself free from him. 'Let me go; don't touch me; I never want to see you again!' I cried.

"'Nevertheless, you shall see me again—and again and again—Star of the Sea!' he answered with a mocking laugh. 'You belong to me, now, and no one shall take you from me. When I want you I will call, and you will come to me, for'—he looked directly into my eyes, and his own seemed to merge and run together, like two pools of liquid, till they were one great disk of green fire— 'thou shalt have no other mate than me, and he who tries to come between us dies. See, I put my mark upon you!'

"He tore my riding-shirt open and pressed his lips against my side, and next instant I felt a biting sting as his teeth met in my flesh. See—"

With a frantic, wrenching gesture she snatched at the low collar of her red-silk lounging pajamas, tore the fabric asunder and exposed her ivory flesh. Three inches or so below her left axilla, in direct line with the gently swelling bulge of her firm, high breast, was a small whitened cicatrix, and from it grew a little tuft of long, grayish-brown hair, like hairs protruding from a mole, but unlike any body hairs which I had ever seen upon a human being.

"*Grand Dieu*," exclaimed de Grandin softly. "*Poil de loup!*"

"Yes," she agreed in a thin, hysterical whisper, "it's wolf's hair! I know. I cut it off and took it to a biochemist in London, and he assured me it was unquestionably the hair of a wolf. I've tried and tried to have the scar removed, but it's useless. I've tried cautery, electrolysis, even surgery, but it disappears for only a little while, then comes again."

For a moment it was still as death in the big dim-lighted room. The little French-gilt clock upon the mantelpiece ticked softly, quickly, like a heart that palpitates with terror, and the hissing of a burning resined log seemed loud and eery as night-wind whistling round a haunted tower. The girl folded the torn silk of her pajama jacket across her breast and pinned it into place; then, simply, desolately, as one who breaks the news of a dear friend's death:

"So I can not marry you, you see, John, dear," she said.

"Why?" asked the young man in a low, fierce voice. "Because that scoundrel drugged you with his devilish incense and made you think you'd turned into a wolf? Because—"

"Because I'd be your murderess if I did so," she responded quiveringly. "Don't you remember? He said he'd call me when he wanted me, and anyone who came between him and me would die. He's come for me, he's called me, John; it was he who attacked you in the fog tonight. Oh, my dear, my dear,

I love you so; but I must give you up. It would be murder if I were to marry you!"

"Nonsense!" began John Maxwell bruskly. "If you think that man can—"

Outside the house, seemingly from underneath the library's bow-window, there sounded in the rain-drenched night a wail, long-drawn, pulsating, doleful as the cry of an abandoned soul: "*O-u-o—o-u-oo—o-u-o—o-u-oo!*" it rose and fell, quavered and almost died away, then resurged with increased force. "*O-u-o—o-u-o-o—o-u-o—o-u-oo!*"

The woman on the hearth rug cowered like a beaten beast, clutching frantically with fear-numbed fingers at the drugget's pile, half crawling, half writhing toward the brass bars where the cheerful fire burned brightly. "Oh," she whimpered as the mournful ululation died away, "that's he; he called me once before today; now he's come again, and—"

"*Mademoiselle*, restrain yourself," de Grandin's sharp, whip-like order cut through her mounting terror and brought her back to something like normality. "You are with friends," he added in a softer tone; "three of us are here, and we are a match for any *sacré loup-garou* that ever killed a sheep or made night hideous with his howling. *Parbleu*, but I shall say damn yes. Did I not, all single-handed, already put him to flight once tonight? But certainly. Very well, then, let us talk this matter over calmly, for—"

With the suddenness of a discharged pistol a wild, vibrating howl came through the window once again. "*O-u-o—o-u-oo—o-u-o!*" it rose against the stillness of the night, diminished to a moan, then suddenly crescendoed upward, from a moan to a wail, from a wail to a howl, despairing, pleading, longing as the cry of a damned spirit, fierce and wild as the rally-call of the fiends of hell.

"*Sang du diable*, must I suffer interruption when I wish to talk? *Sang des tous les saints*—it is not to be borne!" de Grandin cried furiously, and cleared the distance to the great bay-window in two agile, cat-like leaps.

"*Allez!*" he ordered sharply, as he flung the casement back and leaned far out into the rainy night. "Be off, before I come down to you. You know me, *hein?* A little while ago you dodged my steel, but—"

A snarling growl replied, and in the clump of rhododendron plants which fringed the garden we saw the baleful glimmer of a pair of fiery eyes.

"*Parbleu*, you dare defy me—*me?*" the little Frenchman cried, and vaulted nimbly from the window, landing sure-footed as a panther on the rain-soaked garden mold, then charging at the lurking horror as though it had been harmless as a kitten,

"Oh, he'll be killed; no mortal man can stand against a *vrykolakas!*" cried Sarah Leigh, wringing her slim hands together in an agony of terror. "Oh, God in heaven, spare—"

A fusillade of crackling shots cut through her prayer, and we heard a short, sharp yelp of pain, then the voice of Jules de Grandin hurling imprecations in mingled French and English. A moment later:

"Give me a hand, Friend Trowbridge," he called from underneath the window. "It was a simple matter to come down, but climbing back is something else again.

"*Merci*," he acknowledged as he regained the library and turned his quick, elfin grin on each of us in turn. Dusting his hands against each other, to clear them of the dampness from the windowsill, he felt for his cigarette case, chose a Maryland and tapped it lightly on his finger-nail.

"*Tiens*, I damn think he will know his master's voice in future, that one," he informed us. "I did not quite succeed in killing him to death, unfortunately, but I think that it will be some time before he comes and cries beneath this lady's window again. Yes. Had the *sale poltron* but had the courage to stand against me, I should certainly have killed him; but as it was"—he spread his hands and raised his shoulders eloquently—"it is difficult to hit a running shadow, and he offered little better mark in the darkness. I think I wounded him in the left hand, but I can not surely say."

He paused a moment, then, seeming to remember, turned again to Sarah Leigh with a ceremonious bow. "*Pardon, Mademoiselle*," he apologized, "you were saying, when we were so discourteously interrupted—" he smiled at her expectantly.

"Doctor de Grandin," wondering incredulity was in the girl's eyes and voice as she looked at him, "you shot him—wounded him?"

"Perfectly, *Mademoiselle*," he patted the waxed ends of his mustache with affectionate concern, "my marksmanship was execrable, but at least I hit him. That was something."

"But in Greece they used to say—I've always heard that only silver bullets were effective against a *vrykolakas*; either silver bullets or a sword of finely tempered steel, so—"

"*Ah bah!*" he interrupted with a laugh. "What did they know of modern ordnance, those old-time ritualists? Silver bullets were decreed because silver is a harder metal than lead, and the olden guns they used in ancient days were not adapted to shoot balls of iron. The pistols of today shoot slugs encased in cupro-nickel, far harder than the best of iron, and with a striking-force undreamed of in the days when firearms were a new invention. *Tiens*, had the good Saint George possessed a modern military rifle he could have slain the dragon at his leisure while he stood a mile away. Had Saint Michel had a machine-gun, his victory over Lucifer could have been accomplished in thirty seconds by the watch."

Having delivered himself of this scandalous opinion, he reseated himself on the divan and smiled at her, for all the world like the family cat which has just breakfasted on the household canary.

"And how was it that this so valiant runner-away-from-Jules-de-Grandin announced himself to you, *Mademoiselle?*" he asked.

"I was dressing to go out this morning," she replied, "when the 'phone rang, and when I answered it no one replied to my 'hello.' Then, just as I began to think they'd given some one a wrong number, and was about to put the instrument down, there came one of those awful, wailing howls across the wire. No word at all, sir, just that long-drawn, quavering howl, like what you heard a little while ago.

"You can imagine how it frightened me. I'd almost managed to put George from my mind, telling myself that the vision of lycanthropy which I had in Smyrna was some sort of hypnotism, and that there really weren't such things as werewolves, and even if there were, this was practical America, where I needn't fear them—then came that dreadful howl, the sort of howl I'd heard—and given!—in my vision in the Smyrna garden, and I knew there *are* such things as werewolves, and that one of them possessed me, soul and body, and that I'd have to go to him if he demanded it.

"Most of all, though, I thought of John, for if the werewolf were in America he'd surely read the notice of our coming marriage, and the first thing I remembered was his threat to kill anyone who tried to come between us."

She turned to Maxwell with a pensive smile. "You know how I've been worrying you all day, dear," she asked, "how I begged you not to go out to that dinner tonight, and when you said you must how I made you promise that you'd call me as soon as you got home, but on no account to call me before you were safely back in your apartment?

"I've been in a perfect agony of apprehension all evening," she told us, "and when John called from Doctor Trowbridge's office I felt as though a great weight had been lifted from my heart."

"And did you try to trace the call?" the little Frenchman asked.

"Yes, but it had been dialed from a downtown pay station, so it was impossible to find it."

De Grandin took his chin between his thumb and forefinger and gazed thoughtfully at the tips of his patent-leather evening shoes. "U'm?" he murmured; then: "What does he look like, this so gallant persecutor of women, *Mademoiselle?* 'He is handsome,' you have said, which is of interest, certainly, but not especially instructive. Can you be more specific? Since he is a Greek, one assumes that he is dark, but—"

"No, he's not," she interrupted. "His eyes are blue and his hair is rather light, though his beard—he used to wear one, though he may be smooth-shaven now—is quite dark, almost black. Indeed, in certain lights it seems to have an almost bluish tinge."

"Ah, so? *Une barbe bleu?*" de Grandin answered sharply. "One might have thought as much. Such beards, *ma chère*, are the sign-manual of those who traffic with the Devil. Gilles de Retz, the vilest monster who ever cast insult on the human race by wearing human form, was light of hair and blue-black as to beard. It is from him we get the most unpleasant fairy-tale of Bluebeard, though the gentleman who dispatched his wives for showing too much curiosity was a lamb and sucking dove beside the one whose name he bears.

"Very well. Have you a photograph of him, by any happy chance?"

"No; I did have one, but I burned it years ago."

"A pity, *Mademoiselle*; our task would be made easier if we had his likeness as a guide. But we shall find him otherwise."

"How?" asked Maxwell and I in chorus.

"There was a time," he answered, "when the revelations of a patient to his doctor were considered privileged communications. Since prohibition came to blight your land, however, and the gangster's gun has written history in blood, the physicians are required to note the names and addresses of those who come to them with gunshot wounds, and this information is collected by the police each day. Now, we know that I have wounded this one. He will undoubtlessly seek medical assistance for his hurt. *Voilà*, I shall go down to the police headquarters, look upon the records of those treated for injuries from bullets, and by a process of elimination we shall find him. You apprehend?"

"But suppose he doesn't go to a physician?" young Maxwell interposed.

"In that event we have to find some other way to find him," de Grandin answered with a smile, "but that is a stream which we shall cross when we have arrived upon its shore. Meantime"—he rose and bowed politely to our hostess—"it is getting late, *Mademoiselle*, and we have trespassed on your time too long already. We shall convoy Monsieur Maxwell safely home, and see him lock his door, and if you will keep your doors and windows barred, I do not think that you have anything to fear. The gentleman who seems also to be a wolf has his wounded paw to nurse, and that will keep him busy the remainder of the night."

With a movement of his eyes he bade me leave the room, following closely on my heels and closing the door behind him. "If we must separate them the least which we can do is give them twenty little minutes for good-night," he murmured as we donned our mackintoshes.

"Twenty minutes?" I expostulated. "Why, he could say good-night to twenty girls in twenty minutes!"

"*Oui-da, certainement*; or a hundred," he agreed, "but not to the one girl, my good friend. *Ah bah*, Friend Trowbridge, did you never love; did you never worship at the small, white feet of some beloved woman? Did you never feel your breath come faster and your blood pound wildly at your temples as you took her in your arms and put your lips against her mouth? If not—*grand Dieu des porcs*—then you have never lived at all, though you be older than Methuselah!"

R UNNING OUR QUARRY TO earth proved a harder task than we had antici-pated. Daylight had scarcely come when de Grandin visited the police, but for all he discovered he might have stayed at home. Only four cases of gunshot wounds had been reported during the preceding night, and two of the injured men were Negroes, a third a voluble but undoubtedly Italian laborer who had quarreled with some fellow countrymen over a card game, while the fourth was a thin-faced, tight-lipped gangster who eyed us saturninely and murmured, "Never mind who done it; I'll be seein' 'im," evidently under the misapprehen-sion that we were emissaries of the police.

The next day and the next produced no more results. Gunshot wounds there were, but none in the hand, where de Grandin declared he had wounded the nocturnal visitant, and though he followed every lead assiduously, in every case he drew a blank.

He was almost beside himself on the fourth day of fruitless search; by eve-ning I was on the point of prescribing triple bromides, for he paced the study restlessly, snapping his fingers, tweaking the waxed ends of his mustache till I made sure he would pull the hairs loose from his lip, and murmuring appalling blasphemies in mingled French and English.

At length, when I thought that I could stand his restless striding no longer, diversion came in the form of a telephone call. He seized the instrument pee-vishly, but no sooner had he barked a sharp "*Allo?*" than his whole expression changed and a quick smile ran across his face, like sunshine breaking through a cloud.

"But certainly; of course, assuredly!" he cried delightedly. Then, to me:

"Your hat and coat, Friend Trowbridge, and hurry, *pour l'amour d'un têtard*— they are marrying!"

"Marrying?" I echoed wonderingly. "Who—"

"Who but Mademoiselle Sarah and Monsieur Jean, *parbleu?*" he answered with a grin. "*Oh, la, la,* at last they show some sense, those ones. He had broken her resistance down, and she consents, werewolf or no werewolf. Now we shall surely make the long nose at that *sacré singe* who howled beneath her window when we called upon her!"

The ceremony was to be performed in the sacristy of St. Barnabas' Church, for John and Sarah, shocked and saddened by the death of young Fred Suffrige, who was to have been their best man, had recalled the invitations and decided on a private wedding with only her aunt and his mother present in addition to de Grandin and me.

"DEARLY BELOVED, WE ARE gathered together here in the sight of God and in the face of this company to join together this man and this woman in holy matrimony," began the rector, Doctor Higginbotham, who, despite the informality of the occasion, was attired in all the panoply of a high church priest and accompanied by two gorgeously accoutered and greatly interested choir-boys who served as acolytes. "Into this holy estate these two persons come now to be joined. If any man can show just cause why they should not lawfully be joined together let him now speak, or else hereafter forever hold his peace—"

"Jeez!" exclaimed the choir youth who stood upon the rector's left, letting fall the censer from his hands and dodging nimbly back, as from a threatened blow.

The interruption fell upon the solemn scene like a bombshell at a funeral, and one and all of us looked at the cowering youngster, whose eyes were fairly bulging from his face and whose ruddy countenance had gone a sickly, pasty gray, so that the thick-strewn freckles started out in contrast, like spots of rouge upon a corpse's pallid cheeks.

"Why, William—" Doctor Higginbotham began in a shocked voice; but:

Rat, tat-tat! sounded the sudden sharp clatter of knuckles against the window-pane, and for the first time we realized it had been toward this window the boy had looked when his sacrilegious exclamation broke in on the service.

Staring at us through the glass we saw a great, gray wolf! Yet it was not a wolf, for about the lupine jaws and jowls was something hideously reminiscent of a human face, and the greenish, phosphorescent glow of those great, glaring eyes had surely never shone in any face, animal or human. As I looked, breathless, the monster raised its head, and strangling horror gripped my throat with fiery fingers as I saw a human-seeming neck beneath it. Long and grisly-thin it was, corded and sinewed like the desiccated gula of a lich, and, like the face, covered with a coat of gray-brown fur. Then a hand, hair-covered like the throat and face, slim as a woman's—or a mummy's!—but terribly misshapen, fingers tipped with blood-red talon-nails, rose up and struck the glass again. My scalp was fairly crawling with sheer terror, and my breath came hot and sulfurous in my throat as I wondered how much longer the frail glass could stand against the impact of those bony, hair-gloved hands.

A strangled scream behind me sounded from Sarah's aunt, Miss Leigh, and I heard the muffled thud as she toppled to the floor in a dead faint, but I could no more turn my gaze from the horror at the window than the fascinated bird can tear its eyes from the serpent's numbing stare.

Another sighing exclamation and another thudding impact. John Maxwell's mother was unconscious on the floor beside Miss Leigh, but still I stood and stared in frozen terror at the thing beyond the window.

Doctor Higginbotham's teeth were chattering, and his ruddy, plethoric countenance was death-gray as he faced the staring horror, but he held fast to his faith.

"*Conjuro te, sceleratissime, abire ad tuum locum*"—he began the sonorous Latin exorcism, signing himself with his right hand and advancing his pectoral cross toward the thing at the window with his left—"I exorcise thee, most foul spirit, creature of darkness—"

The corners of the wolf-thing's devilish eyes contracted in a smile of malevolent amusement, and a rim of scarlet tongue flicked its black muzzle. Doctor Higginbotham's exorcism, bravely begun, ended on a wheezing, stifled syllable, and he stared in round-eyed fascination, his thick lips, blue with terror, opening and closing, but emitting no sound.

"*Sang d'un cochon*, not that way, Monsieur—this!" cried Jules de Grandin, and the roar of his revolver split the paralysis of quiet which had gripped the little chapel. A thin, silvery tinkle of glass sounded as the bullet tore through the window, and the grisly face abruptly disappeared, but from somewhere in the outside dark there echoed back a braying howl which seemed to hold a sort of obscene laughter in its quavering notes.

"*Sapristi!* Have I missed him?" de Grandin asked incredulously. "No matter; he is gone. On with the service, *Monsieur le Curé*. I do not think we shall be interrupted further."

"No!" Doctor Higginbotham backed away from Sarah Leigh as though her breath polluted him. "I can perform no marriage until that thing has been explained. Some one here is haunted by a devil—a malign entity from hell which will not heed the exorcism of the Church—and until I'm satisfied concerning it, and that you're all good Christians, there'll be no ceremony in this church!"

"*Eh bien, Monsieur*, who can say what constitutes a good Christian?" de Grandin smiled unpleasantly at Doctor Higginbotham. "Certainly one who lacks in charity as you do can not be competent to judge. Have it as you wish. As soon as we have recovered these fainting ladies we shall leave, and may the Devil grill me on the grates of hell if ever we come back until you have apologized."

Two hours later, as we sat in the Leigh library, Sarah dried her eyes and faced her lover with an air of final resolution: "You see, my dear, it's utterly impossible for me to marry you, or anyone," she said. "That awful thing will dog my steps, and—"

"My poor, sweet girl, I'm more determined than ever to marry you!" John broke in. "If you're to be haunted by a thing like that, you need me every minute, and—"

"*Bravo!*" applauded Jules de Grandin. "Well said, *mon vieux*, but we waste precious time. Come, let us go."

"Where?" asked John Maxwell, but the little Frenchman only smiled and shrugged his shoulders.

"To Maidstone Crossing, quickly, if you please, my friend," he whispered when he had led the lovers to my car and seen solicitously to their comfortable seating in the tonneau. "I know a certain justice of the peace there who would marry the Witch of Endor to the Emperor Nero though all the wolves which ever plagued Red Riding-Hood forbade the banns, provided only we supply him with sufficient fee."

Two hours' drive brought us to the little hamlet of Maidstone Crossing, and de Grandin's furious knocking on the door of a small cottage evoked the presence of a lank, lean man attired in a pair of corduroy trousers drawn hastily above the folds of a canton-flannel nightshirt.

A whispered colloquy between the rustic and the slim, elegant little Parisian; then: "O.K., Doc," the justice of the peace conceded. "Bring 'em in; I'll marry 'em, an'—hey, Sam'l!" he called up the stairs. "C'mon down, an' bring yer shotgun. There's a weddin' goin' to be pulled off, an' they tell me some fresh guys may try to interfere!"

"Sam'l," a lank, lean youth whose costume duplicated that of his father, descended the stairway grinning, an automatic shotgun cradled in the hollow of his arm. "D'ye expect any real rough stuff?" he asked.

"Seems like they're apt to try an' set a dawg on 'em," his father answered, and the younger man grinned cheerfully.

"Dawgs, is it?" he replied. "Dawgs is my dish. Go on, Pap, do yer stuff. Good luck, folks," he winked encouragingly at John and Sarah and stepped out on the porch, his gun in readiness.

"Do you take this here woman fer yer lawful, wedded wife?" the justice inquired of John Maxwell, and when the latter answered that he did:

"An' do you take this here now man to be yer wedded husband?" he asked Sarah.

"I do," the girl responded in a trembling whisper, and the roaring bellow of a shotgun punctuated the brief pause before the squire concluded:

"Then by virtue of th' authority vested in me by th' law an' constitootion of this state, I do declare ye man an' wife—an' whoever says that ye ain't married lawfully 's a danged liar," he added as a sort of afterthought.

"What wuz it that ye shot at, Sam'l?" asked the justice as, enriched by fifty dollars, and grinning appreciatively at the evening's profitable business, he ushered us from the house.

"Durned if I know, Pap," the other answered. "Looked kind o' funny to me. He wuz about a head taller'n me—an' I'm six foot two,—an' thin as Job's turkey-hen, to boot. His clothes looked skintight on 'im, an' he had on a cap, or sumpin with a peak that stuck out over his face. I first seen 'im comin' up th' road, kind o' lookin' this way an' that, like as if he warn't quite certain o' his way. Then, all of a suddent, he kind o' stopped an' threw his head back, like a dawg sniffin' th' air, an' started to go down on his all-fours, like he wuz goin' to sneak up on th' house. So I hauls off an' lets 'im have a tickle o' buckshot. Don't know whether I hit 'im or not, an' I'll bet he don't, neether; he sure didn't waste no time stoppin' to find out. Could he run! I'm tellin' ye, that feller must be in Harrisonville by now, if he kep' on goin' like he started!"

TWO DAYS OF FEVERISH activity ensued. Last-minute traveling arrangements had to be made, and passports for "John Maxwell and wife, Harrisonville, New Jersey, U.S.A.," obtained. De Grandin spent every waking hour with the newly married couple and even insisted on occupying a room in the Leigh house at night; but his precautions seemed unnecessary, for not so much as a whimper sounded under Sarah's window, and though the little Frenchman searched the garden every morning, there was no trace of unfamiliar footprints, either brute or human, to be found.

"Looks as if Sallie's Greek boy friend knows when he's licked and has decided to quit following her about," John Maxwell grinned as he and Sarah, radiant with happiness, stood upon the deck of the *Île de France*.

"One hopes so," de Grandin answered with a smile. "Good luck, *mes amis*, and may your *lune de miel* shine as brightly throughout all your lives as it does this night.

"*La lune*—ha?" he repeated half musingly, half with surprise, as though he just remembered some important thing which had inadvertently slipped his memory. "May I speak a private warning in your ear, Friend Jean?" He drew the bridegroom aside and whispered earnestly a moment.

"Oh, bosh!" the other laughed as they rejoined us. "That's all behind us, Doctor; you'll see; we'll never hear a sound from him. He's got *me* to deal with now, not just poor Sarah."

"Bravely spoken, little cabbage!" the Frenchman applauded. "*Bon voyage.*" But there was a serious expression on his face as we went down the gangway.

"What was the private warning you gave John?" I asked as we left the French Line piers. "He didn't seem to take it very seriously."

"No," he conceded. "I wish he had. But youth is always brave and reckless in its own conceit. It was about the moon. She has a strange influence on lycanthropy. The werewolf metamorphoses more easily in the full of the moon than at any other time, and those who may have been affected with his virus, though even faintly, are most apt to feel its spell when the moon is at the full. I warned him to be particularly careful of his lady on moonlit nights, and on no account to go anywhere after dark unless he were armed.

"The werewolf is really an inferior demon," he continued as we boarded the Hoboken ferry. "Just what he is we do not know with certainty, though we know he has existed from the earliest times; for many writers of antiquity mention him. Sometimes he is said to be a magical wolf who has the power to become a man. More often he is said to be a man who can become a wolf at times, sometimes of his own volition, sometimes at stated seasons, even against his will. He has dreadful powers of destructiveness; for the man who is also a wolf is ten times more deadly than the wolf who is only a wolf. He has the wolf's great strength and savagery, but human cunning with it. At night he quests and kills his prey, which is most often his fellow man, but sometimes sheep or hares, or his ancient enemy, the dog. By day he hides his villainy—and the location of his lair—under human guise.

"However, he has this weakness: Strong and ferocious, cunning and malicious as he is, he can be killed as easily as any natural wolf. A sharp sword will slay him, a well-aimed bullet puts an end to his career; the wood of the thorn-bush and the mountain ash are so repugnant to him that he will slink away if beaten or merely threatened with a switch of either. Weapons efficacious against an ordinary physical foe are potent against him, while charms and exorcisms which would put a true demon to flight are powerless.

"You saw how he mocked at Monsieur Higginbotham in the sacristy the other night, by example. But he did not stop to bandy words with me. Oh, no. He knows that I shoot straight and quick, and he had already felt my lead on one occasion. If young Friend Jean will always go well-armed, he has no need to fear; but if he be taken off his guard—eh bien, we can not always be on hand to rescue him as we did the night when we first met him. No, certainly."

"But why do you fear for Sarah?" I persisted.

"I hardly know," he answered. "Perhaps it is that I have what you Americans so drolly call the hunch. Werewolves sometimes become werewolves by the aid of Satan, that they may kill their enemies while in lupine form, or satisfy their natural lust for blood and cruelty while disguised as beasts. Some are transformed as the result of a curse upon themselves or their families, a few are metamorphosed by accident. These are the most unfortunate of all. In certain parts of Europe, notably in Greece, Russia and the Balkan states, the very soil seems cursed with lycanthropic power. There are certain places where, if the unwary traveler lies down to sleep, he is apt to wake up with the curse of were-wolfism on him. Certain streams and springs there are which, if drunk from, will render the drinker liable to transformation at the next full moon, and regularly thereafter. You will recall that in the dream, or vision, which Madame Sarah had while in the Smyrna garden so long ago, she beheld herself drinking from a woodland pool? I do not surely know, my friend, I have not even good grounds for suspicion, but something—something which I can not name—tells me that in some way this poor one, who is so wholly innocent, has been branded with the taint of lycanthropy. How it came about I can not say, but—"

My mind had been busily engaged with other problems, and I had listened to his disquisition on lycanthropy with something less than full attention. Now, suddenly aware of the thing which puzzled me, I interrupted:

"Can you explain the form that werewolf—if that's what it was—took on different occasions? The night we met John Maxwell he was fighting for his life with as true a wolf as any there are in the zoological gardens. O'Brien, the policeman, saw it, too, and shot at it, after it had killed Fred Suffrige. It was a sure-enough wolf when it howled under Sarah's window and you wounded it; yet when it interrupted the wedding it was an awful combination of wolf and man, or man and wolf, and the thing the justice's son drove off with his shotgun was the same, according to his description."

Surprisingly, he did not take offense at my interruption. Instead, he frowned in thoughtful silence at the dashboard lights a moment; then: "Sometimes the werewolf is completely transformed from man to beast," he answered; "sometimes he is a hideous combination of the two, but always he is a fiend incarnate. My own belief is that this one was only partly transformed when we last saw him because he had not time to wait complete metamorphosis. It is possible he could not change completely, too, because—" he broke off and pointed at the sky significantly.

"Well?" I demanded as he made no further effort to proceed.

"*Non*, it is not well," he denied, "but it may be important. Do you observe the moon tonight?"

"Why, yes."

"What quarter is it in?"

"The last; it's waning fast."

"*Précisément*. As I was saying, it may be that his powers to metamorphose himself were weakened because of the waning of the moon. Remember, if you please, his power for evil is at its height when the moon is at the full, and as it wanes, his powers become less and less. At the darkening of the moon, he is at his weakest, and then is the time for us to strike—if only we could find him. But he will lie well hidden at such times, never fear. He is clever with a devilish cunningness, that one."

"Oh, you're fantastic!" I burst out.

"You say so, having seen what you have seen?"

"Well, I'll admit we've seen some things which are mighty hard to explain," I conceded, "but—"

"But we are arrived at home; Monsieur and Madame Maxwell are safe upon the ocean, and I am vilely thirsty," he broke in. "Come, let us take a drink and go to bed, my friend."

W ITH MIDWINTER CAME JOHN and Sarah Maxwell, back from their honeymoon in Paris and on the Riviera. A week before their advent, notices in the society columns told of their homecoming, and a week after their return an engraved invitation apprised de Grandin and me that the honor of our presence was requested at a reception in the Leigh mansion, where they had taken residence. ". . . and please come early and stay late; there are a million things I want to talk about," Sarah penciled at the bottom of our card.

Jules de Grandin was more than usually ornate on the night of the reception. His London-tailored evening clothes were knife-sharp in their creases; about his neck hung the insignia of the *Legion d'Honneur*; a row of miniature medals, including the French and Belgian war crosses, the *Médaille Militaire* and the Italian Medal of Valor, decorated the left breast of his faultless evening coat; his little, wheat-blond mustache was waxed to needle-sharpness and his sleek blond hair was brilliantined and brushed till it fitted flat upon his shapely little head as a skull-cap of beige satin.

Lights blazed from every window of the house as we drew up beneath the porte-cochère. Inside all was laughter, staccato conversation and the odd, not unpleasant odor rising from the mingling of the hundred or more individual scents affected by the women guests. Summer was still near enough for the men to retain the tan of mountain and seashore on their faces and for a velvet vestige of veneer of painfully acquired sun-tan to show upon the women's arms and shoulders.

We tendered our congratulations to the homing newlyweds; then de Grandin plucked me by the sleeve. "Come away, my friend," he whispered in an almost tragic voice. "Come quickly, or these thirsty ones will have drunk up all the punch containing rum and champagne and left us only lemonade!"

The evening passed with pleasant swiftness, and guests began to leave. "Where's Sallie—seen her?" asked John Maxwell, interrupting a rather Rabelaisian story which de Grandin was retailing with gusto to several appreciative young men in the conservatory. "The Carter-Brooks are leaving, and—"

De Grandin brought his story to a close with the suddenness of a descending theater curtain, and a look of something like consternation shone in his small, round eyes. "She is not here?" he asked sharply. "When did you last see her?"

"Oh," John answered vaguely, "just a little while ago; we danced the 'Blue Danube' together, then she went upstairs for something, and—"

"Quick, swiftly!" de Grandin interrupted. "*Pardon, Messieurs*," he bowed to his late audience and, beckoning me, strode toward the stairs.

"I say, what's the rush—" began John Maxwell, but:

"Every reason under heaven," the Frenchman broke in shortly. To me: "Did you observe the night outside, Friend Trowbridge?"

"Why, yes," I answered. "Its a beautiful moonlit night, almost bright as day, and—"

"And there you are, for the love of ten thousand pigs!" he cut in. "Oh, I am the stupid-headed fool, me! Why did I let her from my sight?"

We followed in wondering silence as he climbed the stairs, hurried down the hall toward Sarah's room and paused before her door. He raised his hand to rap, but the portal swung away, and a girl stood staring at us from the threshold.

"Did it pass you?" she asked, regarding us in wide-eyed wonder.

"*Pardon, Mademoiselle?*" de Grandin countered. "What is it that you ask?"

"Why, did you see that lovely collie, it—"

"*Cher Dieu*," the words were like a groan upon the little Frenchman's lips as he looked at her in horror. Then, recovering himself: "Proceed, *Mademoiselle*, it was of a dog you spoke?"

"Yes," she returned. "I came upstairs to freshen up, and found I'd lost my compact somewhere, so I came to Sallie's room to get some powder. She'd come up a few moments before, and I was positive I'd find her here, but—" she paused in puzzlement a moment; then: "But when I came in there was no one here. Her dress was lying on the chaiselongue there, as though she'd slipped it off, and by the window, looking out with its paws up on the sill, was the loveliest silver collie.

"I didn't know you had a dog, John," she turned to Maxwell. "When did you get it? It's the loveliest creature, but it seemed to be afraid of me; for when I went to pat it, it slunk away, and before I realized it had bolted through the door, which I'd left open. It ran down the hall."

"A dog?" John Maxwell answered bewilderedly. "We haven't any dog, Nell; it must have been—"

"Never mind what it was," de Grandin interrupted as the girl went down the hall, and as she passed out of hearing he seized us by the elbows and fairly thrust us into Sarah's room, closing the door quickly behind us.

"What—" began John Maxwell, but the Frenchman motioned him to silence.

"Behold, regard each item carefully; stamp them upon your memories," he ordered, sweeping the charming chamber with his sharp, stock-taking glance.

A fire burned brightly in the open grate, parchment-shaded lamps diffused soft light. Upon the bed there lay a pair of rose-silk pajamas, with a sheer crêpe negligée beside them. A pair of satin mules were placed toes in upon the bedside rug. Across the chaise-longue was draped, as though discarded in the utmost haste, the white-satin evening gown that Sarah had worn. Upon the floor beside the lounge were crumpled wisps of ivory crêpe de Chine, her bandeau and trunks. Sarah, being wholly modern, had worn no stockings, but her white-and-silver evening sandals lay beside the lingerie, one on its sole, as though she had stepped out of it, the other on its side, gaping emptily, as though kicked from her little pink-and-white foot in panic haste. There was something ominous about that silent room; it was like a body from which the spirit had departed, still beautiful and warm, but lifeless.

"Humph," Maxwell muttered, "the Devil knows where she's gone—"

"He knows very, exceedingly well, I have no doubt," de Grandin interrupted. "But we do not. Now—*ah? Ah-ah-ah?*" his exclamation rose steadily, thinning to a sharpness like a razor's cutting-edge. "What have we here?"

Like a hound upon the trail, guided by scent alone, he crossed the room and halted by the dressing-table. Before the mirror stood an uncorked flask of perfume, lovely thing of polished crystal decorated with silver basketwork. From its open neck there rose a thin but penetrating scent, not wholly sweet nor wholly acrid, but a not unpleasant combination of the two, as though musk and flower-scent had each lent it something of their savors.

The little Frenchman put it to his nose, then set it down with a grimace. "Name of an Indian pig, how comes this devil's brew here?" he asked.

"Oh, that?" Maxwell answered. "I hanged if I know. Some unknown admirer of Sallie's sent it to her. It came today, all wrapped up like something from a jeweler's. Rather pleasant-smelling, isn't it?"

De Grandin looked at him as Torquemada might have looked at one accusing him of loving Martin Luther. "Did you by any chance make use of it, *Monsieur?*" he asked in an almost soundless whisper.

"I? Good Lord, do I look like the sort of he-thing who'd use perfume?" the other asked.

"*Bien,* I did but ask to know," de Grandin answered as he jammed the silver-mounted stopper in the bottle and thrust the flask into his trousers pocket.

"But where the deuce *is* Sallie?" the young husband persisted. "She's changed her clothes, that's certain; but what did she go out for, and if she didn't go out, where is she?"

"Ah, it may be that she had a sudden feeling of faintness, and decided to go out into the air," the Frenchman temporized. "Come, *Monsieur,* the guests are waiting to depart, and you must say *adieu.* Tell them that your lady is indisposed, make excuses, tell them anything, but get them out all quickly; we have work to do."

JOHN MAXWELL LIED GALLANTLY, de Grandin and I standing at his side to prevent any officious dowager from mounting the stairs and administering home-made medical assistance. At last, when all were gone, the young man turned to Jules de Grandin, and:

"Now, out with it," he ordered gruffly. "I can tell by your manner something serious has happened. What is it, man; what is it?"

De Grandin patted him upon the shoulder with a mixture of affection and commiseration in the gesture. "Be brave, *mon vieux*," he ordered softly. "It is the worst. He has her in his power; she has gone to join him, for—*pitié de Dieu!*— she has become like him."

"Wha—what?" the husband quavered. "You mean she—that Sallie, my Sallie, has become a were—" his voice balked at the final syllable, but de Grandin's nod confirmed his guess.

"*Hélas*, you have said it, my poor friend," he murmured pitifully.

"But how?—when?—I thought surely we'd driven him off—" the young man faltered, then stopped, horror choking the words back in his throat.

"Unfortunately, no," de Grandin told him. "He was driven off, certainly, but not diverted from his purpose. Attend me."

From his trousers pocket he produced the vial of perfume, uncorked it and let its scent escape into the room. "You recognize it, *hein?*" he asked.

"No, I can't say I do," Maxwell answered.

"Do you, Friend Trowbridge?"

I shook my head.

"Very well. I do, to my sorrow."

He turned once more to me. "The night Monsieur and Madame Maxwell sailed upon the *Île de France*, you may recall I was explaining how the innocent became werewolves at times?" he reminded.

"Yes, and I interrupted to ask about the different shapes that thing assumed," I nodded.

"You interrupted then," he agreed soberly, "but you will not interrupt now. Oh, no. You will listen while I talk. I had told you of the haunted dells where travelers may unknowingly become werewolves, of the streams from which the drinker may receive contagion, but you did not wait to hear of *les fleurs des loups*, did you?"

"*Fleurs des loups*—wolf-flowers?" I asked.

"*Précisément*, wolf-flowers. Upon those cursed mountains grows a kind of flower which, plucked and worn at the full of the moon, transforms the wearer into a *loup-garou*. Yes. One of these flowers, known popularly as the *fleur de sang*, or blood-flower, because of its red petals, resembles the marguerite, or daisy, in form; the other is a golden yellow, and is much like the snapdragon. But both have the same fell property, both have the same strong, sweet, fascinating scent.

"This, my friends," he passed the opened flagon underneath our noses, "is a perfume made from the sap of those accursed flowers. It is the highly concentrated venom of their devilishness. One applying it to her person, anointing lips, ears, hair and hands with it, as women wont, would as surely be translated into wolf-ish form as though she wore the cursed flower whence the perfume comes. Yes.

"That silver collie of which the young girl spoke, *Monsieur*"—he turned a fixed, but pitying look upon John Maxwell—"she was your wife, transformed into a wolf-thing by the power of this perfume.

"Consider: Can you not see it all? Balked, but not defeated, the vile *vryko-lakas* is left to perfect his revenge while you are on your honeymoon. He knows that you will come again to Harrisonville; he need not follow you. Accordingly, he sends to Europe for the essence of these flowers, prepares a philtre from it, and sends it to Madame Sarah today. Its scent is novel, rather pleasing; women like strange, exotic scents. She uses it. Anon, she feels a queerness. She does not realize that it is the metamorphosis which comes upon her, she only knows that she feels vaguely strange. She goes to her room. Perhaps she puts the perfume on her brow again, as women do when they feel faint; then, *pardieu*, then there comes the change all quickly, for the moon is full tonight, and the essence of the flowers very potent.

"She doffed her clothes, you think? *Mais non*, they fell from her! A woman's raiment does not fit a wolf; it falls off from her altered form, and we find it on the couch and on the floor.

"That other girl comes to the room, and finds poor Madame Sarah, trans-formed to a wolf, gazing sadly from the window—*la pauvre*, she knew too well who waited outside in the moonlight for her, and she must go to him! Her friend puts out a hand to pet her, but she shrinks away. She feels she is 'unclean', a thing apart, one of 'that multitudinous herd not yet made fast in hell'—*les loups-garous!* And so she flies through the open door of her room, flies where? Only *le bon Dieu*—and the Devil, who is master of all werewolves—knows!"

"But we must find her!" Maxwell wailed. "We've got to find her!"

"Where are we to look?" de Grandin spread his hands and raised his shoul-ders. "The city is wide, and we have no idea where this wolf-man makes his lair. The werewolf travels fast, my friend; they may be miles away by now."

"I don't care a damn what you say, I'm going out to look for her!" Maxwell declared as he rose from his seat and strode to the library table, from the drawer of which he took a heavy pistol. "You shot him once and wounded him, so I know he's vulnerable to bullets, and when I find him—"

"But certainly," the Frenchman interrupted. "We heartily agree with you, my friend. But let us first go to Doctor Trowbridge's house where we, too, may secure weapons. Then we shall be delighted to accompany you upon your hunt."

As we started for my place he whispered in my ear: "Prepare the knock-out drops as soon as we are there, Friend Trowbridge. It would be suicide for him to seek that monster now. He can not hit a barn-side with a pistol, can not even draw it quickly from his pocket. His chances are not one in a million if he meets the wolf, and if we let him go we shall be playing right into the adversary's hands."

I nodded agreement as we drove along, and when I'd parked the car, I turned to Maxwell. "Better come in and have a drink before we start," I invited. "It's cold tonight, and we may not get back soon."

"All right," agreed the unsuspecting youth. "But make it quick, I'm itching to catch sight of that damned fiend. When I meet him he won't get off as easily as he did in his brush with Doctor de Grandin."

Hastily I concocted a punch of Jamaica rum, hot water, lemon juice and sugar, adding fifteen grains of chloral hydrate to John Maxwell's, and hoping the sugar and lemon would disguise its taste while the pungent rum would hide its odor. "To our successful quest," de Grandin proposed, raising his steaming glass and looking questioningly at me for assurance that the young man's drink was drugged.

Maxwell raised his goblet, but ere he set it to his lips there came a sudden interruption. An oddly whining, whimpering noise it was, accompanied by a scratching at the door, as though a dog were outside in the night and importuning for admission.

"Ah?" de Grandin put his glass down on the hall table and reached beneath his left armpit where the small but deadly Belgian automatic pistol nestled in its shoulder-holster. "Ah-ha? We have a visitor, it seems." To me he bade:

"Open the door, wide and quickly, Friend Trowbridge; then stand away, for I shall likely shoot with haste, and it is not your estimable self that I desire to kill."

I followed his instructions, but instead of the gray horror I had expected at the door, I saw a slender canine form with hair so silver-gray that it was almost white, which bent its head and wagged its tail, and fairly fawned upon us as it slipped quickly through the opening then looked at each of us in turn with great, expressive topaz eyes.

"Ah, mon Dieu," exclaimed the Frenchman, sheathing his weapon and starting forward, "it is Madame Sarah!"

"Sallie?" cried John Maxwell incredulously, and at his voice the beast leaped toward him, rubbed against his knees, then rose upon its hind feet and strove to lick his face.

"Ohé, quel dommage!" de Grandin looked at them with tear-filled eyes; then:

"Your pardon, Madame Sarah, but I do not think you came to us without a reason. Can you lead us to the place where he abides? If so we promise you shall be avenged within the hour."

The silver wolf dropped to all fours again, and nodded its sleek head in answer to his question; then, as he hesitated, came slowly up to him, took the cuff of his evening coat gently in its teeth and drew him toward the door.

"*Bravo, ma chère*, lead on, we follow!" he exclaimed; then, as we donned our coats, he thrust a pistol in my hand and cautioned: "Watch well, my friend, she seems all amiable, but wolves are treacherous, man-wolves a thousand times more so; it may be he has sent her to lead us to a trap. Should anything untoward transpire, shoot first and ask your foolish questions afterward. That way you shall increase your chances of dying peacefully in bed."

T HE WHITE BEAST TROTTING before us, we hastened down the quiet, moonlit street. After forty minutes' rapid walk, we stopped before a small apartment house. As we paused to gaze, the little wolf once more seized Jules de Grandin's sleeve between her teeth and drew him forward.

It was a little house, only three floors high, and its front was zigzagged with iron fire escapes. No lights burned in any of the flats, and the whole place had in air of vacancy, but our lupine guide led us through the entrance way and down the ground floor hall until we paused before the door of a rear apartment.

De Grandin tried the knob cautiously, found the lock made fast, and after a moment dropped to his knees, drew out a ringful of fine steel instruments and began picking the fastening as methodically as though he were a professional burglar. The lock was "burglar-proof" but its makers had not reckoned with the skill of Jules de Grandin. Before five minutes had elapsed he rose with a pleased exclamation, turned the knob and thrust the door back.

"Hold her, Friend Jean," he bade John Maxwell, for the wolf was trembling with a nervous quiver, and straining to rush into the apartment. To me he added: "Have your gun ready, good Friend Trowbridge, and keep by me. He shall not take us unawares."

Shoulder to shoulder we entered the dark doorway of the flat, John Maxwell and the wolf behind us. For a moment we paused while de Grandin felt along the wall, then click; the snapping of a wall-switch sounded, and the dark room blazed with sudden light.

The wolf-man's human hours were passed in pleasant circumstances. Every item of the room proclaimed it the abode of one whose wealth and tastes were well matched. The walls were hung with light gray paper, the floor was covered with a Persian rug and wide, low chairs upholstered in long-napped mohair invited the visitor to rest. Beneath the arch of a marble mantelpiece a wood fire had been laid, ready for the match, while upon the shelf a tiny French-gilt clock beat off the minutes with sharp, musical clicks. Pictures in profusion lined the walls, a landscape by an apt pupil of Corot, an excellent imitation of Botticelli, and, above the mantel, a single life-sized portrait done in oils.

Every item of the portrait was portrayed with photographic fidelity, and we looked with interest at the subject, a man in early middle life, or late youth, dressed in the uniform of a captain of Greek cavalry. His cloak was thrown back from his braided shoulders, displaying several military decorations, but it was the face which captured the attention instantly, making all the added detail of no consequence. The hair was light, worn rather long, and brushed straight back from a high, wide forehead. The eyes were blue, and touched with an expression of gentle melancholy. The features were markedly Oriental in cast, but neither coarse nor sensual. In vivid contrast to the hair and eyes was the pointed beard upon the chin; for it was black as coal, yet by some quaint combination of the artist's pigments it seemed to hide blue lights within its sable depths. Looking from the blue-black beard to the sad blue eyes it seemed to me I saw a hint, the merest faint suggestion, of wolfish cruelty in the face.

"It is undoubtlessly he," de Grandin murmured as he gazed upon the portrait. "He fits poor Madame Sarah's description to a nicety. But where is he in person? We can not fight his picture; no, of course not."

Motioning us to wait, he snapped the light off and drew a pocket flashlight from his waistcoat. He tiptoed through the door, exploring the farther room by the beam of his searchlight, then rejoined us with a gesture of negation.

"He is not here," he announced softly; "but come with me, my friends, I would show you something."

He led the way to the adjoining chamber, which, in any other dwelling, would have been the bedroom. It was bare, utterly unfurnished, and as he flashed his light around the walls we saw, some three or four feet from the floor, a row of paw-prints, as though a beast had stood upon its hind legs and pressed its forefeet to the walls. And the prints were marked in reddish smears—blood.

"You see?" he asked, as though the answer to his question were apparent. "He has no bed; he needs none, for at night he is a wolf, and sleeps denned down upon the floor. Also, you observe, he has not lacked for provender—*le bon Dieu* grant it was the blood of animals that stained his claws!"

"But where is he?" asked Maxwell, fingering his pistol.

"*S-s-sh!*" warned the Frenchman. "I do not think that he is far away. The window, you observe her?"

"Well?"

"*Précisément.* She is a scant four feet from the ground, and overlooks the alley. Also, though she was once fitted with bars, they have been removed. Also, again, the sash is ready-raised. Is it not all perfect?"

"Perfect? For what?"

"For him, *parbleu!* For the werewolf's entrances and exits. He comes running down the alley, leaps agilely through the open window, and *voilà*, he is here. Or leaps out into the alleyway with a single bound, and goes upon his nightly hunts. He may return at any moment; it is well that we await him here."

The waiting minutes stretched interminably. The dark room where we crouched was lighted from time to time, then cast again into shadow, as the racing clouds obscured or unveiled the full moon's visage. At length, when I felt I could no longer stand the strain, a low, harsh growl from our four-footed companion brought us sharply to attention. In another moment we heard the soft patter-patter, scratch-scratch of a long-clawed beast running lightly on the pavement of the alleyway outside, and in a second more a dark form bulked against the window's opening and something landed upon the floor.

For a moment there was breathless silence; then: "*Bon soir, Monsieur Loup-garou,*" de Grandin greeted in a pleasant voice. "You have unexpected visitors.

"Do not move," he added threateningly as a hardly audible growl sounded from the farther corner of the room and we heard the scraping of long nails upon the floor as the wolf-thing gathered for a spring; "there are three of us, and each one is armed. Your reign of terror draws to a close, *Monsieur.*"

A narrow, dazzling shaft of light shot from his pocket torch, clove through the gloom and picked the crouching wolf-thing's form out of the darkness. Fangs bared, black lips drawn back in bestial fury, the gaunt, gray thing was backed into the corner, and from its open jaws we saw a thin trickle of slabber mixed with blood. It had been feeding, so much was obvious. "But what had been its food?" I wondered with a shudder.

"It is your shot, Friend Jean," the little Frenchman spoke. "Take careful aim and do not jerk the pistol when you fire." He held his flashlight steadily upon the beast, and a second later came the roar of Maxwell's pistol.

The acrid smoke stung in our nostrils, the reverberation of the detonation almost deafened us, and—a little fleck of plaster fell down from the wall where Maxwell's bullet was harmlessly embedded.

"Ten thousand stinking camels!" Jules de Grandin cried, but got no further, for with a maddened, murderous growl the wolf-man sprang, his lithe body describing a graceful arc as it hurtled through the air, his cruel, white fangs flashing terribly as he leaped upon John Maxwell and bore him to the floor before he could fire a second shot.

"*Nom de Dieu de nom de Dieu de nom de Dieu!*" de Grandin swore, playing his flashlight upon the struggling man and brute and leaping forward, seeking for a chance to use his pistol.

But to shoot the wolf would have meant that he must shoot the man, as well; for the furry body lay upon the struggling Maxwell, and as they thrashed and wrestled on the floor it was impossible to tell, at times, in the uncertain light, which one was man and which was beast.

Then came a deep, low growl of pent-up, savage fury, almost an articulate curse, it seemed to me, and like a streak of silver-plated vengeance the little she-wolf leaped upon the gray-brown brute which growled and worried at the young man's throat.

We saw the white teeth bared, we saw them flesh themselves in the wolf-thing's shoulder, we saw her loose her hold, and leap back, avoiding the great wolf's counter-stroke, then close with it again, sinking needle-fangs in the furry ruff about its throat.

The great wolf shook her to and fro, battered her against the walls and floor as a vicious terrier mistreats a luckless rat, but she held on savagely, though we saw her left forepaw go limp and knew the bone was broken.

De Grandin watched his chance, crept closer, closer, till he almost strad-dled the contending beasts; then, darting forth his hand he put his pistol to the tawny-gray wolf's ear, squeezed the trigger and leaped back.

A wild, despairing wail went up, the great, gray form seemed suddenly to stiffen, to grow longer, heavier, to shed its fur and thicken in limbs and body-structure. In a moment, as we watched the horrid transformation, we beheld a human form stretched out upon the floor; the body of a handsome man with fair hair and black beard, at the throat of which a slender silver-gray she-wolf was worrying.

"It is over, finished, little brave one," de Grandin announced, reaching out a hand to stroke the little wolf's pale fur. "Right nobly have you borne yourself this night; but we have much to do before our work is finished."

The she-wolf backed away, but the hair upon her shoulders was still bris-tling, and her topaz eyes were jewel-bright with the light of combat. Once or twice, despite de Grandin's hand upon her neck, she gave vent to throaty growls and started toward the still form which lay upon the floor in a pool of moon-light, another pool fast gathering beneath its head where de Grandin's bullet had crashed through its skull and brain.

John Maxwell moved and moaned a tortured moan, and instantly the little wolf was by his side, licking his cheeks with her pink tongue, emitting little pleading whines, almost like the whimpers of a child in pain.

When Maxwell regained consciousness it was pathetic to see the joy the wolf showed as he sat up and feebly put a groping hand against his throat.

"Not dead, my friend, you are not nearly dead, thanks to the bravery of your noble lady," de Grandin told him with a laugh. Then, to me:

"Do you go home with them, Friend Trowbridge. I must remain to dispose of this"—he prodded the inert form with his foot—"and will be with you shortly.

"Be of good cheer, *ma pauvre*," he told the she-wolf, "you shall be soon released from the spell which binds you; I swear it; though never need you be ashamed of what you did this night, whatever form you might have had while doing it."

JOHN MAXWELL SAT UPON the divan, head in hands, the wolf crouched at his feet, her broken paw dangling pitifully, her topaz eyes intent upon his face. I paced restlessly before the fire. De Grandin had declared he knew how to release her from the spell—but what if he should fail? I shuddered at the thought. What booted it that we had killed the man-wolf if Sarah must be bound in wolfish form henceforth?

"*Tiens* my friends," de Grandin announced himself at the library door, "he took a lot of disposing of, that one. First I had to clean the blood from off his bedroom floor, then I must lug his filthy carcass out into the alley and dispose of it as though it had been flung there from a racing motor. Tomorrow I doubt not the papers will make much of the mysterious murder. 'A gangster put upon the spot by other gangsters,' they will say. And shall we point out their mistake? I damn think no."

He paused with a self-satisfied chuckle; then: "Friend Jean, will you be good enough to go and fetch a negligee for Madame Sarah?" he asked. "Hurry, *mon vieux*, she will have need of it anon."

As the young man left us: "Quick, my friends," he ordered. "You, Madame Sarah, lie upon the floor before the fire, thus. *Bien*.

"Friend Trowbridge, prepare bandages and splints for her poor arm. We can not set it now, but later we must do so. Certainly.

"Now, my little brave one," he addressed the wolf again, "this will hurt you sorely, but only for a moment."

Drawing a small flask from his pocket he pulled the cork and poured its contents over her.

"It's holy water," he explained as she whined and shivered as the liquid soaked into her fur. "I had to stop to steal it from a church."

A knife gleamed in the firelight, and he drove the gleaming blade into her head, drew it forth and shook it toward the fire, so that a drop of blood fell hissing in the leaping flames. Twice more he cut her with the knife, and twice more dropped her blood into the fire; then, holding the knife lightly by the handle, he struck her with the flat of the blade between the ears three times in quick succession, crying as he did so: "Sarah Maxwell, I command that you once more assume your native form in the name of the Most Holy Trinity!"

A shudder passed through the wolf's frame. From nose to tail-tip she trembled, as though she lay in her death agony; then suddenly her outlines seemed to blur. Pale fur gave way to paler flesh, her dainty lupine paws became dainty human hands and feet, her body was no more that of a wolf, but of a soft, sweet woman.

But life seemed to have gone from her. She lay flaccid on the hearth rug, her mouth a little open, eyes closed, no movement of her breast perceptible. I looked at her with growing consternation, but:

"Quickly, my friends, the splints, the bandages!" de Grandin ordered.

I set the broken arm as quickly as I could, and as I finished young John Maxwell rushed into the room.

"Sallie, beloved!" he fell beside his wife's unconscious form, tears streaming down his face.

"Is she—is she—" he began, but could not force himself to finish, as he looked imploringly at Jules de Grandin.

"Dead?" the little man supplied. "By no means; not at all, my friend. She is alive and healthy. A broken arm mends quickly, and she has youth and stamina. Put on her robe and bear her up to bed. She will do excellently when she has had some sleep.

"But first observe this, if you please," he added, pointing to her side. Where the cicatrix with its tuft of wolf-hair had marred her skin, there was now only smooth, unspotted flesh. "The curse is wholly lifted," he declared delightedly. "You need no more regard it, except as an unpleasant memory."

"John, dear," we heard the young wife murmur as her husband bore her from the room, "I've had such a terrible dream. I dreamed that I'd been turned into a wolf, and—"

"Come quickly, good Friend Trowbridge," de Grandin plucked me by the arm. "I, too, would dream."

"Dream? Of what?" I asked him.

"Perchance of youth and love and springtime, and the joys that might have been," he answered, something like a tremble in his voice. "And then, again, perchance of snakes and toads and elephants, all of most unauthentic color— such things as one may see when he has drunk himself into the blissful state of delirium tremens. I do not surely know that I can drink that much, but may the Devil bake me if I do not try!"

The Hand of Glory

1. The Shrieking Woman

"T H' TIP O' TH' marnin' to yez, gintlemen." Officer Collins touched the vizor of his cap as Jules de Grandin and I rounded the corner with none too steady steps. The night was cold, and our host's rum punch had a potency peculiarly its own, which accounted for our decision to walk the mile or so which stretched between us and home.

"*Holà, mon brave*," responded my companion, now as ever ready to stop and chat with any member of the gendarmerie. "It is morning, you say? *Ma foi*, I had not thought it much past ten o'clock."

Collins grinned appreciatively. "Arrah, Doctor de Grandin, sor," he answered, "wid a bit o' th' crayter th' likes o' that ye've had, 'tis meself as wouldn't be bodderin' wid th' time o' night, ayther, fer—"

His witticism died birth-strangled, for, even as he paused to guffaw at the intended thrust, there came stabbing through the pre-dawn calm a cry of such thin-edged, unspeakable anguish as I had not heard since the days when as an intern I rode an ambulance's tail and amputations often had to be performed without the aid of anesthesia.

"*Bon Dieu!*" de Grandin cried, dropping my elbow and straightening with the suddenness of a coiled spring released from its tension. "What is that, in pity's gracious name?"

His answer followed fast upon his question as a pistol's crack succeeds the powder-flash, for round the shoulder of the corner building came a girl on stumbling, fear-hobbled feet, arms spread, eyes wide, mouth opened for a scream which would not come, a perfect fantasm of terror.

"Here, here, now, phwat's up?" demanded Collins gruffly, involuntary fright lending harshness to his tones. "'Tis a foin thing ye're after doin', runnin' through th' strates in yer nighties, scarin' folks out o' their sivin senses, an'—"

The woman paid him no more heed than if he'd been a shadow, for her dilated eyes were blinded by extremity of fear, as we could see at a glance, and had de Grandin not seized her by the shoulder she would have passed us in her headlong, stumbling flight. At the touch of the Frenchman's hand she halted suddenly, swayed uncertainly a moment; then, like a marionette whose strings are cut, she buckled suddenly, fell half kneeling, I half sprawling to the sidewalk and lifted trembling hands to him beseechingly.

"It was afire!" she babbled thickly. "Afire—blazing, I tell you—and the door flew open when they held it out. They—they—*aw-wah-wah!*—" her words degenerated into unintelligible syllables as the tautened muscles of her throat contracted with a nervous spasm, leaving her speechless as an infant, her thin face a white wedge of sheer terror.

"D.T.'s, sor?" asked Collins cynically, bending for a better view of the trembling woman.

"Hysteria," denied de Grandin shortly. Then, to me:

"Assist me, Friend Trowbridge, she goes into the paroxysmal stage." As he uttered the sharp warning the woman sank face-downward to the pavement, lay motionless a moment, then trembled with convulsive shudders, the shudders becoming twitches and the twitches going into wild, abandoned gestures, horribly reminiscent of the reflex contortions of a decapitated fowl.

"Good Lord, I'll call the wagon," Collins offered; but:

"A cab, and quickly, if you please," de Grandin countermanded. "This is no time for making of arrests, my friend; this poor one's sanity may depend upon our ministrations."

Luckily, a cruising taxi hove in sight even as he spoke, and with a hasty promise to inform police headquarters of the progress of the case, we bundled our patient into the vehicle and rushed at breakneck speed toward my office.

"MORPHINE, QUICKLY, IF YOU please," de Grandin ordered as he bore the struggling woman to my surgery, thrust her violently upon the examination table and drew up the sleeve of her georgette pajama jacket, baring the white flesh for the caress of the mercy-bearing needle.

Swabbing the skin with alcohol, I pinched the woman's trembling arm, inserted the hypo point in the folded skin and thrust the plunger home, driving a full three-quarter grain dose into her system; then, with refilled syringe, stood in readiness to repeat the treatment if necessary.

But the opiate took effect immediately. Almost instantly the clownish convulsions ceased, within a minute the movements of her arms and legs had subsided to mere tremblings, and the choking, anguished moans which had proceeded from her throat died to little, childish whimpers.

"Ah, so," de Grandin viewed the patient with satisfaction. "She will be better now, I think. Meantime, let us prepare some stimulant for the time of her awakening. She has been exposed, and we must see that she does not take cold."

Working with the speed and precision of one made expert by long service in the war's field hospitals, he draped a steamer rug across the back of an easy-chair in the study, mixed a stiff dose of brandy and hot water and set it by the open fire; then, calm-eyed but curious, resumed his station beside the unconscious girl upon the table.

We had not long to wait. The opiate had done its work quickly, but almost as quickly had found its antidote in the intensely excited nervous system of the patient. Within five minutes her eyelids fluttered, and her head rolled from side to side, like that of a troubled sleeper. A little moan, half of discomfort, half involuntary protest at returning consciousness, escaped from her.

"You are in the office of Doctor Samuel Trowbridge, *Mademoiselle*," de Grandin announced in a low, calm voice, anticipating the question which nine patients out of ten propound when recovering from a swoon. "We found you in the street in a most deplorable condition and brought you here for treatment. You are better now? Good. *Permettez-moi*."

Taking her hands in his, he raised her from the table, eased her to the floor and, his arms about her waist, guided her gently to the study, where, with the adeptness of a deck steward, he tucked the steamer rug about her feet and knees, placed a cushion at her back and before she had a chance to speak, held the glass of steaming toddy to her lips.

She drank the torrid liquid greedily, like a starving child gulping at a goblet of warm milk; then, as the potent draft raced through her, leaving a faint flush on her dead-pale cheeks, gave back the glass and viewed us with a pathetic, drowsy little smile.

"Thank you," she murmured. "I—oh, I remember now!" Abruptly her half-somnolent manner vanished and her hands clutched claw-like at the chair-arms. "It was afire!" she told us in a hushed, choking voice. "It was blazing, and—"

"*Mademoiselle!* You will drink this, if you please!" Sharply, incisively, the Frenchman's command cut through her fearful utterance as he held forward a cordial glass half full of cloudy liquid.

Startled but docile, she obeyed, and a look of swift bewilderment swept across her pale, peaked features as she finished drinking. "Why"—she exclaimed—"why—" Her voice sank lower, her lids closed softly and her head fell back against the cushion at her shoulders.

"*Voilà*, I feared that recollection might unsettle her and had it ready," he announced. "Do you go up to bed, my friend. Me, I shall watch beside her, and should I need you I shall call. I am inured to sleeplessness and shall not mind the vigil, but it is well that one of us has rest, for tomorrow—*eh bien*, this poor one's case has the smell of herring on it and I damn think that we shall have more sleepless nights than one before we see the end of it."

Murmuring, I obeyed. Delightful companion, thoughtful friend, indefatigable co-worker that he was, Jules de Grandin possessed a streak of stubbornness beside which the most refractory mule ever sired in the State of Missouri was docility personified, and I knew better than to spend the few remaining hours of darkness in fruitless argument.

2. The Hand of Glory

A GENTLE MURMUR OF VOICES sounded from the study when I descended from my room after something like four hours' sleep. Our patient of the night before still sat swathed in rugs in the big wing chair, but something approximating normal color had returned to her lips and cheeks, and though her hands fluttered now and again in tremulous gesticulation as she talked, it required no second glance to tell me that her condition was far from bordering on nervous collapse. "Taut, but not stretched dangerously near the snapping-point," I diagnosed as I joined them. De Grandin reclined at ease across the fire from her, a pile of burned-out cigarettes in the ash-tray beside him, smoke from a freshly lighted Maryland slowly spiraling upward as he waved his hand back and forth to emphasize his words.

"What you tell is truly interesting, *Mademoiselle*," he was assuring her as I entered the study.

"'Trowbridge, *mon vieux*, this is Mademoiselle Wickwire. *Mademoiselle*, my friend and colleague, Doctor Samuel Trowbridge. Will you have the goodness to repeat your story to him? I would rather that he had it from your own lips."

The girl turned a wan smile toward me, and I was struck by her extreme slenderness. Had her bones been larger, she would have been distressfully thin; as it was the covering of her slight skeletal structure was so scanty as to make her almost as ethereal as a sprite. Her hair was fair, her eyes of an indeterminate shade somewhere between true blue and amethyst, and their odd coloration was picked up and accentuated by a chaplet of purple stones about her slender throat and the purple settings of the rings she wore upon the third finger of each hand. Limbs and extremities were fine-drawn as silver wire and elongated to an extent which was just short of grotesque, while her profile was robbed of true beauty by its excessive clarity of line. Somehow, she reminded me more of a statuette carved from crystal than of a flesh-and-blood woman, while the georgette pajamas of sea-green trimmed with amethyst and the absurd little boudoir cap which perched on one side of her fair head helped lend her an air of tailor's-dummy unreality.

I bowed acknowledgment of de Grandin's introduction and waited expectantly for her narrative, prepared to cancel ninety percent of all she told me as the vagary of an hysterical young woman.

"Doctor de Grandin tells me I was screaming that 'it was burning' when you found me in the street last night," she began without preamble. "It was."

"Eh?" I ejaculated, turning a quick glance of inquiry on de Grandin. "What?"

"The hand."

"Bless my soul! The *what?*"

"The hand," she returned with perfect aplomb. Then: "My father is Joseph Wickwire, former Horner Professor of Orientology and Ancient Religion at De Puy University. You know his book, *The Cult of the Witch in Assyria?*"

I shook my head, but the girl, as though anticipating my confession of ignorance, went on without pause:

"I don't understand much about it, for Father never troubled to discuss his studies with me, but from some things he's told me, he became convinced of the reality of ancient witchcraft—or magic—some years ago, and gave up his chair at De Puy to devote himself to private research. While I was at school he made several trips to the Near East and last year spent four months in Mesopotamia, supervising some excavations. He came home with two big cases—they looked more like casket-boxes than anything else—which he took to his study, and since then no one's been allowed in the room, not even I or Fanny, our maid. Father won't permit anything, not even so much as a grain of dust, to be taken from that room; and one of the first things he did after receiving those boxes was to have an iron-plated door made for the study and have heavy iron bars fitted to all the windows.

"Lately he's been spending practically all his time at work in the study, sometimes remaining there for two or three days at a time, refusing to answer when called to meals or to come out for rest or sleep. About a month ago something happened which upset him terribly. I think it was a letter he received, though I'm not sure, for he wouldn't tell me what it was; but he seemed distracted, muttering constantly to himself and looking over his shoulder every now and then as though he expected some one, or something, to attack him from behind. Last week he had some workmen come and reinforce all the doors with inch-wide strips of cast iron. Then he had special combination locks fitted to the outside doors and Yale locks to all the inside ones, and every night, just at dusk, he sets the combinations, and no one may enter or leave the house till morning. It's been rather like living in prison."

"More like a madhouse," I commented mentally, looking at the girl's thin face with renewed interest. "Delusions of persecution on the part of the parent might explain abnormal behavior on the part of the offspring, if—"

The girl's recital broke in on my mental diagnosis: "Last night I couldn't sleep. I'd gone to bed about eleven and slept soundly for an hour or so; then suddenly I sat up, broad awake, and nothing I could do would get me back to sleep. I tried bathing the back of my neck with cologne, turning my pillows, even taking ten grains of allonal; nothing was any good, so finally I gave up trying and went down to the library. There was a copy of Hallam's *Constitutional History of England* there, and I picked that out as being the dullest reading I could find, but I read over a hundred pages without the slightest sign of drowsiness. Then I decided to take the book upstairs. Possibly, I thought, if I tried reading it in bed I might drop off without realizing it.

"I'd gotten as far as the second floor—my room's on the third—and was almost in front of Father's study when I heard a noise at the front door. 'Any burglar who tries breaking into this house will be wasting his talents,' I remember saying to myself, when, just as though they were being turned by an invisible hand, the dials of the combination lock started to spin. I could see them in the light of the hall ceiling-lamp, which Father insists always be kept burning, and they were turned not slowly, but swiftly, as though being worked by one who knew the combination perfectly.

"At the same time the queerest feeling came over me. It was like one of those dreadful nightmares people sometimes have, when they're being attacked or pursued by some awful monster, and can't run or cry out, or even *move*. There I stood, still as a marble image, every faculty alert, but utterly unable to make a sound or move a finger—or even wink an eye.

"And as I watched in helpless stillness, the front door swung back silently and two men entered the hall. One carried a satchel or suitcase of some sort, the other"—she paused and caught her breath like a runner nearly spent, and her voice sank to a thin, harsh whisper—"the other was holding a blazing hand in front of him!"

"A *what?*" I demanded incredulously. There was no question in my mind that the delusions of the sire were ably matched by the hallucinations of the daughter.

"A blazing hand," she answered, and again I saw the shudder of a nervous chill run through her slender frame. "He held it forward, like a candle, as though to light his way; but there was no need of it for light, for the hall lamp has a hundred-watt bulb, and its luminance reached up the stairs and made everything in the upper passage plainly visible. Besides, the thing burned with more fire than light. There seemed to be some sort of wick attached to each of the fanned-out fingers, and these burned with a clear, steady blue flame, like blazing alcohol. It—"

"But my dear young lady," I expostulated, "that's impossible."

"Of course it is," she agreed with unexpected calmness. "So is this: As the man with the blazing hand mounted the stairs and paused before my father's study, I heard a distinct *click*, and the door swung open, unlocked. Through the opening I could see Father standing in the middle of the room, the light from an unshaded ceiling-lamp making everything as clear as day. On a long table was some sort of object which reminded me of one of those little marble stones they put over soldiers' graves in national cemeteries, only it was gray instead of white, and a great roll of manuscript lay beside it. Father had risen and stood facing the door with one hand resting on the table, the other reaching toward a sawed-off shotgun which lay beside the stone and manuscript. But he was paralyzed—frozen in the act of reaching for the gun as I had been in the act of walking down the hall. His eyes were wide and set with surprise—no, not quite that, they were more like the painted eyes of a window-figure in a store, utterly expressionless—and I remember wondering, in that odd way people have of thinking of inconsequential things in moments of intense excitement, whether mine looked the same.

"I saw it all. I saw them go through the study's open door, lift the stone off the table, bundle up Father's manuscript and stuff everything into the bag. Then, the man with the burning hand going last, walking backward and holding the thing before him, they left as silently as they came. The doors swung to behind them without being touched. The study door had a Yale snap-lock in addition to its combination fastenings, so it was fastened when it closed, but the bolts of the safe lock on the front door didn't fly back in place when it closed.

"I don't know how long that strange paralysis held me after the men with the hand had gone; but I remember suddenly regaining my power of motion and finding myself with one foot raised—I'd been overcome in the act of stepping and had remained helpless, balanced on one foot, the entire time. My first act, of course, was to call Father, but I could get no response, even when I beat and kicked on the door.

"Then panic seized me. I didn't quite know what I was doing, but something seemed urging me to get away from that house as though it had been haunted, and the horrifying memory of that blazing hand with those combination-locked doors flying open before it came down on me like a cloud of strangling, smothering gas. The front door was still unfastened, as I've told you, and I flung it open, fighting for a breath of fresh outdoors air, and—ran screaming into the street. You know the rest."

"You see?" asked Jules de Grandin.

I nodded understandingly. I saw only too well. A better symptomatized case of dementia praecox it had never been my evil fortune to encounter.

There was a long moment of silence, broken by de Grandin. "*Eh bien, mes amis*, we make no progress here," he announced. "Grant me fifteen small minutes for my toilette, *Mademoiselle*, and we shall repair to the house of your father. There, I make no doubt, we shall learn something of interest concerning last night's so curious events."

He was as good as his promise, and within the stipulated time had rejoined us, freshly shaved, washed and brushed, a most agreeable odor of bath salts and dusting-powder emanating from his spruce, diminutive person.

"Come, let us go," he urged, assisting our patient to her feet and wrapping the steamer rug about her after the manner of an Indian's blanket.

3. The House of the Magician

THE FRONT ENTRANCE OF Professor Wickwire's house was closed, but unfastened, when we reached our destination, and I looked with interest at the formidable iron reinforcements and combination locks upon the door. Thus far the girl's absurd story was borne out by facts, I was forced to admit, as we mounted the stairs to the upper floor where Wickwire had his barricaded sanctum.

No answer coming to de Grandin's peremptory summons, Miss Wickwire tapped lightly on the iron-bound panels. "Father, it is I, Diane," she called.

Somewhere beyond the door we heard a shuffling step and a murmuring voice, then a listless fumbling at the locks which held the portal fast.

The man who stood revealed as the heavy door swung back looked like a Fundamentalist cartoonist's caricature of Charles Darwin. The pate was bald, the jaw bearded, the brows heavy and prominent, but where the great evolutionist's forehead bulged with an intellectual swell, this man's skull slanted back obliquely, and the temples were flat, rather than concave. Also, it required no second glance to tell us that the full beard covered a soft, receding chin, and the eyes beneath the shaggy brows were weak with a weakness due to more than mere poor vision. He looked to me more like the sort of person who would spend spare time reading books on development of willpower and personality than poring over ponderous tomes on Assyriology. And though he seemed possessed of full dentition, he mumbled like a toothless ancient as he stared at us, feeble eyes blinking owlishly behind the pebbles of his horn-rimmed spectacles.

"*Magna Mater . . . trismegistus . . . salve . . .*" we caught the almost unintelligible Latin of his mumbled incantation.

"Father!" Diane Wickwire exclaimed in distress. "Father, here are—"

The man's head rocked insanely from side to side, as though his neck had been a flaccid cord, and: "*Magna Mater . . .*" he began again with a whimpering persistence.

"*Monsieur!* Stop it. I command it, and I am Jules de Grandin!" Sharply the little Frenchman's command rang out; then, as the other goggled at him and began his muttered prayer anew, de Grandin raised his small gloved hand and dealt him a stinging blow across the face. "*Parbleu*, I will be obeyed, me!" he snorted wrathfully. "Save your conjurations for another time, *Monsieur*; at present we would talk with you."

Brutal as his treatment was, it was efficacious. The blow acted like a douche of cold water on a swooning person, and Wickwire seemed for the first time to realize we were present.

"These gentlemen are Doctors Trowbridge and de Grandin," his daughter introduced. "I met them when I ran for help last night, and they took me with them. Now, they are here to help you—"

Wickwire stopped her with uplifted hand. "I fear there's no help for me—or you, my child," he interrupted sadly. "They have the Sacred Meteorite, and it is only a matter of time till they find the Word of Power, then—"

"*Nom d'un coq, Monsieur*, let us have things logically and in decent order, if you please," de Grandin broke in sharply. "This sacred meteorite, this word of powerfulness, this so mysterious 'they' who have the one and are about to have the other, in Satan's name, who and what are they? Tell us from the start of the beginning. We are intrigued, we are interested; *parbleu*, we are consumed with the curiosity of a dying cat!"

Professor Wickwire smiled at him, the weary smile a tired adult might give a curious child. "I fear you wouldn't understand," he answered softly.

"By blue, you do insult my credulity, *Monsieur!*" the Frenchman rejoined hotly. "Tell us your tale, all—every little so small bit of it—and let us be the judges of what we shall believe. Me, I am an occultist of no small ability, and this so strange adventure of last night assuredly has the flavor of the superphysical. Yes, certainly."

Wickwire brightened at the other's words. "An occultist?" he echoed. "Then perhaps you can assist me. Listen carefully, if you please, and ask me anything which you may not understand:

"Ten years ago, while assembling data for my book on witchcraft in the ancient world, I became convinced of the reality of sorcery. If you know anything at all of mediæval witchcraft, you realize that Diana was the patroness of the witches, even in that comparatively late day, Burchard, Bishop of Worms, writing of sorcery, heresy and witchcraft in Germany in the year 1000 says: 'Certain wretched women, seduced by the sorcery of demons, affirm that during the night they ride with Diana, goddess of the heathens, and a host of other women, and that they traverse immense spaces.'

"Now, Diana, whom most moderns look upon as a clean-limbed goddess of chastity, was only one name for the great Female Principle among the pantheon of ancient days. Artemis, or Diana, is typified by the moon, but there is also Hecate, goddess of the black and fearful night, queen of magic, sorcery and witchcraft, deity of goblins and the underworld and guardian of crossroads; she was another attribute of the same night-goddess whom we know best today as Diana.

"But back of all the goddesses of night, whether they be styled Diana, Artemis, Hecate, Rhea, Astarte or Ishtar, is the Great Mother—*Magna Mater*. The origin of her cult is so ancient that recorded history does not even touch it, and even oral tradition tells of it only by indirection. Her worship is so old that the Anatolian meteorite brought to Rome in 204 B.C. compares to it as Christian Science or New Thought compare in age with Buddhism.

"Piece by piece I traced back the chain of evidence of her worship and finally became convinced that it was not in Anatolia at all that her mother-shrine was located, but in some obscure spot, so many centuries forgotten as to be no longer named, near the site of the ancient city of Uruck. An obscure Roman legionary mentions the temple where the goddess he refers to by the Syro-Phœnician name of Astarte was worshipped by a select coterie of adepts, both men and women, to whom she gave dominion over earth and sea and sky—power to raise tempests or to quiet them, to cause earthquakes, to cause fertility or sterility in men and beasts, or cause the illness or death of an enemy. They were also said to have the power of levitation, or flying through the air for great distances, or even to be seen in several places at the same time. This, you see, is about the sum total of all the powers claimed for witches and wizards in mediæval times. In fine, this obscure goddess of our nameless centurion is the earliest ascertainable manifestation of the female divinity who governed witchcraft in the ancient world, and whose place has been usurped by the Devil in Christian theology.

"But this was only the beginning: The Roman chronicler stated definitely that her idol was a 'stone from heaven, wrapped in an envelope of earth,' and that no man durst break the tegument of the celestial stone for fear of rousing Astarte's wrath; yet to him who had the courage to do so would be given the *Verbum Magnum*, or Word of Power—an incantation whereby all majesty, might, power and dominion of all things visible and invisible would be put into his hands, so that he who knew the word would be, literally, Emperor of the Universe.

"As I said before, I became convinced of the reality of witchcraft, both ancient and modern, and the deeper I delved into the records of the past the more convinced I was that the greatest claims made by latter-day witches were mere childish nonsense compared to the mighty powers actually possessed by the wizards of olden times. I spent my health and bankrupted myself seeking that nameless temple of Astarte—but at last *I found it.* I found the very stone of which the Roman wrote and brought it back to America—here."

Wickwire paused, breathing in labored gasps, and his pale eyes shone with the quenchless ardor of the enthusiast as he looked triumphantly from one of us to the other.

"*Bien, Monsieur,* this stone of the old one is brought here; what then?" de Grandin asked as the professor showed no sign of proceeding further with his narrative.

"Eh? Oh, yes." Once more Wickwire lapsed into semisomnolence. "Yes, I brought it back, and was preparing to unwrap it, studying my way carefully, of course, in order to avoid being blasted by the goddess' infernal powers when I broke the envelope, but—but they came last night and stole it."

"*Bon sang d'un bon poisson,* must we drag information from you bit by little bit, *Monsieur?*" blazed the exasperated Jules de Grandin. "Who was it pilfered your unmentionable stone?"

"Kraus and Steinert stole it," Wickwire answered tonelessly. "They are German *illuminati,* Hanoverians whose researches paralleled mine in almost every particular, and who discovered the approximate location of the mystic meteorite shortly after I did. Fortunately for me their data were not so complete as mine, and they lost some time trying to locate the ancient temple. I had dug up the stone and was on my way home when they finally found the place.

"Can you imagine what it would mean to any mortal man to be suddenly translated into godhood, to sway the destinies of nations—of all mankind—as a wind sways a wheatfield? If you can, you can imagine what those two adepts in black magic felt when they arrived and found the key to power gone and on its way to America in the possession of a rival. They sent astral messengers after me, first offering partnership, then, when I laughed at them, making all manner of threats. Several times they attempted my life, but my magic was stronger than theirs, and each time I beat their spirit-messengers off.

"Lately, though, their emissaries have been getting stronger. I began to realize this when I found myself weaker and weaker after each encounter. Whether they have found new sources of strength, or whether it is because two of them work against me I do not know, but I began to realize we were becoming more evenly matched and it was only a matter of time before they would master me. Yet there was much to be done before I dared remove the envelope from that stone; to attempt it unprepared would be fool-hardy. Such forces as would be unleashed by the cracking of that wrapping are beyond the scope of human imagining, and every precaution had go be taken. Any dunce can blow himself up handling gunpowder carelessly; only the skilled artillerist can harness the explosive and make it drive a projectile to a given target.

"While I was perfecting my spiritual defenses I took all physical precautions, also, barring my windows and so securing my doors that if my enemies gave up the battle of magic in disgust and fell back upon physical force, I should be more than a match for them. Then, because I thought myself secure, for a little time at least, I overlooked one of the most elementary forms of sorcery, and last night they entered my house as though there had been no barriers and took away the magic stone. With that in their possession I shall be no match for them; they will work their will on me, then overwhelm the world with the forces of their wizardry. If only—"

"Excuse me, Professor," I broke in, for, wild as his story was, I had become interested despite myself; "what was the sorcery these men resorted to in order to force entrance? Your daughter told us something of a blazing hand, but—"

"It was a hand of glory," he returned, regarding me with something of the look a teacher might bestow upon a backward schoolboy, "one of the oldest, simplest bits of magic known to adepts. A hand—preferably the sinister—is cut from the body of an executed murderer, and five locks of hair are clipped from his head. The hand is smoked over a fire of juniper wood until it becomes dry and mummified; after this the hair is twisted into wicks which are affixed to the finger tips. If the proper invocations are recited while the hand and wicks are being prepared and the words of power pronounced when the wicks are lighted, no lock can withstand the light cast by the blazing glory hand, and—"

"*Ha*, I remember him," de Grandin interrupted delightedly. "Your so droll Abbé Barham tells of him in his exquisitely humorous poem:

Now open lock to the dead man's knock,
Fly bolt and bar and band;
Nor move nor swerve joint, muscle or nerve,
At the spell of the dead man's hand.
Sleep all who sleep, wake all who wake,
But be as the dead for the dead man's sake.

Wickwire nodded grimly. "There's a lot of truth in those doggerel rimes," he answered. "We laugh at the fairy-story of Bluebeard today, but it was no joke in fifteenth century France when Bluebeard was alive and making black magic."

"*Tu parles, mon vieux*," agreed de Grandin, "and—"

"Excuse me, but you've spoken several times of removing the envelope from this stone, Professor," I broke in again. "Do you mean that literally, or—"

"Literally," Wickwire responded. "In Babylonia and Assyria, you know, all 'documents' were clay tablets on which the cuneiform characters were cut while they were still moist and soft, and which were afterward baked in a kiln. Tablets of special importance, after having been once written upon and baked, were covered with a thin coating of clay upon which an identical inscription was impressed, and the tablets were once more baked. If the outer writing were then defaced by accident or altered by design, the removal of the outer coating would at once show the true text. Such a clay coating has been wrapped about the mystic meteorite of the Great Mother-Goddess, but even in the days of the Roman historian most of the inscription had been obliterated by time. When I found it I could distinguish only one or two characters, such as the double triangle, signifying the moon, and the eight-pointed asterisks meaning the lord of lords and god of gods, or lady of ladies and goddess of goddesses. These, I may add, were not in the Assyrian cuneiforms of 700 B.C. or even the archaic characters dating back to 2500, but the early, primitive cuneiform, which was certainly not used later than 4500 B.C., probably several centuries earlier."

"And how did you propose removing the clay integument without hurt to yourself, *Monsieur?*" de Grandin asked.

Wickwire smiled, and there was something devilish, callous, in his expression as be did so. "Will you be good enough to examine my daughter's rings?" he asked.

Obedient to his nodded command, the girl stretched forth her thin, frail hands, displaying the purple settings of the circlets which adorned the third finger of each. The stones were smoothly polished, though not very bright, and each was deeply incised with this inscription:

"It's the ancient symbol of the Mother-Goddess," Wickwire explained, "and signifies 'Royal Lady of the Night, Ruler of the Lights of Heaven, Mother of Gods, Men and Demons.' Diane would have racked the envelope for me, for only the hands of a virgin adorned with rings of amethyst bearing the Mother-Goddess' signet can wield the hammer which can break that clay—and the maid must do the act without fear or hesitation; otherwise she will be powerless."

"U'm?" de Grandin twisted fiercely at his little blond mustache. "And what becomes of this ring-decorated virgin, *Monsieur?*"

Again that smile of fiendish indifference transformed Wickwire's weak face into a mask of horror. "She would die," he answered calmly. "That, of course, is certain, but"—some lingering light of parental sanity broke through the look of wild fanaticism—"unless she were utterly consumed by the tremendous forces liberated when the envelope was cracked, I should have power to restore her to life, for all power, might, dominion and majesty in the world would have been mine; death should bow before me, and life should exist only by my sanction. I—"

"You are a scoundrel and a villain and a most unpleasant species of a malodorous camel," cut in Jules de Grandin.

"*Mademoiselle*, you will kindly pack a portmanteau and come with us. We shall esteem it a privilege to protect you till danger from those *sales bêtes* who invaded your house last night is past."

Without a word, or even a glance at the man who would have sacrificed her to his ambition, Diane Wickwire left the room, and we heard the clack-clack of her bedroom mules as she ascended to her chamber to procure a change of clothing.

Professor Wickwire turned a puzzled look from de Grandin to me, then back to the Frenchman. That we could not understand and sympathize with his ambition and condone his willingness to sacrifice his daughter's life never seemed to enter his mad brain. "But me—what's to become of me?" he whimpered.

"*Eh bien*, one wonders," answered Jules de Grandin. "As far as I am concerned, *Monsieur*, you may go to the Devil, nor need you delay your departure in anywise out of consideration for my feelings."

"Mad," I diagnosed. "Mad as hatters, both of 'em. The man's a potential homicidal maniac; only heaven knows how long it will be before we have to put the girl under restraint."

De Grandin looked cautiously about; then, satisfied that Diane Wickwire was still in the chamber to which she had been conducted by Nora McGinnis, my efficient household factotum, he replied: "You think that story of the glory hand was madness, *hein?*"

"Of course it was," I answered. "What else could it be?"

"*Le bon Dieu* knows, not I," he countered; "but I would that you read this item in today's *Journal* before consigning her to the madhouse." Picking up a copy of the morning paper he indicated a boxed item in the center of the first page:

Police are seeking the ghouls who broke into James Gibson's funeral parlor, 1037 Ludlow St., early last night and stole the left hand from the body of José Sanchez, which was lying in the place awaiting burial today. Sanchez had been executed Monday night at Trenton for the murder of Robert Knight, caretaker in the closed Steptens iron foundry, last summer, and relatives had commissioned Gibson to bring the body to Harrisonville for interment.

Gibson was absent on a call in the suburbs last night, and as his assistant, William Lowndes, was confined to bed at home by unexpected illness, had left the funeral parlor unattended, having arranged to have any telephone calls switched to his residence in Winthrop St. On his return he found a rear door of his establishment had been jimmied and the left hand of the executed murderer severed at the wrist.

Strangely enough, the burglars had also shorn a considerable amount of hair from the corpse's head. A careful search of the premises failed to disclose anything else had been taken, and a quantity of money lying in the unlocked safe was untouched.

"Well!" I exclaimed, utterly nonplussed; but:

"*Non*," he denied shortly. "It is not at all well, my friend, it is most exceedingly otherwise. It is fiendish, it is diabolical: it is devilish. There are determined miscreants against whom we have set ourselves, and I damn think that we shall lose some sleep ere all is done. Yes."

4. The Sending

However formidable Professor Wickwire's rivals might have been, they gave no evidence of ferocity that I could see. Diane settled down comfortably in our midst, fitting perfectly into the quiet routine of the household, giving no trouble and making herself so generally agreeable that I was heartily glad of her presence. There is something comforting about the pastel shades of filmy dresses and white arms and shoulders gleaming softly in the candle-light at dinner. The melody of a well-modulated feminine voice, punctuated now and again with little rippling notes of quiet laughter, is more than vaguely pleasant to the bachelor ear, and as the time of our companionship lengthened I often found myself wondering if I should have had a daughter such as this to sit at table or before the fire with me if fate had willed it otherwise and my sole romance had ended elsewhere than an ivy-covered grave with low white headstone in St. Stephen's churchyard. One night I said as much to Jules de Grandin, and the pressure of his hand on mine was good to feel.

"*Bien*, my friend," he whispered, "who are we to judge the ways of heaven? The grass grows green above the lips you used to kiss—me, I do not know if she I loved is in the world or gone away. I only know that never may I stand beside her grave and look at it, for in that cloistered cemetery no man may come, and—eh, what is that? *Un chaton?*" Outside the window of the drawing-room, scarce heard above the shrieking of the boisterous April wind, there sounded a plaintive mew, as though some feline Wanderer begged entrance and a place before our fire.

Crossing the room, I drew aside the casement curtain, staining my eyes against the murky darkness. Almost level with my own, two eyes of glowing green looked through the pane, and another pleading miaul implored my charity.

"All right, Pussy, come in," I invited, drawing back the sash to permit an entrance for the little waif, and through the opening jumped a plump, soft-haired angora cat, black as Erebus, jade-eyed, velvet-pawed. For a moment it stood at gaze, as though doubtful of the worthiness of my abode to house one of its distinction; then, with a satisfied little cat-chuckle, it crossed the room, furry tail waving jauntily, came to halt before the fire and curled up on the hearth rug, where, with paws tucked demurely in and tail curled about its body, it lay blinking contentedly at the leaping flames and purring softly. A saucer of warm milk further cemented cordial relations, and another member was added to our household personnel.

The little cat, on which we had bestowed the name of Eric Brighteyes, at once attached himself to Diane Wickwire, and could hardly be separated from her. Toward de Grandin and me it showed disdainful tolerance. For Nora McGinnis it had supreme contempt.

I T WAS THE TWENTY-NINTH of April, a raw, wet night when the thermometer gave the lie to the calendars assertion that spring had come. Three of us, de Grandin, Diane and I sat in the drawing-room. The girl seemed vaguely nervous and distraught, toying with her coffee cup, puffing at her cigarette, grinding out its fire against the ash-tray, then lighting another almost instantly. Finally she went to the piano and began to play. For a time she improvised softly, white fingers straying at random over the white keys; then, as though led by some subconscious urge for the solace of ecclesiastical music, she began the opening bars of Gounod's *Sanctus*:

Holy, Holy, Holy,
Lord God of Hosts,
Heaven and earth are full of Thy Glory . . .

The music ended on a sharply dissonant note and a gasp of horrified surprise broke the echoing silence as the player lifted startled fingers from the keys. We turned toward the piano, and:

"*Mon Dieu!*" exclaimed de Grandin. "Hell is unchained against us!"

The cat, which had been contentedly curled up on the piano's polished top, had risen and stood with arched back, bristling tail and gaping, blood-red mouth, gazing from blazing ice-green eyes at Diane with such a look of murderous hate as made the chills of sudden blind, unreasoning fear run rippling down my spine.

"Eric—Eric Brighteyes!" Diane extended a shaking hand to soothe the menacing beast, and in a moment it was its natural, gentle self again, its back still arched, but arched in seeming playfulness, rubbing its fluffy head against her fingers and purring softly with contented friendliness. "And did the horrid music hurt its eardrums? Well, Diane won't play it any more," the girl promised, taking the jet-black ball of fur into her arms and nursing it against her shoulder. Shortly afterward she said goodnight, and, the cat still cuddled in her arms, went up to bed.

"I hardly like the idea of her taking that brute up with her," I told de Grandin. "It's always seemed so kind and gentle, but—well"—I laughed uneasily—"when I saw it snarling at her just now I was heartily glad it wasn't any bigger."

"U'm," returned the Frenchman, looking up from his silent study of the fire, "one wonders."

"Wonders what?"

"Much, by blue. Come, let us go."

"Where?"

"Upstairs, *cordieu*, and let us step softly while we are about it."

De Grandin in the lead, we tiptoed to the upper floor and paused before the entrance to Diane's chamber. From behind the white-enameled panels came the sound of something like a sob; then, in a halting, faltering voice:

"Amen. Evil from us deliver but temptation into not us lead, and us against trespass who those forgive we as . . ."

"*Grand Dieu—la prière renversée!*" de Grandin cried, snatching savagely at the knob and dashing back the door.

Diane Wickwire knelt beside her bed, purple-ringed hands clasped before her, tears streaming down her cheeks, while slowly, haltingly, like one wrestling with the vocables of an unfamiliar tongue, she painfully repeated the Lord's Prayer backward.

And on the counterpane, it's black muzzle almost forced against her face, crouched the black cat. But now its eyes were not the cool jade-green which we had known; they were red as embers of a dying fire when blown to life by some swift draft of air, and on its feline face, in hellish parody of humanity, there was a *grin*, a smile as cold and menacing, yet wicked and triumphant as any mediæval artist ever painted on the lips of Satan!

We stood immovable a moment, taking in the tableau with a quickening gaze of horror, then:

"Say it, *Mademoiselle*, say it after me—*properly!*" commanded Jules de Grandin, raising his right hand to sign the cross above the girl's bowed head and beginning slowly and distinctly: "Our Father, which art in Heaven, hallowed be Thy name . . ."

A terrifying screech, a scream of unsupportable agony, as though it had been plunged into a blazing fire, broke from the cowering cat-thing on the bed. Its reddened eyes flashed savagely, and its gaping mouth showed gleaming, knife-sharp teeth as it turned its gaze from Diane Wickwire and fixed it on de Grandin. But the Frenchman paid no heed.

". . . and lead us not into temptation, but deliver us from evil. Amen," he finished the petition.

And Diane prayed with him. Catching her cue from his slowly spoken syllables, she repeated the prayer word by painful word, and at the end collapsed, a whimpering, flaccid thing, against the bedstead.

But the cat? It was gone. As the girl and Frenchman reached "Amen" the beast snarled savagely, gave a final spiteful hiss, and whirled about and bolted through the open window, vanishing into the night from which it had come a week before, leaving but the echo of its menacing sibilation and the memory of its dreadful transformation as mementoes of its visit.

"In heaven's name, what was it?" I asked breathlessly.

"A spy," he answered. "It was a sending, my old one, an emissary from those evil ones to whom we stand opposed."

"A—a sending?"

"Perfectly. Assist me with Mademoiselle Diane and I shall elucidate."

The girl was sobbing bitterly, trembling like a wind-shaken reed, but not hysterical, and a mild sedative was sufficient to enable her to sleep. Then, as we once more took our seats before the fire, de Grandin offered:

"I did not have suspicion of the cat, my friend. He seemed a natural animal, and as I like cats, I was his friend from the first. Indeed, it was not until tonight when he showed aversion for the sacred music that I first began to realize what I should have known from the beginning. He was a sending."

"Yes, you've said that before," I reminded him, "but what the devil is a 'sending'?"

"The crystallized, physicalized desires and passions of a sorcerer or wizard," he returned. "Somewhat—as the medium builds a semi-physical, semi-spiritual body out of that impalpability which we call psychoplasm or ectoplasm, so the skilled adept in magic can evoke a physical-seeming entity out of his wicked thoughts and send it where he will, to do his bidding and work his evil purposes. These ones against whom we are pitted, these burglar-thieves who entered Monsieur Wickwire's house with their accursed glory hand and stole away his unnamable stone of power are no good, my friend. No, certainly. On the contrary, they are all bad. They are drunk with lust for the power which they think will come into their hands when they have stripped the wrapping off that unmentionable stone. They know also, I should say, that Wickwire—may he eat turnips and drink water throughout eternity!—had ordained his daughter for the sacrifice, had chosen her for the rôle of envelope-stripper-off for that stone, and they accordingly desire to avail themselves of her services. To that end they evoke that seeming-cat and send it here, and it did work their will— conveyed their evil suggestions to the young girl's mind. She, who is all innocent of any knowledge of witchery or magic-mongering, was to be perverted; and right well the work was done, for tonight when she knelt to say her prayers she could not frame to pronounce them aright, but, was obliged perforce to pray witch-fashion."

"Witch-fashion?"

"But certainly. Of course. Those who have taken the vows of witchhood and signed their names in Satan's book of blackness are unable to pray like Christians from that time forward; they must repeat the holy words in reverse. Mademoiselle Diane, she is no professed witch, but I greatly fear she is infected by the virus. Already she was unable to pray like others, though when I said the prayer aright, she was still able to repeat it after me. Now—"

"Is there any way we can find these scoundrels and free Diane?" I interrupted. Not for a moment did I grant his premises, but that the girl was suffering some delusion I was convinced; possibly it was long-distance hypnotic suggestion, but whatever its nature, I was determined to seek out the instigators and break the spell.

For a moment he was silent, pinching his little pointed chin between a thoughtful thumb and forefinger and gazing pensively into the fire. At length: "Yes," he answered. "We can find the place where they lair, my friend; she will lead us to them."

"She? How—"

"*Exactement.* Tomorrow is May Eve, Witch-Night—Walpurgis-Nacht. Of all the nights which go to make the year, they are most likely to try their deviltry then. It was not for nothing that they sent their spy into this house and established rapport with Mademoiselle Diane. Oh, no. They need her in their business, and I think that all unconsciously she will go to them some time tomorrow evening. Me, I shall make it my especial duty to keep in touch with her, and where she goes, there will I go also."

"I, too," I volunteered, and we struck hands upon it.

5. Walpurgis-Nacht

COVERTLY, BUT CAREFULLY, WE noted every movement the girl made next day. Shortly after luncheon de Grandin looked in at the consulting-room and nodded significantly. "She goes; so do I," he whispered, and was off.

It was nearly time for the evening meal when Diane returned, and a moment after she had gone upstairs to change for dinner I heard de Grandin's soft step in the hall.

"Name of a name," he ejaculated, dropping into the desk-side chair and lighting a cigarette, "but it is a merry chase on which she has led me today, that one!"

I raised interrogative brows, and:

"From pharmacy to pharmacy she has gone, like a hypochondriac seeking for a cure. Consider what she bought"—he checked the items off upon his fanned-out fingers—"aconitum, belladonna, solanin, mandragora officinalis. Not in any one, or even any two places did she buy these things. No, she was shrewd, she was clever, by blue, but she was subtle! Here she bought a *flaçon* of perfume, there a box of powder, again, a cake of scented soap, but mingled with her usual purchases would be occasionally one of these strange things which no young lady can possibly be supposed to want or need. What think you of it, my friend?"

"H'm, it sounds like some prescription from the mediæval pharmacopœia," I returned.

"Well said, my old astute one!" he answered. "You have hit the thumb upon the nail, my Trowbridge. That is exactly what it is, a prescription from the *Pharmacopœia Maleficorum*—the witches' book of recipes. Every one of those ingredients is stipulated as a necessary part of the witch's ointment—"

"The what?"

"The unguent with which those about to attend a sabbat, or meeting of a coven of witches, anointed themselves. If you will stop and think a moment, you will realize that nearly every one of those ingredients is a hypnotic or sedative. One thoroughly rubbed with a concoction of them would to a great degree lose consciousness, or, at the least, a sense of true responsibility."

"Yes? And—"

"Quite yes. Today foolish people think of witches as rather amiable, sadly misunderstood and badly persecuted old females. That is quite as silly as the vapid modern belief that fairies, elves and goblins are a set of well-intentioned folk. The truth is that a witch or wizard was—and is—one who by compact with the powers of darkness attains to power not given to the ordinary man, and uses that power for malevolent purposes; for a part of the compact is that he shall love evil and hate good. Very well. *Et puis?* Just as your modern gunmen of America and the *apaches* of Paris drug themselves with cocaine in order to stifle any flickering remnant of morality and remorse before committing some crime of monstrous ruthlessness, so did—and do—the witch and wizard drug themselves with this accursed ointment that they might utterly forget the still small voice of conscience urging them to hold their hands from evil unalloyed. It was not merely magic which called for this anointing, it was practical psychology and physic which prescribed it, my friend."

"Yes, well—"

"By damn," he hurried on, heedless of my interruption, "I think that we have congratulated ourselves all too soon. Mademoiselle Diane is not free from the wicked influence of those so evil men; she is very far from free, and tonight, unconsciously and unwillingly, perhaps, but nevertheless surely, she will anoint herself with this witch prescription, and, her body shining like something long dead and decomposing, will go to them."

"But what are we to do? Is there anything—"

"But yes; of course. You will please remain here, as close as may be to her door, and if she leaves the house, you follow her. Me, I have important duties to perform, and I shall do them quickly. Anon I shall return, and if she has not gone by then, I shall join you in your watch. If—"

"Yes, that's just it. Suppose she leaves while you're away," I broke in. "How am I to get in touch with you? How will you know where to come?"

"Call this number on the 'phone," he answered, scratching a memorandum on a card. "Say but 'She is gone and I go with her,' and I shall come at once. For safety's sake I would suggest that you take a double pocketful of rice, and scatter it along your way. I shall see the small white grains and follow hard upon your trail as though you were a hare and I a hound."

OBEDIENT TO HIS ORDERS, I mounted to the second floor and took my station where I could see the door of Diane's room. Half an hour or more I waited in silence, feeling decidedly foolish, yet fearing to ignore his urgent request. At length the soft creaking of hinges brought me alert as a fine pencil of light cut through the darkened hall. Walking so softly that her steps were scarcely audible, Diane Wickwire came from her room. From throat to insteps she was muffled in a purple cloak, while a veil or scarf of some dark-colored stuff was bound about her head, concealing the bright beacon of her glowing golden hair. Hoping desperately that I should not lose her in the delay, I dialed the number which de Grandin had given me and as a man's voice challenged "Hello?" repeated the formula he had stipulated:

"She goes, and I go with her."

Then, without waiting for reply, I clashed the monophone back into its hooks, snatched up my hat and topcoat, seized a heavy blackthorn cane and crept as silently as possible down the stairs behind the girl.

She was fumbling at the front door lock as I reached the stairway's turn, and I flattened myself against the wall, lest she descry me; then, as she let herself through the portal, I dashed down the stairs, stepped soft-footedly across the porch, and took up the pursuit.

She hastened onward through the thickening dusk, her muffled figure but a faint shade darker than the surrounding gloom, led me through one side street to another, gradually bending her way toward the old East End of town where ramshackle huts of squatters, abandoned factories, unofficial dumping-grounds and occasional tumbledown and long-vacated dwellings of the better sort disputed for possession of the neighborhood with weed-choked fields of yellow clay and partly inundated swamp land—the desolate backwash of the tide of urban growth which every city has as a memento of its early settlers' bad judgment of the path of progress.

Where field and swamp and desolate tin-can-and-ash-strewn dumping-ground met in dreary confluence, there stood the ruins of a long-abandoned church. Immediately after the Civil War, when rising Irish immigration had populated an extensive shantytown down on the flats, a young priest, more ambitious than practical, had planted a Catholic parish, built a brick chapel with funds advanced by sympathetic co-religionists from the richer part of town, and attempted to minister to the spiritual needs of the newcomers. But prosperity had depopulated the mean dwellings of his flock who, offered jobs on the railway or police force, or employment in the mills then being built on the other side of town, had moved their humble household gods to new locations, leaving him a shepherd without sheep. Soon he, too, had gone and the church stood vacant for two-score years or more, time and weather and ruthless vandalism taking toll of it till now it stood amid the desolation which surrounded it like a lich amid a company of sprawling skeletons, its windows broken out, its doors unhinged, its roof decayed and fallen in, naught but its crumbling walls and topless spire remaining to bear witness that it once had been a house of prayer.

The final grains of rice were trickling through my fingers as I paused before the barren ruin, wondering what my next move was to be. Diane had entered through the doorless portal at the building's front, and the darkness of the black interior had swallowed her completely. I had a box of matches in my pocket, but they, I knew, would scarcely give me light enough to find my way about the ruined building. The floors were broken in a dozen places, I was sure, and where they were not actually displaced they were certain to be so weakened with decay that to step on them would be courting swift disaster. I had no wish to break a leg and spend the night, and perhaps the next day and the next, in an abandoned ruin where the chances were that anyone responding to my cries for help would only come to knock me on the head and rob me.

But there was no way out but forward. I had promised Jules de Grandin that I'd keep Diane in sight, and so, with a sigh which was half a prayer to the God of Foolish Men, I grasped my stick more firmly and stepped across the threshold of the old, abandoned church.

Stygian darkness closed about me as waters close above the head of one who dives, and like foul, greasy water, so it seemed to me, the darkness pressed upon me, clogging eyes and nose and throat, leaving only the sense of hearing—and of apprehension—unimpaired. The wind soughed dolefully through the broken arches of the nave and whistled with a sort of mocking ululation among the rotted cross-beams of the transept. Drops of moisture accumulated on the studdings of the broken roof fell dismally from time to time. The choir and sanctuary were invisible, but I realized they must be at the farther end of the building, and set a cautious foot forward, but drew it quickly back, for only empty air responded to the pressure of my probing boot. "Where was the girl? Had she fallen through an opening in the floor, to be precipitated on the rubble in the basement?" I asked myself.

"Diane? Oh, Diane?" I called softly.

No answer.

I struck a match and held the little torch aloft, its feeble light barely staining the surrounding blackness with the faintest touch of orange, then gasped involuntarily.

Just for a second, as the match-head kindled into flame, I saw a vision. Vision, perhaps, is not the word for it; rather, it was like one of those phosphenes or subjective sensations of light which we experience when we press our fingers on our lowered eyelids, not quite perceived, vague, dancing and elusive, yet, somehow, definitely *felt*. The molding beams and uprights of the church, long denuded of their pristine coat of paint and plaster, seemed to put on new habiliments, or to have been mysteriously metamorphosed; the bare brick walls were sheathed in stone, and I was gazing down a long and narrow colonnaded corridor, agleam with glowing torches, which terminated in a broad, low flight of steps leading to a marble platform. A giant statue dominated all, a figure hewn from stone and representing a tall and bearded being with high, virgin female breasts, clothed below the waist in woman's robes, a scepter tipped with an acornlike ornament in the right hand, a new-born infant cradled in the crook of the left elbow. Music, not heard, but rather felt, filled the air until the senses swooned beneath its overpowering pressure, and a line of girls, birth-nude, save for the veilings of their long and flowing hair, entered from the right and left, formed twos and stepped with measured, mincing tread in the direction of the statue. With them walked shaven-headed priests in female garb, their weak and beardless faces smirking evilly.

Brow-down upon the tessellated pavement dropped the maiden priestesses, their hands, palms forward, clasped above their heads while they beat their foreheads softly on the floor and the eunuch priests stood by impatiently.

And now the groveling women rose and formed a circle where they stood, hands crossed above their breasts, eyes cast demurely down, and four shaven-pated priests, came marching in, a gilded litter on their shoulders. On it, garlanded in flowers, but otherwise unclothed, lay a young girl, eyes closed, hands clasped as if in prayer, slim ankles crossed. They put the litter on the floor before the statue of the monstrous hermaphroditic god-thing; the circling maidens clustered round; a priest picked up a golden knife and touched the supine girl upon the insteps. There was neither fear nor apprehension on the face of her upon the litter, but rather an expression of ecstatic longing and anticipation as she uncrossed her feet. The flaccid-faced, emasculated priest leaned over her, gloating . . .

As quickly as it came the vision vanished. A drop of gelid moisture fell from a rafter overhead, extinguishing the quivering flame of my match, and once more I stood in the abandoned church, my head whirling, my senses all but gone, as I realized that through some awful power of suggestion I had seen a tableau of the worship of the great All-Mother, the initiation of a virgin priestess to the ranks of those love-slaves who served the worshippers of the goddess of fertility, Diana, Milidath, Astarte, Cobar or by whatever name men knew her in differing times and places.

But there was naught of vision in the flickering lights which now showed in the ruined sanctuary-place. Those spots of luminance were torches in the hands of living, mortal men, men who moved soft-footedly across the broken floor and set up certain things—a tripod with a brazen bowl upon its top, a row of tiny brazen lamps which flickered weakly in the darkness, as though they had been votive lamps before a Christian altar. And by their faint illumination I saw an odd-appearing thing stretched east and west upon the spot where the tabernacle had been housed, a gray-white, leprous-looking thing which might have been a sheeted corpse or lichened tombstone, and before it the torch-bearers made low obeisance, genuflecting deeply, and the murmur of their chant rose above the whispering reproaches of the wind.

It was an obscene invocation. Although I could not understand the words, or even classify the language which was used, I felt that there was something wrong about it. It was something like a phonographic record played in reverse. Syllables which I knew instinctively should be sonorously noble were oddly turned and twisted in pronunciation . . . "*diuq sirairolg.*" With a start I found the key. It was Latin—spoke backward. They were intoning the fifty-second Psalm: "*Quid gloriaris* . . . why boastest thou thyself . . . whereas the goodness of God endureth yet daily?"

A stench, as of burning offal, stole through the building as the incense pot upon the tripod began to belch black smoke into the air.

And now another voice was chanting. A woman's rich contralto. "*Oitani-mulli sunimod* . . ." I strained my ears and bent my brows in concentration, and at last I had the key. It was the twenty-seventh Psalm recited in reverse Latin: "The Lord is my light and my salvation . . ."

From the shadows Diane Wickwire came, straight and supple as a willow wand, unclothed as for the bath, but smeared from soles to hair-line with some luminous concoction, so that her slim, nude form stood out against the blackness like a spirit out of Purgatory visiting the earth with the incandescence of the purging fires still clinging to it.

Silently, on soft-soled naked feet, she stepped across the long-deserted sanctuary and passed before the object lying there. And as her voice mingled with the chanting of the men I seemed to see a monstrous form take shape against the darkness. A towering, obscene, freakish form, bearded like a hero of the *Odyssey*, its pectoral region thick-hung with multiple mammae, its nether limbs encased in a man's chiton, a lingam-headed scepter and a child held in its hands.

I shuddered. A chill not of the storm-swept night, but colder than any physical cold, seemed creeping through the air, as the ghostly, half-defined form seemed taking solidarity from the empty atmosphere. Diane Wickwire paused a moment, then stepped forward, a silver hammer gleaming in the lambent light rays of the little brazen lamps.

But suddenly, like a draft of clear, fresh mountain breeze cutting through the thick, mephitic vapors of swamp, there came another sound. Out of the darkness it came, yet not long was it in darkness, for, his face picked out by candlelight, a priest arrayed in full canonicals stepped from the shadows, while beside him, clothed in cassock and surplice, a lighted taper in his hand, walked Jules de Grandin.

They were intoning the office of exorcism. "Remember not, Lord, our offenses nor the offenses of our forefathers, neither take Thou vengeance of our sins. . . ."

As though struck dumb by the singing of the holy chant, the evocators ceased their sacrilegious intonation and stared amazed as de Grandin and the cleric approached. Abreast of them, the priest raised the aspergillum which be bore and sprinkled holy water on the men, the woman and the object of their veneration.

The result was cataclysmic. Out went the light of every brazen lamp, vanished was the hovering horror from the air above the stone, the luminance on Diane's body faded as though wiped away, and from the sky's dark vault there came the rushing of a mighty wind.

It shook the ancient ruined church, broke joists and timbers from their places, toppled tattered edges of brick walls into the darkened body of the rotting pile. I felt the floor swaying underneath my feet, heard a woman's wild, despairing scream, and the choking, suffocated roar of something in death-agony, as though a monster strangled in its blood; then:

"Trowbridge, *mon brave*; Trowbridge, *mon cher*, do you survive? Are you still breathing?" I heard de Grandin's hail, as though from a great distance.

I sat up gingerly, his arm behind my shoulders. "Yes, I think so," I answered doubtfully. "What was it, an earthquake?"

"Something very like it," he responded with a laugh.

"It might have been coincidence—though I do not think it was—but a great wind came from nowhere and completed the destruction which time began. That ruined church will never more give sanctuary to wanderers of the night. It is only debris, now."

"Diane—" I began, and:

"She is yonder," he responded, nodding toward an indistinct figure lying on the ground a little distance off. "She is still unconscious, and I think her arm is broken, but otherwise she is quite well. Can you stand?"

With his assistance I rose and took a few tottering steps, then, my strength returning, helped him lift the swooning girl and bear her to a decrepit Ford which was parked in the muddy apology for a road beside the marshy field. "*Mon Père*," de Grandin introduced, "this is the good physician, Doctor Trowbridge, of whom I told you, he who led us to this place. Friend Trowbridge, this is Father Ribet of the French Mission, without whom we should—*eh bien*, who can say what we should have done?"

The priest, who, like most members of his calling, drove well but furiously, took us home, but declined to stay for refreshment, saying he had much to do the next day.

We put Diane to bed, her fractured arm carefully set and bandaged. De Grandin sponged her with a Turkish cloth, drying her as deftly as any trained hospital nurse could have done; then, when we'd put her night-clothes on her and tucked her in between the sheets, he bore the basin of bath-water to the sink, poured it out and followed it with a liberal libation of carbolic antiseptic. "See can you withstand that, vile essence of the old one?" he demanded as the strong scent of phenol filled the room.

"WELL, I'M LISTENING," I informed him as we lighted our cigars. "What's the explanation, if any?"

He shrugged his shoulders. "Who can say?" he answered. "You know from what I told you that Mademoiselle Diane prepared to go to them; from what you did observe yourself, you know she went.

"To meet their magic with a stronger counter-agent, I had recourse to the good Père Ribet. He is a Frenchman, therefore he was sympathetic when I laid the case before him, and readily agreed to go with me and perform an exorcism of the evil spirit which possessed our dear Diane and was ruled by those vile miscreants. It was his number which I bade you call, and fast we followed on your message, tracing you by the trail of rice you left and making ready to perform our office when all was ready. We waited till the last safe minute; then, while they were chanting their so blasphemous inverted Psalms, we broke in on them and—"

"What was that awful, monstrous thing I saw forming in the air just before you and Father Ribet came in?" I interrupted.

"*Tiens*, who can say?" he answered with another shrug. "Some have called it one thing, some another. Me, I think it was the visible embodiment of the evil thing which man worshipped in the olden days and called the Mother Principle. These things, you know, my friend, were really demons, but their strength was great, for they drew form and substance from the throngs which worshipped them. But demons they were and are, and so are subject to the rite of exorcism, and accordingly, when good Père Ribet did sprinkle—"

"D'ye mean you actually believe a few phrases of ecclesiastical Latin and a few drops of holy water could dissipate that dreadful thing?" I asked incredulously.

He puffed slowly at his cigar; then: "Have it this way, if you prefer," he answered. "The power of evil which this thing we call the *Magna Mater* for want of a better name possesses comes from her—or its—worshippers. Generation after superstitious generation of men worshipped it, pouring out daily praise and prayer to it, believing in it. Thereby they built up a very great psychological power, a very exceedingly great power, indeed; make no doubt about that.

"But the olden gods died when Christianity came. Their worshippers fell off; they were weakened for very lack of psychic nourishment. Christianity, the new virile faith, upon the other hand, grew strong apace. The office of exorcism was developed by the time-honored method of trial and error, and finally it was perfected. Certain words—certain sounds, if you prefer—pronounced in certain ways, produced certain ascertainable effects, precisely as a note played upon a violin produces a responsive note from a piano. You have the physical explanation of that? Good; this is a spiritual analogy. Besides, generations of faithful Christians have believed, firmly believed, that exorcism is effective. *Voilà*; it is, therefore, effective. A psychological force of invincible potency has been built up for it.

"And so, when Père Ribet exorcised the demon goddess in that old and ruined church tonight—*tiens*, you saw what happened."

"What became of those men?" I asked.

"One wonders," he responded. "Their bodies I can vouch for. They are broken and buried under tons of fallen masonry. Tomorrow the police emergency squad will dig them out, and speculation as to who they were, and how they met their fate, will be a nine days' wonder in the newspapers."

"And the stone?"

"Crushed, my friend. Utterly crushed and broken. Père Ribet and I beheld it, smashed into a dozen fragments. It was all clay, not clay surrounding a meteorite, as the poor, deluded Wickwire believed. Also—"

"But look here, man," I broke in. "This is all the most fantastic lot of balderdash I've ever heard. D'ye think I'm satisfied with any such explanation as this? I'm willing to concede part of it, of course, but when it comes to all that stuff about the *Magna Mater* and—"

"*Ah hah,*" he cut me off, "as for those explanations, they satisfy me no more than they do you. There *is* no explanation for these happenings which will meet a scientific or even logical analysis, my friend. Let us not be too greatly concerned with whys and wherefores. The hour grows late and I grow very thirsty. Come, let us take a drink and go to bed."

The Complete Tales of Jules de Grandin by Seabury Quinn
is collected by Night Shade Books in the following volumes:

The Horror on the Links
The Devil's Rosary
The Dark Angel
A Rival from the Grave
Black Moon